Tontine

The Eye of Providence

by
Brian Darr

Tontine
The Eye of Providence

Library of Congress Control Number: 1-1456601371

ISBN-13: 978-1499127447

ISBN-10: 1499127448

10 9 8 7 6 5 4 3 2 1

First Edition United States

To Jennifer Darr, who supports me, motivates me, makes me laugh, and said 'yes' when I asked if she'd marry me. I don't know how the book thing will turn out, but you're proof I did something right.

All that I know of tomorrow is that Providence will rise before the sun.
-Jean Baptiste Lacordaire

Chapter 1

1

The wedding was small. It wasn't flashy or exotic, but Victor Stone was disappointed it happened at all. The man Abby Patterson married was someone Victor was not. What that something was, Victor wanted to understand. He was never insecure, but there had been something special about Abby—something he was drawn to. He'd offered her the world, and she shot it down, publicly embarrassing him. He'd been willing to change, but in the end, she chose another man.

She chose Charlie Palmer, who Victor had never heard of, but made a point to get to know, and as he did, his frustration increased as he obsessively questioned what Charlie was able to offer that Victor wasn't.

When they were married and Abby was gone for good, Victor stayed true to his word. He wrote Abby and Charlie into his will, though he'd struggle with Charlie's name until the day he died. Victor understood how unfair this was for Charlie and how little control he was giving a man who had no idea he'd wronged Victor. He liked Charlie's name on the will, but believed one day he'd remove it. Unfortunately, he never got around to it.

It was easy for people to believe they'd have all the time in the world to finish unfinished things—to start working on their bucket list, or apologize to someone they hurt. Abby and Charlie needed time to work through their marriage, just as Victor needed time to reconsider his actions.

Victor took a long look at the wedding photo, squinting at the small specks in the newspaper that formed the larger image. Charlie looked happy standing next to the only woman Victor ever truly wanted. He never believed himself to be a man who could be disliked so immensely. He'd spoken with Abby in a way he hadn't spoken to any other woman, telling her about his life and who he was. She'd been special.

Of all Victor's flaws, one glaring shortcoming was the belief that there would always be time. Everything was cut short, from removing her name from his will, to removing the innocent bystander she married who was caught in the cross-hairs, to making a final decision on whether or not to even submit that draft at all.

Charlie had been unknowingly placed into something he had no control over, and for a man who'd displayed many moments of weakness in his life, it would be hard to predict how he'd respond when faced with the truth: Victor was out to get him because the woman he wanted fell in love with Charlie instead. It was on the day Abby married Charlie that Victor added both names.

Like Victor, Charlie counted time too. He valued efficiency. He timed every procedure, tried to top himself constantly, and measured success by progression. He bragged that he once removed a bullet lodged in a child's brain within five minutes, and it was true. Charlie's precision and confidence in the ER caused him to be an asset to Banner General.

Victor fell for Abby after one date. He decided to change his life within a month, and he didn't forget her for two years. Charlie hadn't counted the dates, or the time he'd spent with her. He was bad with anniversaries, but when it came to his trade, he was great with the numbers. He might have kept count if he ever really felt like Abby was his. Even after "I do", the only count he ever kept was the days until the end, until she was sick of him or found someone better. To Charlie, Abby was just a phase—not by choice, but a phase like everything else. The only thing he could truly count on in life was his own skill, his own practice, something he'd perfected because he had complete control. When he performed a surgery, he did a dance, and nothing made him more sure of himself. He'd looked at the times for every surgery, counted and categorized them; he was a machine in the ER, methodically and swiftly going through the motions without hesitation.

Charlie's confidence at his job and his insecurity in his personal life was what defined him. Most people saw one side or the other; rarely had anyone seen both. No one had a full understanding of what was...

...in his brain. The patient was Jeremiah Breckenstein and his two month headache turned out to be a two pound tumor. Charlie's eyes moved along the edge of the tumor with fascination. He knew he could fix it. His chief of surgery, Joel Everson, watched silently, admiring Charlie's delicate form and steady hands.

After a successful surgery, Joel tiredly cleaned up, noticing an upbeat Charlie and envying the days when he had the energy and eagerness to conquer surgery with success and get a high off it.

"What did you think of that?" Joel asked.

"A little hard to stomach."

Joel nodded, knowingly. *"That's about as bad as it gets. Don't focus on the display in front of you. Focus on fixing the problem. It gets easier."*

"I know," Charlie said, showing some doubt.

"You'll see. You did good in there. If you're nervous, it doesn't show when it matters the most."

Charlie nodded, pulling his surgical gloves off and tossing them into a trash bin.

"So what are you gonna do with the rest of your day Dr. Palmer?"

"Sleep."

"How about after?"

"I don't know if I'll wake up today."

"Set an alarm. I've made plans."

"What, uh..?"

"Carol and I are going to dinner and she insisted I find a date for her sister."

"I can't."

"Carol will have me in the doghouse if I don't come through."

"You can't find someone else?"

"Bartlett's married. So is Erickson. I'm not asking Forke."

"I'm not single." Charlie said. He hadn't considered Abby his girlfriend until this moment, and he hadn't really known for sure, but he knew he wanted her and going out on a date could potentially ruin that, even if it would please his boss. He hadn't mentioned Abby to his co-workers because he'd assumed the relationship would be short, but she'd seemed interested and always willing to go on another date, and she kissed him like she liked him, though it'd gone no further than that.

"That's not the word around here," Joel said. *"You were highly recommended."*

Charlie couldn't help but feel uncomfortable knowing that they spoke about him behind his back, even if it was flattering.

"It's nothing serious now, but I like her and I don't think going on dates with other women would be right. We're not fully established, but she seems to be into me too so I don't wanna chance it."

"It wouldn't be a date Dr. Palmer. She just wants entertainment. We can work out an exit strategy so it goes no further than dinner."

"I really can't. I'm sorry."

"Don't apologize. I respect loyalty, even if I don't believe this other girl exists."

"She does, and frankly I find it odd that everyone else gossips about it instead of asking me."

"We work side by side, hours at a time. I assumed you didn't have much to say—not that you were private. Just in case though..." Joel

scribbled a number on a pad of paper and handed it to Charlie. "Her name's Tanya and she's stunning, so if you're still unsure about your imaginary girl and you don't want to pass a good thing up, give her a call."

Charlie pocketed the number. He had every intention of tossing it in the garbage as soon as he was free from Banner General. "Will do," he said...

...After 45 minutes of waiting, when the silence hit him, Charlie called the police.

In those 45 minutes, he waited quietly, tears in his eyes, forcing himself through the moments as he passed the point of no return. He went through every emotion in that time, mostly regret. Numerous times, he almost backed out. He could open the door, save his wife, and be a hero, if not for the fact that she'd already seen him walk away.

Those 45 minutes were endless. He heard nothing through the door and feared opening it only to find Abby staring at him, her eyes filled with hurt and disappointment. He didn't prepare himself to justify his actions. He'd make no excuses. He made a mistake, and did it because he wasn't strong enough to carry a marriage that was broken. He was defeated and would always carry this with him, but ultimately had to do it to avoid a future of hurt that was inevitable with Abby.

The darkness in the hallway enveloped him. He was sweating immensely and his fingernails dug into his palms. He wondered whether anyone would ever know what had happened. He could say he slept through the gunshot or tried to save her. Both required theatrics.

Then there was the shooter.

The shooter would be caught eventually. If he was, the truth would surface. He'd been face to face, but he'd seen nothing, other than a height and a weight range, and he moved like a young man. If it had been a beneficiary, he knew it was the kid who sat quietly in the back throughout the duration of the will reading. If he were tracked down, he'd spill his guts to everyone, and the time-line wouldn't add up, and so Charlie needed a truth that fit being in the hallway while Abby died, which would also fit the shooter's truth. The longer he waited, the less likely the truth would be believed. He had to force himself to his feet and see this through. He had to walk in the room and call the police. He put his knuckle on the ground and pushed himself to his feet. It was when he stood that he saw how surreal the whole thing had been.

He opened the door.

He closed his eyes at the thought of her. She'd been so innocent—so good to him. The only anger he could direct toward Abby was the anger he invented in his head for whatever future misdeeds she'd had yet to do. Regret had already set in. It was a sign of things to come. He'd have to convince the police, his coworkers, his family, her family, their friends...everyone would have to see genuine sadness—genuine anger at whoever did this, and if and when someone asked "what about the husband?" he would have to convincingly respond with the right emotion, or the lie would be detected.

Charlie was immediately a suspect. Police always looked at the spouse first. His trauma was real and helped sell his version of what happened. What he hadn't anticipated was the guilt he'd feel as people gave him their condolences, knowing he didn't deserve the kindness offered. Everyone felt sorry for him, and only Charlie mourned his actions silently. When the investigation turned no solid suspect, the detectives in charge circled back to the beginning and some of the unanswered questions only Charlie could answer.

It was detective Phillip Weizmann who first began scratching his head at what Charlie had to say. Charlie couldn't be at home because it was too hard to be near the bed—to stand in the room where it took place. He'd checked into a motel and spent his nights watching old flicks and reading medical textbooks, anything to take his mind off Abby.

Weizmann arrived at Charlie's hotel unexpectedly one night. He startled Charlie, and something about his nervous reaction registered wrong with the hardened detective. Whether Charlie did it or not, he suspected he wouldn't like Charlie much under ordinary circumstances, and translated that fact into believing Charlie guilty. He began by asking questions Charlie had answered a hundred times before, hoping he'd slip up, grow tired, or get a little too comfortable. If a liar is left to talk long enough, eventually he'll stumble over his own story. He wrote down everything, another scare tactic, so Charlie would speak slower and think harder.

"Let's work on an exercise," Weizmann said. "Focus on the shooter's mannerisms."

"I told you everything I saw."

"Most people see more than they think."

"It happened fast. It was dark."

"Small details are often more essential than you'd think."

"He walked in the door and fired a shot at Abby. I jumped out of bed and he ran. I would've gone after him but I stayed to help her."

"For forty-five minutes..."

"I don't know how long it was!" Charlie yelled, abruptly.

"Mr. Palmer, I understand your frustration, but what we're doing right now is to bring your wife's killer to justice."

"I've cooperated. I've given six different detectives a description. I've listed Abby's friends, anyone who could be an enemy..."

"You've been vague about yourself."

"What about me?" Charlie's heart seemed to stop as Weizmann waited for an answer.

"Your friends. Your enemies. A shooter walks into your bedroom in the dark and fires a shot into the bed, yet, you assume he wasn't there for you."

"I haven't thought about who it was," Charlie said. "I don't believe it was personal."

"You got enemies?"

"No one that would do this."

"You weren't robbed..."

Charlie shook his head.

"The shooter came into the house in the night. No one was in his way. He went directly to the bedroom and fired a single shot while you were sleeping." Weizmann watched Charlie's reaction slowly, but he got exactly what he expected: no reaction. "Mr. Palmer, you've spoken with six detectives, because no one's satisfied with how forthcoming you've been. Now I've got a pot-pie getting cold at home and enough paperwork to keep me busy through the night..."

"I've answered everything."

"...But what concerns me most," Weizmann kept going, trampling over Charlie's words, "...is the time-line."

"Then what do you think happened?"

"I think it's time we go back to the station."

Charlie finally showed a sign of life as the idea set in of further scrutinizing. "I didn't shoot her," he said.

"I'm not saying you did. I just think we need to answer more questions."

Weizmann had a partner at the station. He'd said his name but Charlie forgot and only referred to him in his head as 'good cop' since the routine seemed to be playing out just as he'd seen on television. Good cop was smaller in size and more neatly dressed, with a fresh shave. He offered Charlie coffee and food and only asked questions for details, not accusing him of anything. Even though the whole thing seemed routine, Charlie preferred good cop's questions because they allowed him to focus. Bad cop was Weizmann, who did most of the talking, which Charlie suffered through, reminding himself along the way that it wasn't Charlie who broke into the house or fired a bullet. The only crime Charlie committed was allowing something to happen, and hopefully the police would find enough evidence of a forced entry, or a murder weapon, or something soon that would shift the blame elsewhere.

"Abby was hurt. She was asking for help. I held her hand and stayed at her side. I told her it would be okay. I assumed the shot woke the neighbors. The police are called for every noise and I don't know…the shock of it all, I guess it seemed to me like the police were on their way. So I focused on the gunshot wound. I applied pressure and talked to her. She wanted me to stay."

"You have a phone on the nightstand?" Weizmann asked. "There didn't come a time when you thought you'd call an ambulance yourself?"

"I did."

"But not the moment you knew it was a fatal shot?"

"I thought I had time. I didn't want to decrease the pressure or she'd bleed out. She asked me to stay and I did."

"Yet, she bled out anyway. You, a surgeon, unsuccessfully stopped her from bleeding out."

"That's forty-five minutes," good cop said, matter of factually.

"It felt like ten."

"It was forty-five. Neighbors reported they heard the shot shortly after eleven…"

"And no one else called the police?"

"They didn't think it was what it was. They heard the shot, but thought nothing of it. Happens often. The only person who knew Abby was shot was you."

Charlie buried his head in his hands. "I should have been faster. I screwed up."

The cops exchanged knowing looks, unsure of the full truth, but only agreeing on the fact that something was off with Charlie's story.

"You didn't just screw up," Weizmann said. "You killed your wife."

2

Abby's death hadn't reached most of the beneficiaries, and for some, it wouldn't for some time. Those who were close and paying attention caught the news. Charlie's detainment came as no surprise and they hoped it had actually been Charlie who killed her, if anything, because that would make the whole thing quick and easy. Knowing a beneficiary was after the money shook things up a bit.

For one of the group, the news came as no surprise, but still struck him hard just the same. His own random attack had been a spark but it'd failed to light. Todd Mason's disappearance seemed like a spark, but no one really knew the truth of where he landed. The death of Abby, for Anthony Freeman, would be the first domino that would make all the others tumble. Victor's will had officially done what it set out to do: Teach them not to mess with Victor Stone. If the remainder of the group survived and no one else died, it didn't change that Victor's plan had worked. He'd successfully killed an enemy posthumously.

"Today's your big day. You ready?" Nurse Darlene Schiable entered Anthony's hospital room with a brown bag from a nearby restaurant. He'd gotten in the habit of paying her to pick up lunch from wherever she ate. He'd become like family to the staff during his recovery and everyone was thrilled by his remarkable comeback.

"I don't know," Anthony said in a daze, his head in the clouds since he'd heard about Abby from another staff member that morning.

"You're gonna do great. You've worked hard. You're like new."

"I know. It's..."

"I know," she said with a sad sigh. "The Palmers. And you were working so closely with her." She sat beside him and reflected on her own encounters with Abby.

"I don't understand how it is that the best of them, those who we think will live many years, fall so young. The least deserving go early while those with nothing to offer, last ages."

"I agree wholeheartedly Anthony. Everyone keeps saying it couldn't have happened to a nicer person. There's such a rumor mill around here about everyone and sometimes I swear no one likes anyone at all, but Abby—there were no bad rumors. People loved her."

"It wasn't a robbery."

"How do you know?"

"I have a friend who's a cop."

"So what does that mean?"

"If you're a burglar choosing a random home, would you go straight to the bedroom where you'd know people are sleeping? And if you wanted something from the bedroom, why break in at night instead of during the day?"

She shrugged. "Some people don't think it through I guess. Some people are dumb."

"Dumb enough to be able to bypass an alarm? Why break in in a professional manner, take nothing, but murder someone, while sparing the husband who would act as a witness?"

"I guess we'll find out as more information comes out."

"I hope so," he said, his mind working.

"I'm sorry. I didn't mean to put a damper on your big day."

"It's not my big day. I'm just checking out."

"Well, you've come a long way and recovered from something that many aren't fortunate enough to live through. It's your day Anthony."

He gave her a warm smile and thought about the last conversation he had with Charlie. Charlie had been upset about Abby and the direction of their marriage. He wondered what Charlie was thinking now, maybe seeing what he took for granted—maybe even slightly...

Relieved?

The thought came to Anthony abruptly, but he pushed it aside. The notion that Charlie was anything but distraught was preposterous, but Charlie's whole demeanor suggested Abby was a pain to him. She may have been the reason Charlie was on Victor's will, but it was her—not Charlie—who ultimately suffered for it. Maybe Charlie was angry or scared. He was probably a mix of emotions. Charlie's wife had been murdered, probably by one of the others, maybe the same person who shoved a knife in his back. He couldn't fathom the idea of more than one killer on the loose right now, but a knife had been used on Anthony. For Abby, it was a gun. Multiple murder weapons meant multiple killers.

He was relieved to be released. He was finally free to walk around again, go back to his career, his favorite coffee-shop where he'd do the daily crossword and flirt with his favorite barista. Most importantly, he had to find a way to analyze Victor's will post-death. Everything had changed with the death of Abby and the sooner they sorted things out, the sooner they could all move on and feel safe. The process of elimination would be easy. He'd studied the minds of every type of sociopath he'd ever come across. Besides Dent, Abby, and himself, there were twelve other beneficiaries, all equally suspect—and he wouldn't rest until he figured out which one was guilty.

3

Good cop asked Charlie for the fourth time if he was hungry and for the fourth time, Charlie told him he was fine. He wanted to leave as soon as possible, and the moments it would take to fetch coffee, or food, would only prolong the process. He'd given them a time-line, play by play, and though it all fit together within forty-five minutes, Weizmann still bombarded Charlie with questions.

"How long do I have to be here?" Charlie asked.

"As long as we have questions."

"I didn't kill her." He'd avoided saying it so directly until now, but couldn't resist anymore. Something in the words was discomforting, as if he was saying it to convince himself.

"Forty-five minutes Charlie."

"I want an attorney," he shot back.

"You'll have to answer these questions either way."

"I stayed with her too long. I thought she'd be okay. After I felt no pulse, I cried a long time, tried to revive her, spoke to her even though she couldn't hear me." Tears stung Charlie's eyes. He thought about Abby laying in the bedroom and all the things he would've said to her if only his story had been true.

"What did you say to her?"

The question blind-sided Charlie, but he kept going. "I kept telling her I loved her and I was sorry."

"Sorry for what?"

"For not being good enough to her." It was easy for Charlie to answer the questions because now they were true.

"Were you fighting?"

"No."

"Witnesses outside the hospital said they saw you fighting."

"We argued. It was a small deal."

"They heard you talking about separation." He read from a notebook, showing it was on the record.

"Yeah, it came up. It did a lot. We made up."

"Were you sleeping next to Abby that night when the shooter walked in?"

"I already told them..." He drifted off as he fully understood what the question meant. It was a question he hoped would never come up, but finally someone was headed in the right direction and Charlie needed to start adjusting the story to coincide with wherever the investigation might end up. He wondered for the first time if the truth would be so bad. Would it actually be murder, or attempted murder, or neglect, or...

"You said you were in bed, correct?" Weizmann went on.

"That's right."

"There were blankets on the couch. Your wife also happened to be positioned in such a way..."

"She was on the right side!" Charlie shouted angrily, knowing this to be true. He'd even noted that night that the space was available to him if he'd only come up. She'd been sleeping on one side of the bed, welcoming him when he was ready. "I was in the bed with her," he added softly, aware that his tone changed drastically when he lied and wishing he hadn't said it. The easiest way to get through this was to find a way to only say what was true and dodge the rest.

"The thing that gets me is that you're a gifted surgeon with a just about spotless record—impressively spotless. I've even looked at your evaluations. Among your strengths: cool under pressure, steady, consistent..." Charlie turned away, and looked at the door as if he was longing for his freedom beyond this room. "So why would this be any different? You knew what to do. You knew how to save her, or at the least, to call an ambulance. You're not an idiot. What was different about this? Other than, of course, the fact that the person who was dying was your wife?"

He swallowed hard. They knew, and they were unraveling the details inches at a time. He thought about that night, searching for an angle. He could tell them about Victor's will and give them the incentive they needed to narrow down the list of suspects, but something held him back; he wasn't sure what yet. Maybe the idea that whoever the shooter was—and he thought he knew who—figured out Charlie's part in the whole thing.

"Are you sure I can't get you a sandwich?" good cop asked.

"I'm not hungry," Charlie's voice was parched. He'd grown exhausted to the point of letting everything out, from the beginning to the end: how he'd been seeing Mindy on the side and how Abby had lied to him constantly, pushing Charlie into a position where he just couldn't take it anymore.

"You sound tired."

It didn't help that Weizmann had been reading his mind all day.

"Some water," Charlie finally said. It occurred to him that everything could be a test, not just the questions about Abby, but every question, designed to reveal his character. Weizmann turned to the two-way mirror and signaled for water before shifting his weight and pulling himself forward as if he was ready for a new round of questions. Charlie was exhausted, but Weizmann looked like he could go all day.

"The witness at the hospital mentioned the argument. He said there was talk about a number you'd been calling. Your phone records verified this. Who were you calling in the middle of the night?"

Charlie knew they knew the answer already. Lying about the affair would be seen as a sign of guilt. It might kill his reputation, but he didn't hesitate to give these answers correctly. "Another woman."

"A mistress?"

"We'd only seen each other a few times. I met her at a conference and we started talking. It was nothing serious."

"But it was more serious than a friendship..."

"We spent a few nights together."

"This is piling up on your head."

"That's fine," Charlie said, dryly.

"It's fine? How's that?"

"Because you'll find out soon enough that this wasn't me. There was no gun, but when you start doing your jobs, you'll trace the weapon to its real source, who by the way, has been running long enough now that you may never catch him. I know you know I didn't break into my house. I didn't shoot my wife..."

"Agreed, but I'm toying with a theory."

"You already know," Charlie said, his voice rising in an effort to humiliate Weizmann in the same way he'd been humiliating Charlie. "You know someone broke in. You're trying to play hero cop and force me to incriminate myself because you can't catch the real killer. That's what you guys do. You can't find the real bad guys, so you frame whoever is nearby."

Weizmann and good cop gave each other an amused smile before Weizmann stood and circled Charlie. "What we need to know is that you had nothing to do with this. Until we know everything that happened, second by second. In every domestic case, the spouse is always suspect number one. As a matter of fact, the spouse is usually guilty, and if they're not, then they set it in motion to some capacity."

"I loved her. I still do," was all Charlie could manage, but he meant it, and his eyes showed it to be true.

Good cop finally spoke up. "I don't think anyone believes you're guilty Mr. Palmer. You're just the best witness we have right now and you hold most of the clues. We just want the details so we can get the right man."

Charlie nodded. It was all tactical, but he was relieved when good cop took the pressure off Charlie as the main suspect. "We had our troubles, and yeah, I was distracted by another woman. Abby and I fought about it. We talked about divorce. Our marriage had become ugly. You want to know about timing?" Charlie found Weizmann's eyes. "This is bad timing. It's a bad coincidence that happened at a time when only I could look guilty, but that's all it was: bad timing. I'm sitting here regretting the other girl, regretting the fights, regretting the fact that I said the word 'divorce' out loud on the same day she was murdered. I sat with her in that time because I was afraid she was going to die. I was afraid I'd walk away and she'd die and her last thoughts would be the course our marriage had taken. I stayed with her so she would know that the only thing that mattered was how much I loved her."

"Weizmann.." An officer leaned into the doorway, interrupting a moment Charlie was proud of. "Mr. and Mrs. Patterson are here. They want to see Charlie."

Charlie knew this moment would come: an inevitable confrontation with the in-laws. He'd managed to keep his fear under wrap until now, but facing the people who raised Abby, who loved her as much as Charlie had, was his biggest fear.

The detectives allowed him to step outside the room where he faced the grieving couple standing at the desk. He watched them closely, wondering if they'd see through him, wondering if they'd blame him for not being there. As he thought about all the reasons they could potentially blame him, he realized most of them to be true. He'd failed to protect Abby. They had every right to blame her death on him.

He walked forward; his legs felt like rubber as he approached them. The first thing Abby's mother did was hug Charlie, wrapping her arms around him and sobbing into his shoulder. The hug was followed up by a handshake by her father and a sad sympathetic nod. Her parents looked at Charlie and saw a man in the same boat.

Charlie looked over their shoulder and noticed Weizmann watching with his arms crossed. He watched Charlie closely, seeing more than just a man who lost his wife. Something in Weizmann's eyes showed that he knew more—that he knew the truth...

...The bell rang and Abby Patterson looked up from her place in the bathroom, a towel wrapped around her and another around her head. She hurried to the peephole, where she was surprised to find Charlie standing on the other end. She hadn't expected company but was happy see him.

She opened the door and waved him in quickly, hurrying back to the bathroom. "I thought you were working," she called out, as she disappeared behind the door.

"We closed up faster than expected."

She finished drying her hair and began to dress. "How did it go?"

"Really amazing. The human brain is so complex. I've seen thousands of diagrams but the real thing is something else."

"Did you get to touch it?"

"No way. I observed. My value doesn't go beyond holding instruments."

She exited the bathroom, a t-shirt hung loosely over her shoulders. She gave him a hug and a kiss, finding his eyes for a moment and smiling. She suddenly felt guilty that she was going to a ball at Stone Enterprises that night with Victor. Charlie saw she was conflicted, and backed away.

"I should go. You seem busy."

"Well, wait..." she said, urgently. "Why are you here?"

"Just seeing if you had plans, and I guess you do."

"Yeah, I do," she said, regretfully. "Sorry."

Charlie lingered momentarily, hoping she'd tell him the plans, but she fell silent, almost as if she was deliberately withholding. "What kind of plans?" he finally asked.

"A friend of mine has a fund raising function I'm supporting. I wish I would've known you were off early. I totally would've blown him off." She

meant it, but Charlie only noticed that she was going with a 'him'.

"That's alright. Just call me sometime. I'm not working Thursday. Or even if your thing ends early."

"Okay," she said, without enthusiasm as if it wasn't expected to end early at all.

Charlie left moments later, but he replayed the encounter in his head repeatedly. He'd been dancing around the issue for too long. The longer their relationship went undefined, the more he wondered what Abby did in her time away from Charlie.

He stood in the hallway after parting and stood outside the door motionless for a long moment before coming to the conclusion that Abby wasn't a one man woman and she didn't see her relationship with Charlie as serious. He pulled his cell from his pocket and dialed a number.

"Joel..." he said. "Is it too late to join you?"

He was glad he gave up on Abby for the night. Tanya was a looker and she was very much into Charlie. She leaned toward him as if Joel and his wife Carol weren't even there. She was practically giving herself to Charlie, and if not for Abby, he might have submitted, but he couldn't get Abby out of his mind.

"So why'd you get into neurosurgery?" she asked.

"Well, when I was ten, I flew over the handles of my bike and hit my head on the pavement."

"Ouch!" Joel said.

"I got up from the accident, walked to the garage, and collapsed in front of my parents."

"Oh my god..." Tanya said.

"I was taken to the hospital because I kept having seizures. They had to drill a hole in my head to release the pressure and I ended up in a coma for three weeks. No one thought I would make it. I finally woke up screaming and fighting the doctors."

"So you're a medical miracle," Tanya said.

"It really puts life into perspective," Carol added.

"Yeah, except it was horrible after that. I suffered from seizures and headaches growing up. I'd become irritated and angry. It caused a lot of problems for me. Of course, in that time, I became fascinated with the human brain because I was constantly trying to diagnose myself so I could fix it later."

"Do you still have seizures?" Tanya asked.

"A few years ago, I had surgery that removed part of my left temporal lobe, which affects my recognition of words and impairs my memory for verbal material. Even though the doctors recommended I shouldn't take

*classes immediately, I went to med school. I still get nervous or frustrated
sometimes, but I function like anyone else."*

"That's amazing," Tanya said with a smile.

*Joel raised his eyebrows at Charlie as Tanya scooted closer to him.
Charlie fidgeted nervously with his silverware, wondering why it was
never this easy when he was single—unless he still was. He thought about
Abby and just what the limitations on dating were at this point. She seemed
to be dating, and this was a date...but how far did her dates go? How far
could his dates go?*

*He asked himself these questions all the way to the parking lot, where
Tanya and Charlie separated from Joel and Carol, who walked to their car
as Tanya lingered at Charlie's side, apparently not ready for the night to
end.*

"Can I offer you a ride?" Charlie asked.

*"I live three blocks away and it's too nice of a night not to walk, but
you can walk with me."*

Charlie considered a moment before nodding and walking with her.

*"There's a tribute to the Beatles at the House of Blues tomorrow night
if you're interested in joining me," she said.*

"Yeah, maybe. Keep me posted. Or I can call."

"You won't call me," she said, rolling her eyes.

"I'm just a little unsure right now."

"Did you not have a good time?"

*"I did. It's just that I don't know if Doug said anything to you, but I'm
seeing someone."*

"Ah, okay. No, he left that out."

*"So don't take it personal. I just need to see where this other thing's
going first."*

"It's a new relationship?"

*"Sorta. Moving slow. Maybe not moving at all. That's what I'm trying
to figure out."*

"I take it you're serious about her anyway."

"I am. Waiting for word from her."

*"If she's not telling you what's going on, then what's the problem with
dating?"*

"I like her."

*"You're out with me." She stepped toward him, seductively close,
allowing Charlie to smell her hair, which smelled like apricot.*

"I can't." he managed to say.

*"Forget I asked then," she said, her whole tone changing. She was
clearly let down—not a woman used to rejection. It took everything
Charlie had to reject her. "Besides, you're a little weak for me."*

"What do you mean by that?" Charlie asked.

"You like a girl but you're waiting to hear from her? I'm more direct. You're dating a girl for how long and she can't throw you the smallest hint? Sounds to me like she's stringing you along and you're one of those guys who allows it."

"I appreciate your diagnosis but..."

"But you're just gonna wait around and be her lap-dog. I offered a sure thing, and you're not interested."

"I'm interested. Believe me. I just really care about her. She could be more direct and I could too, but I'm just enjoying getting to know her. It might be nothing, but if it's not, then being here with you could ruin it."

"I think you probably don't have a chance with her and that's probably what you like about her."

"Wow," Charlie said. "Rejection doesn't suit you well."

"Not when I'm five drinks in and was promised a cute available doctor, who turned out not to be."

"Cute or available?"

"A little of both."

Charlie smiled and nodded. She was prodding him but he'd stood his ground and felt good about it. The more he was around Tanya, the better Abby looked. She was a handful, and a bit of a diva, the kind of girl that probably doesn't see many second dates.

"Okay then," he said, and turned to walk away.

"You love her or something?"

He'd tossed the L word around quite a bit but hadn't truly defined his feelings. He could count on one hand the times in his life he thought he loved someone, but in hindsight, he'd always known it was a blind attempt to move things quickly so he could keep what he had. He wasn't sure what love really felt like, but believed the old cliché that said he'd know it when he was there. With Abby, something was different—something that could be love. He knew there weren't a lot of girls who could squeeze so many dates out of him and still keep him hoping for more. He would've given up on anyone else by now.

He slowly shrugged, to let her know the idea was on the table.

"You know, you shouldn't just sit back and do nothing," Tanya said, suddenly becoming a voice of reason. "If you sit back and wait—if you don't take action—you're going to lose her. I'll walk the rest of the way alone. Make sure not to call me..."

..Doug and Layla Patterson sat side-by-side, holding hands. Charlie sat across from them. Charlie knew they weren't all going through the same thing. Any guilt or regret that Doug or Layla were experiencing was nothing compared to what was going on in Charlie's head. That, and fear. As Layla recounted memories of Abby, Charlie watched the officers from a distance, stealing glances in his direction as if keeping tabs.

Layla asked Charlie if he was okay three times before he finally looked up at her. She waited, concerned about her son-in-law and whatever he was going through.

"I don't know yet," he said.

"You look like you need to eat," Doug said. "Let us buy you lunch."

"I can't leave."

"Why can't you leave?" Layla said.

"They're questioning me. They're trying to get me to remember what I can so they can find the shooter."

"You're not a suspect, are you?" Doug asked. Suddenly, he was on his feet, ready to tell off any officer who was willing to point their finger at Charlie.

"I'm not a suspect. It's just what they have to do."

Doug turned to Charlie, who gave him a reassuring look, though he knew at any moment, Weizmann could come over and slap handcuffs on his wrist.

"They have no real evidence. It's all protocol. The guy who did it aimed his gun right at me and pulled the trigger. I think so anyway, because he was confused and suddenly ran. The gun jammed, or maybe it was empty, but he was scared."

"Have you told the police that?"

"Yeah, but he didn't steal anything. He came to kill us. No one knows a motive and there has to be a motive if it's not robbery. I'll be fine. I'm sure. I should go back."

You shouldn't just sit back and do nothing. If you sit back and wait—if you don't take action—you're going to lose her.

Charlie remembered the words, but they held a new meaning. He tried to hide the fact that he would've saved Abby, telling himself she would've died no matter what, but a gun-shot wound to the stomach wasn't fatal—not if you acted fast.

"When will they release you?" Doug asked.

"I don't know, but you need to hear this from me now because it's part of the problem: Abby and I fought earlier that day. They're making a thing out of it. They think I could have saved her if I'd acted quicker."

Layla paused for a long moment, registering what Charlie said, wondering if there was truth to it. Charlie saw her doubt—doubt he couldn't afford for other people to have. "It happened fast. She wanted me with her and she died. I did everything I thought I was supposed to do. I wanted to be with her but I should have acted faster."

Layla buried her face in her arms while Doug turned over his shoulder and shook his head in disbelief. Charlie hoped the man wouldn't start wondering about Charlie too. He didn't know how much accusation he could take. Finally, her father turned back to Charlie and sized him up.

"She really thought the world of you. Don't let those cops bully you into saying something stupid. You understand son?"

Charlie nodded. Abby had thought the world of him. Somehow, no matter how insecure he'd been, he always knew she adored him. She loved him in ways he didn't deserve. Her last moments were proof of that. He closed his eyes as he thought about those forty-five minutes—what she must have been thinking while he sat outside the door waiting. She probably died hating Charlie. She knew he was cheating. She knew he'd over-reacted with Victor. Her husband: the murderer.

"I have to go," he said, quietly.

He walked back to the interrogation room, the notion of confessing crossing his mind for a moment. *Confessing what? You didn't shoot anyone. You just didn't react. Is that illegal?* He arrived at the room where Weizmann and good cop sat waiting for him. He entered without a word and sat.

4

Richard Libby learned of Abby's death the next morning, and was unable to speak the rest of the day. He sat in shock, avoiding confrontation with Benjamin and trying to sort out how it could make sense that something finally happened—especially to Abby. Richard's worst fears had always involved the boys battling it out with guns—never a defenseless woman while she slept.

Brian Van Dyke heard the news moments after Trish Reynalds. Brian was sitting in front of his television, a bag of fast food in front of him. Trish was arriving at the station, only to hear the news from Carlos, who didn't even know Trish knew who the Palmers were, but only gossiped that the husband was being brought in for questioning. "It's always the husband," He said.

Aileen Thick was at work, having begged for her job back, despite Jason's best efforts to stop her from working in a strip club. Jason, on the other hand, wouldn't find out for some time, as he sat with Erica Drake on a beach in Maui, detached from the rest of the world.

Royce Morrow saw it on the news, as did Maria Haskins, who thought back to a time when she'd had a similar vision—a time when she'd warned Abby about Charlie—though the news was reporting her death as a break-in.

Christian Dent may have seen the story, but wouldn't remember. He was distraught over the death of Ira, who'd managed to get nowhere on his mission to take out the whole list. Dent expected his old mentor to at least have done a little damage, but by the looks of it, he was taken down before he could even handle one—and by two police officers nonetheless—one being the officer who was an everlasting pain in his ass.

Tarek Appleton was the last to hear and sat silently in disbelief. The hustle and bustle of his day brought him back to life and he didn't think about her for quite some time.

In his last moments in the hospital, the staff wouldn't stop talking about Abby and what a remarkable woman she was, a fact Anthony knew and wanted to forget. He'd spent a lot of time with her in physical therapy, and the crush he pretended to have on her was the product of an extension of his real admiration for her. She was a girl who hadn't let the world get her down. Call her naïve. Call her stupid. Call her 100% positive. She simply had been a happy and trusting person, a person he'd almost watched Ira kill only hours before. He'd gone back to his room that day and let out a breath of relief for Abby, who he'd believed was too young, too innocent, too colorful of a personality to be wasted to a violent convict. His relief only lasted until he woke up the next day, the news all over the hospital. She'd escaped a certain death only to find another. It was a waste of the top one per-cent of the cream-of-the-crop in the human race. Abby, who spent her life helping people, inch by inch, pound by pound, taking the time to fix people who were broken, gunned down in her own home in the middle of the night.

Just as Anthony had been stabbed.

He closed his eyes and winced, trying to erase the image he'd conjured of the pinch, the pain, his weakness, and the moment he fell to his knees as he felt his back drenched in his own blood.

"Ready for your freedom?"

He opened his eyes to find the nurse in his doorway with a wheelchair in front and a bubbly smile on her face.

Freedom. It was a funny word. He was ready for freedom, but he was also re-entering a world that was different than the one he remembered. It was a world post-death, void of Abby.

"I won't need that," he said, without any cheer. The wheelchair was an insult to him. He wasn't a hundred per-cent. He knew that. But he was walking out on his own two feet.

"Is anyone coming to pick you up?"

"I don't need a ride. I'll take the bus like I always have."

"You know what? I'm on lunch in ten minutes. I'll take you home."

"No."

Her smile faded. His tone was brash. The man who'd been friendly, appreciative and taking every opportunity he could to charm the staff and visitors, just so he'd have someone to interact with, was gone. The man he'd been replaced with was a man who wanted to get out of there and get away from the world. She saw it ever since Abby died. They'd all been sad and all leaned on each other, but Anthony had grown quiet and isolated.

Outside his room, a small gathering of doctors and nurses gathered to see him off. They wandered away, breaking up the party as they realized it wouldn't be in order. He was just another patient who they'd brought back to life and sent out into the world. They'd mistaken him for a friend. In half an hour, he'd be out of their lives.

Anthony grabbed a small pile of his belongings, leaving the flowers and balloons and gifts behind. He winced as he got to his feet, but began walking, trying to move quickly, counting each step until he was finally free of Banner General. He'd grown claustrophobic in his room, and tired of being in one place all the time. He was ready to get back to the world, though he had no idea what would be next. Most of all, he wanted to get away from the place he'd spent so much time getting to know Abby.

One death. Maybe the best one of them all. Richard had his lawsuit and Trish had her gun and badge. There were efforts being made, but they hadn't been enough. They hadn't stopped the first death. Anthony was free to finally bring something of his own to the table. Fourteen people remained standing and a good handful of them most definitely didn't stab him or murder Abby. Anthony was the brains of the group—the brains of every group. He was a psychology major and taught behavioral science and sociology for over a decade. There were thirteen other living beneficiaries out there—all were just average people.

It won't be hard to figure this out, he thought, as he winced when a spasm of pain shot through his back.

5

Weizmann and good cop sat reclined in their chairs, sipping on coffee, a burger in Weizmann's hand, and a patient countenance that told Charlie they wouldn't be done anytime soon.

"When is this over?" Charlie asked.

"If you're done answering questions, I have to take you in as a suspect."

Charlie closed his eyes, debating in his head what the consequences of his actions would be—trying to decide whether or not it was better to spill the truth now than be caught later. It came down to a question of whether or not they could prove his story. The more he thought about it, the more he knew they couldn't. They could call him a poor decision maker, or a bad husband, and even dumb, but no one was in the house within that time other than Charlie and Abby. No one in the world could possibly know what Charlie was doing for forty five minutes.

"I didn't do it," he said.

"It's still protocol."

"No, it's not. I haven't lied. I know what you guys do here. You scare innocent people into saying things so you can bring in a suspect. You call it filling in blanks, but you keep people until they're tired and sick of the game and say something you need them to say so you can take it to court and lock them up. Forget the fact that the real killer is running around and may kill again. You guys don't give a shit about that. You just want convictions because it looks good on your record. So do me a favor and don't pretend like this is justice or like you're sad about the fact that someone murdered my wife. If you gave a shit, you'd be doing your job and catching the real killer instead of trying to lock me up just so the public doesn't call the police department the joke they are."

"Alright," Weizmann said, with a wave of his hand at good cop, who quickly stood.

"We have evidence of a third person in the house." Good cop helped Charlie to his feet, his whole demeanor having changed. It seemed as if they were just waiting for him to break or to expose their trap. Instead of rubbing it in further, or calling them names for what they were putting him through, he decided to take what he could get.

"You can't go too far of course," Weizmann said. "You're still going to be needed if anything comes up. And if you remember anything helpful, just give us a call."

"Thank you," Charlie said, letting out a tired breath, only thinking about his bed and how badly he needed to sleep before he could fully process everything that had happened. Good cop escorted Charlie to the door, who walked away without turning back. Weizmann watched him closely as he disappeared from the building. Good cop sat across from Weizmann and threw his feet up on the table.

"What do you think?"

"There was a third person, like I said. But ya know, I've done this same kinda scenario six times now. We question the spouse. They have to deal with the death of a loved one while dealing with the accusation. Six times...I've had to let someone go. They scowl or swear or demand an apology from the department. Charlie Palmer just thanked me."

"What are you saying?"

"He might not be guilty, but he's not innocent either"...

...He paced back and forth, scratching his head, his eyes watching the clock. He stared at his phone, having regretted ditching Tanya only to come home to an empty apartment. He didn't know what else he expected. Abby hadn't called or texted. She was probably still out at whatever function she had for the night, maybe with a guy, holding his hand, kissing him, going home with him...

He closed his eyes, his body frozen as he felt the sting of being rejected repeatedly by a girl he liked...maybe more...like Tanya said.

Tanya.

He suddenly grabbed the phone and pulled Tanya's number from his pocket. He began to dial, but his eyes jumped at a light knock at the door. He slowly set the phone down and listened closely, his eyes finding the clock. It was after midnight but he was sure he'd heard a knock. He waited, until he heard it again.

He approached the door and opened it slowly, seeing her eyes first, and then the black dress which hugged her perfect figure. Abby pushed the door open the rest of the way. She looked beautiful. Her eyes were tired, but looked at Charlie with something he'd never seen before.

Relief?

"I love you," she said.

He almost choked on the words before saying it back. A moment after he did, she stepped in and kissed him, her hands moving up to his face and holding her hand gently against his cheek as their lips met. He reached his arm around her back and pulled him close to her. They moved from the doorway to the bedroom. She tugged at his shirt while he pulled the dress over her head. They made love that night and the next morning.

Charlie was happy. If he'd gone home with Tanya, he would've missed the moment. He had never been great with commitment, but Abby was different, and he knew in that moment that he would make the effort and do whatever he had to do to hang onto her. He would suppress the part of him that sabotaged previous relationships, the part that was so possessive—so insecure.

As he lay staring at her, plotting the course of their relationship, he didn't acknowledge how late it was, why she'd suddenly showed up to tell him she loved her, what events led them to this moment. It wouldn't be until years later, after they were married, that Charlie would learn that the very first time they made love was the night Abby dumped Victor Stone...

...”Charlie. Wait up!”

Charlie stopped dragging his feet on the sidewalk and turned, not thrilled to be sidetracked from his plan to go straight home and to sleep. “I wondered if I'd see you,” he said as Trish Reynalds hurried to catch up to him.

"Are you okay?" she asked.

"I don't know."

"I want you to know that I'm looking into this."

"I appreciate that."

It was the last thing he needed. Trish had the advantage of a narrowed down list of suspects. If Weizmann saw the will, he'd have a good list of suspects.

"I thought about the others..."

"What others?"

Trish wondered if Charlie was playing dumb, or actually wasn't smart enough to connect the dots.

"The others from Victor's will," she said, obviously.

"Right. What about them? You think this has something to do with that?"

Her eyes narrowed. *Of course it does, you idiot.* She watched him closely, alarms going off in her head. She'd heard about the forty-five minutes. She'd heard about the fight outside the hospital. Charlie was no killer. She could see it by looking at him. He was distraught. But there was more to this than she'd originally thought.

"Your security alarm was disarmed. That's not an easy thing to do. No one even tried to get in any other way. There was no signs of forced entry."

"What's that mean?" He already knew.

"Do you remember the kid who sat in the corner? Young and goth looking? Real quiet?"

Charlie nodded.

"His name is Adlar Wilcox and he's missing. Recently ran away from home and has a bit of a record. He also knows computers and electronics, so I figured it was him. When I heard you had a description, I checked to see how close it would be to him. Adlar's short. You said the shooter was tall. Adlar's skinny. You said portly. Adlar's 22. You said in his 30s or 40s."

"Then it's not him."

"I thought that too when I read the report. Then I got to thinking that everything you said was the opposite. If it were one or two things, I wouldn't have thought twice, but the description was the complete opposite of Adlar, as if it was deliberate. So it got me to wondering why you wouldn't want Adlar to get caught."

Because Adlar Wilcox knows the truth.

"I don't know what you're trying to..."

"Just listen." He shut his mouth. "If he turns up dead, you're the first person I'm coming after."

Charlie couldn't play this game with Trish. She knew, and nothing would change that, and Charlie had every intention of making sure Adlar turned up dead. He found Trish's eyes. "He killed Abby." His voice was rigid, but calm. He watched her expression, which didn't change.

"You can't make this about revenge. You know what's at stake when this snowballs."

"It already snowballed. You think I give a shit about the others? The only person I care about is dead, and if that was Wilcox in my home, then we're all safer without him."

"Abby would have cared."

"Abby was too trusting. She kept telling me nothing would happen and I kept expecting something. Being too trusting isn't..." His voice broke as he thought about Abby and her peppy rose-colored attitude. He always held it against her, and he was right in the end, but he couldn't say he would've changed it. She made a miserable world colorful for him.

"Todd Mason's funeral is in a week. When that happens, his death certificate is signed. That's two. If something happens to Adlar, that's three. Anthony Freeman wasn't stabbed by Adlar. You need to figure out which side you want to be on if it all hits the fan."

"What do you expect?"

"I expect you to tell the truth. Help us catch him. I'll personally make sure he's locked up forever. The others will see that trying to take matters into their own hands is futile."

Charlie thought about her resolution. If things had been different, it might be an option worth exploring. "I told everything as it was." He turned and began walking as Trish took a step forward, done being pleasant.

"Or maybe you don't want Adlar arrested for other reasons."

He closed his eyes in frustration, wondering again how many people could see through him. He turned to her, giving her a perplexed grimace. "Care to tell me what that means?"

"Forty-five minutes Charlie. Even I can speculate on that. For an average person, that's suspicious. For a surgeon who would know exactly what to do, it's worth a conversation. Maybe not everything happened the way you said. Of course, you've thrown everyone else off of Adlar, but I'm betting I'll be able to find him. What story is he going to tell?"

He stared at her endlessly. This was getting to be too much to carry. He was lying on a level he'd never had to before. It wouldn't just be Adlar thrown in jail if the truth was pieced together.

"The point is that I don't care what happened Charlie. I care about locking up the threats in the group so the rest of us can live in peace. If Adlar is dangerous, I need to know now, because if I have to find him and prove this myself, and you hide from it, I'll find the whole truth and make sure you share a cell with him. Then...you can deal with him."

"Deal," Charlie said, and turned again. This time, he didn't turn back. Trish had all her cards on the table. She knew the truth, and would race Charlie to prove it. Adlar would confirm everything if she brought him in. Charlie had come face to face with Adlar once but Charlie froze. He swore it wouldn't happen the next time. Trish called out to Charlie, but he kept walking, his face set and determined. He was no longer tired. He had no time to be tired. He had to find Adlar Wilcox.

Chapter 2

1

"How has your recovery been?" Rickers asked, facing Anthony Freeman.

He sat uncomfortably in the chair, shifting repeatedly. He cleared his throat. "Very well. Thank you for asking."

"Do you feel ready?"

"To educate? It's the least physically restraining thing I can think of at the moment. I sit on a stool and read from a book."

Rickers nodded with a skittish smile. Anthony saw his skepticism.

"Have you heard from the police lately?" Rickers asked.

"No suspects." It took all of Anthony's self-control to control everything he said and did. He wanted to stand up and pace. He wanted to hurry outside and get some air.

"I read the file of every student who would have possibly been here that day. I have a hard time believing it was one of our own."

"I agree."

Rickers nodded again. "Anyway," he said, getting down to business. "When I heard you wanted to be back among the living, I almost said 'not yet', but I decided to allow it if you agree to meet with a counselor, who will sign off on it."

"How long will that take?"

"Once a week for a month. You're allowed in the classroom throughout the duration as long as he agrees that you're of sound mind. We want to be sure there's no prolonged effects."

Anthony was disturbed by this, but in trying to seem his chipper normal self, nodded and signed a dozen forms. It was just a formality. Anthony taught about men in similar circumstances—men who spent their childhoods going through unfathomable trauma, who didn't recover—who sometimes grew up to be the worst of the worst that society had to offer.

Anthony would return. Everything would be fine. To prove it to himself, he walked back to the room where he'd been stabbed, looked straight at the spot on the ground where he'd been, shouting for help before he passed out. He headed in that direction, familiar faces greeting him with large smiles as he passed. He'd have to get used to being an attraction for a while. Everything would normalize in time. He stopped abruptly upon seeing the doorway that led into the room—a doorway he'd unsuccessfully tried to reach from the inside coming out. If he kept walking, the room would reveal itself and in a matter of moments, he'd see where it'd happened. Maybe he'd even see himself, lying there, in a pool of...

His face went white and he swallowed hard.

"I believe everyone who knows me, will tell you I've handled myself well."

Anthony twiddled his thumbs during the awkward silence as the doctor listened and mentally assessed everything he said.

"Have you had a lot of interaction since the incident?"

"Of course. I got to know the staff at Banner well. I had visitors constantly."

"Family? Friends? Students?"

"A little of each."

"I see." He wrote something down. Anthony wondered what. "Have you been sleeping okay?"

"Better than ever."

"No nightmares? Daydreams?"

"Nothing relevant to the incident."

"Have you allowed yourself to relive it?"

"It's all I did initially."

The doc watched him closely. It was the most important question of all, and the one Anthony was prepared for—prepared to lie about. He'd relived the attack in segments, but he hadn't allowed himself to replay every moment. To relive it meant he was past it. To hold back meant it was on the horizon, only Anthony already knew the psycho-babble behind trauma and knew he could avoid it altogether. He was the most intelligent person he knew. He studied and analyzed the mind for a living. He knew how to control the conversation.

"Have you talked to anyone else?"

"Hospital staff. Visitors." *Abby Palmer.*

"Family? Loved ones?"

"I don't have many remaining. I'm an old man."

"Do you feel there's been closure on what happened to you?"

Another challenging question. It was another way of asking if he'd relived the incident. The doctor was trying to trick him, but Anthony was able to track where he was going before he went there. Instead of telling the doc what he wanted to hear, Anthony gave him the truth, which seemed harmless enough. "I feel fine. I don't believe closure is possible until whoever did this is found and justice served."

"What's your definition of justice?"

"Balance."

"What would bring balance?"

"That's for a judge and jury to decide."

The doc nodded.

"Do you have any feelings of revenge?"

"No."

"Nothing you'd like to say to your attacker if you came face to face?"

"I'd tell him he failed. I'm alive. He took nothing from me."

"Nothing at all?"

"No. In fact, he may have given something to me: perspective."

"You give good answers. One might even say you give all the right answers."

"In that case, I'd conclude that I'm ready to get back to work."

"I agree Mr. Freeman, and I'm not going to stand in your way. I just want to tell you that no matter how intelligent you are, you can't hide from the emotional consequences of violent trauma. You may have a talent for seeing your situation from the outside. You may not feel it now, but certain feelings surface in time. No one can suppress forever. If you can, I advise you find an outlet."

"Educating is my outlet," he said simply...

"...Why did you want to end your life?"

Anthony leaned forward in a plush chair, facing Karen Stark at her desk, a copy of a book: Goodbye Cruel World, displayed between them with his name stenciled in golden letters at the bottom right corner. He nervously twiddled his thumbs while he pressed his hands together, seemingly rocking as he thought about the answer.

"It's hard to pinpoint one thing. It was a combination of misfortune and a very poisonous isolation that effected my outlook on many things. For a very long time, a much darker version of myself controlled me."

"We're all very happy you overcame those feelings." Karen smiled, compassionately while a studio audience applauded. Anthony smiled and nodded, touched by their empathy and appreciation of his book. She went on, addressing the crowd. "Again, the book is Goodbye Cruel World, and the author is Anthony Freeman, who's sitting with me today. Thank you for your time Mr. Freeman."

After the show, he mingled with a line of fans while autographing their copies of his book. He made small talk, answered questions, and politely gave those in similar situations words of encouragement. Anthony had once felt alone, but as it turned out, writing a self-help book brought all kinds of people out of the woodwork—people who needed people just like themselves to relate to.

He turned for a moment and caught a stranger watching from a distance—a young girl wearing a stocking cap with strands of golden hair popping out. She was skinny and pale, and lingered as if waiting, but looked too frightened to approach. Her demeanor would surely haunt him if he didn't invite her over or approach her. He kept his eye on her during autographs and when the crowd thinned, he excused himself and approached. She stood waiting, as if she'd hoped for this a one on one encounter without the crowd.

"Anthony Freeman?" she said. "Are you hungry?"

He wondered if she was infatuated with him. It wouldn't be the first time. He almost brought up her age but she assured him this was something different. "Your book saved my life, but I can't keep going." Her voice trembled, and somewhere in her eyes, he saw she'd cried too many tears and had none left. He dismissed his assistant and thanked the remaining crowd before hurrying off with the girl, who told him her name was Natasha before they found an all-night restaurant where they ordered coffee and breakfast.

She didn't want to initiate the conversation, instead asking him about his own experience. He told her everything about his suicide attempt, and followed it with all the reasons he was relieved it didn't happen. "One thing I took away from it all was how much I would've missed out on that I've experienced since."

"Yeah, well, I can barely remember happy times, and there's no good days."

"No one knows the future, so why assume nothing will change?"

She fidgeted, and looked at him with sad eyes, and spoke as straight-forward as she could. "There's no point to me."

To her surprise, he laughed, took a sip of coffee, and set it down while he searched for words. "Don't get me started on purpose. I asked the same question, but who chooses their fate? We do the best we can."

"What if my purpose is to die? To serve as an example or warning to others not to copy my actions, and my suicide is meant to show the result of the choices we make."

"If you fundamentally believe that, sure, but it sounds like a cop-out to me."

"Not if it's the only sense I can make of it. Maybe, humanity will look back on the choices of those who chose to end it all, figure out how things

go wrong, and work to progress to the next stage of human mental evolution. Who's to say there's no positive outcome from my death?"

"You're speaking hypothetically. It's not the act of a martyr and it's not for the betterment of society. It's because you feel trapped and it's still wrong."

"Technically, it isn't wrong if your perspective is that it's right. Wrong is relative. It's only because the majority say it is, which is the precedent in which morals are determined. Ethics are an invention of man, but they aren't universal law."

"How old are you?" he asked.

"Sixteen."

"You not only contemplate suicide, you research and rehearse to justify it. You know, there are cultures that applaud suicide under certain circumstances? The problem is being able to gauge whether or not life is bad enough to warrant such an irreversible act. There are some joys and experiences, not yet lived, that are immeasurable. To willingly give these up because of perceived hopelessness is beyond tragic. You're trying to make sense of death. Have you ever turned that logic on its head and tried to make sense of living?"

"Of course. That's all I've done."

"I try finding a moral philosophy that works. The 'meaning of life' comes from acting in a way to sustain that. There's a good list of reasons to choose from: to be duty driven, live for a greater good, Social Contract, following the will of God. It's up to each one of us to find an individual plan that's acceptable to us."

"I don't believe in anything." Her voice cracked, and she swallowed hard, covering her emotions well, but Anthony saw the truth.

"You need what we all need: something to look forward to. I'd be willing to help you by inviting you to be a part of a project I'm working on. I've created a suicide support group that meets Thursday nights. It's a place to come and relate to others with similar situations."

"My parents wouldn't let me."

"Let you what? Go out an hour a week? You're out now."

"I snuck out."

"If they knew you were helping people..."

"They still wouldn't."

He let out a breath and took a sip of water, while tapping his finger on the table. "I'll write down the address. If you can make it, you'll see that you can be part of something bigger. Just promise me you'll find a reason to wake up every day. Someday, I promise you, you won't have to search anymore..."

...Fifteen names on the list...
Abby Palmer was shot...
Fourteen remain...
I'm innocent. That's all I know. I could narrow it down further. I'd written off Brian. Trish had always been on my side.
But I'm smarter than that...

His own voice interrupted his thoughts. "U.S. women experienced intimate partner violence almost seven times more frequently than men. Statistics for last year showed that more than five times as many females were victimized by an intimate than were males." He looked up. They were blurs.

"I don't think that's right." It was the voice of Simmons, the number one instigator in class debate. "I read that women hit at about the same rate men do, or even more often. Studies don't show what's not reported."

"The source please?" Her name was Judy. She always offered a rebuttal to Simmons.

"I don't remember, but it's still true. Women who slap men or throw things increase their chance of being hit in return."

"Yeah, but a man slapping or shoving a woman is much more likely to inflict injury than a woman hitting a man."

"That's my point. The statistics are impossible to record because women provoke as often or more often than men. Women are only victims because they sustain greater injuries."

Anthony looked up to find all eyes on him, awaiting his two cents.

"Go on," he said, simply.

"What are your thoughts?"

"I think you're also omitting women will be twice as likely to report being injured. Men face ridicule and isolation. Who do men talk to when they're abused?"

"True actually," a student said. "I had a girlfriend who hit me with a frying pan once and I was bleeding pretty bad. I didn't tell anyone because I figured everyone would assume I hit her first or deserved it, but I didn't."

Abby wouldn't have touched anyone. She wasn't close to being a threat. In fact, logically, killing Abby makes no sense—not from a self-defense standpoint. So why choose Abby? That's the key. Who of everyone would make sense of Abby being the first?

A book in the hallway hit the ground, sounding an echo throughout the auditorium. Anthony's thoughts abruptly ended as he looked up suddenly, a cold sweat forming on his forehead. The pinch in his back surfaced and shot a pain that went straight up his spine and into the back of his head. He winced as he leveraged himself with a hand on the podium in front of him.

"Women usually hit men out of fear," Judy continued, oblivious to Anthony's episode.

"They poison men out of greed for their money or because they found a new lover."

"So do men!"

The shouting in the room sounded entirely different in Anthony's head. Instead, he heard himself shouting for help, gasping for breath, Abby lying in bed while Charlie tried to save her—Charlie the surgeon who waited too long to call an ambulance. His eyes glazed over as he stared blankly at the wall. His jaw clenched and he closed his eyes, the sounds of screaming overtaking his mind—the pain in the back of his skull expanding to his eyes.

"When you think about it..." Simmons said, already showing how proud he was of his train of thought, "...Women shelters probably save more lives of men than women. Women have an option when they're scared, but men don't."

"Yeah," a student chimed in, "...remember when that lady in Newport shot her husband in the back of the head in front of her kids and then took him outside and burned the body? Turned out she was having an affair all along. That's not fear."

Judy fumed, tired of being teamed up on. It seemed the only people who wanted a part in the debate were two other males, and Anthony hadn't been much help.

"Excuse my language, but..." She happened to turn to Anthony at that moment and stopped mid-sentence. Everyone followed her gaze to find him standing still, his face white and his hands shaking. "Mr. Freeman?"

A bunch of students stood, and slowly made their way toward him with concern. He stood frozen for a long moment before simply saying "I need water" before running from the room. The students stared in shock, all knowing the repercussions of what happened to Anthony went beyond physical pain.

As they forgot the argument and began discussing Anthony's frame of mind, he ran to a fountain and drank water before splashing a little on his face. What he really wanted was a glass of Maker's Mark, the only medicine that could cure him, but also the medicine he was forbidden from so long ago.

He took a long moment to catch his breath and suppress the temptations. The world came into focus and was suddenly quiet. He closed his eyes and tried to find peace. *I'm crazy. I'm crazier than the people I analyze and pick apart in class. I've become the kind of man I once loved to put under the microscope...*

He understood what was happening. He was reliving the incident, only now it was mixed with thoughts of Abby—of the faces of the list of suspects. His own mortality had been called into question so many times and he'd cheated death without deserving it, while Abby took one shot to the stomach and bled out for an hour.

He caught his breath and went back to class.

2

When he learned his attempt on the Palmers' life was only halfway successful, Adlar Wilcox went through a moment of grief, followed by shock, followed by immense fear. He ran into the woods and hid under a bridge to lay low until trouble passed, and so far, he was safe. He missed his Internet, the roof over his head, but mostly, his freedom. He had to be cautious. At least until he knew he was in the clear.

He'd faced Charlie, and he'd relived the moment various times since the night he'd walked into their bedroom and taken a single shot into the lump in the bed. He was sure she'd survive, but the shot hit its target and though it took her forty five minutes to die, he did the job. Unfortunately, Charlie wasn't there, and when he did run into him, the gun jammed.

He was faced with what to do next. He'd ventured out for food, stopping in gas stations and hiding his face as he made his purchases. He'd stolen a few items, but mostly did whatever it took to be invisible. As time passed, he grew more comfortable going out in public. He'd also realized that hiding would make him seem guilty. All they'd have to do was discover the beneficiary who was acting shady. Being nowhere to be found was a sure sign of guilt. He would have to act normal, which meant eventually going back to life as it was. If the police ever happened to show up, he'd need an escape, but for now, he had to at least go back to the world. Luckily for Adlar, he'd run away from home before the incident, and so his parents wouldn't find his behavior to be unusual.

His first bold move was going back to his stomping grounds at the Internet cafe, where he dropped two dollars an hour to read headlines on Abby's death. It repeatedly mentioned suspects, which was good news because as far as he could tell, no one had tried approaching Adlar. If Charlie had really seen Adlar, he would've been mentioned somewhere. Every moment that passed, he found new doses of optimism. Soon, he'd have to see Toby O'Tool to find out what to do next.

After infiltrating the LAPD's website and finding his name nowhere, he decided to do what he'd wanted to do from day one: go back to the scene of the crime. He started four blocks away, slowly making his way step by step, closer to the Palmer home. *This is where it happened*, he kept thinking to himself. He'd been relieved he'd never had to see the look of horror on her face. Shooting into a lump in the bed was easy. Looking into the victim's eyes wouldn't be. He hoped she didn't suffer, that she'd never seen his face and known what he did, but most of all, he found himself hoping somehow that she deserved it, that he didn't deprive the world of a great person. Everything he knew about her said she was, but everyone was bad in some form.

He made his way down the block, which was empty and quiet. The people who lived in the neighborhood were working, running errands, or hiding inside in front of the television. He stared at the Palmer home, which looked much different in the sunlight. It was hard to believe someone died inside.

"Hey."

Adlar turned to come face to face with a boy on a bicycle. He'd stopped, interested in Adlar, who sized him up. Adlar hated people who were comfortable enough to strike up conversations with strangers.

"You know Abby Palmer?" the boy asked.

Adlar suppressed a sudden panic, but the boy was only curious. He was probably just a kid who knew vague details and wanted to gossip. Adlar had an opportunity to gather information. "The lady that died?" he asked, playing along.

"Yeah, the police have her husband now."

Adlar wasn't surprised Charlie was being questioned. "So was it his fault?" he asked.

"I dunno. My dad heard a gunshot in the middle of the night and then the police came later."

"Did he call the police?"

"No. No one did. That's why she died."

"What?" Adlar asked.

"Because if her husband would've called an ambulance, they would've saved her. She wasn't shot that bad but no one helped her."

"But why?" Adlar asked, hoping desperately that the boy knew more. "Who called the police?"

"Her husband. It just took too long. And he works at the hospital too."

"So they think it's him?"

"I dunno."

Adlar's fraction of hope increased significantly. He wondered if anyone would ever point a finger at him. Charlie's survival could be the best thing that happened to him if Charlie was taking the heat for what he should have done differently when Abby was dying.

The boy wanted to stay and talk, but Adlar hurried past him. The last thing Adlar wanted to do was draw attention to himself, but he had to know what he had to work with. Not only were the police not searching for

Adlar: they were pinning her death on the wrong person. As bad as it sucked for Charlie to go down for what Adlar did, it still beat the alternative. He wondered if Toby would be proud. He couldn't wait to talk to him.

The one question that failed to cross Adlar's mind in all the excitement was: Why hadn't Charlie simply saved his wife?

3

Anthony reflected on how poorly his return was executed. He was taken off guard by his own trauma. He never expected to find himself face to face again with the doc, who'd warned him this might happen. Anthony tried to deny he was traumatized, but now was all about damage control— finding the fastest way to come back to his job and recover according to the University standards. This time, Dean Rickers sat in as the doc listened to their conversation.

"There's no trauma," Anthony insisted with a laugh.

"What you're doing is damaging to yourself Anthony," the doc said with compassion that felt fabricated to Anthony. "Your medical background raises questions."

Anthony froze up. It seemed the doctor and dean had done their homework. He swallowed hard and forced himself to find the dean's eyes, but spoke to the doc. "Anything I've been through has made me stronger and wiser. I had a brush with death and it opened my eyes."

"Just how many times have your eyes been opened?" Rickers asked.

"What's that supposed to mean?"

"You've been self-destructive in the past."

Anthony narrowed his eyes and nodded at the doc as if sizing him up for the first time. The doc was smart and Anthony underestimated him, but there was no way he was getting the best of Anthony.

I'm smarter than him. I'm always smarter than the room. "Are we done?" was all he was able to muster.

The doc turned to the dean, who shook his head to signal what the doc had expected. Before the doc could go head to head with Anthony, Rickers stepped in. "You're not ready to be back."

"What exactly have I done? I showed up. You think it was easy for me to make this decision?"

"Which is why you need more time. We're doing this for you. I know you can't see that now. I'd like to make myself available for counsel if you'd like it."

Anthony hastily got to his feet. "No thanks. I'll talk to someone with a real job."

"Mr. Freeman, what I do..."

Rickers waved him off dismissively, shutting him up, but Anthony got his jab in. Rickers knew it was coming. Anthony was a conspiracy theorist who happened to think every psychologist was a fraud and that the whole profession was catering to people who refused to take responsibility for their actions.

"Anthony," Rickers said, calmly. "While we appreciate everything you've done for us, and deeply sympathize with what happened to you, right now you're a liability to your students and yourself."

Anthony stood and took a breath. He nodded his head, accepting his position...

...Mostly children sat in a circle and silently waited their turn. Natasha was among them and watched as a boy named Miles stood and controlled the floor. Miles was short, with strands of hair that nearly covered his eyes, which were red around the edges from tears. His voice was shaky as he spoke. A year ago, if someone told me I'd be this upset over a girl, I would've laughed. I mean, I used to hate guys like myself, but for some reason, I really fell for this one."

"She left you for your friend?" Anthony asked, listening intently and displaying as much empathy as he could, for Mile's sake.

"Yeah."

"Sometimes, it's not the breakup that hurts. It's the pride that's been wounded in the process. No one wants to feel like they weren't good enough and that someone else was better. Especially, a friend or family member who you consider an equal."

"That's just it," Miles said, thoughtfully. "I was never good enough for her."

Natasha suddenly sat forward, abruptly enough to catch everyone's attention. She had something to say and she was able to steal the floor with one quick movement. "You need closure," she said. Anthony sat back, allowing Natasha to take the lead.

"She won't talk to me."

"Well, stop trying to win her back."

"I'm not," Miles said, defensively.

"Yeah, you are. You barely cut your wrist and called her. That's not suicide. That's a cry for help. You wanted her to see a world without you so she'd see how much she'd miss you when you were gone. You staged a scenario, hoping her emotional reaction would bring her back to you, but it didn't work and now you're humiliated and things are worse. You're gonna keep doing it until you accept that she's no good and move on."

"Yeah," Miles said, embarrassed to have been analyzed so bluntly.

"Seriously, if you really think a girl who cheats on you with a friend is a good enough reason to die, then you're just dumb. She doesn't even sound like a good person."

"She is though. Other than what happened, she was very good to me."

"She's just another slut."

Some of the others, including Anthony, smiled at the comment. Even Miles lightened up and giggled a little to himself. Anthony watched Natasha deal with Miles for another ten minutes and when they walked out of the building that night, a fire was lit under his ass. Anthony caught up to Natasha, who hurried away.

"What is it about some of the most amazing minds that makes them think the world's better off without them in it?" he asked when he was close enough.

"What are you talking about? Me?"

"Yes, of course. You have a gift. You connect with people."

"That was all just common sense. It's annoying watching people who don't have real problems act like life is hopeless."

"You can have impact on a large scale. You need a platform."

She smiled to herself, flattered to earn such high praise from a man she admired.

"Let's grab a pizza," he said. *"I'm buying."*

"I can't."

"How about a coffee?

"I have to be home."

"I don't understand your rush."

"I just have a lot to do."

"I get it," Anthony said with good-humor. *"I'm a creepy old man."*

"No. Just...my parents will be mad."

"They know where you are, don't they?"

"Not really. They think I'm at the library."

"Are they highly influential stress factors in your life?"

"They take my future seriously."

"How seriously?"

"They want me to succeed."

There was an awkward silence. Anthony stopped walking and took a deep breath. *"I'll talk to them,"* he said.

"No."

"Maybe they need an outsider's opinion on what's important in your development. Sometimes it's difficult for parents to understand our needs."

"I appreciate the gesture, but please don't."

He told her he wouldn't, but thought it would be harmless to at least drop in and see her father. If he seemed like a reasonable man, Anthony *would work it into the conversation and reach him. He did some research and discovered he worked for a car dealership. It would be easy enough to strike up a friendly conversation with a man trying to sell him a car.*

"You looking to buy or just browsing?" a man asked, as he strolled over to where Anthony stood, pretending to check out an automobile.

Anthony sized up the man with the Texas drawl and cowboy getup. Natasha's father was the owner of Lee's Auto, Lee Hayward, and he was every bit as present as Anthony had expected after talking to Natasha. No man couldn't be reasoned with. He just needed an outside perspective that wasn't a part of whatever broken relationship the man had with his daughter. Lee seemed friendly enough, and Anthony knew he'd proceed.

"Lee Hayward?" Anthony asked.

"I am," he said, as if proud to be called by name.

"I'm here to talk about your daughter."

Lee's whole demeanor changed. The car salesman left his body and was replaced with a concerned father. "She do something she shouldn't?"

"Not at all. Quite the opposite actually. I met her a few weeks ago and we've befriended."

Lee sized Anthony up quickly, trying to run through his head all the ways his daughter could know a man like Anthony. "And how's that?" he asked.

"I'll let her explain if she'd like. She actually asked me not to come speak with you, but I felt it was best." Lee frowned and grasped for words. He suddenly didn't even seem like a concerned father anymore. Now, he seemed slightly angry. "It's platonic. We're part of a support group."

"Support for what?"

"Again, you should talk to her. I just came by because I get the impression that Natasha doesn't feel a lot of support at home. I'm not here to shake my finger at you, but just to make you aware."

"Excuse me?" Lee asked, getting in Anthony's face. "Am I being lectured now?"

"I'm playing messenger to help her. Obviously, if she doesn't feel comfortable talking to you, there's an issue. She's a good kid. She wants to excel and move forward. I was hoping I could make you more aware. I'm sure you want what's best for her."

Lee rubbed his temples as if he had a headache. "Tasha been telling you about us then?" he asked, with an edge in his voice.

"Not at all. It's something I picked up on. If anything, she speaks highly of you. She said you work hard and have been a loyal husband and father. My concern was her feelings of isolation."

"I see," Lee said, turning his head away and nodding.

"I just want to make sure she lives up to her potential."

"Of course," Lee said, impatiently. "If you're not looking to buy a car, I need to git."

"I appreciate your time."

Lee nodded and walked away with a short glare over his shoulder. Anthony stood for a long moment, trying to decipher what exactly Lee's reaction had meant. He took a deep breath...

...A car backfired, causing Anthony's heart to stop in his chest momentarily. He stopped in his tracks, right outside his doorstep, and caught his breath. He continued up his steps, grunting as he pulled his old body closer to his door. He reached the door and caught his breath again before entering and getting into the elevator to take him to his twelfth story penthouse.

He entered his apartment and tossed his keys on the nightstand. A gust of wind blew the curtains from his balcony inward and they rippled in the wind.

His eyebrows suddenly furrowed as he realized he'd left the window open. In fact, had he even opened his door with a key, or had it already been open? He quickly turned the lights on and scanned the room with his eyes. It was quiet, but something was off. His eyes fixated on the balcony and he slowly approached it, step by step as if his shoes had weights in them. As he got closer to a full view of his balcony, a shape began to take form. A man, standing on the ledge, looking down.

"I called the police," Anthony called out. The man didn't move. It was as if he was in the wrong place, troubled, consumed by something else. Yet, he'd gone through a lot of trouble to be in that exact spot. "Excuse me!" Anthony shouted.

"Fine," the man said, responding to the threat. His tone was one of defeat—the tone of a man who had nothing to lose. Anthony had heard it many times before.

"Why are you here? Can I help you?"

"You—you were supposed to be the first," the man said, his voice cracking. The color drained from Anthony's face as he realized he was facing the man responsible for his attack.

"I don't know what you're talking about," Anthony said.

"You were supposed to die first," the man said again, crouching down as if his body was coming undone with uncontrolled movements.

"Who are you?"

"Vince. I'm so sorry." Tears formed in his eyes.

"Sorry for what?"

There was a long silence. Vince finally turned, but only partially.

Anthony had never seen the man before in his life.

"For trying to kill you."

4

When Toby O'Tool heard of Abby's death, he was shocked. Something deep inside told him that Adlar Wilcox didn't have it in him. He'd hoped he did and he'd shaped him the best he could, but Adlar had been a weakling. He was no doubt destructive, but Toby didn't think he'd have the goods to pull it off.

Then there was the execution, which frustrated Toby to no end. If Adlar had it in him to kill, he might as well have it in him to kill well. Killing only Abby seemed like a waste. Charlie was alive, and therefore, could spill everything he knew about the will. Abby and Charlie had always seemed like one beneficiary. If Adlar was going to have the balls to break into their home with a gun, leaving one standing was pointless. He guessed what also happened to be true: that Adlar only had it in him to fire a shot in the dark and run away. This left numerous issues that Adlar would have to deal with, and if Adlar had to deal with them, he could implicate Toby. Suggesting Adlar pursue the money wasn't a crime. He hadn't paid or even helped beyond giving advice. He pointed Adlar in the right direction, and even that went off-course. Toby was under the impression Adlar was going to go after Tarek Appleton, but he'd picked the Palmers instead—a couple of the most harmless people on the will. To make matters worse, Adlar was on the run without even having been accused of anything yet.

Toby regretted recruiting a lowlife like Adlar the same way he usually regretted partnering up with anyone on any of his endeavors. What happened to Abby was bittersweet. On one hand, everything changed. Creating panic set the snowball in motion. On the other hand, Adlar was now a danger to Toby. In hindsight, Toby wished he could have dragged things out a little longer, prodded at Adlar from a distance and made him think it was his idea all along while Toby pulled strings behind the scenes. The best cons made their targets believe they owned their actions. Adlar wouldn't own what he did at the Palmer house. He'd been pushed, and he knew who pushed him.

Toby knew Adlar would show up at his door eventually. The frantic knock on the door startled him, but he'd expected it. He opened the door where Adlar stood, his shirt wrinkled and covered in dust and grass stains, his hair a cropped mess. His eyes were red in the corners, as if he hadn't slept. Toby stepped aside, inviting him in.

"You did it," he said.

Adlar let out a breath and nodded. "I'm in trouble."

"Why? No one's looking for you. You're fine. You're in trouble if you don't maintain control."

"That lady's husband is alive."

"What were you thinking walking into a house with two people? I thought you were going after Appleton."

"I never said who. You said to kill the hardest one."

"Right, but why them?"

Adlar shrugged, but Toby saw it in his eyes and in a moment of realization, Toby knew Adlar had gone after the Palmers because they were a couple—because they reminded him of his own parents.

"Alright," Toby said with a sigh, trying to find the right words. "It was dark?"

"Yeah."

"Fingerprints?"

"No, but the guy was there and he saw me. I tried to shoot him, but my gun jammed, so it wasn't my fault."

"You put yourself in a bad place. You never go into a room with two people and only take care of one."

"I didn't know," he whimpered.

"He see your face?"

"I don't know."

"He hasn't said anything yet, unless the police are withholding details."

"So what do I do?"

"Stop acting guilty. Go home. Charlie saw what you saw: A dark unrecognizable figure."

"Can't I just stay here?"

"I don't want a roommate Wilcox."

"But you were the one that asked me to do this."

"I didn't ask you to do shit, so stop telling that story."

Adlar cowered like a wounded puppy. He thought he did the right thing, but not only had the impact of what he did set in, now the mentor he thought was his only friend in the world was turning against him.

"Look," Toby said, taking a deep breath. "I can hook you up with an apartment. You ran away from home before this happened. If you go missing, it's not the worst thing in the world. At least until the heat dies down."

Adlar released a breath of relief. All he needed was guidance. If Adlar were his enemy, he could do real harm. If Adlar thought they were friends and out of the way for a while, he could still utilize him—maybe persuade him to move onward.

"I'll drop you off at a place I know and leave you with a few parting gifts. I've got a cell you can use and we can communicate via email. At least until this blows over."

"What about food?"

"I'll give you a little cash, but I'm broke. There's plenty of restaurants with dumpsters in the alleys. Tough it out for a little while. You'll compensate later when you're the last standing."

Having restored Toby's confidence was all Adlar needed. He'd been struggling with whether to continue onward. He'd even grabbed the gun a time or two with the intention of picking another and taking them out. Something inside told him it'd be too much, too fast.

"I'm proud of you kid," Toby managed to say with a straight face. If it wasn't so necessary, if Adlar didn't hang on his every word, he might have stopped himself. "You took a leap. Everything from here gets easier."

Adlar nodded, swallowed hard, and before Toby could stop him, moved in and wrapped his arms around his waist. Toby would've pushed him away, but the hug was a response to his guidance, and allowing Adlar to look up to him was essential. Earning his loyalty meant everything when the time came. Pretending, at least for a little while, like they were in an after-school special and Toby was the cheesy know-all platitude-spewing voice of morality, would pay off.

After a long enough moment, Toby was able to wriggle free from the hug. "Okay kid. Let's get you out of here. You feeling okay?"

"Yeah."

"You gonna be able to keep doing this?"

"Yeah, cause..."

Toby's eyes narrowed. Adlar wanted to say something, but held back—something Toby wanted to hear.

"Cause what?"

"Remember the arcade? The game where we were shooting and it was fun? I know this was real, but it was like that."

"Was like what exactly?"

"I liked it," Adlar said. "It was fun."

5

Vince stared at the traffic. One leap would send him to the ground.

Anthony stood frozen. He tried to seem as non-threatening as possible. "Who are you?" he asked.

"It wasn't my fault," Vince said.

"Why don't you come down and tell me what happened?"

"I can't. My life is finished. Nothing you say changes that."

"I need to know why you did it."

Vince struggled with the words. "About a month ago, a guy comes to my workplace. He approaches me and my co-workers with a proposition."

"What co-workers? Who was he?"

"It was some guys I work with—friends. This guy comes to us and says he's created a lottery for us and he's giving away a large sum of money if we want to play. He had a list of people. You were one of them."

"What were the terms?" Anthony asked.

"It's like this game we used to play. It was some morbid shit. Everyone picked ten celebrities—people who may not make it—old and washed up or whatever. Only this was a specific list. Fourteen names. Everyone gets to pick who they think will die first. We took turns picking. I was second and I picked your name."

"Did he tell you to kill us?"

"No. Not a word about that. But the stakes were high. He showed us the money and everything."

"Did he say his name?"

"No. You were the oldest so I thought picking you was a good bet."

"Then what? That's why you tried to kill me? To win the lottery?" Anthony asked in disbelief. He wanted to talk Vince off the ledge but was furious.

"He called it a tontine—like an insurance thing. No one thought we were supposed to tamper with anyone—we'd just hope we picked the right guy so our dividends increase when you all…" he trailed off and moved on. "We were gonna forget about it. We figured no one was gonna die for some time but that a few years down the road, he'd come back to one of us and raise our shares. We even made a mutual agreement among some of us to split it if one of us won. I admit the guy did a shitty thing, but it didn't seem dangerous then."

"Until you stabbed me…"

"I wasn't gonna do anything. Then I made some bad bets. I have debt. I got five kids at home and I was desperate. So I…you know…" Vince looked away and wiped his eyes on his sleeve before turning back to him. "You lived though. And then someone else died. And the guy who picked the girl that died—up and disappears. Took his money and ran. And I got nothing."

"You placed bets on lives," Anthony said with disgust.

"It seemed alright, but now I get it, and I thought the others would too, but now they're placing bets again. I wanted nothing to do with the second round."

"You were set up to do someone else's dirty work. You should have understood the objective."

"Why?" Vince asked, his eyes welling again.

"You and your friends were manipulated by a man who wants that specific list of people dead for his own benefit. He tempted you all to kill us and you took the bait. He's doing it again and if you help me, we can prevent further damage. You said there were fourteen names, but there are fifteen of us. If you can recite the list, I will know who did this. I can stop him."

"He didn't do anything wrong. He never said to kill."

"But that was the whole point."

"I didn't mean it," Vince said. Anthony could see he wanted to come down but couldn't bring himself to believe that the man he'd shoved a knife into would forgive and forget. No matter what Anthony said, Vince wouldn't find that trust. He was stuck between Anthony and the ground. One way meant prison and a life facing his crimes. The other meant a quick fall and eternal resolve for him.

"You didn't do this," Anthony said quickly. "Who could blame you for how you acted? Someone put this in front of you. If I speak with your friends and they give me the names, I can sort this out. I can find the man missing from the list. Was there a man named Royce?"

Vince shook his head, indicating there was. "How would you know that?" he asked.

"You need to trust me. Come down so I can explain." Though Vince was softening and Anthony's focus should have been on bringing him down from the ledge, he couldn't help but eliminate suspects. "What about Tarek? You remember that name?"

"The talk show guy. Yeah."

"Good. You're doing great. You see? I know the names, but I know fifteen. If I read them to you, there will be one you don't recognize. Come down and we'll figure this out together. I'll help you with your debts and get you through this. We can stop this before it happens again. I'm alive. No harm done." Anthony put his arms out, palms facing up, in a desperate attempt to show he was harmless.

Vince watched him closely, and for a moment, Anthony believed he was going to come down. In the next moment, without a word, Vince turned and jumped...

...Her face was bruised, her lip cut and eye black. Her right cheek was swollen and she walked with a limp. Natasha was broken in everywhere— most of all, internally.

"What the hell happened?" Anthony asked. He already knew the answer. Her father had been enraged by Anthony's visit—something she'd warned him about, but Anthony didn't get the hint. Or maybe he did and

he'd thought he was too smart. There were words for every occasion: Words to make a woman fall for you, words to earn forgiveness, words to talk a man down from a ledge. There were always right words, and Anthony's talent to a fault was having them. He'd gone to Natasha's father with the belief that he was a man who could be reasoned with—a man who only needed to hear the right words.

"Did your father do this to you?" he asked as she came closer. He observed the extent of the damage.

"I told you not to talk to him," she said. He'd expected pain in her voice, but it came out as rage instead.

"I tried to help. And I still can. What he did to you can easily be resolved."

"I fucking told you!" she screamed. He could see the distance between them lengthening. It'd been there from the moment he met her, but he could see in her eyes that she desperately wanted to close the gap. Instead, he'd betrayed her trust and lost her forever.

"You have to report this. It won't change until the victim steps up."

"Stop acting like you know what's best."

"You came to me for a reason. We can help people, but you have to help yourself first."

"I made a mistake when I came to you."

"You didn't. You don't realize your potential, but I do."

From behind a van, her father took a step out with his hands in his pockets, waiting for Natasha to finish telling Anthony to stay out of her life before taking her home. Home, where he could continue his routine of abuse and damage her beyond repair. "Go ahead and get in the car sweetie," he said. Natasha hesitated, but walked toward her father.

"I'm calling the police," Anthony said.

"Good luck with that, asshole."

"I don't believe I'll be the one who needs luck."

"You'd believe it if you knew who you were talking to."

"And who am I talking to?"

"A guy with friends in high places. I can bury you with one phone call."

"What have I done other than show concern for your daughter? More concern than you show, I might add."

"How about profiting on the pain of others?"

"I don't know what you're implying."

"There's profit in selling books. Nice little idea you had. Write a suicide note, publish it, make money off the weak-minded."

"Are you implying my suicide was a farce?"

"The Getaway had no record of your stay that night."

"And how could you possibly know that?" Anthony asked. A bad feeling consumed him. Something was off about the situation. Lee wasn't just upset about his impeding. Apparently he'd done his homework.

"Check it out for yourself," he said. "Come near Natasha again, and I'll expose you."

Anthony turned to Natasha, who stared at him with disappointment. "It's not true Natasha. I've been honest about everything. You came to me. I only wanted to help."

Lee turned to his daughter and gave her a look Anthony couldn't see. After a moment, she disappeared into the car. Lee turned back to Anthony with satisfaction, gave him a long look as if to say he'd been beaten, and...

...held a small crowd of onlookers back as police observed the body of Vince, laying crookedly on the ground, a pool of blood surrounding his body. Anthony stood side to side with Trish Reynalds, who stared forward, all color drained from her face. Anthony called her, told her of the encounter with Vince, and his departure from the world. Trish listened silently, told him to wait, and hurried to see for herself.

"You have nothing to worry about," she said. "We'll get an ID, figure out where he works and who was in on this. It won't be hard to figure out who set the whole thing up."

"Whoever the ring-leader is, they have money. And they're still playing this game. You won't get them to talk. They've got their bases covered." Anthony's voice was drained of optimism. His charisma was gone, his analytical self no longer contemplated the many scenarios that could play out. Instead, he only felt doom. "We have to protect ourselves."

"You're the one who said from the start that everyone was going to be okay," she reminded him.

"Is Abby Palmer okay?" he snapped. She stepped back, surprised to see he'd been so hostile. Anthony had suffered a good deal of trauma, but he'd always been one of the strongest and most practical of the group. The last thing she wanted to see was defeat. "I was wrong," he said, softening.

"You weren't wrong. You were optimistic."

"We can't control what happens. We can't hypothesize the outcome."

"I'm going to find out who Vince was tied to and we'll straighten it out. You have my word."

"It won't matter," Anthony said. "This will kill us all..."

...He showed the manager behind the counter his identification, made up a story about his significant other doubting his loyalty to her, and asked for a receipt of his stay at the Getaway on the fateful night of his near-suicide. The manager was suspicious, at first telling him he couldn't give

out guest information. *After Anthony convinced him that all he needed was*
anything that indicated he'd spent one night there almost a year ago, the
manager reluctantly ran a search for their transaction.

The manager grew confused, searched again, and stared at the screen
for a long moment as if trying to figure out what was going on. "Have you
always gone by the name on your I.D.?" he asked.

"I have. Why?"

"You sure this is the right motel?"

"Of course."

"And you paid with your card? Didn't bribe the guy at the counter
with cash or anything like that?"

"I would never do that."

"Your name's not in our system sir. I think you're mistaken or there's
been some kind of miscommunication."

"Check again," Anthony said, his frustration growing. Lee hadn't only
beat him. He'd stumbled on a truth that wasn't true at all, and if it ever
reached Anthony's readers, it would expose him as a hack. Somehow, any
trace of proof that Anthony had been where his book claimed he was on the
night had disappeared—or never existed at all.

The manager checked again, shook his head, and said the words
Anthony didn't want to hear. "Sir, you've never stayed in this motel."

Chapter 3

1

"We're shutting Stone Enterprises down."

Lawrence Curatola stood with his arms akimbo and faced Michael and Andy, his captains of the operation. Lawrence was Director at the Department of Institutional Integrity. He'd spent three decades investigating the policy and ethics of major corporations. Stone Enterprises had been on his radar for quite some time and as he began pushing around the idea of retirement, he'd decided to execute his career-long fantasy of bringing them down. Some companies were too big to go after, and Victor Stone ran one of them. The days of avoiding the big dogs were behind Lawrence.

"We'll conduct a thorough investigation, get the warrants, and take them down," Lawrence said.

"I don't agree with this," Andy said. Michael kept quiet, a team player all the way, even though he believed Lawrence was in over his head.

"They keep records somewhere that haven't been doctored."

"They won't see the light of day. I'm sure they're well aware that they're under scrutiny. We've done this already. We had Kustov."

"Kustov was two years ago. His whole staff is new."

"They've covered their tracks," Andy said.

"Right," Michael said, adding his two cents. "But what you can't cover up is income. Everything has to be accounted for. Even the doctored books will have gaps."

"I'm not saying we're going to find anything," Lawrence said. "Stone Enterprises deals under the table. We all know it's true. If we kick down their doors and flash warrants, we'll find nothing."

"And if we place another agent inside, the same will happen. They know what they're doing over there. I think our resources would best be utilized on other things. We're not even certain there's anything to find."

"*I ever tell you guys I spent my last two college years blissed out on pot, hash, and pills?*" *Lawrence said.* "*We sold party bowls brimmed with Valium, Seconal, and Black Beauties, while our speakers blasted The Dead and Janis Joplin. We started selling hash to fund the good times. The timing was fortuitous. Eleven states had reduced the penalty for pot possession making it tantamount to receiving a parking ticket, while thirty other states had eliminated jail for first time offenders. So, of course, we believed we were invincible, but when you believe you're invincible, you let your guard down. You get sloppy and your weaknesses are exposed.*"

"*Victor Stone and Bernard Bell aren't blissed out college kids. They cover their bases.*"

"*I thought we had too. Then my roommate sold me out and bought himself immunity. He was my partner from the beginning. If memory serves me, the idea to sell was his from the start. But freedom can be bought, and he bought his at the cost of mine.*"

"*Stone Enterprises is the exception to that rule.*"

"*What does exception to the rule mean? If there's an exception to a rule, then it's not a rule. Even the largest company trickles down, all the way down to the mail-room clerks. There's always an intern, an outcast, or an ex-employee with an ax to grind. You think I'd bring you my proposal if I didn't already have my rat?*"

Andy and Michael stared at Lawrence, waiting for the rest.

"*Who's the rat?*" *Andy finally asked.*

On the sixth floor of Stone Enterprises, one floor below where business was conducted, and far from reach of human contact beyond an occasional janitor, Adlar Wilcox stared at a computer screen, not noticing as Cory entered without invitation. Adlar looked up suddenly as Cory's shadow covered his work area.

"*I didn't hear you knock,*" *Adlar said, skittishly, as he covered his computer screen.*

"*I didn't knock.*"

"*But...this is my office.*"

"*It's not an office. It's a room we let you use.*"

Adlar quickly shut his mouth, afraid to confront the man.

"*Victor wants you to start logging what you're doing; time started and stopped and a description of the task.*"

"*I've been working. I swear.*"

"*We need to see it.*"

"*Fine,*" *Adlar said, slouching in his seat. He'd been gaming, but there was nothing else to do. If he had to invent tasks to keep them happy, it would take extra time, but was doable.*

"And make sure you're on time from now on."

"I never had a schedule."

"Not my rules," Cory said, throwing his hands in the air, pretending to disown the rules, which actually were his. In fact, he hadn't spoken with Victor at all.

"How come you're picking on me?" Adlar asked. He looked up and watched Cory's face become skewed with confusion. It wasn't like Adlar to become confrontational, but it had been on his mind for some time. He'd jumped through every hoop with respect and he was still being harassed.

"I earned my way," Cory said. "You cheated your way. You don't deserve to be here and I won't kiss your ass."

He left Adlar on that note, which rolled off him easily. The constant insults and bullying had become common, and didn't even come across as threatening anymore. Still, Adlar preferred to command a little respect. After the virus incident, he'd hoped they'd find him useful.

He grabbed his laptop and stuffed it in a back-pack, exiting the building without a word to anyone. The hallway to the elevator was empty and took him to an elevator, which brought him to the parking garage, where he exited and walked to a bus-stop every day. From the bus-stop, it was a six block walk back to his home, with one detour on the way: a comic book store.

He entered just before close and flipped through comics, wishing he were the characters on the pages—usually the villain, but sometimes the hero—depending on the day. The best stories had the most evil of villains—the guy you wanted to root against.

"You gotta buy it Wilcox! You can't just read em!" a man behind the counter shouted without moving from his post.

"I'm not! Geez. I'm gonna buy it. I just wanna make sure I want it first," he muttered to himself.

"You're reading it!" the man shouted.

"I'm not!"

Moments later, Adlar finished the page, set it back, and edged out the door as the man called out to remind Adlar they weren't a library. He picked up his pace, trying to escape the sound of the man's voice, and suddenly came to a halt, nearly running into a man. He looked up to find Lawrence standing in his path. Before he could maneuver around him and continue on his path, Lawrence put his hand on his shoulder.

"Adlar Wilcox..."

Adlar stopped and sized Lawrence up, trying to place him. He wore a dark suit and tie and a business-like expression was plastered to his face. Adlar thought about running, but if this meeting wasn't by chance, he'd probably see him later anyway. Aside from that, his curiosity would eat at him if he didn't at least find out how the man knew his name.

"I'm here to talk to you about Stone Enterprises."

"Okay?" This could be better than he'd expected. Lawrence was friendly, and he certainly didn't work for Victor. Maybe he was the competition, poaching Victor's people. Maybe Adlar would even wind up in a comfy position where people treated him like he mattered.

"Are you aware that Stone Enterprises is running illegal business practices?"

Adlar tensed up. It made no sense for anyone to be talking to him about something like this.

"He is, and the DII is closing in."

"So what? What did I do?"

"Nothing, which is why you have nothing to worry about."

"Then what do you want?"

Lawrence offered Adlar a cigarette. He rejected it.

"Stone Enterprises is about to crumble. When that happens, a lot of people will go down."

"When?"

"Soon. Hopefully sooner with your help."

"I only do on-line security."

"I know. You're also working on your own floor away from operations, being paid a very low wage, without a future."

"What do you want? I need to go."

"I want you to help me bring down Stone Enterprises," Lawrence said.

"Can't you just get someone else?" Adlar asked.

"We don't want someone else," Lawrence said.

"So what do you want?" Adlar asked after an awkward pause.

"We believe Stone Enterprises uses compromised credit cards to buy electrical goods, which they have delivered to a double layer of mailbox addresses to reduce the connection between fraudsters and the goods, and then later sell them on-line both inside and outside the UK. They also used the stolen card details to set up on-line gambling accounts and divert the winnings, directing stolen money to hundreds of bank accounts. Most of these accounts are fake, and they use them to filter money."

"Nice," Adlar said, impressed.

"No, it's not nice at all. It's illegal."

"I just mean it's smart."

"If you like going to prison, it's smart."

"Just saying. Geez..."

Lawrence took his glasses off and wiped them with his shirt as he continued. "Police ran an investigation and then raided the company two *years ago, issuing an arrest warrant for a man who worked for the company who went by the name Peyton. This resulted in a raid which resulted in the arrest of a man named Estonian Aleksei Kusov, but not before Kusov was able to trigger a system that encrypted the records held on the company's computers. Despite police IT expert efforts, the data has not been decrypted."*

"How did he trigger it?"

"He had a switch on his desk. All he had to do was flick it. He was ready for us."

Adlar laughed, unable to hide his admiration.

Lawrence continued. "And now we have nothing and please, this isn't funny."

"There's nothing I can do," Adlar said, shrugging his shoulders.

"Everything in Stone Enterprises filters through their systems, but we can't get to it. You're new, young, and smack dab in the middle of it all. You have your life ahead of you and you have more to gain in helping us than sticking with them. Ask yourself if you want to be caught in the bust when we kick their doors in."

"I didn't do anything wrong."

"Maybe not before, but now you're an accomplice."

"I didn't know anything until you told me, and I still don't know for sure that it's true."

"Now that I've spoken to you, I don't doubt you'll look for yourself for confirmation. Then, it's up to you how you want to proceed, but if you go down with the company, and it will go down, then you'll never have credibility again. You want that on your record?"

The blank stare on Adlar's face showed Lawrence he didn't really care much about his record, so he took another approach.

"They won't have the Internet in prison. If you want to buy yourself some good will, then help us out."

"When those guys find out, they'll kill me."

"Forget them. Your name would never have to come up. I'll see to it that they're put away and that your reputation isn't tarnished."

"That's probably the best job I'll ever have."

"With me in your good graces, you'd have nothing to worry about. If everything goes as planned, you wouldn't even have to testify. You'd never be revealed."

"So I just have to decide now?"

"Of course not, but I'm on the edge of my seat here. We're ready to set this thing in motion, so we're waiting on you to do what you do best. Use your Internet savvy to find the paper-trail and get it to me."

Adlar thought for a long moment. Lawrence waited patiently, hoping to bring an answer back to the bureau.

"Immunity," Adlar said, unexpectedly. Lawrence looked up, trying to conceal his excitement. "And a job. And you gotta write it down so I know..."

Lawrence nodded, putting Adlar's demands into perspective in his head. For now, he could agree and iron out the details later. They needed Adlar, who other than sitting in a dark room and being on Victor Stone's payroll, would be insignificant to him. Adlar Wilcox, who somehow managed to increase his value by wedging himself directly between Victor Stone and Lawrence Curtola. Adlar Wilcox...

...stood in a gathering of trees and watched as cars passed by outside the gates. He was surrounded by tombstones, disrespectfully walking on the grass where those who'd passed were buried. He shoved his hands in his pockets and slowly followed the line of parked cars to where a funeral was in procession.

The casket dangled above the ground with Abby Palmer's body securely inside. The gathering was large; friends, family, clients, co-workers, and Charlie Palmer in front and center—the man who Adlar failed to kill when his gun jammed. He was unable to catch a glimpse of anything he'd hoped to see, though he didn't know what that was. He was disappointed the crowd was so large, so sad...

He tried to make sense of what he'd hoped for. Ever since Abby died, he'd followed the news, only to constantly have it rubbed in his face how perfect she was. He was aware of the fact that only good words were spoken when someone passed, but with Abby, it was ridiculous. She was the woman who could do no wrong—a woman without so much as a bad rumor to her name.

He turned away from the funeral, paranoid at the idea of being spotted, and followed the stone fence that surrounded the cemetery. He stopped at a monument when he passed another boy, about his age, leaning against a wall with a cigarette in hand. He looked up at Adlar.

"Hey," the boy said. "Want one?"

Adlar almost refused and walked away, but the boy seemed to want company, and Adlar was curious as to whether he had been at the funeral.

"Sure." He took a cigarette from the boy and gently put it between his lips and inhaled as the boy lit it.

"I'm Brandon."

"Adlar."

"Are you here for the funeral?"

"What funeral?"

"Never-mind."

Adlar knew Brandon was supposed to be at Abby's funeral and decided to prod. It wasn't as if he'd know more than the news had to offer, but he was searching for something else—some dirt, a rumor, something that would indicate Abby wasn't as perfect as everyone made her out to be.

"Whose funeral?"

"Friend of my mom's from work. She was murdered."

"Really?" Adlar asked, feigning curiosity. He was afraid the boy would look up and see how bad of a liar he was, but he was in his own world, obviously dwelling on what happened to Abby.

"Why aren't you there?"

"Barely knew her. Funerals are boring."

"Who killed her?"

"Don't know. I know sometimes cops keep information from people so the person who did it doesn't know they're onto them. But it might be the husband."

"Why you say that?"

"I dunno. I guess he was there with her. Whoever did it got away."

Brandon didn't have all his facts straight. Charlie had been on the couch.

"I wonder why someone wanted to kill her," Adlar said, prying for information.

"Yeah, she seemed cool."

"So you liked her?"

"I only met her a couple times, but she was nice. Pretty hot too actually. Everyone else liked her. No idea why someone would kill her. Fucked up world with a bunch of fucked up people."

Adlar's eyes narrowed for an instant, but he pulled himself away from taking it too personally. Showing he was offended would come across as a sign of guilt for sure. Instead, he sucked on his cigarette, closing his eyes as he took it in.

"Hope they find them," Adlar said, wishing the opposite in his head.

"Husband said he didn't see a thing. He woke up to the shot and said the guy ran off before he could even get out of bed."

Brandon really didn't have his facts straight, but Adlar started wondering if the misinformation was coming from somewhere else. Adlar followed the news, but couldn't remember the minimal details that seemed unimportant. If he reread the articles, he wondered if it was written that Charlie was in bed with Abby. If he'd said that, Adlar wondered what that could mean. It had seemed pointless to speculate on all the details the news had gotten wrong, but this seemed somewhat significant.

Charlie's telling the police he was in bed with Abby. In fact, there was no mention of him coming face to face with me before the gun jammed.

Adlar wanted to hurry back to the apartment Toby set up for him, do more research, and figure out what else was happening in the house that night. If everything worked out the way he hoped, he just might learn that Abby wasn't so perfect after-all.

If he only knew that, he'd be content with what he did.

2

Richard Libby's initial reaction to Abby's death set off a series of emotions that ended in anger. He replayed the events as they unfolded when he set out to invalidate Victor's will. He might have succeeded, which might have prevented this incident, if not for his attorney who'd stalled to save his own career when Toby O'Tool propositioned him. He'd meant to pay Toby a visit for some time, but got wrapped up with service, event-planning, and a recent bout of vandalism that had gotten out of hand—the culprit still unknown. Finally, when Richard had enough breathing room, he took an afternoon. He drove a long time, trying to wrap his mind around how he felt and what he wanted to say.

Toby was the instigator—there from the beginning, pulling the strings that ultimately prevented Richard from his goal, making Toby equally guilty. Unable to shake an inevitable confrontation from his mind, Richard journeyed to Toby's side of town to see him in person, finding him in his usual hangout with his friend William at his side, beers in both hands. Before Richard reached the bar, Toby spotted him and hopped from his stool, meeting Richard halfway.

"We need to talk," Richard said, wasting no time.

"Am I being framed again?"

"Abby Palmer."

Richard turned and walked outside while Toby stood in the middle of the bar for a moment, gathering his thoughts. He joined Richard outside and waited for his lecture.

"This have something to do with you?" Richard asked.

"What? Abby? Of course not. You challenged me on the ledge and I passed."

"This is what you wanted."

"I didn't want people to be murdered. I wanted to outlive everyone."

"For the will to be profitable, people have to die."

"You never understood this at all Richard. I just wanted to have the security. I didn't want it to go away. Everyone dies. I have a one in fifteen shot of outliving everyone like everyone else. And don't assume that her murder has anything to do with the will. Charlie Palmer's the suspect and that sounds domestic to me."

"One stabbed, another disappeared, and now one dead. You knew I was trying to stop this. I don't understand how this doesn't bother you."

"Maybe because I don't carry the weight of the world on my shoulders. If I'm pulling the trigger, I guess I've got a problem, but I didn't. I just wanted to be in the running like everyone else. You think I deserve the first degree every time something happens to someone?"

"All I know is that of everyone in that room, you were the only one who openly expressed your desire to inherit the money."

"The key word being 'openly'. I was sad when she died, okay Richard?" Toby practically shouted it. He was a great liar and everything he said sounded convincing, but telling Richard he mourned for Abby's death convinced even Toby that the height of what happened bothered him a little. It wasn't guilt, or regret, or any admittance that Toby had done something wrong. It was simply an emotion that resembled sadness because Abby had seemed okay—like the girl he wouldn't want to hurt because she probably had a personality underneath her beauty.

Richard held his tongue, ready to scold Toby further, but held back. He just needed someone to take his anger out on, but there were too many people to blame. Going after Toby was a crutch. This was the work of Victor, whoever broke into the Palmers' home, and everyone who secretly hoped to profit off Victor's death. Toby only wanted his name on the will, a sentiment that the bulk of the world would want in the same situation.

"Look, Richard, I'm seriously bummed about Abby. I felt bad about what I did."

Richard watched Toby closely, wondering just how good of a liar he was. "Let me ask you this: Now that we've seen proof of what can happen, would you be on my side if the opportunity arises?"

"Of course." Toby didn't flinch or hesitate, his voice was even and convincing. It was a convincing act. "But let me tell you something about human behavior. At this point, you can't prove Victor wasn't of sound mind. Yeah, he was accused of some bad shit, but nothing sane people don't do all the time. You wouldn't have won that thing anyway. So if you've got a new plan, it's gotta be better than that."

By the look on Richard's face, there wasn't anything in the works. Satisfied that Richard wasn't going to be asking Toby for help, it made it easier to agree to help if needed. Toby desperately needed the other beneficiaries to see him as one of the good guys. Being on team Richard was the right move. "But yeah, I'm with you if something comes up."

"Toby..."

"Yeah."

"What would you say to the person who killed Abby if they were standing in front of you?"

It was a test, and Toby found it interesting—a question designed to trap him. The best he could give Richard was an answer that wouldn't incriminate himself, but was also true.

"I'd tell them..." Toby said, pretending to think. "...She was a poor first choice."

3

Adlar entered his new living space, and opened his laptop on the bed. He stole a nearby Internet connection and plugged in. He pulled up every news website he could find and searched Abby Palmer's name, looking for every piece of history he could find on her. She'd never been arrested or picked up for anything remotely negative. Every story featured her winning an award in sports or medicine or accolades for community service work.

The more research he did, the more he realized he chose the wrong person. He chose a perfect person—the one who seemed to do no wrong. It was just like the world to throw this burden at him when he was already overwhelmed with the stress of how to get away with murder. Not only did he have to duck the police and hide his guilt, but he had to cope with the fact that he took the life of the most perfect person he'd ever run across. Even a shell of a person, who didn't fully comprehend the moral implications of his actions; how could he ever forget the girl from the newspaper clippings, who everyone loved while they called her killer a monster?

Because I'm a monster.

He shook the thought. Whatever made Abby perfect, Adlar never had those resources. Whether it was good parents, friends, or her natural beauty that opened doors, Adlar lacked those luxuries.

He needed to hide.

He wanted to keep moving through the list. He wanted to get the whole thing over so he could move on.

Instead, he was numb. He was unable to think of anything except Abby. All he needed was to know she wasn't so perfect, so he could convince himself he wasn't a monster...

...Since his encounter with Lawrence, Adlar searched records of the mysterious man, finding that he was well known in his work. He sat in his small office and searched every avenue for information that could tell him more about what he was dealing with. Most affairs within agencies like his were well covered and discreet.

As he was finishing up for the day, there was a light knock at the door. He let out a breath of relief when he found it was only Victor standing in the door-frame with a bottle of whiskey in one hand.

"*May I join you?*" he asked, with a slur. Adlar looked around the room as if Victor could possibly be talking to someone else. Normally, the man was intimidating, but there was a sort of defeat in his demeanor.

"*Uh, sure,*" Adlar said after a pause. He hated that he couldn't give quick answers and instead would always talk to everyone like it was a dumb question with an obvious answer, but caught himself too late every time. Victor didn't notice though. He took a few steps before stumbling and standing near Adlar's desk and sliding a finger across the edge while he observed Adlar's trinkets. He came across a comic book that Adlar wished he'd hidden.

"*X-Men. Mutant Massacre,*" he read, straight from the cover.

"*I just have that here cause I like it. I don't read it while I'm here.*"

Victor ignored his excuse. "*You're working late.*"

"*I was just shutting down but I had a lot to do. I wrote it all down.*"

"*You wrote it all down, huh?*" Victor said, teasing him in a mocking tone. He picked up a clipboard and scanned it without reading before tossing it back onto the desk. What's this?"

"*Everything I did today. Starting and stopping times.*"

"*Why did you do that?*"

"*Cory told me to,*" Adlar said.

"*Why?*"

"*He told me you said to.*"

"*Cory's an asshole,*" Victor said with a chuckle. "*You'll waste more time writing all that than anything.*"

"*That's what he told me,*" Adlar said, defensively.

"*Just do your work. You don't answer to him.*"

Adlar watched Victor with fascination, finding something he liked for the first time. He'd sided with Adlar—even over something minimal—over his trusted associate. Maybe Victor was tired of his equals, or maybe Adlar had grown on him. Either way, Adlar was beginning to feel like he had an ally for once. It heightened his amusement to find Victor flipping through the comic book.

"*I liked Iron Man,*" Victor said. "*Have a few collector issues from years back.*"

"*Really?*"

"*Does that surprise you?*"

"*Kinda. I didn't think you would like that.*"

"*What's not to like?*" Victor asked, his mind wandering. "*Comics have better themes than anything else you'll find. Good versus evil, twists and turns, double identities, heroism, ordinary people living extraordinary lives—fulfilling a life the rest of us fantasize about.*"

"You'd like that issue then," Adlar said.

"Who was Warren Washington?" Victor asked, noticing he was the most prominent character in the issue.

"Archangel," Adlar said. "He was my favorite. In that one, he has his wing injured and they had to be cut off. But then they grow back and they're metallic. Then he renames himself Death and fights against the X-Men."

"I was under the impression Archangel was a protagonist."

"He was, and he becomes good again after that issue."

"Interesting," Victor said, studying the pages.

"See, he hated his wings because when he first got them, he thought he was a freak. Then he realized he could use them for good."

"Every comic book hero turns bad and fights his friends at least one time," Victor said.

"Maybe. I dunno. It's still good."

"Yes, it is," Victor agreed. He took a drink from his bottle and stared at the wall.

"How come you came to see me?" Adlar asked.

"Are you aware that Stone Enterprises is a sinking ship?"

Adlar frowned, unsure of what to say. The honesty was blunt, and not well placed. Adlar was the last person Victor should be venting to, but here he was. "It'll probably be fine," Adlar said, awkwardly.

"It's in the air Wilcox: a sense of inevitable doom..."

"I'll stay," Adlar offered with some optimism. "Not that you want me to." Victor held his stare at the wall. "What are you gonna do?" Adlar asked.

"Find direction. It seems we've lost sight of what's important. It's good to be reminded—to become grounded now and then."

"I guess..."

"I saw you watching the other night at the party." He turned to Adlar, who gave him a blank stare. "My confrontation with Ms. Patterson. You're the only person who saw that conversation—or rather—that side of me."

"I didn't mean to. I was just nearby."

"I was dumped, and I responded like a High School boy. I was hostile and it wasn't a conversation I would ever want made public."

"I won't say anything. I wasn't gonna anyway."

"We all lose sight of ourselves and when we do, we slip. I've done it...Archangel...we all have. What's important is that we find our footing again—that we re-evaluate our goals. There's hope for you Wilcox. You get yourself straight and work for it and there will be hope for you."

"I don't get it."

"If and when a day comes when you're forced to choose between *everything you are and someone else, ask yourself if they'd do the same for you."*

"Okay," Adlar said, not understanding.

"Hell, you read comic books so you're a leg up on most people. You already know the most important thing: Anyone can be the bad guy."
Victor walked to the door, never turning on the way out. He said something over his shoulder, but Adlar barely caught it. Something about throwing the clip-board away. Adlar couldn't wait for the next time Jones tried to tell him what to do. Victor was in his corner and even confided in him. Victor had treated him like—well—a friend.

He thought about Lawrence again, a man who'd asked Adlar to bury Victor, an offer that sounded too-good-to-be-true until now. In the top drawer of his desk, a flash-driver sat, waiting to be used to transfer data that would end Victor and his corporation once and for all. Adlar considered the advice Victor gave him.

He took a long look at the flash-drive, considering his options. He slid the drawer shut...

...Adlar stumbled over a curb, almost falling flat on his face, but he caught himself just in time. He looked over his shoulder as if the momentary stumble might draw attention. No one was in sight—at least no one paying attention to him. For the first time, he wondered if being invisible wasn't such a bad thing.

He pushed through a door to a tavern and spotted Toby taking a drag from a cigarette and tossing it aside before going back to his drink. He stared at Toby for a long moment; the man he looked up to, the man who would get him out of this mess. To Adlar's surprise, Toby didn't seem to be working hard at all. He didn't seem to care about anything other than his drink and the blond at the end of the bar. He wondered just what else Toby was doing other than motivating Adlar to do the dirty work. He was moral support, but Adlar didn't understand why Toby needed him at all. If he really was dying like he said, why waste his time on Adlar or Victor's will at all? If it hadn't been for Toby, Adlar would have never found the ability that brought him to the Palmers' doorstep. He'd put all his trust in a man who seemed not to give a shit about anything or anyone.

He swallowed hard and approached Toby. After a moment of hesitation, he tapped him on the shoulder. Toby turned and shook his head in disbelief. "We can't meet like this," he said, the annoyance in his voice thick. "I need you out there doing your thing so I can cover you from the sidelines."

"I have to talk to you. It's not...I can't keep..." He shook as he tried to say what was on his mind.

"Use your words."

"She was a good person," Adlar said, his voice wavering.

"I didn't expect this shit from you."

"I know, but she was," Adlar insisted.

"Look, I know it's hard to believe now, but you did a good thing with the Palmers. Of course you're going to feel guilty, but you can't turn back now. That's why you had to go after the hardest one. Everything from here becomes easier. Either way, what's done is done."

He sucked in air, finding it hard to swallow. "Everyone liked her."

"So what? You think you've deprived the world? You haven't."

"I'm serious. I was reading about her and..."

"Reading what? The paper? Everyone talks up the dead. It's all fake. It's like how your parents didn't want you to cry in public and told everyone what a great kid you were when you weren't around, but when you are, they want you to shut your face-hole and leave them alone. Because the real you is an embarrassment to other people. We're all a bunch of assholes. Even Palmer."

"No, but I met her too. That's why I picked her. I met her once and she was nice to me when no one else was."

"Look," Toby shifted in his stool, trying to find the words. "I'm going to give you some good news and some bad news. The bad news is that nobody deserves to die. The good news is that everybody deserves to die. You following?"

"No," Adlar said.

"We're all dying. Every day is one day closer to death. In a hundred years, no one will know who she was. No one will know who you are. In the grand scheme of things, none of this matters. There's no such thing as everlasting consequences. We all go to the same place. Knowing that we're not all the Brady Bunch makes it easier to care less. A building blows up or a country does itself in in a civil war and it's tragic, but in all of time, it's just a moment—a small moment. Knowing that, makes it easier to improve the quality of your own life, because it's all you get: A speck in time. People will get over Abby, and tomorrow you'll be one day closer to your own demise, so in the big picture, who cares? All you can do is make your fraction of time as rewarding as possible."

"Maybe she deserved it more than me," Adlar said.

"Trust me: Everyone has skeletons. Even Abby."

Adlar nodded, unsure, but with a new perspective to hold him over until he could find a reason to be content with what he did.

Toby leaned in and became very serious. "But now you have to take out Charlie."

Adlar shook his head frantically. "No."

"He's a witness."

"I can't."

"You have to finish what you started. Your ass is on the line."

"What about you? I thought you were helping."

"I'm keeping the cops off of you, but I can't say the same about Charlie. If he saw you, he'll want revenge. You killed his wife. If you face him again, he'll kill you if you don't kill him first."

Adlar frowned thoughtfully. He'd come face to face with Charlie and there were so many things he'd expected in the days to follow which hadn't happened. He'd never considered Charlie might be protecting his identity so he could take care of Adlar himself. It sent a chill through Adlar to think that a single man would come for him—a man who hated him enough to hunt him down and kill him. He suddenly wished Charlie was dead—not for his own protection—but so that someone in the world didn't hate him so much.

"Adlar," Toby said, bringing him to attention. "It's too late now. You need to keep going or her death was for nothing. It only gets easier from here."

"How would you know?" Adlar asked.

"I know because we're going through the same thing. I liked her too. I'm responsible too. You and me. We're in this together." Adlar looked up at him, remembering why he liked Toby. "You want my advice? Talk to Charlie—from a distance. See what he has to say. Try to find out why they were fighting."

"They were fighting?"

"They had a big fight outside the hospital the same day you did the deed and it started long before that."

"How do you know?"

"I know everything about all of you. Whatever was happening between them, someone was at fault. They're not the couple you saw on the surface. He's not perfect and neither was she. The closer you get to this, the more you'll see that she wasn't the person you've been reading about in the papers."

"But you want me to talk to Charlie?"

"Yeah, I do."

"What does that do for me?"

"It's going to open your eyes. You're going to find contentment."

4

Richard needed a distraction to help him forget what happened to Abby. His distraction came in the form of a 19 year old named Joshua

Wylie. His long-time partner at the church, Benjamin, brought him something he described as right up Richard's alley. Joshua's family name was deep rooted in the church. Alan and Rhonda Wylie were devote followers and well known to the congregation. They'd been regular church-goers weekly until their other son Wallace died. He was the only casualty of a small earthquake which was barely notable on land, but generated enough power to create a wave that pulled Wallace into the ocean. The body was never found, the seas settled, and the Wylie family never fully recovered, least of all Josh, who became known as a troubled young man in the community.

Richard knew of Josh, and while tragic, kept himself out of the family affairs. Then, one day after church, Benjamin had a talk with Alan and Rhonda, who were fed up with Josh and wanted him to have guidance. Benjamin didn't hesitate to assign Richard to the case.

"What am I supposed to do with him?" Richard asked.

"Josh's parents say he disappears all day. He flunked out of High School and just comes and goes. They don't want to kick him out, but he has no drive. They were hoping someone could talk to him and try to inspire him."

"I doubt I'll have a new perspective," Richard said. "He's upset about what happened to his brother. We won't change that."

"Let's try to keep an open mind."

"What do I do?"

"Josh agreed to meet you here tomorrow at ten. Just talk to him. See what he wants to do and see if you can start an ongoing relationship."

"You know I've done this kind of thing before…"

"I know."

"You weren't crazy about it then."

"And I was wrong. You're a good man Richard. That's why I came to you. You care about bettering people."

"They have to want to be better."

"He's coming to see you," Benjamin said. "Start there."

5

Adlar sat where he was most comfortable: In front of his laptop. He wasn't in his usual routine though. Instead, he continually researched Abby. He stopped with interest at a new article. He played the video along with the link. It highlighted the usual points on the shooting with very little new footage.

A newswoman stood near the Palmer home, which was surrounded by police tape.

On the television, she read the highlights. "The shooter likely obtained the weapon illegally and only fired one shot. The police arrived at midnight to find Abby dead from a gunshot wound to the stomach. Her husband, a surgeon at Banner General, tried to save her but was unsuccessful."

Then suddenly, Adlar understood everything. He'd heard the details repeatedly, and he'd sensed something was off. The police hadn't pieced it together yet, but having been in the house that night, Adlar had access to more intimate details. He knew the time he'd fired the shot. He'd kept track of everything that happened down to the minute so he could work out his story if it was ever needed.

...Police arrived at midnight...

I fired the shot shortly after eleven. Charlie was there and awake and staring me in the face. Charlie was downstairs.

...her husband wasn't hit...

He wasn't even there. I fired the shot...

...midnight...

At...

...11:14 when Adlar returned from lunch. He was fourteen minutes late, but with Victor in his corner, it didn't matter anymore. Cory and Jones and the whole gang of assholes who stood by Victor's side could bully him all they wanted. In the end, they'd never be able to touch him.

He strolled past the cute receptionist who gave him a wave and a smile, which he returned awkwardly. He was at the door that led to the staircase when Cory saw him and hurried across the lobby, calling out to him in a friendly enough tone to make Adlar feel comfortable enough to stop.

"Wilcox," he said with a smile, which faded and became serious. "I haven't seen your work reports for the last two days."

"What work reports?" Adlar asked, feigning confusion.

"What you're doing. When you're doing it? Ring a bell?"

"Oh..." Adlar turned to the cute receptionist, who was pretending not to eavesdrop. A few other employees stood by, curiously watching the exchange. On another day, Adlar would tense up, but Victor had his back. He could tell Cory what Victor said, and it would make him look like an asshole. "I thought it didn't matter anymore."

"Why wouldn't it matter anymore? We had this discussion less than a week ago."

Suddenly, Adlar spotted Victor on the tier above from the corner of his eye and felt safe—even courageous. He turned back to Cory, maintaining his strongest composure. "I'm always working, okay?"

"It's not okay. We take things seriously here. The company doesn't pay

you to download porn all day."

"That's not what I do."

"Okay, play Space Avengers then."

"There's no game called Space Avengers. How can I play a game that doesn't exist? You're just not..." Adlar stopped himself before he could finish his statement, but it was too late.

"I'm not what?" Cory said, getting in Adlar's face. *"Speak up."*

"...Not smart," Adlar said. *"You act like I don't belong here, but what do you do? I'm way smarter than you."*

For once, Cory was speechless. He was a tough man, but being called *"not smart"* in front of a crowd of people at Stone Enterprises by Adlar Wilcox; worst of all: it was an insult that Adlar sincerely meant. Through Adlar's eyes, Cory was intellectually inferior and if they were to go head to head, it could turn out to be true.

Victor stepped forward, interested to see where the encounter would end. It wasn't every day that two opposing people stood head to head like Wilcox and Cory were. It was like a scene from a western, both gun-men facing off at high noon while the sun beat down on them. Only this was real life and Cory was a loose cannon and Adlar, so easily disposable.

"What did you say?" Cory asked in a low enough tone that no one in the room heard him.

"You're not smart," Adlar said, his voice shaking, mostly because what he was prepared to say next—what he'd been gunning for from the moment he saw Victor. *"And fuck yourself."*

The receptionist's eyes went wide. Robert Baily, custodian in training, stood at their side and almost coughed up his gum. Laughter was withheld. Coughing was suppressed. Everyone waited on edge to see what would come next.

"Let me tell you--" Cory began before Adlar tried to interrupt him again. Then, Cory exploded, his face red and his fists shaking. *"LOOK AT ME WHEN I TALK TO YOU!"* Adlar looked up suddenly, his face white. *"You answer to me! You do what I say! You're a fucking twig in this place! You got that? You're an extension of an extension of an extension and you mean shit! You don't disrespect me! You do what you're told! You're a loser! You get that?"*

Adlar tried to hide his face, but Cory was right there, leaning in. There was no escape.

"You gonna cry? You were a tough guy a second ago. What happened? You need to cry now? That it?"

It was true. Adlar could have burst into tears—maybe for the first time since he'd seen Dumbo as a child. He looked up instead, hoping to find his hero—his archangel. Surely, Victor would stand by what he'd said about

Cory and the likes of the bullies at Stone Enterprises. Surely, he'd rescue Adlar and tell everyone that he didn't answer to anyone. Instead, Victor stood watching, his arms crossed in front of him as if creating a barrier between himself and the confrontation.

"Then go back to your basement and cry, and fill out a time card for the last three days, you fucking embarrassment."

Adlar tried to turn and walk to the door but his knees shook as his feet somehow managed to carry him. Everyone held their breath as he disappeared. He walked through the staircase, almost tumbling with each step, his breathing heavy and his composure broken. He'd never felt this way before—so ready to crack and lose control. Thoughts of violence and terror flowed through his head. The thought of ending everyone who'd treated him that way—those who watched and snickered behind his back and believed they were better than him because of the way they carried themselves. When he finally got to his office, he fell apart, burying his head in his arms and sobbing uncontrollably.

Then, as suddenly as he'd fallen apart, his sadness transformed into anger, but a very controlled anger. He couldn't go crazy and lose himself in front of everyone. He'd be escorted from the building by security within seconds. Instead, he filled out three days' worth of time cards and emailed them to Cory with a brief apology. He pulled the memory stick from his drawer and plugged it into his computer and suddenly, everything Victor had ever done—corrupt or not—was on one drive.

He hid the drive and left Stone Enterprises through an underground tunnel that led him to the parking garage so as not to be seen. He stopped home, contacted Lawrence, and an hour later, stood next to him at a fountain in Heritage Square, a popular shopping and clubbing center. Adlar's eyes were still red and glossed over. He walked and talked expressionless, as if all signs of life had been taken from him. Lawrence stood with his hands in his pockets, partly satisfied and slightly concerned.

"Someone lit a fire under your ass, huh?"

"There was a lot to copy."

Lawrence nodded, trying hard to keep from jumping with joy. "We have paperwork for you to sign. I want you to know that I honor my deals. I hope you do the same."

"I do, but I have new terms."

"Okay?" Lawrence said, taking a step back and pulling his hands from his pockets. Whatever the terms were, he could likely honor them, but Adlar wasn't completely there right now. Whatever they had to talk about should have waited a day. His eyes were glazed over and he spoke in a monotone.

"I don't need you to protect me when I do this. I want them to know it

was me that brought them down..."

"...Charlie?"

Charlie waited a moment. He looked at the time, bewildered by the late night call. He stared at his watch and leaned up against his car, staring into the cemetery where he'd finished sitting at Abby's grave for hours. There was no sound on the other end. Everything felt wrong.

I'm being called by whoever...

"This is Adlar Wilcox."

Charlie swallowed hard, and quickly looked over his shoulder and from side to side. There were too many shadows in the trees that surrounded the cemetery. He slipped into his car and locked the doors. "Adlar Wilcox," he said, buying himself a moment to comprehend what was happening.

"Yeah, we met once. I knew your wife kinda."

"You knew my wife?" he asked, doubtfully.

"I saw her when she was dating Victor Stone once."

Charlie's eyes filled with tears.

"She um...she was a nice lady."

"Yeah, she was," Charlie said, trying to hide anything in his tone that might indicate he knew he was talking to the shooter.

"I um, there was this time I had a really bad night and I think she did too because it was the night they broke up..."

"You were there the night they broke up?"

"Yeah, cause she broke up with him at this party and I was there. He asked her to marry him in front of everyone and she walked out. He followed her and she dumped him and I was nearby and saw it."

It was the first time Charlie ever heard evidence of the truth, and though he was hearing it from his wife's killer, he believed every word. He could have appreciated it under other circumstances and suspected he'd be thinking about it later with regret.

"Why are you calling me?" he asked.

"Because they broke up and..."

"Why?"

"What?"

"Why would she dump him?"

"I don't know. For you. She told him about you."

Charlie's grip loosened and his mouth went dry. He closed his eyes and his actions the night of her death suddenly flashed before his eyes as he filled with shame.

Adlar continued. "She passed me that night and she was happy but I wasn't. And she smiled like, she knew I wasn't, and then I went home. But that's how I knew her and I thought that was nice of her. Cause no one else thought I should go to that party, and then she didn't want to be there and she acted like I was okay." Adlar lingered silently for a moment while Charlie silently held his eyes closed. "So, I'm...sorry."

And then Charlie's eyes snapped open. "Sorry for what?"

"Just...that she died."

"Why are you calling me like this? At this time? Where are you?"

"I'm..." he fumbled. "I'm at home."

"You haven't gone home."

Silence. "How would you know?"

"Because it was you," Charlie said, coldly.

"What was? No it wasn't."

"I saw you." The silence after that was long. Charlie thought maybe Adlar hung up. It was satisfying to know Adlar was clinging onto some hope that he wasn't seen and in that moment, Charlie was able to tell him the world of shit he was really in. "And I'm going to find you," he said.

"I wrote a letter," Adlar burst. "If something happens to me, it'll be read."

"Who gives a shit?"

"You told everyone you were in bed with her and that wasn't true."

This time, Charlie grew silent. It seemed the only person in the world who knew his deep dark secret was the same person who only Charlie could identify as the killer. "I was in the kitchen, having a glass of milk."

"No, the lights were off. There was a blanket on the couch. You weren't with her and you called the ambulance way later. Like an hour."

"Forty five minutes."

"So then maybe what happened..."

"You better stop right there."

"I just think that you shouldn't try to find me," Adlar said. "Because my letter says all this."

"I'm going to take this phone call as a confession."

"Why did you want your wife to die?"

"What did you say to me?" Charlie asked, fuming.

"You could save her. You weren't with her. You let her die. But Abby was perfect. Why would you let her die?"

Charlie's eyes darted to the trees again, from one place to another. Adlar held more cards than he'd expected—as harmless as the timid boy in the room when Victor's will had been—he'd wound up being Charlie's worst nightmare. "Where the hell are you?"

"What did she do wrong?"

"You're digging your grave you son of a bitch."

"I just want to know..."

"So what? You can tell yourself it was okay to murder her? Are you hoping I'm going to tell you she was a bad wife or a selfish bitchy woman? She wasn't. You took the life of an angel."

"No. If that were true..."

"I didn't let her die. She died immediately and I cried. I sat and cried at what you did. You've got nothing Wilcox."

"I have to go."

"Don't."

"I have my letter. It says everything I know. So you have to let me go."

"That won't stop me," Charlie said.

"It was your fault. You could've saved her and if you hurt me, everyone will know that. You did it as much as me. And you knew her and I didn't hardly. You knew her and you didn't want her to live either, so you're worse."

Charlie opened his mouth, but before he could say more, the line clicked on the other end. Charlie threw his phone and pounded on the steering wheel, the windows, anything he could break. When his tantrum was over, he was left breathless.

On another side of town, Adlar hung up his phone, unusually happy. The conversation was therapeutic. Charlie really was an unlikable man and Abby married him. No matter how many articles said otherwise, someone else wanted her gone—the closest man to her as a matter of fact.

Toby was right. There were no good or bad people. People just did what they did. Sometimes good. Sometimes bad. All Adlar did was cut a life a little shorter, and it hadn't just been his doing. Ultimately, her life was in Charlie's hands. He was the real murderer. Adlar was a stranger—Charlie, her husband.

She wasn't an angel. He wanted her dead.

Adlar walked back to his hideout with a new confidence and a fresh perspective. Charlie would be after him and Adlar already started something he couldn't finish. Before he could move on to the next beneficiary, he had to get Charlie out of the way. Assuming, of course, that Charlie didn't find him first.

Chapter 4

1

"It really can't wait," Richard Libby told Victor Stone outside Stone
Enterprises after catching him on his way in. "I came down here only to
tell you one thing."

Victor turned and raised an eyebrow. Richard was unusually stern.
The relationship between Victor and Richard had been friendly in the
beginning, but even Victor could see that underneath the banter Richard
was displeased with Victor's way of life.

"Of course," Victor managed a smile. "I can always make time for
you."

"I wanted to return this." Richard handed Victor a check for five-
thousand dollars, made out to the church.

"Was there something wrong?"

"We don't need it."

"Come on up to my office," Victor said with a smile. "We can talk
more on the way."

"That was really all I had to say."

"You've rejected my donation. You're upset. Walk with me."

Richard hesitated, but followed. He'd hoped to avoid confrontation. It
was months since Victor officially joined the church, and weeks since
Richard had endorsed Donald Jackson as a favor to Victor. In that time,
Victor had continued to be a no-show, but sent checks in the amount of
five-thousand dollars weekly.

He followed Victor to an elevator and rode halfway up to the seventh
floor in silence. Finally, Victor spoke.

"You're disappointed in me."

"Yes," Richard said without pause.

"Tell me why."

"I appreciate your generosity, but I was clear about what I wished of
you."

"What you wished…"

"What I want and you need."

The elevator opened and Victor walked out at a brisk pace, contemplating his words. "What do I need?"

"To attend."

"I haven't shut the church out."

"You're also not present."

"My life is busy. Accept my donation and don't worry about me."

"If you want to be a member, don't do it for publicity and pictures. You should do it to believe in something."

"I'll be there if and when I can."

Victor's tone was cold, but Richard pushed on anyway. All their cards were already on the table.

"You really like to play it safe, huh?" Richard asked.

"Richard, you're my friend…"

"I don't think you see it that way at all. I endorsed your candidate. I've welcomed you time and again, despite how members feel about you and what they see in the news and the papers. You know what I believe I am to you? A way to compensate for the way of life you really prefer. Booze, women, money, and as long as you send a check once a week, you buy your way."

"Excuse me?" Victor said, turning to face Richard. "I do what I do because you knocked on my door and asked for money."

"I was sent to do it, and you didn't give me money because I asked. You gave it to me because you're conflicted."

"I guess you know me better than I know myself."

"I know you can change. You can be a good man and earn your way on merit. You can't cover your bases with money. It means nothing when you're gone. Come back. Get involved. Get to know us."

"That's enough." Victor closed his eyes, frustrated, and took a deep breath. Richard watched him closely, seeing the inner turmoil. Victor was lost, and Richard was fighting the good fight, but judging by Victor's demeanor, it would have to be another day. "I'll be there if and when I can," Victor repeated, slowly.

Richard stared at Victor and decided in the moment to make a statement. He ripped the check up in front of his eyes and dropped it on the ground. "You either put everything into it, or nothing at all." He turned and walked away…

…Joshua Wylie ran away from home on average once a week. He lived close to the church, and though he had no idea what faith meant or even what religion he was, he found comfort going there. It always tempered him to sit in a row to the side near the candles and gaze at the statues on the wall, the colorful stain glass windows, and a light that shone down from the roof onto a cross on the wall. He wasn't sure what he really believed but the doors were always open and it was a quiet place to temper himself when he was in his worst condition.

He found comfort in the church, but was conflicted by that. He wanted to be angry at God for taking someone important from his life and disrupting the harmony that existed when his family was whole. He still attended, in search of answers, and though his questions were only met with silence, he'd always leave church, go home and apologize to his parents, and all would be well for a while.

Then, Josh's parents forced him to meet Richard. Josh kept him at a distance. He didn't want to be preached to. Somewhere deep inside, he knew the answers. The answer was always something along the lines of "God has a plan. Bad things happen, but we have to have faith. They're in a better place now." Those things might be true, but they weren't what Josh needed—or wanted—to hear.

That meeting ended, and Richard was surprised when Josh agreed to meet him again the next day in one of the meeting rooms where a luncheon was to be served. Josh almost didn't go, but decided to see it through. His parents forced the first meeting with Richard, but hadn't followed up. Josh wanted to get out of his house, and Richard offered opportunities through missions to other countries that he could potentially pull strings to get Josh into since Josh expressed that he wanted to be as far away from home as possible. Another place, completely unfamiliar, could help him figure out what to do next.

He pulled into the church parking lot and walked through the church double doors. He nodded to a greeter who smiled and handed him a pamphlet, before moving on to the meeting room where the luncheon was served. He looked around for Richard, but he was nowhere to be seen. He sat and waited.

If Josh had arrived ten minutes earlier, he would have caught Richard, and Richard would have stayed if not for a phone call from someone he never expected to hear from again.

"Richard," a voice on the other end said. "It's Phil Cunningham. How have you been?"

"Phil...I'm..."

"You got a sec?" Phil asked, excited and out of breath.

"What is it?"

"You're going to love me."

"Why?"

"I got you a one on one meeting with Judge Proctor."

"I don't know who that is."

"I've been trying to make things right. After what happened, I owe it to you and I'm not charging a dime. I started looking into your case and the insane thing, I didn't see that happening, but I talked to a judge and he was interested. He made me a deal."

"I can't go through this again," Richard said.

"There's nothing to go through. I took care of everything. Drop what you're doing. We need to meet."

Richard turned to the door but didn't see Josh. He probably wouldn't even show up.

"Another day," Richard said.

"It's gotta be now. He's headed out of town tonight. Trust me. You're gonna want to hear this. But he wants to meet you."

"You couldn't have said something sooner? This isn't my battle to fight," Richard said, trying to hide the irritation in his voice.

"It happened fast, and you have no idea how long it took me to track you down. It's ten minutes with the judge."

Richard contemplated for a long moment, wondering what Josh would think. He asked Phil for the details and made it clear that the news better be good. From the tone of Phil's voice, he supposed it really was something he wanted to hear. Maybe things would work out in the end after-all. The insane approach never was promising, but the chain of events that followed led to this moment. If not for Richard's idea, based on Micky Miller's words, Toby O'Tool may not have propositioned Phil, which would later ruin his marriage and career and generated enough guilt for Phil to pursue Richard's case on his own and find a new loophole—a loophole which might actually be promising.

By the end of the day, he could have good news about the will. He couldn't wait another moment. Even if Josh showed up, he'd be just like everyone else—unwilling to change his life. He was forced to meet him once. That didn't mean he'd keep seeing Richard, and if he did, then what? Save him like he saved Micky?

He grabbed his keys and left the church.

Phil Cunningham led Richard to a table where judge Proctor sat, scanning paperwork above his reading glasses. He had a full gray beard, but no hair left on his head. Deep frown lines had set in on his forehead and when he spoke, his voice mixed with a series of grunts and groans. He pushed his chair back upon seeing the men and stood to greet them. After ordering a round of burgers, they got to the point. Proctor asked questions about the aftermath of Victor's will, adding the events in his head as

Richard recounted them.

"What's next then?" Proctor asked when he finished. Richard wasn't sure he understood the question, but wanted to make sure the judge knew their situation was serious.

"Things have gotten overwhelming. We've been through one death and another missing—probably dead. I tried once to invalidate the will, but that plan was blocked."

Phil looked away as Richard shot him a glance.

"What do you want to happen now?" Proctor asked.

Phil spoke quickly, making sure to have Richard's back. "Richard's a good man. He's taken it upon himself to help the others."

"How many did you say?"

"Fifteen," Richard said. "Thirteen when you exclude Mrs. Palmer and Mr. Mason."

Proctor scratched his beard. "I knew Mr. Stone and let me tell you right now that it's improbable he was able to accomplish what he did in his life if he were insane."

"I understand," Richard said.

"Not for nothing, it was an admirable undertaking and I think we can handle this here, but we can't throw this aside without causing a fuss."

"I'll do whatever it takes," Richard said.

"Then bring me a majority."

"Majority?"

"How many of the remaining thirteen do you believe to be corrupted?"

"Two or three."

"Then it shouldn't be a problem. Thirteen living beneficiaries, including yourself. Get me seven supporters. Anything less, you're outnumbered and I let it go."

"That's it?"

"That's it."

"What happens with the money?"

"Most likely goes back to the system. Maybe the family."

Richard nodded. He'd hoped the offer would be a split pot for the supporters, but beggars can't be choosers. Richard had no interest in the money, but hoped to be able to offer incentive to throw support behind his cause.

"Good enough," Richard said. He turned to Phil, who smiled proudly.

"I sympathize with your problem and never thought much of Mr. Stone, but I need to know the group feels the same as you before causing a stir. One month from this date, bring me half, and I'll see to it that this will is wiped out forever."

2

In his mind's eye, he saved her life earlier the day she died. He'd walked back into Anthony's hospital room and delayed Ira from killing him long enough for the police to get there. Abby had shown up and involved herself in his rescue attempt. There had been no thank yous, or even an admittance that they were wrong for assuming Brian Van Dyke to be a suspect.

It all seemed pointless now. Abby must have been destined to die that day, having walked away from one close call only to be murdered in her home. It hit Brian hard. He'd thought no one would go after Victor's money, but between Ira, whoever broke into the Palmer home, and Anthony's attack, he realized he was in a very real situation—a situation where small acts of heroism were meaningless. Brian would never throw himself in front of a bullet and he'd never wrestle a bad guy to the ground. All he had in him was to pretend to be a nurse with the belief he could pull it off. He only did it because he thought he could—because it felt safe.

Brian needed that kind of comfort. He needed to feel rewarded. Since he didn't find comfort in people, he turned to other things—usually food. He'd gained ten pounds since Abby's death. He was on task to end up where he began: three-hundred and fifty pounds. Victor couldn't coach him. He'd once set Brian on a journey that he may have completed if Victor hadn't died. Now, with Abby dead, Brian was left to contend with his love for Victor versus what Victor set in motion. He assumed Victor intended on something else—that he didn't actually want anyone dead— just to fight temptation. Victor always knew what he was doing. It felt wrong to believe Victor didn't consider the possibility of actual casualties. It could have just as easily have been Brian. His door had less security than the Palmer's did. Victor left Brian unprotected.

The only way to cope was to eat.

He found a restaurant he liked. It was all around American food: burgers, steaks, pizza...anything and everything Brian liked to eat. His routine was an appetizer, a large entree with a side of soup, and dessert. He'd refill his soda twice and order everything with extra condiments. The fries were dipped in ranch and were already covered in cheese and bacon. The appetizer was usually a combo tray. The waitresses remembered him. He disgusted them. They talked about him behind his back. He was one of those guys who was fat and deserved it. He earned it. In fact, it was shocking he wasn't fatter. He ate fast and didn't chew much. His fingers would still be covered in grease before he moved on to the next item.

Brian could have stayed that course, but it was a few blasts from his past that snapped him out of it—two faces he hadn't seen in a while and hoped he wouldn't for quite some time—especially in his shameful condition. Miranda and Neil entered the restaurant that day, holding hands. Brian noticed them right away, and his face flushed with embarrassment. He was finishing his appetizer when they arrived. He'd hoped when he saw Miranda again, he'd be a better version of himself. Instead, he'd gone backward. She used to run with him. She'd doubted him and turned out to be right: He was weak.

Victor would've known what to do.

Their faces lit up when they saw him. They hurried over, grabbing a couple seats at the table without invitation. He tried hiding his plate but they saw it. Miranda's face displayed an awkward look, as if she could feel Brian's shame. The waitress brought the entree, which made Miranda grow even quieter, but Neil couldn't resist ribbing him.

"You got a family of four joining you?"

"No," Brian said, turning red. "I got some to go for later," he said. He'd need a to go box.

"You still downtown?" Miranda asked.

"Yup. Same old..."

"I heard you dominated that place," Neil said.

"Where did you hear that?"

"Your manager told Tobin and he tells us."

"Yeah, well, my coworkers are slow and they don't do much, so it's not that hard."

"Nice! So Miranda and I are dating." Neil said it as if he'd forgotten Brian had a huge crush on her.

"Yeah, I always thought you guys would be a couple," Brian said.

"I told her how you originally wanted her," Neil said with a laugh. Brian froze and turned to Miranda, who gave him a comforting smile.

"I figured anyway," she said. "It's sweet."

"K."

"Yeah, and how you called dibs," Neil said, laughing obnoxiously. Brian once liked Neil quite a bit, but found himself disliking him more by the moment. "But don't worry Bri. I always tell her to hook up her single girlfriends with you."

"You already tried that," Brian said.

"Yeah, and you flaked man. Didn't hear from you after that. It was cool if you didn't like her. We wouldn't have cared."

"That wasn't it. I just don't really like being set up with people I don't know."

"We can still find ways to have you meet Miranda's girlfriends."

"I don't have girlfriends," Miranda said.

"You trust that?" Neil directed to Brian. "Girls who don't have girl friends? I don't think that's a good thing. Guys always have guy friends. Must be a jealousy thing."

Miranda rolled her eyes. Brian wasn't sure they were a good couple. She didn't seem to appreciate the way Neil dominated the conversation with his booming voice and demeaning comments. She'd chosen Neil over Brian, and what did that really say about Brian? It meant that even as annoying and incompatible as they were, she still preferred Neil.

"You should come back Bri," Miranda said. "We miss you. You should ask. We could use the help."

Brian suddenly liked her all over again. She was sweet, and made him feel important.

"Yeah, man," Neil said, leaning halfway across the table as he grabbed food off Brian's plate. "Tell your boss you wanna come back or you'll quit."

"You should seriously say something," Miranda said. Brian saw she was serious. She wanted him to come back, which was something. He reminded himself that she used him in the past.

"I'll bring it up," Brian said.

"Do you even still want to come back?"

Miranda saw through him. He hoped she didn't see everything he was thinking. She probably wouldn't care if she did. She'd likely be upset if she read Brian's thoughts about how she'd picked the wrong guy and Neil and her won't work out. How she was compatible with Brian.

"Of course I do," he said.

"The waitresses there hotter or something?" Neil asked. Miranda shot him a look she'd shot him many times before. Neil couldn't take any situation seriously.

"The adults are talking," she said. Neil turned to Brian with a smile, begging for approval.

"It's different here, but I like it. It's more serious, but that's probably a better move for me."

"They want me back at the other store," Brian told Bob that day as Bob sat at his computer, trying to hide the screen.

"What? The uptown Wasp?"

"Yeah, remember? I was supposed to only be here a day."

"Yeah, I know, but you were a good fit so I talked to your boss over there. We worked out a better salary for you."

"K," Brian said, unable argue—unable to tell Bob he wanted nothing to do with this place, or training, or working with two power-tripping employees in the kitchen that fought for control with Brian in the middle. "I live close to there," he said.

"If this is about money, I can take a look at see what can be done. Unless you just don't like the team here."

Bob read Brian's mind, which he could never confess. "I like it here. I just was used to it there. I worked a lot of hours and they needed me."

"Don't worry about them."

"I was told I should come back."

"They shouldn't be poaching my employees.

Even though you poached me first?

"K," he said instead. He walked away, dragging his feet, thinking about Miranda and Neil and their relationship that was falling apart and how soon she'd need a shoulder and Brian could be there for her and finally redeem this terrible direction his life was headed. It had to be for something. He lost Victor and his cozy job at Stone Enterprises and his rebound job for the dingy hole-in-the-wall diner. There had to be a light at the end of the tunnel.

Then, just as he was thinking he needed something new in his life— something good—someone entered his life and set him on a new course.

The new waitress.

Brian prepared for his shift. He tied an apron around his waist, hardly able to reach both ends together, his stomach sticking out more than ever. He grabbed a handful of his stomach and squeezed, trying to gauge whether he'd gained a lot or a little lately. He was able to grab two whole handfuls below his belly, which wasn't a good sign. He tugged at his fat for a moment as if he could shake it off. Decidedly disgusted, he let go and hurried to the grill where Guy pointed toward the lobby to redirect him.

"You see the new girl?" Guy asked.

Brian looked out into the lobby and saw her: Jet black straight hair, a strand dangling over her eye, full lips, a dimple on one side of her face when she offered a crooked smile. She wasn't the type he usually went for, and she certainly wouldn't like him, but she'd be fun to look at.

It turned out, Eve Chaplan was easy-going. She immediately got along with everybody, and didn't care if she didn't.

When she came face to face with Brian, she narrowed her eyes as if thinking of where she saw him before. Then, after she remembered, she said his name and told him they went to High School together. She was a freshman when he was a senior. He didn't remember her, but she remembered him. "Sorry," he said, unable to place her face.

"I was super-goth back then. My hair was much shorter and black with red streaks."

"K," he said.

"Yeah, I can't believe that I used to think I was that cool and edgy."

"Oh man," he said. "I can't believe that was you. I remember you now." He didn't.

"Yup, those were my messed up days. I was Ms. Victim-of-Everything. Ran away from home at least once a month and hung with some pretty bad influences—not that I was any better."

"You're different than I remember. That's for sure."

"Different good, or different bad?"

He paused for a moment. She was compliment fishing, giving him a window to flirt with her. He'd kick himself later if he was reading her wrong, but she seemed to want only one answer. "Different good."

She gave him a quick smile and walked away. Brian thought she looked nervous. In that moment, he kind of liked her. He liked her enough to be a little excited. He smiled to himself at the thought of things to come. He'd been downgraded twice since Victor's death, but may have ended up exactly where he needed to be.

3

Richard drove back to the church with a smile plastered to his face. He counted the beneficiaries in his head, eager to start making calls to secure their support. Unless he'd pegged everyone wrong, he'd have no problem securing seven. He'd completely forgotten about Josh by the time he walked through the door where Ben looked up at him and shook his head with disbelief.

"Where were you?" he asked.

Immediately, Richard knew he screwed up. "He showed, didn't he?" he said, with disbelief.

"Yeah, and left. And who's going to explain this to his parents?"

"What did he say?"

"Nothing. I saw him leaving and hurried to catch up but he ran off."

Richard shrugged. "I sat down with him already."

"Right," Ben said. "And agreed to meet again."

"I learned all I needed to when we met. He doesn't have much interest in anything other than running away. He doesn't need me for that."

"What's wrong with you?" Ben asked. "Usually, you're helpful to a fault. Usually, I can't get you to give up these causes."

"I have a cause that actually matters," Richard said, simply. "I don't need to save a guy who doesn't want to be saved just because you're worried his parents will spread bad things about us."

"That's not what this is about."

"What's it about then?"

"You ignoring your responsibilities for the last several weeks. Your lack of dedication."

"I'll dedicate myself to something I can manage," Richard said.

"You're dangerously close to being pushed out of here."

"Because I'm not babysitting?"

"Because you don't care," Ben snapped back.

"I had something come up," Richard said. "It's not as if you've never told me to…

…change your plans for today." Benjamin turned to Richard, straightening his collar in front of a mirror as he addressed his partner. "Save your sermon for next week. We have a financial adviser, Harry Wallace, speaking."

"Why?" Richard asked.

"Our accountant walked me through the numbers. We're bleeding."

"I thought we were okay."

"Me too, but we didn't expect the steep decline in membership this quarter and donations have decreased with the younger crowd."

"How much damage?"

"Over thirty thousand."

"Whoa…"

"Yup. You talk to Victor Stone lately?"

Richard turned to him, analyzing the question. "I haven't seen him in a while."

"He's been absent. He stopped giving. Probably busy. You're his friend. Maybe you should have a discussion with him."

"You want me to get a check?"

"Or some ideas. Unless there's something going on that I don't know."

Benjamin could be hard to read. It was as he could predict what was happening, but appeared to be guessing at the same time.

"I haven't been impressed with him." Richard said. "He's in the news for questionable things. He's not a good role model."

"Who says he needs to be a role model? Besides, those are all rumors."

"There's a lot of them."

"Regardless, I think you'd agree that there are more important things, like church upkeep, congregational gatherings…"

Richard nodded, wondering if he was being selfish. Other things were slipping, and his own quest to save Victor was cutting into that.

"We're looking at major cutbacks," Benjamin continued. "Four churches went under in L.A. Last month. People are losing faith."

"Victor Stone's money doesn't save their faith. It's always been about

the message first. Cutting sermons to bring in financial advisers to talk about responsibility never seemed to do much good."

"Then what do you suggest?"

"The first time I met Victor, he told me I was a salesman, selling a product. He only gave what he did because he wanted me to sell it to him. I grew, I suppose, a little aggressive. He took to it. I think we should take a page from his book. People invest in products they trust that are reliable. Has the church been that for them? Why are they leaving? What haven't we sold them on yet?"

"Hey, I agree with you Richard, but it's not up to me. Can't reach people if we're no longer in business."

Richard nodded with consideration. "I'll talk to him, but he can't be our only lifeline."

"Of course not," Ben said, seemingly relieved that Richard was on-board. Richard turned and found himself facing a mirror, observing his own reflection as if he were staring at a version of himself he wasn't proud of. Influence always boiled down to money. He hoped that wouldn't always be the case, but it had to be now.

"I was rude and I'm sorry," Richard said, facing Victor with embarrassment.

"I'm not upset," Victor said calmly. From the look on his face, it was true. Victor wasn't easily offended. He dealt with people wanting things all the time.

"I still owe you an apology."

"Why are you really here Richard?"

"I stand by my convictions," Richard said. "I want you to know that. I believe that to be a member of the church, you should contribute—and not just with money. With your presence, to hear the word."

"Richard..."

"But you made a donation and it was very generous and I'm very gracious. What you saw this morning was a frustrated man taking out his personal issues on you."

"I see," Victor said.

"Still, I like to think I've come through on my end where I could. I helped with the endorsement of Donald Jackson and have welcomed you to the community."

"You've done an excellent job Richard."

"My message remains, but I would like to express it differently. I'm asking for one hour a week. And I don't ask for myself. I ask you for your own well-being. I'm not about the bottom line Victor."

"I know you're not."

"I'm telling you this because I want you to know that the last thing I want from you is money."

"Money's what you need though. And money is driving you in this moment."

Richard looked down. His pitch ultimately had to lead here. He only hoped Victor knew that someone else was pulling the strings. *"This isn't up to me,"* he said.

"Benjamin?"

"He's concerned for our future."

"Then I'll present him with a check." Victor pulled open a drawer and out came a checkbook. Richard watched, struggling with what was happening. He'd make the check out to Ben and Ben would take the credit while Richard was forced to do the dirty work.

"It should be made to the church," Richard said.

"Benjamin wants the donation. You don't."

"I was sent. There's no reason to..."

"Credit him?" Victor asked, knowingly.

"Yes."

"Do you mind if I'm blunt?"

"Please."

"I'd like for you to give up on me."

"Give up on you?"

"I made up my mind a long time ago about who I was. You won't change that. I'm not a part of your scenery. I don't do potlucks, soup kitchens, or picnics, nor do I believe those things extend their influence beyond a few dollars and relief until the next time you need a check."

"I don't understand."

"I write a check because that money will do more for the church's survival than my presence will."

"And we appreciate it, but I'm telling you on a personal level that God doesn't judge you by how much money you have."

"What then?"

"What you do. Acts of service."

"Your attendance is dropping. Your congregation isn't giving enough. You think I don't notice?"

"I know. Everyone notices. It's concerning."

"Yet, here you are asking me—one man—to save you. You rely on me to breathe life into the church and still have the audacity to ask for more than that—to give more of myself. What have you done about the members you've lost? What about those who don't feel the same about the church as they once did? Why aren't you saving them?"

"I try to help everyone."

"You help the wealthy first. You help me because you want me in your corner. You're no better than Benjamin. When all is said and done, no matter what you claim your intent is, you're sitting here asking me to save you and claiming you're here to save me." Victor ripped the check from the checkbook. "This will be in the mail today."

Richard had nothing more, except what he felt would happen—what he couldn't prove just now but hoped Victor would remember later.

"Someday, you're going to know that you don't have everything Mr. Stone. Someday, you'll understand that your empire wasn't enough..."

...Richard knocked on the Wylie's door, but there was no answer. A car in the driveway told him they were home—maybe hiding—but apparently they didn't want to talk to Richard. He hoped it wasn't because he flaked on Josh, but he still had no regrets. He simply wanted to apologize, see if Josh was interested in rescheduling, and start working on his list.

"What do you want?" a voice behind him said.

Richard turned to find Josh walking up the sidewalk with a gym bag in hand, drenched in sweat.

"You work out around here?" Richard asked.

"Do you actually give a shit whether or not I work out around here?"

"Alright," Richard said. "I'm sorry I wasn't there today. I didn't think you'd show up. In my experience, people don't usually want help, and something came up."

"I don't want your fucking help."

"First of all, watch your mouth. Second, you wouldn't have been there if you didn't want help, which tells me there's more to your situation than a couple of parents who want to fix you. It tells me they can't reach you but you want to be reached."

"Okay thanks. What do I owe you for the therapy?"

"You got friends?"

"Yeah."

"How you going to tell your friends a Reverend kicked your ass?"

Josh opened his mouth, but closed it immediately and couldn't help but smile. Richard nodded with a smile, clearly pleased with himself.

"I get it," Josh finally said. "You're going to try to come down to my level so I can relate and..."

"I'm only here because I've been forced to talk to you," Richard said, bluntly. "I did this on my own a long time ago...tried to fix people who were clearly broken, but I came across too many people like you and in the end, even when it seems as if I break through the exterior, they go back to being pissed off and feeling sorry for themselves. I'm here because I'm taking heat from my associate because your parents are high society. I'm not into that. I don't like sucking up and jumping through hoops for guys like you. Do me a favor and pass a message to your parents: Tell them if they want to fix you, to do it themselves. I've got nothing to offer."

Richard turned to leave, but Josh spoke immediately, stopping him in his tracks.

"They're the problem," he said. Richard turned back to face him.

"Then what's the solution?"

"To get the hell out of here."

Richard watched Josh closely as his face faltered for a moment, as if he could easily fall apart if his mouth kept running. He was ready to burst, and it scared Richard. He knew he would try to help and get invested, and if history repeated itself, he was in for a lot of trouble. But no matter what happened, ridding the world of Victor's will was first priority.

"I can help you get in with a team," Richard said. "But I don't want you committing to something until you're doing it for the right reason."

"Fine, whatever," Josh said, submitting to his terms. "I want to help people too. I just want to get out of here."

"I have a project I'm going to be taking on," Richard said. "It's not church business. It will take some time. I've got a group going to Haiti in a month and a lot of my time will be on this other thing."

"That's fine. Just point me in the right direction and I'll get in."

Before Richard could go on, his mind wandered, considering the time-frame he was working with. One month from that day, he needed the majority support to end the will. In 29 days, he could send Josh off if he felt he was ready. He wanted to spend time with Josh—at least make an attempt. He needed to take on both projects without compromising either.

"How would you like to help me with my personal project?" Richard asked.

4

Toby O'Tool kept himself in check after Abby's death. He broke every rule in his own book by being so connected through Adlar.

He'd tried to steer clear of the other beneficiaries, with the exception of Brian Van Dyke, who just happened to work at the diner he frequented often. Running into Brian on an almost daily basis had never been a tactical ploy. He'd tested him once, but realized Brian was neither a threat, nor a tool to be used. He was the most useless beneficiary—a waste of the air around him. He was forgettable, other than to insult for sport.

Toby had been a patron for years, and was thrilled when Brian showed up, and was also aware of other staffing changes. He'd noticed the new waitress, and noticed Brian noticing her. Toby caught Brian checking her out while her back was turned. Oh, the fun Toby could have if he really wanted to screw with Brian.

She arrived at his table. "That guy training you?" Toby asked, pointing in Brian's direction.

"Yeah, why?"

"We're old friends."

She sized Toby up, baffled that Brian and someone like Toby could possibly be friends. The differences between the two were astounding, and Toby had a smug look on his face that told her there was more irony in what he was saying than truth.

Brian noticed they were staring at him, and came out to greet them, giving Toby a smile that was less awkward by the day. Brian was warming up to Toby, if only because he was a regular who knew him by name and chummed it up with him. "How's it going Toby?"

"Just ducky," he said, finishing his coffee, while Eve waited for back-story. "I was just about to tell this young woman what a hell of a nice guy you are for a registered sex offender."

"I'm not," Brian said, instantly turning red. As foolish or unbelievable as Toby's insults were, it still made him awkward and defensive. Brian didn't want people looking too deep. He was afraid of what they'd find.

"No, he's not. But he's a big-shot. He tell you that?"

"No," Eve said, confused.

"Worked for the man himself. Ever heard the name Victor Stone? Took silver shits in golden toilets. How can you not brag up credentials like that BVD?"

Brian tried to hide by shrinking in place, but only made himself more noticeable. Eve saw how embarrassed he was and almost did him a favor by walking away. Instead, her curiosity got the best of her. "How did you work for Victor Stone? What did you do?"

"He was his driver," Toby chimed in, before Brian could find his answer.

"He's dead now, right? Wasn't he the one who died in the fire?"

"Well, yeah," Toby said, with an obvious tone. "That's why Brian works at The Wasp. Victor had a significant dip in errands since he died."

"How did you end up doing that?" Eve asked.

"Delivered a pizza to him once and he needed someone. I think just cause I knew my way around town. It wasn't a big deal."

Toby feigned a proud smile. "From pizza boy to big-shot at Stone Enterprises and back to waiter..."

"This is temporary," Brian said. He didn't want to make Eve aware of the giant leap back he'd taken. It was fun telling people why Victor hand-picked Brian to be his personal driver. Explaining how he ended up slinging burgers in a dainty diner wasn't so fun.

"Nowhere to go but up," Toby said.

"Well, he's great at his job here. Don't know what I would've done without Bri," Eve said, giving him a smile. She saw him struggling and wondered again what the true nature of Brian and Toby's relationship was. Whatever it was, Toby was making him visibly uncomfortable.

"No doubt," Toby agreed. "I was even thinking I'd get your manager's name and put in a good word."

Brian almost deflected the conversation, but Eve spoke up before he could stop her. "Bob."

"Bob," Toby said, making a mental note.

Brian didn't know why, but he wished in that moment that Toby didn't know Bob's name. He wished Toby didn't know anything about Brian. He knew too much, and he wanted to know too much, and Brian didn't know why.

"You don't have to do that," Brian said.

"I want to. I want to jump-start your career. I'm no billionaire who needs to be taken places, but I've got influence. Customer's always right."

"I don't want to advance here," Brian said, bluntly.

"Of course you don't. I just think you gotta do well at your plan B until something better comes along."

Brian didn't know if Toby was referring to his career or hinting that he knew about Brian's complicated situation with Eve and Miranda. Was that what he'd been doing? Going after Eve in the hopes that she'd lift him to Miranda's level? He wondered who he'd choose if both girls wanted him. As things were, only one seemed to, and Eve wasn't so bad.

Guy appeared in the window and tossed a plate out with ticket in hand. "Pick it up!" he shouted, cuing Eve to hurry off. Brian breathed a sigh of relief when saved by Guy, but before Brian could get away, Toby spoke up again.

"Sad about the Palmer girl."

"Yeah," Brian said, awkwardly.

"I guess Victor knew what he was doing after-all."

"Uh, maybe," Brian said. "If one of you guys did this, I don't really think Victor wanted that. He loved Abby Palmer."

"Well, he got her killed."

Toby studied Brian's reaction. His face became skewed, unsure of what to say, displeased to have Toby talking trash about Victor but unsure he was able to dispute it. Victor had, in a way, been responsible— assuming it really was one of them that did it. He suddenly wondered if the blame was placed on him, as he'd been suspected by Anthony.

"Did you hear about what happened earlier that day?" Brian asked, eager to let Toby know he was one of the good guys.

"Ira Moore? Yeah, I heard. Escaped death to be killed hours later," Toby said. Then, he did Brian a favor and did what any guy in the same situation would do for another guy. "Pretty girl," he said, eyeballing Eve. "When you gonna hit that?"

"Brian?" Eve called later. "You can come sit with me." She laughed at him, sitting alone at a booth with his burger and fries. He preferred to eat alone because he ate fast and often took too large of bites, or shoved too many fries in his mouth simultaneously. He knew an outsider would watch him with disgust. If he sat with Eve, he'd have to slow it down, count the seconds between bites. He pulled himself from the booth with great effort, and sat across from her.

"So was that all true?" Eve asked.

"Some of it. He was exaggerating. I had a pretty good job before. It wasn't even a really good job. Just a job working for a good company."

"That's still something. Before I worked here, I was in rehab."

"Really?" Brian asked with sudden interest. She'd said it carelessly, as if there was no shame in it. Brian couldn't even be himself eating in front of other people, but a girl can say she was in rehab like other people say they're going to the store.

"Yeah, I always had some pretty bad influences in my life in the friend department. Not that that's a good excuse, but my friends all the way back to kindergarten were trouble. I finally got sick of it. I was living in a place with nine other people and it was crowded and trashy and no one ever had money. They were all just high and drunk and getting in fights with each other and sleeping with each other's boyfriends or girlfriends. I just got sick of it and checked myself in."

"So, you just got out?"

"Yup. Wasn't that long ago."

"Damn. Sorry to hear that."

"Don't be. I'm glad I went through it. Made me stronger."

"I admire that kind of thing."

She smiled. "Thanks."

Brian became aware of how many fries he was about to stuff in his mouth and almost dropped them back onto his plate. Instead, he looked her in the eyes and ate them the way he would if he was alone—multiple fries at one time. Eve showed no judgment. Neither would he. Surprisingly, she only gave him a smitten look. She liked Brian, disgusting habits and all. Maybe it took one broken person to like another. Eve's recent addiction to drugs didn't scare Brian away. Even Toby failed to sabotage him. She simply liked him.

"I smoked a few cigarettes," he said. "But never got addicted. I drink sometimes but I've never been drunk."

She laughed to herself and shook her head. "I gotta say Bri: even though I don't do it anymore, I still think there's something to be said for at least experimenting a little. You gotta try it and get it out of your system."

"It's not like I'm afraid," he said. "I just haven't had a lot of opportunities."

"I work tomorrow, but afterward we'll go shoot some pool and get you trashed."

"What?"

"Shoot pool and drink."

"I'm bad at pool."

"So am I. It's not about pool. It's more about getting trashed."

"I can go out for a drink."

"Oh jeez," she said, rolling her eyes. "If I beat you, who cares?"

"I don't want to be someone who gets you back into the things you got away from."

"I wasn't an alcoholic. I'm just talking about a few beers. My gosh, you're so afraid to have fun."

"No, I'm not. I said I'd go."

"You'll go and get trashed."

"We'll play it by ear. I work tomorrow."

"Don't worry," she said with a devilish grin. "I'll have you home by curfew. What else you gonna do Bri? Go home and watch TV?"

As a matter of fact, that's what I'd do.

"Okay, let's do it," he said. It would be harmless. He'd be bad at it, but they'd be drinking and laughing and it seemed with Eve, he couldn't fail. She liked him. Maybe because he was nice. Or safe. Or maybe he represented the opposite side of the tracks; he wasn't one of the pricks she was used to who would always make her wind up in rehab.

The events of the upcoming night played out in his head. They'd have fun, have a little to drink. They'd kiss. Maybe he'd even get laid. Of course, he'd stop her before it went too far and he'd be the gentleman he always was and tell her he wanted to take it slow. He'd cuddle with her in his bed and stroke her hair and they'd wake up together and call themselves a couple. And at some point, Miranda would find out and know Brian moved on without her. And he wouldn't care because Miranda would be forgotten and replaced with his new crush.

They finished their work and the night progressed exactly as Brian had seen it in his head.

5

Excluding himself, ten beneficiaries responded when Richard called them together. Adlar Wilcox didn't bother to show, Christian Dent was absent, and Todd Mason was still missing.

Richard greeted them one by one as they arrived, but the tone was different. They all silently mourned the loss of a one in the group. Richard was unsure whether Charlie would join, but he arrived and sat by himself in a corner until he was joined by Trish Reynalds. They talked about Abby for a few moments before the conversation shifted to Trish's daughter Shiloh.

Anthony arrived like a man on a mission, eager to expedite the process, but discouraged when Richard announced it would be 28 days before the end. Anthony invited a happy Brian to sit with him, apologized for the way their last meeting went down, and was happy to hear Brian met a girl and they'd started dating.

Royce Morrow was willing to help, but kept his eyes on the door, watching to see if Adlar would arrive, relieved with every passing moment that he didn't. Maria Haskins sat near him, too timid to start a conversation, but Royce initiated a discussion with her instead. She thought he was polite, and eased as they talked.

Tarek Appleton sat alone until Aileen Thick arrived and sat nearby, trying to flirt with him. Tarek leaned in with interest, but Aileen knew he was just being friendly. She stopped mid-conversation when Jason Stone walked through the door. He looked relaxed and had a nice tan. She smiled to herself, overwhelmed by his presence—especially because he looked happy—maybe for the first time.

Richard watched them all, a smile on his face. They sat together in their circles, enjoying conversation, laughing, getting to know each other, seemingly...friends. In that moment, Richard wondered how he could have ever worried about this group being dangerous. He reminded himself that Todd wasn't among them, neither was a man in jail for murder, who'd already attempted to kill them from behind bars. He watched as Anthony shifted in his seat and winced, still in pain. He watched Charlie listen to Trish, but with a solemn look in his eyes. He watched the group carry on, maybe the only mutual bond between them, the doom they all recently felt. Maybe they were coping.

"You didn't think I'd show," Toby O'Tool said, falling into the seat next to Richard.

"I assumed you would."

"Whatever I can do to help."

"Will you be here in a month? When it really counts?"

Toby nodded, but the clock began ticking in his head. One month. One month and part of this group would either need to change their mind, or this meeting would have to be prevented. Richard was one persistent pain in the ass and this time around, he'd be expecting Toby to sabotage his efforts. All Toby could do was lay low and play along and search for a window of opportunity from behind the scenes.

Everyone quieted when Richard began explaining what was happening. Most were pleased, but some were skeptical, as if trying to decide where they really stood.

"I hope I can count on everyone's support," Richard said in conclusion.

"Where will his money go?" Aileen asked.

"His executor would take control of his estate. A large portion would go to his son."

Jason closed his eyes. The last thing he wanted was Victor's money, and he certainly didn't appreciate that Aileen asked.

"Should we be worried about what may happen in the coming month?" Royce asked.

"I would keep your eyes peeled," Richard said. "Obviously, by now we all know there has been an incident." He turned to Charlie, who looked down. "Whoever did what they did could very likely be hiding, or maybe among the group, and they're either too scared to act again or they'll be more aggressive. There's no way of knowing."

"I'm investigating what happened," Trish said. Everyone nodded with comfort.

"What else?" Richard asked.

"Is this a sure thing?" Brian asked.

"Is what a sure thing?"

"You really will make this go away? The judge won't change his mind?"

"It's a sure thing, as long as we're all here."

"I thought you only needed the majority," Brian said.

"I do, but I think we should all be here."

"But that was his will," Brian said. "That's like, the last thing he wanted."

Toby cocked his eyebrow curiously, while the remainder of the group fell awkwardly silent. And then Richard surprised them all, by turning to Brian and with a straight face, he said, "When I die, how would you like my will to wish death on you?"

Brian shrank in his seat, without a response.

"What else?" Richard asked.

"Why you?"

Richard turned to Anthony, who leaned forward, curiously.

"You knew I was doing this," Richard said.

"But why you? Why do you feel so strongly about this?"

"Because," Richard said, thinking to himself for a moment, "I knew Victor was doing this, and I tried to talk him out of it, and I almost did, but I failed. You've all been asking yourselves what he was thinking, whether or not he wanted to hurt us or give us an opportunity—whether or not he wanted to scare us or actually wanted us to kill each other…"

Everyone listened intently, especially Jason, who leaned in.

"…He was angry," Richard said. "But he was teetering. I don't know how many drafts of his will he had, but he had more than one. I know that much. He changed it often, adding names, subtracting names, but one thing I know is that he was never set on going through with it. Victor died unexpectedly; his life was cut short before he had the opportunity to find what he really wanted. He created his will because he was angry, but I don't believe he ever had the chance to shred it, and I believe he wanted to destroy it. In his last moments, I believe he tried to open his safe which held his will, because I believe he wanted to destroy it. So in answer to why I'm doing this, in answer to your question Mr. Van Dyke, no one else needs to die, and we don't need this money, and if Victor was the man I believe he wanted to be, then I believe he would support this too…"

…Victor stood with Benjamin on the altar, surrounded by the congregation. Richard watched from a side door, watching as everyone applauded the hefty donation that exchanged hands. Benjamin took it proudly, and managed to hug Victor which brought laughter and more applause from the crowd. Suddenly, Benjamin was the center of attention.

It was the following Saturday that Richard watched Victor walk through a crowd and to a podium where a group of men handed him an award. A banner displayed behind him announced he'd become the humanitarian of the year. Richard sat in the crowd, forcing himself to smile and applaud.

"I'm requesting no further donations. I don't want anything. Not in the baskets, not through the mail, not in your will," Richard said, standing over Victor's desk the following Monday. Victor looked up slowly, displeased to see him.

"You know Richard, as a child, my father said he had two puppies. They were brothers—inseparable. They loved each other and were loyal to each other in every way. One day, my father left town for a week and asked

the neighbors to feed the dogs, but they didn't. When my father returned, one dog was dead, killed for food by the other. Sometime in the duration of that week, one dog realized its own life was more important than his loyalty to his brother."

Richard shifted, uneasily. He didn't know how Victor had gotten so off-track, but it was concerning. It wasn't the macabre story he was telling, or the fact that it had little relevance. It was how little focus he had when threatened—how angry he sounded, even as he spoke steadily. Victor did not like being told what to do.

"My life reminds me of those dogs at times. I'm surrounded by friends, family, co-workers, your congregation, the people I've helped... They're all loyal until their own interests suddenly become more important. Perfectly good people who, if I were to put them in a room with one serving of food for a week, would tear each other apart just to better their existence a little longer. One dog died and one dog lived. The dog that died may have fought back, but I'd like to believe that some dogs have loyalty that goes beyond a meal—that he laid down and sacrificed himself so his brother could live, but in my life, I never really know who wants a piece of my success and who is grateful for what I've given them. I suppose I'll go to my grave without knowing the difference."

"If I've implied that I've ever wanted anything other than to help you grow in your faith, then I apologize. We're all tested Mr. Stone. We're all faced with a choice between right and wrong and no matter how hard it is..."

"I won't add you to my will Richard."

"I'm sorry?"

"You're a decent man. I would never include you."

"I don't understand what you're saying."

Victor grew distressed and suddenly began pacing, looking out into nothing in the distance. *"I've been considering actions I'm not proud of—things directed at those who I believe are the very people who turn their backs..."*

"Confess your sins and I will absolve you. Victor..."

"I created a will Richard," Victor said, his eyes glossing over. His distress was replaced with a darkness in his countenance. *"For those who have betrayed my trust and our relationship. I've created a way to reenact the incident in my father's youth with those dogs—maybe once I wasn't serious, but this feeling has only grown and the more they betray me, the further I take it, the more names I add..."*

"Rip it up," Richard said. He didn't know at the time what it entailed, but he knew the look in Victor's eyes. *"I'll do you one better: disclose who makes you feel this way and I'll talk to them. I'll show you that people can*

Brian Darr|93

be reached."

Victor took a long moment to think about the proposition, and then, to Richard's surprise, Victor challenged him. "I've just added a fourth heir to the list, an associate who once worked for me and has harassed me since I let him go. Recently, he pushed me too far. I won't settle for less than an apology and a promise that he'll never come near me again. If I don't have that, he will never be released from my will."

"What's his name?" Richard asked. "Give me a chance to show you my way."

"You won't reach him. He won't apologize, but I'll accept your challenge Richard. We've butted heads enough. Prove to me that this man can find his redemption," Victor said. "His name's Stanley Kline. If you succeed, I'll burn my will."

Chapter 5

1

Victor sat along-side Jones, an open portfolio in his lap. While Victor sat silently, Jones relayed his weekend activities.

"The Hyatt had this club and I was just going for a drink and maybe pick up a girl," Jones said. "No expectations at all, and you know who I end up with?" Victor sat silently, without acknowledgment, but Jones kept going, as if the end of the story would win him over. "A porn-star."

He waited for a reaction, but Victor was expressionless. His expression indicated he may not have been listening at all.

"She had the whole package: Curves, beautiful face, wicked sense of humor; she was a solid ten. I was intimidated, but she said she was used to these druggie assholes with mutated cocks and she just wanted a normal— mind your own business perv!" he suddenly shouted, looking up at the driver.

Victor jumped at the unexpected outburst, and realized it was directed toward the front of the car.

Brian Van Dyke's eyes went wide and diverted.

Jones muttered something and reached for the switch to roll the partition up.

"What are you doing?" Victor asked.

"Closing the partition. Van Dyke was eavesdropping."

"We're not talking business. It can stay open."

"Yeah, but it's personal."

"It doesn't sound personal at all."

"Not personal with you, but to the driver? No offense Vic, but you should be able to see this kid doesn't fit the mold. I don't know if you went through an agency on this one or what..."

"I hired him personally. He's a driver, which he's doing just fine."

Victor looked up to find Brian watching. He liked the partition down because he had made a habit of chatting with Brian over random topics—usually new restaurants in town.

"Been to Fonzellis yet?" he asked. Jones' eyes darted back and forth between them in disbelief. Victor was a known womanizer and Jones assumed he'd impress the man, but Victor would rather speak to a driver about food than a friend about women.

"The Italian place?" Brian asked.

"That's right."

"I haven't yet."

"They've got gourmet pizza to die for. Toppings you've never heard of."

Brian smiled, his eyes glazed over at the thought of pizza.

"Thai, Mediterranean, you name it. It's unbelievable."

"Nice!" Brian said, enthusiastically enough that Jones cringed.

"This is the real deal."

"Cool," Brian said. Talking food with Victor made him hungrier than he'd already been.

"First chance we get, we'll do lunch."

"K," Brian said, in his own world, wondering how he went from slinging pizzas to driving one of the richest men in the world around and being invited to gourmet lunches. Jones was right though. All he did was drive, and he did that well, but he wasn't business material. He saw the others talking behind his back, the way Victor's associates looked at him sideways and whispered things to each other and laughed. Jones was finally expressing his annoyance and Brian wondered if this was the beginning of the end. Usually people liked him, but not in Victor's world. No one liked him here. No one but Victor. He was protected now, but it would last until Victor talked everyone into accepting him, or realized Brian didn't fit the company profile.

They arrived at Stone Enterprises and Victor exited and met a woman outside. She walked him into the building while Brian watched, wiping sweat from under his hairline. Jones exited the car shortly after, and Brian eased up. Being alone with Victor's buddy made him uncomfortable. From a distance, Cory noticed Jones and hurried over.

"How was Vegas?" he asked, lighting a cigarette.

"It was great. Hey, you meet the new driver?" Jones asked, glaring at Brian. Brian pretended not to notice as Cory sized him up and extended his hand.

"What's up bud? I'm Cory."

"Brian Van Dyke," Brian said with a smile.

"It's Vic's gopher," Jones said, hoping Cory would hate Brian. "Speaking of which, do me a favor Pud..."

"Pud?"

"Short for Pudge. It's just friendly ribbing. Unless you're not okay with that?" He raised an eyebrow, challenging Brian. Brian suspected he had no choice but to be okay with it.

"It's fine."

Cory turned away to hide a smile. It was like Jones to antagonize people he didn't like. A little mean for Cory's taste, but funny to watch.

"Do me a favor and stop stuffing fast food bags under the seats."

"That's..." Brian thought for a moment about whether admittance or denial was the route to go. "...not me."

"Of course it's not. It's Victor Stone stuffing his face and hiding the evidence. Everything food related is you Pud."

Cory stepped forward. "I'm going inside. Nice meeting you."

Brian didn't want Cory to leave, but he was finally alone with Jones.

"Anyway Pud, Vic likes the partition down, so you need to tune us out when we talk."

"K. Sorry. I just liked your story."

"Oh, it's no story."

"Well, I mean..."

"It's guy talk, so know your place. You're the equivalent of the janitor at NASA. We want you around so the floor shines, but we sure as shit don't need your input."

"K."

"Unless you have a real contribution. You nail a porn-star lately?"

Brian shook his head slowly, to tell him no.

"Models? Actresses?" Brian pretended to think for a moment. "Yeah, didn't think so. Stop putting your trash under the seats."

"That's not..." he cut himself off, knowing the effort was futile. Before he could defend himself further, Jones was gone. Brian released a breath and closed his eyes.

He took a large bite of a third pound cheeseburger, which fell apart as he ripped into it, lettuce and sauce dribbling down his chin. He stared at the passing people in tuxedos and gowns as they entered a gallery which lit up the night with bright lights, lining the roof and soft music filling the night. He watched wide-eyed, enjoying the sights, dreaming about being among them; Someday, when he moved up within Stone Enterprises and lost a hundred pounds. Victor kept him waiting outside the gallery while the party played out. A good deal of Brian's job was waiting. Waiting and watching. Watching and hoping. It was motivating, but Brian was well aware that the cheeseburger in his hand was a sign that he hadn't yet been motivated enough for a change.

This crowd wouldn't give a minute of time to Brian, and he certainly wasn't a hit with women, but when a drunken blond by the name of Angela stumbled from the gallery and found her way to his car, he assumed at first that she was there to meet Victor. He spit a mouthful of chewed burger into his napkin, rolled it up, and tossed it in his fast food bag. He stuffed it under the seat and rolled the window down, trying to keep himself cool as she leaned down and gestured for him to talk to her.

"You got a light?" she asked, her voice slurred.

"No, sorry," he said, after some thought. He wished he did.

"In the car..."

"No, I don't. Sorry." The words were barely out of his mouth when he realized she was referring to the car lighter. "Oh, wait..." he said quickly, covering his tracks. He fumbled with the lighter and handed it to her. She lit her cigarette and while her eyes were diverted, he took the opportunity to stare at her chest. She handed it back and stood in place while she smoked.

"How's the party?" Brian asked.

"Boring."

"That sucks. So you're leaving or something?"

"When my cab gets here." Then, she had a thought as she observed the limo, the driver, and the empty seats. "You could give me a ride."

"I wish. I have to wait for my boss."

"Who's that?"

"Victor Stone," he said, proudly.

"I count in his building."

"Count?" he asked, confused.

"No. Account. I'm an accountant."

"Oh, gotcha. Sorry."

"Don't say sorry. You're not sorry." She said it with such a straight face, he wasn't sure whether she was joking or not.

"Sor..." he started, but stopped himself. "K."

"I don't live far. You can stay for a glass of wine."

Brian considered, tempted as ever, trying to decide what world he was living in that a woman like Angela was hitting on him. Maybe it was the power he seemed to have as Victor's private driver, maybe he really was attractive to her, or maybe she was wearing the highest prescription beer goggles any woman had ever worn, but he suspected if he took her home, he'd go inside. If he went inside, he'd get lucky. In the end, it would be a little bit of fun at the risk of his job. And she'd wake up sober and take a look at him and say something that would make Brian cry later and try to start a diet which would last half a day.

"Sorry. I really can't. Maybe another time?" he asked. Another time *she'd be sober, but she really seemed to be into him.*

"Yeah," she said with a smile and pulled a card from her purse. "Ask for Angela." She gave him a look over her shoulder that told him she most definitely wanted him to call...

...Miranda stood in the hall outside Brian's apartment, looking in at Eve, a confused look on her face. Eve didn't question her presence and invited Miranda in. Eve was hospitable and chummy with strangers—even females.

"Is Brian here?" Miranda asked.

"Yeah, he's in the bathroom. One sec."

Miranda waited while Eve walked to the kitchen and buttered her toast. She didn't call for Brian—just waited while Miranda slowly entered the suite. After a long moment, a toilet flushed, and Brian emerged from the bathroom long enough to notice Miranda, before hurrying back in and closing the door.

"Hey, Brian," Miranda called out.

"What are you doing here?" he asked from behind the door.

"You're off today, right?"

"Yeah..."

"I figured I'd ask you to go on a jog. I can't seem to get a hold of you, so I came in person. I didn't know you had company."

Brian finally exited the bathroom and looked from Miranda to Eve and back again. Eve was the only one who didn't feel awkward. In fact, she felt too comfortable in situations that others didn't. Brian didn't know why he wanted to hide her, but for some reason he didn't want Miranda knowing he had a girlfriend. Eve passed them on the way to the couch, and put her feet up, simultaneously flipping channels and eating toast.

"She's a friend," Brian said with a hushed voice. "But yeah, my boss called me in, so I actually do work. Or, not even work. He just needed to talk to me but I don't know why, so it shouldn't take long."

"I can wait to run if you wanna go later."

"Can I call you later?"

"I could stop by The Wasp," Miranda said.

Miranda was insistent. Uncharacteristically insistent. He could see that this was more than that. She had something to tell him. Maybe something about Neil. Maybe something unfortunate for some but fortunate for others about the current status of their relationship.

"She's pretty," she said, changing the subject suddenly.

"You think so? Yeah, she's cool."

"I didn't know you were with someone."

"We're not together. We're just friends. Well, I dunno yet. We'll see."

"So Neil and I got into a pretty bad fight."

There it was. She had a problem and she was at Brian's door. How convenient for her. Later, Brian would think of all the ways he could appropriately tell her to stop using him for a shoulder while dating his nemesis. Instead, he did the opposite—the route that lacked integrity that he'd wind up kicking himself for later. "You can tag along if you want. We could chat on the way."

"Sure," she said, brightening. "I'll drive."

Brian told Eve he was leaving and she muted the television. "Hey, my friend Miller's coming by. He's cool."

"Okay. Sure. Who is he?"

Here he was with the girl he wanted, hiding his relationship status with Eve, while Eve mentioned another guy and made Brian insecure again— especially if he was a guy from Eve's past. Eve's confidence was far advanced and he didn't want to know anyone in her life from the days pre-Brian.

"He's an old friend."

Old friend. Alarms went off in Brian's head. As far as he knew, Eve's old friends were bad news.

"Yeah, I'll be back," he said, making sure she knew he'd return soon and walk in at any minute. If Miller and her started feeling frisky, he'd show up. Or maybe they'd just go at it right there in front of him and he'd feel obligated to say something, but never would because he didn't have the balls to tell Miller he was the schlep she was dating.

Eve went back to the television, blocking Brian out. He stood in the doorway, about to leave with a very attractive girl, and Brian was jealous over an old friend he'd never met. When he thought about it, it really was foolish. If she wasn't going to make it a thing, he couldn't either. Besides, Miranda wasn't a threat. Unless, she happened to make a move, which she'd never do, but if she did...

I over-think, he thought. *I'm even thinking about how I over-think.*

His own thoughts were constantly in the way of what was next. He'd always been his own worst enemy, unsure of how to act or who to be or what to say. He never knew how to go with the flow, instead presenting himself as the guy that everyone needed to like—and if you didn't, then something in him had to change.

I should be stronger. Victor wanted me to be stronger. I should say something. But to who and what? Miranda's using me. Eve's going to go back to her old ways. I should stand up and say something...

He lingered in the doorway between two women—the one he was with and the one he tried to tell himself he no longer wanted.

I should be stronger.

Someday I'll fix that.

2

Prison had become routine, just as Ira Moore claimed it would be. Christian Dent began blending in, which he despised more than anything. It was a relief to know things, to understand operations, know how to get around the guards and inmates. He'd find ways to buy himself out of trouble, selflessly handing out candy and cigarettes when he happened across them. He'd been brutally beaten twice, and had regular encounters in the shower which he didn't easily submit to. This was the life he'd expected, prepared for, and accepted.

For now.

He focused on survival. People were killed for being stupid. Integrity, pride, manhood—all words without meaning. Ideas that standing behind only meant shortening your time. Dent refused to die and he refused to stay.

Wayne Dalton replaced Ira Moore as Dent's cell mate. They hadn't said a word to each other until the day Dent learned of Ira's death. He silently said a prayer, but looked up when he saw Wayne praying too. When Wayne caught Dent looking, he looked up and simply said, "Respect to the man who was here before."

And then they started talking. Dent didn't like Wayne because Wayne wasn't all that intelligent. He had nothing to teach, but they got used to each other.

When Wayne had the go-ahead to talk, he talked. That became the problem with Wayne. Ira was a talker too, but his words had substance. Wayne told him once, "I can talk about anything. Sports, current events, movies, music. I like to talk. If you don't like to talk, I don't need to talk. See what I'm saying? I don't plan on fighting or asking for anything. Not drugs. Not hand-jobs. I can be quiet. I can be talkative. I'm a chameleon."

Wayne wanted his time to be easy. He was willing to be as accommodating as possible.

"You can talk," Dent said. "Don't expect much in return."

"Good. Gotta pass the time however I can. I got stories. Lots of em."

"You done time before?" Dent asked.

"Enough times to know my way around."

"How long you in?"

"Two years at best."

"Hey…"

Both men turned to find the tier guard standing outside looking in. Neither man heard him coming, despite his large husky frame. The guard was Donovan Willis, who was physically built for the job. Even his shadow nearly drowned out the light in the room.

"You ladies staying smart?"

"Couple of geniuses in here," Wayne said with a smile.

"Couple of dummies who got lucky is how I see it," Donovan said. "Another time and place, we'd just save the taxpayers their hard earned money and execute you in the street. These places get awful packed. Always looking to thin the population. Being smart means being in my good graces. Being in my good graces means you're allowed to breath. Course, means you also say 'yes sir' to anything I say."

"Thinning the population..." Christian said, trying to comprehend.

"I need to explain myself dumb-shit?"

"No, sir," Dent said. "I understand. You murder the inmates."

Dent let himself fall back on his bunk as Donovan tried to grasp what Dent had meant putting it so bluntly. He'd simplified it, and it was true, yet Donovan knew he'd said it aloud so he could hear it—so he could hear that he was a murderer. Dent had effortlessly brought Donovan down to his level. He could have opened their cage right then and beat him within an inch of his life—maybe even another inch from there. Instead, he clarified for Dent, mentally noting he'd do it only once. "Call it what you want. Nothing wrong with ending a miserable life. Better than killing some innocent like you two done."

On the outside, Dent would've given Donovan a brutal critique of his grammar. Here, he had to find a way to play by their rules without completely losing himself. If he ever lost himself, all hope was gone. He'd walk the thin line between being a problem and being cooperative. Playing dumb was the way to go. When people thought you were ten times dumber than you really were, you could get away with just about anything.

"I'm innocent," Dent said, causing an outburst of laughter from Donovan. As much as Dent hated to make a ridiculous statement, he was satisfied to have shown Donovan he was just another inmate with no sense of reality. Every inmate came in proclaiming their innocence.

Donovan's laugh went on and on to the point that Dent knew he was just laughing just to be heard laughing. "Sure you are," he said before moving on.

"Who's the hookup on contraband?" Dent asked Wayne the next day while they worked out.

"There's a ton. Some better than others. Best to stick with trading until you know the market."

"Why?" Dent asked. He suspected Wayne tried to sound smart, without logic behind the things he said.

"You don't just show up and start asking for shit. That's all. Make time for introductions. You build a reputation as trustworthy. Usually, they come to you when they find out you're holding a deck or candy or something."

"I've got nothing to trade."

"You've never got nothing to trade. Favors are worth more than anything here."

"And if I need something fast?"

"I'd ask what the hurry was, but I don't really give a shit if you're gonna ask around either. Just don't say my name."

"You have no connections?"

"Nothing I've needed. Ain't no rush round here unless you're a junky, and they trade favors. They're always good for it."

"Who's the number one guy?"

"Don't know for sure, but there's a guy, Ziggy, who seems to be one of the better merchants. If you've gotta ask someone, I'd go to him, but I still wouldn't do it like that if I were you. You're gonna turn heads at you and that's the last thing you want."

"I just want a few items. I can pay."

"You think it's that simple, be my guest. I'll point the guy out, but that's it. He's got long hair and usually wears a black wife-beater. He's hard to miss. One of the fattest guys in here."

Dent found a place with the old-timers at Kern—the guys who didn't give you a hard time to sit with them, but knew you wouldn't last long. If you had no friends, you sat with them until you found a gang to associate yourself with, or wound up in the ground.

Dent observed Ziggy from a distance before making his approach. Ziggy was seated near his table, talking shop. One of the men who everyone called Dozer turned to Dent as if he was the gatekeeper of the group.

"What you want?"

"Talk to Ziggy."

"Got an appointment?"

Everyone stopped, including Ziggy, and watched Dent as he jutted his jaw in thought. "Appointment?" he asked, trying to suppress a laugh. "Why we talking about merchants and appointments? Who are we kidding? We all trying to believe we're beyond these walls? Let's call it what it is: give and take. You help me and I pay you. Whatever trust you need to build so I can use your services...let's just get that out of the way."

"What you looking to buy?" Ziggy asked.

"I'd rather tell you in private."

"I wanna hear it now."

"Why?"

"It makes a difference. The only bond we share is we were busted. If you were caught at a park with your pants down—well I don't think I want anything to do with you cause I've got a couple kids of my own."

"What if I tell you it's nothing you'll disapprove of?"

"Not good enough."

"Double homicide," Donovan said, hovering over the group from out of nowhere. Ziggy and the boys turned to him, immediately acting like everything was cool. "Christian Dent. New to Kern. Killed a couple business-men. Stabbed them to death. Ask him why. He wouldn't tell the courts. Maybe he'll tell you."

"It's no secret why I'm here," Dent said.

"I know more than that. Before they're loading the buses, I'm looking at the roster. Names, ages, background—every man that comes through here. Figure I'll be spending every moment with y'all, so might as well know what kind of shit-heap I'm dealing with. You're trying to gain some trust with the merchants here, so how bout you offer a little something to them? Why did you kill those two boys?"

Everyone fixated on Dent, waiting for him to say something. No one really cared why he became a murderer. Everyone's story in Kern was the same. Motivation meant nothing.

"I'm talking to Ziggy," Dent said.

Donovan faked a loud laugh. "Oh boy. I like the attitude around here. Most of these guys are smart enough to keep to themselves and not smart mouth authority. Every now and then, we get some dumb shit with too much of an ego to respect the chain of command. Love when guys like you show up. It's fun for a little while anyway. Never too long. Just until they end up in the morgue. You're looking for a victory—something in the way of telling the boys around here how you got smart with a guard so you can get some respect. But believe me, the little battles you think you win don't mean shit. I go home to a woman, a steak, a couch with a remote control and hundreds of channels. Your little battles don't mean shit. I'll just beat your ass and go home at the end of the day. That's free perspective for you Dent. I win every day whether we cross paths or not, and no matter how many cigarettes you score from the merchants today, you still lose. The winners and losers are separated by where we sleep at the end of the day."

3

Brian sat silently in the passenger seat as Miranda made her way through downtown traffic to The Wasp. She opened up about her relationship with Neil and one thing led to another before she was full-out ranting.

"He gets so paranoid like I'm doing something wrong just because I'm focused on school."

"He's insecure. Most guys are."

"You're not."

Brian almost laughed, but suppressed it. He'd always been his best version of himself around her, but if she didn't think he was insecure, she'd pegged him wrong at his very core. "Why would you say that?" he asked.

"You just don't seem like it. Your girlfriend's having a guy over and you don't seem to care."

"Probably cause she's not my girlfriend and she told me he was a friend."

"Neil would assume somethings going on. Like every guy's a threat or something. He even worried about you."

Brian couldn't decide if that was an insult or if he should be flattered. "Want me to talk to him?"

"No, but thanks. We haven't been going out long enough to be fighting like this."

"Yeah," Brian said, secretly hoping she'd already decided to break up with Neil. He could help her make that decision or he could support her. He hadn't decided where he wanted to steer the conversation.

"Are you supposed to go home after this?"

"Um, no. Why?"

"We should do something."

"K," he said. It wasn't so long ago that the situation had been turned on its head. Brian and Miranda spent time together before she ditched him for Neil. Now, the more she got sick of Neil, the more she wanted Brian around.

He tried to sort his feelings as Miranda waited for him in the lobby and he hurried to Bob's office, who sat at his desk, messing around on the Internet with a letter sitting open at his side. He turned when he saw Brian and gave him a half smile that told Brian that whatever he was here for wasn't good news.

"Tell me what this is about," Bob said, handing Brian the letter without so much as saying 'hi' to him first.

"I don't know," Brian said.

"I'll read it and then you can explain."

Brian grew uncomfortable at once. He couldn't imagine what the letter could possibly say, but Bob was clearly unhappy.

Bob read: "To whom it may concern: I frequent your diner often and felt there was a matter that needed to be brought to your attention.

Oftentimes, there is no consistency in quality and this depends on who is cooking the food. The only one pulling his weight is Brian Van Dyke. It seems to me his co-workers often do nothing. Please take this letter as a concerned customer informing you how great Mr. Van Dyke is. I'd like to believe that he earns more than those he works with. I'd also like you to consider adding tater tots to your menu as an alternative to fries."

Bob looked up and Brian shrank in his spot. Assuming the letter was real, it seemed Bob drew the same conclusion that Brian feared he'd draw: Brian wrote it. Only, Brian hadn't. Bob waited for an explanation, studying Brian's face, waiting for him to deny or admit it. Finally, Bob said, "I can talk to Guy and Mandy about smoke breaks but this is no way to go about things."

"What?" Brian asked, baffled...

"I'm not stupid. You wrote this Brian."

"No, I didn't."

"It has your full name on it. And Mandy said you mentioned tater tots."

"You told them about the letter?" he asked, panicked. It was bad enough that he was being blamed. Now Guy and Mandy would think he complained about them and boosted himself with a fake letter. Bob nodded, verifying his fear. Brian needed to think fast. He had to find a convincing way to communicate the truth to Bob. What was the truth? He already knew. He knew the moment the letter was read. Toby O'Tool liked to push his buttons. He didn't know why he did it. Maybe because that was his personality. He enjoyed watching people squirm, but he'd embarrassed Brian many times just to play. He wondered if the letter was meant to hurt Brian in the exact way it had.

"I think it's a customer," Brian said. "I might have mentioned some things to him, but I didn't tell him to do this."

"I see," Bob said, doubtfully. Even with Brian's input, the story wasn't convincing.

"Really. I know it was him."

"So you asked a customer to write it. Look, Brian, I've had no problems with you. I think you do great. In fact, this letter pretty much nails it. Mandy and Guy can do better. You're up for a raise soon. I'm sorry you don't make more now. You don't have to admit you wrote the letter, but if you have any problems in the future, I want you to talk to me."

"K, fine," Brian said, in defeat. "Can I go home?" He stared at Bob, not making his usual effort to be nice. It was bad enough that everyone pushed him around and he took it. He blamed himself for being the guy who tried to be accommodating, even when people didn't deserve it, but this was something new. Not only had his hard work and loyalty given him no reward—it ultimately hurt him. It was the same when he'd made an effort to save Anthony's life after being called a suspect for having stabbed him. When he'd left Banner General that day—the same day the Palmer woman was killed—he'd considered himself a hero. No one else did. Then, Richard called him out in front of everyone, as if he was one of the bad guys. All he did was second guess the goal to relinquish Victor's last wishes.

"Mind working a few hours since you're here?"

"It's my day off," Brian said.

"Had a waitress quit."

"Which one?"

"Julianne."

"I can't."

"Why not?"

"It's my day off," he said, obviously.

"If you don't have anything going on, I don't see why you can't be a team player. If you can't, you're really putting us in a bad spot."

Moments later, Brian stood in the pantry, tying an apron around his stomach. The strings barely reached. He tensed up as he heard footsteps nearby. It was Guy—the last person he wanted to run into. If Guy knew about the letter, there would be a confrontation.

"You're in front," Guy said without love, "We need a waiter."

"I'm not a waiter," Brian said.

"You are today."

"And we're not getting tater tots," Mandy said, appearing from nowhere with her arms crossed. Brian tensed up and withheld a breath. He felt like he was going to breakdown....

...A clerk stared at Brian doubtfully, but turned toward an office which was apparently Angela's. The clerk recognized the look on Brian's face. It was hope, a boy with a crush, except Angela was a fit, classy, and gorgeous girl. This guy was fat and nervous. Whatever impression he had, it was clearly wrong.

"Have a seat," the clerk said.

Brian picked up a magazine while the clerk went to track Angela down. When Angela saw Brian sitting in the lobby, his face came back to her. He was even fatter outside the car, and suddenly she felt more shame than she ever had. She realized in that moment the magnifying capabilities of her beer goggles and swore of drinking forever. She slowly approached and confronted him with all the courage she could manage.

"You're the driver, right?" she asked, trying to make their meeting as informal as possible.

"*Yeah, I thought I'd stop by since you told me to.*"

Angela signaled Brian away from eavesdropping range of her coworkers. "I'm at work," she said with a hint of irritation.

"*Yeah, but you told me to come by and gave me your card.*"

"*Well, you should have called,*" *she snapped. He backed away suddenly.*

"*Sorry,*" *he said.*

"*Don't apologize.*" *He opened his mouth to instinctively apologize for apologizing, but snapped it closed again. "You shouldn't just stop by someone's work. I could get in trouble.*"

"*K, well then real quick: tonight I'm going to a show and wanted to see if you would wanna go. It's like an Elvis tribute thing.*"

"*I can't,*" *she said, in an obvious tone.*

"*K, well I'm pretty much free any night after six, so if there's a better night...*"

"*How about I call you if I'm free?*"

"*Sure. Or I could call you if...*"

"*No,*" *she said, bluntly. Brutal honesty was all that remained. "Don't take this the wrong way, because I really am a nice person...*"

"*K..?*" *he said, slowly.*

"*Are you really going to make me spell it out for you?*" *she asked. She waited while he stared at her, apparently wanting it spelled out. "I was drunk. When I drink, everyone's my type. When I'm sober, hardly anyone is.*"

"*Ah,*" *Brian said, trying to play it cool, though inside his heart stopped beating.*

"*You'll have to settle for friends.*"

"*K,*" *he said. She studied his face for a moment. She turned to leave. "Do you wanna go to the Elvis thing as friends then?*" *he asked.*

She stopped in her tracks and shook her head in disbelief...

...Miranda.

There she was, sitting in the lobby reading a book as she waited for Brian. She noticed him watching and met his eyes for a moment before offering a smile. He liked her more than ever. No matter how many things had worked against him, the way he felt when he saw her smile hadn't changed at all. His legs carried him into lobby. He wanted to see her up close and gaze into her eyes. He didn't care if she knew he liked her. He wanted it to be in the open.

"Shouldn't be much longer," he said.

"That's fine."

"You sure?"

"I'm enjoying myself."

"K."

She smiled. She was content, just sitting there waiting for him.

He opened his mouth to say more, but Guy interrupted as he tossed Brian an apron. "Need you in the kitchen," he said.

"I'm cooking now?"

"Just while we're on break."

Brian turned to Miranda, who was buried in a book. She either didn't hear them or was pretending not to.

Brian walked out of Miranda's range with Guy. "You said I could leave at noon," he said.

"We're swamped."

Brian looked around. It wasn't swamped at all. It was only swamped to someone who didn't want to do the job.

Brian grabbed the apron and walked to the kitchen, which was the only thing that stood between himself and spending the day with Miranda.

Then there was Eve, who was back home, maybe with her guy friend. Still, he didn't care. He cared about Miranda—and getting away from the diner.

I'm going to tell her today, he thought. *I'm going to tell her I like her.*

As if she heard his thoughts, she looked up from her book again and caught his eyes in the window.

When Guy finally told Brian he could go, he lingered for a moment, working up the need to leave on his own terms—to let Guy know he was pissed off and did them a favor by being there. It was bad enough he was taking the heat for the note, but being treated like shit all day long...

"You're welcome," he said, under his breath. Guy didn't respond.

Brian walked back to the dining area to get Miranda, but when he rounded the corner, Miranda was there with Neil, and every problem she'd had was apparently forgotten. They were happy, laughing, flirting, Neil's arm around her.

"Hey Bri," Neil said.

"Hi Neil."

"Neil and I have to hurry," Miranda said. "We're catching a movie and it starts in fifteen. Any chance you can get a ride?"

There were dozens of things he could have responded with—all of them would run through his mind later—but today was bad, and if it got worse, maybe it would light the fire under his ass that he so desperately needed. He needed to embrace how shitty life was right now and use it as fuel.

"Yeah," he said.

"You sure?" Neil asked. "We can catch a late show."

"I can get a ride. It's not a problem. Go ahead."

Moments later, they were out the door. Before she disappeared from Brian's life again, she mouthed the words "thank you". And then Brian did the last thing he really wanted to do: went back to the kitchen and asked Guy for a ride.

Half an hour later, they sat side by side in silence as Guy drove, keeping his eyes on the road.

"You know," Brian finally said with a sigh. "I tried to tell Bob, but I didn't write that letter. I think someone did it as a prank...one of our regulars. I think you guys do fine. I have nothing bad to say."

"I know," Guy said, to Brian's surprise.

"You do?"

"Bob told me. You asked someone to write it for you."

"That's not true either," Brian said with a sigh.

"You never liked being downtown, so you're trying to get out. You're always whining."

"That's not what I'm doing. It's just farther away and it pays less and some good friends of mine work there."

"What about Eve? You're hitting that, right?"

"We just hang out."

"I know what hanging out is. You're hitting it. And she's here. You hitting any of the waitresses there?"

"No."

"Man, I was a cook on a Naval ship for a crew of two hundred. You think I like being in this shithole?"

"Really?" Brian asked. It was probably the first time Guy had ever revealed anything about himself.

"I got no better offers than this and I got three kids. I'm happy to bring in a paycheck."

"I had a better job before this too."

"Yeah, I know. You live in Skyline Apartments. That place ain't cheap. I don't even wanna know how you're living there on a cook's pay."

"My old boss took care of my living expenses for a while. After that, I'm on my own."

"You see? We're both working in the armpit because we got nowhere better to be. If we did, we'd be there. And I don't know what you complain for. You're living large and fucking the waitresses."

"There's no future with Eve. There's someone else."

"You hitting her?"

"No. One of my friends is," Brian said, realizing how foolish it all sounded.

"A friend? A friend at the other store? Man, you need to learn your place in the world Van Dyke."

"What do you mean?"

"You got a friend hooking up with your girl in that place. You're hitting the girls here. You think you belong over there and you're above this place? Sounds to me like you're exactly where you should be."

"I'd rather fit into something else."

"Don't wanna give up the fancy condo life? Well, guess what: your old job ain't your job anymore. This is. You're not the guy for the girl you want. You're the guy for Eve and she's not bad. I'm twice your age and I'm not the one living in the ritzy apartment and I ain't going back to the Navy anytime soon. You and I don't have that life anymore. Our best days are behind us. Lower the bar Van Dyke. Learn your place in the world and accept it."

4

Dent was grabbed outside his cell in a swift movement. Dozer wrapped his arms around Dent and held him against the wall, his face pressed against the brick. It happened too fast for Dent to react, but he quickly submitted. When he was secure, Ziggy appeared from behind a cement pillar. Though it didn't seem like it would be a happy encounter, it was the kind of face time he was looking for. The area was conveniently cleared of all life, other than Ziggy, Dozer, and his gang.

Ziggy stepped forward and sized him up. "Christian Dent, infamous drug dealer, snatched outside his home and resurfaced fifteen years later."

"Why the need for hierarchy?" Dent asked. "When will you ask yourself when all the cons in all the prisons would work together instead of fighting each other and rise up. There's a hell of a lot more of us than there are them, but they keep us fighting. Why do you think that is?"

"The fuck you talking about?" Ziggy asked, with a laugh, but there was something curious in his tone.

"They're afraid of us because we have nothing to lose. They're forced to keep order because they know there's consequences if they don't play by the rules. Not us. For us, we all die here anyway. Why wait? I talk to you today and the guard wasted no time preventing us from becoming allies, because we have a chance of getting out if we're together."

"I know I'm not hearing you talk about escaping."

"For a man who serves a role in a cage, I know you don't want to stay here forever."

"See what I mean?" Ziggy said, talking to his posse. "Thinks he owns the world."

"I want supplies."

"Then go get some. Shit, boy. There's plenty of dealers. Even dealers that will deal with a shit-stain like you. You come to me again, and I'll take that as a sign that you don't give a shit about your life."

"What's it take to earn trust? You want Donovan out of the way?"

Everyone laughed, but there was still that curiosity. Dent had a way of sounding convincing, even when he spewed nonsense.

"Yeah, we want Donovan out of the way," Ziggy said with a laugh.

"Done," Dent said. Nobody laughed. If he was planning on killing Donovan, it would be futile. Ziggy licked his lips and looked around at his posse, too curious to let Dent walk away without seeing what he had in store.

"Shit, I'll honor that. If you're gonna try to hurt that motherfucker, you're dead and I'm entertained for a while. So yeah Dent, take Donovan out of the equation and I'll get you a pack of gum. But don't show your face around me while you're doing it, because I watch the drama. I ain't a part of it."

Dent extended his hand, but Ziggy didn't shake. "I'll be asking for more than a pack of gum," he said.

Christian laid in his bunk, his face buried in his pillow, trying to drown out all light. When his eyes were closed and his face buried, he could be almost anywhere. When he'd open his eyes the next day and be reminded of where he really was, it would be all the motivation he needed to find his way out.

"You're not gonna last," Wayne's raspy voice said from the bunk below.

"I didn't ask."

"No, but you need to know. You're okay Dent. Knew it from the moment we met that you were okay. I don't want you replaced with a rapist or sick mental case with his brain fried. You got an ego. You think you're invincible. Not a good habit to have around here."

"I've heard."

"Then how about enlightening me as to just what's going on?"

"I'm not going to sit around with my thumb up my ass."

Wayne blinked, wondering if Dent was just stupid or if he had something unique in how he was wired—if there was some kind of substance to what he was saying. "You're stuck here like the rest of us. Don't go thinking you're special."

"Every problem has a solution."

"Ain't that a smart thing to say? You're in a cage with a few dozen armed guards and they stand on higher ground just itching for a reason to put one in your head."

"Like I said, I didn't ask for advice."

"You fixing on an escape? Tell me what you've got going on and I'll give you the history of who's tried and why it didn't work. You think every man in here hasn't attempted to get out through every hole in the wall? They give up when they know it ain't possible and the ones who don't, end up dead."

"Good work takes time. Climbing the fence when you think no one's looking, trying to hitch a ride on a truck or dress up as a guard or pay someone to lower a helicopter into the yard—that's predictable. I solve problems. Every safety precaution they've put in place was the result of an attempt. Every guard on every post has been strategically placed there based on history. As our methods evolve, they evolve to keep up. The only way to be successful is to be ahead of their evolution—to be an innovator—to find the next hole that has yet to be filled, to expose a flaw in their system when it's too late for them to fix."

5

Brian opened the door to his apartment to find Miller sitting with Eve on the couch. They were close, but nothing indicated anything intimate happened. If Brian had come home later, that might not have been the case. Currently, they seemed perfectly happy getting high together on the couch. Miller wore a black wife-beater, which was one size too small for his bulky body. He acknowledged Brian with a momentary glance and a nod before going back to what he was doing. As Brian came closer, he saw the blade on his dining room table and the rolled up dollar bill. He'd never seen something like this in person, only in the movies.

Eve made a half attempt to cover the evidence, but realized it was too late. She raised her eyebrows at him as if asking for permission. And though it bothered him somewhere inside, he knew this was going to happen and he wouldn't object. Eve waited for him to make his next move. Then, Miller looked up again.

"You Brian?"

"Yeah."

"Grab a seat bro," he said making space.

Brian turned from Miller to Eve. They weren't going anywhere and if Brian did, this night would end with Brian crying into his pillow while Miller banged his alleged girlfriend. And he wouldn't be able to say a word against it because Brian and Eve hadn't established just what they were.

He took a seat while Miller prepared a hit.

"Sure you don't want some bro?" Miller asked, passing Brian a joint.

"I better not. I work tomorrow. Sorry."

"No need to apologize. It's cool." Miller turned to Eve. "So you remember when we went off-roading with that Donnie kid and we tried driving up that huge pile of dirt by Burkes Pond?"

Eve burst into laughter. "I forgot about that. His jeep turned upside down."

Eve and Miller shared laughter while Brian awkwardly smiled, desperate to be included.

"His dad shows up at four in the morning with his truck," Miller said. "He was so pissed off. That guy was crazy." Miller began to pass the joint to Eve, but Brian leaned forward and intercepted it.

"You care if I try?"

Miller's eyes met Eves, as if asking permission.

"You really don't have to," Eve said.

"I just wanna try it. I've never done it before, so..." he trailed off.

"It's cool bro," Miller said, passing Brian the joint.

Brian hesitantly put the joint in his mouth and inhaled...

"...The best Polish dumplings I ever had were in Krakow," Victor said, meeting Brian's eyes in the mirror as Brian glanced from the mirror to the road as Victor talked. "They were in a restaurant just on the mini-square. I could hardly walk afterward. Poland is worth a trip if you ever get a chance. I'd say it's the most beautiful place I've ever been, except it suffered terribly because of the war and Russian occupancy. There are still some beautiful cities such as Krakow though."

Brian nodded, listening intently. He didn't always follow what Victor said, but appreciated that he was saying it.

"Take a left up here."

Brian's eyes narrowed as he thought about where they were going. An idea came to mind. "Where am I taking you tonight?"

"Just take a left."

Moments later, they were in the parking lot of Fonzellis. This trip was for him; Victor was treating Brian. Brian was overwhelmed, but maintained self-control. Showing Victor just how excited he was might make Victor see him as pathetic. These days, Brian had enough of people seeing him in his real light. The message was clear: Brian had to change.

"You coming?" Victor asked, standing outside the car.

Brian stared at the restaurant, eager to enter, but unsure. He'd spent all his self-control drinking water and eating vegetables since his encounter with Angela. He wondered what Victor's intentions were. Would Victor try to have a conversation with him? At some point, he'd recognize that Brian didn't match his intellect or come near his success. Brian wanted to be close to Victor, but he had to change first—to earn the right to be in the position he was lucky enough to have.

Inside was nice. It was the kind of place Brian would bring a girl on a first date, if it were ever to happen. The menu was foreign. Most of the ingredients listed were things Brian hadn't heard of. If he'd looked at the menu a week ago, the desire to experiment would be strong, but he'd already decided he'd have to learn to love salads.

A waiter approached and asked if they were ready to order. Brian tried ordering an arugula salad with sesame ginger before Victor asked the waiter for another minute. The waiter hesitated and walked away. Brian had no idea what was happening. He drank his water, trying to fill up so his hunger decreased. What really sounded good right now was fast food—a couple burgers and mozza sticks and...

"You know Brian," Victor began. "Most of my associates and friends waste our conversation kissing up and trying to impress me. I hear who slept with who, who made a killing in the stock market this week; it's all very irritating to me, but it's part of my profile. It's what to expect when your name is on the building."

Brian shifted in his seat, trying to track what Victor was saying, but with every word, he couldn't decide if this was a lecture or if Brian was doing something right.

"The partition between the driver and the passenger is always down. It stays down because believe it or not, you keep me grounded. You're the closest thing to a real life that I have, and if I didn't have that, I'd probably go crazy being submerged in the hollow world that comes with my territory. Sometimes, I prefer to be normal. You're my normal."

"Thank you," Brian said, exasperated. Suddenly, everything about Brian's employment made sense, down to the fact that Victor defended him in front of his own friends. Ultimately, Victor preferred Brian's company. And that gave Brian value—more than he knew.

"Don't thank me. Understand me."

"What..."

"You can order a salad. You can order nothing at all. You can order a penne pasta and a couple slices of tomato basil that I highly recommend. Whatever you order, order what you want. If you decide to change, don't change in the way they think you should, the way people want you to change. Change when you want to, when you're ready. Because if you change for them, and that one bit of normalcy in my life converts and you're like every other fabricated relationship I have, striving to impress me because you think what makes you a man is your status, then the partition goes up...

...Hey, you," Eve said, entering the diner to find Brian at the counter drinking coffee. The high lasted all night and into the morning, and then he crashed with six hours left to go of his shift. Eve looked equally as dreary, but was better at carrying herself as if nothing happened. They managed to exchange smiles. "Last night was fun," Eve said, giving him a kiss; short but seductive.

"Me too, but we should talk." He dragged himself from his seat and pulled Eve to the side, out of hearing distance from the kitchen. "That's not something I can do again."

"I know," she said in agreement.

"It's just that...I liked it. It was fun, and last night I was thinking about the next time we should do it and this morning I realized how easy it would be to just keep going, ya know? And I don't wanna change or get caught up in something. I know it will be bad for me if I do. I just can't."

"Brian," she said with sincerity. "It's fine. I don't wanna either. I shouldn't have in the first place. That's the old me. It was a one-time thing."

"Really? Cause I don't want to ask you not to do something that you want to do."

"I don't want to. I'm recovering, remember? Miller was an old friend and I just fell into it because it was what we knew. That part of my life is behind me."

"K, good. That's a relief. Cause I dunno...you said you were in rehab and I don't wanna help screw that up."

"You don't have to explain. I'm a big girl. I can handle it. But it's sweet that you care. It was a one-time thing, alright?"

"K."

She moved in and wrapped her arms around him, holding him close. He sucked in his gut as they stood in a long hug. Neither let go, letting each other know everything would be okay—that there was nothing to be worked out—just a lapse of judgment. They stood in the nearly empty diner for a long time, clinging together like they would never be separated. In that moment, Brian knew Eve was what he'd been looking for, and he knew if she had wanted to continue getting high every night, he would have been right there alongside her. But they were the same—two people who could easily be tempted and swayed into the wrong things if they didn't stay strong—if they didn't stick together. He knew he had to accept that he was exactly where belonged.

From the other side of a wall, another person analyzed the situation from another perspective—only he wasn't interested in Eve's addiction. He was interested in Brian's addictive personality and his need to fit in—to cave under peer pressure. He'd only come for his usual breakfast, but Toby

O'Tool stumbled on a way to bring Brian down—to take out one of Richard's supporters. He pulled out his cell phone and dialed William's number. After a few rings, William groggily answered.

"What do you want Toby?" he asked, without so much as a greeting.

Through a forkful of eggs, Toby smiled as Brian and Eve still held each other on the opposite end of the wall. "You still want to help me with the inheritance thing? I found your first task." He turned to a 'now hiring' sign displayed in the window with a smile. "Polish your resume. You're getting a job."

Chapter 6

1

Christian Dent was face down in the shower when they found him. The water splashed on his back, mixed with the blood and swirling to the drain. In his back was four stab wounds, the homemade knife still protruding from between his shoulder blades. He murmured incoherently, asking for help.

Five minutes later, he was taken to the prison hospital, his hands bound as doctors worked on him.

When Warden Reggie Sunjata heard the news, he hurried to Dent's block and began asking questions: Who saw him last? Who found him? What enemies did Dent have? It was procedure to gather details when an inmate was attacked and survived. It didn't happen often, but when it did, the survivor became a liability. Sunjata needed to put a face to the attacker, and fast. If Dent survived and it happened to be a guard or a security error, it would be a shit-storm on his shoulders. Sunjata didn't condone most of what went on in Kern, but lived by the creed that if he didn't hear about it, it was okay.

Sunjata found Alvin Knight, the nearest guard to the incident. Knight told him that no one should have been in the showers at that particular time.

"How bad was it?" the warden asked.

"No idea but he was stabbed four times. I doubt he'll pull through."

"He say who did it?"

"He was trying to talk."

Sunjata walked away and straight to the hospital, giving one word answers as other guards approached with issues. Nothing, at the moment, was more important than Dent. To Sunjata, Dent's arrival at Kern was noteworthy. In his own way, Dent had been a celebrity—a man destined to one day be locked up for his crimes. His past had put him on a road that he'd never strayed from. He was a victim of a lapse that interrupted his youth, and he'd never found his way out of the lifestyle he was forced into. After brutally murdering two of the elite at Stone Enterprises, he'd found his way to Kern and according to some, wasn't doing a very good job of laying low. Dent was reputed to be intelligent, but nothing about his stay so far had lived up to that reputation.

He found Dent strapped to a gurney, his face white and barely able to speak.

"Nod if you understand me," he said.

Christian slowly nodded in small jerking motions.

"Did you see who did this to you?"

Just as he asked, Donovan appeared in the doorway, watching Dent closely. Dent's eyes warily found him there and he raised a finger in his direction. Sunjata turned and eyed Donovan before turning back to Christian.

"I didn't do this," Donovan said, fearing the wrath of Sunjata if this fell on him. If he was lucky enough to keep his job, he'd be transferred from his block, probably pencil pushing for the better part of the next decade.

Sunjata found the homemade knife laying on a table and picked it up, turning it in his hands. He turned to Dent, wondering if the man was taking his last breaths. Dent's eyes watered as they glazed over and he passed out...

...He ran as quickly as his spry legs would take him. Christian was days from becoming a teenager, and was at the peak of speed. It took four men to chase him. Among them, Mitch struggled to keep up, frustrated that Dent was still running after all this time. He was always running, always trying to escape, and as he grew and matured, he was becoming a handful. Mitch would never kill him though. He'd gotten beyond that point as over the years, Dent grew on him. He would never kill him—only hope one day he'd come around, and every time he thought he'd made progress with Dent, he ran.

Christian turned his head to find them closing in. The gap was closed within a few more yards before one of Mitch's guys grabbed Christian's collar and pulled him to the dirt. Christian struggled, but all four men held him down.

"Calm down!" Mitch shouted, watching Dent's anger temper as defeat settled in. They were too big. This attempt—something around attempt number fifteen—was a failure. They dragged him to his feet and carried him back to their compound, a fortress which housed Mitch and his crew. He'd come a long way since the days when he was doing petty kidnappings

and rigging elections. He turned drug-runner and found success, along with a crew who became family. Along the way, he'd managed to hang onto Dent. Cutting him loose had been a risk in the early days, but he'd grown fond of the boy, thinking at some point he'd grow fond of Mitch in return. So far, his plan hadn't worked and Mitch understood that there would come a day when Chrissy had a choice—when he was too old to keep on a leash without being a threat. Until that day came, he'd hold onto him and raise him in the luxurious life they'd grown accustomed to.

He pulled Dent by his arm to his room and handcuffed him to a vent where he'd been handcuffed numerous times before.

"Enough is enough Chrissy."

"It's not enough until you let me go."

"You know I can't do that. It's been a long time. You don't want to go back. Trust me. Your father gave up searching," Mitch said. "He didn't do what we asked and he stopped searching. You know where he is? He's back home in town hall, raking in the dough. He hasn't thought about you in years."

"You don't know that."

"If you go back, you'll end up wishing you were here. You know what's waiting for you? School, homework, an office job, and a daddy who doesn't give a shit about his boy. Your American dream is over-rated."

"So?"

"So? You kidding me with that shit? Those other kids are sitting around glued to their TVs. You wouldn't believe the garbage on the tube these days. It's violent and disturbing and glorifies being an asshole to the lowest common denominator. A hundred years ago, people idolized guys like Einstein. Now, it's pregnant teenage girls who live with their mums. You're living more than most people ever will. You ever get out of here, you'll regret it."

"No, I won't."

"Keep telling yourself that. You have no way of knowing. Most people have the same foibles kid. They overvalue the things they have that don't matter, they overeat food in containers that are too large, and they overestimate the probability of improbable events. But most importantly, they don't miss the things they don't know they love until they're gone. You following this?"

Christian nodded, but had no idea what Mitch was saying. Mitch saw through him.

"You will someday." Mitch tossed a book toward Christian. It landed with a thud at his feet. The book was entitled Human Anatomy. "You're going to start reading a book a week."

"Why?"

"Because I said so."

"Can I pick the book?"

"No."

"How come?"

"Because the best way to expand your knowledge is to find a topic you know nothing about and read a book about it. It'll smarten you up."

Christian tugged at his handcuffs hopelessly and picked up the book, his eyes scanning the cover. He wasn't even sure he knew what human anatomy was, but was about to find out.

"Do I ever get to go?" he asked.

"If you ever truly want to go, I'll let you." Mitch gave Christian a sly smile and walked out the door, leaving Christian perplexed by the statement. He already wanted to go. Mitch was playing another mind-game, designed to baffle Christian.

Later, he held the book in his lap while the sun hit his face in the front of Mitch's speedboat. Mitch sat across from his right hand man Darryl, sunglasses covering their eyes and cigarettes dangling from their lips. Dent was handcuffed to a rail, his arm being pulled constantly as the waves pulled the boat from side to side. As Mitch and Darryl spoke of things Christian couldn't comprehend, he stared out at the open sea and thought about his father, somewhere far away.

"You like it out here on the water Chrissy?" Mitch asked, noticing Christian's interest in the ocean.

"Thought the kid was a boy," Darryl said with a laugh. He had no love for kids and would have preferred to let Christian loose. He was oblivious to Mitch's interest in Christian's well-being.

"My name's Christian," the boy said, sternly.

"I know you're a boy dummy. You're a boy with a girl's name is all."

"My daddy called me Mitchel and I hated it," Mitch chimed in.

"You're not my dad," Dent shot back.

"Oh, right," Mitch said. "You're daddy's out campaigning and trying to make another thousand dollars so he can live it up."

"At least my dad isn't a criminal like yours and you."

Mitch and Darryl exchanged amused smiles. "That so?" Mitch asked. "You think our parents should be judged based on who we are?"

"Your dad did what you do," Dent said. "My dad helps people."

"My father never left my side. Not once," Mitch said in all seriousness. "He gave me the life that you got a piece of. For now."

"You're a criminal."

"Yeah? What kind of criminal am I?"

"Huh?" Dent asked as Darryl cracked open a beer and handed another to Mitch.

"There's more than one type of criminal Chrissy. See, there's the kind that guns down a convenience store for the money in the register, or the type like your daddy who stays safely on the border between crime and an honest life to benefit his pocketbook. There's also the kind of criminal who sells people the things they want and can't get anywhere else. That's the kind of criminal I am. Free enterprising, servicing those in need of the fix that the law won't allow. Hardly even call myself a criminal—only by their definition."

"You won't make me believe the shit you're saying."

Darryl and Mitch broke into laughter. Dent had a lot of attitude for such a small boy.

"You got a mouth on you Chrissy," Mitch said. Dent silently glared at him. "When I was your age, my daddy gave me a loan to buy some Mexican bricks from a pair of local distributors. We sold it lickety-split, but people kept asking me for Colombian which was supposedly free of the lung killing pesticides that Uncle Sam had started spraying on Mexican land. Problem was, it was becoming a big deal back then and they were cracking down. Most men in that game got themselves arrested."

"We were lucky," Darryl added.

"No, not luck," Mitch said with a wag of his finger. He turned to Christian and pointed to his temple to indicate brains drove the operation. "Through a connection, we got a new gig: running a Winnebago full of Colombian weed from an entry point in the Florida Keys to the parking lot of a major Miami mall, where I'd leave the keys on a back tire for the driver to find. The ride up the road swarming with local law-enforcement agents was a reputation maker for me. Suddenly I was making six figures a year—enough to buy a house for my mother, who not only knew where the money was coming from, but fundamentally believed in the business."

"If my mom were still here, she'd shit a brick if she knew what I did," Darryl said.

"What'd your mama do?"

"City clerk."

"I bet she made next to nothing."

"Less than that."

"You see? Good honest living—just like Chrissy's father made before he turned politician."

"What's wrong with that?" Christian asked. He knew the men he was with were intelligent. He'd even picked up on a few of their viewpoints, but he didn't understand politics. He knew politicians wrote the laws and made all the money, but he'd always believed that to be honorable.

"You don't know the enemy," Mitch said. "That's what's wrong."

"Yes, I do."

"You think I'm the enemy?"

Christian nodded.

"How sad. You don't know the nature of your enemy. You don't know who your enemy is. The mere mention of mystery schools or secret societies probably has you baffled. We're all screwed and you don't even know why. Learn, just learn for one day about who your enemy really is. It's a domestic problem, and no, it's not the government either. Elements in the government? Elements in the military? Elements in the intelligence gathering organizations? Absolutely! But it ain't me."

"What about the cops?" Christian asked.

"What about em?" Mitch asked, laying back to let the sun hit his chest. *"They do what they do. If they think there's something respectable in keeping order to the best of their abilities, more power to em. The law don't change my reality. Because of my father, I rent penthouse suites on Biscayne Bay where the cocaine comes in softball sized mounds and the prostitutes stay for days. It's a fucking thrill. We're running week long benders through the Caribbean."*

"Kings of east coast smuggling," Darryl said, raising his beer. Mitch let his beer clink against his partners' before leaning forward toward Christian again.

"I'm introducing you to the world of ten ton payoffs, and the job? Oil tankers to the Caribbean Islands, parceled out to private sailboats being moved north to the Chesapeake Bay, Cape Cod, the Hamptons... You go to school and get a job like your daddy's got and you'll be saving your whole life for a vacation half as good as that."

Christian looked down, ashamed to find romance in what they were doing. The open sea was nice—the sunlight—how easy it all was. Every day, he felt like he was coming around, and he felt guilty for it.

"One time, we paid a friend a thousand dollars to get lost so we could use her home on Long Island. We counted a million dollars in the living room, right where we sat that night for Thanksgiving. That was a trip. All I'm saying is my daddy gave me a life I wouldn't trade. Who says yours is better just because a bunch of assholes wrote a bunch of laws about what we should and shouldn't do? We can do whatever the fuck we want."

"Then why can't I go home?" Christian asked, challenging Mitch. *"Why won't you let me go if I can do what I want?"*

"Hey, Chrissy, don't let me stand in your way. You can go anytime you want—if you really want. If you really want your freedom...

...One week before he was stabbed, before Dent lay in a pool of watery blood, he stood in the yard, taking in his surroundings, person by person. He'd been watching Ziggy from across the yard, plotting a way to approach him. He needed a hook-up. He didn't have time to build a reputation, and frankly, wasn't in the mood.

Wayne had warned him. Worse yet, Donovan had warned him and had his eyes on Dent, who was just another play-toy to him. Anyone who had a vendetta against Donovan would come to regret it later in life when they wound up on his block. Christian hadn't said much to offend Donovan, which spoke volumes for the world he was now in. The hard truth was that it didn't take much in prison to be on someone's shit list. A small jab, the wrong look, even a rumor.

What was even harder was gaining respect, a feat that took time and self-control—even a good deal of humility. What Christian needed was to prove himself with a gesture. Considering he thought himself smarter than everyone else in Kern, he didn't think it would be so hard and had developed a plan for some time—something that was unheard of in a place like this—something that would have repercussions. As long as he wasn't killed, he'd come out a champion.

Step one was approaching Ziggy in plain daylight for all the world to see, to do something forbidden by the meanest guard in the place, if only to show his determination—his persistence to get what he wanted, even at the risk of death.

He took a deep breath and headed in Ziggy's direction. Ziggy stopped the conversation long before Christian approached, watching him the whole way. He looked up to see Donovan's eyes on Dent, realizing he was being approached by a dead man.

"The fuck you want?" he asked, before Christian could say a word.

"You know what I want. I want to make a deal."

"What did I tell you? We only have a deal if you make Donovan go away, and you haven't come through," Ziggy said, in disbelief. "I'm surprised. Surprised at just how dumb you really are, but not impressed."

"Is that what I'm supposed to do? Impress you?"

"You need to do a hell of a lot more than that."

"Tell me what to do."

"Scram."

A feeling of doom consumed the group. Dent was going to get himself killed because he didn't know any better. It happened all the time. People died because they didn't know their place. Ziggy took a step forward.

"Who the fuck you think you are? What you here for? Life? You need a deck of cards or some cigarettes, then adjust and learn to be patient. There's no hurry around here. You need a fix, then too fucking bad. Don't get caught next time. You're not my problem."

"What's he want?"

The conversation stopped. No one had been aware that Donovan had approached. He showed up from nowhere with a hard look on his face and a bone to pick.

"He's just talking," Ziggy said.

"Bullshit. No one just talks here."

"Yeah, well he's a dumb-shit. He doesn't know how things are."

"Got that right," Donovan said, sneering at Dent, who waited patiently for Donovan to go away. "Don't be thinking I don't know what you're good for around here."

"Yeah, boss. I got that. I'm just saying he doesn't want anything important and I told him to scram. He's just looking to pass the time."

"Pass the time..." Donovan repeated, doubtfully.

"Nothing out of the ordinary."

Dent stood through the long silence. There was an unspoken bond between cons when it came to the guards. The worst of enemies silently chose each other over any guard. The moment Donovan's back was turned, Ziggy would be telling Dent to get lost. In those few moments, they were allies.

"I see anything moving through the walls, I'm taking it," Donovan said. "I've turned my back to you for too long Ziegfried."

"What the fuck boss? I'm not helping the guy out."

"You're talking to this piece of trash and I don't like it." Ziggy shot Dent a look. Donovan watched the display, pleased with himself. "You're going out of business," Donovan said before he strutted away, leaving Ziggy seething. Most guards didn't give a shit what Ziggy did. They even welcomed it, usually getting a cut for their own services. In fact, most guards smuggled the contraband in. There was a lot of profit to be made when a man would pay just about anything for a cigarette and just about every guard had a finger in the pie.

"Get away from me," Ziggy said, steadily, seemingly using all his self-control not to strangle Dent. Dent nodded, turned, and followed Donovan. The men would later say there came a dreadful moment when they realized he was trying to catch up to the guard, and a heavy silence filled the yard. They'd say that was the moment they knew he was dead.

"Hey..." Dent said. Donovan stopped and paused, as if he'd never expected a man to approach him from behind in the yard and call out to him. He turned over his shoulder to find the impossible had happened. Dent stood five yards away, challenging the man.

"What the fuck you..."

Before Donovan could finish, Dent swung his fist, connecting to Donovan's jaw, which cracked as he nearly toppled to the ground. Dent turned to walk away, but many things happened at once. The yard was an uproar. Guards rushed from their posts and others stood on high grounds, positioning their weapons on Dent.

Donovan quickly recovered from momentary shock, and grabbed his club, hurrying after Dent, who paced himself as if he didn't expect what would happen next. Donovan swung at him, first hitting him across the back of the neck with a whack. The second swing sent Dent to the ground, who shielded himself as Donovan brought the club down brutally, trying to hit Dent in every exposed area he could. Dent let out an oomph at every hit, waiting for the beating to end. It lasted no more than fifteen seconds before the guards pulled them apart.

"The hot box! A week!" Donovan shouted, a line of spit falling from his lower lip as he lashed out with uncontrolled rage."That was a mistake," Donovan said. Dent didn't react. He didn't care. What bothered Donovan the most was how Dent had calculated his reaction—had known exactly what he was doing. It was as if he didn't realize the ramifications and did it anyway.

From a few yards away, Ziggy watched the display, his eyes darting between the men as if he couldn't believe what was happening. People could say what they wanted about Dent, but one thing that was certain was that he had balls. Ziggy shook his head and turned to one of his guys. "Never gonna see him alive again."

2

The migraines came on fast and didn't stop. The pulsating thumping inside Shiloh Reynald's head was growing more intolerable by the day. It was beyond any flu she'd ever had. As Shiloh's grades began to suffer, her mother, Trish Reynalds, began suspecting there was more to her story than just the flu.

When Shiloh stayed home for the day, Trish would come home on her lunch break and end her shift early. Her frustration at home began bleeding into her work, and soon, Carlos began questioning her about it. She told him about Shiloh's headaches and he tossed out potential diagnoses, trying to solve the problem for her, though in her opinion, it was just a simple case of her daughter staying up late, watching TV. Carlos continually threw out solutions until she got fed up with his input.

"I'm not an idiot," she said. "I know the obvious symptoms. It's only headaches and some weakness. She doesn't do her homework and then she plays hooky as a solution."

"You let her stay home? Even when you know she's faking?"

Trish shrugged. "Benefit of the doubt," she said. "All I know is she never used to get sick this often or for this long. I don't understand what's going on."

"You've been working more."

"So what?"

"Hard to know what she's getting into while you're not around."

"Why don't you just say you think I'm a bad mom?"

"Nah. A bad mom wouldn't give a shit at all," he said. "I'm just saying that she could be eating junk food all day or smoking cigarettes and you'd have no way of knowing because our job is demanding."

"She doesn't smoke. What's your point?"

"Point is you don't know what's going on. I see you struggling because you know it too. You're not sure you know your own kid."

"What am I supposed to do about that?"

"I'm sure it won't be easy, but find more balance."

Her cell rang and she answered, relieved to end the conversation until the caller turned out to be the school nurse, who told her Shiloh passed out at school. After a short conversation in which Trish pressed the nurse to guarantee her daughter would be fine, she ended the call and turned the car around.

"I have to drop you off at the station. Can you let Frank know I'm taking a personal day?"

"What's going on?"

"Shiloh fainted," she said. She suddenly felt guilty for doubting her daughter.

"Don't drop me off. That's a twenty minute detour for you. Go straight to the hospital."

"Carlos…"

"Just go. I'll hitch a ride with the medics to the station."

"That could take a while."

"It gets me out of work. I wanna make sure she's okay too," he said, sincerely. "You've got no reason to worry though. Kids faint in school all the time. Probably got nervous around a cute boy or something."

"She warned me about this. She said she's been having headaches and I've been yelling at her and accusing her of faking."

"Still could be. I fake fainted once to get out of sex ed."

She laughed. "That explains a lot."

"Explains nothing. I picked up on that shit like a pro."

She didn't respond—only had another thought. She'd been occupied with side projects in her free-time and hadn't made much time for her daughter. They all related to the will and the other beneficiaries. Richard would bring an end to the will within the month, but until then, she wanted to guarantee the safety of the remaining beneficiaries. The focal point of her investigations had remained on Anthony, though she frequently checked in on Cynthia Mason, and she'd kept close tabs on the remaining members of the group in the previous days. She made sure Brian was going to work regularly, and he was. Charlie wasn't back to work yet, but he'd spent his time in a hotel or at the cemetery. Adlar was unaccounted for, but he wouldn't have had the resources to pull off the lottery. Few people could. Royce Morrow and Tarek Appleton had the money, but neither seemed interested in the money and had their full support behind Richard. Even Jason Stone came from Maui to show his support. Whoever operated from behind the scenes was still there, probably relieved no finger had ever been pointed at them. Trish had no leads and no theories. She only had the hope that time would pass without another incident. Richard would end the will. Whoever was responsible for Anthony's attack would lose. Maybe they wouldn't be caught, but they'd lose.

As she thought about everything she'd been doing for their safety, Anthony called and told Trish he had a lead. She didn't know how he stumbled on it, and he was vague with the details, but her intention that day had been to escape Carlos and talk to Anthony. After some thought, she asked Carlos a favor. She wanted to be with her daughter, so she asked Carlos to meet with Anthony and gave him a contact number.

"What's the deal with this guy?" Carlos asked. "Why you so interested in this?"

"I've looked into his case."

"That case was never yours and you said you barely knew him."

"I know Carlos, and obviously there's more to it than that. The whole thing at the hospital, and my interest in Todd Mason's disappearance, and Abby Palmer's murder…"

"That's all connected?" he asked, taken aback.

"Yeah," she said and swallowed hard, ready to tell him everything. "Victor Stone."

Carlos agreed to talk to Anthony. In fact, when he learned what Victor's will really was, he became visibly upset and motivated. Trish didn't know if he was concerned about her safety or was just willing to help her, but he suddenly was interested in nothing more than helping find the man who propositioned the group. He took five minutes to make sure Shiloh was okay before taking off.

When Trish was alone with the nurse, she got up to speed on what happened. Shiloh said there had been a migraine and a dizzy spell. She grew light-headed, stood to see if she could go to the restroom, and her knees gave out under her. Trish cringed as the nurse finished with, "She said she's been feeling this way since yesterday. When was the last time you took her in for a checkup?"

Trish apologized to Shiloh on the way home and told her she had no idea it was as bad as it was. Shiloh gave her the silent treatment, which made her feel worse. She wondered for a moment if she really had faked fainting just to teach her mother a lesson but dismissed it. Shiloh's face really did look pale. "We'll schedule an appointment," she said. "Last time we saw your doctor, he said you were healthy and that wasn't long ago."

"You believe him over me," Shiloh said, accusing her mother.

Trish took a deep breath. "Shiloh, I already apologized. I told you we're going to schedule an appointment."

They rode in silence for a while before Shiloh innocently asked, "Do you think I'll be okay?"

Trish assured she would be, but wondered. She'd be the first to admit she would never be mom of the year—that sometimes it seemed like Shiloh was raising herself. She'd always wanted there to come a day when everything would change and she'd be able to make her daughter the center of her life. The job had simply been too demanding and when Paul stepped out of the picture, it only became harder. She couldn't help but wonder if she was being punished. Whether Shiloh wasn't getting enough sleep, or there was something to seriously be concerned about, the timing couldn't be worse. Richard was rounding up supporters and trying to hang on to them, and Trish needed to back him up, to put the scare into anyone who tried to prevent his success. On top of that, she was consumed by Anthony's case and Abby's death. The incidents were piling up so high that Trish was having a hard time counting them in her head. And now, her daughter was sick. Her daughter, who barely saw her mother now needed her full attention. Trish hated herself for feeling that Shiloh was a burden but maybe this was what would finally force her to prioritize.

Carlos was meeting with Anthony. She'd have to allow that to be enough for now and focus on Shiloh. She scheduled an appointment with her doctor, Dr. Neomin, and made a mental note to forget everything related to Victor until her daughter was okay.

3

When Dent was released from the hot-box, he emerged a different man. He was tired and appeared to have aged years over the course of the week. His eyes had deep grooves under them which deepened when he squinted in the sunlight. The hot-box was jail within jail. As if prison wasn't bad enough, a place had to be built inside to isolate a man more. A long disconnect worked in favor of authority. No man—no matter how tough—wanted to go back.

Wayne stood against a fence with his hands behind his head, trying to get a tan. Wayne didn't bother to turn toward Christian as he approached and joined him at the fence, letting the sunlight hit his face.

"You're still alive. I'll be damned," Wayne said with a chuckle.

"What will Donovan do?"

"Shit, men have disappeared from this place for doing less than you done."

"Do the guards approve of what he does?"

"Some do. The ones that know, don't care. Those that would care, don't know."

"Does the warden know?"

"Everyone knows deep down. Can't do anything bout what you can't prove though. You get shanked in here, and the cons will be the first they finger. No arm of the law gonna come here and believe your story over his."

"No decent guards ever have the urge to speak out?"

Wayne chuckled again. "Not a witness in the world for that guy. He cleans his messes up. When he wants someone dead, they're dead. Always an accident. No way to prove an accident."

"He's got a temper. If he were to explode in front of the right people, he'd be gone. If he's angry enough, he won't think."

Wayne chuckled again. That why you decked him in the yard?"

"Something like that," Dent said. "I'll need your help."

"You got last words you want passed? Or bum a cigarette? Some of these guys don't think you got half a day left."

"I'll bury him before he gets the chance."

Wayne closed his eyes and shook his head, ready to be rid of Dent for good. Being around him was dangerous.

Dent stared forward, slowly adjusting to the light...

...He sat behind the wheel of an inky blue Mercedes Sedan, speeding along a gravel road. Years have passed. Mitch has traded in his hippie garb for Miami white pants, a mesh shirt, a Rolex, and a coral ring.

Next to him, Christian stared forward in his seat, a book in his hand. It had been long ago he'd attempted to run. Mitch had taken notice of Christian's change in personality. He'd become quieter and less resistant. He even seemed content at times. Mitch was afraid to let his guard down though—afraid Christian had been waiting all this time and one day he'd wake up and he'd be gone. Mitch wondered if that was such a bad thing— maybe it was time.

"You haven't asked to leave in some time," Mitch said, interrupting Christian's book about string theory.

"Same answer every time," Christian said in a monotone.

"If I let you out of the car, what would be your plan? Just curious. What you think you'd do?"

"Don't know."

After some silence, "You know, I don't blame you for being scared of me."

"I'm not scared of you."

"And I know why you feel the need to act like a tough guy. No one prepared you for what happened. Most things in life happen without preparation. I didn't say bye to my father either."

"Why not?" Christian asked.

"Because this business comes with risk. The positive is we know that. We can plan ahead. Sometimes that's not enough though. It wasn't for him."

"Is he dead?"

"No. One of his crew was caught. FBI made a deal with him and he gave them names. Among them was my father, who's spending the rest of his days in Leavenworth."

"Why can't you see him?"

Mitch shook his head and thought about the question. Finally, he shrugged. "Maybe I'd be disappointed. Maybe he would. I don't need any earth-shattering revelation on why what I'm doing is wrong. I know it is by most standards, but I'm good at it."

"You should visit him," Christian said.

"Yeah?" Mitch asked, turning to Christian, who looked up at him from where he sat, a serious look on his face. Mitch was cracking the kid, and that had always been the objective, but more important than that, he really liked having him around. "Maybe I should someday."

"And you should let me go," Christian said, smiling to himself.

Mitch sighed heavily. "It's a sign of weakness, letting emotion stand in the way of progress. People's ethical decision making is strongly driven by gut emotions rather than rational analytic thoughts."

"So what?"

"So my father got caught because he was loyal to the man who turned him in. I learned from his mistakes and you should too."

"I will, but you won't let me do anything but follow you around."

"That won't be forever."

Christian's mind wandered and he finally asked the question that had been on his mind for quite some time. "Are you going to kill me?"

Mitch let out a burst of laughter. "No. For nothing, no. I don't kill for nothing."

"You killed your wife."

Dent's reminder brought Mitch back to the day he brutally beat his wife to death in front of him. "Yeah, well that wasn't for nothing. She'd pushed me too far. You can only push a guy so far. She made me angry."

"I make you angry."

"You don't make me angry."

"You yell at me all the time."

"You're a kid. You're supposed to be annoying. If the day ever comes that you turn on me, and you get a chance to put me down, then I'll kill ya without a thought. But not for nothing. You never kill for nothing..."

…Dent looked up, following the looming shadow of Donovan, who blocked the sun, depriving him of sunlight. Donovan looked up toward the sky and smiled, teasing Christian with words. "You really pack a punch, ya know?"

"Sure do."

"You should be feeling nothing but doom and regret."

"Maybe," Dent said, smiling as if mesmerized by the memory of what he did. "But the thought of your busted up face got me off every night in the hole. Hell, if I use my imagination, maybe think about your whole body broken and bleeding, I could last years in there. It'd be like a vacation."

"Donovan nodded with a smile, careful not to show weakness. "I met a guy like you once. Outside, he was respected and very established, so when he was busted for tax fraud, he arrived thinking he was smarter than the rest of us. He couldn't handle the shame he brought to his name and decided he'd rather be dead than spend his life in here. Came to me one night and made some crack about my mom. You can guess the rest."

"Wish I could shake his hand."

"You'd need a shovel for that. Maybe I can arrange for you to see him another way."

"The first time you implied you'd kill me, I got the idea. How many ways you plan on saying it?"

"Here's the thing Dent," he said. "You just don't strike me as a man who wants to die. So as much as I fantasize about cutting your fucking head off, I'm also wondering what you're really up to."

"Keep wondering."

Donovan stared him down a long moment before reaching into his belt and tossing something to the ground. Christian looked down, the shine of a homemade knife drawing him in. It's the same knife that would later be found protruding from Dent's back in the shower.

"There's a dozen ways I can kill you, but you're gonna make it easy for me. You're gonna come at me. Give it your best shot. Hell, I bet your ego even makes you believe you'll beat me."

Dent's eyes fixated on the knife, barely hearing anything Donovan said. He got the gist of it. It wasn't the first time Donovan had propositioned an inmate, giving them the chance to attack, only to end up six feet under. It was too tempting for the cons to pass up: Either be beaten by Donovan whenever he felt like it, or be given the chance to defend himself. And when he wound up dead, that's exactly what Donovan would claim: he defended himself.

"I won't give you the luxury of killing me in self-defense," Dent said.

"I guess you're not the fighter I thought. You can come at me, or I can come at you and you won't have a fighting chance. Your choice. After the shit you pulled, the only way you live is if I die."

Dent finally looked up to find a sly smile on Donovan's face, a smile that reminded him who was in charge. Donovan left him there, staring at the knife, pondering how he'd make it through the week alive.

"How many inmates have died on his watch?" Christian asked in the cafeteria to Wayne and a couple other guys who already dismissed him as deceased.

"Too many to count," one man said. "Probably more than we know."

"How many you know for sure?"

"If you ask around, you'll get different numbers. I know for a fact of only two, but I don't ask a lot of questions. Others around here are gonna tell you a dozen or so. I can tell you I know how he did it. Gave you a weapon, right?"

Dent nodded, unsurprised Donovan's tactics were common knowledge.

"That's what he does. That's his big plan. Everyone knows he's a hard-ass so it ain't hard to believe a man would want to kill him. Especially when they think their life is on the line."

"I know."

"Yeah, well here's what you don't know," Wayne said. "In here there's a lot of egos and you're about par for the course when it comes to the guys who don't last long. If you think you can take him, you're dumber than a rock. And if you did, killing a guard here is a death sentence in itself. He put you in a lose lose situation. That was the point."

"What would you do?" Christian asked.

"What I'd do is shut my mouth in the first place, so I'd never be in your shoes."

4

"I think she's fine," Dr. Gregory Neomin said, though not with complete assurance. "I ran a few tests. We did find an abnormal spot on an x-ray on her skull. It doesn't look like anything, but I'd rather be sure. I'm going to prescribe some medication for the headaches and have her come back in a couple days. I'll have results by then and can run her x-rays by the attending."

"Why would she pass out?" Trish asked.

"Many reasons could have been attributed to that. Fatigue, dehydration, lack of sleep and nutrition. She admitted she doesn't get as much sleep as she should."

Though Neomin only spoke positively of the results, Trish couldn't keep her mind off the x-ray. She asked various questions, but Neomin was trained to give vague answers. He gave her his personal number and told her to let him know if there were further issues.

Shiloh was tired, and picked at her mom on the way home. All they did was fight when they were together—which wasn't often—and Trish hoped being together in a potentially traumatic time would change that, but Shiloh was angry at her mom for reasons Trish didn't understand. When they were home, Shiloh stormed into the house without a word, leaving Trish outside her car, shaking her head and rolling her eyes. She took a deep breath and tried to gather her thoughts. She needed someone to talk to, someone to vent to…

Suddenly, she pulled her cell phone and dialed a number. Carlos picked up after two rings. She took a few seconds to consider what to say. She wanted to talk about Shiloh, about how much her life was unraveling, about how she could manage being a single parent who was able to pay the bills and raise a child to hopefully one day have some character. Instead, she discussed something she didn't really care about anymore.

"Hey Carlos. I was wondering if you met with Anthony Freeman?"

"Yeah, you got time to hear what's going on?"

"Yeah, go ahead," she said.

"First of all, what do you plan on doing with this whole Palmer thing?"

"I'm doing all I can."

"Victor's will isn't common knowledge," Carlos said. "When the department is investigating a crime against someone on that list, you're withholding evidence by keeping to yourself."

"The station will follow guidelines and nothing will get done. Nothing ever does. The other beneficiaries and I have mutually agreed to protect the names."

"Fair enough," he said, letting the matter drop. It seemed Carlos didn't want a repeat of his earlier issues with Trish. Maybe he was coming around. Maybe he didn't want to fight. Carlos went on. "So you know about the lottery. You've got a mystery ringleader propositioning a group of ex-cons to bet on who will die first. The cons work for a place called

Gelatin Steel, which mostly employs ex-cons because it's cheap labor. Winner gets the cash, which is incentive to control the outcome. Vince bets on Freeman, thinking he's old and odds are in favor of his death being the first. Vince becomes desperate for money and stabs Freeman, but later regrets his actions. Then, one of the other people on the list is killed—Mrs. Palmer—and the money goes to another con and leaves Vince desperate, broke, and filled with regret. You know the rest."

"Is that all? What's the lead?"

"One of the cons who was there for the betting said they're placing new bets—playing the game again with the remainder of the group."

"Great…" Trish said. "Mystery ringleader tempts these assholes into killing us again."

"Well, mystery ringleader is where we're hung up. Not one con saw his face or can describe anything about him. Guy just showed up, offered the bet, came back to pay up, and disappeared. This Friday, he's returning. That's when we get him."

"Alright," Trish said. She'd swore to herself she'd put Shiloh's medical issues first, but she could squeeze in a trip to Gelatin Steel to arrest the man responsible for Anthony's attack. "I've got this thing going on with Shiloh, but get back to me with solid details and I'll try to be there."

"Try to be?" Carlos asked, surprised. "What's wrong with Shiloh?"

"I don't know. Maybe nothing. But she hates me enough already. I need to back up a little and start spending some time at home."

"I agree, but be there for this. If you're keeping that list of names secret, then you're all the backup I have. If you're not there, I go to the department with this information and we look at some of these cases with a narrowed down list of suspects."

They said their goodbyes and Trish took a few more minutes to enjoy the fresh air before going back in the house. When she entered, the lights were off. Shiloh was probably in her room with the door locked pretending to be asleep so she wouldn't have to talk to Trish. She started walking to her bedroom, but stopped. If she didn't tell Shiloh she loved her—even if Shiloh didn't say it back—she wouldn't be able to sleep.

She was surprised the door was unlocked, and more surprised to see the light on and Shiloh's bed empty. "Shiloh?" she asked, stepping into the room. As she cleared the bed, she saw her daughter's legs—then her body, sprawled out on the ground, her arms at her sides and a pool of vomit at her mouth.

Dent stood in the corridor outside the shower facilities. In his hand, he held the knife. Donovan's footsteps echoed throughout the corridor. In a matter of moments, they'd be alone in the room. Dent had a weapon and a choice, but he was at odds with his ego. Was it worth throwing away the little freedom he had left? Or was there a way he could keep his promise to Ziggy, stay alive, get the guards off his back, and gain some respect at Kern without tarnishing his integrity?

Donovan appeared around the corner. He was vulnerable, weaponless, a man armed with only the knowledge of who held the power. He'd done it many times before—looked into the eyes of the men he'd given an ultimatum to—men who believed they could get the best of him.

"Day's fading fast," Donovan said.

"You've killed more men than anyone in here," Dent said. "Makes you a criminal—bad as the men you condemn."

"The scum in here are lower than rodents, and it ain't illegal to kill a rodent. No one's throwing up much of a fuss when your kind goes down."

"Maybe not, but what kind of man does what you do? Why not sit in an office or be a day trader? You do what you do because they give you a gun and it gets you on a power trip. You're a loser outside this place. I'd bet a thousand cigarettes you were a dumb-ass in school and the bigger kids took your lunch money. You're getting revenge on the world for being a lowlife."

Donovan let out an uncontrolled laugh that sounded like a yelp. "You got balls Dent. I'll give you that."

"Shoot me and finish this."

"I won't need a gun."

"You will if you're facing me."

Donovan took a step back, letting his guard down momentarily. He reminded himself that he was talking to a dead man. There was nothing to be afraid of. "A couple of fellas who never lost a fight," he said. "That's all we are. You're about to find out there's always someone better."

Dent grimaced and shook his head at Donovan. He was too cocky. He was too power-hungry. The kind of power-hungry Dent hated. Behind the weapon and under the uniform, he was just a marshmallow. Dent met his eyes and extended the knife. He let up on his grasp and let it fall between them to the ground with a clink. Donovan's brow creased.

"I'm not coming after you," Dent said. "Stab me in the back, but make sure I'm dead."

"Oh, I'll be sure," Donovan said, trying to remain in control, but his voice faltered.

Dent didn't stand down. He stared at Donovan with a sly smile and confidence in his eyes.

"Have it your way," Donovan said. "Same result in the end."

Dent turned and entered the showers. Donovan watched him with a sneer on his face, bent and picked up the knife.

Five minutes later, Dent was found in a pool of blood...

...Mitch, Darryl, and a crew loaded crates from a ferry into inflatable rafts. Christian stood next to Mitch, watching curiously.

"They'll handle distributions from here," Mitch said.

"What's distribution?"

"They rent safe houses and store the loads there where they'll carve them up for local dealers."

"Oh..."

Another boat pulled up to the dock and Darryl jumped in and got behind the wheel, revving it up.

"This isn't just a business Chrissy. This is a fail-safe. Most buyers have a fraction of the operation we have. That's the key."

"What is?"

"Think big. See, we're one step ahead of the competition. In ten years, they'll do it the way we do it now, but we're the innovative ones, so no one's looking in our direction." Mitch lit his cigarette and hauled a large rope into the boat. "See, we cover our bases. We have an out for every scenario..."

Christian squinted his eyes and caught lights in the distance coming toward the pier. Mitch noticed Dent's gaze and followed it toward the streets where a dozen police cars were coming their way. He turned toward the crew on the boat. "Start the boat!" he screamed.

Mitch grabbed a duffel bag with one hand and Christian's arm with the other, pulling him toward the boat. Gunshots fired in the distance as one of the crew further down the pier tried holding them back.

The ferry started and changed direction, causing the life-rafts to tip. The contents spilled into the ocean.

Mitch pulled Christian into the boat and quickly slapped the handcuff onto the rail, securing Christian in place. He turned to Darryl and gave him an urgent look. He turned back to Christian, who tugged at his handcuff as the boat picked up speed. The engine kicked in and the boat pulled away from the dock.

Mitch and Darryl turned toward the pier to be sure they were at a safe distance. The police were a good block away from the dock, but there was a bigger problem to tend to. Mitch's eyes went wide when he saw Christian was gone and the rail unhinged. Mitch searched the water until he found Christian pulling himself from the water onto the dock.

"Stop the boat!" Mitch yelled.

"Mitch!" Darryl shouted with the urgency in his voice.

"Stop the fucking boat!" Mitch shouted back.

Darryl let the boat idle, ready to high-tail it again if given the word. He watched Mitch closely. He had always wondered what would happen when the day came when Mitch could either let him go free, or end his life to protect the operation. Mitch didn't pull his gun. He didn't even go near it. He only watched Christian stand on the docks. "We really gotta go," Darryl said, keeping his cool.

Mitch nodded, gave Christian one last look, and turned away.

From the dock, Christian returned the gaze, and in one instant, he was filled with regret. All at once, he realized the police would scoop him up, return him home, and he'd live his life the way he was supposed to, with his father, mother, friends at school, some fame for having been the boy who was abducted—and to his surprise—none of it sounded good. He wanted to be on the boat with Mitch.

Before he could talk himself out of it, he was in the water, swimming back to the boat.

Mitch heard the splash and turned to see Christian headed his way. Darryl didn't need to be told. He idled long enough for Mitch to reach down and grasp Christian's hand. He pulled him up just as the squad cars were coming to a stop at the docks and their doors opening.

Christian tumbled over the edge. Mitch turned and left him there, in a pool of water. He didn't show Christian he was relieved, that he was more than just a prisoner, that he was attached.

But in that moment, Christian knew...

...His eyes opened two days later. He was patched up by the doctors. His situation at first had looked helpless, but with all his stab wounds, nothing major had been punctured. All were near the heart, but not one was fatal and major arteries were missed. He was lucky. He was alive. Most importantly, the event would serve as the incident that would define every incident after. With Donovan, Ziggy, Wayne, the whole yard, and it even caught the eye of the warden, who hadn't given Dent a second look until now.

Now, the warden leaned against the wall, waiting for Dent's world to come into focus. When it did, he stepped forward and sized him up. "You're lucky," he said.

"Yeah," Dent said, weakly. "Lucky." He'd tried to be sarcastic but couldn't find the tone.

"You were stabbed multiple times and from what I've been told, he missed the jugular, the brachial, and every major artery. Someone did a piss-poor job of killing you. You should be dead."

"Might as well be."

"You've got nothing to worry about. There will be a criminal investigation handled by the Attorney General's office, and with your testimony that Donovan was behind this...well, he won't work in Kern, or any prison in the state ever again."

Dent closed his eyes, relieved they knew the truth, but more importantly that they cared about it. "Until then?" he asked, though he suspected no one would let Donovan near him during that time.

"He's behind a desk. He'll have no access to you."

Christian's head fell back against his pillow with relief.

The warden watched Christian closely, who didn't react. "I like to keep this place under control, and this isn't the first time Donovan has been a problem. I want you to know you'll have my full support, as long as I have your cooperation. I've never liked his methods and he's a liability. You're the only inmate who's lived to turn on him. He's going to say he wasn't there, but video in the corridor places him there moments before we found you."

"The knife will have prints," Christian added.

"I know. We've already sent it to a lab to verify that. You were lucky. Don't make me regret this." With that, he turned and exited.

Dent closed his eyes.

He was free. He walked with a limp, but even in the confinements of the prison walls, it was nice to walk again. There were a hundred reasons why a convict needed to watch his back in prison, but the guards was no longer one of them. Heads turned. There was no admiration—only disbelief. Most thought he was lucky, but stupid. He'd lasted longer than anyone expected, and deep down, the best of them knew that maybe there was something beyond luck. Maybe Dent was an asset.

For the first time, Ziggy approached Christian, meeting him by the fence, where Christian stared out beyond the walls of Kern.

"Didn't expect to see you again," Ziggy said.

"You ready to deal?" Dent asked.

"Why would I be ready to deal?"

"Donovan's out of the way."

"If you think Donovan was the reason I wasn't doing business with you, you weren't listening."

"He was hurting business. I took care of him. We had a deal."

Ziggy laughed. "You don't win points for being stupid."

"I can pay you generously."

"On delivery?"

"When I'm free."

Ziggy shook his head. He'd heard more than his share of guys trying to score drugs and other paraphernalia on their word that one day they'd make it right. Once a man left Kern, no one ever saw him again. "You might have impressed a few of the boys in here and that might go a long way with them, but not with me. You antagonized a guard and you almost got yourself killed. Only thing in the way of that was luck. You're a stupid lucky man. That's it. Won't take you far." Ziggy turned to walk away.

"I'm breaking out. Thinking I'd take you with me."

Ziggy laughed. "You just topped yourself."

"I have resources on the outside. I want the layout of Kern, everything around it, the geography of the land..."

"You listening to me at all?"

"Yeah, but I'm hearing you call me lucky and that's not what it is."

"Donovan didn't finish the job. You can't take credit for that."

"That's not true."

"What ain't true about it?"

"My cell-mate got me a knife."

"No one else was there. Donovan set you up like he's done to everyone else who ended up in a box and took you down in the shower...."

"Yeah, just the two of us..."

Ziggy studied Dent, trying to track where this was headed. Even though there were no alternatives to the truth as he knew it, Dent's face told him there was more to it. "You got something to explain, start explaining."

"Donovan and I were the only two in the room and it wasn't Donovan."

Ziggy frowned. "Not possible."

"I wedged the handle in a crack in the wall. Ran my body into it."

"A man can't stab himself in the back four times. Even if he could, he'd still kill himself."

"Not if he knows what to hit—what not to hit."

"Yeah, and how could he know?"

"I just know. I'll do whatever it takes to get out of here. I asked you for a favor and you told me to take care of Donovan. I heard you were a man of your word."

Ziggy's mouth dropped. He stared in disbelief. "You framed him..."

"Got him off both our asses."

Just like that, there was trust between them. The disbelief faded and Ziggy got right down to business, speaking discreetly by habit, though no one was around. "You run all details by me. You got that? I'm a part of this now, and you better have a real plan because everyone talks escape and no one's got shit. Your cell-mate know?"

"Not everything, but he will. I need him."

"Anyone else?"

"No."

"Keep it that way," Ziggy said. When they were done talking business, Ziggy took a moment to reflect. He looked at Dent and shook his head again. "Consider me impressed."

Sunjata had been positioned in Kern a long time. What happened to Donovan wasn't shocking, but he had every reason to question it. Donovan was careful. He'd always known what he was doing. Most of the men who died on his watch didn't need four attempts to get the job done. They needed one. Dent was stabbed four times and survived. Everything was red flags.

After some thought, he walked through the corridor, to the holding area, and went straight to Dent's cell. In the dark, Wayne looked up at him with curious eyes.

"Your cell-mate survived. He'll be returning within the week."

Wayne nodded, surprised to hear this. He didn't have time to register how it was possible before the warden had his cell door open and stood in the center of the room. "You're up for parole in six months. You think you'll be approved?"

"Never have been. Never will be."

"Yeah, well things change. Politics and such. Parole board is looking for reasons to depopulate prisons. They're lowering the bar on potential releases."

Wayne swung his legs over the bed and was suddenly on his knees looking up at the warden desperately. "Sir, if you can get me out of here, if you can give a good word..."

"How about you show me you can be an upstanding member of society so you'll have my stamp of approval come parole?"

"Of course. Whatever it takes," he said, desperately and with gratitude.

"I'll give you something to start with..."

"Anything."

"Your cell-mate, Dent, I want to know what he's up to. I know who he is. I know what he's capable of. He's already causing a stir and I don't like it."

"What do you want me to do?" Wayne asked. He felt slightly guilty, acting as a rat on one of his own. It was a carnal sin in Kern.

"You tell me what he's doing and you're home free. I ain't stupid, so don't think about treating me like I am. I find out you've got something and you're holding back, you won't just be here forever. You'll have every privilege taken from you. You'll be thrown in with the real pieces of shit."

Wayne nodded. He understood completely. He understood so well that when the warden turned to go, he realized the warden didn't know Wayne already had information. That, or it was part of his game. Wayne was desperate.

"Sir..." Wayne said.

The warden turned.

"I may know something."

Chapter 7

1

Anthony and Carlos stopped by the station-house to research the layout of Gelatin. Anthony insisted they know exactly what they were getting themselves into, down to the history of the building. For the most part, it was reformed ex-cons, as explained. Few went on to have records. They kept their noses clean with few exceptions. They were hard-working and willing to earn a paycheck when most other companies wouldn't hire them. It was easy to see how someone with money could walk into the establishment, offer a hefty sum of money, and expect them to act.

"Looks like at most a dozen employees working the night shift, give or take," Carlos said, scanning the page. "All criminal records."

"What will you do with them?"

"I'm not there to do anything to them. I want the ringleader."

"What kind of plan are we looking at?"

"Trish and I bust in the doors when he's there tonight."

"And if Ms. Reynalds won't join you?"

"I do it alone."

"Without backup?"

"No choice. This isn't exactly sanctioned by the department and this may be our only chance at nailing the guy."

"He's gone to great lengths to cover his identity. If we pressure him, he may be unpredictable."

"Then I'll rely on Plan B: The element of surprise."

Anthony hoped everything would be as simple as Carlos was trying to sell it, but nothing had gone as predicted. "It's important that nothing goes wrong," he said.

Carlos looked up, all serious. "We'll get this guy."

Shiloh Reynalds sat on a gurney. A numbing pain shot through her forehead between her eyes, deep down to the brain. She closed her eyes, trying to suppress the throbbing. She reached over to a tray table, looking for something to pass the time, and put her fingers on a tool.

"Don't touch that honey," Trish said, from her seat in the corner.

Shiloh sighed and snatched her hand away, looking up at her mother, who sat in a chair, using all her effort to be patient as they waited for a doctor to come back.

"This is taking forever," Shiloh said.

"I know. Doctor tests always do."

Her cell phone rang and she reached to silence it until she saw it was Carlos. She hurried outside to take the call.

Carlos knew Trish needed the morning to be with Shiloh, but there had been too many developments related to the lottery to ignore. She'd once pursued Anthony's case with a passion that faded the moment her daughter was sick. Carlos figured she'd see a doctor who would tell her it was mono or just the flu and she'd be back to work. Carlos sat in his squad car with Anthony sitting passenger, listening intently to one side of the conversation.

"How's it going with Shiloh?" Carlos asked.

"It takes forever to find anything out. We're still waiting."

"You'll let me know?"

"Yeah."

"I have Mr. Freeman with me. We're meeting a guy named Dale Turntile in half an hour. I could still use the backup."

"Go without me. I'll meet you later for Gelatin."

"You sure?"

"Anthony will help. He knows what's going on. Do whatever you have to do to get the name of whoever set the lottery up."

"Sounds good. And I'm serious. I wanna know how Shiloh's doing."

"You'll know when I know. Thank you."

"Don't mention it."

Carlos shut his phone and watched the streets silently. Anthony kept quiet, on the edge of asking what was happening with Trish. He knew it was none of his business, but felt obligated to see to it that her well-being was intact. "Will officer Reynalds be joining us?"

"No," Carlos said. "Her kid's sick. She'll meet us for Gelatin."

Anthony nodded. He was disappointed. Carlos was helpful. He just didn't understand the extent of what was happening. He was outside the problem and didn't have as much invested as the beneficiaries did.

"Has she explained the situation to you?"

"The will?" Carlos asked. "Yeah, I think I get it. Victor Stone was a prick."

"He certainly found a way to immortalize himself."

It made him uncomfortable knowing that others beyond the original fifteen knew of Victor's will, but supposed many of the others had told people less trustworthy than Carlos. In fact, somewhere, a warehouse filled with ex-cons was betting on the deaths of the remaining beneficiaries. It was good Richard was bringing an end to this disease since it seemed impossible to manage.

They arrived in a run-down manufacturing area, which was empty from the outside, except for a single car where a man sat waiting for them. They exited the car and walked toward him. Dale had a pot-belly and a bald spot that covered most of his head. He shoved a wad of chew under his lip before shaking hands with Carlos and Anthony, sizing up the unlikely duo.

"Mr. Turntile?" Carlos asked.

"Yup. Who's this?" He nodded toward Anthony.

Anthony introduced himself and waited for a reaction, which he got in spades. Dale took a step back and put his hands in the air, defensively.

"This wasn't my doing. You gotta know that. Vince did what he did on his own."

"Vince put the knife in my back. You and your friends gave him incentive."

"That guy was a loose cannon. No one planned on doing a thing. If I thought it was gonna come to that, I wouldn't have been a part of it."

Carlos stepped between them. "If you mean that, you'll tell us everything we need to know. We only want the person or persons who propositioned you."

"No one knows his name."

"Then what are we doing here?" Carlos asked.

"He's coming back tonight to settle and place new bets."

"Does he know you're talking to us?"

"I don't even think he knows who I am. Gelatin hires ex-cons because it's cheap labor. The guy came to us because he knew we didn't have much and we had a history of, you know, violence and whatnot. Except most of these guys don't want to go back to the joint. We're reformed. Even Vince was a decent guy but he got himself in too deep with a bookie. We were shocked at what he did to you."

Anthony withheld his anger, burning inside at mention of the lottery.

"Alright," Carlos said. "Here's what's gonna happen: You go to work like this conversation didn't take place. Tonight, the ring-leader shows up and we bust him. You have a problem with that?"

"What happens to me?" Dale asked.

"Nothing. You didn't do anything illegal. You're a sick bastard but that's not a crime and you're not my target. Just make sure you keep your little family of co-workers clean after we bust this guy so we don't have to come back. I could throw a wire on you and turn this into a big operation, but I'm going to make this simple because I don't feel like being buried in the politics. Tonight I'll come by uninvited and make sure this guy gets the message. If what you're telling us is something other than what you say it is..."

"It's not," Dale said, adamantly.

"Why are you telling us?" Anthony asked, wary of Dale's motives.

"Just didn't like what they did. Don't agree with it. Found my faith in the joint. Trying to do what's right. Almost talked to the police after the thing was offered to us."

Anthony turned to Carlos to see if he was buying Dale's story. Carlos seemed satisfied and didn't push Dale for any further details. When they were back on the street, Anthony was unusually silent. Carlos held his cell to his ear, hoping Trish would answer while Anthony stared out the window.

"Trish is gonna be happy about this."

"If it's legitimate."

Carlos shook his head, irritated by Anthony's pessimism. He closed his phone and thought about his partner and whether or not she was okay.

Trish saw the call, but ignored it, still waiting with Shiloh. She had put so much effort into policing Victor's experiment but it slipped away from her. Carlos and Anthony were working on the lottery. Abby's killer was being hunted by Charlie Palmer which was beyond her control. She hated to think like this, but there were two large mysteries hanging over their heads and she didn't have the time or energy to pursue either. The only thing that mattered now was that her daughter was okay.

She sat patiently, rereading the certificates on the wall for the tenth time, waiting to hear what came next...

...Shiloh was cradled in her arms as Trish looked down at her face. Her eyes were barely open, her nose was just a nub, and a tangle of dark hair sat atop her head. Trish held her close and took her in. The rest of the world faded around her—the flowers and balloons, the doctors outside; Nothing else mattered in that moment.

Then Paul Reynalds interrupted her after missing the twelve hour birth. He knocked at the door, looking in with a mixture of happiness and guilt. She gave him a cold stare, which surrendered into something else quickly. She signaled him over with the tilt of her head and he silently approached and knelt at her side.

"I'm so sorry," he said, directed at Shiloh, but spoken to Trish.

He turned to her with regret in his eyes. He was torturing himself, and she wanted to let him off the hook, but she couldn't.

"*How could you let this happen?*"

"*She's three weeks early. I was gone half a day. I'm so sorry. The timing was terrible. I know that's not a good excuse, but...*"

"*No, it's not.*"

"*It was a fluke. I can't help what my job demands. Come on Trish. I've got a job that I used to think was a pipe-dream.*"

Trish didn't know the true nature of his job. The details were always vague, and she couldn't share Paul's excitement as long as he worked for a man like Victor. She couldn't find a way to make him walk away from something he loved so much. She secretly hoped missing the birth of his daughter would be the wake-up call he needed.

"*Is it worth it? Look what you missed for that damn job.*"

"*I'm Chief Financial Officer. We've been over this. I sometimes have to run at the drop of a dime, remember?*"

"*And I haven't complained, despite how I feel about him. He sends you to God knows where over the weekend when we have plans. And even that's fine, but Paul...*"

He looked down at his daughter and stroked a finger across her small forehead, brushing a strand of hair to the side.

"*If I could go back and do it over, I would. She was early. Much earlier than we expected.*"

She didn't respond. Only looked lovingly at Shiloh. After a long moment, she looked up at Paul with a smile as if to tell him everything was okay.

"*You know who I ran into on the way in?*" *she asked.*

"*Who?*"

"*Debbie Brown.*"

"*Debbie Brown...*" *he said to himself, trying to place the name.*

"*She runs a day-care out of her home and lives three blocks away.*"

"*Right,*" *he said.*

"*We got to talking...If I went back and worked days...*"

"*Why?*"

"*Why what?*"

"*Why work if you don't have to? Am I not making enough?*"

"*You're making plenty. That's not it.*"

"*Then why work?*"

"*I don't know. I didn't see my life turning out like this. That's all. I always wanted to be a cop. Always planned on it.*"

"*And you were.*"

"*For what? Four years? Enough time to figure out what I was doing. Suddenly I'm pregnant and a stay-at-home mom.*"

"Nothing wrong with that."

"Maybe not to you."

"Shiloh will appreciate it someday. With all the stories you see on the news these days, who knows who you're giving your kid to?"

"Yeah, well I know Debbie."

"I know you feel a sense of obligation or feel like you have some kind of feminist responsibility..."

"Hold on," she interrupted. "This isn't like that. I just want to work. It's not a gender issue. You sound like a sexist when you use that word by the way."

"Yeah, well it has real meaning and if the shoe fits..."

"It doesn't."

"I just don't want you to look back and wish you'd been home more."

"What about you? When you gonna be home more?"

"I'm sorry, but my job isn't a set schedule. I'll never be able to give you a specific time."

"You can at least let me know when you'll be late, or give me notice when you leave for a weekend. If I go back to the station, we need to coordinate schedules. We need to know who's picking up our daughter and when."

Paul sighed. "I'm taking on more. You can't go back. You don't need to."

"I never said I needed to. I said I wanted to."

"I can't come to terms with that."

"With what?"

"You want to be a cop. You want to put your life in danger, yet you have a husband and kid back home."

"Yeah okay Paul, I <u>want</u> to be in danger."

"Sure sounds like it."

"I want to help people."

"Yeah, but that's not what happens. Your job is demanding and there's too much risk."

"There's risk in everything."

"We're set for life on my salary and there's nowhere to go but up. We have a daughter now. Most women today don't get the luxury you have. There's no reason that you have to have a side hobby that will add strain to our lives."

"This isn't up to you."

"Maybe not, but I've been working steadily. If you want your little hobby, you find a daycare or a sitter and you pay them out of your pocket. Makes no sense to me, so if this is what you're set on, you can deal with the problems you're creating..."

...You might want to sit down."

Dr. Neomin stood between Shiloh and Trish with a chart in his hand. Trish waited silently to hear what she'd already suspected: It wasn't just headaches and dizziness.

"I've reviewed the results of the CT scan. I did find an abnormal growth of cells on the posterior cranial fossa, which in children is a red flag for a brain tumor."

"Wait," Trish said, stumbling over her words as she tried to register what he was saying. "No, hold on. Just wait. But she's healthy. She's always been."

"I know," he said, sympathetically.

"So what? You're saying my daughter needs surgery?"

"Based on my diagnosis, yes. But I'd like to run more tests and consider our options. Depending on the size and exact location of the tumor, she may need radiotherapy."

"Okay, so..." she trailed off, in disbelief. There were too many questions.

"I need to run more tests. It will take time."

"How much time?"

"We'll contact your insurance carrier with what we can and can't do. Like I said, we have to run more tests so we can pinpoint this exactly. There's ground that needs to be covered before I can lay out solid options. If it helps, I don't believe this isn't treatable."

She gathered herself and turned to Shiloh, who stared forward as if this was meaningless.

Her cell buzzed, but she ignored it. It was probably Carlos, pushing her to pursue things that didn't really matter. Suddenly, she resented Anthony. She resented everything she'd prioritized. She'd been so busy doing her job in relation to Victor's will that she'd ignored the pain her daughter had been in. She'd tried to police a situation that had spiraled out of control. Anthony could handle his own problems. She'd lost touch with what she was supposed to be first: A mother.

She turned her phone off and turned to Neomin. "What do we do next?"

2

His first trip back to Los Angeles meant nothing to Jason. He attended Richard's meeting and left without any feelings about what the group was trying to do. It all sounded great, but he wouldn't consider it over until after the fact. He didn't bother to stop at Stone Enterprises, but caught a glimpse of the building on his flight out of the city. When he landed in Maui, Erica Drake picked him up at the airport and took him back to their beach-front property. He passed out right after and awoke ten hours later. Erica was gone.

He sat up, looking out the windows at the sun overhead, and wondered what to do next.

Every moment in Maui had been a mistake. He kept thinking he'd eventually adapt and learn to love his new surroundings, but he had yet to come around. Erica was excited he moved there and gave him a tour of her favorite places on the island, but then disappeared in the following days. She spent her days on the beach, playing volleyball, going for drinks at local clubs. She'd tried to get him to come along, but Jason stayed back, unable to dive into the party scene. He'd hoped she'd get tired of the endless parties, but she stayed out every day, and after some time, he concluded that he was foolish for being there.

They had sex sometimes, but it seemed meaningless, like he was there when she needed it. Despite the detachment, Erica wanted him there. She allowed him to live with her and treated him well when they were together. They weren't defined, which is where the problem rested, and Jason wasn't sure he wanted to be anything more than friends. He couldn't keep up with her, and didn't agree with her reckless lifestyle. Every so often, he'd get it in his head that maybe he could adjust his habits, but he wasn't there yet—maybe never would be.

He tried calling her twice, but she ignored her cell—or his call. After his trip to Los Angeles, he realized it was time to have a chat with Erica about where they were going. He'd made a decision without analysis. It wasn't the way Jason operated, but the damage was done. It was nothing he couldn't undo, but he needed some footing with wherever they were headed.

She came home later that night, but was only stopping by to shower before going out again. She invited him along and he turned her down. She didn't look disappointed. Maybe she only asked because she knew he'd say no. Maybe she didn't want him there.

"You should stay in tonight," he said. "We could have dinner and watch a movie."

"Already made plans," she said.

After she hurried out the door without a hug or a kiss or a "see ya later," his mind began turning. He could only wonder how he got here—what he was thinking. His mother put it in his head to do something spontaneous to be happy. He had no problem with spontaneity. He just wasn't sure the end result was that he was happy. He now resided in the most beautiful place in the world, but he was isolated—just as he was back home, except back home he knew his role. Here, he didn't know what to do when he woke up in the morning.

He went to the gym, worked out harder than usual, and stopped home before leaving again. He walked down the beach, stood in the ocean, had dinner at a bar, had a few drinks, and sat outside. He stared forward, club music and the sound of people enjoying themselves in the distance.

He struggled to find his way home, mumbling the whole way. He had something to say to Erica, but when he arrived at the condo, the lights were off and the place was still empty.

He thought about Victor, the almost surreal upbringing he had, the loveless relationship they had as father and son, partners in business, shortened by a tragic death. He wished he'd known him better. He wished he'd known him in a different way. He wished he knew his father in a similar situation—what Victor could have done if he was vulnerable and lost, but he never was. That part of the apple fell far from the tree. Jason Stone had a chunk of personality that his father never came close to resembling.

Leave Erica and take what's yours.

Jason's eyes began to close as he heard Victor's voice.

You can have anything you want, but it's time to step up. It's time to be the leader you were born to be.

He tried to keep his eyes open, but drifted in and out, intent to stay awake until Erica came back and gave him a piece of her mind, but less than ten seconds after his head hit the pillow, he was out. As he passed out, the last thing he heard was his father taunting him. If he'd remembered it the next morning, he'd remember how real it sounded.

3

"Shiloh okay?" Carlos asked. Trish stood against the wall with her arms crossed, irritated to see her partner and Anthony. They had tried to get a hold of her all day but she'd ignored every call.

"I don't know yet," she said.

"It's taking a long time."

"Yeah, I talked to the chief. I don't know when I'm coming back. I need to see this through."

"What's going on?" Carlos asked with genuine concern. Behind him, Anthony stood fidgeting.

"Nothing. What did you find out?" she asked.

"We have a contact. Guy who worked with Vince and participated in the lottery."

Anthony stepped forward. "Tonight we have a window of opportunity to meet the man who set the whole thing up." He waited for her reaction, but she was seemingly unaffected. "I don't know what has you tied down Ms. Reynalds, but it may need to be put on hold so we can prevent this from happening."

"On hold?" she asked, suddenly cold. He'd hit a nerve.

"We're all targets if we don't stop this from happening."

"The lottery isn't our only problem. What about Todd Mason? Abby Palmer..."

She knew there was more than one thing at play, but she'd made a promise to herself that she'd put Shiloh first. At least until she knew she was okay. "Let it go," she said, dryly.

Anthony and Carlos exchanged glances. Carlos signaled Anthony to back off and turned to Trish. "All we have to do is arrest him. Doesn't matter how we do it."

"Then go alone. Or talk to the department. I won't be there. I'll be here."

"I'm here if you need to talk about Shiloh or anything else."

"I know," she said. "I'd rather you just stay away from this. I shouldn't have said anything. It has nothing to do with you and I don't care what happens…"

…Paul may have been bluffing or giving her a guilt trip, but as soon as she was able, she went straight to the station. No matter what the reason, she had no intention of letting his attitude stop her. She went to her chief, who hadn't seen her since she was eight months pregnant. He gave her a look up and down, impressed she'd dropped her baby weight. He stood from behind his desk and hurried around for a hug.

"Look at you. Lose a little weight Reynalds?"

"Six pounds. Eleven ounces."

"Very good. Congratulations. We got the pics you sent. Cute kid."

"Thank you."

"You sure Paul's the father?"

"Pretty sure."

"Cause she's too cute to be Paul's."

"She's his."

"We can do some DNA testing to be sure."

She smiled at the chief, but he saw through it. Something was on her mind. "What brings you in? You coming back to us?"

"That's what I'm here to talk about. There still a spot?"

"Always. Especially for you. What you looking for? Your old beat?"

"I need a few adjustments. I need to be home by five every day. That's the best I could do."

"Done," he said, without hesitation.

"That was easy."

"If that's what it takes..."

"Thank you," she said, sincerely. "And really, if all you have is desk duty..."

"Nah, we'll get you on the street. Got a transfer in who needs a partner anyway. Just let me know when you're ready. You sure you don't wanna stay home with the baby? I don't know if leaving her with Paul is such a good idea."

"I need to work. He'll be okay."

As she exited the office, she spotted the rookie cop the chief mentioned sitting outside the office with a folder in hand. Carlos was still ironing out the last of his paperwork and readying himself for a career on the force. He had that look that all cops had when they first arrived—eager, but scared. He was probably thinking about how he couldn't wait to learn the ropes and then prove what a hero he could be. She sat across from him, and smiled.

"I'm Trish Reynalds."

"Carlos," he said.

"You the new guy?"

"First day."

"Couldn't make it as a firefighter?"

"No ma'am. This was my first choice."

"You should have weighed your options."

"I'll give it some thought," he said, unsure how to respond to hazing.

"I'm going to be your partner," she said. "So I'm sizing you up...checking you out... This is first impressions, so be careful." She maintained a straight face, and he cowered. "This moment is monumental. I'll decide right now whether or not I'm coming back and it's completely dependent on you."

"What am I supposed to do?"

"Just seem like a decent enough guy that I can spend most days in a cramped car with you. You shower daily?"

"Yes ma'am. Where'd you go?"

"What?"

"You said you might be coming back. Why'd you leave?"

"I have the option of being a stay at home mother, or refilling my old position. Just tell me why you're a cop."

He nodded and laughed to himself. "Cause I used to be the guy the cops chased. I know the neighborhood and I speak the language."

"Your hair's burned," she said, pointing at a spot on Carlo's head where a patch of hair was frazzled. Carlos tried to turn and block it from

her view, slightly embarrassed.

"Yeah, that's nothing."

"It doesn't look like nothing," she said, smirking.

"Not nothing. I mean, my uncle Sal cuts my hair and he screwed it up. He was wetting down the side of my head behind my ear with some sort of lotion and then he stood back and I smelled butane and I felt a flash of heat and I realized he'd lit my hair on fire. He didn't use clippers or a razor. He just singed the hair right off. I've been to a lot of places, but I've never seen a barber anywhere use fire except my uncle Sal."

Trish laughed and decided she liked Carlos. "There are plenty of places you can get it done cheap without being lit on fire."

"Yeah," he said. "You like the job then? Take it over staying home and all?"

"Of course."

"The rest of these guys cool?" he asked, looking around the station.

"Yeah. You've got nothing to worry about. There's a camaraderie between cops. You meet someone outside this place, in plain clothes, and find out they're a cop...you've made a new friend. Doesn't matter where you are or what kind of cop. There's an unspoken bond between them." She stopped suddenly and realized in the moment that she'd given herself advice. Her words applied to her life and she wished she was able to find the words with Paul as she had been able to with Carlos. "You know what?" she said. "A lot of people think we're the bad guys, but we've all got each other. It's really great."

"So I shouldn't have been a fireman?"

"Oh, you should have been a fireman," she said with a smile. "But this works too..."

…She entered her daughter's hospital room to find her in surprisingly good spirits. The color in her face was back, and for a moment, Trish felt that everything would be okay.

"Hey sweetie," she said.

"Can we go?" Shiloh asked. She was bored, and had been texting friends. Her only objective was to see a movie that night with a group of friends, including a boy she liked.

"Not yet."

"I'm fine."

"They're not done."

Shiloh's good mood faded and she looked down, visibly bored and frustrated from the long stay at the hospital. "Are you going back to work?"

"Of course not," Trish said, surprised she'd believe that was possible.

"Not until I know you're okay."

"I was sick last week and you went to work."

"I didn't know how sick you were then."

She didn't want to explain that Shiloh was sick once a day every other week since she could remember. Every conversation seemed to get heated, so she avoided the topic altogether and offered to grab her something from the vending machine instead.

A few minutes later, Trish walked through the double doors to the parking lot to let out a deep breath. From the lobby, Dr. Neomin saw her outside and joined her. "Just tell me what's happening," she said.

He contemplated for a moment. "Shiloh has what's called an optic nerve glioma."

"Cancer?"

"No, it's a tumor. Untreated, in time there will be peripheral loss of vision in one or both eyes."

"Does she need surgery?"

"That's one option, but we have a lot to talk about before moving forward."

"Then what can we do now?"

"I'd like to start her on Corticosteroids and consider Radiation Therapy."

"What will that do?"

"It kills rapidly producing cell DNA. The downside is that it may also kill healthy cells, but it will shrink the tumor so we can be ready for surgery if it's something we need to do."

"It has to be done, right?"

"Yes."

"Then I want it done."

4

Jason woke the next morning to find Erica hadn't come home. He nursed his hangover and called her number but she didn't pick up. By noon, he thought about calling the police, but didn't want to raise concern if she was just out with friends or another guy.

She arrived home shortly after noon and by then, Jason lost all motivation to talk. Instead, he'd packed a suitcase which sat promptly at his side, staying to say goodbye as a courtesy. Erica entered through the kitchen screen door, dragging her feet. She hadn't gone to bed yet. The sight of her demeanor confirmed his decision.

"I shouldn't have come," he said.

She looked up, suddenly aware he was sitting there. Her eyes darted to the suitcase. "Why would you say that?"

"We don't know each other."

"I'm the same girl you met in L.A."

"I know. It was my mistake. I don't expect anything."

"Mistake? Okay Jason. Go ahead and go then."

"You have no reason to be upset."

"We have everything you could possibly want here and then some."

"What 'we' are you referring to?"

"You and me. Who do you think?"

"You and me," Jason said with a laugh. "What is this relationship to you exactly?"

"You're always invited. I've made that clear. But you'd rather mope because you love being unhappy."

"Then why are you with me?"

"I don't know. You tell me," Erica said. "Who are you exactly? Because the guy I met seemed to want a better life and I liked that guy. And I have money, and he happened to have money, and so we could basically live in paradise for the rest of our lives, but he's looking for another job and more responsibility and just needs to be miserable so he doesn't have to feel guilty for being happy. I'm just waiting for you to get here. You moved, but you're not here."

"So what are you telling me? That you've been waiting for me to lighten up? That you've been loyal to me? You're not out fucking other guys?"

"I meet people."

"And then what?"

"Are you asking if I've been having sex? Yeah, I've had sex."

"Then what am I doing here?"

"I don't know," she said with a sigh.

"I have a pretty good idea. I'm security. Sooner or later, your money will run dry. Then, you'll cozy up to me, tell me you love me, stick around for a few nights, and disappear."

"Believe it or not, not everyone in the world wants you for your money."

"Alright," he said, getting to his feet. "We're done with this."

"Wait," she said, changing her tone. She reached forward and grabbed his arm. He turned to her, as if she was joking, saw she wasn't, and softened. "You have to be able to see that this was a bad idea."

"I know it was," she said, suddenly breaking down into tears. "But I'm pregnant."

5

"Her head's clouded," Anthony said, as the squad car rolled through neighborhoods. "She should be here."

"She's removing herself from the situation and I agree with her," Carlos said. "It's too dangerous."

"What's wrong with her daughter?" Anthony asked, abruptly. It had been on his mind that Shiloh didn't have the flu. Maybe there was actually something wrong with her.

"I don't know," Carlos said.

"Why has she been at the hospital all morning?"

"She's been passing out and having dizzy spells. Fainting, throwing up..."

"You know, Trish came to see me at the hospital after I was attacked. She had been looking for alibis. She expressed fear of herself...of her capabilities."

"What's that mean?"

"If she wanted that money, she could have it. She was aware of that and it scared her."

"She's a good person."

"When a person commits a horrid crime, there's intent. Is it a bad thing to steal food to feed a starving family? You ever ask yourself if a moral person desperately in need of money should be held to the same standard as a morally bankrupt person who wanted it?"

"She'd come to me if that was on her mind."

"Bad things are happening Carlos. I've been attacked. Another killed. Another presumably dead. No one's behind bars. There's a meeting tonight in which a dozen ex-convicts will be placing bets on lives...and Trish is one of them."

Carlos nodded, his eyes glazing over as he considered.

"Knowing that...and knowing her head is somewhere else, you don't feel like it's your responsibility to protect her?"

"Maybe she was right," Carlos said. "We have no reason to be there. We need to include the department. If we don't do this by the book, no charge is gonna stick."

"We don't have that option. You draw him out and leave him to me," Anthony said, his face rigid.

Carlos suddenly hit the brake and pulled to the side of the road. He turned to Anthony and studied his face. Anthony was serious. "What are you suggesting?"

"It's better you don't know."

Carlos thought hard for a moment. He took a breath and closed his eyes. "This is how it's going to go down: I go in and claim there was a distress call from the factory and I'm there to investigate. While I'm there, I get names. All we need is names. We can work outside Gelatin without raising suspicion."

"If they suspect anything, you put yourself at risk."

"I'll get a name and you may do as you wish, but I don't wanna hear about it. Then my hands...Trish's hands...washed of this. Anyone turns up dead or harmed, you'll have no protection from me."

Anthony smiled to himself. If everything went as planned, he'd easily find who was behind the lottery and expose them. Then, when the Reverend disposed of the will once and for all, the mystery man would be left to contend with himself and what he had done forever. "Deal," Anthony said...

...Miss Reynalds," Victor said, calmly. "Have a seat."

Trish stood in the doorway leading into Victor's office as he poured himself a drink and offered one to her.

"No thanks. This won't take long."

"This is about Paul," he said, taking a sip from his glass.

"It must seem ridiculous that I'm coming to you with this."

"It seems motherly. Does Paul need to be taken care of?"

"No."

"You would like him home more."

Trish couldn't stand how Victor wanted to figure everything out on his own. "It would be nice if Paul could find the time to be around for, oh I don't know, his baby being born and stuff."

"Is there another on the way?"

"No, but he's got one to take care of. I'm going back to work. We'd like to keep the option open of having another baby and I don't really appreciate that you make Paul choose between work and family just because you'd rather count your money than see your own son."

Victor ignored the dig. "Why are you going back to work?"

"I like what I do."

"You'd rather be a beat cop than secure your daughter's future?"

"Haven't you heard the news?" Trish asked. "Cops make money too."

"Paul's a great addition here. There's nothing in life that you will need badly enough to justify a career with LAPD."

"Money can buy comfort. Not contentment. My happiness correlates with my causes and relationships. Not my net worth."

"What's stability worth to you?"

"I don't need your kind of stability. I don't need to have the biggest house or most expensive item on the menu. There's a difference between

greed and stability."

"Is that right?" he said with a smile.

She nodded.

"And you associate greed with evil..."

She nodded again.

"I see," he said, rounding his desk and leaning against it, facing Trish as he spoke slowly. "Nearly every great achievement in history has been the result of someone trying to achieve or create something for their own desires. Greed, without immoral acts, is extremely beneficial. If someone works hard for everything they want and deal and trade peacefully without using violence or defrauding people, then a person is offering services people want, which is empirically verified because people are paying for that service."

"Stone Enterprises is a revolving door of employment."

"You don't trust Paul's job is secure..."

"Nope. You hired him to get to me. You'd let him go for the same reason."

"What if I gave you assurance?"

"Depends on what you want."

"About two months ago, I had a heart attack. Only twelve people in the world know that. You're number thirteen."

"Does Paul know?"

"No and I ask you respect that. It got me thinking about what will happen when I'm gone—what would come of Stone Enterprises." He slid a paper to the center of the desk. Trish leaned forward, unable to read what it said, but curious nonetheless. "This is my living will. It's a burden dividing my worth."

"Give it to charity."

"I've never found one worthy. Most are very self-serving when you dig deep enough. I've written a few friends in, some family, but it's unsatisfactory. I have yet to find one person deserving of what I have to offer. Even my son seems to want nothing to do with my legacy." Victor's eyes scanned the paper sadly before he looked up. "If I die today, it holds up and I suppose it's good enough, but I've been thinking about a second draft."

"I don't want your money."

"You don't want security? I could give you two percent of my worth and you'd be set."

"Then I have two reasons to celebrate when you die."

"What exactly is your problem with me?"

"I don't have a particular problem with you."

"I'm not dumb Miss Reynalds."

"We're different. We hold different values. You take by force and intimidation. Most people earn respect. You demand it."

"I built everything I have from the ground up. I'm a first generation millionaire and I provide jobs and wealth to the community. How exactly does that not demand respect?"

"It's too much. You always want more, but there's a line you cross when you have too much. You don't care about money Mr. Stone. You want power and it ruins everyone around you. I see it in Paul, just as I see it with the jerkoffs that come in and out of your building."

"How many people think they're secure and later fall on hard times?"

"I'll manage."

"I offer options. How would you like to retire by the time you're forty and spend the rest of your life tending to your child's needs? One day, you may find you wish you had that option."

Trish got to her feet and shook her head dismissively. "All I want is for you to give Paul some wiggle room so I can work. And take care of him without demanding too much. He's stressed. He was never high-strung until he started working for you. Stop poisoning my husband's priorities. Not everyone has to be as miserable as you."

"Offer ends when you walk out the door."

Trish made a point to stand and walk to the door with exaggeration. His lips pressed together and he controlled his breathing steadily. He didn't like being rejected. He especially didn't like disapproval of everything he stood for. As she grabbed the doorknob, he got to his feet.

"Why do you want to be a cop so badly?" he asked.

She turned and a smile crept across her face. "To put guys like you in prison..."

...They parked the car four blocks from Gelatin and sat in the parked car for five minutes before either said anything. The neighborhood was a ghost town. Most buildings had been abandoned for the day.

They watched the building as one by one, men arrived in their vehicles and entered the building for the beginning of their shift. After eight, no more cars arrived. They sat silently anyway, neither man wanting to be the one to initiate the confrontation.

"I'm going in," Carlos finally said.

"What happens if he's not there?"

"We'll bust some heads until we get a name. Stay put."

Carlos exited the car and walked to the building, surveying his surroundings as he approached the entrance.

Anthony heard music in the distance. He turned and saw lights on down the block. His eyes fixated on a small tavern filled with people laughing and having a blast. His eyes filled with envy.

The ex-convicts who work the night shift at Gelatin Steel turned their heads as Carlos entered the building. Everyone froze reflexively upon seeing a cop. He could be there for any one of them. Carlos walked through the factory, looking from man to man as if searching for the right face.

A supervisor spotted Carlos and hurried over. "Can I help you officer?" he asked with a fake smile. He was breathless from his hurry to intercept Carlos before he walked too far.

"I received a distress call from this location."

The supervisor looked around the room. "I doubt that."

"This is where the call came from. Police procedure to check it out."

The supervisor looked past him nervously, checking to see if Carlos was alone. "I can ask my guys, but we just started shift. If someone butt-dialed you, it was an accident."

"You sure about that?"

"Yeah. Heard some fighting outside when I got here. Domestic dispute of some sort. Maybe that was what the call was about."

"What's your name?"

"Matt."

"You got a last name?"

"Yeah, Smith."

Carlos nodded, watching his eyes closely. "You got a guy by the name of Dale here?"

"Nope. No Dale." He shook his head. Carlos couldn't spot the lie—assuming it was a lie.

"You mind if I look at your time cards?"

"Do you have a warrant?"

"I can go back to the station and get one, or you can get the time-cards. If I have to get a warrant, I'll figure you have something to hide. All I want is time-cards. With a warrant, I tear this place apart."

"Fine. I don't care. You're mistaken. There's no Dale here."

As the night supervisor walked toward the office to grab the time-cards, Carlos looked around the factory. He hadn't expected Matt's reaction. He clearly didn't want an officer in his factory but when Carlos asked about Dale, the supervisor seemed confused. If there was no Dale, then the lie began outside Gelatin Steel. The lie began with their informant.

Anthony's eyes glazed over as he walked slowly toward the bar. He came upon the large window that separated him from the crowd inside. A drunk at the bar turned his way and they made eye contact. The drunk gave him a nod and raised his glass as if to offer a toast. Anthony returned the gesture with a smile.

Just then, an explosion ripped through the air. Anthony turned in time to see the windows burst outward at Gelatin. His eyes went wide and his knees weak. They were set up.

Before he could do anything more, he called for help. A crowd was already gathering to find the source of the explosion. Soon, the police would be here. He thought about Carlos with sudden terror. There couldn't be any survivors.

He pulled his cell out of his pocket with shaky hands and dialed. He waited for her to answer. "You need to get here now..."

An hour later, Trish stood in the middle of a crowd of police, firefighters, and paramedics. A crowd nearby watched as water cascaded onto what was once the steel company. Trish's face was tired, lifeless, and streaked with tears through the dust on her face.

Anthony stood behind her, giving it time to sink in. He waited a long time, but she remained motionless.

"Carlos came here to protect you," he said. "I want you to know that. We were set up. Clearly, the man who orchestrated the lottery wants to eliminate those of us who know. The man said his name was Dale. If we can trace his number, or if I could identify him, we can find him."

Trish turned to him slowly, her brow wrinkled and a quick shake of disbelief. Too much was happening. She didn't want to talk about Dale, or Victor, or the beneficiaries. "There were only fifteen of us," she said. "We've been trying to protect the lives of fifteen people."

"We don't have another option."

"More than fifteen have died."

"I understand, but more will die if we don't stop these people now, before it gets out of control."

"No," she said, shaking her head. "Let it happen. More have been killed than were at the reading. What's the difference between them and us?"

"Those men were criminals," he started.

"No!" she shouted unexpectedly. "Carlos was in there. He was better than...!" She trailed off.

"And I want justice the same as you. I didn't do this."

"You're on your own," she said. "I don't owe anything to any of you."

"Someone will win," he said calmly. "At the expense of our lives, someone will win."

"I'm the one who deserves it!" She shouted so loud, others stopped and looked from nearby.

"What are you saying?" Anthony asked.

"Victor took more from me than any of you."

"That may be so, but you don't want it. This is what he wanted. You're giving in to a man you hated."

"It should have been you inside..."

"Trish..."

"No, don't..." she said, backing away from his reach, "It should have been you. It's not like you ever gave a shit about your life anyway."

Anthony looked down. He saw the statement coming before it was out of her mouth. His suicide would haunt him forever. He was viewed as a man who didn't deserve to live while other people who respected life were dying all around him. "You don't want the money," he said, quietly, ignoring what she said.

"If it means my kid lives, then yes I do," she said, her voice trembling as she looked him in the eyes to show just how serious she was. All the time she'd spent away from work, the way her head hadn't been in the game, her short temper...it was all on the table. Every failed attempt to thwart whoever was behind this, Carlos' death...Trish had warned Anthony about this when she'd visited him in the hospital, but he'd never believed it could happen until now.

Trish's daughter was dying, and to save her, it would require a good deal of money.

Anthony watched her walk toward the factory as a gurney was brought out by her fellow officers. She began to break down shortly before she reached it. Carlos was gone and her daughter was dying. Anthony dreaded the realization that Trish no longer cared what happened to the group. She may have even realized how to solve her problems.

Chapter 8

1

In his 20s, Jason Stone still hadn't grown accustomed to the mansion he'd shared with his father for so many years. Every morning, he stood in the kitchen and listened to silence and wondered what it was about having so much space that people envied. He rummaged the cabinets, searching for a blender, which was promptly put in a cabinet built specifically for it. Everything had its own place.

He blended a power-shake and drank straight from the blender as a shadow passed behind him. He turned, expecting to see Victor, but came face to face with Bridget Bloom, dressing herself and pulling her hair back in a pony-tail. She stopped abruptly and put her hand over her heart, startled to find Jason standing there. She let out a breath as she realized who she was facing.

"Hi," Jason said.

"I'm so sorry. I didn't think you'd be awake."

"It's no problem," he said, smiling knowingly.

"I'm Bridget."

She extended her hand and they shook. Jason offered her a shake, which she surprisingly took, immediately giving Jason the impression that they were buddies.

"So I take it from your reaction that Victor didn't warn you about me."

"Uh, sorry, but I haven't seen him since yesterday, so..."

"We've been dating a month," she said, matter-of-factly. "But it's okay. I get it."

Bridget seemed too smart to be so naïve, but if what she was saying was true, Victor wouldn't see just anyone for a month. He liked the way Bridget carried herself and spoke. Most women he'd encountered snooping around weren't like that. Maybe Victor saw in Bridget what Jason saw. If he did, and Victor was ready to commit to something long term, it might open up the possibility to fill the house a little—build a family.

As he thought about Victor, Victor entered the kitchen, joining them, working his tie into a perfect knot.

"Good morning," he said, sizing up the duo. Jason nodded and watched Victor approach Bridget and gave her a quick kiss.

"Sorry if I woke you," she said. "I tried to get up quietly."

"I was awake. You met Jason."

"I did. We were just talking."

"Is that right?" Victor said. He looked at Jason, who smiled and nodded.

"Sweet kid you got."

"I agree," he said. Jason wondered if he meant it or if he was being agreeable to impress his alleged girlfriend. Jason smiled awkwardly, trying to grow accustomed to the rare scenario. "You need a ride to school?"

"Nope," Jason said.

Victor turned to Bridget. "Do you have time for breakfast?"

Jason almost laughed. He couldn't remember the last time—if ever—Victor wasn't rushing a woman out the door in a manner that seemed as if he wanted to never see them again.

"I have a client in an hour," she said.

"Boscos on the corner is fast. We've got time and you need to eat."

"Love to, but I'll take a rain-check. I'm going over briefings. I'll get in touch later."

"Okay," Victor said.

They kissed again and she hurried to the door, looking over her shoulder with a smile. "Nice meeting you again Jason." Jason smiled and waved, still stunned by their interaction.

"How about you?" Victor asked.

"How about me, what?"

"Boscos?"

"The restaurant? What about it?"

"Are you hungry?"

"Sure," he said slowly.

"Get your shoes…"

…Jason stood with his feet in the ocean and a frown set on his face. He spent the better part of the morning wondering how he got to where he was. He walked out the night before, unable to fathom the idea of being bound to Erica forever with a child. Every move he made was wrong. So much for being spontaneous with his life.

After Erica broke the news, he walked out and went to the gym, where he worked out harder than he ever had in his life. After his workout, he stood in the men's room, staring into a mirror. He thought he saw Victor in the reflection for a moment, but upon observation, he reassured himself it was only Jason, and though the physical resemblances were strikingly close—closer every day—his father only haunted him in features and mannerisms.

After the gym, he walked straight to the ocean and stood knee deep in the water, staring into the distance.

I'm not ready to have a child. I haven't done anything yet.

He wondered if this is how Aileen felt. Maybe even his father. After all, Victor barely raised him. He just gave him entertainment to pass the time. He was all about business, and allowed Jason to be self-sufficient.

He turned to the sound of music in the distance and watched the action at a bar called Kea Lani. He slowly walked to the bar, ready to let loose, just as Erica always recommended. He stayed in the bar until last call, staring at the mirror across the bar. As his vision blurred, his eyes sunk in until the shadows covered his face completely.

"Ready to go back and take your place?" a voice said.

Jason didn't turn and wasn't surprised his father sat next to him. He tried to ignore what he knew he was conjuring, but couldn't avoid the sight of Victor sitting on the stool at his side in the mirror.

"You're dead," Jason said matter of factually.

"Apparently I'm more productive dead than you are alive. What are you doing with your life?"

"Getting as far away from your bullshit as possible," Jason said.

"You're doing everything wrong."

"Yeah, I know. You want me to be a rich asshole like you and die alone and hateful."

"Is that your reality?"

Even his dream—or whatever it was—was criticizing him, commanding his obedience the same way his father had. He shifted his eyes, running a script of ways he could tell his father off, but it would only satisfy him until he sobered up and realized he'd given a piece of his mind to a bar-stool.

"Tell me why I should go back," Jason said.

"Because it's in your blood. You're supposed to be a leader, and I saw hints of leadership throughout your life, but you held back. It doesn't matter what you do with Stone Enterprises, but you have to go back."

"Why is that?"

"Because you know there's a river of corruption in Stone Enterprises."

"That you started."

"You don't know how things unfolded. You shouldn't have left it in Bell's hands."

"If you didn't want it in his hands, then why did you keep him around?"

Victor didn't answer. Instead, he stood and turned away from Jason.

"This woman—she was wrong and you know it. You knew it all along. You ran so you wouldn't have to face me, but there are things that are more important than whether or not I raised you right."

Though Victor was a figment of his imagination, he struck a nerve. He wasn't saying what Jason would imagine him saying. He was talking cryptically, giving Jason substance that was beyond the father he knew—or maybe memories were coming back. Things Victor said in his final days were making sense. Even in his drunken state, he found clarity. Suddenly, he realized he wasn't supposed to leave—there were things left undone, things in motion that needed attention.

"Wait," Jason said, turning toward Victor's voice. "What is Bell..?"

He trailed off. No one was there.

2

Jason tried calling his mother. He didn't know why. He didn't usually need to vent, but he wanted to hear her voice. She didn't notice her phone buzzing. She kept it in her locker during her shift and didn't usually get important calls anyway. She was consumed by business on her Friday shift. Lights flashed, women danced on-stage, and men hooted and hollered whether the dancing was good or not.

A bottle smashed at Aileen's foot and she hopped away as alcohol splattered her leg. She'd dropped a lot of bottles lately and Tyson usually ignored it, still honoring his agreement with Jason. He watched from across the bar as Aileen hurried away from the mess, leaving it for the busboy. His eyes narrowed. He couldn't take it much longer. He thought about his encounter with Jason. He wouldn't hit Aileen, but he couldn't let her continue to break the bottles and give out free drinks. She was costing him money and he couldn't stay quiet any longer.

"What the hell is wrong with you?" he asked, grabbing her arm much harder than he'd intended. "You know how much waste we've had because you're a klutz?"

"It's one beer."

"One in the last five minutes. What's the point of having you here if you're burning my money? I don't care about the broken bottles so much as the free drinks you constantly give out. I've got about a case per night missing according to inventory."

"You said to give free drinks now and then. I'll cut back."

"Yeah, why don't you do that?" Tyson said, sarcastically before walking away.

She couldn't focus after that. Her hands were shaky and her knees were weak. She looked at the clock. *Five hours left.*

Most men didn't pay attention to the waitresses. They were always in too big of a hurry to talk. The strippers made flirting part of their job. Sometimes the guys at the bar would try to pick up the waitress because they were sharp enough to know they had better odds of taking one home. Alfonso Romero had his eyes on Aileen since he entered, and he sat at the bar, occasionally stealing a glance in her direction. He saw her drop the bottle and eavesdropped on the following encounter between her and Tyson. While she took a breath, preparing for a second wind to push through her shift, he took the opportunity to make himself known.

"Why don't you take a break?" he said, nodding to the stool at his side.

"We're busy. Sorry baby-doll."

She tried to slip past.

"Maybe you need a new line of work," Alfonso said.

"Excuse me?"

"All night, I've seen these drunk assholes treat you like dirt. I saw a guy grab your ass an hour ago and you didn't flinch. You don't get paid like the girls on stage."

"This whole place is eye candy for men. Not just on-stage, but thanks for the concern." She started to walk away, but stopped, sizing him up. He had dark hair and amber eyes. He had a well-groomed beard and dressed with style. He wasn't the typical clientele. "You have a name?" she asked.

"Alfonso Romero."

"Well Alfonso, your shtick is pretty transparent."

"What shtick is that?" he asked, eager to hear how she perceived him.

"Exploiting the assholes behavior so you can be a knight in shining armor. You sit at the bar like you're not interested in the women and come to their defense when someone takes it too far. We're all on display and you're here for the same reason as everyone else: To get your rocks off."

"I like the scenery from the bar."

"Well, you have no need to stalk me," Aileen said. "I'm married."

"No ring."

"I don't wear it during my shift."

"Just listen for a second, because I'm out of here in five minutes anyway. Tomorrow night, I'm attending a fundraiser for muscular dystrophy research. Do you have a dress?"

"That's a little forward. You don't know me."

"That will change if you have a dress."

"If you get to know me, you won't like me."

"Does that attitude work in your favor often?"

"I'm being honest."

Alfonso wrote on a napkin and handed Aileen his information. "I'll leave the invite open."

"You know what? I can't make it, so don't stop yourself from finding another date."

"If you want to change your life, you'll be there. Heritage Square, nine o'clock. Don't bother showing up if you're truly married, don't have a dress, or still employed here."

Aileen laughed, but their eyes met and she saw he was serious. She carelessly folded the napkin and stuffed it in her jean pocket. She didn't intend to go, but she wanted the option. Something in Alfonso's eyes told her he already knew what she would do. He was probably a guy who always got his way, and she looked forward to shocking him by rejecting his invite.

She watched him exit carelessly. She looked around the club, taking in the filth and disdain as her eyes darted from one patron to another, to the girls on stage, to Tyson. There was nothing here but a paycheck, and the unknown was exciting. She reached in her pocket, intent on throwing the napkin away, but when her hand came out, it was empty.

3

Jason hurried home to break the news to Erica. He couldn't live in Hawaii. He couldn't be a father. He was going to catch the first flight out and never look back. He'd pay her for the trouble and give her contact information so he could be sure the child was raised right. The lingering question though—the one that really ate at him was—how could she know the baby was his? In her nightly excursions, it seemed as if she'd slept around often. Suddenly, she was pregnant, and brought it up conveniently at the moment Jason wanted to leave.

But if it wasn't his baby, why did she want him to stay? Anyone could see the differences between them.

No matter where the truth lie, he still owed her the truth, and it would have been painless if she'd been there when he arrived. Instead, as usual, she was gone. He shook his head in disbelief.

If you're pregnant, why are you always out? Why aren't you taking care of yourself?

He couldn't partner up with someone who would make the kind of mother she was shaping up to be. He tried calling her cell, but got no answer. Instead of sitting and waiting, he went out to find her. The sooner he could break the news, the sooner he could move on to…to what? He wasn't sure, but there was something waiting for him back home. Something within Stone Enterprises. He thought about the last conversation he had with his father. It was bizarre to say the least. He thought about the desk—about what Bernard told him: Victor carved into it—to add Bernard. In his last moments, Victor's mind was…

He had go go back so he could complete the thoughts, give them framework, iron out the dirty details.

Erica was on foot. She always was. There were multiple bars within walking distance, but he'd find her. He worked his way down the beach for an hour, popping into every venue long enough to make a once through and realize she wasn't there. Then, she called him to see if he was okay. She confirmed she was out and gave him the location. He was twenty yards away and found her while they still were on the phone. She was surprised to see him, and by the look on her face, not too thrilled. Probably because she had a man at her side.

She hung up the phone when she saw him and met him halfway across the bar. Jason knew she hadn't been loyal to him, but there was a man, in the flesh, whose arms had been wrapped around her. Maybe, hopefully, the father.

"What are you doing here?" Erica asked.

"What do you think I'm doing? After what you told me last night…"

"Yeah, and you walked out."

"To get my thoughts straight."

"Are they straight now?"

"Yeah."

"So what are you going to do?"

"I want to know why you're pregnant and sitting in a bar."

"I'm not drinking."

"That's not the point. What's your plan here? Go out all night and day like you've been doing and pretend like this isn't happening?"

"When the time comes, I will take care of…"

"Is the baby even mine?"

"Of course."

"It doesn't make sense. How you'd know for sure, or the likelihood."

The man approached. Shane Tikani, the bar manager with a solid tan and strong physique. "This guy bothering you Erica?"

Erica hesitated to answer, and Jason beat her to it. "I live with her. I'm the father of her baby."

Shane didn't seem surprised. He either knew already or didn't care. "What's all the hostility about?" Shane asked.

"We're having a conversation. Go back to the bar," Jason said.

All 220 pounds of Shane lit up. He didn't like being told what to do, and he especially didn't like the way Jason had come in and confronted Erica. Shane's whole body flexed and he positioned himself toe to toe with Jason. "Get out of my bar."

Erica tried to break them up, but she was long forgotten. Shane's friends at the bar were ready to pounce if he gave them the nod.

"This is between her and I," Jason said. He tempered himself and controlled his breathing, and just as he was about to make peace with Shane so he could have a final conversation with Erica, Victor appeared at his side.

"If he knew who he was talking to, he would back down," Victor said.

Jason turned for a fraction of a second, aware of how crazy he'd seem if he responded. Instead, as Shane towered over him with his fists clenched.

"You're intimidated?" Victor asked. *"By a bartender?"*

Jason swallowed hard and fixated on Shane. "This is none of your business," he said. His eyes darkened and any intimidation Shane was supposed to project didn't sit with Jason.

"No, but it's my bar," Shane said. He called his friends and before Jason could react, his arm was pinned behind his back and a foot wedged behind his. A kick to the back of the knee sent him to the ground. Jason looked up and caught a glimpse of Erica with a pained look on her face, but she didn't intervene. Suddenly, he regretted giving her the courtesy of a goodbye.

Shane crouched and met Jason's eyes. "If you're going to come into my bar and talk down to my customers, then you're gonna get your ass booted.

Jason gasped, but managed to get the only message he wanted to relay out. "Go fuck yourself."

It was short and sweet, and he'd held it in a long time. He'd wanted to tell Brian off at his father's funeral, Bernard when he'd campaigned to take over the company, and Aileen when she told him he was to blame for her life going wrong. It had been brewing for some time—inspired by Victor, and as Victor stood by watching—or whatever Jason's mind had created—he knew he'd disappointed him. He had all the money in the world, all the power, but no control. He wasn't the leader his father wanted him to be. He couldn't be proactive and take care of problems as Victor did. He tried to look up into his father's eyes, but Shane didn't take his words well. The last thing Jason remembered before waking up face down in the sand, was three guys overpowering him with blows to the face....

...Victor's smile was genuine. It wasn't the fake, lips pressed together grin that he showcased for the cameras every time he attended a party or cut a ribbon.

And it was for Bridget.

And she returned the gesture.

She really liked him.

And Jason liked her.

"I got one," Bridget said, while preparing a fajita at a Mexican restaurant. "When I was about seven, I went with my family to Scotland. One night, everyone went to bed and I couldn't sleep so I started to get bored and was messing around in my room. I decided it would be fun to climb inside my suitcase and do up the zipper to scare my parents when they finally entered my room. Low and behold, the zipper gets stuck and I'm stuck in a suitcase. Seeing as how everyone was sleeping and couldn't hear my muffled cries for help, I had to spend the night curled up inside. It wasn't until the next morning that my parents found me there."

Jason and Victor laughed. Jason's eyes shined at how vibrant she was when she talked—how happy—and how it rubbed off on Victor. It was almost as if Jason had stumbled upon a family by accident.

"What about you Jason?"

"Nothing like that. I mean, I dunno..." he said, trying to think of a story. But he came up blank. Not because there was nothing embarrassing or funny or interesting. Jason had spent his life in a mansion with structure and a schedule. There was never room for odd happenings.

"You ever been to Europe?"

"Nope."

"Really? I figured you would have been by now." She turned to Victor, who had talked about Europe on more than one occasion. She'd always assumed it was for pleasure, but...

"I've only been there on business," he said. "But we should think about planning a vacation." He directed the comment at Jason, whose excitement faded. Trips to Europe were business, and they would never have been anything else if Bridget hadn't entered the picture. He resented Victor playing father when there was suddenly someone around to impress.

"Paris is unbelievable," she said.

"We'll need a tour guide," Victor said.

"So you don't do vacation?"

"Not since I was a child," Victor said. "I soak in the culture. I try the food and I always have a hotel with a view. Beyond that, there's not a lot of time."

"You went on vacation in Europe as a child?" she asked.

"When I was nine. My mother died."

Jason sat straight and became attentive. Victor's eyes went to another place and time.

"She was close to the end and she wanted to see the mountains. So we went to see mountains. My mother was funny. She made me laugh, even in the last days. I mostly feigned laughter because I was sad I was going to lose her, but I was captivated by her attitude in death. One day, I asked her how she can be so funny during those times. She told me she doesn't want to feel like she's winding down—fading away. She said she didn't want to do what she would be bad at—dying. It was a good explanation at the time, but in hindsight, I know she was putting on a front. She didn't want me to see her fading."

Bridget squeezed Victor's arm, while Jason wondered what world he was living in to have heard his father tell such a personal story.

"She might have been doing it for my sake, but there was something to what she said. My father was very good at over-complicating our lives. She had a way of simplifying it that made me feel like everything would be okay."

Jason learned a lot about his father that night and for once was in awe of his old man. Victor had always been tough. Tonight, he was vulnerable. The thick shell that contained any resemblance of a human being, hadn't just been cracked. It had been ripped away entirely. It was perfect until Victor answered his phone and made a brief exit, reminding Jason that business always came before family.

"You're shy," Bridget said, observing Jason as he sat silently.

"I'm not shy. This is new," he responded.

"You know, your dad is image on the outside. He has to keep up appearances to be successful. But inside, he's a big softy."

"Yeah," Jason said with a smile. If that same statement had been made at any other time and place, it would have baffled him, but apparently there was more to Victor than he understood.

"He's not usually my type. His type, I mean. I was intrigued and told myself to just go with it. To my surprise, we connected."

"Good. I like seeing him like this," Jason said. He didn't mean to say it like he did, but he couldn't help but put a little truth on the table. To imply Victor only behaved this way with Bridget in his life.

"What about you?" she asked, not responding to the implication.

"What about me?" he asked.

"What's your calling? Or don't you know?"

"I haven't the slightest idea."

"You have time."

"I'm supposed to inherit Stone Enterprises at some point."

She laughed in a few short bursts. "Is that what you want?" It was as if she saw right through him. He wasn't very subtle with his tone, but most people assumed anyone would want Jason's inheritance.

"Sometimes. I watch him work and sometimes it seems almost glamorous. I mean, he composes himself in a way I admire and makes it seem easy. On the other hand, I have no idea what he's doing or how he does it. I may not even have a knack for business."

"You can learn anything in time sweetie."

When she called him sweetie, it brought comfort to him. It was as if she was his mother. The ideal family scenario was creating itself in front of his eyes.

"People look at me like I'm destined to follow in his footsteps," he said, talking slowly. "I don't seem to have a choice. Yet, my one option is something no one would pass up."

"You don't only have one option."

"It's easy to say that."

"You're a bright guy sweetie. You can't let everyone else steer you. You just have an advantage. That's all it is: an advantage. You can use it or you can find something else to pursue. I find that when I need to figure out what direction to take, I just need to look for the signs. They're there. They'll interrupt your plans and put you somewhere you never expected to be. You just have to pay attention…"

…He didn't know how long he was out, or if he was ever out at all. He heard murmurs and felt a constant stinging sensation in his face. Moving only made it worse but he couldn't bring himself to open his eyes yet. The world was dark and out of sorts. It was the perfect rock-bottom moment to get Jason to reflect over the last months. He'd lost his father. The will was read. Everything changed. He met a girl. He made a drastic move. He wasn't in character. He questioned his choices. He regretted his choices. He was confrontational and hostile. He was laying on the ground with a mouthful of sand. He didn't know where to go from here.

What would Victor do?

It was the question he kept trying to avoid, but somehow it resurfaced.

I have to stop avoiding it.

Stop avoiding it. He didn't fully comprehend where he was aiming, but he knew that the one thing Victor always did right was avoid ending up in a position like this. Victor was always in control. Jason had no idea what he was doing.

The world slowly came into focus as Jason struggled to open his eyes. People walked past, looking down at him knowingly. He slowly rolled to his back, sand cascading off his clothes and the ocean crashing near his feet.

Anger began pulsing inside as he opened himself up to what his father would do. When the world came into focus, he was there again: Victor stood over Jason, shaking his head with disappointment. "I won't do it your way," Jason said, ignoring the strange looks people gave him while he talked to himself.

Victor seemed real, but Jason knew better. He'd conjured him, only he'd done it with precision. He'd envisioned all the right expressions—all the right words. He was able to channel his father and still be on the receiving end of advice that he didn't want—but advice he needed.

"You're doing everything wrong," Victor said.

"Then tell me what's right," Jason said.

Victor turned toward the ocean and looked out into the distance before turning back to his son. "Stop fighting me."

"Then tell me what you'd do!" Jason yelled, earning more strange looks.

"I'd be in control. I'd start with honesty. That's always your starting point. But when they fight you, disrespect you, you move on to alternative solutions."

"What do I do about Erica?"

"Forget Erica. You're one of the wealthiest people in the world and you were just tossed out of a bar into the sand. Start there."

Jason sat across from a man in a suit and waited for him to speak. The suited man stared at a piece of paper with a number scribbled on it, trying to decide whether the stranger in front of him was joking, or if he really was making him an offer he couldn't refuse.

"I wasn't looking to sell," the suited man said.

"I made my offer," Jason said. "If you don't want to accept, I'll look elsewhere."

"I may be a fool for saying this out loud, but that's a high offer."

"I know."

"Mind if I ask why?"

"I want the property."

"You planning on renovating?"

"Does it matter?"

"Trying to figure out your motives here."

"My money's good."

"Maybe, but this is a little too good to be true, and you know what they say about that."

"Then accept."

The man studied Jason's face for a long moment before reaching across his desk and offering a handshake. "As long as the paperwork is in order and your check clears, it's yours. You bought yourself a bar."

4

Heritage Square mostly served as a ballroom but was considered a square because of the streets surrounding it that were lined with old-style shops. The area was always filled with people, but only the crème de la crème would ascend the stairs and pass the fountain that led into one of the grandest of rooms in the city. It was the venue for every prestigious fundraiser or party.

As Aileen crossed the room, the familiar feeling of deja vu overcame her. Though short lived, there was a time when Victor wasn't ashamed to escort her through rooms like this. It was a brief time of their relationship that she'd considered promising—even happy.

Alfonso stood at the top of the stairs, finding her in the crowd, and smiling at the sight of her. They met near the fountain and he kissed her hand. "You put on a convincing act," he said. "I had it in my head that maybe you wouldn't show."

"I was bored."

"You look beautiful," he said.

She smiled wide and mouthed "thank you." The wall was down. She always tried to resist, but the right gesture or words always convinced her that she was talking to a man different than every other man. "So...muscular dystrophy, huh? Is this close to you or is this all for show?"

"My organization does this every year. My partners parents both suffered from it. It's a chance to do something good, although most of these people truly are here to mingle and kiss ass."

"Should I donate something?" she asked slowly.

"No obligation. You do what you can. But it's not necessary. I made a donation in both our names."

"You did not."

"I didn't know if you'd come, but I treated the night as if you would. Just in case."

"Wow," she said, taken aback. "So you're like, a nice guy then."

"Don't tell anyone," Alfonso said, feigning secrecy.

"And so hanging in strip clubs is your cover?"

"I actually feel no shame in admiring a woman's form."

"You're admitting you go for the girls?"

"The difference between men going to a strip club and going to a bar is a very thin line. Most men have the same objective, no matter what amount of clothing their prey is wearing. Does this surprise you?"

"A little. I mean, not that you were there for the girls, but that you don't have some made up excuse."

"I'm an honest man."

"I've dated men that I met there," she said, rolling her eyes. "They say they're at a bachelor party or just there for a drink."

"Ah, so you prefer the honest pervert."

"All men are perverts, so yes, I prefer honesty."

"Me too," he said, meeting her eyes.

She instinctively looked down, smiling a little. She tried to cover it up. "You're not gonna like me."

"You keep saying that. What's it mean?"

"That you shouldn't expect more than just a date tonight."

"I wasn't."

"Good."

"I do have a dinner I would like you to accompany me to on Friday though."

"I better not."

"Why?"

"Because you're not gonna like me."

"I like you now."

"You think you like me now."

"Spare me the baggage. I'll decide for myself."

Her eyes met his and she felt the spark. It was familiar, but Alfonso really was a nice guy. "Okay," she said, weakening. "Did you know I was married once?"

"Doesn't matter."

"I was Victor Stone's ex."

Alfonso stepped back and sized her up with a smile. "I knew you were familiar."

"There were two sides to that relationship."

Alfonso chucked. "I wouldn't defend Stone," he said, as if the notion was foolish.

"Good."

"In my business, Stone's name has come up more than once."

"I wouldn't be surprised if he purchased boob jobs for every woman he was with."

"You'd be surprised," Alfonso said, confirming it had happened at least a couple times. "Never on his dime, but I did at least five or six augmentations on women who claimed to be with him."

She rolled her eyes.

"I'm a little intrigued by you now," he said.

"Why?"

"A man like that doesn't settle down. He married you though."

"For a very short time, yes."

"That puts you ten steps ahead of every other woman he dated."

"I was pregnant," she confessed. "He had to. Believe me, if I could do it over, I would. People find out I was married to him and it puts me on another level."

Alfonso nodded, unsurprised. "I found you in a strip club with no ambition, or confidence..."

"Okay?" she said, irritated.

"Your face is recognizable and not in a way that suits you."

"I'm pretty much branded for life."

"You don't like who you are. You don't like who you see in the mirror."

Aileen swallowed hard. Nothing truer had ever been spoken. She appreciated Alfonso for knowing it.

"Flip through this," he said. He reached in his inner pocket and came out with a pamphlet.

She thumbed the pages, each featuring a before and after picture of a woman. No after resembled the before. All were vast improvements. "Wow, some of these women you can't even tell it's the same person."

"That's the idea. Ordinarily, people come to me and I ask them why they desire a change. Most are already beautiful. I do a lot of reconstruction on burn victims and facial deformities. I rebuilt a face for a woman who was attacked by a dog. Her face was completely warped. Those are the cases that I got in the game for, but mostly, I deal with people who have no real reason to change."

"I'm impressed," Aileen said. She never fully understood reconstructive surgery, but seeing examples displayed in front of her brought new light to Alfonso's career.

"I like you Aileen. I enjoy your company."

"Me too."

"And I think you're beautiful."

"But you don't want Victor's ex," she said, finishing his thought.

"I didn't say that. What I do believe is that you no longer need to be Victor's ex. You need a new label. I can make that happen."

"What would you do?" she asked, fearing the answer.

"You show me who you want to be and I will make your vision a reality. We can change your appearance—your name. I can turn you into a woman you like to look at in the mirror and you can put your past behind you."

"I'll still be me."

"Under your skin, you have nothing to be ashamed of."

"You don't know that."

"Then start over. Live a new life..."

"It's so drastic."

"People do it every day Aileen. Most look at themselves and see their imperfections because they can't hide from them. They have to learn to accept their flaws. You look at yourself and you don't see idiosyncrasies. You see one big imperfection."

Her mind wondered. She smiled at the concept. She'd only miss her face because she was used to it, but she hated having to hide from everyone constantly. She hated knowing people saw her as the crazy lady Victor tossed aside.

"Take some time," Alfonso said. "Think about it."

5

Jason watched Shane exit bar in a hurry, fuming. He knew better though. Jason beat him with his secret weapon: Money—an easy win in any situation. Jason bought the bar and booted Shane. Then, he sent an invite to Erica. She arrived, confused, but immediately knew what he did upon arrival. Only Jason sat behind the bar. She entered, her hands crossed in front of her. "What did you do?" she asked.

"I'm the proud new owner of this place," he said. Too bad I won't be staying long enough to run it into the ground, but I'll eat the cost."

"This is really who you are?" she asked.

He put his palms up in mock surrender. "I'm having fun. That's what you wanted, right? Hell, maybe I'll buy every bar a mile down the coast. Free drinks every night, easy one night stands when we want. You can have the baby and we'll buy someone to raise it."

"I told you, I'm not going to keep doing that."

"Is that right? Then you're with me?"

"I hoped so."

"Where were you last night when I was having the shit kicked out of me? Standing by?"

"That's because Shane's a violent drunk asshole and I was afraid, and you were being a dick to him. You brought it on yourself. But you know what else I know about him?"

"What he's like in the sack," he said, with a smile.

"No, asshole. He's got a wife and three kids. Do you feel better about yourself knowing you put him out of a job?"

"He'll find another."

Jason knew in that moment that wherever Victor was, down below or up above, or standing behind him, he was smiling proudly at his son. He'd be even prouder with Jason's next statement. "I'm going back to run the business."

"So you're not going to stay and raise your baby?"

"Prove to me it is my baby," he said, challenging her. She backed off, and he knew his answer.

"You were the only one I was with at that time."

"How about since? You can't talk one of your new flings into moving in with you?"

She slapped him suddenly. It threw him off guard and his cocky attitude faded. He saw the woman in front of him who he'd hurt just because she hurt him first, and maybe everything she said was true, and maybe Shane really was a family man whose life he'd ruined. It had all been so easy when he had an endless supply of cash at his disposal. In that moment, he never felt more like Victor in his life. He hadn't felt this connected since…

…He exited his car and walked up the driveway, ready to hit the pillow. He was distracted by the sound of sobbing and heels clacking on the pavement moving away from the mansion. He turned to find Bridget hurrying away. It was a visual he'd seen many times: a distraught woman running away from his father, but this time was different. Bridget had been different. This wasn't supposed to happen.

"Bridget!" he called out. She didn't respond, so he hurried after her. "Stop!"

She turned hastily. "What do you want?"

"What's wrong?"

"Your father."

"Let's talk. I think this is a mistake."

"I'm going home. Good luck with him."

She tried to move along, but he hurried around her and stood in her path. "You live too far away to walk."

"I can get a cab."

"No, I'll drive you."

"No…"

"Please," he insisted. "Let me."

She sniffled and hung her head, submitting to him. She nodded quietly.

Moments later, she sat curled in the passenger seat of Jason's car as he hurried through the neighborhood. She watched out the window, blocking him out as he glanced at her, unsure of what to say. "I'll talk to him," he finally said.

"Believe me, he made it clear."

"Made what clear?"

"He told me not to come back."

"It's a mistake. He likes you."

"That's what I thought."

"Did he tell you why?"

"His performance at work is suffering. Apparently, your father can't balance a social life and a career."

Jason already knew this all too well about his father, but had hoped Bridget would open his eyes. Apparently she had, just not in the way he'd hoped.

"I was stupid. I heard what he was and I thought he'd change."

"He did. There's still a chance. Give him a day to think about this."

"We can't come back from this. I'm not playing his game. I'm not going to be the girl who falls for him and gets dumped every time he has a bad quarter."

"I'll miss you," Jason said.

"Do me a favor?"

"What's that?"

"Just be your own person."

"I am," he said.

"No, you're not, but I hope you will be."

"I don't..."

"You try to please him constantly. You pattern his mannerisms. You laugh when he's not funny. You agree when he's wrong."

"I don't think I do those things."

"You're seeking his approval. Right now, that's all it is, but someday you're going to realize that you've been trying to impress him for so long that you've become him."

Jason stormed up the driveway on the warpath, running the dialog he would have with his father through his head. He stopped on his way to the door as he heard the clink of a bottle around the house where the pool was. He circled and as his father came into view, he saw Victor had a drink in his hand and was sprawled out on a lawn chair. Before Jason could hang back and watch, Victor turned and caught sight of him. He smiled and patted the seat next to him.

Jason approached and took the seat. It would be easier giving Victor a piece of mind if he was drunk, but suddenly all courage was gone. Instead, he sat in silence, waiting for his father to have the first word.

"Is she okay?" Victor asked.

"Yeah."

"You got her home?"

"I didn't think she should be walking."

Victor nodded and struggled to find the right words. *"She wanted too much," he finally said.*

Jason made a point to avoid sympathy—to not allow his father the luxury of understanding his angle.

"She liked the money too much."

Jason let out a breath and turned to Victor. Something in his eyes told Jason he was pained by the decision, that maybe he wasn't sure he did the right thing. "She's just a girl," Jason said.

"You liked her..."

"It's not my decision."

"It's your problem though."

"No."

"Yes, Jason it is, because your life is my life. You're old enough to find meaning in my relationships. You can hold conversations with my friends, my dates, my coworkers."

"Is that a bad thing?"

"It is."

"Why?"

"Because it's not the life for you."

"Dad, you have everything."

"No, I don't."

"You can though."

"At an expense. For me to do well, others suffer. That's the central dogma to my success."

"It's just business," Jason said.

"It is...It is. And day to day, I make dozens of decisions at the expense of someone else, and that's fine and I live with that. It's easy when it's a name on a piece of paper; Close a bank here, tear down an apartment complex there. All I hear is numbers, you know, sixty residents, two hundred employees on payroll. It means nothing to me."

Jason leaned in and narrowed his eyes, listening intently.

"But then one day, all these numbers, all these meaningless decisions, one day, out of the blue, they have a face. You look a friend in the eyes and see what you took from them, and you have to know you've done the same thing a thousand times over." Victor paused a long moment before turning to his son. "Today it had a face. I let a close friend go. You met him once—Stanley Kline. He was a good man, but a liability. And his reaction surprised me. He cried. Told he had a family and nowhere to go from here. And I couldn't do anything. So today, something I've done a thousand times finally had a face, and I wondered if I've done more harm than good in this world. Don't follow my footsteps Jason. When you can, run as far away as you can."

"I wouldn't know what to do," Jason said.

"I like to think we take something away from every relationship we have. Bridget was wonderful. Take what we can from her."
"She said a lot of things."
"She told you to follow the signs," Victor said. "Follow the signs…"

…Jason sat on an outcropping of rocks sitting in the tide, his arms wrapped around his knees, looking into the distance. The sun was coming up through the clouds and the tide was growing stronger. He looked at the one way ticket he held in his hands. He reminded himself he should be at the airport in an hour, but he looked out into the distance, realizing for the first time how beautiful it really was here. Maybe one day he'd come back. Right now, there was no reason to be here. He'd made a mistake. He'd misread what he thought he was supposed to do.

Half an hour later, he exited his house with one suitcase. Erica was nowhere to be found. She didn't want to say goodbye. Maybe later she'd really prove he was going to be a father and he'd make it right, but he wasn't going to be with her. That was one thing his father got right—you don't stay with someone you don't love. If Victor hadn't married Aileen in the first place, maybe she wouldn't have turned out to be so damaged.

He waited outside for the cab and when it finally pulled up, Jason took a last look at the house before entering the cab. He caught the driver's eyes in the mirror and before he could say "to the airport," both men stopped in shock at the sight of one another.

Jason believed that sometimes coincidences happened, and would even be caught saying "it's a small world" once or twice in his life, but nothing prepared him for the complete unlikeliness of who he'd just run into thousands of miles from home. Jason almost choked on the words, but needed to confirm the man wasn't an illusion.

"Todd Mason?"

Todd turned, his eyes narrowed in disbelief. "How the hell did you find me?"

Chapter 9

1

It was her last day as Aileen Thick. She woke up and looked around to find herself in an empty bed. Alfonso was gone. She brushed her teeth, shaved her legs, and applied makeup to her face. She tussled her hair, styled it, and stared at herself in the mirror, saddened by the reflection staring back.

She only went back to her apartment for the mail. When she was bored enough, she'd take the bus straight across Sunset and walk the two blocks to her place. The mail usually overflowed, mostly with junk. Today, a handwritten letter from Richard awaited her. She opened the letter and read. Everyone probably received one, but it was personalized. Richard's letter was optimistic. It claimed the end of the will was near, and only served as a reminder to be there on the right date and time.

Instead of making a decision or sending a letter back in the self-addressed stamped envelope, she visited Richard. She had the time, and it was surprisingly refreshing to have someone take the time to write a letter which was polite and asked questions about how she was doing. The man was a preacher, and not typically the kind of person who would be so polite to her. Right now, she needed polite. It was hard to tell who had ulterior motives in her life. Even Alfonso was set on changing her appearance, and ever since she'd agreed, he began the process of mapping out her new look. She didn't know Richard well, but he'd given her a window of opportunity to show her face one last time and be treated with respect. At least, until she told him why she was really there to visit.

Richard stepped aside and invited her in when she arrived at his home. He hurried across the room and shut off a television, making her feel as welcome as possible. It seemed the only thing on his mind was seeing his letter's proposition through.

"I received your letter," she said. "I'm sorry I didn't just send it back."

"No," he said. "I'm happy you're here."

She turned to her and saw a teenager sitting at a computer, eavesdropping on the conversation. Richard noticed. "Aileen, this is Josh. Josh, Aileen. Josh is helping me move the process along. He stuck the stamp on your envelope."

She managed a smile and a nod in Josh's direction. "So, anyway," she said. "I read your letter."

"Good. I hope I can count on your support."

"Um, no," she said.

Richard stood, frozen in place, while her refusal registered.

"I was under the impression that you and Victor weren't on good terms."

"We weren't."

"You want his money?"

"I don't think it's your place to decide what happens with it."

Richard sighed deeply. She hadn't been the first surprising refusal on the list. In fact, it was nearly split fifty-fifty, which made Richard increasingly uneasy. "I'm not deciding what happens with his money. I'm trying to prevent his production from playing out. I don't care if we all split it."

"You can do that, but it's not my place and I won't be there."

"You know, the day the will was read, I recall everyone in the room growing uncomfortable and displeased with what Victor had done. I've gotten an overwhelming lack of support from the group and I can't say I'm not disappointed. In hindsight, I see the fear and anger was just a facade. You all want the money and you don't care what happens to innocent people to get it."

"You can be as disappointed as you want," Aileen said, offering no rebuttal.

"Why are you here Ms. Stone?" he asked, no patience left in his voice.

"It's Thick. I've never gone by that name."

"I apologize," he said. "The judge seems to be flexible. I'd like to suggest we split it fourteen ways with the option of opting out."

"That won't work," she said, shaking her head.

"I assume you're not concerned about what happened to Abby Palmer?"

"It has nothing to do with them. I'm taking steps and soon, no one will be able to find me. I'm not leaving town or anything like that, but I'm starting over with some things and I want to detach myself from Victor and all his shit. Excuse my language."

"You're telling me you've taken steps to protect yourself and you hope to outlive everyone."

"Richard, I want you to understand something. Even though Victor wanted this, that money should have rightfully gone to his family. I wanted you to know because..."

"You don't want me to have the wrong impression?" he asked, finishing her sentence. "My impression is that you're selfish."

Aileen held back, blinking her eyes to hold back tears. She hadn't expected so much hostility from Richard. He was clearly frustrated but she couldn't deal with the thought of the will being invalid and the money being distributed to people who didn't deserve it—who Victor wouldn't and shouldn't have given it to. "I shouldn't have come," she said, her voice breaking.

"People have died. It doesn't matter what should have happened. And you should be worried. I assumed there would be one or two bad apples, but I'm struggling to even find a majority against this."

"I have to go."

Richard waved his hand dismissively and turned his back. She watched him for a long moment before turning to Josh, who watched the display confused. She felt a little better about her decision not to throw her support behind Richard. He had been kind at the reading, but watching him now, she realized he was just another person who considered himself above Aileen. He wouldn't hear her out, find out why it was too hard for her to help, why she...

...reluctantly joined her father, Eugene Thick, on the couch as he sunk into the bulk of the couch, a blob of a man who was unkempt in every way; unshaven, unbathed, and a frame that grew thicker by the day. Denise Thick had given up on him and everything else long ago. She was still prim and proper, ready to make an excuse for her husband at the drop of a dime. She kept everything at right angles and if they weren't, she threw a fit. They were the poster-parents for why kids wanted to run away from home. Aileen walked on egg-shells around them for years, and had gotten pretty good at it, but being five months pregnant had forced her to open up new lines of communication—new issues for the family to deal with.

"Who left their laundry in the dryer?" Denise asked, in a sweet tone, though Aileen tensed up at the question. Everything started sweet with her mother and escalated into a hysterical fit. It was best to apologize quickly or have a believable excuse.

"I thought they were still drying," Aileen said.

"Then the dryer must be broken because it's not making any noise," her mother said, laying the sarcasm on thick.

"I didn't know it was done, okay?"

"Maybe you should use your ears."

"I didn't know!" she snapped, fed up with a long line of lectures. Being pregnant made Aileen feel more grown-up—more capable of making her own decisions. Surprisingly, Denise let it slip, but her father gave her a look that begged permission to bring on his brand of punishment. Her mother ignored him and handled Aileen herself.

"And when you finish your laundry, I need to see how you're doing."

"How I'm doing with what?"

"School. I haven't seen anything in a while."

She bit her lip for a moment, and then blurted what she'd held onto for months. "I dropped out."

Denise suddenly stood and gasped for air, dramatically showing her disbelief in what she'd just heard. "What?" she asked, dragging it out in a long exasperated breath. Eugene turned the volume on the television up, ignoring them. He didn't care what she did, as long as she didn't disrespect him. "Turn it down!" Denise yelled. As threatening as Eugene was, the one person who could control him was his wife. "Did you hear what she just said? She dropped out of school!"

"I had no choice."

"No choice?"

"Financial aid didn't come through. I'll pick it up again after the baby is born."

"Is that why you've been doing nothing around here? All you do is sit around. You couldn't have gotten a job?"

"I'll go back but right now there's too much going on."

"Like what?" she practically screamed. She put her hands on her hips and waited. Aileen almost answered but broke down in tears instead.

"Can't you just support me?" she asked, wavering between sobs.

"Support what? Your laziness? Your stupidity?"

"I can't believe you. My friends' parents stand by everything they do. You know nothing about parenting! Everything I do, I have to figure out on my own. God forbid I can have a child that could be proud to have grandparents."

Eugene rose suddenly, towering above Aileen, even at a short stance.

"I didn't mean to yell," Aileen said, suddenly aware of what would happen—what happened dozens of times before, only this time, Aileen carried a child. He gave her a blank stare, ready to bolt toward her in a moment. Her mother cutting in was the only thing that saved her.

"You need to go find out how to get back in your classes."

"They don't just let you back in," she whimpered.

"Then what's your plan hot-stuff? Get knocked up and ask your baby daddy for money?"

"I'm looking for a job. I'm going to find work and save money and

next year I'll go back to school. I'll even get a dorm so you won't have to keep me here."

"Oh, that's just great. Up and leave even though school's five minutes away."

"I'm doing it to help."

"Help by leaving?"

"You won't have to take care of me anymore," Aileen said, almost pleading with her mother to allow her to go.

"Some mother you must think I am, leaving me after all I do. Dropping out of school and doing God knows what when you're not here isn't enough freedom for you?"

"Mom..." Aileen pleaded harder. Denise stormed out of the room, slamming a door, as her father winced and turned the volume of the television up again. It was the first time in her life that she realized...

...she just wanted to be somebody else.

Alfonso and his partner Brent sat together at an upscale hotel restaurant, Aileen seated across from them with her arms folded neatly in her lap. They finished going over the final details of what the day would bring, what Aileen should expect.

As they waited for their check, Brent made small-talk while Alfonso sat back. "Where did you go to college?"

"CCA."

"What did you study?"

"Fine arts."

"Ahh," he said with a nod. "An artist. Alfonso hadn't mentioned that."

"She never told me," Alfonso said, carelessly.

"It's a little embarrassing."

"What's embarrassing about art school?" Alfonso asked.

"That I'm not actually an artist."

"Sure you are," Brent interjected. "When you strive to create anything that's never existed, you're creating art."

"I don't even strive."

"I'd love to see a piece."

"I have nothing. See, that's what's embarrassing. I mean, people ask what I studied and I say art, and they ask what I do, and it's not art. So..."

"Hey, I drank through college," Brent said with a laugh. "I don't remember a thing. How did that happen?" He shrugged his shoulders and mocked a guilty face. "There's no shame in shifting your goals."

"Or maybe you could pick it up again," Alfonso said, in all seriousness.

"I don't think so."

"Why not?"

"It's not something I can just pick up after thirty years. Just getting back to the point I was when I left off would take another twenty. But yeah, I had a kid."

"Ah.."

"He is an adult now?" Alfonso asked. "Able to take care of himself?"

Aileen turned to Alfonso, who gave her a stare as if to say she was foolish—to call her out on the fact that she was only making excuses. "Yeah, he's an adult," she said.

"Then I would say your kid is no longer an obstacle."

"No," she said, coldly. "I guess not."

The table fell awkwardly silent all around. Alfonso seemed satisfied to have stumped Aileen, and Aileen became suddenly aware of his true feelings for her. He was with her because she looked good on his arm, but he was like everyone else: ashamed of her. And as much as she wanted to hate him for it, she understood.

She had one last consultation. Alfonso and Brent went over some of the details of what she'd go through psychologically. Afterward, they walked away to have their own meeting. She waited, staring at the shiny tools displayed in front of her. In a matter of hours, those same tools would be cutting into her flesh and rearranging her into something...someone Alfonso would want.

"You take a good long look at yourself in the mirror today?" Alfonso asked as he entered the room.

"I tried not to."

"The hardest part will be the unfamiliarity. It may seem surreal. Traumatic even. Seeing yourself without recognizing yourself can be hard to accept. A number of people have tried to undo their surgery when it was too late."

"I'll be fine," she said.

"I know you'll be fine."

She paused for a moment, contemplating what would come next. "Alfonso?"

"What?"

"Are you okay with this?"

"I support your decision."

"It was my decision, but your suggestion."

He nodded, picking his words carefully. Aileen was searching for an ego boost—but he wanted who she was, only in another body with another name. "I wouldn't put it that way. I like you and want to know you better. You're a stunning woman, but yes, you don't have a reputation that meshes well with my life. I don't need people recognizing you from filthy clubs or the street."

"What do you mean the street?" she asked, but she already knew, and he didn't have time to answer before she backed away, offended. "I never did that."

"But you understand..."

She found his eyes. There was no love. He wanted her, and for Aileen, sometimes that had to be enough. He smiled with satisfaction and assurance when she nodded. "Good," he said. "Enjoy your last hours as you."

2

Abby Palmer's tombstone was covered in flowers. It stood out from afar, which made it easy to find. Maria Haskins fixated on the flowers, noting how much it spruced up a cemetery that was otherwise dreary. Her mind wandered to the last time she saw Abby—how she'd tried to warn her but regretted it later because her friend reminded her that she was a fraud— a woman who tried to control the fate of others based on how her own life was shaping up.

Medication or not, she'd been onto something. There was something within that needed to surface, and maybe her problem had always been her unwillingness to explore beyond basic medium tactics. She'd always played it safe, dealing with cold readings and matters that would have no significance to anyone and therefore not be important enough to truly analyze whether or not she'd been right or wrong.

She sold the old shop for a hefty sum of money. Her new shop was bigger and better. It was flashy, with more trinkets and a brighter atmosphere. It was more welcoming and warm. It was different, but that's why she liked it. The way she'd practiced in the past hadn't worked, and so she'd extended her gift beyond readings. She'd begun meditating silently ever since she saw the apparition that was Victor Stone—or posed as him. It didn't matter. She saw something in the cemetery and it spoke to her. Pop-premonition was no longer in the cards. She practiced as a medium now, speaking to the dead and learning from them. It was new, but it was bigger than anything she'd practiced and there was a higher demand for speaking to loved ones beyond the grave. Her shop was always busy, and the people were friendlier and walked away happier.

When she told Kisha she was relocating, Kisha expressed concern for why she was still practicing at all.

"I've evolved into something so much deeper," Maria said, passionately. She hoped she could convince Kisha that she was a newer, better version of herself.

"Are you sure that's what you want? The last time we spoke, I was under the impression you were enlightened."

"I appreciate your concern and maybe some of that was true then, but Kisha, I know I have a gift. I've seen things that came to be true."

"Of course you have. You're bound to."

"I've seen things that are impossible to see. I was haunted and told what to do. I didn't listen because I doubted myself. If I would have listened, I could have prevented something horrible from happening. I can't make this mistake again."

Maria wondered what the locals would be like. It wasn't long before she found out. "Knock knock," a cheery voice said. Maria turned and spotted two women smiling in at her. They looked and acted alike. Dana White and Karen Salazar could have been sisters. When meeting them, Maria spotted a mole near Dana's ear and used it to differentiate between them. "Hey neighbor," Dana said, never losing her smile.

"Welcome to the neighborhood," Karen chimed in.

Good God. They even sound the same.

"Thank you," Maria said, sweetly.

"So you're the mind reader, huh?" Karen said. "That's neat!"

"I don't read minds," Maria said.

"Oh, I'm so sorry. I don't mean to offend you. I guess I've never seen this before," Karen said.

"She's another kind of psychic, aren't you dear?" Dana said.

"Yes. There are different ways to practice as a spiritualist."

"What is it you do exactly?" Karen asked. Maria could see the doubt in her eyes. Karen was the skeptic. As for Dana, she was just happy—too happy to form an opinion, and therefore impossible to read.

"Tarot readings, crystal, aura and Chakra readings, spiritual cleansing, I can turn negative karma into positive, remove spells, help you reconnect with friends, family, lovers..."

"Oh my," Karen said, flustered by the extent of all she didn't know.

"Has business been good?" Dana asked.

"Very good."

"I should come by and you can do what you do with me," Dana said.

"Oh!" Karen said, delighted. "We can both stop by before work tomorrow!" She turned to Maria. "We run The Baby Boutique on the corner. If you ever need baby supplies, you know where to go."

"I'll recommend you if anyone asks," Maria said. She'd almost laughed at the concept, but didn't know them well enough to decide whether they'd be offended or not. "But I'm not a mother."

The women looked at each other, a mutual message passing between them that Maria couldn't decipher.

"We can always cross market," Dana said.

"We know a lot of people in the neighborhood," Karen said. "Maybe we can give you some gossip before sending people your way. We've got your back."

What does she mean by gossip?

"Gossip?"

"Doesn't it help for you to know a few things before your clients show up? To convince them?" Dana asked. She waited for an answer, genuinely curious. Maria couldn't even be offended because the woman was truly dumbfounded. She didn't know any better.

"I wouldn't need gossip," Maria said. "It would cloud my work."

"Oh, sure," Dana said. "I mean you use what we tell you to break the ice with them and then do your own thing. Don't let me tell you how to do your job. I really know nothing about this."

The conversation hit a brick wall, and all the women stood around, awkwardly waiting for one another to say something to get the ball rolling again. Finally, Karen stepped forward. "Maria, it was great meeting you. We should get back."

"We'll pop in tomorrow," Dana added.

Maria could see it in their faces, and if they only understood the way Maria worked, they might have tried to hide it better. Maria's neighbors were uncomfortable and had no intention of coming back. Life for Maria was about to cycle back to the way it had been, unless she found a way to fit in fast, to connect to the community instead of sit in the dark constantly.

And this time would be different. She needed to project more confidence, and standing in the middle of the cemetery and staring at Abby's tombstone made her believe she was capable. She'd called it. Maybe she hadn't hit it on the nose, but she was close enough. There was no denying that her encounter with Abby would have ended better if Abby had believed her.

Not again, she thought. *This time will be different.*

3

Aileen laid in a bed, fidgeting nervously. She stared up at a light fixture. Her hands slowly rose to her face and she started running her fingers over every familiar bump and valley. It was her face as she knew it. She knew she was beautiful from an early age. It was good genetics. There were many reasons to change your appearance. She once knew a man in college who got a nose job because he had the misfortune of having something that looked like a beak on his face. While his family had told him to love himself as he was, it was hard not to understand his need to rid himself of something that grabbed anyone's attention that he was facing.

Aileen usually looked down on people for this act—especially women. Breast implants, tummy tucks—it was all pointless. Most women looked fake after having work done. She'd always liked her natural beauty. This was something else entirely. She would miss her features. She wouldn't miss her celebrity in having them. There were people in the world who gained fame by going to trial for a high profile murder of a spouse or a child and got off free. The world would always be outraged, but those people never seemed relieved. She always knew why. They had to walk around the world with a recognizable face. They'd be spit on, or talked about, but no matter what it was, they were never really free. They would always be branded for what they did, and sometimes deservedly so, but you can't rewind life. If you could, Aileen supposed a lot of people would go back and prefer not to be recognized.

She wished she could go back too. She wished she could go back to when...

...The interviewer was Peter Drat—a man who judging by his appearance, had been completely swallowed up and digested by the art world. He had a long beard, colorful clothes, and thick glasses with a red tint. He shuffled through her portfolio, observing her work with an unreadable expression.

"Hmm," he said, with a deep frown on his face.

Aileen smiled awkwardly at his unpredictable reaction to each painting. He set them down and stared blankly at the pile for a moment, as if his inner thoughts were the only things left in the world. Finally, he said "You've got something here."

"Really?" she asked, trying to conceal her relief.

"You could strengthen a thing or two, but nothing beyond repair."

"I feel like I've come a long way," she said, eagerly selling herself. "Every piece feels like I've picked up something from the one before."

"Very good. It's a never-ending process. If you're not evolving, you're doing something wrong. So let's talk about a job. You'd be working quickly, sometimes under a lot of pressure. Is that a problem?"

"Not at all."

"Very good. Being away from home...problem?"

She shook her head, actually smiling inside at the concept. Being away from home sounded glorious to her. Then she remembered the baby.

"What if I would need a few weeks off at some point?"

"Depends on when."

"December."

"Not December. January, maybe. After that, no problem."

She nodded, but her enthusiasm was gone. Maybe this was a sign. She didn't really believe in signs, but now would be a good time to start. She was faced with the decision between her dream job, and living with her parents and her fatherless baby. It was really pretty simple. And Peter was making it simpler by the moment.

"I wasn't going to make a final decision today, but I'm offering you a spot because I like what I see. You're ahead of the other candidates when it comes to technique and honestly, attitude. I can make you a sensational artist, and the sooner the better." He noticed she was staring at the wall with a blank look. "Aileen?"

She snapped out of it, aware she needed to hide her thoughts from him. "Sorry. Just excited."

"What do you say? Do you want to commit to this?"

After a moment of thought, she said with optimism, "Can I let you know tomorrow?"

"Yeah," Peter said, taken aback. "But this really isn't something you should let slip away. I'm not saying I'm going to take the offer back, but..."

"I know. I promise I won't blow you off. I'll call tomorrow."

"Tomorrow by five?"

"Yes."

He extended his hand and shook it delicately. "I look forward to hearing from you."

Later, she sat cross-legged on a bed across from Becky in her pajamas, with a bowl of popcorn between them. Life was always best sitting with her best friend, chatting about whatever was on their minds, but ever since Aileen had become pregnant, it was always at the forefront of her thoughts. Every decision in life had to revolve around how to make it work with a baby in the picture. And soon, she'd have to tell everyone. Becky knew it too.

"You can't hide this forever Aileen."

"I won't."

"You have to do it fast and get it out of the way. Like ripping a band-aid."

"My parents flip out over the smallest things. They won't handle it well."

Becky shrugged, considering what she said. "Maybe they'll want grand kids. You never know."

"Not them. They'll just see it as more kids to support."

Becky fidgeted, considering telling Aileen what she was afraid to say: The elephant in the room. Aileen saw her toying with an idea. "What?"

she asked.

"I'm sorry to bring this up, but he's rich."

"Becky," Aileen said, warning her with her tone.

"I'm just saying..."

"I know, but I'm not telling him."

"He does have the right to know."

"Well, to be honest, I haven't decided if I'm even going to have it yet."

Becky couldn't hide her disappointment. "Oh..."

"Don't say it like that. It's not you that's in this situation. You don't know what it's like."

"I didn't put you in this situation. You made your own choices."

"Please, you sleep with any guy that compliments you. I slip up one night..."

"Yeah, well I'm careful."

"I was too."

"Look," Becky said sincerely, "your parents will help you. And if they don't, he'll have to. And if he doesn't, you can handle it. You're strong."

"I'm going to be a bad mother."

"How can you say that?"

"I'm going to be like my mom: miserable, impatient..."

"Or you can learn from her mistakes."

"People say that, but this is ingrained in you. The things I don't like about her, I see those things in me. Not as strong, but they're there, and they might develop."

"Oh, so what? You can be any type of mother you want to be."

"I was offered the job," Aileen said abruptly.

Becky fell speechless for a moment. "The gallery thing?"

"Yeah..."

"Why didn't you tell me? You're not excited?"

"If I have this baby, I can't take it."

"Oh," Becky said, understanding her situation a little better.

"Between my parents and the job and the fact that I don't have a plan, I just don't think I can."

Becky fell back in Aileen's bed, her head hitting the pillow with a plop. "Oh, Aileen," she said, showing some compassion.

"I can't let one mistake ruin everything I've worked for," Aileen said, biting her lip as if she was in the middle of making up her mind once and for all...

...She closed her eyes after catching a reflection of herself in a monitor at her side. She focused on the positive side of what was going to happen. As much as she'd grown to disdain her appearance, she couldn't help but feel as if what was about to happen was tragic.

Alfonso entered the room and began organizing his instruments. He didn't say a word. He didn't even acknowledge her. It was as if he was in a hurry—a hurry to transform her into someone he could be seen with. Without looking up, he said, "after this operation, when you recognize someone, it won't be acceptable to expose yourself anymore or strike up a conversation."

"I know."

"Good," he said.

She paused for a long moment. "What's your problem?" she finally asked. Under other circumstances, she might not have been so confrontational, but this meant something to her. She was about to take the biggest step of her life just to help a man cope with being seen with her.

Is that why I'm really doing this?

"I'm just going over some details."

"It's not an easy thing to...seriously, what's your problem?"

"I'm just confused. I thought we were moving forward. I thought you wanted to change who you were. This part of your life, where you think it's romantic to be a starving artist, going after your dream while mooching off others who are supposed to support you...that's supposed to be over."

"You pushed me into this," she said, rigidly. "This is because I brought up painting this morning?"

"I'm trying to fix the things you admitted you hate about yourself."

"Yes, but Alfonso, it's scary. It's a big thing for me. I want to do it, but I want you to understand that."

"You think I don't get that? I have to coach everyone who comes in here and prepare them for the psychological ramifications. But in the end, you have to detach. Otherwise, what's the point?"

"Detach from what exactly?"

"From yourself."

Her eyes filled with tears as she suddenly grew emotional. He'd pursued her, and when he had her, he began to shape her. And nothing he ever said was wrong, but why he'd pursued her in the first place was what she was hung up on. "How can you chase after me and then try to change everything about me?"

"Because when I met you, I didn't know you were Victor Stone's leftovers. I didn't know you were a gold-digger and a whore."

"What?" she asked, exasperated.

"It's my fault. You were a stripper. I knew what I was getting into..."

"I wasn't a stripper!" She stood abruptly, wiping her eyes with the back of her hand. "You don't know anything about me."

"Sit down," he demanded. "Your appointment's in ten minutes. If you're not there..."

Before he could finish, she was out the door.

4

The shops that lined the market were bright and busy. There was a juice shop on the corner, two banks, a sushi joint, a bookstore, a video-store, a coffee shop, and the Baby Boutique which sat right on the corner. She eyed the shop before turning a sign in her door that announced she'd be back in half an hour. She wandered down the street, looking through windows, observing her neighbors as they worked. Everyone seemed warm and friendly—people she wanted to know. She hoped they wanted to know her too.

She wandered into the Baby Boutique and browsed the aisles, rummaging through clothes and books and electronic rockers that had multiple motion settings. The store was nearly empty, except for two women working the counter who watched her, ready to jump in to assist her if she needed.

She approached Dana and Karen, who stood with another woman, Jacqueline. Before Maria could introduce herself, Karen brought Jacqueline up to speed on what Maria did.

"I don't know about all that," Jacqueline said, disapproval in her tone. "Sounds to me like you're tampering with things you're not supposed to get into." Maria dealt with doubters and mockery her whole life, but the one encounter she feared was the one who claimed to be moral authority, claiming Maria did the devil's work.

"It's safe," she said. "What I do is not unlike the work of a psychiatrist, but most people's therapy comes from within. I help them draw it out."

"I'm not telling you what to do hon," Jacqueline said. "I just think God wouldn't approve."

Maria was speechless. Dana and Karen stood by silently with no desire to come to her rescue. Finally, Dana stepped forward. "Maybe Maria's talent is a gift from God and she's supposed to use it."

With the shades drawn, Maria slumped in her chair, resting her forehead on her arm in misery. She loved the new shop, the new life, she loved it all...but the sinking feeling always came back. When she got too high, she'd catch herself falling, and there was never a reason for it. Maybe that true happiness wasn't in the things she'd been chasing after. She'd never had it all. She'd never had the non-physical: Approval, praise, acceptance.

The door opened, letting a line of sun shine through, which didn't brighten the room much. Dana popped her head in with her usual toothy smile. "Maria?"

"Hi Dana."

"Hi. I thought I'd stop by for...you know...just to help you out."

"Have a seat," Maria said, defeated. She wanted to tell Dana she didn't need assistance—that people came to her because they were seeking something and she gave it to them. Everyone had a way of calling Maria a scam artist without actually using the words.

"It looked like you weren't open," Dana said.

"Sometimes I close the door and shut the blinds. I like a dark atmosphere."

"Oh, I'm sorry dear. Is this a bad time?" She picked up on the silence and saw the look in Maria's eyes. "Is something wrong?"

She responded with an expressionless shrug. "Some say I'm fake. Most of the time, they'll pretend to believe me in the beginning. Then, I see they don't."

"I've always believed it was a bit much to take in, but I never say I know something until I really know for sure. I figure, as many people out there who say they see UFOs or ghosts—maybe there's something to it. But I want to ask you a question without offending you." Maria looked up, curiously. For such a fake cheery persona, Dana was shaping up to have a more honest approach than most. "This isn't just directed at you, but why don't you just prove yourself? People would be a lot less skeptical if they saw proof."

"I have no interest in helping those people. I cannot work on skeptics because there must be a bond that can only be formed if I am connected to someone who is open to all possibilities. The largest revelations come to me from those who allow me in. There was a woman. Her and I were two of fifteen in a group. We all shared an acquaintance. He hated us. He wanted us to be cursed. He wanted to turn us against each other."

"Oh my..." Dana said.

"And because he cursed us, one of the group has passed. This same woman I formed a bond with."

"You need to talk to the police Maria."

"The man who cursed us did so through death. He reached out from beyond the grave and used his power to turn those he didn't like against each other. One has passed. More will follow."

"How can you know?"

"When we all learned of the curse, there was fear. I saw visions of what would happen, but they were not clear. I'm not always right Dana. Sometimes I read my visions wrong, but when they are strong, my instinct is right. In baseball, if a hitter is batting three hundred, he's a star. Four hundred, he's immortal. But he's still hitting less than half. I don't hit every time—sometimes not even half—but when I do, it's paramount."

"I understand," Dana said. And she did. And she believed Maria, but still watched in fear, wondering what else in the world was beyond her religious upbringing. Maria's passion was too deep to be faked, and she understood her own limits—not like most mediums who claimed to be one hundred percent real deal.

"So what happens when you're wrong?" Dana asked.

"I don't want to be wrong. I want to develop. If I learn to understand my visions, I can trust myself. If I trust myself, I can prevent things from happening. I did it once as a child."

"You said there are others? Others in danger?"

"Yes," Maria said, envisioning their faces.

"Then maybe since this is significant, you can use that. If you can't stop the man who cursed you, maybe you can prevent him from doing more harm. If he did this in death, then maybe he's still with you, and maybe you can prove to him that he can't do these horrid things to you."

"Yes," Maria said. She'd felt Victor's presence since her encounter at the cemetery. Victor had always believed in her, and even when he wrote her into his will, he must have believed she was legit. The inclusion of her name was proof enough.

"Do you have family that supports you?"

"I have a brother. He's a year older than me. He lives in South Dakota. That's where we grew up."

"Are your parents still there?"

"My father is. My mother passed."

"And what brought you to Los Angeles?"

"My career."

"And what does your father think of what you do?"

It was a loaded question. "He wanted me to do something else."

"So what brought you to our block?"

"Before the woman died, I was discouraged—doubted myself. I stopped liking what I did. And then a man came to me and wanted to buy my shop. I saw it as a sign and I sold. I was going to take the money and quit. But then she died. She was murdered. No one knows who the killer is. But I know."

"You need to go to the police dear."

"The police don't listen to me. They refuse to hear me. The news said it was a break-in, but there's more to it. I know. But I said the wrong thing when she came to me. I told her he was dangerous and he was going to hurt her."

"If only she would have listened to you."

"I downplayed it because I didn't want her to hate me, but I thought I saw what happened before it did. I saw in my vision but I couldn't tell her."

"She should have listened."

"I couldn't make her hear me."

"It's not your fault dear."

Maria cleared her throat and dismissed the memory. "No more self-doubt. I tell people what I see. If I don't have visions, I give them spiritual guidance."

Maria swallowed hard and realized she'd broken a barrier. Dana seemed to feel sorry for her. But more importantly, while talking, she'd had her own revelation. She really had been right about the Palmers. She saw what was going to happen, and she knew something that it seemed no one else knew: Charlie was behind it.

Later, she stood outside the Palmer home. There was no movement, as if the whole residence died with Abby. The shades were drawn and the lights were out. It was likely Charlie wasn't there, but she was cautious anyway. The last thing she wanted was for him to recognize her in his neighborhood. She circled in a wide arc, and then moved in, circling again, getting closer to the house with every pass. Finally, she was in a position to look in the windows. After deciding the house was empty, she rang the doorbell. She didn't have a plan if anyone answered, but she'd already decided there was no chance of it. The silence resumed. She tried twisting the knob, not expecting much. It didn't move.

She walked around the house, looking for anything that was out of place, anything that could give her any kind of premonition. She found her way to the door leading into the garage in the back of the house. The security alarm that Adlar had once broken through sat displayed in front of her with two wires hanging out. She tried the knob, but it didn't twist. She closed her eyes and let her mind drift to that place.

Her eyelids fluttered for a moment as she found her focus. And then a flash of light and scattered moments. She didn't recognize the killer, but she recognized the man lying in a pool of blood. And suddenly she knew who would be next.

5

Josh slouched in a chair with a book displayed in front of him. The book was a mundane novel about the joy of giving and community service. Richard was making him read it before they moved forward. He told Josh it was in preparation, but it seemed like Richard was looking for ways to distract Josh while he went about his business. When Richard wrote his sermons, Josh always wanted to inject his own logic into them. There were opportunities wasted, but Richard wasn't receptive to Josh's advice. He only zoned in on getting him on the next flight out of the country. To help him, maybe. But he clearly didn't want to invest the time in Josh. In fact, he seemed to deflect him as much as he could without letting him run away. He had the look of a man weathered and worn—like maybe he'd already met Josh in another life and had been disappointed. Maybe, to Josh's surprise, they had that in common.

He greeted Aileen as she closed the door behind her and stood against it for a long moment as if trying to decide whether or not to come in.

"He said he won't be long," Josh said, relaying Richard's message. The muffled sounds of one end of a conversation drifted in from Richard's office, where he was on the phone. He didn't sound happy.

Aileen nodded and took a look at Josh, noticing what looked like a smear of makeup near his eye. She tried not to seem suspicious as she approached slowly and squinted her eyes to confirm. "Did something happen to you?" she asked.

Josh quickly spotted where her eyes were fixated and diverted away from her, trying his best to cover. "What?" he asked, buying time. Instead of pressing him, Aileen dropped the subject.

She took a seat while Josh buried his face in his book. He didn't look to be reading. He looked to be hiding. She knew the motion. She'd been in the shoes. She...

...held her stomach.

Eugene sat at her side, teetering between consciousness and sleep, his own snoring waking him every couple of minutes. She turned to him with disgust but quickly became attentive as Denise entered the room in a hurry, as if she needed to make it known that she was overwhelmed. "I see you're home," she said.

"I went to Becka's"

"Didn't bother saying a word to me. Is it too much for you to call?"

"I didn't want to wake Dad."

On cue, Eugene stirred and woke with a grunt, sitting up as if he wasn't sure where he was for a moment.

"Don't pretend you care about us," Denise said.

"Fine."

"No, it's not fine. It's not okay. You're a college drop-out."

"I might have a job."

"You're going back to school. I don't need a daughter with no education out doing drugs and whoring."

Aileen couldn't take any more. It was as if her mother wasn't hearing a word she said. She certainly wasn't addressing it. "I don't!" she screamed in her face. She turned and ran to her room, hoping it wouldn't do the damage she knew it would.

Sure enough, she heard her father struggle from his chair as she entered her room, slamming the door behind her. She broke down in tears as the door cracked open and he shoved through.

She tried to dodge the old man but he towered over her, allowing little room around. He grabbed at her with his large hands and finally got a hold of her wrist. His body barreled down, pinning her as she tried to break free. Every attempt she made, she grew weaker. He raised his fist high. She closed her eyes. "Hit my face! I'm pregnant!" she screamed, breaking down into louder sobs.

Eugene stopped his hand midair, trying to decide what he should do. If he did hit her stomach, there could be irreparable damage. Instead, he loosened his grip and let go. Aileen took the moment of freedom to squirm away from him and run for her door. She passed her mother in the living area and before she could say a word, Aileen was out the door.

She didn't stop running, never bothering to hop a bus or hail a cab. Instead, she let herself cry until she couldn't anymore, but she never stopped moving, walking three hours across town until she finally stood outside Victor Stone's gate. Before she could knock, the gate slowly began to open. He, or someone, had seen her on the cameras—probably had seen the state she was in. As she made her way up his driveway, his door opened and he approached, watching the wreck in front of him, unsure of what he was supposed to say or do.

"What happened?" he asked when he was close enough.

"I'm pregnant," she said, finding she had more tears.

Victor stood still a long moment as the scenario he'd feared so many times before finally became a reality and in the most unlikely of places: a one night stand who he'd taken all precautions with. He set his hand on her arm. "Let's go inside."

"…Come in," Richard said. Aileen entered his office.

She entered silently and walked around, looking at pictures on the wall. He waited while she stalled. Finally, she turned. "That kid out there…are his parents okay?"

"Yes," Richard said with a shrug. "Why?"

"He's covering a mark on his face."

"Really?" Richard asked. He considered for a moment. "How do you know?"

"Look closely. He's trying to cover it. When I asked about it, he denied it and wouldn't look at me."

"His parents are good people."

"Okay," she said, doubtfully. "So what's he doing here?"

"He's one of our volunteers. He's moving overseas for the summer."

"Starting over…" Aileen said to herself, still thinking about how close she came to getting away from herself. Suddenly, she felt small again and wondered if she made the right choice.

Richard watched her from across the room. "Are you okay?"

"You called me selfish," she said.

"I was frustrated. I didn't mean to judge you. It's a delicate situation. I understand that you were his family and rightfully it should have been…"

"No, I wasn't, and I wasn't talking about myself." She ran the back of her hand across her eyes. "I don't know why he didn't give it to Jason."

"I don't know," Richard said with a shake of his head.

"He never wanted me. But Jason...that's his son."

"Aileen, there's no way to understand why people do what they do. I try to live by one simple creed. When I die, will I have made the world a better place?"

She nodded and the corner of her mouth turned up in a half smile. "You know, I don't regret Jason."

"Good. You shouldn't."

"I mean, I regret things, but not him. Sometimes I think people think I do, but I don't."

"Does he know that?"

"I don't know."

"You should tell him."

"I will," she said. "And if you need support with your court thing, I can help."

Richard smiled. He assumed that was the real reason for her visit, but it was refreshing to hear, especially because Aileen had turned out to be a good egg after-all.

"I doubt me being there makes a difference, but…"

"Actually, it does. I just got off the phone with another who informed me I won't have support."

"Why? Who?"

"One of the others is a self-proclaimed psychic. She wants us to stop. You know why?" Richard shook his head in frustration. "She believes if we move forward, meeting Judge Proctor will get another one of us killed."

"And she thinks we're safe if we don't?"

"That's what I asked, and she didn't have an answer. All she said is she can see what's next. She can see who's next. And if we do this, she said it will set events in motion that will lead to Royce Morrow's death."

Chapter 10

1

Royce Morrow didn't believe in mediums, black magic, or a paranormal world of any sort. Part of his success relied on pragmatism. He'd made a point never to deal with what could be and instead focused on what was. When he'd met Maria Haskins at the reading of Victor's will, he'd given her a friendly nod. He did the same at Richard's trial run but hoped to avoid a conversation. He was too polite to tell her he wasn't into the whole mind-reading mumbo-jumbo, and if pushed, he would've likely offended her.

Most people chose a psychic encounter, whether for amusement, guidance, or just plain old curiosity. Royce didn't want to know the future. He wanted to live in the present, enjoy it, and do what it took to evolve into a better person tomorrow. It had always worked for him and there was no need for anything more.

He likely would have lived the rest of his life without any sort of supernatural intervention if Maria hadn't reached out. She sat on the fountain outside his corporation, waiting early in the morning until she saw him pull into a parking lot close to the building. She had to run to catch up to him and as she got closer, he turned, hearing her footsteps closing in. After a double-take, he stopped and turned completely, waiving a finger at her as he tried to remember her name.

"You're..."

"Maria Haskins."

He nodded and smiled before attempting to move on.

"Do you work around here Ms. Haskins?"

"I came to speak with you."

"What can I do for you?"

"This is hard to explain."

"Walk with me."

He began walking toward the building and she followed close behind, looking up at the tower before her. A strong feeling of deja vu overcame her as she found herself once again standing with a powerful man, ready to share with him and hope he didn't laugh in her face. Royce had a kind face and a warm tone. He wasn't intimidating like Victor was. She suspected he would be civil—even if she had to deliver horrible news.

"I think you are in trouble," she said.

"What kind of trouble?" he asked.

"I had a vision."

He picked up the pace.

"I know to you that sounds foolish, but I've practiced a long time."

He stopped and turned, his face not as kind as she'd remembered. She backed away, seeing something in his eyes—something dark. He was a kind man who was going through something heavy, which only assured her that her vision had been right.

"Why don't you go ahead and call my secretary and set up a time we can do lunch? I have a meeting that started a minute ago."

"You're going to die," she said. To her surprise, he took a deep breath and stood still.

"Because of the will?"

"Yes."

"Three and a half weeks and this is over. Soon, there will be no money to gain from this charade. Why on earth do you fear for me?"

"Richard doesn't have the names he needs. He needs more."

"Did he tell you this? I was under the impression the majority were in favor of what he's doing."

"It's split. He'll need my help, but you need to listen first."

"What do you want Ms. Haskins?" he asked, defeated.

"Only a few minutes of time."

"Get behind what Mr. Libby is doing and we'll talk."

"If I get behind it, I believe you'll die as a result."

"I don't have time for this," Royce said, turning to walk away. "Make an appointment next time. Until then, help Richard. We'll talk on that day when we both throw our support in his favor."

"You don't care about your life?"

"If my life is the only one on the line, then it's still a win." He kept walking, not bothering to turn back this time. Maria watched him enter his building, biting her lip, conflicted. If there was something she was sure of, it was that her intuition was correct. The building was doomed, and just like Victor, Royce would be inside when it fell. She'd never seen something so complex, so clearly. It frightened her, but there was also validation in such a powerful vision. Like the Palmers, Royce was a completely random name to appear on her radar, and this time her gift was enhanced. But what was missing from her visions was what would happen to the others if Royce were to live.

She turned and walked back to her car, climbed inside, and turned the key...

...She drove through the city, her face expressionless. Kisha tried not to look at her passenger, whose hair was disheveled and her head turned away in humiliation. She'd silently picked Maria up from the hospital and had driven her ten miles without a word before she decided she deserved more than just a call in the middle of the night telling Kisha her friend was in the hospital, her stomach having just been pumped of over twenty pills.

"We should talk about this," Kisha said.

"No."

"I'm worried about you."

"Don't be. Please."

"You tried to kill yourself again."

"I can't talk about this now."

"I told you if you ever feel that way to call me."

"It was a moment of weakness. I made a mistake."

"Evan came to see me." At Evan's name, Maria's face shriveled in pain. "He said he just broke up with you."

"It was mutual," Maria said, defensively. She wasn't sure why she was lying. Kisha would never believe it, and it was irrelevant. What happened, happened. Kisha would see past any excuse Maria gave her. What went down was pretty clear cut and it wasn't the first time.

"He said he broke it off," Kisha said. "And that you called him right before you swallowed the pills—that you warned him you would."

"I don't want to talk," she said, closing her eyes with shame. She'd hoped the news wouldn't reach Kisha, but the hospital didn't have an emergency contact number and searched through her work. Kisha was the only person who could be connected to her name.

"What happens if you do this and really die? No one is worth dying for. Not even Evan."

"He fooled me. He said he was in love two days ago."

"I met him once and even I could see he was in it for sex. He targeted you because you gave it up for the right words."

"You weren't there."

"No, but you're sharper than this. You're supposed to keep your mind open to signals. How you didn't see his intent was beyond me. Open your eyes Maria."

"I don't want to talk about this."

Kisha slammed on the brakes, fed up with her attitude. The car came to a screeching halt along the side of the road. Suddenly, everything was quiet, except for the cars that zoomed around them. Kisha leaned in, confronting Maria face to face. "Then don't use suicide as a way to get attention and guilt someone into staying with you. You complain because I care, but this is what you asked for. It's not right."

"That's not what I did."

"Evan said the last thing you told him is if you can't have him, you refuse to go on. You wanted him to come find you there and save you, and when he didn't, you called the ambulance yourself."

Maria turned away, ashamed for what she'd done. "Please take me to my shop," she said, her voice trembling.

"I think you need to go home."

"My shop," she insisted. Kisha shook her head in disbelief. Maria shouldn't have been dealing with people, but Kisha was anxious to be rid of her. She was tired of the games she played. She kept silent the remainder of the ride and respected Maria's wish and dropped her off at her shop where she exited the car silently and walked inside without a word.

The door swung open and she stood in the darkness for a long moment, thinking about Evan and the new low she'd shown him. It was bad enough that he didn't like her as she was, but she went and outdid herself with her cry for help. He still didn't care enough to show up and save her. She reached for the switch. The lights flickered on as she dragged her feet to her desk where she tossed her keys.

Her answering machine displayed a number, which was unusual. She immediately knew it was Evan but was afraid to listen. She reluctantly pushed the button and closed her eyes, expecting the worst. Instead of Evan, Victor Stone's voice projected throughout the small room.

"Maria, I stopped by. You weren't there. I was under the impression you had set hours of operation. Do me a favor and stop by my office this afternoon anytime. Tell my secretary you have an appointment. I need to talk to you."

The machine beeped and the machine rewound while an electronic voice told her there were no more messages.

She sighed, wondering why the only person in the world that seemed to value her was one of the wealthiest. She opened a drawer and pulled out a prescription bottle. She popped the cap and downed a couple pills. She took a seat and waited until they took the desired effect.

Two hours later, she sat across from Victor Stone, her hair and makeup redone and a smile on her face, as if the previous night didn't happen.

"Is everything okay?" Victor asked, as if he sensed a problem. She nodded. "Please accept this as constructive feedback from one business *professional to another. It's bad business not to have structure."*

"Something came up," she said.

"You sure everything is okay?"

"I'm sure," she insisted. "Your message sounded urgent."

"A little. I've appreciated your outlook. Your method of thinking is based on instinct non-factual notions. I haven't always accepted what you've told me, but when I do, I'm generally pleased."

She smiled warmly.

"I'm constantly surrounded by about a dozen or so less than trustworthy people. Their minds operate the same."

"I don't understand."

"I've tried to stay grounded, but there are repercussions to things that have happened. Things are resurfacing that I've buried. Things that can hurt myself and my colleagues."

"Do you want to tell me about it?"

"The less I say, the better." Maria nodded, accepting his discretion. "Something is happening that could bury everything I've worked for, and one single action could make it go away. It requires crossing a line I've always tried to avoid."

"I can't advise you commit a crime," she said.

"I'm asking you to do what you do—to close your eyes and search for an answer."

"But if you do something wrong..."

"There are always gray areas Maria. I'm asking you to do what you do, and tell me if there's a chance that a decision I have to make will do more harm than good. I'm asking you to search within a gray area."

She stared at him for a long moment. She knew a thing or two about gray areas. They were typically an excuse people used for bad actions. Victor was trying to justify something, and Maria couldn't help but wonder what.

"Have a seat please," she said.

"Should we be in your shop?" he asked.

"It's not necessary. It's you who gives off an aura."

Victor hesitantly sat.

"May I turn off the lights?" Maria asked.

"Whatever you need."

She did, and then sat and let herself become comfortable. She took her time, preparing for what might be the most significant reading to date. Other than April Lovelace, of course. Victor watched closely as she closed her eyes. "I need you to envision your problem. I need you to think about the deed as if you're doing it."

Victor held his eyes closed and shifted uncomfortably. He swallowed *hard, hoping she'd start talking. Every sound was illuminated by the silence, and his discomfort would become apparent if she didn't move on.*

"Do you see it?" she asked.

"Yes."

She couldn't decide whether or not he was lying, but it didn't matter. He'd put his trust in her hands, and after the day she'd had, there was value in Victor's faith in her ability. She closed her eyes, searching for answers, but all she found was darkness. She read nothing, but she could fish for information and give good advice.

Victor was talking about doing something undo-able—something he wasn't capable of, but was trying to do anyway—his gray area. Maria would ordinarily steer him far, somewhere safe in the black and white world most people lived. She'd always played it safe with Victor, and the last thing she wanted him to see her as was a fraud—a fraud giving him the safe route time and time again until one day he realized she was just telling him what anyone would. The only way to sustain her time with him—to keep her shop—was to be something more. Something unexpected and special. She needed to tell him what he didn't expect to hear. She needed to speak like a woman with a vision instead of just a woman fending off a problem.

She opened her eyes and stared blankly.

"Nothing?" Victor asked.

"No. I have no answer now."

"Maria," he started, doubtfully, "this is something I won't do if I don't believe there is a greater good..."

"I think you should do it," she interjected before he could go further.

"Do what?" he asked, taken aback.

"What you don't believe you can do."

"Even knowing..."

"You have to."

He stared at her a long moment. Her face gave nothing away. "What did you see?" he asked.

"I saw a greater good. Bad things happen with all decisions, and they will with yours, but there will be a greater good."

She'd made it so simple. He didn't know if she'd seen something, or if she was telling him what he wanted to hear. Either way...

...nothing happened.

She tried again several times, but the car didn't start. She popped the hood and took a look, though she had no idea what she was looking for. She considered her options, wondering if she had triple A and how much they'd be able to do for her.

"You need help?"

She looked up and her eyes stopped on a handsome man who was already rolling up his sleeves. A good Samaritan, who appeared out of nowhere just as she needed help the most—and he was easy on the eyes too—a knight in shining armor. He gave her a smile and their eyes met for a moment, making her blush.

"Do you know much about cars?" she asked. "Because I don't."

"Depends on the problem," he said with a smirk, exposing his dimples to her. "I'm Henry."

"Maria."

"What's happening? Is it trying to turn over at all?"

"No. No noise."

"Any previous problems?

"No. It started fine when I left."

"Probably just something knocked itself loose." He held up a spark plug. "Like this. Your spark plugs are encrusted with a buildup of residue and it probably just shook them loose. Just scrape it off and you're good to go, but I'd invest in some new ones at some point if I were you."

"Are you sure?"

"Yup. I've owned quite a few lemons in my day. This is actually a cheap fix compared to what it could have been. Try her now."

She entered the car and started it without a problem, smiling to herself at the fact that a good looking man showed up and saved her day. She shut the engine off and climbed out, facing him.

"I want to give you something for your trouble.

"What trouble? Two minutes of my time? Forget about it." He looked up to see where she came from. "You work for Morrow?"

"No. Just in the area."

"Same. I bank across the street actually. What do you do, Maria?"

She liked him too much to blurt out the truth. Henry arrived on a white horse and made a gesture from the kindness of his heart. He was different than anyone she'd ever dated within five minutes of meeting. For the first time in her life, she not only feared approval from a man for who she was. She outright didn't want him to know.

"I cut hair," she said. "Stylist," she quickly added.

"Nice. You have a card?"

"Not on me."

"Where you located?"

"Um, well, how come?"

"In case I need a haircut," he said, obviously.

She laughed a little and took a step toward her car, retreating. He was too good for her. She needed to run before they even got started. "Thanks again for your help."

"No problem. Get the spark plugs changed."

2

If the story leaks, never give the public the names.

It was the simple creed Tarek Appleton held and struggled with. Tony pushed him to make those revelations and even Tarek toyed with the concept of free publicity and a brighter spotlight. In the back of his head, he wondered if someday he'd use it—if someday those names would slip. He had less than a month to let that happen. That time would fly and that fear would be behind him.

He was late to The Cave. He'd spent the night before with a woman he met at the club and didn't bother to set his alarm. He hurried into the room, prepared to defend himself against a frustrated crew, but the tone was something else entirely. What was going to be an apology transitioned into a "what happened?" when Tarek read their faces.

Tony slid a paper toward him. "You got a death threat. This one's morbid."

"So what?" Tarek asked.

Tony pulled the paper back and read, "I will be waiting for you at your home so I can put a bullet in your fat head."

Tarek frowned as they awaited reaction. "You guys think my head is fat?" he finally asked.

"It's pretty fat," someone said. Tarek feigned offense.

"We're cutting Westboro jokes for a while," Tony said.

"We're not pulling back from anyone," Tarek said. "In fact, do the opposite. Take every group, make twice as many jokes and make them heavier. Declare war on everyone. I'm serious."

"The guy mentions Victor Stone," Tony said.

Tarek paused and finally asked. "What about him?"

"Said he knows the truth. That's all. We watched old footage of Victor on the show. I wanna say the letter comes from Victor, but he's dead."

"How about we keep this in the room?" Tarek said, his voice growing soft. "If it leaks, someone will lose their job."

"A second ago, you declared war on everyone," someone said. "What makes this different?"

"Nothing. It's a non-story. Just people who want money."

"So you know what this is about?"

"It's a personal issue between me and old acquaintances of his. It's nothing. If it hits the news, people will care."

"If people know and you ignore it, you breathe life into the story."

"It's a letter. No one knows."
"Hopefully, it's only a letter."

Deon Horowitz was in the business of laughter, but hadn't cracked a smile in over ten years. He wore a suit, moved quickly, constantly stared at numbers, and fired people. He ran the company that owned the studio that ran the show that housed The Cave where Tarek worked. Tarek and the writers got their ratings from the news or had data passed down the line. Usually, bad numbers meant try harder. Good numbers meant try harder. The message was always try harder. It was a fairly run-of-the-mill routine until Tarek was called to sit in on a board meeting.

The room was filled with men who looked and acted like Deon. Angry men with deep thought lines on their faces who seemed displeased at the direction of the numbers. The meeting went on as if Tarek wasn't there. Nothing indicated he should be there. Nothing was new, or enlightening, or even interesting. Most of it was above his head.

Deon sat at the head of the board with a printout in hand. "Of the 9.7 million viewers that tuned in to watch the beginning of the show, two million changed the channel before the hour ended. The series also held on to just 47 percent of the viewers from its lead-in. Sound grim to anyone else?"

And then, most heads turned to Tarek and he realized why he was there.

"The jokes are fucking terrible," Deon said. "They're not smart, witty, or anything that resembles what a joke should look like. The interviews aren't edgy. The network is calling for fresh writers. And I'm with em. Now, Mr. Appleton, bring me the heads of your three weakest links."

Tarek froze long enough to realize that not giving an answer with some sort of substance without turning against his own crew was going to make him feel very small in a room full of hot-heads. "We don't have weak links," he said.

"Loyalty will get your ass nowhere. I understand you don't know there's a fucking problem because you think the audience is laughing at your jokes and not at the applause sign flashing in their faces."

"I take the blame."

"You should. You oversee the staff. We give you too much freedom to make the show your own because you were strong coming in. But, now the audience is used to you. You don't outdo yourself or take comedy to a higher level while it evolves all around you. But it's still your face they want to see which is why you need fresh voices in the writing room."

"I believe that we have the right people, but they're overworked. Rick was one of the hardest working writers we had and he was using on the side. Without him, we're already spread thin."

"If anything, you're overstaffed."

"Everyone in that room contributes to the show."

"That's not what I'm hearing. I'm hearing there's too many cooks in the kitchen down there."

"I'll rally them."

"Decision's already made. I need three names. Get the guys who aren't getting any jokes on the air."

"I don't have weak links."

"I hope you have weak links, because if the show that's been airing is everyone's best foot, we're in trouble. Peggy Wheeler hasn't had her name on anything."

"Peggy took three months off for maternity leave."

"Haven't seen her name on anything since."

"Their names aren't always on the jokes, but they've contributed to the line of thought behind many successful bits."

"We don't attribute success to who was in on brainstorming. Zero jokes Appleton. They're being paid generously for nothing."

Tarek leaned in and quieted his voice. "If you ask me to fire someone, it's broken and we fall apart. It comes undone."

"Then we'll replace those that can't handle the change. There's a long line of people who would be grateful just to work in late night, and what we need is an overhaul. Ratings suck. Television's changing. I don't think your family environment is cutting the mustard. They might be angry, but they'll cash their paychecks anyway. This is the best gig of their lives, and no one has a guaranteed shelf life here. Not you or me, and sure as fuck not a writer who gets nothing on the air."

Tarek nodded. Dean was right. The Cave was in show business. People were lining up outside the studio just begging for a job. The Cave did have a tendency to be ungrateful for the opportunities they were given.

"You're better than the quality has been Appleton. This show is your baby. You should expect nothing but the best and we both know the writing is suffering."

"I won't fight you," Tarek said. "Your call. I won't approve, but you're the guy.. You know, Peggy was the eleventh man in a ten man sitcom writing group."

"Who was fired..."

"Fired because her jokes were too smart for the show and they didn't know it. She's a legend in that room."

"Doesn't have to be Peggy. Stop road blocking me Appleton. We can't keep moving in this direction. If you can't find three, how you gonna feel when everyone's out of business because the show gets the ax?"

"Alright, well, tell me what to do and I'll do it."
Deon pointed his finger at Tarek's chest. "Do better."

3

Toby O'Tool recruited his bar buddy William to infiltrate lives.
William suggested they bring more in, but Toby didn't want a staff of guys
he couldn't control. He didn't know too many trustworthy people, so when
William proposed Toby have a staff of three—William and two others—
Toby agreed on the grounds that Toby approve of William's recruits. One
agreed to come by later in the day after he got off work. The other didn't
work because he was fresh out of a twelve year stint in prison after
murdering his wife.

Sal Blovik was a mountain of muscle and flesh attached to a six foot
five frame. Within all the muscle and fat, there was no sign of a brain.
William believed there was a place for Sal. Toby didn't.

The bar became their boardroom. Toby and William met daily, going
over strategic ways to bring down the beneficiaries. William was
trustworthy. He'd gotten a job at The Wasp effortlessly, and made his
place as a useful asset in the kitchen. He hadn't interacted with Brian Van
Dyke much. He'd only made a point to be nice and observe his behavior.
He'd infiltrated the enemies base. Phase two was to gain the trust of the
enemy. Enough, anyway, to be influential. Today, William realized that
after working in the diner for a week, he was tired of the job already. Every
day felt less like an assignment, and more like actual work.

"I don't see how flinging burgers can be hard," Toby said, directing all
conversation toward William as if Sal wasn't sitting at his side.

"It's harder than you'd think," William said. "You'd have to actually
work to understand."

"If dentists, a job that's infinitely harder than making burgers, by the
way, are forced to provide flawless service, why can't burger makers do
something as easy as giving a person what they ask for? Your recipes
probably hang on the wall."

"We're not burger makers. We're chefs.."

"If you're going to sensationalize the job title, then you could at least
sensationalize the work by doing it right."

"Going back up to your dentist remark: When a dentist screws up the
filling in your mouth, they open themselves up to a lawsuit for causing
unnecessary damage or pain to your body and putting your medical future
in jeopardy. When the burger place screws up your order, all they're
putting in jeopardy is having limp-dick losers whine about their food to
people who are smart enough to bring a bottle of their own hot sauce into

the restaurant and apply it themselves."

"When it's on the menu, you have to honor that. That's a written contract. Would you deduct the cost of the hot sauce if I'm supplying it from my own home?"

"I'm not a cook Toby. You made me do this. You can't complain because you got one bad burger."

"Van Dyke never screws up. I'll tell you, the biggest regret I'll have when he's dead will be the deprivation of properly manufactured burgers."

"I honestly don't give a shit about your burger," William said.

"Not just the burger numb-nuts. This goes to the very core of what you're doing. You get fired and what next?"

"They really don't take much pride there. I couldn't get fired if I tried."

"Just keep things moving. You have three weeks to stall. We don't need anyone turning up dead until after the trial. When am I meeting your other guy?"

"He'll be here later."

"I should have met him by now."

"He wanted to prove himself to you. You can trust him. He's smarter than both of us and charming as hell."

"I could give two shits about charming. He needs to know how to play people against their vices and it's time consuming. Your buddy wants to prove himself? Sounds aggressive. The last thing we need is aggressive."

"He knows. He's not dumb."

"If he so much as carries a gun..."

"I know."

Toby nodded. "What about Sal? What's the story on this ugly looking thing?"

"What?" Sal asked. He looked up, surprised to finally be acknowledged.

"You're ugly as sin. Don't be offended by something I have no doubt you already know."

William turned to Sal. "I told you he can be blunt. Just listen to him."

"I don't care if you're a delicate flower," Toby said. "I have an objective here and it includes blending in. This isn't the kind of job where we can just bring in hideous giants. You'll stand out. You have to be able to play the rancorous cynic or affable romantic, blue-blooded sophisticate or rustic commoner. You have to be able to inspire trust and confidence in those you deal and misdeal."

"I do that," Sal said.

"No, you can't, because people will take one look at you and flee, like they would from a burning building."

"There's a place for him," William said. "He might not be able to get involved on the same level as we do, but there's got to be ways of utilizing him."

"I don't know if William told you or not, but I was in prison fifteen years for killing my ex," Sal said, as if bragging.

"Yeah, he told me."

"So you know I'm not afraid to kill."

"This isn't about killing."

"Isn't that what this is all about?" Sal asked, confused.

"Killing requires one take the life of another. When this is through, we won't have taken one life, there will be no weapons or violence. Confidence games are an art where one uses words to persuade others to do the work for them. What we're doing is nothing more than a petty crime that no one even cares about, except the victims, who will never know anyway."

"You're underestimating me Mr. O'Tool," Sal said.

"I hope so. Because this isn't about guns. I don't care that some woman was unlucky enough to marry you because of your murderous tendencies and just the simple fact that she had to wake up next to you every day before you put her out of her misery. But yeah, I got something you can do for now. I don't see a whole lot of use for you though."

Toby looked at William, as if to ask what he was thinking by bringing Sal in on what they were doing.

"Good," Sal said, "because I don't appreciate people busting my balls for nothing."

"I wasn't busting your balls. You need to work on your sensitivity level."

"I can stay cool."

"Good. Go learn to play poker."

"I know how to play."

"Don't learn the mechanics. Learn how to keep a straight face. If you're emotional, learn to kill it. Not people. Use your brain."

"Give me an assignment. I'll prove myself."

"No," Toby said. Sal waited for Toby to say more. Toby noticed, and grew irritated. "'No' is a complete sentence."

Toby's real irritation was behind a call he received earlier in the day. Richard Libby seemed to be testing Toby on a regular basis ever since Toby told him he had his back. First, he was forced to show his support at the trial run. Now, Toby was expected to be Richard's voice when he needed to persuade other beneficiaries to be there. It seemed Maria had backed out, after a ridiculous premonition told her Royce Morrow would be killed if they moved forward. Richard needed Toby to talk some sense into her. It was impossible for Toby to work behind the scenes to sabotage Richard's efforts if Richard continued forcing his help. Richard picked him up outside the bar and Toby stepped inside without a word. Richard asked him to put out his cigarette, but otherwise, the ride was silent. Richard didn't know what to say and Toby played potential courses in his head. He was searching for a way to cooperate and still come out ahead in the end. Richard tried making small talk, but Toby responded with one word answers. Finally, Richard decided he needed to get a grasp of whether or not Toby was truly on-board.

"I spoke with Royce Morrow. He's a good guy. It's hard to believe what Maria said about him."

"What does this have to do with me?"

"Maria believes she has visions. I may not be someone she'll listen to. Our faith comes from very different ends of the spectrum."

"I'd think you'd get along. You both worship your imaginations."

"You know, guys like you who don't believe in anything they can't see are so cynical. Your outlook might be brighter if you believed there was more to life than what's in front of you."

"I was thinking guys like you might be a little less naïve if you stopped telling yourself there's more to life than what's in front of you."

Richard smiled nonsensically at Toby's logic. "Either way, you have a gift. You probably don't see it this way, but the power of persuasion is a gift."

"I absolutely see it that way."

"Good."

"I once used my gift to bag blond twins in one night."

"Today, you'll be using it for good."

"You know, you've got me pegged all wrong."

"How's that?"

"I get my way by verbally abusing people and blackmailing them."

"Okay," Richard said, awkwardly. "Do what you have to do. Getting through to her is more important than her feelings at this point."

Toby nodded, with a smirk. He didn't like what they had to do, but he liked the method in which he was going to do it. Maria was such a weakling and nothing would be more fun than taking her down a peg, even if it meant gaining her support. He still had plenty of time and energy to undo any progress he made in Richard's favor. This was just one of those moments he had to cooperate. It was one of those…

"…*gray areas,*" Maria said. "*That's what he called it. So I thought maybe there was positive and negative outcomes to his decision.*"

"*How can you say that?*" Kisha asked, softly.

"I saw it," Maria explained.

"If someone asks permission to do the wrong thing, always say no."

"If we go against our instincts, what's the point?"

"You must learn to read what your mind tries to tell you. Sometimes our premonitions are not easy to see clearly—especially when we want so badly to do what we want. This does not sound like an insignificant decision."

"I know this."

"From what I know about Mr. Stone, your advice could mean life or death and you directed him to do as he pleases. You gave him assurance that it was okay to make a decision that could mean doom. You must reverse what you've done."

"I can't," Maria said.

Kisha rubbed her temples, and shook her head hopelessly. "You just got out of the hospital. You're a wreck."

"That's not what this is about."

"How can you know?"

"Have you ever seen me so sure of myself?"

"I know sometimes we're wrong."

"You don't know what I saw. What if there's a greater good? What if someone told you to kill a child and you believed it was wrong, but you knew the boy would become an evil dictator? To outsiders, the death of a child is tragic, but we see further. We can see unchosen paths that others cannot."

"Horrid things happen every day that no visionary was able to prevent."

"How do you know?"

"Because fate doesn't allow pick and choose moments. The best we can do is hear what the heart wants and show how they can change their own fate. We can only steer people to make better choices and change negative outcomes."

"That's what I did," Maria said, quietly.

"What you did was help a man decide to kill someone."

"For a greater good."

"You can tell yourself that until you die but the only fact, the only thing you'll ever know with absolute certainty, is the harm you've done. You must stop him from acting, or this will haunt you forever."

"What I said..." Maria told Victor later. "I think I was wrong."

"You were sure," Victor said.

"I didn't see the whole picture, but I do now. I changed my mind."

"What's the whole picture?"

"It's wrong."

"Maria," he said, leaning forward and taking her hand. "You don't know the details. You haven't aided in anything. All you did is what you're paid to do."

"I only told you it was okay because I assumed there would be balance. I believed more good would come than harm."

"You don't know the situation well enough to know there won't be. Forget I confided in you Maria. I shouldn't have put this on your shoulders and I apologize.."

"No, I can't offer my blessing. I wasn't right that day. I was in a dark place. I don't know what overcame me."

"It's already been done."

She closed her eyes, distressed. Whatever was done was set in motion by Maria. Whatever came of it was rooted in her visionary expertise.

"You come to me and blindly listen to what I say. You hadn't made your mind up until we sat together, and when we spoke, I wasn't in a good place. I said..."

"Relax Ms. Haskins. There's a greater good to this. That's all you need to tell yourself."

"You have to be sure that is true," she said, taking his hands and pleading.

"I will."

"You must do something—a gesture or a good deed—something to provide balance. The next chance you get, you must make up for what you're about to do. You must intervene in a positive way to reverse the negative deed..."

...The last people Maria expected to see were Richard and Toby walking through her door. Richard approached her desk while Toby walked through the area, observing the place. When Richard greeted her, she managed a smile, her eyes darting suspiciously toward Toby.

"I'm here to talk about Royce," Richard said.

"Have a seat." She gestured to a chair and Richard sat. He glanced back at Toby, who was deeply consumed by Maria's belongings, seemingly allowing Richard to handle her alone. He turned his attention back to Maria.

Toby watched Maria out of the corner of his eye as she drank from a glass of water, her eyes watching the glass instead of Richard. He raised his eyebrows in thought as Richard addressed her.

"Maria, you seem like you sincerely want to help, but you do realize that you're preventing us from ending this."

"It was implied that we have time to consider."

"I'm trying to get all my ducks in a row now."

"I would be happy to help, but what you're doing brings more bloodshed."

"Doing nothing brings bloodshed It already has. Maria, that makes no sense. I don't understand how what you do works, but is it possible you're mistaken?"

"I don't choose what I see. You don't know what we go through and you don't want to know what we see."

Toby's eyes perked up and before Richard could say a word, he intruded on the conversation. "Yeah, and please don't tell us because I'm sure it will be boring."

Richard closed his mouth and let Toby have the floor.

"Seriously, I can't even feign enough interest in this conversation to make a joke at your expense using my B material."

"You mock what I do," she said.

"No, I just think you need an intervention before your television tells you to kill the neighbors. You are, by far, the loneliest woman I've ever met."

"I'm not..."

"For starters, you're nervous around strangers. Your awareness is heightened because you can't trust yourself to do something you've done hundreds of times before, like taking a drink of water without having to pay attention to what you're doing. It's a matter of unconscious competence, but you still can't take your eyes off the glass. Your eyes, by the way, which dilated within moments of our arrival, which indicates you were either watching out the window, or you're high on amphetamines."

"I believe we should..."

"And you turn down ownership of your problems by using pronouns like 'we', as if you're in a club of psychics who are victims to the burden of having to save the world. You get your personal mail here. Not at home. You also have a vast variety of magazines, mostly geared toward men, so you can read them based on what they pick up when they wait, but also as a personal indicator of what kind of catch they are. How many men have you asked to leave their wife just so they'd be available? Or maybe it's just to give happy people a taste of the misery that's your day to day life."

"I never..."

"And like any good poker player with a good hand, you manipulate the situation by pausing and pretending to think when you're asked a question that you easily know the answer to. If you have a bad hand and you're bluffing, you answer quickly, pretending to be confident in the answer. You've done both of these things in less than a minute."

Maria held her lips together, afraid of what might come out and how

Toby would interpret it.

"I'm not surprised the room is dark and decorated in blue shades. You're sad. Makes sense."

"How can you know anything about me?"

"Cause I see the future!" Toby said, crazily. "Or maybe anyone can be read in a second. Sadly, you probably actually believe this shit that you sell. I'm just as sure as I am that Richard here has been feeling guilty all day for canceling on some kid he promised to meet today."

Richard's face twisted in confusion. The last thing he wanted was to be a target in Toby's assault.

"So I guess the question is whether we should respect the charlatans who strip sad lonely people of their savings in return for vague false messages of hope from the dead, who camouflage their highly infallible opinions in the guise of facts as they taught themselves to do, even though in thousands of years of faith versus science, there's been not one instance of proof that supports a sixth sense of any kind."

"You couldn't understand the impact I've had."

"Post hoc ergo propter hoc. It's Latin for 'after this, therefore because of this'. It's a common fallacy that occurs when people assume that if event A proceeded B, then A caused B. For example, you buy a rabbit's foot and then pass a driver's test. You think you passed because you bought the rabbits foot. Royce Morrow's not in trouble because you envisioned it. If Royce were to die, it's because you set it in motion by putting us in danger."

Maria was dumbfounded.

"You tell someone to leave their wife, or their job and they listen without knowing any better, and they think they did it for the best because a fortune-teller told them so, and they probably always believe that, but only because you plant seeds that tell them the alternative would have been worse. Your readings become true because you lead them on that path and you make them believe you're right. But you're not right. You're a con-woman. You lie to sound special. You interfere to seem important, because the truth is: you're probably not special and you know it. So you invented your sixth sense so people would listen, so you'd have something no one else had and no one could disprove."

Maria's guard was down. She weakened with every word.

"It's a vicious cycle. Your misery creates misery. Why don't you try telling someone something positive? Maybe you'd feel good for once in your pathetic life and be rewarded."

"What do you want me to do?" she asked, willing to do whatever it took to get rid of them.

"Support what Richard's doing."

She nodded, numbly.

"You know why con artists always accuse each other of cheating?" Toby asked. "Because a person looks at the world as a reflection of themselves. When you see the world as corrupt, that's how you see yourself. When you quit interfering in everyone's happiness, you won't be so miserable."

"I've been right."

"And you've been wrong. Same odds as everyone else. You're nothing special."

After the slaughter, Richard and Toby sat silently in the car, driving in the opposite direction. Toby was in his own head and Richard was trying to find a way to be grateful without Toby rejecting it.

Finally, Richard turned to him. "I don't know if we changed her mind."

"Everyone wants the money," Toby said, carelessly.

They sat in silence a moment longer, before Richard asked what had been on his mind for quite a while. "How did you know about the kid?"

"What kid?"

"The one I canceled on today. You were right."

"I flipped through your day planner when you were buying coffee and Cheetos."

Richard looked down where his planner was wedged between the seats. He put a hand on it, protectively. "Would you mind not looking through my personal belongings?"

"Sure."

"He'll understand. He knows what I'm doing."

"You don't have to defend yourself to me.

"You said I let him down. I'm just telling you that's not the case."

"However you need to justify it."

Richard sighed. "You don't know everything."

"Maybe not, but all your prayers and all your faith and you're so sure that you have all the answers, and you still relied on my dirty tactics for your project, and you're so hung up on my opinion of a kid I don't even know. Frankly, I'm concerned that you're hanging out with kids at all."

"Just this kid."

"Seems shady to me. I read the news."

Richard chuckled. "You really try to hit a nerve with people."

"Did I?"

"No."

"You angry about Maria?"

"What you did needed to be done."

The car pulled to the side of the road.

"Is this the place?" Richard asked.

"No, one more block. There will be a neon outline of a woman and Girls Girls Girls written next to it."

Richard smirked as they pulled up to their destination. "You're not so bad when you use your powers for good."

Toby's face momentarily froze. He wasn't crazy about what he was doing behind Richard's back. He couldn't accept compliments while he had his own plots in motion. "Wanna come in and have a drink?" he asked.

"No thanks."

"You sure? They go full nude in here."

"Not my scene."

"Well, there's nowhere in the area that does Bingo. Otherwise, I'd buy you a fifty cent popcorn and try our luck."

"I don't like Bingo."

"Alright."

Richard didn't move. He'd surprisingly enjoyed his time with Toby and appreciated his feedback. He was sharp and brought something to the table that Richard couldn't. They made a good team. "You think she'll help us?" he asked.

"Of course I do," Toby said with confidence. "Honestly Richard, I could turn them all in your favor if I wanted to. Even Dent."

Before Richard could respond, Toby hurried from the car and walked to the entrance. Richard smiled to himself.

4

"No comment" Tarek said, trying to deflect an oncoming reporter named Katy Malloy.

"I haven't asked a question," she said, catching up to him, notebook in hand.

"Go ahead."

"What was the nature of your relationship with Victor Stone?"

Tarek stopped, taken aback. "He's my long lost brother."

"I'll print that."

"Go ahead. What's he have to do with anything? I owe my career to him. I'm grateful. If you want to spit on his grave, make up your own rumors."

"I think you know what I'm referring to."

"If you already know the truth, why you asking me questions about my relationship?"

"How did he feel about you?"

"Why don't you ask him?"

"He's dead," Katy said, confused.

"Oh right. I forgot. I assumed no human being would disrespect the memory of the dead by trying to tarnish their reputation. I'm sure you would have understood back when you were a person."

"I'm not disrespecting," she said. "Is there a reason he'd want you dead?"

Tarek held it together. He wanted to set her straight, but that's what they wanted. If not the truth, an outburst. Instead, he stopped walking and calmly faced Katy. "If you have questions for Victor, like I said, I'm not him. Why don't you go back to your tabloids and photo-shop a picture of Victor's ghost or something?"

"Because I've moved up in the world. I'm with TMZ now and since I can't ask him, I'm asking you."

"You must be under the impression that Victor and I drove around the city on a bicycle made for two, then hold hands and skip up a hillside to have a picnic on a hillside of marigolds. Surely, even someone like you should know that I can't speak for another man."

"But you can speculate..."

"Yes, I can."

She waited a moment, but Tarek said nothing. "And?"

"No comment," Tarek said with a wicked smile before turning his back.

"It's quitting time," Tarek said, entering the room and messing up the pages in front of Tony. "Let's grab a drink."

Within the hour, Tarek was three drinks in and Tony had a buzz.

"We celebrating?" he asked, observing Tarek's good mood.

"We're talking. Maybe meeting girls."

"Sounds good," Tony said, and it really did.

"I don't want you to think I'm angry."

"About what?"

"You talk to the press?"

"About what?"

"Victor Stone."

"No. Do they know something?"

"You talk to anyone about him?"

"Not at all."

"I was asked by Katy Malloy about my relationship with Victor."

"She ask about the will or Victor?"

"She hinted at the will."

"What did you say?"

"Nothing," Tarek said. "You know our ratings are dropping? I've been assigned to pick three writers to can. We're not holding the audience, so the powers that be are saying we need to reinvent the show and get rid of the weak links. We're not funny anymore."

"Then we'll write funnier jokes."

"We need a new approach," Tarek said. "The self-deprecating humor doesn't work. Funny comes in waves. What was funny in the fifties, we scoff at now. Same will be said in the next decade. Television's evolved into a war of who can hold the most shock value. Toilet humor, self-mutilation, drama..."

"What are you saying?"

"I'm saying ratings are generated by publicity. Maybe I've got publicity without doing anything wrong. I'm a victim."

"I don't know what you're saying."

"People would tune in just to see if I'm alive day to day."

"Is that what you want? To be reality TV?"

"I wanted to be funny. If I stepped on a head or two in the past, I did it for a laugh. If I thought it could potentially get someone killed, you think I'm gonna do it? In a few weeks, this will be over and the moment will have passed. I have a chance to turn heads."

"You're not thinking Tarek. You're watched by millions of people every night. You make fun of one person on the air and they see it. You know what that does to that person? This is the same thing. Trust me. In grade school, I was forced to wear thick glasses and I had buck-teeth and a stutter. There's nothing worse than public humiliation. People hang on your words. How many jokes have you started that are replayed and suddenly we're hearing the insults in public being aimed at other people? And I get it. That's just the nature of the beast, but we already know we have an audience that hangs on our every word. If they know about the will, you're going to make life a living hell for those people."

Tarek sipped his beer and stared forward. It was flattering to know that his viewers stayed tuned for Tarek and not just for the laughs and gimmicks, but if keeping people happy meant exploiting the drama in his life, then he had some things to think about. Tarek's career was at a stalemate. The late night show wasn't going anywhere, he was being forced to throw friends under the bus, and when it all fell apart, there would be no coming back.

He had a way of fixing it all. He needed something newer, better—he needed to rethink the path he was on. That meant looking inside—finding what was holding him back. He'd been resistant too long, holding out to protect the others on Victor's will, but maybe there was no danger. Maybe Tarek could use this tidbit from his personal life for a boost in ratings.

He had to decide fast. If he was going to do this thing, it had to be soon.

5

The Baby Boutique was packed with women from the neighborhood. Most were married, but escaped the confinement of their home once a week to meet and talk about random subjects which usually revolved around recipes, gossip in the neighborhood, and their pets. As Maria stood within the circle of women, she wondered to herself how people could be entertained by the same generic conversations.

"In the 90s, I had a Bichon named Snowy," a woman named Janine said. "We loved her dearly but she had kidney problems and couldn't digest normal dog food, so we had to feed her chicken and rice. I was wondering if anyone else had issues with that."

Four women tried to talk at once, but only one rose above them. "I feed my kitty an all raw food diet. All raw meat and bones."

Maria wanted to escape. She didn't have a pet, she didn't have gossip, she simply didn't fit in.

"My mom has a dog who loved vegetables, which I thought was odd for dogs," Karen said. "One of them even eats pickles! But I've heard feeding dogs meat and rice is quiet healthy. I used to have a half spaniel half setter mix. That dog loved carrots! Carrots!" she exclaimed to the delight of the room, who laughed heartily. "Every time we peeled carrots, she got the peelings. We used to joke that she used it as a beauty treatment to keep her coat nice and red."

The woman continued chatting. Maria loved animals, but didn't understand the need to domesticate them and give them people names. Dogs shouldn't have names. Being given a name and led on a leash made them slaves to humans. She couldn't take any more of the conversation. With the whole room consumed in conversation, she took the opportunity to slide out of the circle. She didn't get far before Karen spotted her. "Do you have to go already Maria?"

Maria looked up, embarrassed. She still couldn't figure out if Karen was really too nice, or just used it as a cover for how mean she really was.

"I have some things to do at work."

"I thought you made your own hours."

"Yes, but I make appointments."

"We're only here for an hour at most," Karen said with a smile, blinking her eyes in a robotic way as if hoping she could hypnotize Maria.

"I don't have any pets," Maria blurted. "I don't really know much about this."

Karen's face suddenly twisted into a dramatically terrified look. "Oh no!" she said, horrified. "We've excluded you!"

"No," Maria said.

"We need to be more hospitable to new neighbors and find topics that everyone can talk about."

To Maria's surprise, every woman nodded in agreement. The room was silent, and Maria's discomfort only intensified. Leaving now was impossible and staying would be worse.

"Maybe you should read someone's palm dear," Dana said softly. She thought she was helping. She was making it worse.

"I can't."

"Sure you can. I saw you work and it was a lot of fun."

There it was again: the non-deliberate jab. As if Maria was running a circus and they were enjoying the rides.

"I usually do one on one. It's a more intimate setting."

"Nonsense. Our hand-prints don't change when we're alone. Show us what you do."

The women fell silent and looked to Maria for a demonstration. There was no way out. She stood for a long while, without a choice. She turned to Jacqueline, who gave her a look of disdain. It was that one woman that changed everything. Suddenly, inside she was angry. Not just that she was forced into this situation, but because now she was facing someone who wanted her to fail—who expected her to fail. Angry because she had a very real premonition and Toby and Richard barged into her place of employment and called her a fraud in the cruelest way possible. Not only was she angry, but she wanted the woman to get a dose of what Maria was going through. She nodded in her direction. "Okay. You...come up."

"Not me," Jacqueline said.

Maria stared at her sternly. "Yes, you."

The women prodded and provoked the situation until the Jacqueline and Maria met in the front of the room. Jacqueline laughed to herself, mocking how ridiculous the situation was, but Maria kept her focus.

"What do I do?" Jacqueline asked.

"Palmistry is more than looking at lines. The practice originated in the far east and most ancient communities were greatly interested in it. There are many techniques that can help with your psychology, holistic healing, and divination. I read the lines and the bumps in your hand to evaluate character and future life."

"What about the lifeline?" she asked with a snort.

"There is a lifeline. There's a line for fate, luck, sex, money...and it is not only lines, but skin texture, color, shape, flexibility of the hand..."

"Well, I don't need a history. Let's just do the lifeline."

Maria could have cold read Jacqueline easily and probably impressed everyone in the room, but she had forced Maria to take another approach. Her face turned serious and she stared at her opponent, concealing the darkness she felt. She smiled instead. "Your lifeline is the largest and simplest to read."

"Yes, it's the long one. Everyone knows that."

"It has nothing to do with length," Maria said, pleased to correct Jacqueline, who only let out a hmph in return.

Maria went on, squinting at her hand as if she was evaluating every valley. She suddenly frowned and looked up into the woman's eyes with fear.

Jacqueline saw the panic. "What is it?" she asked, her voice slightly shaky. She cleared her throat, so as not to let Maria know she was buying into it.

"One moment," Maria said, quieting her.

Jacqueline turned to the crowd and smiled nervously, rolling her eyes in another attempt to cover her real expression.

"Something's wrong," Maria said.

"Okay, that's enough of this. You can't tell how long my life will be by looking at my hand."

Maria stared at her with a blank expression as if she didn't know what to say. The woman's disgruntled look slowly transitioned into fear again.

"Is it saying she has little time left?" a woman from the crowd yelled.

"Her lifeline is barely visible," Maria said "It's not deep. As if she's sick."

The woman turned her palm upward and searched for her lifeline. "Which one is it?"

Maria pointed to a spot as the woman squinted at her hand, doing her best to decipher what she saw.

"I'm so sorry," Maria said, sympathetically.

"That's barely a line!" the woman said.

"That's why I'm worried."

As the women in the room reacted with concern, Maria realized she'd taken the game too far. She'd only meant to teach Jacqueline a lesson, to show her that the magic that she claimed foolish was the same magic that she was afraid of. But something had happened. Everyone in the room was scared—everyone but Maria. She could say she made a mistake, or downplay the importance of the lifeline, but what she really wanted to do was laugh in her face. She wanted Jacqueline to know that Maria's sinful ways could reach her—that even the most faithful could buy into it if they were in the limelight.

"Your lifeline is here," Maria said, pointing to a crevice in her palm, a nice long deep line that ran the length of her hand. The woman stared in horror as the room fell silent. No one knew what was happening. In that moment, she regretted not simply saying she'd made a mistake. She hoped her explanation would be good enough. "I saw your doubt and I wanted you to understand how powerful this is."

"You lied to me?" Jacqueline said, exasperated. All eyes in the room waited for an answer, but Maria found no words.

"Maria?" Karen said.

Maria turned to the crowd, apologetically.

"That was a mean-spirited thing to do," Dana said.

Maria slowly made her way to the door. She almost ran and didn't turn back, but she couldn't leave them there without something. "It's just...it's real. That's all. People think it's not real, but it's real."

As Maria reached the door, Dana said the most profound thing anyone had ever said to Maria—something that would sit with Maria for a long time after. "Just because you're unhappy, you don't have to spread your negativity on us..."

"...Make yourself at home," Maria said as a handsome man named Evan entered her apartment. She hugged him, but he barely returned it. It was the first time he'd seen her since she faked a suicide attempt for his attention.

"Don't go through any trouble. I'm leaving. I wanted to check in."

She stopped and looked deep into his eyes, moving close to him. "Stay," she said.

"I wanted to tell you not to call me, not to bother me. I'm back with Rosy."

"What did I do wrong?"

"Nothing. We're just not on the same wavelength."

"I can't go on without you."

"This again?" he asked, frustrated.

"I mean it."

"You're not my responsibility. If you do something stupid, you only have yourself to blame."

"I can't help it."

"Most people break up and it sucks, but they get over it. Ya know, when you called me that night, you only confirmed that I did the right thing. People that do what you do—that childish end of the world shit because you can't be alone—it really gets under my skin. You think because you're unhappy, the world has to stop. If you're hurt, you have to guilt me and make me feel responsible, like I'm going to blame myself if you die. It's pathetic. What if you actually died? Do you ever consider

that? You'd end your life to make someone feel bad? Do you know how low that is?"

"We can't just leave it like this. We need to talk."

"No. I have to go. I just wanted to see that you're alright and make sure you know I don't want to be bothered anymore."

"I'm not alright."

"Well then..." he said, with a dismissive wave. "You're on your own..."

...She held the phone, her mind wandering. She considered everything Toby told her, ready to call Richard if she could only make up her mind. After a long pause, she set the phone down and let out a breath, satisfied with her decision.

"Maria?" a voice said from the doorway.

She looked up, shocked to find the man from earlier that morning looking in with a smile on his face. Henry stepped inside in amazement. "Is this your place?" You cut hair here?" he asked with a knowing smirk.

"I lied about that. It's just..."

"No, I get it, but you should have told me. I love this stuff."

"Really?"

"Yeah, I took intuitive practitioner classes and studied the metaphysical for two years. I heard a place opened here and—well this is a huge coincidence. You know that?"

She nodded at her white knight, wide-eyed. "Do you want to sit? I won't charge you anything if you want to see what I do."

"Would love to, but I'd actually be interested in discussing this over lunch. I'd love to pick your brain. It's been awhile since I dabbled in this, but the topic fascinates me."

She stared at him, beaming.

Toby sat with William in a strip club, speaking over the music. "We're on a time-line now," he shouted.

"Why didn't you just sabotage the whole thing?" William asked.

I didn't have a choice. I'm laying low, working behind the scenes, but Libby's ambitious."

"How about we work on him then?"

"There's no way to work on Richard. Believe me. It's gotta be one of the supporters."

"Why not just convert them to our side?"

"Because Richard will find another way. He has to think he has it in the bag. He has to believe he's won. Then, we pull the rug out from under him last second."

"What about Wilcox?"

"He's my last resort."

"We need to focus on one of the others."

"Just stay with Brian."

"We don't have the time to..."

"It's you I'm waiting on, alright? You said you had guys. Fine. But you said it a week ago and the only introduction you've made is that piece of shit you brought in this morning who you've already said too much to. Now I'm stuck with him."

"You'll like my other guy. He just walked in," William said with a nod. He looked over Toby's shoulder and Toby followed his glance. From behind them stood Henry, sporting a satisfied look on his face. Henry approached the table and sat across from Toby, sizing him up.

"What is this shit and why is he smiling as if he thinks I'm impressed with him?" Toby asked.

"This is Henry," William said. "You converted Maria today. We can convert her back. Henry's already secured a date with her. Remember your theory on how to rid the world of the medium? Henry's the perfect guy to do it."

"You should have talked to me about this," Toby said, though he was pleased they'd already started. Henry was good looking, and carried himself in a way that didn't appear to be a problem. Henry was the ying to Sal's yang. He might even be a bigger asset than William.

"No problems then?" Toby asked.

"No," Henry said. "She's not bad looking. Guess the job comes with perks."

"Don't enjoy her too much."

"You won't need to babysit me," Henry said. "I get what you're doing and it's going to be cake..."

...Victor sat in his car outside the motel. He waited, his eyes carefully watching a room at the end of the building, his breathing carefully controlled. He sat conflicted, struggling with where he was and what was happening.

Two figures come his way, approached the car, and crouched into the light, Victor nodded to Stanley.

"He's not saying a word," Stanley said. "I don't think this guy will keep his mouth shut."

Victor took a deep breath and thought to himself, unable to decide on what to do. Despite what Maria had told him—giving him the okay—he was about to cross a line he hoped never to cross—a gray area.

"Tell us what you want us to do," Stan said.

Victor looked into Stanley's eyes, then behind him, where Brian Van Dyke stood nervously with a blank expression on his face. The color had drained from his face. "Don't let Brian be there. He's not ready."

"Not a problem. That a go?"

"Everything can't just come to an end because of this one guy."

"Say no more," Stanley said, as if pleased to have the go-ahead. Stan turned back where he came.

Victor rubbed his temples and took deep breaths. Movement two motel rooms to the left caught his attention. An old man stood in the light outside his room with a bundle of papers in his hand. He laid them neatly outside the door and looked out into the night, wiping his eyes. Victor leaned forward. The man was distraught. His mannerisms were weak. Inside the room, Victor thought he caught the sight of a rope hanging over a beam, a noose tied to the end.

Maria had given him permission to do a wrong, but only if he could make a right. In the very moment that Stanley was fixing a problem for him, a stranger was about to take his life. As dangerous as it was for Victor to make his presence known that night, he couldn't get Maria off his mind. If you take a life, you might as well breathe life into another. The world balances. All will be okay.

He exited his car and walked to the motel, looking down at the manifesto on the ground below. On the cover, the words "Goodbye Cruel World" were written. He picked up the pages, hesitated for a moment, and knocked on the door.

Chapter 11

1

"A celebrity is only known for being well known," Tony said backstage as they waited for the show to start. "People are enthralled by reflections of reality. Not reality. By the pretense of substance without the actual substance. Hollow facades illuminated by publicity. Anyone who's been to high school knows that being popular and being talented are two different things. There's a group of people who are entertaining the world with their personal lives and a group of people entertaining with talent. You have to figure out which one you really are."

"You don't think I have talent?"

"My point is that you do. You don't need to throw your personal shit out there for everyone to hear. What got you here? This isn't what got you into show business. When you started, you didn't care about the rules. Now you're so afraid of public opinion that you have to resort to this shit with Victor?"

The crowd applauded when the band began to play. Tarek hurriedly spoke, before his entrance. "I'm forced to fire three of our crew, ratings are dropping, jokes aren't hitting. We need to be saved. This is it. Short-lived drama that will get everyone excited, scared, and most importantly, tuned in. Believe me, because I was dead set against this before it was coming to an end, but I wouldn't be doing this if I didn't believe it was safe."

The master of ceremonies called his name. Tarek raised his eyebrows at Tony as a signal that all would be well. Then, he turned and ran onstage...

...Thunderous applause rewarded Tarek for a show well done. He took a bow from a stage where a large audience greeted him. Victor's hook-up had found Tarek the right agent—the kind of agent that sculpted his client into the perfect money-making product. All it took was the right clothes, hair-stylist, a voice coach, and a man whose soul job was to teach Tarek

how to walk and stand still onstage.

Levi Katz was the perfect agent, with a perfect agent's name. He even had the rapid talk. If Tarek let his mind wander for a second, he'd lose track of the whole conversation. Levi was especially fast-talking since Tarek was pulling in positive reviews and quickly making a name for himself on the comedy scene.

"They love you," he said, grabbing Tarek's shoulder as he entered his office. He was touchy-feely, but Tarek liked it. On another person, it might have been creepy, but this man was quickly paving the way for fame and if he wanted Tarek on his knees, he'd likely obey.

"I'm loving it!" Tarek said, falling into a seat and putting his feet up.

"And you're mixing it up more. You've got stage presence. You looked good tonight."

"I'm writing a ton of material these days. I can do something new every night if I wanted to."

"Don't do that."

"I know," Tarek said, obviously. There was a rule for comedians. Start with what works. End with what works. Experiment in the middle. Tarek relived the best moments of the night—the biggest laughs. Levi suddenly slapped his desk, snapping him out of it. "This is good. Real good. I've been holding onto something that I was unsure of before, but I'm gonna lay it on you."

Tarek leaned forward as Levi pulled a script from a stack and looked the cover over for a moment as if contemplating his next move. "Didn't think much of this when it first hit my mailbox. This is a pilot. And it was suggested with you as the lead..."

"Are you serious?" Tarek asked in disbelief. It was every comic's dream to have a sitcom, but this was all so fast. It didn't seem like so long ago that crowds were booing Tarek offstage and throwing ice cubes at him.

Levi nodded, his eyebrows raised. He allowed Tarek to bask in his success, but only for a moment. "Keep your pants on. There's no guarantee and the worst thing that can happen now is a sitcom that fails six episodes in. I had a good feeling when I read it though," Levi said.

"What's it about?"

"A failing actor who picks up a talk show to replace a host who walked out while it's on its last week on air. The show is failing and so is his career, so he sabotages it with careless antics and his own wacky crew. Anyway, in his attempt to make the show into a joke, the ratings jump and it becomes a hit. So it's this regular loser guy and his crew of misfits who are stuck with a Jerry-Springer-type talk show."

Tarek smiled to himself, envisioning the synopses at its best. He liked the concept, but most shows were so much more than concept. The writing, the actors, the crew, the marketing...All he had was an offer. It could fail, and if it did, it could be the end of his rise.

"Anyway, the pilot's good."

"So what do I do? Should I accept?"

"Slow down. Read it. Make sure you like it. Don't accept something because it's something. I want you to feel good about it. It will reflect in your work if you believe in it. Too many of these wide-eyed wannabes show up in town and take everything thrown at them—good career boost or not. Their careers go nowhere. In fact, what it does is give them the impression they're headed somewhere and they blow their wads on junk and wash out. Be smart. Use your intuition."

Tarek nodded quickly, letting everything Levi said register.

"This is different from stand-up," Levi said as he smashed a cigarette on a homemade ashtray at the corner of his desk. "You're answering to others. It's no longer a solo act. You're going to have to take your talents and learn to intermix. Some people aren't so good at sharing the spotlight. You'd be the star, but no star holds the show."

"I understand."

"Good. If it's right, you'll feel it." With that, he slid the script across his desk to Tarek, who handled it carefully as if it was breakable. "If you're the real deal—and I think you are—you'll be careful to always make the right move. Be passionate." It was the slowest Tarek had ever heard Levi speak when he said those two words, enunciating them for emphasis.

Be passionate...

...The crowd watched silently.

It was unusually packed with people who waited for what it was Tarek was going to say. People were so used to jokes—to a persona—that moments like these held value. Few moments in television came down to a man breaking character and addressing people as himself.

Tarek was on the verge. They basked in it. They cherished it. They hoped it would make television history so they could say "I was there."

He let the moment drag, allowing everyone to fully appreciate what he had to say. They knew of the will. They knew there were names. They wanted to know something personal. They wanted to know why everyone's favorite late night host's life was in danger. They wanted to know what he was a part of.

"Today," he started slowly. "Channel 6's Katy Malloy asked me if we'd have a show tonight." He turned to his side where Katy stood with her arms crossed, listening intently. "I'm proud to say that we've never missed a show for any reason. We never will."

The crowd applauded, but it was underwhelming. They didn't care if there was a show. They wanted something else.

"I'm sure everyone's familiar with Katy and her work. I've known Katy awhile and I've always had a theory that she once met a genie who granted her three wishes. She wished for fame, talent, and sex appeal..."

To the side, Katy smiled to herself. It sounded as if Tarek was sucking up, but she liked the shout-out regardless.

Tarek continued. "...But the genie was cunning and only gave her fame." The audience laughed as Katy turned red and stepped back to hide herself from view. Tarek turned to her, drawing attention, and smiled proudly. The audience laughed harder as they saw her reaction.

"The reason she approached me though is that lately I've been dodging a very important rumor in the air: the nature of my friendship with Victor Stone."

The applause fell silent. Katy stepped forward, the insult forgotten.

"Now, no matter what I say here tonight, unless I address this, I don't think anyone will hear anything else. And because our writers spend fifteen hours a day, every day, working on the show, I want to be sure they're heard. And because of that, I've decided to get this out of the way so we can go back to business."

Several crew members stared at their screens in disbelief. Most of the city shared the same reaction as they waited on pins and needles to know the names of those included in Victor's will. It could be a bluff, or another joke. No punch-line came. Instead, Tarek pulled a paper from his inner pocket and unfolded it.

"I was listed as a beneficiary on Victor's living will. The rumors are true. The last living among this list inherits everything."

What he was about to do was against everything he'd ever said. He wasn't dumb enough to believe that if he read the names, none of his deranged fans would try to impress him. Everything Tony said was true, and if he spoke another word, he'd be compromising the lives of thirteen innocent people.

Finally, he spoke. "Tomorrow night."

Tarek straightened his tie and stared at his reflection in the mirror. He ran his finger over his teeth as if to polish them momentarily and practiced a smile, satisfied with what he saw.

His assistant popped her head in. "Do you have time to see him now?"

"Yeah. Send him in."

She rushed out and a moment later, Anthony Freeman entered his office. Tarek stood and greeted him with a handshake. "Let's grab lunch," Tarek said. They ended up at a deli across from the studio, their plates piled high with roast beef sandwiches and chips

"I've been watching your show," Anthony said. "You've gone to great lengths in the past to avoid giving us away. Would you mind if I ask why you you've chosen to endanger us now?"

"Because by the time anyone gets anything in their head, we'll all be safe."

"I wouldn't be so sure this will end."

"We were all there," Tarek said. "All but a couple anyway."

"That doesn't mean we'll all be there in three weeks. You're doing what you're doing for ratings."

"You know," Tarek said, shaking his head and desperately trying to stand up for himself. "There have obviously been some incidents. The one guy's missing, the girl's dead, you had your thing, but I've sat back without a word. I mean, obviously we don't know who did what, but I've stayed out of it. I haven't been involved in the least, and I never will be. But this thing leaked somehow—again, not me that leaked it—and now people won't shut up about it, and they'll probably figure it all out anyway because if someone leaks what the will is, then someone will probably be leaking the dirty details too."

"Then allow them to do it, but don't hurry it along."

"Hurry what along? We're not going to die," Tarek said.

"How can you be sure?"

"Because I don't walk around assuming the worst will happen. I don't say 'I'm not going to drive today because I could be in an accident,' or 'I'm not going to live my life, because I'll put myself at risk'."

"This is…"

"Look Anthony, if you feel there is real danger out there, work on the guys with the guns and knives. I've constantly got cameras on me. I'm not going to stop doing what I do just because you're cynical."

Anthony dropped the subject, hurriedly ate his sandwich, and said a quick goodbye to Tarek. Before he walked out the door, he turned to Tarek again and asked him to please not spill the names. Tarek didn't respond.

From outside, a man watched them finish their lunch. He watched their mannerisms and knew the content of the conversation. He recognized both and though he knew Tarek was on Victor's will, he'd finally discovered a second name. Stanley Kline watched Anthony walk away with a knowing smile. He'd leaked the news of the will to the press. He'd threatened Tarek in written death threats. He'd put a lot of pressure on Tarek from afar and finally, Tarek was on the cusp of spilling the names. As a bonus, before he got the chance, he'd led Stan to another name from Victor's past. Stan hoped to be sitting in his living room with a notebook and pencil the next day while watching Tarek's show, but just in case

Tarek changed his mind, a new plan would develop. He'd followed Tarek for quite some time, but as his plan developed, so did his direction. While Tarek finished his chips, contemplating what he would say on tomorrow's show, Stan left in the same direction as Anthony.

2

Two beneficiaries weren't watching Tarek's show and had no idea the list was going to be revealed. Jason Stone and Todd Mason sat together at a restaurant on the coast, where pelicans passed their feet and picked at scraps that fell from the tables. A waiter dropped off a couple plates of food and the check.

"I'll take it," Todd volunteered, grabbing the check before Jason could get his hands on it. He thanked the waiter, who hurried off.

"I can give you some money," Jason said. It was a rarity to have someone else buy lunch.

"I did the inviting. I don't need you flashing your money around..."

"That's not what I'm doing," Jason said, defensively. He watched Todd fish through his wallet, thinking about the last few days—since he ran into Todd randomly. There had been suspicion, some accusations, some hostility, and finally, both accepted it was a coincidence and went their separate ways. Though they had no intention of getting together for lunch, something about his encounter with Todd made him stay. Then, Todd contacted him and told him he wanted to sit and chat. The talk had been civil, but Todd wouldn't let up on Jason about why they were in the same place, and how Todd was run out of town, and why Jason would allow his father proceed with the will. There was no reasoning with Todd, but Jason was drawn to him. Maybe it was because Todd was the ultimate victim of his father's wrath. Maybe he just needed a friend. Whatever it was, he was careful not to say too much. He let Todd dominate the conversation, hoping he could learn more about one of the strangest inclusion on his father's will.

"So what happens if all the rest of em show up in Maui?" Todd asked with a laugh.

"Then I'll admit there's a conspiracy."

Todd let out a laugh and Jason smiled. He'd broken through. "I'm harmless Todd. And if you want to walk the other direction when you see me, feel free. I've told you this before: I'm not my father. You got father issues?"

"My dad was a mechanic and a damn good one. Died young. Had a heart attack while he was working on a car."

"Well, Victor wasn't such a great dad. And I knew it from a very young age. That's what I was thrown into. I get it. You think I worked for him and lived with him and somehow that influenced me. I didn't agree with what he did. I was ashamed of it. It's part of why I'm here."

"Alright," Todd said, to let Jason know he got the point.

"You know, I didn't know if it was appropriate to tell you this," Jason started. He took a sip of water and contemplated the words. "Some of the others back home are trying to invalidate the will. Looks like they're going to do it too."

Todd frowned as he took Jason's words in. His curiosity was piqued. An end to the will meant an end to his problems.

Jason continued. "If they do, hell even if they don't, my opinion is that you go back."

"It's too late now," Todd said, but he wasn't sure.

"Too late to what?"

"Make things right with Cynthia."

"If you ran off to protect her, she'll get it."

"You don't know Cynthia," Todd said.

"Yeah, well I know you'd be happier knowing you died protecting your family than spending your life without them." Jason stood. He began to walk away.

"Hey..." Todd called out.

Jason turned.

"I know a place with live Jazz. You like Jazz?"

"Yeah," Jason said with a shrug.

"Wanna check it out?"

Todd watched with disappointment as a band blasted a country tune. At his side, Jason enjoyed the music. Both had drinks in hand.

"This was supposed to be Jazz," Todd said.

Jason turned a table tent, which displayed the locale's events. "Every other week."

"That's not what it said in the paper."

"This isn't so bad."

"Can't stand country."

"What is it about country that people either hate it, or can't get enough of it?" Jason asked.

"It's called the "anything but country phenomenon.""

"Oh yeah? It's got a name?" Jason asked, bemused.

"It caters to middle America. I find it particularly odd that so many people can find likable artists and bands in every other genre except country."

"There's two schools of country. The old school with lots of twang and rhinestone cowboy boots, and new contemporary that is identical to pop."

"I feel, and many of my friends agree with me, that 95% of country is formulaic carbon copy shit," Todd said. "And I have listened to a great deal of it, and I've heard what up and coming and independent country artists sound like, and the majority of those artists sound like the mainstream artists. In other words, shit."

"At least you don't feel too strongly about it."

"I'm just saying it's odd. That's all. Like the Wal-Mart phenomenon. Everyone complains about it, but everyone shops there."

Jason laughed. "Not the types of things I usually think about."

"This is all I ever did back home with my crew. Work with a bunch of guys all day long and all you get is sports, complaining about wives, and random bullshit. We spent a whole day talking about microwaving ice cream once. One of my buddies does it. Another doesn't. It damn near started a war."

"There's work like that here."

"I know. I just landed a job painting houses."

"Cab driver yesterday, painting houses today. What's the plan Mason?"

Todd shook his head. "Pass the time."

Jason sat quietly for a moment. "Todd...do yourself a favor and go back. You're lonely. You miss your wife and kids. You miss your job."

"I'm not going back until my name's no longer on the list."

"Have you even bothered to look yourself up? They called off the search after they drained the pier where they found your car. They think you're dead. They may have even declared it by now. You remember what Bell said? They need fourteen death certificates. Whether it's invalid or not, you'll be free to go home, assuming Bell doesn't pull the certificate when everyone realizes you're alive."

Todd only heard part of what Jason was saying. "They think I'm dead?"

"Yeah, and yours won't be the first death certificate."

"What do you mean?" Suddenly, Todd was genuinely concerned.

"Abby Palmer—the girl with the doctor—the newlywed; someone broke into her home in the middle of the night and shot her. The threat is real Todd, and they'd probably like your help, but whether you want to be there or not, you have no reason to be here. You're the only one who claims to have been chased off. Why you? Doesn't it kill you being here while everyone thinks you're dead? Doesn't it kill you knowing that someone beat you so easily?"

Todd's eyes narrowed. Jason was right.

3

When Tarek stepped into the street, he was bombarded with questions from the press. Among them was Katy, who stepped ahead of the line, ready to rip Tarek to shreds.

"I need to make this quick," Tarek said, beating her to the punch."

"Are you really going to release the names?" Katy asked.

"Yes, of course."

Katy waved her cameraman over as everyone else prepared for his statement. "Mr. Appleton, people are saying this is just a publicity stunt designed to boost ratings. Do you have a comment on that?"

"I believe that's true."

"You do?" she asked, surprised.

"Absolutely. Everything the press pushes is for ratings."

"I'm talking about your show."

"I've kept this a secret until you forced it out of me Katy. Question the source of the leak if you want motive."

"I received a telegram."

Tarek had no response. This was similar to the prostitute he had a fling with. Someone set out to sabotage Tarek from afar. He wondered who had to gain, and more importantly, was it just a ploy to get him to say the names? If so, should he really be doing this? He tried to track where it all led, but he couldn't find the advantage in anyone making the names public.

"I'll expect an apology for what you said about me," Katy said.

"I didn't say anything I don't believe to be true. My apology would be meaningless. You used a personal and delicate situation and turned it into entertainment. I realize that you get a bigger paycheck when you exploit the worst in life, but..."

"It's not entertainment," she said, cutting him off. "It's information."

"Where's our information on your life?"

"I'm sorry?" she asked.

"I want to know how many of you are cheating on your spouse, abusing your kids, or..."

"That's absurd," she said.

"I'm going on air tonight to read fourteen names and you will circle them like vultures."

"Well," Katy said with a smug smile. "That's why we prefer to be behind the camera."

"Maybe I won't say the names."

"Don't do it," she said, calling his bluff. "You've already promised you will. See how your fans react when you back out..."

...Tarek stood in the center of a line of actors. They took a curtain call and the crowd cheered as they raised their arms in the air. It was the first of what would hopefully be many curtain calls. At his side, his co-star stood holding his hand. Cindy McPherson was blond and beautiful and had the making of a star with her bright smile and twinkle in her eyes. On their side was the supporting cast, Margie Manhattan, Brandon Merce, and Deke Shepherd.

After the taping, they stayed on set where a photographer took pictures for TV Guide. It was a large step—the final straw that put them over the top. They were stars. The show was a hit. And in the middle of it all was Tarek...an overnight success.

The photo shoot was followed by the after-party. The cast meshed together well. They befriended, hung out, did lunches, trips to Vegas, and multiple crowd pleasing visits to shake hands and sign autographs. The chemistry, the rise to fame, the overwhelming sensation of realizing they'd struggled and come out famous instead of homeless—it was splendid.

Tarek and Cindy were the perfect stars. They were good-looking and had an on-screen chemistry that had the fans rooting for their relationship from the pilot. Because of this, they kept themselves at a distance off-screen, but still walked arm in arm and held a strong friendship for the fans.

The after-party was filled with guests—the execs, friends, family, cast and crew, but all eyes were on Tarek and Cindy. Deke was the comic relief of the show. Every line got a laugh, and there was no denying his talent. Like Tarek, he was a failed comedian turned actor and he'd found his niche. He found Tarek and Cindy in the crowd and approached with a look of awe. "This is insane."

"Isn't it great?" Tarek said.

"I mean, seriously insane. I actually have fans."

"This is how it is now."

"It will never get old."

"You say that now," Cindy said. She was a little more accustomed to this. She'd been on two failed sitcoms, and though they went nowhere, she'd already built a fan base who had tried to revive every failed project. She was used to having fans—just not a show that was a success.

Tarek spotted Victor Stone across the room mingling with one of his producers—likely one of his contacts that helped hook Tarek up with the sitcom. For the millionth time since his career took off, Tarek regretted the game he'd played in the beginning—using puppets to mock Victor and his associates. He'd made fun of a man who ultimately made his career, even if it was the same reason Victor helped him build his career. Still, the man was good, and Tarek saw that now. He owed him everything.

"I'll be back," Tarek said, walking away and moving through the crowd toward Victor. When he approached, Victor turned his attention to Tarek, smiled, and shook his hand as if Tarek had always been his buddy— never a pest who he had to buy with an agent.

"Very nice job tonight," Victor said.

"Thank you," Tarek said. "Without you, this wouldn't be possible."

"I saw potential. That's all," Victor said. Tarek wanted to be appreciative, but that was a lie. Victor wanted to shut Tarek up. He'd never believed Tarek would become this big.

"I hope I'm living up to your expectations."

"I admit, you surpassed them."

Finally, something honest.

"How's the cast treating you?" Victor asked.

"Great. After one week, we were best friends. Deke and I are like brothers."

"How about Cindy?"

"Same deal. She's probably the most talented person I've ever known."

"Introduce me to her."

Tarek frowned, confused. *Was Victor looking for a date? Tarek wasn't sure this was a conversation he wanted to be a part. of.* "She's like a sister to me," was all he managed to say.

"Introduce me," Victor said. It sounded like a demand, and Tarek wasn't so sure what the outcome of saying 'no' would be, but he couldn't help Victor pick Cindy up. The cast was tight and if Tarek were to be Victor's buddy, it could make him an outsider.

"I'll talk to her," Tarek said, numbly. Victor nodded his approval as Tarek turned and walked slowly through the crowd, back to the group who seemed to have their eyes on him and grew silent as if he'd been the topic of their discussion.

"Were you talking to Victor Stone?" Deke asked.

"Yeah," Tarek said.

"Why?" Deke asked, unable to contain the disgust in his voice.

"Why not? Do you know him?"

"I know of him. He's an asshole."

"Why do you say that?"

"It's true Tarek," Cindy said. *I had a friend he tried to get with and she wasn't interested, so he flashed his money around like he could have whatever he wanted just because he's wealthy.*

"Yeah," Deke cut in. "I know so many people who hate the guy because he pretty much buys and replaces people like they're nothing."

"I didn't know that," Tarek said. The situation was bad. He was in the middle of his friends and the man who made him, forced to choose and betray one half of the equation.

"How do you know him?" Deke asked.

"He knew my agent. Met him once when I did stand-up."

"Be careful," Deke said as if he knew something Tarek didn't. Cindy nodded her agreement. It didn't seem as if Tarek would be playing Cupid tonight. At some point in the night, Tarek would have to track Victor down and make up an excuse about how Cindy was seeing someone or focused on her career, but deep down, he suspected that wouldn't be good enough. All Victor told him to do—or commanded him to do—was introduce him. Whatever Cindy told Victor, he knew Victor would have a way around it. He'd used his money to try to win over Cindy's friend, just like he used his money to shut Tarek's act up.

Tarek watched Victor from a distance, the guilt eating at him. Surely, Victor would have to understand the need to blend into the group. He hoped Victor would forget, and as time passed, Tarek's hope to avoid Victor was increased.

It wasn't until Tarek stumbled drunkenly into the bathroom that he ran into Victor again. Victor entered shortly after him, and it seemed convenient—as if Victor had waited for a moment he'd be alone. Victor went to the sink and ran the water, cleaning himself up as Tarek stayed at the urinal, quietly going about his business in the hopes that Victor wouldn't say anything—and if he did—that it wouldn't be about Cindy.

"Have you gotten around to setting up an introduction?" Victor asked.

Tarek closed his eyes with frustration and zipped his fly. He turned to Victor with an assuring smile. "Yes, and sorry. It turns out she's taken."

"I never asked if she was taken. I asked to meet her."

Maybe it was harmless. Maybe he was just a fan who wanted to shake her hand. Something in the back of Tarek's head told him that guys like Victor always had one objective and that words like 'date' meant nothing. The word 'introduction' was the only word with meaning. It was a word that would always end in Victor's bed.

"Yeah, I mean, she's seeing someone."

Victor nodded and found Tarek's eyes. He saw through him, or so it seemed. Victor was smarter and more powerful. It seemed pointless to lie or play games, but he certainly couldn't play messenger between his new friends and the man who made him—especially when the two wouldn't mix.

"I can talk to her again if you'd like," Tarek said.

"That won't be necessary."

"Alright," Tarek said, standing awkwardly at the mirror. He didn't *know if he had permission to walk out then. The relationship felt unhealthy, as if owing Victor his career was exactly what Victor intended—that Victor could ask anything, anytime he wanted.*

After a few moments, without a word, Victor walked out, depraving Tarek any words of departure. Tarek looked at himself in the mirror. "You're an asshole," he said to himself...

...Tony stood watching the stage as Tarek walked back and forth. The audience laughed and applauded and from Tony's perspective, it all seemed wrong. Tarek was being rewarded for bad behavior.

There was scattered laughter, followed by silence.

"Aren't we all more odd than we are normal? Aren't so many of us one bad experience away from a mental health diagnosis that could limit us? I don't want to be followed around and judged any more than any of you would, but it's the price I pay for stepping on a stage." Tarek took a deep breath. "Victor Stone discovered me at an open mic. I owed him everything, and then my infamous interview with him on this show broke us apart. I disrespected a man who gave me this life. When he died, he did have a suggestive will, and I was listed among fourteen people who all profit by outliving the rest of us..."

Anthony sat in a bar, sipping a club soda. He watched the television, his body numb as each moment passed. On the television, Tarek promised the world he would give them a list of names. He considered what would happen afterward. He considered getting on a plane and...

"This is wild stuff," a voice said.

Anthony turned to his bar-mate, who hunched over the bar with his large frame. He looked like the kind of man who couldn't find comfort seated anywhere.

"What are you referring to?" Anthony asked.

"Appleton. This thing he's claiming with the guy with the will."

"Right," Anthony said. "I wasn't really paying attention."

Stan smiled to himself. Sure he was. At the next commercial, Stan took the opportunity to strike up a real conversation with Anthony, and half an hour later, the conversation flowed.

Anthony leaned in, listening intently as Stan spoke. "When I was six or seven, I spent most of a summer trying to replicate Batman's grappling hook. That was probably the first time I noticed in myself the obsessive compulsive 'I will solve this problem' gene, or whatever it is. My obsession with mechanics became acute. I sometimes consider the complex neuromuscular choreography involved in every single movement and I become overwhelmed."

Anthony chuckled. "I was the opposite. Analytical, yes, but never obsessive."

"You come across as rather intelligent," Stan said.

"I was, but never like I wanted to be. I think it was my senior year that I finished third in my class after long nights struggling to be on top. I was beaten by a couple guys who had a social life, which I was void of, so it cut that much deeper."

"For some people, it comes naturally."

"I didn't take it well. Sitting in the audience with five hundred other students, I had the unsettling awareness that I had already been consigned to a life of mediocrity by the very fact that I had not been the one chosen to stand on the podium. I had one shot to be at the top of that moment, and missed it. I will forever be indistinguishable from all others in the audience. I was just one of five hundred. One of five hundred million. I am the addressee."

"Look on the bright side," Stan said. "You could have been the dumbest."

"I always had a problem with second place. You know, when the Internet was still finding its footing, I happened across this fan site and found myself interacting with aspiring writers. Somehow, I got to talking to this young man who asked me to read some of his essays. So I did. He was intense. I read everything he sent, on the edge of my seat, and I wouldn't put it down until I was done. He was better than me. One day his computer must have broken because one of his friends sent me an email and asked me if he can send some more writing for his friend. So I responded and said something like: Make up an excuse. This kid keeps sending me his work and I can't stand reading it. Tell him my email changed."

"The kid whose writing you liked..." Stan said, trying to comprehend.

"I don't know why I did it at the time. I suppose it's harder to believe the people you're talking to on-line are real. I never heard from either of them again, which was worse than a simple email telling me to fuck myself. The worst thing was that he was good. Most likely he was eager for an opinion...to share his beautiful writing. And I suppose what it came down to was jealousy."

"Would you do it again today?"

"I've learned too much to make that mistake again. It's torture wondering what happens when you do that to someone and never see them again. After a while, I got to wondering if this kid stuck with it. I'd look up his name now and then. A few years back, when I hadn't even been searching for him, I come across a newspaper article about this kid. He put a noose around his neck and hung himself from a beam in his barn."

Stan nodded. "You believe you caused this..."

"There are usually numerous problems in any individual life, but there's a nagging chance that it was the incident with me...maybe it threw him off-course or made him believe he didn't have the talent he had. I never even met the kid. He struggled to succeed and ran across the man who took him down a peg. There's no logic to this course of events...only tragedy."

Anthony looked up at the TV as Tarek interviewed a guest. Stan followed his gaze.

"What do you think will happen if he reads the names?"

"I don't know," Anthony said, telling another lie. He believed he did know, but in the interest of downplaying the situation, he tried to seem uninterested.

Stan watched him closely, ready to celebrate when the list was finally revealed. And then, it wouldn't matter that he knew Tarek was a beneficiary, or more recently, Anthony. He'd have a buffet of beneficiaries to choose from. He offered to buy another beer. Anthony politely declined. They quietly watched the show from their bar-stools.

4

Todd had a storage locker and a gym membership under his name. In fact, he'd worked out at the same gym that Jason did, but never crossed paths. Todd worked out early in the morning. Afterward, he'd shower and shave, and head to the beach. He filled his day with odd jobs. At night, he slept on the pier. He could have rented an apartment, or bought a house, but he couldn't commit to Maui, and when he fell asleep at night under the moon, he'd never felt more comfortable—more at peace. If he couldn't be home with his wife and boys, this was the next best thing.

It was a routine he'd grown to depend on. He lived one day at a time, trying to distance himself from the world he came from. Every day was easier, until Jason came along. Jason didn't come across as such a bad guy. In another life, they might have been friends. After their time together, the first thing Todd did was seek out a Wi-Fi connection. He'd avoided news of his disappearance for too long, and he supposed he should have known what would happen eventually, but when Jason told him he was declared dead, his awareness was awakened. Someone ran him out of his home. Someone was sitting back with a satisfied smile, having gotten the best of him. Todd followed every command; he allowed himself to be beaten.

When he found his way to the Internet, his fingers froze over the keyboard, unable to type his own name. When he found out he was dead, then what? Instead of searching himself, he searched Cynthia Mason and quickly found multiple stories of his disappearance and presumed death. There had been a funeral, less than a week ago. His sons were listed. Friends and representatives from his time in the military talked about him. He was called a hero, which made him feel ashamed. They mourned his passing while he was living in paradise. They called him heroic, when he'd been a coward. Then, a thought came to him.

I can go back.

He didn't believe it when Jason said it, but now he understood. He was run out of town because his name was on a list. It would no longer be there, and even if the death certificate hadn't been submitted, he'd tell Bernard to do so anyway and take his life back.

He hurried back to the beach and to the storage facility where he kept his belongings. He almost went straight to the airport, but decided to tell Jason first. They met by the ocean, where Jason reluctantly shook his hand. It was right for Todd to go back, but bittersweet. For the first time since Jason arrived on the island, he'd found a reason to stay. It was a short-lived and mismatched friendship, but Jason liked it.

"If things don't go well for you there, if she doesn't forgive you, or if there's too much heat…"

"I won't be back," Todd said. "I already called Bell. He wasn't surprised I was alive at all and is willing to keep my death certificate in the files."

"Well…" Jason said, extending his hand, "nice meeting you under better conditions."

Todd shook before making his exit. As his flight took off, he shut his window, blocking the view. He closed his eyes and thought about Cynthia.

5

The final guest finished his interview, but no one listened. They waited. Tarek was aware of the electricity in the theater, the anticipation of what was to come. Katy was right: There was no backing out now, but when he did this, the wrong people would lose. He didn't know the beneficiaries well. They seemed nice enough.

He tried to remember what Abby Palmer and Todd Mason looked like, but their faces escaped him. He'd always believed himself to be the least corruptible of the bunch, but wondered if his actions could potentially bring about the deaths of others. He'd pleased the execs who congratulated him on his success, but what exactly had he done? He was a comedian who hosted a comedy show. Where exactly was the success in his real life drama?

They came back from the final break and the cameras started rolling.

Tarek paused for a long moment, and began slowly. "I can't say the names," he said. The crowd began ranting and raving and suddenly Katy Malloy took a step toward the stage, as if she would rush it. "I won't apologize because my apology would be meaningless," Tarek said. "Apologies play like vaudeville. The extravagant remorse of disgraced televangelists, the snarled 'I'm sorry' of celebrities who exude regret at being caught rather than being wrong, the artful admissions of politicians who want credit for their confessions without any actual cost. We've learned to peel them apart with tweezers, find the insincerity and self-interest. Apologies are drained from their healing powers. A stiff apology is a second insult, repentance offered in exchange for immunity from further prosecution. I'm not sorry, but you should be."

Tarek's eyes found Katy, whose mind worked a mile a minute. The press would be upset, and they'd declare an all-out war on Tarek. They'd find the names eventually and Tarek would lose and get nothing out of this. For once in his life, Tarek had to control the story.

He tried calming the crowd. He signaled the cameraman to keep filming. All this would be cut seconds before it aired. The executives would be angry. He'd have to fire three friends. The press would be out for blood. He'd have gotten millions of hopes up and tomorrow, they'd tune out.

Everybody could win. Everybody, except for Katy.

"Okay okay," Tarek said with a smile. "The people have spoken."

Tarek stood and circled his desk and walked to the edge of the podium. "You want the names?" he asked.

The crowd went wild.

After a minute, it faded into silence. He waited quietly, giving the cameras a signal: Keep going. This is happening.

"As we all know, fourteen other people are on this thing and in the end, there can be one. I've stalled enough, and I am sorry," Tarek said. Katy watched suspiciously. Tarek was up to something. His change of heart happened quickly and without conflict.

Tarek went on. "Besides myself, of course, the fourteen names of those I'm up against are...Gale Williams, Brent Jacobson, Chester Maclebee, Katy Malloy...

...My name's not in here at all," Tarek said to himself as he sat on the stage reading a script as crew members constructed the set. He panicked as page after page, his character was missing. When he finished, he ran straight to his agent and slammed it down on his desk.

"I'm not in it," he said.

Levi flipped the episode and began listing his theories without much thought. "They're probably shifting focus for an episode." Then, without pause, he rebutted himself. "No one explained this to you. That's concerning."

"Yeah."

"You're not in this at all. For some sitcoms, that's workable, but the show has one set and you can't do a show without the host. This makes no sense at all. Let me make a few calls and find out what's going on."

Later, Tarek paced back and forth on the set, forcing himself not to consider the possibility that he was being cut from the show. Finally, he pushed the thought aside and headed up the aisle toward the exit. Standing near the rear doors, Victor stood with his arms crossed. Tarek nodded and passed, but turned back.

"What are you doing here?" he asked. He froze, aware that all strange events are connected.

"How are things?" Victor asked.

Tarek stopped. "Well, I don't know. Good, I think. Just not sure the direction the show is taking."

"I see."

"I'm a little worried about the long range plans for my character. It's complicated." Though Tarek was testing Victor, he didn't seem to take the bait, or show any indication that he was behind the script changes. In fact, it was silly to think that Victor could pull those kinds of strings in the first place. He went on. "Stand-up was simpler. You control your world. Around here, one bad script and all the fans say you've jumped the shark. Before, I was on my own. It was easier."

"You used puppets," Victor said, as if to point out how obviously far Tarek had come.

"At least it was me."

"No, Tarek. It wasn't. You didn't have material of your own. You didn't tell jokes. You had an act, but it wasn't you. You were pulling strings. Now, you're a part of something. You need to learn to adapt to loss of control. When you learn to work with a team, I'm certain you'll succeed."

"My puppets didn't really have strings. You're thinking of marionettes."

"Nonetheless, it's not your world anymore."

Tarek understood the moral of the story. He had no control. Victor did. Victor asked Tarek to do something and when Tarek didn't do it, he lost.

They taped a week later. Tarek kept his mouth shut and so did everyone else, afraid to ask if Tarek was on his way out. At the cast party

Tarek sipped wine and sat silently as the remaining cast celebrated the show.

"Hellooo?" a voice said. He turned and found Cindy trying to get his attention. She laughed at his blank expression and took a step toward him. "Hello in there."

Tarek snapped out of his daze. "Walk with me. I want you to meet someone."

She followed him as he led her across the room, unable to look in her eyes as he concentrated on where he was headed. He focused on the mission at hand and let himself avoid the internal struggle he'd faced all night. It had to be like this.

"Slow down," Cindy said.

He slowed his pace. She caught up and walked at his side, smiling at others as they passed. Finally, Tarek zoned in on Victor and after a moment, they stood face to face. Victor smiled and waited for Tarek to initiate the conversation, which caused an awkward moment between the trio. Finally, Tarek spoke. "Cindy, I want you to meet Victor. This is the man who discovered me and is responsible for my success."

She reached forward and shook Victor's hand politely. "Nice to meet you." She covered whatever disgust she had for the man well. Tarek supposed it was part of being famous. Most fans were annoying, but you always smile and tell them you appreciate them. Victor took her hand and found her eyes, laying on the charm.

"You're an agent?" she asked.

"No," Tarek said, cutting in. "He's..."

"I knew some people," Victor said. "I met Tarek when he was a ventriloquist."

Cindy laughed. "No way you were a ventriloquist," she said, directing the conversation toward Tarek. She clearly wasn't into Victor, but there was plenty of chemistry between Cindy and Tarek.

"Yeah, I was."

"Not a good one," Victor said. "I told him to meet my friend and to stop with the puppets. Now, here we are."

"I can't believe you didn't tell me this."

"It's embarrassing," Tarek said. "It was a pretty horrifying act."

"Pulling strings wasn't his niche," Victor said.

Tarek corrected him, slightly irritated that Victor was trying to dominate the conversation and taking jabs at Tarek. "Puppets don't have strings."

"Nonetheless..."

"I'm going out for some air," Tarek said, unable to withhold his frustration any longer. "I'll catch up with you guys later." He walked *away, completely unaware that Cindy didn't want to be left alone with Victor. Before she could move, Victor was there, blockading her from following Tarek. She watched Tarek walk away, into the crowd, wounded...*

"...Unbelievable," Anthony said, his mouth wide open in shock.

"What happened?" Stan asked, trying to piece it together. Tarek read the names. Anthony wasn't one of them. The names were recognizable. Something went wrong.

"Those names," Anthony said, and caught himself before he could expose what he really knew. "They're all members of the press."

"So what?"

"Appleton is infamous for going after the press. They're not the real names. He's just getting them riled up."

"That will put the wrong lives at stake," Stan said, trying desperately to withhold his anger.

"It would seem that way, but I have a little inside information," Anthony said. "Won't matter soon anyway."

"Why not?" Stan asked. His mind was spinning. Too much was happening too fast and nothing was going as planned. Even the concept of teaming with Anthony seemed to be fading with every moment.

"The list of people allegedly challenged Stone's will. They have a date set to have it invalidated. Enough show up, and it's over.

A number of reactions passed through Stan's mind: Rage, panic, blind destruction...but then he started thinking.

All they had to do was show up. A group of people—all set on ending the will. Anthony would be one of them and would lead Stan directly to their nest of support. Not only would he expose the group. They'd all be in one place. "I have to go," Stan said. "Thanks for the company."

Anthony turned and shook his new friend's hand. He didn't pay attention to the newly eager man who exited the bar with a new plan in mind. Minutes later, Anthony finished his last club soda and walked to his car. As he pulled his keys from his pocket, Stan stepped out of the shadows behind him and stuck a needle in his neck. Anthony's eyes rolled back and he began to fall, but Stan easily pulled his body up and over his shoulder. He placed him in the back seat and drove away from the bar. He laughed to himself as he thought about Tarek opening hunting season on the press. He loved chaos. He loved destruction. Every mass killing, natural disaster, freak accident with dozens, hundreds, thousands of casualties, brought joy to his miserable life.

He brought Anthony to his workplace. The lights were out and the doors locked. He had his own key, his own garage, his own set of tools. He laid Anthony on a table and stuck another needle in him. He'd be knocked out awhile. Long enough for Stan to work. He grabbed a scalpel and began cutting.

Chapter 12

1

*While Helen waited for Todd Mason back home, he was halfway
across the world in a jungle. He never regretted leaving, nor did he love
where he ended up. He simply went with the flow, which had taken him
outside the action, in a clearing where he held a base, hoping they were
never called to action. For a while, he felt out of place. The men in his
squad were tougher and built for the army. Todd was smart enough to fit
in, but he was there for his own reasons and wondered if anyone else was
really as lost as him, or if they were born wearing camouflage and a desire
to shoot and follow orders.*

*Most of the men in his platoon had loved ones back home, who lived
the life of an army family, waiting to see their fathers in small increments
every few years. For Todd, it was different. He was here to prove
something, to Helen, to his family, to himself. He would come back and be
able to say he did something—fought for something; fought for something
he didn't understand, but stood in the trenches and got his hands dirty.
Only, Todd hadn't seen any danger and wasn't sure just how much of a
fighter he really was—or would be.*

*Every man had his own tale to tell. Some had seen a lot, been shot at,
sometimes shot. Bombs exploded, friends died, they'd taken lives.*

*Taipan Won had seen enough action to fill a dozen lifetimes, and loved
every minute of it. He was one of the hardest men in Todd's squad and
made up for his muscle in lack of brain cells. Since he was five, his parents
had considered the fact that their boy might actually be handicapped, but it
turned out he was just plain dumb and didn't care to be anything else. He
grew up on war movies, watching The Longest Day or A Bridge Too Far
hundreds of times in awe, while envisioning his time in war, running from
explosions and gunning down Nazis.*

*He was born for the army and easily made his way in, the perfect
soldier who would salute and follow orders faster than anyone else. He*

quickly earned respect among the others, who embraced him, giving loyalty to a man who would take a bullet for anyone. They'd only give him a hard time as he did stupid shit like try to give himself a tattoo. Some of the men silently snickered as they watched Taipan poke himself with a needle. Only their sergeant, a tough as nails fellow who went by Barnett, would make no secret of how dumb Taipan was.

"Taipan!" he shouted, hurrying over to a bench where Taipan sat in the sun. "What the fuck you think you're doing?"

"Inking myself," Taipan muttered.

"Go see the doc and have your blood tested for bacterial infection. Then have yourself tested for Hepatitis."

"I'm using Indian ink. It's not poisonous."

"Indians never made tattoo ink. Indian ink is toxic liquid that you're supposed to use on paper you dumb-ass," Barnett said as if he was talking to an idiot. "Go see the doc you fucking numb-nuts."

The others laughed as he followed the order. He knew he was dumb, but didn't understand how half of what he did warranted so much heat. He walked to a medical tent, which other than doctor Miles Cranton, the only soldier laying in a cot was Todd, who had a cold cloth over his forehead.

"What's wrong with Mason?" he asked the doc, though Todd was wide awake.

"Nothing. Stomach flu maybe."

Taipan gave Todd an unsure look. Todd was military, which made him a brother in Taipan's eyes, but he was clearly in the wrong place. He wasn't like Taipan—not a guy to get behind and trust with your life. Everyone else had a sense of duty, a sense of responsibility to the men around them. Todd was too inward to see where his loyalties lie. No one was sure of why he was really there, and when they asked, he'd give half answers.

"I thought only kids play hooky," Taipan said.

"I passed out. I've got heat-stroke."

"We're all under the same sun," Taipan said, making an obvious observation that the doc found to be quite profound.

Miles took a look at Taipan's arm and chuckled. "You do this to yourself?"

"Yeah, Indian ink."

"No such thing," Miles said as he grabbed supplies from a cabinet. "If you're trying to kill yourself, do it in battle."

"It's just ink doc."

Todd leaned in and took a look at Taipan's arm, where a crudely drawn skull was etched. "Not much of an artist," he observed.

"Fuck you. It's symbolic."

Todd followed the lines on his arm, unsurprised to find the only symbolism Taipan to be capable of to be something so morbid.

"You got one?" Taipan asked with genuine curiosity. Todd pulled up his shirt and exposed a black and white albatross. Taipan stared in awe.

"It's an albatross," Todd said.

"Why an albatross?"

Todd shifted in his seat and hopped from his gurney, taking a moment to let the dizziness pass. "I used to have reoccurring dreams. The dreams were always different, except there was always an albatross."

"You got a tattoo cause of a fucking dream?"

"I met a guy who did dream interpretation and he told me the albatross symbolizes a warning of difficult situations. Bad decisions and bad luck—just hanging over your head."

"You unlucky?

"Yeah."

"You're in the wrong place then. Unlucky over here is dead."

"I came here to change my luck."

"No, Mason. This place is gonna make it worse."

"Yeah, well if I die doing this, it will beat dying in a shitty dead end life."

"I'm gonna die here," Taipan said, matter of factually. Todd frowned at him and watched the man, his head in the clouds as he thought about his own demise. He seemed to get pleasure from the thought. "That's the plan, but you can bet your ass I'll kill me a few of them on the way to the dirt."

"You got a wife or family back home?" the doc asked, joining the conversation. Todd had wondered the same thing, but assumed Taipan was a loner.

"Nothing much worth a damn. I'm like Mason. Nothing there so I'm here."

"I'm not here to die," Todd said.

"No one drops themselves in the middle of this cause they wanna change their luck. That's stupid. You have a bird burned into your skin and you say you're unlucky, like you're proud of that and gotta show it off. You're here to die because if you don't die here, you'll put a gun in your mouth back home." Taipan thought nothing of the comment, but there had been a glimmer of truth in it, which sat with Todd. He watched as Miles stuck a needle in Taipan's arm, who closed his eyes, seemingly enjoying the pain.

Todd had been down on his luck for a long time. He wasn't sure he knew how to be anything else anymore. He never intended on putting a gun in his mouth, but he hadn't fully observed what it was he really wanted in the military. He didn't want to die and he didn't want to kill. He wanted to *get away and prove something, but he never knew what. Helen had told him she wanted a fighter, but dropping into the middle of a war didn't make him a fighter. It just meant he was there, hoping she knew it and waiting for him to return. And when he did return and she told him she was proud of what he did, he didn't know what he'd say. He sat on a post, waiting for the day the war was over. If he saw battle, he'd either die, or quite possibly, if he knew himself well enough, run.*

Taipan loved the pain. Todd only wanted to...

...sit comfortably in Bernard Bell's office, waiting and watching out the window. Bernard entered, sizing him up with a look of disbelief. "Back from the dead," he said, shaking his hand. It seemed this meeting would be much friendlier than the last. Bernard already was given the details of Todd's return. He was told where he had been and that he wanted to come back. He knew about Abby's death and Anthony's attack. He was tired of hiding. He wanted to see Cynthia. He wanted to know his official death had removed him from Victor's will.

"If there's a death certificate and it's been submitted. I need to know if my return undoes that," Todd said.

"I don't know if I'm the guy you need to talk to."

"You're the executor. You're exactly the guy. I need to know if I've been removed and what happens now."

"That was your plan? To die, be removed, and return?"

"It was a perk. None of this was ever my plan," Todd said.

"Well, Mr. Mason, you've picked a fabulous time to resurface. I haven't submitted your death certificate yet, but only because I haven't gotten around to it. I assumed I had the time, but you've left me with a predicament."

"There's no predicament. Submit so I can return."

"So you can return to what? You've already run from your family. There's no job waiting for you here."

"I don't see how this is your concern."

"It is because if you decide to stay, you're alive. Victor's terms were specific. Now, I have no problem submitting the thing, but who's to say you don't change your mind one day, or suddenly everyone's dead and you come back to prove you're alive and deserve the money? This isn't only up to me."

"What do you do if I go back? I'm officially dead."

"I'm honoring my client's final wishes. Believe it or not, despite the content of Mr. Stone's final will, I'm doing the ethical thing."

"Your client was an asshole and his final wishes were shit."

"Look in the mirror Mason. Consider the pain you've caused. How exactly will you explain this to Cynthia?"

"The truth. Someone ran me away."

"The truth doesn't play out in your favor."

"Tell me what you think my options are."

"Stay and you're in the running. Go back and you're dead and I submit and never tell a soul. Those are your options and they're non-negotiable."

Todd clenched his fists, ready to leap across Bernard's desk and strangle him with his tie. The man was getting off on their pain, honoring a crazy man who was set on breaking up families and letting people kill each other.

"The playing field shifted when Mrs. Palmer passed away. You were right all along to be paranoid. You're dealing with a serious problem and staying won't fix it, but anyone can disappear and be dead. It doesn't seem like a way out to me. It seems like a tactic. And Victor said it would be you who pulled this kind of stunt."

Todd took a step forward, coming face to face with Bernard. "That's bullshit. He didn't know me."

"We've already had this conversation and I won't have it again."

"What do you get out of this?" Todd asked, a dangerous edge in his voice.

"Hey, I'm not the only one overseeing this. I couldn't help you if I wanted to. Faking your death and coming back doesn't mean you get to still be dead. What you did was illegal. If you're smart, you'll go back."

"Then what?"

"Never come back. Let your family get over the misery you've caused. Or you can stay, beg for forgiveness, and put their lives back in danger while you go to prison. Nothing changed since the last time you were here. The only thing that's changed was someone broke into the Palmer home and killed the wife. Coming back solves nothing for you." Bernard leaned forward, taking a long serious look at Todd. "No matter what you do, let me be clear: I will not help you find a way out of something that everyone else has to confront."

2

Malcolm Wallflower detected enough action on Adlar Wilcox to justify meeting his client with new information. For Royce Morrow, he'd decreased the time spent on other assignments and went all-out trying to track Wilcox. Royce paid him well, but for a stupid kid, Adlar was unusually hard to track. In fact, he hadn't found his exact location. He'd only been able to prove Adlar was alive and in the city. It was better than nothing.

Royce realized the extent of his mistake when his old friends from the street visited him to inform him that the man who offered to fix his problem wanted two hundred thousand dollars. Royce paid the fee and then realized he'd made a mistake. He'd assumed for a long time that he lived in a world where 'taking care of someone' meant sending them far away or threatening them. After the money exited his bank account, he realized what it really meant.

He'd been naive, but when all was said and done, Royce knew he set something in motion that he didn't really want. He tried to ignore it. He tried forcing optimism: *Adlar will be sent to a farm up north.*

Two hundred thousand dollars isn't the kind of money you pay for a threatening conversation.

Royce hired Malcolm to track Adlar down. Malcolm came to his home dressed in jeans and a t-shirt, hiding his face with a ball-cap and glasses. There was little small-talk before Malcolm fished a notebook from his inner pocket and flipped through some pages.

"Parents haven't see him," Malcolm said.

"Has he been reported missing?"

"No, because they know he's fine."

"How?"

"Internet activity."

"Is he in contact with them?"

"His dad tracks him on an interactive. His father plays, but only to observe that his son is playing. I suppose the idea is that as long as Wilcox is playing video games, he's somewhere safe."

"That shouldn't be hard to trace, right?" Royce asked.

"Maybe. Don't know yet. Ordinarily, yeah. He's gifted with computers. He's using firewalls to keep me out."

"Then you can't trace it?"

"Not the easy way, no. But that's just my guy and he's not as good as Wilcox. I'm working on bringing in a more computer savvy guy to see if we can't pinpoint his location."

"No credit cards?"

"No paper trail at all. I'd say he's made himself another identification or he's had help. His name's definitely off the grid. If he's still hacking, he's stealing on-line information and using it to support himself, but nothing in large numbers. Whatever the case, he's taken measures not to be found."

Royce nodded, thoughtfully. He wondered if this was for the best. He could pay Malcolm now and let him walk away. Adlar was scared, hiding, and that made him non-threatening. If his P.I. couldn't find him, no one could. There was no reason to move forward—unless Adlar got tired of hiding. If and when that day came, he'd have nowhere to go. He could come back to the world of the living, more dangerous than when he left it.

Malcolm read Royce's thoughts. He wanted to keep going with his investigation. Royce was an easy payday. "He's young. When it ends up being a runaway, they eventually return home. Without a steady stream of income, he won't hide forever."

"That's it?"

"Sorry there's nothing more. I should have called. I didn't mean to waste your time."

"It's not a waste of time," Royce said. "I'd like to find him."

"Not to pry, but is he a friend? Relative?"

"You already know the answer to that."

Malcolm nodded. Royce knew his job was to know everything about his assignment, and he'd surely looked into the connection between Adlar and Royce and found nothing. It was genuine curiosity. None of his business—just a man wanting to know just what it was he was tracking.

"I apologize for asking. It seems to me he's hiding. Maybe someone wants to hurt him."

Royce didn't respond. He stared forward, listlessly.

Malcolm studied him for a long moment. "Anyway, he's been under a rock a few weeks, but when he comes out, I'll make sure you're the first to know."

The moment Malcolm left, Royce got in his car and drove down University in search of Judd and the gang. They'd moved locations, which sent Royce into a panic. What if he never saw them again? He couldn't let go of that time in his life, even if his friends didn't want anything to do with him anymore.

And what if he could never pass the message back to their contact? What if, down the road, whoever this guy was, was able to track Adlar down and...

As he pulled his car through his gated driveway and came to a stop, short of his mansion, he saw a man sitting on his front steps. He looked harmless, but unfamiliar. Royce tried to be cooperative and let the professionals do what they did, but coming to his home was unacceptable. He wanted to give the man a piece of his mind, but if he was the man he was paying to take care of Adlar, this was his chance to hit the brakes on the whole thing.

The man was scrawny with pale skin and a wiry frame. There wasn't a pound of fat on him. The man was so average that Royce questioned what role he could possibly have in their affairs.

"Royce Morrow?" the man asked, casually.

"How did you get in here?" Royce asked.

"I'm with Manny. I do the leg-work. You can call me Bedbug."

"Who is Manny?"

"Your guys visited him with a request. I was under the impression you were funding it."

"Those guys and I are old friends. We all have the same problem, but they jumped the gun in how to handle it."

"The money came from you," Bedbug said.

"Is there a problem?"

"A couple. One is we can't find Wilcox. The other is you. You hired a private investigator to find him too."

Royce was taken aback. He didn't think hiring someone would upset anyone, but it was apparently an issue. What frightened him was just how close of tabs they must have been keeping on him. "I did."

"Why?"

"Because he's missing."

"That's our problem. Not yours."

"You mentioned you couldn't find him..."

"Which you've just learned. Why you trying to find him? You having second thoughts?"

"Of course I am. I didn't even know what I was funding."

"If you don't want this done, you talk to us."

"And just like that, it's over?"

"Of course not. It would cost you, but you don't have to go through with it if you cancel the contract."

"Why would it cost to cancel it?"

"We maintain a schedule. You put strain on that."

"How much?"

"That you'll have to talk to Manny about."

"I see."

"I'm thinking your mind's not made up though. Otherwise, you would have come to us by now."

"I didn't know where to find you."

"Believe me, we know the stress people go through making these decisions. Before you decide to do anything, talk to Manny. Like I said: we have a schedule. If we'd found Wilcox, he'd already be dead, so keep us in the loop. Whatever this kid took from you, whatever damage he's done, we can take care of it. If you're worried about your safety, don't be. We cover our tracks. Never had a problem."

Royce nodded. "How do I set up a meeting with Manny?"

"He's got the day off, so he'll be home."

"What's his other job?" Royce asked, curiously.

"We don't give you those kinds of details for obvious reasons. You wanna go see him now? I'll take you." Bedbug led the way to his car and

Royce reluctantly followed.

"Should we be seen together?"

Bedbug laughed.

"What's funny?"

"Like I said: our tracks are covered."

3

It could have been yesterday that Todd last sat in his car, taking a last look at the home he and Cynthia had bought together weeks before they were married. He'd last stared at his own front door over two months ago, but being back felt right—it felt as if he hadn't even been to Maui—like it was all a dream. He kept the engine running, contemplating his next move. There was no way to just knock on the door and pretend nothing happened. There was no explanation in the world that would make her happy. She'd cry, scream at him, hit him, or—God forbid—have a rebound.

And as the thought crossed his mind, a car pulled into the driveway—a car Todd had never seen before, and a man he'd never seen exited with a bag of groceries. The man knocked on the door. Moments later, the door opened.

Todd only caught a glimpse of his wife as she invited the man in…

…He tried to catch his breath as he and Taipan moved through the marsh which blanketed the jungle. The heat beat down on their faces and their clothes were drenched in sweat. It didn't seem to faze Taipan, who recited a string of dirty jokes without shame. Everyone laughed. Taipan was animated when he spoke, the curses rolling off his tongue as if was part of a vocabulary he'd had since he was born. Finally, after some silence, he changed the subject. "Mason tell you he has a little birdy tat?"

"Yeah," Todd said. "I have a little birdy tat. Right next to my unicorn."

"He has a little Nancy-boy tat. Don't let sarcasm make you forget that."

"It's an albatross."

"A Nancy albatross."

"Yup," Todd agreed again. Taipan was trying to be a bully. The only way to shut him up was to carelessly agree.

"You got a boyfriend back home Mason?"

Some of the others laughed quietly, unsure where it was headed. Guys in every unit had a way of ribbing each other that came across as semi-serious. Every so often, it was.

"Your sister," Todd shot back.

"You're not her type. She don't like Nancys. You married?"

"Nope."

"Engaged? Fuck buddy?"

"I left a girl for this."

"Sure it wasn't the other way around?"

"Little of both."

"Why"

"Believe it or not, politics. She's with an activist. Some hippy who writes for a small-town paper and calls himself a political activist."

"What the fuck is that? A man who shits on us?"

"Something like that. She liked his cause though."

"His cause is shit."

"This isn't much better."

"What you talking about?"

"Twelve of us out here to do what? Recover a vehicle? Every day, we go out and do things that are worthy of his stupid cartoons. That's the worst thing. They talk about how we're here doing nothing, and we fight them, but what have we done?"

"We follow orders dummy."

"Yeah, well our orders are just orders. They don't mean much to us. We die doing this and we don't even have the courtesy of knowing why."

"You think anyone wants to be here? This is what you sign up for. You don't question shit. If you wanna sign up and question shit, go work the drive through at Fat Burger. That's small-time mindless shit. We're the real deal over here. Life changing shit. Not like your activist who thinks he's making a difference."

"Maybe none of us make a difference no matter what we do."

"Maybe. Maybe not. What did you think? You'd go home a hero? Make your little girly all wet for you and kick the activist out? Jesus Mason. I just figured out why you're here. You're a dumb asshole."

"You're far off."

"Nah, I think I'm close. I dated this tramp a couple years ago. Mostly just fucking. Then, before my tour, she tells me she has six kids and another bun in the oven. Suddenly, I get to be a dad because number seven is mine, and I have to be dad to all of em. Probably six different dads. Probably don't know who each one is."

"The new one yours for sure?"

"Who knows? Probably. Couldn't care less."

"When we're done, you going back to her?"

"Fuck no. World's already got too many people and she's popping out kids once a year? It's a vagina. Not a clown car. Stop making babies. All women wanna do is have babies. More babies. They just love em to death."

Todd began to laugh, but was interrupted by gunfire.

Everyone reacted quickly, grabbing their weapons and ducking to the ground. As they searched through the scopes of their guns, the uselessness of the situation revealed itself. They were completely ambushed from every side. As the soldiers held their ground and fought back, Todd up and ran. Not far from where they stood was a thicket of trees. They were outnumbered, and there was no point in sticking around for the inevitable outcome. He sprinted for the trees. A few others followed his lead. He never saw them, but heard their footsteps behind. And then there were no longer footsteps—just thuds as their bodies hit the ground, picked off one by one.

And then, sharp pain as a bullet ripped into his thigh. He fell to the ground and closed his eyes, waiting for the moment he'd be finished.

Instead, he was pulled to his feet. He opened his eyes, afraid of who would be there. It was Taipan, acting as his legs. In moments, they broke through the line of trees and into the thicket. As Taipan helped him move away from the enemy, Todd caught a glimpse of where they came from. Bodies were strewn in the spot he'd been standing—moments before...

...Irving Cameron lived at the end of a dusty road in the middle of nowhere. From his patio, all there was to be seen was the occasional car passing. He knew the mailman and a waitress at a breakfast nook nearby. His family and friends were forgotten long ago, and he was okay with that. When a car he didn't recognize turned into his driveway, he squinted his eyes in the sun trying to catch a glimpse of the driver. It was likely just someone asking for directions. He watched the car approach slowly, kicking up dust from its tires. Irving's deep wrinkles and sun-blotched skin twitched in the sun as he waited.

Instead, a ghost of the past stepped out—a ghost he'd hoped to never see again. Todd stood in the sun, staring at Irving, trying to find the proper greeting.

"Christ almighty," Irving said.

"Irving Cameron," Todd said, managing a smile.

"Thought you were dead Mason."

"Not dead. Just gone."

"Helen know?" Irving asked, stuffing a wad of tobacco in his mouth and pushing it around with his tongue.

"I'm not with Helen. Married another girl. How about you?"

"What do you want?" Irving asked, suddenly tired of small-talk.

"I wanted to talk about the days following our return."

"Days after we returned? What you need to know about that?"

"Our condition."

"You were a goddamn nut is what you were. Didn't know your head from your ass. I figured I'd mess you up real good for what you did, but you were already so far gone. Figured karma caught up with you."

"Look Irv, there's a guy. I got on his bad side and I don't know why. Maybe I blanked some things out."

"Ah," Irv said, pleased to hear of Todd's misfortune.

"If I was a liability, or a problem for anyone, it had to be in that time."

"You think I know shit about what happened to you? I had my own shit to deal with. So goddamn happy to hear things worked out for you Mason, but some of us are still dealing with the fallout."

"I know," Todd said. He was desperate for answers and Irving was the only one who was there who knew the trauma they went through. "Someone wants me dead. That's why I got out of here but now I'm back."

"You wanna come back from the dead?" Irving laughed out loud to no one at all.

"I do."

"To the wife? The baby?"

"Two boys."

"Two boys," Irving repeated.

"I need to know if you remember those days—if you remember how I would have known Victor Stone."

"The entrepreneur?" Irving asked.

"Yeah, the Stone Enterprises guy. He's dead, but before he died, he sent people to kill me."

"I haven't got the slightest damn clue."

"I need to know if I did anything to..."

"Last I knew of you those days, you talked it through and moved on. You were one of the lucky ones. You left us behind in the war and you got good and fixed up and left those of us remaining behind to battle our demons. Now, you show up at my doorstep years later—uninvited—and you're asking me to help fix your problems so you can resurface? You don't resurface."

"I have to."

"You left two boys behind and faked your death?"

"To protect them."

"To protect yourself Mason!" Irving shouted unexpectedly. "Just like in the jungle. You know I'm the only one left? The head doctor worked you over and the rest of those guys—they all wound up in jail or took their own lives. They couldn't deal with it. But don't matter how many times I bring them up, is it? You don't want to remember what happened..."

Todd swallowed hard. He'd expected a dose of what Irving was saying, but Irving wanted to bring back every last memory. Maybe that's what Todd needed—to remember again.

"You found yourself a cozy job and a family. Ran away from that shit too. I say they're better off. You're a coward. You were a coward then. You did it to protect you, cause you sure as hell didn't do it for your family, or for Danson, or Duffy, or Thomson. Maybe Stone wants you dead because you left one of his buddies to die!"

"I get it!" Todd screamed. He walked in a small circle, putting his hand to his forehead before falling to his ass and resting. Irving watched him for a moment, curiously. It seemed Todd hadn't forgotten. He only wanted to.

"I'm just saying: what makes you think you have the right to come back?"

Todd shook his head, unable to find the answer.

4

Manny sat across from Royce on a dainty couch. Manny was six foot, in his early 40s, but with a head filled with gray hair, which he combed back. He had a full beard and dark splotches around his tobacco stained teeth. They waited for Manny to speak. Finally, he did. "I'm not happy the two of you met."

"He came to me," Royce said. "I've been trying to get in touch with you and haven't been able."

"We wouldn't have kept tabs on you, but it seems you asked us to do something that wasn't as easy as we figured it'd be. People leave trails, unless they're trained to disappear. I've looked at his profile. He's smart, but doesn't have the intelligence for that. Is it possible Wilcox is dead?"

"Supposedly not. He plays a game and his avatar is still active."

"You should have come to us. Not some P.I. You're drawing attention to yourself. Adlar turns up dead and your name comes up."

"I wanted to talk to you about that," Royce said.

"Bedbug already told me."

Royce turned to Bedbug, who offered an insincere apology.

"I'm not sure this is something I can go through with," Royce said.

"You don't have to do anything, so I don't see the problem, but make up your mind fast."

"It's easier if I just forget it."

"It's costlier too," Manny said.

"I'm prepared for that," Royce said.

"Mr. Morrow, you've made every rookie mistake in the book. Three times in our career, we've turned the target on the client. You know why?"

Royce shook his head.

"Interference. We handle our jobs. Bedbug's nickname, well you can guess where that came from."

"If you're upset, I understand."

"Not upset. Not at all. What I'm trying to say is that we do our jobs nicely because we are able to divert attention. I expected you to sit back and wait, and I meant it. Because what will happen is we'll find Adlar and we'll take care of him and no one will ever ask you a question about it. But you start asking questions, coming to us, tracking him down, and you've exposed yourself. You understand?"

Royce nodded.

"Those three times it went sour, it's because attention was turned on us, because people have second thoughts. So I'm telling you right now that I'll give you two days to decide whether or not you want this to happen. But that's it."

"Thank you," Royce said with relief.

"If you do, you drop your investigator and shut your mouth for the rest of your life. Because if you interfere, and something goes south, that's your problem. If you don't, pay us for the inconvenience, go on your way, and we forget any of this ever happened. But rest assured, when your decision is made, it's made, and there's no backing out."

"I understand."

They shook hands.

"I appreciate you coming here and composing yourself in a respectful manner," Manny said. "Bedbug will take you home."

Moments later, Royce sat uncomfortably in the passenger seat while Bedbug whistled along with the radio. He suddenly turned it down and turned to Royce. "What you thinking?"

"I'm thinking I'll put this behind me and pretend it never happened."

Bedbug shook his head, disappointed to hear this.

"Seems like it's beneficial to everyone if we let it end here."

"I don't want to know what Mr. Wilcox did, so don't tell me, but I will say this: You may think a weight has been lifted, but you came to us for a reason. You just may sleep better at night knowing he's not out there."

"Do you mind if I ask questions about your methods?" Royce asked.

"Would knowing my methods make a difference?"

"Maybe. I don't see any reason he should have to suffer. This isn't like that. It's not revenge. He's simply a liability."

"You know why they call me Bedbug?"

Royce shook his head.

"I'm there. You can't see me, but I'm there. I'm quiet. I'm the fatal equivalent of dying in your sleep."

"And if someone asked you to do the opposite?"

"I'd decline. There's no investigation if there's no crime. I carry a gun for protection, but I never use it. If I start shooting everything up, people look for trails. And I'm smart, but there's plenty of smart people in the FBI. I'm not looking for a battle of wits if the repercussions mean prison. I live a nice lifestyle doing what I do and I get away with it because I'm cautious."

"That's refreshing," Royce said. He meant it.

"You won't know he's dead. Forget about him. Forget about us. Someday you'll look him up out of curiosity and find out he slipped and fell or choked on a peanut or some dumb thing. The funeral was nice. He'll always be remembered. Da da da da."

"You want me to go through with it?"

"I don't form opinions."

"Do you prefer your clients to say yes or no?"

Bedbug laughed at the question before giving it serious thought. "Yeah, I dunno. Most of the time, the victim is a piece of trash anyway. Am I proud of what I do? I don't celebrate bring my daughter to work day, but yeah, there's something thrilling about the impact of the job. Sometimes it's good and sometimes not so much. But one thing it comes with is impact. You don't get that sitting in a cubicle your whole life. You might push a lot of buttons on your keyboard, but add up the events in your life and you've either greatly changed the world or you've just been along for the ride."

5

Bernard hurried to his car, briefcase in hand. He fished through his pocket for a wad of cash he'd use as blackjack money. Bernard was feeling lucky, until he came upon Todd waiting outside his car. "Tomorrow Mason. I've got things to do."

"I won't be here tomorrow."

"Back to Hawaii?" he asked, a pleased smile on his face.

"Yeah."

"Good for you," Bernard said, giving Todd's shoulder a squeeze as if to say "atta boy".

"Don't submit my death certificate. If you do, I'll return."

Bernard suddenly stopped, the bounce in his step turned into a slow stride. "Then what the hell's the point in all this?"

"There's no way for me to come back and make things right. I'm dead to them. They'll live their lives thinking that. They'll die thinking that. It's not right."

"I'm not telling people you're alive."

"You don't have to. I already sent letters to all local news outlets and friends in the area."

"I don't understand."

"What's to understand?"

"You have an out Mason. Last time I saw you, that's all you wanted."

"I lost everything for Victor's last wishes. If I can't have my life, I won't submit to whoever did this. Someone wants my name off the will, to disappear forever. I'm not going to make it easy. They chased me out of town. That's all they're getting."

"Then you want the money?"

"Absolutely not," Todd said. "But whoever does will still have to deal with me someday. If you submit my death certificate, I'll make sure everyone knows I'm alive and you'll be legally responsible for overseeing his will is honored the way he wanted."

Bernard took a deep breath and rubbed his temples. "If they know you're alive, they know you abandoned them."

"I'm taking care of that..."

...He was still alive.

But moving.

or...

Being carried.

Then he remembered where he was and what happened. At some point, he'd blacked out—some point after Taipan hauled him over his shoulder and ran into the thicket. He had no idea how long he'd been carried, but Taipan was tired and the sky was darkening. Being set on the ground was what had awakened Todd. If they were taking a breather, Taipan must have decided he'd put distance between himself and the enemy.

Taipan said nothing when he noticed Todd awaken. Instead, he shifted Todd to his side and started working on his wound.

"What..?" Todd asked as he gritted his mouth in pain at Taipan's touch.

"I gotta take the shell out of your leg."

Todd tried not to make noise as Taipan stuck a knife in the wound and fished around. Todd managed to keep his grunts at a sufficient level, but he squirmed on the ground, making it nearly impossible for Taipan to do his job without hacking Todd's leg to oblivion.

When it was over, they rested against a tree. Todd caught his breath for what seemed like hours. "I thought I was dead," he said, trying to sound grateful.

"Not sure we're not."

"How far are we from camp?"

"Farther than before. They're between us and camp and they know we're here. The way I see it, we gotta make a wide circle around them and we got no idea what's out there."

Todd let Taipan take the lead, but he wanted desperately for him to come up with a more optimistic plan. *"What do we do?"* he asked, making it known he'd submit to whatever Taipan had planned.

"We keep moving so we stay ahead."

As the bullet was extracted from his leg, Todd closed his eyes and clenched his jaw, trying not to scream out in pain. Finally, Taipan held a bullet in front of his face with a smile. *"We survive, you impress your girl back home. You took a bullet. You're not gonna be such a Nancy after all."*

"I don't want her," Todd said, letting out a breath. He was surprised to have said it. Something changed, but he didn't know what. The thought of Helen used to be what carried him through. Now, he just wanted to go home, and Helen wasn't in the picture.

"You just want her to feel bad," Taipan said. *"She ran you off, you took a bullet, and you're gonna give her a big old guilt trip."*

"Fuck you," Todd said.

"You're one-upping the activist. You came out here to prove a point to a woman. That's fucked up Mason. Your patriotism is bullshit."

"Look at you," Todd shot back. *"Girl and baby back home and you're putting your life to the test. At least when a guy like me is here, he's not abandoning his responsibilities."*

"Told you the girl was a whore."

"Yeah, another whore with a bunch of children taking over the next generation and you come here to fight and die for them but they've got no one back home."

"Not up to me asshole. This is my third tour. They keep sending me. After the first, I thought I was done and wanted to be home, but it wasn't the same when I did. When I heard an alarm go off in the morning, first thing I did was reach for my gun. This shit damages you for life, and if you're here once, you're here forever. After the second tour, shit, I just about choked her to death one night cause I had a nightmare. You never go home Mason. Your body does, but your mind is always here."

"Then what you gonna do when the war ends?"

"There's always a war to fight. No sir. Damage is done on me. You, not yet. In time. You're young and dumb and haven't seen enough shit yet. What you saw today is nothing. I'd be no good back home. I'd father a bunch of kids and I'd smack em around until one of em got big enough to smack me back. The girl's okay on her own. And she's probably not on her own anymore. She's a freak. Freaks are never on the market long. But if I hadn't run off like I did, she'd be sitting there waiting for me to come home

and that's no good. You got away so you'd be missed. I got away because she wanted me around. In the end, she would have regretted that. Some guys are built to die doing this. Others raise kids. If she's waiting for me to come back and play daddy, she's dumb as a rock. I almost choked her to death. Almost killed her. With me out of the way, she's probably whoring it up with every guy in town, but they ain't gonna kill her. I could though."

Todd nodded, understanding what he was saying and suddenly wishing he hadn't made such a drastic move to make a point to the woman he loved. It had lasting effects that went far beyond what he'd wanted. It was true. He wasn't built for this. He wouldn't have carried a man over his shoulder or pulled a bullet out of anyone. He wasn't sure he could even draw a weapon and return fire.

"This place turned me into someone no one should be around no more," he muttered as an afterthought.

Before Todd could say another word, the bushes moved, and the crackle of leaves underfoot made both men look up to be faced with two men with guns held on them. Taipan would have reached for his weapon if four more hadn't suddenly appeared at their side.

Todd froze in fear, all weapons trained on him and Taipan. If any one man decided to pull the trigger, everything was over.

Sweat fell off Todd and Taipan as they were marched through the jungle by their captors. They had been walking for an hour, cooperatively. Todd reacted out of fear, but Taipan allowed his captors to spend time realizing they were scared, allowing them to lower their guard.

"Be ready Mason," he said under his breath.

"For what?" Todd whispered.

"The upper-hand."

Todd's eyes darted past Taipan. The man at his side had his gun openly exposed within Taipan's grasp, and there was no doubt Taipan could successfully extract his weapon, but then what? They couldn't take out six armed guards by themselves. Todd wanted to stop Taipan, but they'd already drawn attention by talking. Just as the guard began to say something to shut them up, Taipan grabbed the gun and in a flash, slammed his fist into the guard's face, knocking him down with one hit. Gun in hand, Taipan fired shots, taking another two down. Taipan half turned, expecting to see Todd in action, but instead found his partner was frozen in fear. "Mason!" he shouted.

Before Todd could react, the remaining men had already pulled their weapons and trained them on Taipan.

"We had them!" he shouted, aware that the end of his life was near. "Damnit, we had them!"

"I wasn't ready," Todd said, choking the words out. His head began to spin. His stomach turned. He fell to his knees and put his hands behind his head, squeezing his eyes shut and muttering to himself. "Please God, please God, please save me. Please..."

Taipan ignored Todd and kept his gun in hand while the guards yelled orders at him in a language they didn't understand but in a tone indicating one movement would get him killed. They had wanted to take them alive, but Taipan wanted to die like this. To Taipan, there were worse things than death: cowardice and submission. Taipan's eyes turned to Todd and he shook his head as if he'd made up his mind. "Goddammit Mason," he said. He raised his weapon but only had his arm halfway in the air before gunshots rang out and Taipan fell to the ground with a thud.

Todd's eyes squeezed tighter and he held his breath...

...He let out a breath when he saw her standing on the riverbank, a note he'd left her in hand. Cynthia Mason looked as beautiful as ever. The note was a map. The directions led her to him. He watched from behind a gathering of bushes as Cynthia found a picnic table and sat, hugging her knees and watching the river.

After he watched her a long moment, he stepped into the open and waited. It seemed like ten minutes passed before she finally looked up, jumping a little at the sight of him. She slowly stood off the bench, a mix of emotions flooding within. She opened her mouth, but nothing came out. She didn't know whether she should be angry or run to him. "Todd?" she asked, needing confirmation she was really seeing what she was seeing.

"It's me," he called back. He strained to keep a steady tone.

She shook her head, taking it all in. She took a step forward and her eyes darted down the river, looking for a way across.

"There's no bridge for miles either way," he said.

"What's going on?" she asked in shock.

"I've been in Hawaii," he said, expressionless. Everything inside wrenched, but he had to maintain his tone.

"Hawaii?" she asked, exasperated. "Why?"

"Another woman."

Her face wrinkled and tears streamed down her face. Everything she'd ever thought was impossible became a reality in that instant. Her world completely changed. She'd tried to believe this was all a misunderstanding for such a long time. In that moment, she realized she never knew her husband at all.

"I never wanted to be married," he shouted. "I never wanted a family. I thought I did for a while..." He stopped himself, unable to keep going. She couldn't hear him anyway. She'd turned away and sobbed in small bursts. He composed himself. He had to keep going. "I wanted you to move on. I didn't know you thought I was dead."

She turned to him suddenly and screamed. "How could you? We've all thought you were gone! We had a funeral!"

"I didn't realize until it was too late," he said.

"Jackson and Keith are heartbroken!"

His composure slipped again. They would never forgive him, but it had to be this way. He stood tall. "I will send my part of their.."

"Go to hell!" she screamed. "I thought you loved me! You're cruel!"

And then he forced himself to say four words he'd prepared to say since he realized he could never come back. He looked her in the eyes, shrugged, and simply said "I don't love you."

Her hands covered her face and her sobs grew louder. She started to walk away but turned back and her tone changed to desperation. "Come to the house so we can talk."

"I can't. I'm going back. Move on. I'm not worth it."

She suddenly ran to the river and tried to cross, stumbling as her feet hit the water. Todd took a step back, ready to run in the other direction. But then she came to her senses. The current was strong and if she tried to cross, it would do no good. She saw it in his eyes. It was over. She stood in the river and stared up at him.

"Bye Cynthia," he said.

She shouted his name repeatedly, breaking down more with each scream. He kept walking and...

...tumbled into a hole in the ground, the wind knocked out of him as he hit the dirt below. He coughed and wheezed, opening his eyes long enough to see the little stream of light from the top of his dungeon get covered with leaves and branches. He fell back and caught his breath, relieved his captors were at a distance. He felt safer in the hole, but it would present a whole new set of problems. Todd had a long road ahead.

He sat up, wincing in pain as his eyes adjusted to the dark. He suddenly felt eyes on him. He wasn't alone. He turned to find himself face to face with a younger, thinner Irving, who sat against a wall sizing him up. "How many with you?" he asked.

"They're all dead," Todd said.

"Anyone know your location?" he asked without a lot of hope. He seemed like a man drained of it.

"We were ambushed miles from here."

Irving relaxed, not surprised to hear the bad news, and not particularly anxious to have another member in the pit. "Anyone looking for you?" he asked, closing his eyes.

"I don't..."

"I'm Irving," he suddenly said. *"Been here I don't know how long. Longer than the rest."*

"I can't be here," Todd said, *looking around frantically. He never felt farther from home—from Helen. He would do anything to go back and undo things. He could have stayed with Helen. She'd given him the opportunity moments before he disappeared. He'd die in the pit and he'd wind up missing in action, forgotten in a year, and a distant memory in ten.*

"What's your name son?" Irving asked.

"Todd Mason." His eyes began adjusting to the dark and he saw the others sitting together. The pit had another two men and one woman huddled together against the wall. They were barely conscious.

Irving noticed Todd staring in their direction. "Guy on the left was tossed in two weeks ago. Had a weapon on him they didn't find. I work in the dirt sometimes, trying to make footholds—something we can use to climb to the top. The footholds are in the shadows. They won't be able to see them, but that's not the hard part. The hard part is out of the pit and back to safe ground from the jungle. We figure we don't have a chance in hell of getting out of here alive, but we're gonna make a run soon. Otherwise, we just die. I'd rather die running and who knows? Maybe we'll get somewhere. The more we got, the better chance we got."

Todd nodded, unsure he'd be able to face the challenge. He thought about Taipan and if they really had a chance to overpower their captors. When the others climbed the pit and emerged from the safety of their prison, they would all be moving targets. It seemed Todd had a little time to decide if he wanted to be one of them.

"Against the wall, that's Thomson, Duffy, Danson..."

"What do we do?" Todd asked. "What do they do to us?"

"Haven't done anything to Thomson yet. Me, Duffy, and Danson, they've got their ways..." he said, trailing off, unable to relive it. "They're going to want intel. They'll take Thomson soon. Then you."

Todd couldn't deal with whatever was next. Irving was right—they probably wouldn't survive the jungle, but Todd saw options with more clarity. He could stay or run. One meant he'd spill intelligence like a coward or face torture. The other meant running with the possibility of living or dying. He turned to his cell-mates. They looked sick, traumatized, like they weren't even able to function.

"What do we do?" Todd asked.

"Get some rest and sit tight. Keep your energy up."

Todd looked up toward the small opening between the leaves that covered their location. The last of the light shining through turned dark as the sun swallowed it up. Todd closed his eyes but he didn't sleep.

Chapter 13

1

When Royce Morrow was living on the streets, he never blamed anyone. He moved to Anaheim when he was eighteen, ready to throw away his scholarships and play for the Angels. It was a hard reality to face when he was told he didn't have the right stuff. He was a jock in High School, and thought he could skip college and the working world. He tried out four times before he gave up and realized he wouldn't be a ball player. He didn't punch a time-card in the time he lived in California. His parents fronted him the money for a studio apartment, which he shared with two other guys. No one was able to come up with the rent, and within two months, they were gone. Royce's father offered to buy him a ticket home, or pick him up—whatever it took to save his son. Instead, he traveled to Los Angeles rather than home to Pennsylvania, and slept under a bridge. Religion was never in the cards because it never crossed his path, but since Maria Haskins told him he would die, he started thinking about karma.

After Maria's visit, bad things began happening in succession. Manny and Bedbug were only the tip of the iceberg. He was given the option to back out of a contract on Adlar's head. All he had to do was send another 200K and everything would be forgotten. After his chat with Bedbug, his intent was to send the money immediately, but he never even got on-line.

Sandra Morrow met him for dinner and told him about Tarek Appleton's show. Royce didn't understand what Tarek was trying to do, but found relief in the fact that it wasn't his name that was read. He didn't need attention now—not when he was already frantically trying to cover up ghosts from his past.

His right hand man at the office, Edward Maplewood, first offered his resignation so he could focus on a career in politics, and then up and died the next day after announcing his run for council. Edward was a friend, and a good business partner. Royce wanted to see him take a seat in the city, but left the election wide open for just anyone to fill the gap. Immediately after Edward died, Morrow Bank and Trust was put under investigation for insurance fraud. Royce had nothing to worry about, but when the feds began turning rocks, it seemed Edward had some questionable dealings in the works. Edward wasn't around to defend himself, so Royce took the heat.

Maria had told Royce she saw him in a pool of blood. He thought it was silly, but things were escalating in such a way that Royce was genuinely worried about the direction life was headed. When Manny and Bedbug sat him down, he realized there were various directions their relationship could take. If he sent the money, he hoped to never see them again, but it could be what brought about her premonition. He brushed the thought from his head and laughed to himself. *I'm dwelling on what a psychic told me.*

Ed's wake was an open casket and everyone from MUBT paid their respects. Ed had a wife and four kids. Their home was paid for. Their vacation home was paid for. Their boat, their kids college, the coffee table in the dining room which cost over ten thousand dollars—all paid for.

Sandra sat at her husband's side in church, holding his hand as Ed's casket was carried to the altar. A prayer was read. Everyone stood. The church was filled with the sound of sniffles and sobs and powerful men checking emails and fantasy football scores.

Royce turned and caught a figure standing near the front to his left. Bernard Bell hadn't known Ed in person, but here he was. He was here to ride Ed's coat-tails. Ed wouldn't mind. He'd be honored. Royce—on the other hand—couldn't fathom the idea of Bernard attending his funeral.

A pool of your own blood.

He shook the thought and reminded himself again that he needed to send the money to Manny. He kept getting distracted. *Or stalling.* He listened to the prayer for a moment, but felt eyes on him. He turned toward Bernard, who offered him a nod. He turned forward without acknowledging it. Bernard and Royce went way back, only Bernard had no idea...

...He smiled as he stared at his reflection. He wondered if he was good looking anymore as he was as a teenager. It was hard to find self-confidence as a bum—but in his day, Royce had his share of girls. That was long before he got tired of parents who hated each other and ran away from home with the hopes of making it big in the city as a pro ball player. That dream felt surreal—a faraway memory. He had no education, no special skills—a guy who couldn't tolerate the mundane routine of an eight to five job and a steady decrease in money. He sold his movie collection, a few boxes of baseball cards, and made it through for a while until he

finally had to give up the apartment, living in his car for a year before he had to give that up too. One day, the car had a boot on the wheel and street cleaning came by a day later. If it wasn't moved, it would be ticketed. A week later, it would be towed. The day the tow-truck arrived, he grabbed everything he'd be able to carry and walked out onto the sidewalk. It went straight. It went left. It went right. Royce didn't have the slightest idea of which way he was supposed to walk. He didn't know if he even could walk. At that point in his life, he could sit right there at the crossroads and sleep. He'd simply moved too fast when he ran away—believed he had whatever special something it took to succeed.

And he didn't.

Until now.

Until he stared at himself in the mirror, a clean wardrobe neatly pressed against his body. He wanted to hold onto that feeling. He never wanted to feel the stink of the streets again.

Judd was shocked when Royce approached. He didn't want to get too close to his friends. He was afraid they'd touch the clothes, rub off on them, and ruin his chances at giving the impression of a respectable man. "Where did you get the clothes?" he asked.

"Rented them," Royce said, bemused by the look on his friend's face, but keeping his distance. "Nice guy just gave them to me."

"Really? Where at?"

"Don't go asking. He almost got in trouble," Rocky said, instantly regretful for showing Judd in fear that he'd go marching into the store begging for his own outfit. Royce couldn't afford the clothes and one of the cashiers at the store stuffed them in a bag and told him not to worry about it. It was possibly the nicest gesture anyone had ever made for him.

"If some guy's handing out free clothes..."

"I can't tell you," Royce said.

Judd watched Rocky as closely. "What's going on with you?"

"Just trying to find work. You should too."

"Where did you get the money?"

Rocky swallowed hard and squared up against Judd. "I've been saving, finding other ways to get things, and collecting money in the meantime. I told you I would."

"The rest of us been sharing."

"I've been passing up everything offered to me."

Judd stared at him, seemingly pained. "Well how much you got?"

"Bout a hundred."

Judd's eyes lit up. He tried to say something, but reminded himself that Rocky had a plan, that splitting the money and buying booze was exactly what Rocky was avoiding.

"I talked to you about this," Rocky said. "You should be doing what I do, but if you won't, I'll do it alone. I'm not asking for anything from you. I don't expect a share in your earnings."

"You've been lying though."

"I've been protecting what I'm doing." Rocky held his breath as he watched his friend wince in pain. On the streets, trust was a heavy part of the pack. Rocky had betrayed it. "Judd, I could still get myself a job and make a living. If I do it, I'll make a regular income. That's a real paycheck."

The words went straight over Judd's head. "I thought you was our friend, Rock." Judd shook his head in disbelief. There was nothing Royce could say to ease his friend's mind. Someday, he'd be able to show him the benefit. Someday, he could come back and help them. Someday...

...a small gathering of men in suits gathered in the back of the church, chattering and laughing as they spoke in remembrance of a man most hadn't even met—only heard of. Royce watched from a distance, wondering why none of those same men had ever showed their faces before Ed's death. There was a who's who list in the city and Ed was on it, just as Royce was. He couldn't tolerate the thought of his funeral as a networking event. Most of the men in the room, he couldn't stand.

Most of all, Bernard, who stood in the middle of a gathering and reminisced undeservedly of Ed, using words he would have used on anyone after their demise.

"You know, I can tell you this from my experience in business," Bernard said. "I've run across a number of big stock operators and leaders. Some were gentlemen and educated leaders with a gift of epigram. Some were foul-spoken who knew as little of grammar as of manners. Some were cool, calculating, steel-nerved and some were fidgety impulsive, and excitable." He took a moment of silence, mostly for effect, feigning emotion. Everyone fell silent. "I've never seen someone who set the tone like Eddie did though. He would have an outrageous unconventional idea and people listened and took his word. Good or bad, he built himself up to be exactly what he wanted to be and he was true to that. As a businessman, I looked up to him."

And then Bernard said something unexpected—something that made sense of why he was here, and which made Royce freeze in shock.

"In his place, I'll be throwing my hat in the ring for governor of this great city."

The men around him hooted and hollered their approval. Royce shook his head with disgust. If he'd closed his eyes, he'd have a hard time believing he was at a funeral and not a rock concert. Bernard found Royce in the crowd, and for just a moment, gave him an icy stare. It quickly faded and he managed a smile. Next to Royce, Sandra's eyes moved from one man to the other as if she was watching a tennis match.

Bernard continued, keeping his eyes on Royce. "I'd like to also offer my condolences to Royce Morrow."

Royce wanted to tell everyone that Bell didn't know Ed at all—that he wouldn't endorse Bell as a candidate if he was the only man running.

Instead of responding, he hurried away from the church. When Bernard saw Royce walk out, he caught up to him.

"Royce!" Bernard called from a distance.

"Please," Royce said, continuing onward without turning. "I prefer to be called Rocky."

Bernard caught up to Royce, who didn't turn, focused only on pushing Sandra forward. "I know this is a hard time for you, but have I done something to upset you?"

"I'm just trying to understand your motivation,"

"I had a lot of respect..."

"You didn't know him. He only knew of you by name."

"On a business level, he and I shared a mutual respect. You of all people should understand."

"You have a political agenda that doesn't coincide with anything Ed planned on pushing. You're not the man to fit his shoes."

Bernard's face went white with humiliation and his tone changed. Now, he was all business. "Then maybe you and I should go over the details of his campaign and hash it out."

"It was no secret that Ed wasn't planning on turning the land south of the Franklin into condos. Stone Enterprises has been looking at that for a while. I can think of a dozen ways that running is self-serving for business."

"Would you excuse us?" Bernard asked, directed at Sandra as if he'd realized for the first time that she was there. She looked to Royce and he nodded. She told them not to worry. She could entertain herself. A moment later, Royce and Bernard stood a few yards away, leaning over concrete ledge that overlooked the church parking lot.

Bernard swallowed hard and picked his words carefully. "I understand your passion for preserving that part of the city. What I'm proposing is we make it more livable for a greater number of people."

"People with money."

"Property costs money. For everyone. You won't find anything cheaper than six hundred bucks out here, so the people you're trying to help are still SOL."

"What's your plan? Kick out the hundreds of people who live there now?"

"Illegally live there. And yes, to make room for thousands. I don't think your biases are a big secret Rocky, but don't pretend like it's in the best interest of the majority to replace a larger number of tax-paying citizens to make room for the homeless. I came here to offer my sympathy."

"You're on a power trip."

"I'm trying to make a change. Don't assume I'm Victor."

"All I know is that this is convenient for you. Filling in last minute for a man you didn't know, in his honor, but spouting off principles that are in your own best interests...Personally, I think you'd be a disaster."

"I came out here as a courtesy. Beyond that, you're with me, against me, or neutral, but it won't change anything."

"Then what are we doing here? You followed me."

Bernard shook his head with disgust. "If you love the poor so much, why the hell did you go so out of your way to become so wealthy?"

Royce opened his mouth to rebuttal but nothing came out. He wanted to answer the question, but he had no answer. Before he could muster anything, Bernard was gone and Sandra was quickly making her way back to Royce. "Is everything okay?"

He stared off into the parking lot, wondering who he was. He did everything in his power to get off the streets, but still defended the life.

"Yeah, I'm okay," he said.

2

Toby O'Tool twirled Royce's black box in front of him, thinking about the many routes he could take. A dozen beneficiaries could be exploited, but to be an expert tactician, he needed to conquer the who and how before he proceeded. With Brian and Maria under his thumb, he could prevent them from being there when the time came to meet the judge. He had a few other tricks up his sleeve, just in case. He toyed with a plan that involved bringing Adlar into the open, but with Charlie somewhere out there, it could be chaos. He would have to tread carefully.

Royce was the only other card he could play, but Royce was strong willed and smart enough to detect an imposter suddenly injected into his life. Brian was oblivious and Maria was desperate, but Royce would look a liar in the eye and know.

But Toby had the box.

He also struggled with how to utilize Sal. Henry proved to be an asset. It didn't take long before Maria fell in love with him. He picked up the game as if he'd played it before, and Toby wondered if he had. William did a good enough job with Brian too, but he wasn't as aggressive of a player as Henry. Both ways would eventually get the job done, and he was satisfied with his crew—except Sal.

He eyed Sal sitting at the bar with his eyes on a couple girls that he wouldn't have a shot with. Sal carried a confidence he didn't deserve. Toby hated when people didn't know their place—didn't know what a loser they were. Sal was textbook loser and because William already told him what they were doing, Toby was forced to use him . He didn't plan on taking Sal with him until the end, but he'd iron out the details later. For the moment, what he really wanted was to control another beneficiary and because of the box, Royce was the guy. Royce, who wouldn't hurt an insect, but had a skeleton in his closet that he'd do anything to keep there.

Toby shook his head with disgust at Sal as he sat two bar-stools away. Sal tried to ignore him. He'd spent the last few days taking nothing but abuse from Toby. At the coaxing of William, he kept his cool. Toby's approach was a huge gesture and he didn't want to blow it.

"I'll get you in on this if you can prove yourself," Toby said.

"What do you want me to do?" Sal asked, facing forward.

"Get a number from any girl in the bar."

Sal wanted to say 'easy', but it suddenly dawned on him that he hadn't actually been with a woman in a while. He was a giant with pockmarks on his face and uninvited body hair coating him. Even the less attractive of the herd usually would flee from him.

"Why?" Sal asked. "What does that prove?"

"It proves everything. A man with a good game can pick up any girl. Why do you think butt ugly fat guys are always walking around with pretty girls, but you never see the opposite? A good game can get you anything."

"Look, I never said I was a smooth talker. I said I'd do anything. You don't need to be conning everyone. You need to eliminate them. I can do that."

"If any one of those people turned up dead, witnesses within five miles of the crime scene will have seen you, smelled you, and heard that sucking sound you make when you breathe. You're not inconspicuous, and even if you were, don't flatter yourself into thinking you're the kind of criminal who can put a bullet in someone's head and get away. You were caught the first time."

"Cause it was my wife. How will they attach my name to these people?"

"It was your wife," Toby repeated. "Which proves that you act on emotion and you're stupid—two things I prefer not to have at my table, but you're here because William made a dumb mistake, and if you want to be used, you'll learn how to do it my way. The only way to commit crime is to make it appear that no crime was committed. We're not covering our tracks or creating alibis and you're not going near these people until you get a phone number."

To Sal's credit, he tried hard. Every girl that walked through the door was approached, but within hours, he knew he wouldn't be able to pull it off. He eyed Toby from across the bar and tried to embrace the words he'd spoken. Toby didn't want attention drawn. It made sense, and even though Sal could specialize in offing people, he could adjust and be the team player Toby needed him to be.

"You win," he said, approaching Toby. "I'm tired of this."

"'Tired' isn't in my vocabulary."

"You asked me to do something you knew I couldn't do."

"Henry could do it in a second."

"You give him too much credit. The girls don't want to be picked up."

"You know how you win this game?"

Sal shrugged. Toby turned and approached the nearest girl, but spoke loud so Sal could hear. "I'll slip you twenty bucks to write seven digits on a napkin and hand it to me."

The girl rolled her eyes, but wrote the digits. Toby grabbed the napkin and walked back to Sal, tossing it in front of his face. "Cheat. Create illusions. If I tell you to get a phone number and you can't get a phone number, you make me believe you got a number. That's how you win the game."

"Okay, I get it. I'll learn."

"Yeah, I got something for you," Toby said, but regretted officially inviting Sal into the group as he was doing it. "A small task to start with. It requires no brains or charm. You'll be perfect."

Sal took a controlled breath. If Toby didn't hold the keys to a fortune, he would've gotten himself strangled by now. In another life, Sal wouldn't have taken this kind if disrespect. "What do you need?"

"A message delivered."

3

Royce's day hadn't bottomed out yet. It hadn't come close. A number of unrelated incidents further convinced him that the past caught up with him and was beating him into submission. His right hand man's death hit him hard, but when a ghost from his past turned up dead, his body went numb. Long before Royce had a dollar to his name, Judd Corby took him into his street entourage, and soon, they were a pair among the group who found friendship among the ruins of their life. There weren't many people

Royce could display his life humility in front of, but Judd listened when Royce talked, as if the frustrations of Royce's life were his own.

On the day his partner in success was buried, his partner in failure died too.

Royce's was canceled. The distractions were endless, and he barely had time to cope with recent events as he tried to make sense of the timing behind them. The last ten years had been a rise to the top. In the last week, it all plummeted.

He learned the whereabouts of where the body was held. Unlike his partner, Judd was housed in a small wooden box in a run-down building. His death would barely cause a stir and would only have a brief mention in the newspaper.

As Royce prepared to leave the office and claim the body, a message came through his secretary, who told him someone wanted to see him about his black box. He let the message register and realized another event, unrelated to all those before, was playing out.

Adlar Wilcox. Should I transfer the money? Should I call it off? Will he haunt me forever if I do?

He'd almost forgotten Manny and Bedbug. He still had until the end of the day. If no money exchanged hands, Adlar would likely be dead quickly. Did it really matter? His secretary gave him an address and a half hour window to be there. He didn't bother to consider whether or not to go. He drove straight to the address. There was never a better day to get in Adlar's face and demand his property back, only, it wasn't Adlar. It was a grotesque man he'd never seen before. A man who tried to seem in control, but came across as nervous and not well-spoken.

Sal never stated his name. He picked his words carefully, so as not to link himself to Toby. It was harder than he thought, and he found he wasn't as slick as when he rehearsed it in his head on the way to see Royce.

"What is this?" Royce asked. Sal was taken aback. He knew who Royce Morrow was, but the man in front of him didn't look like the Royce he'd seen in public.

"I'm blackmailing you," Sal said. Royce frowned at his choice of words. "That thing you've got coming up where you're going to help that guy stop the money thing…"

"I have no idea what you're saying," Royce said.

"You know what I'm saying. I have your box."

"You get that from Adlar Wilcox?"

"None of your business."

"He took it from me, so I'll assume you're here for him."

"I'm not."

"I'll pay you double whatever he's offering you."

"You can't afford it. I know what I can make."

Royce chuckled. "What you can make? By doing what? Are you even aware of what you're supposed to do? There are about a dozen of us. You've got police and celebrities and you've got a man in prison. What's your plan exactly? I can offer you money now to give my property back and run away before you get yourself arrested or killed."

"I'll take my chances."

"Then you're making a mistake. What exactly are you blackmailing me for? What's the trade?"

"I don't show everyone the box and you don't go to the thing to stop this."

"Are you talking about our meeting to invalidate the will?"

"Yeah, that."

"First, if you're coming here to make a point, pick words I can understand or you'll get nowhere. Second, you're not here to kill me. You're here to secure the lifeblood of Victor's will. When do you plan on getting paid for this? Why not kill us all and be done with it?"

"Yeah, well, that's what I want too, but for now…"

"So you've got Wilcox telling you to hold off and wait—make sure we don't let the will become invalid—hope we all die of old age so you can be rich, and you're turning down what I have to offer for that?"

Royce made a good case, and he'd turned out to be harder to handle than Sal thought. Sal really wanted to come across as intimidating, but he'd walk away having lost the conversation. Part of him wanted to do whatever it was the black box would do by getting his hands on it and releasing the contents. Royce didn't seem worried or want to talk about that at all, and Sal could never get his paws on the box. Toby had the box. Toby made the rules. Toby wanted him to come to Royce with blackmail instead of killing people—as Royce suggested. Toby…

Royce had no tolerance for Sal, and though Sal's visit raised questions, he walked away with the upper-hand. Sal looked dangerous, but his demeanor stunk of an amateur and his words sounded like bluffs. If Adlar didn't want Royce to be with Richard on that day, he had plenty of time to think it over—or dispose of Adlar.

Don't send the money. Don't call it off.

It was a struggle he needed to save for another day. The sidetrack felt surreal—like a higher power was trying to put too much on Royce's shoulders and there was a message to decipher. He forced himself back on task and went to where Judd's body lay. Only one man was in the room filling out forms.

"You family?" the man asked when Royce entered.

"A friend," Royce said, approaching the box and setting his hands on the wood with ease. Judd looked peaceful, more peaceful than he'd ever seen him. The box was unimpressive. It was no respectable final resting place for anyone.

"I have to take the body with me," the man said.

"Will he be buried in this?"

"Yes, he will."

"Was there no family to claim him?"

"Unfortunate as it is, usually the homeless have all their belongings on them. We followed leads and the only family we found were deceased or didn't respond when we reached out."

Royce nodded. No human being deserved to be tossed in a box and disposed of without anyone to mourn. "Will he have a proper burial?"

"He'll be in Highland Hills Park."

"No tombstone?"

The man shook his head.

"His name won't be displayed..." Royce said, talking to himself.

"He wasn't a veteran. He had no bank accounts. The city pays for it. A prayer will be read."

"But otherwise, he slips through the cracks?" Royce asked.

"Most people do…"

...He stared at himself in the restroom mirror, a sight that only he could be amused by. Rocky Morrow groomed nicely with his hair combed, his face shaved, and a shirt, tie, and slacks. He'd forgotten how good looking he was. He'd forgotten that at one time, he'd looked like an average guy.

He left the gym and walked a mile to Young & Associates, a small law firm where he'd managed to land an interview. It was nothing impressive— only some cleaning and landscaping, but it was a start. He entered the lobby. A receptionist looked up at him and smiled. It was a warm smile. It wasn't the usual unwelcoming, disgusted look he often got.

"Do you have an appointment?" the receptionist asked.

"Yes. I'm Rocky Morrow," he said.

She looked at her agenda. "Is it Royce?"

"Oh, yes," he said nervously.

Moments later, Royce sat in a seat across from a man named Earl who studied his resume. He set it down and smiled at him the best he was able to manage. "I filled this position a month ago Mr. Morrow."

"Oh..." he said. "I thought I..."

"It's still running in the trades. We buy an ad and it displays for a

month."

Rocky nodded and let out a breath. He got to his feet and shook Earl's hand. They said their goodbyes and Royce readied himself to exit before turning back. "Is there anything else open?"

"There's nothing you'd be qualified for," Earl said, oddly. It was a strange question, a question of desperation. He'd seen it in Royce, but he didn't want to say anything. He wanted to tell him to get lost, but Royce was polite and respectful.

"I understand," Royce said.

"Maybe work on your resume and resubmit at a later date," Earl said.

"My resume says everything there is to say. Couldn't add much without lying."

Earl chuckled to himself and scanned the resume again. There really was nothing he could use. "What can you do? Any skills at all you haven't listed?"

"I read. I write."

"Can you operate a calculator?"

"Yes sir."

"You live around here?"

Royce fell silent and shook his head. He refrained from speaking so he wouldn't have to lie.

"I'm not asking you where you live. I'm asking if you live around here," Earl said, knowingly. Earl saw straight through him, but it didn't seem to faze him.

"Are you a quick learner?"

"Yes sir."

"I get a lot of applicants fresh out of college. Their resumes are built, but they lack a certain ambition that's not taught in school. I need someone who represents something that everyone thinks they will be when they go to grad school but have the creative spark bored out of them by endless math. Namely, I need a kind of intellectual detective to solve problems."

Royce leaned forward eagerly.

"Mr. Morrow, I have a hot dinner waiting for me at home but I want to sit with you again. Can you be back tomorrow at nine so we can pick up where we left off? At the very least, I can help you strengthen your resume."

"I was just looking for work," Royce said. "If you're looking to fill a high position, I don't..."

"I've got foot-in-the-door and the only qualification is to be a quick learner. We've established you are. Come back tomorrow. The worst that can happen is you're back to square one. The best that can happen though...could be the opportunity you're looking for..."

...Royce walked out for air, but when he was outside, he wanted to keep going and get as far away from business as possible. He loosened his tie, which was suffocating, and took deep breaths. He kept going, sure he'd never go back. He wanted to go back in time, before he was forced to choose between two lives, but he'd already lived both and neither had appeal.

Against everything he believed, he edged his way little by little toward Maria Haskin's part of town. He sat on a bench across the street from her shop and stared for half an hour before entering. The shop seemed lifeless on the outside, but the door was open and a man lay on the couch sleeping. Maria was nowhere to be seen. Royce wondered how she could mismanage a business and stay open.

Henry opened his eyes slowly as Royce stepped into the room. He sat up quickly. "She's not here at the moment," Henry said. "If you want to set up an appointment..."

"Do you know when she'll return?"

"She's running errands. Did you have an appointment?"

"No, she's an acquaintance."

Henry sized Royce up, and noted that he didn't seem to be typical clientele. "Really?" he asked, skeptically.

"Would you mind telling Ms. Haskins that Royce Morrow stopped by?"

At mention of the name, Henry was suddenly on his feet. Royce wandered the shop so aimlessly, without knowledge that he was in the room with one of the men who had access to his secret. He was selective of his words and actions.

"Do you work here?" Royce asked.

"Maria and I are seeing each other."

"Let me ask you something," Royce said. "Is she legitimate?"

"What do you mean?"

"Where do you believe she gets her information?"

"Depends on what she told you."

"I was under the impression that psychics use vague suggestions and cold readings."

"Don't tell her that," Henry said with a laugh. "What did she do? Deliver bad news?"

"She approached me and told me I would die. It seemed out of character for her profession. I saw no other motive than her actual belief in the notion."

"She say how or why?" Henry asked, suddenly curious.

"No, but there's a reason that only her and I would understand."

It was time for Henry to be bold—to really go after him. "Victor Stone's will?" he asked.

Royce nodded, and sized Henry up again. He wondered how many strangers out there knew the truth. Henry seemed indifferent.

"Yeah, she told me," Henry said. "You one of em?"

"Unfortunately."

"Ah, the competition," he said, with a smile. "I won't lie and tell you the money wouldn't be nice."

"There's no crime in desire. Only how one attains their goals."

The comment struck a nerve. If only Royce knew who he was talking to. "True," Henry said, "but currency passes through death. Clean living is as imaginary as the tooth fairy."

"If you're going to justify his will, find an analogy tantamount to murder."

"I didn't say a word about murder," Henry said, defensively.

Royce took a seat. He was interested in Henry. Maybe it was because he was a stranger, impartial to the workings of Royce's complicated life. He was tired of the opinions of those around him, trying to gain what they could from his power. "Did Maria explain to you that one of us has died?

"She did."

"Then you understand."

"Are you afraid she's right? That why you're here?"

"I've thought about it. I believe I'm being pushed."

"What do you mean?"

"Pushed to change. To atone for my past."

"And what did you do?"

"Profited from a crime."

Henry leaned forward. "You know, my father had one of those jobs where you destroy old money. He and four other guys spent their whole day eliminating legal notes from circulation. So they had a lot of time to sit around and come up with their own life mottos. They weren't that deep, but there was something my father said once that I liked. He showed me a crisp dollar bill that he'd gotten from an ATM; never used. Not a crease in it. He told me that everyone starts out like that. Money is flawless when printed; no wrinkles or smudges or graffiti, or fading in the ink from rubbing against your wallet." Henry reached in his pocket and came out with a dollar. "But over time..." He wrinkled it, crushed it, bent it every which way... "Over time, we make little mistakes. We find ways to break the rules or cheat and lie. He said it better than I do, but his point stands. There's a whole list of crimes against man that we become guilty of in time. It's like the wrinkles on your face when you laugh or squint that form landscapes that can't be erased over years of missteps. Physically, mentally, emotionally...we can only be damaged, and when the damage is done, it's always there. Like the dollar bill, we all break, crease by crease, and we're never repaired. Maybe you think you did everything right, but probably not. Otherwise you wouldn't act like you're being punished. But there's no way to fix that. By the time that money was in my father's hands, most of it had blood on it, traces of cocaine, sweat, tears... It was all creased, crumpled, and fuzzy. Then, it was destroyed."

"That's a cynical position."

"Depends on how you look at it I suppose. My father used to talk like this, and I bought it, but I had a hundred dollar bill once with an actual blood spot on it and all I could think about was what he said about money being tainted, and I'm thinking it could still feed a family of four. Not everything is destroyed...just tainted. You can be permanently scarred, but useful. You can be damaged, but hold value."

"Turn your dollar over," Royce said.

Henry found Royce's eyes. Henry turned the dollar over and studied the back as Royce spoke. "I understand what you're trying to say. Money with blood is still money. You're right. I don't deny it or the value of it. But what I'm talking about goes beyond the value of currency. I'm talking about higher power. I don't care if you worship a god or Buddha or the sun. We all experience pleasure and pain. We know how to treat the inhabitants of this planet. Take a look at the pyramid."

Henry's eyes took in the Great Seal as Royce spoke.

"The Declaration of Independence states that we mutually pledge to each other our lives, our fortunes, and our sacred honor. On the top of the pyramid on every dollar bill they put a symbol as a reminder of just what that means. It means there are non-monetary things that hold more value than money. Call it whatever you want, but the all seeing eye at the top of the pyramid is always on us, judging whatever endeavor we utilize the symbol for. It means divine guidance by whatever power exists. The motto on the seal reads 'Annuit Coeptis' which translates to 'he who approves of this undertaking'. You're right in what you say. Most money is tainted over time. Hardly anything is passed down without being compromised, but what kind of man won't stand up for what's right just because the majority won't? What kind of man becomes corrupted by a system instead of being the opposing voice against it? Sure, doing what benefits yourself is easy, but no matter how you slice it, you will still have to answer to the all seeing eye; the eye of providence."

Henry swallowed hard. Before he could respond, Royce's cell buzzed, bringing him out of the moment. He liked talking to a stranger, and didn't want to be interrupted, but no moment could last too long without reality slapping him in the face. "I have to go," he said.

"I'll tell Maria you came by," Henry said. As he said Maria's name, he was suddenly ridden with guilt.

"That's not necessary," Royce said. "Thanks to our conversation, I no longer need to see her. I think I've accidentally stumbled on the answer."

4

Adlar Wilcox waited silently in the corner of the bar as Toby and William sat two booths down. Adlar was recruited to give Richard hope. His job was simple: Tell Richard he'd be there the day they meet the judge and then be a no-show. Richard would tally him in as support and when Toby orchestrated the absence of others, Richard's confidence would fade when his easy win faded away in the eleventh hour.

Adlar waited impatiently. He'd been stuck in a small apartment with a low ceiling ever since he was on the run. He had his laptop, but was otherwise bored and tired of waiting. Toby promised there would come a day when the coast would be clear and they could move on to the next step, but as the days passed, cabin fever set in and Adlar's mind began working. Toby recruited him with a pitch that began with Toby's lack of interest in the money. He said he was dying—but the man in the booth looked healthy and determined. Something deep inside knew he'd been played all along, but he went along with it because he wanted someone in his corner. He still did. That's why he planned on doing whatever Toby said, but he continually tried to make sense of what part he had to play in Toby's production.

A large hideously ugly man entered the bar. Adlar watched as the man sat across from Toby and next to William. Toby had recruits, which decreased Adlar's value further.

Sal noticed Adlar momentarily. After taking his seat, William brought him up to speed on who Adlar was and why he was there. After that, Sal didn't hear much. He looked over his shoulder at the boy, young and filled with angst. He was another tool that Toby must have been utilizing in his fifty point plan. Sal could handle the list in a day if Toby would give him the go-ahead. He wondered why Toby would team up with another. He may have had William and Henry fooled, but Sal could see with perfect clarity: Toby's plan was too complex, and Sal had no future in it.

"What happened with Morrow?" Toby asked.

Sal recounted the events for Toby, who sat unimpressed until the end. He tried to listen expressionless, but he smirked knowingly as if the story was amusing. When Sal finished recounting the conversation, Toby paused a long moment before he said "Tell me again, word for word."

"I did what you asked. He got the message. Why you gotta assume I did something wrong?"

"Just tell me again what you said."

Sal's face was red with rage.

Toby didn't stop. "I'd kill to be a fly on the wall watching you try to be intimidating. How did he react when he saw your face?"

"What are you talking about?"

"Was he horrified?"

"He was afraid because we have his stuff."

"Right, but what about when he saw your face?" Toby leaned forward, listening intently, seemingly interested in the answer. Sal only responded with cold dead eyes. "Come on. What did he do?"

That's when Sal snapped. Within an instant, he grabbed Toby by the hair with one hand and pulled a gun with the other. He pressed the muzzle against Toby's temple.

"Whoa Sally. Calm down!" Toby said.

Adlar watched from his booth, trying to duck out of sight while William got to his feet.

"You got anything else to say about my face?" Sal asked.

"I wasn't trying to be rude," Toby said, frantically.

"I've listened to this horse-shit enough!" Sal shouted. "You make fun of me and you're the one who doesn't know what you're doing."

"I have a plan."

"So do I. What's the guy's name?"

"What guy?"

"The preacher-man."

"Sal, just listen..."

"What's the name!" he screamed, grasping Toby's head in his paws and pressing the gun harder. Toby squinted his eyes and broke into a sweat. He looked to William for help, but he watched the display quietly, afraid to interfere and escalate matters. William finally managed to find words.

"Put the gun down Sal. This isn't going to accomplish anything."

"It's drawing attention," Toby said, in a tone as if to tell Sal he was an idiot.

"I want his name," Sal said again.

He cocked the trigger, but Toby sensed the bluff. No way would Sal murder him in front of witnesses. He wasn't about to say the name, but suddenly Adlar crawled out of his booth and blurted it instead. "Richard Libby," Adlar said.

Sal gave Adlar a long look and repeated the name twice to store in his memory. Toby looked up from his position and scowled at Adlar. "What are you doing kid?"

"If he kills Richard, we get to keep going," Adlar said, cowering. "Maybe we need the help."

"You're as dumb as Sal's face is…" Before he could say 'ugly', Sal brought the gun down on his head. Toby's eyes rolled back and he fell to the ground in a heap. Sal raised his gun and pointed it at William, who backed up and instinctively put his hands up to show he was no threat.

William looked down on Toby's unconscious body and back to Sal, pleading. "I know he's been harsh, but the way he's doing this makes sense. He's playing it safe because if we get eager, we'll make mistakes. It takes patience."

"My way's fast," Sal said. He backed to the door, holding his gun the whole way. He looked up at Adlar. "Toby's not going to help you kid. You already know he needs you dead eventually. Come with me. I'll do the dirty work. You cut me in for half."

Adlar nodded quickly and hurried toward the door.

Sal looked down at Toby's unconscious body, and looked up at William. He was one step away from the door. "You'll thank me later," he said. And then he and Adlar were gone.

5

"I think I'm being punished," Royce told Sandra at lunch. "I think I'm being pushed to come clean about what happened to Lucas."

"You're not being punished. You're a good man."

"A psychic tracked me down a week ago and told me I was going to die."

"What? That's ridiculous. You're not going to die."

"Do you believe in karma?"

"I suppose in some way. I believe in balance."

"What if I told you I deserve this?" he asked. He looked deep in her eyes with a dark look. She found his gaze and saw there was a hint of something there—something that wasn't the man she loved. "There's nothing you've done that you can't undo. You can go feed a poor family for life if you want to. If karma exists, and it owes you anything, it's good fortune."

"Judd died today," he said.

"Who?" she asked.

His eyes met hers as if accusing her, and she knew in an instant who Judd was and regretted forgetting. "Oh no..." she said, but it was too late.

"Same day as Ed's funeral. You don't think that's strange?"

"It's a big coincidence, but I wouldn't read in to it."

"I don't think everything Ed did was right," Royce said. "He was sure made out to be a hero today."

"I thought you loved him."

"I did," he said. "That doesn't make it right."

"You don't know anything for certain."

"I'm tired Sand. I'm tired of bending at everyone's will. I've always done what I had to do to get to the next level, but it's never enough."

"You're too hard on yourself."

"There's been no good outcome to my life."

"You're not happy?"

"I made it this far for what? What influence do I truly have? To be blackmailed, investigated, mocked, disrespected...What's the point?"

"It's in your head. You're afraid to do what you really want to do."

"I don't know what that is."

"You want to fight," she said, bluntly.

"I don't want a fight."

"I see how disgusted you are by this city and how it operates. You want to fight, but you're too afraid to step forward and ruin perceptions of you."

"How can you believe that?"

"I believe it because it's true. Everyone loves you and they love what you've done, and you can't stand it anymore. You're not upset because you're bending at their will. You're upset because they're not bending at yours. You've always been at their mercy and stood by while this city deteriorated around you. Change it," she said, leaning in with passion in her voice.

"What am I supposed to do?"

"Forget whatever dirt they'll find in the past. Don't think about the obstacles, or the people who will step forward to tear your life apart. Just pick a fight."

"This is what you want?" he asked, doubtfully.

"It's what you want. And you're on the right side, and that's why I love you. But you're never going to be satisfied sitting back and watching people who cheated to obtain power. You'll never be content because you deserve it more and you know it. You deserve to be the example. And any rocks they try to overturn, we'll deal with that when it comes."

His eyes meet hers and his whole demeanor became relaxed. "I don't know what I'd do."

"You've never been a small thinker Rock. Don't start now."

Royce smiled as an idea developed.

Bernard wiped a piece of lettuce from his lip as he scanned a newspaper, a mouth filled with food. An associate entered the room. "Bad news Bernie. It won't be as easy as we thought."

"What won't?" he asked. He already knew the answer, and dreaded it…

…You can call it quits." Earl said, watching Rocky struggle with a stack of papers, trying to understand what was in front of him.

"I think it's right," Rocky said.

"You think?"

"I'm pretty sure," Rocky said, trying to project confidence.

"Good. I'll take a look at it in the morning."

Earl began digging through his desk drawer and came up with an envelope. He handed it to Rocky. "Week's pay."

Rocky held it delicately, as if the paper in his hand was fragile. "I'll get better," he said, apologetically. He couldn't help but feel as if he didn't deserve a paycheck.

"It's just a week's pay," Earl said with a chuckle.

"I know, but I've made mistakes."

"You show up every day early, and yes, I can see you struggle, but you're getting it. Your learning curve isn't unusually slow or anything."

"You've helped me a great deal."

"I like you Royce."

"Why me?" he asked. As badly as he wanted the job from the beginning, Rocky had a hard time making sense of his boss's motivation.

"We enter this world with about as much social charm as an ax murderer. We are complete egotists, selfish, greedy, answering to our emotions. Without guidance from others, we would lack the social feeling that is intended to transform us into hard-working, unselfish, public-minded individuals who are willing to sacrifice our own interests for those of others."

"I don't understand."

"Why you? Because you walked through the door at exactly the right time. You were lucky. I take chances on people and believe with the right attitude, anyone can become whatever they want. I only have guidance to give."

"And if I fail?"

"It won't reflect on who I am or my actions. As long as you're not stealing from me, lying to me, and show up and make an effort, you won't fail."

Royce stood against the wall of the alley, watching his friends eat pizza and sip beers. He didn't participate. He was on a streak, due to his ability to avoid temptation.

"Get in on this Rocky," Judd said, his mouth filled with food.

"Earl brought lunch," Rocky said. "I'm good."

"Hey, you think that guy could find work for me too?" one of the others said, taking a step forward.

"You'd have to ask," Rocky said, hoping he wouldn't. What he wanted to say was 'find your own guy'. Rocky hoped they'd find ambition, except not to piggyback off of him and sabotage a good thing.

"Rocky got a check today," Judd interjected.

Everyone stopped. "Don't you need a bank account?" someone asked.

"I think I still have one," Royce said. "Haven't used it in years."

"Go to one of them places that cashes it for you. They charge a fee, but it's the best way to get your cash."

"I'm planning on hanging onto it," Royce said. "Throw it in an account and let it earn interest."

Silence spread through the group and glances were exchanged. Finally, Judd stepped forward. "What are you trying to do?"

"Rebuild my life."

"You know the cheapest apartments in the city are at least six hundred a month, plus a down payment?"

"We lost everything once, but we can start from nothing and get it back. We don't have to live here if we don't want to."

"I applied for everything," Judd said. "They make you wait until some construction crew comes along and they pick a few guys out of about fifty. You get maybe one day working a week, if you're lucky. Anything else, you need computer skills or some kind of degree. I'm not going back to school."

"Then get some skills," Rocky said.

"No time for that."

"All we have is time."

Judd looked up at him, as if he didn't even recognize his friend anymore. "You act like you're better than us Rock."

"I don't want to have more than you. I want us all to have more. There's no secret to it. I convinced someone to take a shot on me."

They were interrupted when officer Lucas rounded the corner, seething, as if he was having a particularly bad day. Before anyone could say anything, the officer's eyes darted to the pizza and beer. "Where did you get that?" he asked.

"We bought it," Judd said.

"Bullshit. Fonzelli's manager said it was taken from the driver's cars."

"That doesn't mean nothing," Judd said. "We didn't take anything."

"Bullshit." He walked to the table they set up and carelessly turned it *on its side. They watched Lucas ruin the rest of their grub and drinks, smashing it into the ground with his shoe and dumping the beer cans. "Theft. Public intox..."*

"Where else we supposed to drink?" a man amongst them asked.

Lucas ignored the question. "Empty your pockets," he commanded.

The group obeyed. A few crumpled dollars and some change fell to the ground and Lucas gathered it.

"How we supposed to buy food if you always take what we got?" Judd asked.

"I don't expect for you to buy food. I expect you to starve and die and empty the streets of your existence. Come on. Empty it all." He approached Judd, who stood in his face, unwilling to comply.

"Rocky has money," Judd said. "He's got a lot."

From his corner, Royce's eyes narrowed as his buddy threw him under the bus.

"Which one's Rocky?" Lucas asked.

Judd pointed. Rocky had been invisible every day before, but now Lucas zoned in on him. "That true?" he asked, walking toward Rocky.

"I wasn't eating the pizza," Rocky said. "Never do. I have a job and I..."

"Let's see it," Lucas said. He didn't care. Royce moved in slow motion, shaking uncontrollably. "Come on. Come on," Lucas said, hurrying him along.

"I earned this," Rocky said, as he pulled the check from his pocket. "Honest work."

"Let me see it," Lucas said.

Royce wanted to comply, but knew what was going to happen. Lucas would make sure Rocky's day ended badly—with nothing in his pocket. Desperate to keep his money, he summoned the courage. "I can't," he said.

"What did you say to me?" Lucas asked.

"No..."

Lucas closed in on Rocky. He grabbed at his arm. Rocky tried to push him away, but Lucas managed to pin him to the wall and grabbed the check from his hand. A struggle ensued, but Rocky was overpowered easily. Lucas was enraged at Rocky's lack of compliance. He grabbed him by the neck and threw him to the gravel.

He held the check high, beyond Rocky's reach. Rocky stood and watched, praying he'd give it back. Then, Lucas ripped it to shreds. Before Rocky could hold himself back, he attempted to lash out, but Lucas grabbed his face and pushed him to the ground, slamming it repeatedly on the pavement.

Finally, Lucas stood and stared down at him with disdain before limping away. Judd and the others watched in horror, regretful for giving Lucas incentive to target the most innocent of all.

Rocky struggled to stand, wincing in pain with every movement.

"Rock..." Judd said. "I didn't know he'd be like that."

Rocky didn't respond. Instead, he walked away from his friends. They watched with blank expressions; no one was willing to say a word. He walked to a gated block and set a cushion in the corner, hidden by tall grass and weeds. He slowly laid down, grunting in pain. He faced the city skyline, deep in thought, no longer part of the group...

...A crowd of onlookers stood by a stage, where Rocky had a microphone set up and a small staff surrounding him. He spoke with passion, working the crowd. Bernard stood with arms crossed, displeased by the sight. Posters announced the candidacy of Royce. If it had been anyone else, Bernard would have laughed it off, but Morrow was ambitious, and out for blood. He would pose a real threat.

Royce spoke with passion. "...There's a sense of purpose I feel to do something heroic, legendary, and trans-formative; to elevate your spirits and give you courage. History is littered with big moments that turned on the pettiness of small men, but if I can go through the door of pain to embrace life on the other side, you can too!"

The crowd applauded and Royce threw his hands in the air. Bernard watched, seething inside.

Later, as Rocky shook hands and greeted the crowd, Bernard approached and took his turn. Photographers rushed to take pictures, but Bernard led him aside discreetly. "I heard you were running," Bernard said. "Congratulations. I lacked a worthy opponent until now."

"You had no opponent until now. Now you're in over your head."

"We're slinging mud I take it? That's not really the Morrow way."

"The media will make it what they want. Stone Enterprises will be exposed to a lot of questions and you'll be the one who will have to answer."

"If you're going to become a combatant, you're going to be scrutinized too."

"I know."

"People like your story Royce. You're an inspiration...from rags to riches. It's the story everyone wishes was their own. That admiration has taken you far. No one's ever tried to dig up the dirt on you. I'm not naïve, and frankly, I've never cared how you made your fortune, but I also wonder what you really look like under the microscope."

"Go at it then Bell," Royce said.

"I plan on. Unless, of course, you drop this thing now. You and I can

find common ground on the condos and work together on any other issues
you're concerned about."

"I'm not interested."

Bernard nodded. "Have it your way. Don't ask me for any favors
later."

"Right back at ya."

"Whatever beef you have with me, you can handle it like an adult."

"You know what always bothered me?" Rocky asked.

"What's that?"

"You and I...we have the same job, the same status in life...hell, we
could be the same person. The difference between us is invisible, but it still
eats at me. Stone Enterprises, unlike Morrow Bank and Trust, was founded
on corruption."

"I didn't build it and it's not mine."

"No, but Jason's gone, which I wouldn't be shocked to find out you
had influence over, and from what I know about Victor, I have a hard time
believing his will was entirely his idea."

"You're overstepping."

"No Bernard, I think you're the man behind the man. I think you've
always been, and I think everything you do is to distract from what Stone
Enterprises really is."

Bernard laughed awkwardly. "And what is that?"

"When I win this election, the first thing I'm going to do is expose the
inner workings and shut you down for good."

Bernard's face grew stern. "You're a reasonable man, and we both
know you're operating on assumptions. You despise me...for more than
this. Yet, you won't say what it is I did to wrong you."

"Start digging," Royce said. "You'll figure it out in time."

"I will, because while everyone turns a blind eye, I'll bury you. Then
we'll see who's in over their head."

The men turned and waved at a swarm of reporters as flashes light up
their faces. Both men shook hands with a smile...

*...In a darkened funeral home, long after it was emptied of mourners,
the only remaining presence was that of the body, and two brothers who
stood looking at their father, laying peacefully. One brother's eyes were
bloodshot, and he hadn't shaken off his rage completely from an earlier
encounter. Sure, he'd used the death of his old man and taken it to an alley
where he let out his hatred on a bunch of fellows that lived there, but the
real cause of his trouble lay in front of him.*

*The other brother finally turned to him and studied his face,
disappointed he'd arrived so long after the wake. "You missed the whole*

thing," Bernard Bell said.

"Relax Bernie. I was working," Lucas replied.

"I guess there's nothing left in this world more important than your job."

"Am I supposed to suddenly care about the old prick just because he's dead? He was an asshole before he died. I could care less."

"He left us everything," Bernard said.

"Us? As in you and me?"

"Yeah, and it turns out he was worth a hell of a lot more than you think."

Lucas turned back to the body, transfixed on his father, and suddenly his troubles disappeared. Bernard and Lucas Bell stood side by side, staring into the face of their father.

"What was he worth?" Lucas asked.

"One hundred and twenty-five million dollars," Bernard said. "Still think Dad's a prick?"

Chapter 14

1

In Studio City, an independent woman named Dina Florentine began a pod-cast that quickly turned into a daytime talk show. Dina was short, but attractive. Her hair was shoulder length and stylish and she carried herself with confidence. Her show was topical—usually something with a victim and an antagonist; Someone the crowd could ooh and aww over and someone they could boo.

On today's show, the victim was played by Heather Harrison, a middle aged woman with a skirt and tight-fitting shirt. She sat quietly while Dina stood nearby with a microphone in hand.

"What kind of things did he do to you?"

"He'd shove books from my hands. He'd call me ugly."

"And you had a crush on him anyway?"

"It was dumb," Heather said, shamefully. "I thought maybe he was doing it because he liked me. Back then, I was a big girl."

The crowd let out a sympathetic "aww" as a picture of Heather in her teens flashed on the screen underneath a caption that read: You made fun of me in High School. Look at me now.

"But look at you now girl!" Dina shouted to the approval of the audience who hooted for her. "And we're gonna show him what he missed out on. Ladies and gentlemen, please welcome to the stage the man who according to Heather, made High School a living hell for all girls: Toby O'Tool!"

The crowd stood and booed—even threw things—as Toby ran onto stage with a large smile displayed on his face. He wore a sport jacket and styled his hair for the occasion. Even with the long sustained "boo," the smile never left his face. He nodded at Heather without recognition and took a seat. After everything quieted, he turned to Heather again and blatantly checked her out.

"Do you know why you're really here today Toby?" Dina asked,

approaching him.

"*I was told someone had a crush on me.*"

"*That's true, but that's not why you're here. You're here because Heather said in High School, you tormented her.*"

Toby registered the revelation in an instant, and as his mind spun, no one in the audience noticed his brain already engineering an escape. The best con-men didn't have to defend themselves, but when backed into a corner, not only could they easily find their way out, they could redirect the blame.

"*Really? Heather said that? I had no idea.*" *He turned to Heather and feigned sincerity that even she was confused to see.* "*Heather, if you had a problem, you should have talked to me.*"

"*Oh yeah, right. And be made fun of?*"

"*Then you claim you didn't make fun of her?*" *Dina asked, followed by another loud disapproval of Toby's game from the audience. Toby sat forward and directed his words at the audience.*

"*High School was a long time ago. I remember my parents were really pushing me to get good grades and that was stressful because we found out later I had a learning disability.*" *All at once, the crowd fell silent, indecisive as to how to proceed.* "*I knew girls liked me, but I was socially awkward and I could never tell. I had a crush on Heather, but I did all that dumb stuff to get attention. I'd throw things or knock the books from her hands. I just wanted her to notice me.*"

"*I asked you to prom,*" *Heather said, growing irritated that the booing ceased.*

"*No, you didn't. I would've remembered that. I was dying for anyone to ask me. No one did.*"

"*You were at the prom!*" *she snapped.* "*You went with my best friend!*"

The audience watched the display, confused. Toby shook his head insisting she was wrong, though he had been there with her best friend and took her best friend's virginity afterward in a cheap motel. "*You have me confused with someone else. My parents didn't let me go. They made me study instead so I could keep up with the class. All I remember was liking you and wishing I could go with you, but you'd be so mean to me about it. I even cried knowing I was home and you were at prom and I wouldn't be able to see you in your dress.*"

Even Dina's microphone fell to her side. Heather began stammering and speaking nonsense as the tables turned. It was unflattering to everyone watching Heather grow spastic on stage.

"*You're lying! That's what he does!*" *Heather shouted.* "*He lies!*"

Toby started to stand. "*If this is going to get out of control, I'm going to have to go. I grew up in a very violent home and I can't be around hostility."*

The audience let out an aww in his favor.

Heather suddenly stood. She spun toward Toby. "Well, I'm here to say look at me now." Five minutes earlier, the crowd would have roared. Instead, there was silence at the misplaced bragging.

Toby took a look and nodded his approval. "You're very beautiful. I didn't think you could outdo your High School self, but you have. The crowd awed again. Heather fumed.

Toby feigned sadness.

Two hours later, Dina straddled Toby in a hotel suite, riding him wildly, while her hair flipped from side to side. He let out a grunt and she screamed in pleasure before falling to his side and catching her breath. They both faced the ceiling quietly for a long moment before Toby ruined it.

"I always figured you were a dyke."

"I'm a dyke like you lived in a violent home."

"You figured me out, huh?"

"Men are easy to read."

"You're such a man-hater on your show."

"You watch my show?"

"No. because you're a man-hater."

"I don't discriminate," Dina said. "I hate all people."

"I gotta hand it to you: You picked the right profession."

Dina rolled out of bed with a smirk and crossed the room to begin dressing. Toby watched her, admiring her body. She turned back to him.

"You don't know what it's like putting on a front for these people. Half the guests we're supposed to feel sorry for, I actually despise." She began rummaging through Toby's wallet, making no secret of it.

"What the hell are you doing?"

"Looking at your stuff."

"Why?"

"I want to see what kind of stuff you carry around. Do you mind?"

"Mind if I go through your purse?"

In answer, she lobbed her purse at him. He frowned, confused by her, but appreciating her all the same. "You're a catch," he said, admiringly as he began sifting through her purse. "I don't think there's a purse in the world that's contents don't make me want to punch the owner."

Dina held up a punch card, ignoring his statement. "You have a punch card for Hair-Biz?"

"Free haircut if I fill it," he said proudly. She tossed it aside with disgust. "At least you know if you're ever quarantined, you have enough

makeup to last the rest of your life," Toby said.

"What's this?"

He turned to her as she held a business card, turning it from side to side. He squinted his eyes, trying to remember what it was for. "I forgot about that," he said, thinking about the time he played poker with a man named Chuck and conned him out of money. In the process, he'd met Victor Stone and held onto his card as souvenir. He didn't know why he did. He'd neatly tucked it in one of the pockets of his wallet and forgotten it until Dina decided to snoop through his things.

"Victor Stone?"

"Yeah, awhile back I was trying to make a point to this douche-bag I met."

"What kind of point? That you could obtain a card?"

"There was more to it than that. It was a challenge...a con."

"A con thing...On Victor Stone..."

"Something like that."

"I wonder how he's coping without his business card," she said, unimpressed.

"Seriously," he said, digging through her purse and ignoring the jab, "you have three tampons in here. Why three?"

"Why not take him for everything you can?"

"I don't feel like pissing off one of the richest men in the world."

"Isn't there a con saying about how a good con artist is never known?"

"I'm a braggart. I don't use that slogan."

"Then do it and brag."

"The guy's got a shit-ton of money and runs half the city. You want a guy like that knowing your name and despising you, be my guest."

"You know most of his money isn't legit, right?"

"I'm not Robin Hood."

"You said you liked the guy. You don't con people you like? Is that it?"

"That would be a hard theory to prove. I don't like many people. When it comes to whether or not to mess with guys like Stone, it's a question of respect."

"Get something better to brag about."

"I'm not bragging. You're the one who found it. I didn't even remember I had it. It's a memento of a thing I did once. Stone wasn't even my target. I'll get something better," he said, unable to resist the challenge.

"You don't have to actually do it. I'm just teasing you. You don't have to impress me and steal something from your BFF."

"No one's above being conned. There's a creed I live by."
"Yeah?" she asked, curiously. "What's your creed?"
"Five words..."

"...Suckers get what they deserve."

Toby held an icepack to his forehead. The hit stung, and when Toby woke up, he had a hard time remembering where he was and what happened. Pieces slowly came back and he realized a destructive man was on the loose—a man linked to him. He'd trusted others in the past, and always regretted it. It was the people who tried to help that always messed everything up. He dialed Richard's number, but it only rang. He wondered if Sal would really to go after Richard and murder him. Maybe he already had.

He looked up at William. Henry had arrived and stood at his side. "I've got time," Toby said.

"We don't understand why this is such a bad thing," Henry said, slowly.

"Is there some kind of learning curve you can't comprehend?" Toby asked in disbelief. "What have I said repeatedly from day one?"

"Yeah, but Sal is only loosely connected to us," Henry said. "One casualty and the meet with the judge problem is solved."

"He'll cover his tracks," William added.

"He's a hothead," Toby said. "And when he kills Richard, he'll come back here. And then he'll kill another and come back here. And then another. And someday someone will ask who that large tool is who is seen at every crime scene and ask where he hangs out, and guess who will be here. There will be witnesses that see him kill. There will be witnesses that see where he goes. Just because you're not on the cover of People magazine holding hands with the guy, don't assume people can't connect him back to us."

"We could let him do his thing, turn him in, and deny any knowledge of his actions," Henry said. He tried not to sound serious, but he clearly had thought it through. Use a man to do the dirty work and let him take the fall.

"Let's go," Toby said. Neither man moved. "You guys in on this or not?"

Nothing.

"Fine. I'll do it myself and rethink the percentages," Toby said, walking to the door. When he was outside, he dialed Adlar's number. To his surprise, Adlar picked up. There was silence on the other end. "You there Wilcox?"

"Yeah."

"You with that guy?"

"Yeah."

"Richard still alive?"

A pause. "Yeah."

"You heading his way?"

"I think so."

"I'll have the cops on you in five minutes if you don't stop this from happening."

"He can kill him," Adlar said.

"I need you to follow through with my plan. It will work."

"I'd be in that apartment another month," Adlar said. "I hate it there."

"I'm protecting you from Charlie Palmer. He's pissed about what you did. If you're out in the open, you're putting yourself at risk."

Before Adlar could say another word, Sal took over the call, snatching the phone from Adlar's hand. "Got a headache?" Sal asked, laughing with amusement.

"What the hell are you doing Sal? You're going to expose everything."

There was a click, followed by silence. Toby threw his phone with frustration. As long as Sal had control over Adlar, Toby wouldn't be able to get through. He quickly reached for his phone and called Richard, but no one answered. Seconds after, Richard sent a text asking what he wanted. He was at a church function and couldn't talk. This was good news. A church function meant a group of people. Surely, Sal wouldn't do anything stupid in front of a bunch of witnesses. Toby hoped not anyway.

He drove to the church. He spotted Sal's red jeep in the parking lot. He hurried inside to where an anniversary party was hosted by the church. Toby spotted Richard across the room and breathed a sigh of relief. What he couldn't see was Sal or Adlar. He dialed Adlar's number again. This time, Sal picked up.

"How's your head?" he asked, laughing again.

"Will that be the only thing you say to me from here on out?" Toby asked. "Can I talk to the guy with some semblance of intelligence?"

"You see that?" Sal asked. "That's why I'm doing this. You've had nothing nice to say to me since day one."

"We're adults. You shouldn't need ego-boosters."

"You went out of your way to exclude me. You tried to run me off."

"I'm at the church with Richard, and I'm telling him what's happening."

"And you call me dumb."

"Where are you?" Toby asked, feeling in control.

"Meet me outside and we'll talk."

Moments later, Toby cautiously walked through the parking lot. Sal's jeep was still there, but no Sal. He picked up his phone to dial again, but was interrupted by Adlar's voice. "Toby?"

Toby looked up to find Adlar weaving toward him, two cars away.

"Where's Sal?" Toby asked.

Then Sal appeared from a row away, his gun held at his side. "You're going to apologize and we're going to work together, or I'm done with you."

"God owes you an apology. Your DNA isn't my fault."

"You're a shitty leader," Sal said.

"I don't want to lead. I just want competent partners. You know why I'm angry?" Toby's frustration poured out. "I'm relatively good at making a point. I can get through to intelligent people. I can get through to your average Joe. I can get through to the elderly, children, men, women, you name it. But you're the one type—the type of person I'm unarmed against. Because my weapon is my mouth, and the very fact that I have to live in the world with a guy like you and share the same oxygen with such a bottom-of-the-barrel, dumb-as-a-rock, clueless, who's who of stupid— there are no words to make you understand—because words don't matter to guys like you. Do you have one redeeming quality? Anything at all? Got some money stashed away or a friend in a position of power? Anything? No, you don't. You're just a hideous paper-weight. And I'm supposed to split billions of dollars with you? You offer nothing I can't get a chimp to do for free. You're a roadblock. There's no way to deal with guys like you. You don't understand a word that I say because you have nothing in your head. And you're on my doorstep. You're my problem and I never asked for you. A guy like me shouldn't have to share my money with a professional footnote."

Sal smiled, but underneath the smile was pain. He walked toward Toby, who found himself with nowhere to run. The man was a giant, barreling down on him quicker than he could escape. He tried to protest, but the butt of Sal's gun come down on his forehead, knocking him to the ground for the second time. The world blurred and darkness overcame.

Sal looked up at Adlar, who cringed at the sight of Toby on the ground. "Forget Richard for now," Sal said. "Let's kill this asshole instead."

2

Trish Reynalds sat across from her daughter in the hospital cafeteria. She helped Shiloh with her homework, trying to focus on her math problems and not on the fact that according to hospital labs, Shiloh's days were numbered. She would continue to become sicker, unless Trish could get her the treatment she needed. They had an appointment with Gregory Neomin that day. He'd called with news—a hint of optimism in his voice. Now, he was with a patient and they were stuck waiting. She wished she could get more information—anything to get her mind off recent events. Carlos's funeral was today, and she was stuck here. It seemed like a good escape. Being there could open the floodgates of guilt she felt—guilt for not being with her partner. But she was with Shiloh, where she was supposed to be. She tried considering all the ways his death could have been prevented, and it came down to one simple fact: Carlos shouldn't have been at Gelatin Steel. He shouldn't have been helping them. He shouldn't have been involved in their personal problems.

Victor Stone killed Carlos.

As did whoever wired the building to explode. Victor couldn't pay, but someone could. Except she was here, where she should be, and there was no time in the foreseeable future that she could pursue that case. She wanted to work badly, if only as a distraction. After Shiloh's appointment, she'd be back to school. Trish considered going to work, but couldn't deal with everyone looking at her with pity—or blaming her for what happened to Carlos.

A familiar movement caught her eye and she looked up and noticed Charlie Palmer entering the cafeteria, dragging his feet. She was surprised to see him, but more surprised to see him in the state he was in. He looked tired. He looked like he was unaware of the world around him, completely inside himself. She wondered how he could even function. "I'll be back sweetie," she said. "I'm going to say hi to someone." Trish crossed the room and approached Charlie, who finished paying a cashier for his lunch before looking up and catching sight of Trish. He didn't smile or say anything. He didn't even react.

"Back to work?" she asked.

"Yesterday."

"Good. It's probably best to keep yourself busy."

"Yeah," he said, expressionless.

"Has anyone spoken to you about..?"

"No. Why?" he asked. "Did something happen?"

"No, I'm nowhere near the case."

"They're not doing shit to find out who did this."

"I doubt that."

"There's no evidence. No motive. No witnesses."

"You're their only witness, but you don't remember anything."

Her observation silenced him quickly. He walked to the table, seemingly hiding his reaction from her.

"Did you tell them about Adlar?" she asked.

"What's to tell? Couldn't be him."

"Are we pretending like our last conversation didn't happen then?"

"What are you doing here?" he asked, slightly irritated.

"Brought my daughter in. We were having lunch."

Charlie looked past her and spotted Shiloh ignoring her homework. His dull expression changed to concern. "She okay?"

"Flu-bug," she said without hesitation.

"You sure about that?" Charlie didn't believe her. He kept his eye on Shiloh for a moment, taking a second to register the fact that she was lying and to explore what that meant later. "Have you talked to Adlar?" he asked.

"Like I said, I'm not on the case and he's not a suspect unless we have reason to think he is. Like a witness."

"I was going to talk to him myself," Charlie admitted. "He's not around though. Ran away."

"You went to his house?"

"To ask questions."

"Just questions, huh?" she said, letting the doubt through.

"No one's seen him, but there's no missing person report. Kinda strange."

"He's over eighteen. He could have moved. Cops aren't looking for him and have no reason to."

"What if I told you there's no listing for him anywhere and no one knows where to reach him at all?"

"I'd tell you I already knew that."

"Then you've looked for him."

"I keep tabs on everyone."

Charlie sighed and shook his head to himself, tired of the game. "What are we going to do about him?"

"I'm not doing anything. If you find him, I want you to tell me."

"Alright," he said, but it wasn't very convincing.

"Charlie..." He gave her his attention as her tone changed. Trish was serious, and Charlie knew that if he took any initiative in carrying out his own justice, he'd have to answer to Trish. "You find out where Adlar is, I want you to call me. You understand?"

He nodded, expressionless.

"Glad to see you're back to work. It will be good for you." She turned and walked back to Shiloh. Charlie watched her, his cooperative expression fading and bitterness overcoming.

Trish finally met with Dr. Neomin and a woman named Laura Wolf, who wore a jacket and carried a folder. She was all business and carried the meeting while Neomin sat at the edge of the table. Laura opened the folder and pulled the appropriate forms, laying them out for Trish to see. After the introductions and small talk, Laura got the point.

"The reason I took so long is because it took a while just to find what's wrong with your insurance."

Trish listened nervously.

"Your daughter was treated six years ago with the same symptoms on two separate dates. Dr. Neomin wanted to run tests at the time and they were denied."

"That can't be right," Trish said. "Paul would have allowed it. I would remember this."

"Is there a chance he wouldn't have said anything to you?"

Trish thought a long moment, trying to comprehend why Paul wouldn't have said anything.

"He signed off on both visits," Laura said. She pointed to Paul's signature. "It's possible he didn't see a concern."

"Our insurance would have covered this. Why would he refuse?"

"You didn't have insurance at that point in time. I think your husband believed he was acting in your best interests."

"No," Trish said. She got to her feet and began pacing. "His best interest was his daughter."

"I can't speak with any knowledge of that Ms. Reynalds."

"So what does this mean? I don't have the money to treat Shiloh?"

"The treatment she needs will be costly. I would recommend you get this sorted out and in the meantime, keep your daughter on medications that are covered and ask about any trial drugs that have high success rates. I'll see what I can do on my end, but this case will go through a dozen people after me who won't meet your daughter or sympathize for your situation. I feel I should be honest about that. The majority of the time, these things do work out. There's always community support, friends, family." She began gathering her things. "Of course, if you have any questions, day or night, give me a ring."

"Thanks," Trish said. Then, an afterthought. "Does this happen a lot? Why would he do that? If Dr. Neomin saw something..."

"Most of us like to believe our children are okay. I have two boys and I fully expect them to outlive me by many years, but every headache and runny nose is a trip to the hospital. Most parents just don't like to hear that it may be more than the common cold. I'm sure your husband didn't know it would come to this."

After Laura left the room, Dr. Neomin gave her a comforting smile. "We'll keep her on the Temodar for now," he said, "but what I'd really like to discuss is clinical trials."

"No. I'd rather not."

"I think this is something you should at least consider. I can give you all the information you need if you want to look it over."

"What do you think?"

"First things first. It can't make it worse. There has been some success, but it's still a trial, which a lot of physicians would not recommend, but a lot of physicians only deal with medical treatment that's been proved. Of course, without trials, nothing would ever be proved, so that's where we're at."

"What kind of success has there been?"

"It's a drug derived from scorpion venom. It's known as TM601. It combines radioactive iodine with a piece of toxin found in the venom of an Israeli desert scorpion. It binds to receptors found on the surface of the glioma cells but not the healthy ones. It essentially targets the tumor. We often talk about targeted therapy, but this is far more targeted than most of what we see."

She nodded with consideration. "If I do this, if it works, will it actually eliminate the tumor?"

"By itself, the toxin is thought to restrict tumor growth by preventing the proliferation of new blood vessels required by an expanding tumor. More important, it transports a lethal dose of radiation directly to the cancerous cells. The radioactive iodine kills malignant cells but causes little damage to nearby healthy cells. I assume the notion of introducing arachnoid venom into Shiloh's brain probably has little appeal."

She laughed as if that was an understatement. "So what do I do? When would it start?"

"One dose once a week for a month to start. At the very least, the tumor will be controlled. Your insurance will cover this too."

"What about the risks?"

"Headaches, vision loss, swelling in the brain, confusion, fatigue..."

She took a deep breath. When she exhaled, she realized how badly she was shaking.

"I'm asking you to think about it. Read the literature I've provided."

"And we're just taking radiation therapy off the table?"

"Maybe, but there's similar risks. This is something you can cover and in theory is as effective—possibly more. Of course, I can't say with certainty."

"And if it doesn't?"

"We try something new. We cross that bridge when it comes."

He gave her a sincere look. She smiled in return, comforted by his assurance. Had she met him at another time and place, she could see herself crushing on him, and maybe when Shiloh was better... She shook

the thought and tried not to think of Neomin when she left the hospital—
the man who was going to heroically save her daughter. He was
compassionate, and handsome, and invested in her daughter's well-being.
More than Paul apparently did.

As she walked to her car, she caught a familiar face in the entry,
smoking a cigarette as he did often. And he was with someone. She
stopped and watched, curiously, as Charlie stood with another woman. She
didn't recognize Mindy, but she recognized the mannerisms of a man and a
woman who were attracted to each other—the elbow touching, the
shoulder brushes...

And then they kissed.

This is too quick. Abby Palmer just...

And they kissed again.

They broke apart and Charlie tossed his cigarette and went back
inside. Trish stood for a long time contemplating what could have
happened between the time Abby died and now—just how much Charlie
moved on.

Or maybe this was in motion before she died.

Charlie had a girlfriend.

How convenient.

3

Toby struggled to open his eyes. The spot on his head where he'd been
hit twice in the last six hours was throbbing. Worse, he couldn't move. As
the world came into focus, he realized his arms were fastened securely in
place. He blinked until he could focus, realizing he was tucked into a ball
with his arms bound to his feet. He tugged, but couldn't move. He was
stored in the back of the jeep, the world passing by as it cruised along a
windy road filled with trees as far as he could see. Sal was at the wheel,
and to his surprise, Adlar sat in the passenger seat, enjoying himself. Sal
caught Toby's eyes in the mirror and smiled upon seeing he was conscious.
He turned to Toby.

"Welcome back! How's your head?"

"Holy shit. Could you stop asking that?" Toby said with irritation.

Adlar turned and found Toby's eyes, but turned away quickly. His
face was filled with guilt, but he'd made his decision. Toby apparently lost
his appeal and Sal filled the void.

"You're with him now?" Toby asked.

"Not really," Adlar said. "He wanted to tie you up. Not me."

"Then untie me."

"I can't," Adlar said after a long pause.

Sal smiled, satisfied to see Toby at a loss. "That's some welt on your forehead," he said, rubbing salt in his wounds. As Sal said it, Toby winced, realizing he had a second gash on his forehead. "You look like hell."

"Hit me a dozen more times and my face will be as fucked up as yours."

"We won't have time for that," Sal said with a smile.

Toby turned to Adlar, who met his eyes in the mirror. "I don't know what he told you Wilcox, but we had a plan."

Adlar forced himself to confront Toby. "With Sal, it's faster. He said he'll kill everyone and I don't think I can do it again. Plus, you lied to me and said you were dying. He said he's going to kill Richard, which is good, right? Cause then we still have a chance?"

"Obviously, we need to talk but you can't let him kill me. We were pals Wilcox."

"He tried it your way," Sal cut in. "He doesn't want to do all the work for you. Wilcox is hiding cause of you. Can't even go out without permission and you're living it up. How's that fair to him?"

The jeep pulled to the side of the road and swerved onto a dirt path. Toby watched, dreadfully, as they approached a bridge crossing a river. The jeep came to a stop and Sal turned with a wide smile. "End of the road for you Toby."

Sal climbed out of the jeep and Adlar followed. Toby watched Adlar closely, his mind working quickly. Adlar looked skeptical. If he was going to talk him down, he needed to think fast...

"...Can I borrow some detergent? "Toby asked.

Daisy Carlson looked up at the only other man in the laundromat and smiled. "Sure," she said. Daisy was cute, with full lips, wide eyes, blond streaks in her hair and a toxic giggle.

Toby opened the washer next to her and loaded his clothes before pouring far too much into the washer.

"Whoa," she said, grabbing the detergent. "Have you even done laundry?"

"Why do you ask?"

"Here..." Daisy held the cap up and showed Toby the concept of measuring. After he nodded, she scooped what she could from his machine using the cap. Their bodies touched lightly as she worked. He didn't bother to move. It was all part of the game. From the moment he learned who Daisy was and where she worked until now, everything was running smoothly. He'd profiled her perfectly, and if the con went right, there would be perks.

"You must have a soapy smell in your clothes all the time," she said

with a giggle and shake of disbelief.

"Actually, I've just started doing my own laundry. I'm learning. Glad you were here."

"Really? Why?"

"Mom did it the first half of my life. My ex took over until a week ago."

"Oh no," Daisy said, sympathetically.

"She's doing some other guy's laundry now."

"Wow," she said, covering a bra out of her basket and tossing it in the washer as if she was shy about Toby seeing her underwear.

"That's funny," Toby said with a nod toward her bra.

"What's that?"

"I've always thought it was interesting how different societal expectations on what is and isn't acceptable to wear in public affects whether someone feels fine wearing certain clothes, but embarrassed if they're in essentially the same amount of clothing for a different use."

"Okay..." she said slowly.

"You covered your bra. Most women don't feel embarrassed to be seen in a bikini, but they're all screams and pepper-spray when I spring from their closet while they're in bra and panties."

Daisy burst into laughter and blushed. "I don't even know what to say to that."

"I'm Dick," Toby said, extending his hand.

"Daisy."

They shook and fell silent, their eyes meeting. She flashed what Toby called 'sexy eyes' at him, and he knew he was in.

"I need to coordinate laundry time with you," he said.

"Yeah? How come?"

"Cause you know what you're doing."

"You'll learn. It's easy."

"What do you do while it's drying?"

"I brought a book."

"I'll take you to lunch instead. My treat."

Five minutes later, they sat in a deli adjoining the laundromat, a clear view of the machines from where they sat. Toby warmed Daisy up, and now she was laughing at everything he said.

"What do you do Dick?" she finally asked, catching her breath.

"I'm a forensics pathologist."

"Really? I love that stuff. I watch all the shows about it."

"Yeah, don't believe that shit."

"Well, I know it's not real."

"Not even close. You know how long it actually takes to get DNA tests *approved? Let alone how long we wait for test results when they are? On TV, it takes minutes. Real life, not so much."*

"It still sounds so interesting," she said. "Have you ever, like, proved someone innocent or anything?"

"All the time, but we frame people all the time too. If we want someone to be guilty, we just switch shit around. Do it all the time."

She was so interested, she didn't realize what he said. He could tell her he was the first man on the moon and she'd be putty in his hands.

"What do you do?" he asked. He'd set her up long enough. Now, it was time to get to business.

"I work in Stone Enterprises. Nothing big. Just a receptionist. It's in the main offices though, so that's cool."

"Really? So you know the guy?"

"I see him every day. I swear."

"Wow. That's funny actually. Kinda a coincidence."

"What is?"

"I probably shouldn't admit this, but a few days ago I'm with some friends and the topic of weirdest sexual encounter came up. My buddies had a few good ones. I had nothing so I made it up completely. I used that."

"Used what? Where I work?"

"I said his office. Played poker with the guy once and was thinking of him, so I used it. It's all I could think in the moment."

"You actually lied to your friends and said you had sex in his office?"

"I did and they bought it."

"Wow," she said, blushing as she turned away.

"I know. Impossible, right? Dumb-asses bought it though."

"Well..." she said, turning back to him as ideas came to her.

"Well what?"

"Not impossible. I have access. I'm one of very few people who could make it possible. Impossible for most people. Not me."

"I'm not talking about his building or his floor. I'm talking about his office."

"I know."

"Really? His office though? Seems kinda careless..."

"I could go up there anytime I wanted," she said, slightly flirtatious. She sipped through her straw and looked up at him. "I mean, I wouldn't without good reason though."

"I'll be damned. Now if I ever have to explain that lie, I'll have inside information."

"Or it doesn't have to be a lie," she blurted.

"Excuse me?"

"If you did it, it wouldn't be a lie."

"You'll get me access if I find someone?"

"You're not understanding what I'm saying. I said I can make it happen."

"Oh," he said, sitting back and pretending to think. "I just got out of a relationship. If I was doing that behind her back, I'd be no better than her for doing it behind mine."

"She did it first and she wasn't single. You are. You're too nice of a guy, you know that Dick?"

"I get that all the time…"

…He stood at the edge of the bridge, a drop from his demise. Sal and Adlar stood facing him. Adlar had the gun and Sal stood by for support. Toby wasn't the type to beg for mercy, but if there was ever a time, this was it. "I've got things in place Wilcox."

"He's got a guy sleeping with one and another working with another," Sal said. "That's not a plan."

"Would you shut up? I'm talking to Wilcox. And I've got more going on than you know."

"What about Royce?" Adlar asked. "And the cop?"

"We'll get them too."

"How? Your way might work for some, but not everyone."

"And all the risk is on Adlar," Sal said. "He does it all and takes the fall."

Toby fell quiet. Adlar's mind was made up.

"I'm sick of hiding," Adlar said, with desperation.

"A couple weeks and this thing with Richard goes away," Toby said. "Then you're on your own again."

"He wanted you to pretend to support Richard, but he's supporting him too," Sal said. "He's making you the bad guy and taking care of himself. You do the killing, and what does he do? You have to lie to the preacher, but he's not. You get your hands dirty while he's clean. He did it to me too."

"Adlar…" Toby said, giving him a look of innocence.

Adlar stood frozen, conflicted between opposing voices.

"With Toby dead, we're free to take down the rest. We don't have to worry about the preacher. In a month, we're rich."

Adlar held the gun up at Toby. "Sorry. I can't keep waiting."

Suddenly, something clicked in Toby's head and he sprang into action. Something that sounded like a disappointed parent came out and the right words came to him. He directed his eyes at Adlar and talked to him as if he was stupid. "You're gonna shoot me?"

Adlar hesitated for a moment, and that's when Toby really started talking.

"I'm tied up. Drown me if you wanna get away with it."

"Just shoot him," Sal said, rolling his eyes. "This is ridiculous."

Toby went on. "My car is at the church. I'll be reported missing."

Adlar turned to Sal for rebuttal. "We'll get rid of his car," was all Sal said, but it was weak in comparison to Toby.

"I can't swim with my hands tied," Toby said. "Here's what you need to do..."

To Sal's annoyance, Adlar paid attention.

"I won't struggle so there's no rope-burn. Drown me and after I'm dead, untie my hands. If you're moving my car, you might want to think about taking my car keys now, and while you're at it, delete the history off my cell. You realize I called Richard on the way to the church? You need to think this through. I'm not dying for a cause that makes no sense."

"What the hell are you talking about?" Sal asked.

Toby looked at Sal as if he was an idiot and increased the volume in his voice for effect. "If you're going to kill me, don't be so stupid. Do it right. Wilcox didn't come this far to get amateur advice. If you're going to take him under your wing, try thinking before you talk."

"I think he's right," Adlar said.

"Don't fall for this shit," Sal said.

"What shit?" Toby asked. "It has to be an accident. Go out and kill them all for all I care, but they still have to be orchestrated as accidents. People have seen us together. They'll come right to you. After I'm dead, you get my car and bring it back here. Make sure you bring fishing gear or something that excuses me being on this bridge. You could stage a suicide if you think it through."

"Are you sure people will think it's an accident?" Adlar asked.

"If the douche-bag guiding you stops putting welts on my face, that would help, but if you cover your trail, those can be excused as collateral damage from a bar-fight."

"Just shoot him," Sal said.

"Listen closely Adlar. Hold my head under water for as long as it takes, but you have to move me downstream so I'm not found for a while. If I'm found later, a lot of the physical evidence, like rope fibers are gone. It's likely fish will eat at me and dispose of evidence. Park my car deep in the woods so it's hidden."

"Think about what he's trying to do," Sal said.

"If I'm dying for something, do it in a way that works!" Toby shouted.

"You're dead either way!" Sal shouted back.

"Do it right! The execution of my death is not going to be riddled with stupidity!"

It was an all-out shouting match. Adlar watched, confused. Sal crouched down to his level. "Give me the gun and I'll take care of him."

"His way would work," Adlar said.

"Just give me the gun," Sal said.

Adlar backed away before Sal could grab at the gun. Sal started toward him but Toby distracted him. "If you're gonna work with him, the least you can do is have his back. You can't collect your money if you put Wilcox in jail."

Sal noticed Adlar was conflicted—maybe even swayed completely—and finally submitted. "Fine. Let's drown him."

Sal started toward Toby. He stopped abruptly at the sound of the gun being cocked. He turned to find it pointed at him. "Kid..."

"He's right," Adlar said. "Get away from him."

"We'll go with his plan then."

"No, he's...he knows what to do."

"What about me?" Sal asked.

"No. I don't care. Untie him."

Sal didn't move. Adlar raised his gun to show he was serious. Sal moved dreadfully, untying Toby. When Toby was free, he circled around the large man and joined Adlar. Sal glared at them, waiting for whatever came next.

"What should I do now Toby?" Adlar asked.

Toby held his hands out toward Sal. "We'll need your keys."

Sal pulled his keys out. Toby grabbed them. "Jump in the river."

"I can't swim."

"Big surprise. Jump in anyway."

"Why?"

"Cause you're dumb as a rock and ugly as sin."

Adlar laughed. Toby smiled to himself as Sal glared at the two of them celebrating their victory over him. "Go on. Take a dip," Toby said.

Sal sighed. "Alright, I'll help you guys with whatever you ask. No more complaining from me."

Adlar trained his gun on him again, more serious this time.

"Your jeep will be waiting back at the bar," Toby said. "But don't bother to come inside. I can think of a dozen ways to have you back in prison by the end of the day."

"Jump," Adlar said, stepping forward with his gun trained on him.

Sal shook his head and laughed to himself before jumping and falling to the river below. He resurfaced after a moment, staring up at the bridge with hatred. Adlar and Toby ran to the jeep and started it up as Sal shouted threats from the river.

Adlar ignored the shouting, except for one remark that Sal made that had always been on Adlar's mind. "He has to kill you to get the money Adlar! He'll turn against you!"

4

A series of shots rang out. When they stopped, a target riddled with holes rolled toward Charlie. It came to an abrupt stop and he studied it. The shots were off center, but not by much. His aim had improved over the last week, and it pleased him. He was on the edge of being ready.

He signed out for the day and exited the gallery, making his way to his car when he stopped at the sight of a familiar face. When Bernard Bell noticed him, he tried passing nonchalantly, but Charlie stopped and addressed him. "Bernard?" he said, forcing Bernard to stop in his tracks.

"Oh, right," Bernard said, pretending to just remember his face. "Mr. Palmer. It's good to see you. I meant to extend my condolences. I felt horrible about what happened to your wife."

"You're sorry?" Charlie asked with a laugh. "There were letters that Victor sent to her and they showed up at our doorstep and caused friction between us. She told me those letters came from you. Know anything about that?"

"I don't know what that's about," Bernard said.

"Sure you don't."

"She said I gave you the letter?"

"Did you?"

"No. It's a misunderstanding."

"Then make me understand."

"I told her who had the letters, but it wasn't you."

"Who left them for me to find?"

"Toby O'Tool."

Charlie paused momentarily. "Who?"

"One of the beneficiaries. The rude one."

"He asked and you just gave it to him?"

"It wasn't so cut and dry. He had a story. I have nothing to gain from any of this. You know how many people come to me asking for assistance? Most of the time, I can't shut them up. Toby was very persuasive. I don't know what his strategy was, but he wanted to know each of you. Victor had a box of belongings that was meaningless. I meant no harm when I gave it to him. Within the contents of the box were personal letters. I assume your wife's letters were among them."

Charlie tried to take this all in. He couldn't understand why Toby would have any interest in driving a wedge between them.

"You don't think he was the one who broke into your home, do you?" Bernard asked.

"No."

"Do the police have leads?"

"No."

Charlie wasn't very convincing. Bernard nodded anyway. "I just wanted to say I was sorry," he said.

"Why us?" Charlie asked, out of the blue.

"Excuse me?"

"Someone went out of their way to ruin our relationship. Then they break into our home. Why ruin it first? Why not just do what they did? The last time I talked to Abby, we were fighting. It was over this. Why ruin our marriage first?"

"From what I know, you're not the only one that's had their life affected by this, but in answer to your question, it sounds to me like you're dealing with two different people. Toby seems to be a manipulator, but this other person is the one to worry about. They're not likely one and the same, but they could be working together."

While Charlie confronted Bernard in the parking lot, Trish managed to follow Mindy from the hospital and confront her outside her hotel. Mindy was busy, but they exchanged information when Trish asked her for help with an ongoing investigation. They met later at the Grove and Trish bought her an ice cream while they took a walk and Trish told her what was happening with the investigation and Charlie's role in it. Mindy was stubbornly vague to protect Charlie, but her curiosity outweighed her loyalty.

"Is he a suspect?" she asked.

"No, I'm just filling in some blanks."

"I didn't know he was married at first. He came clean eventually, but he was unhappy with her."

"And you didn't care?"

"Hey, I'm not married. Being the other woman isn't a crime."

"Was the fling between you and Charlie becoming serious?"

"I know where this is going," Mindy said with a knowing smile.

"Where's it going?"

"I have an alibi."

"You're not a suspect."

"Then what blanks are you trying to fill?"

"I'm trying to figure out if Abby knew you existed."

"I don't think so. He didn't think so. He was discreet until the end."

"You talked on the phone in the middle of the night."

"Yeah."

"When he wasn't working."

"So?"

"I don't understand why Abby wouldn't suspect anything. I'm sure she heard the phone in the night."

"Charlie and Abby weren't getting along," Mindy said. "He told me it was okay to call and I did ask him if she'd mind."

"What did he say?"

"He said not to worry. He was sleeping on the couch downstairs. He told me if that changed, he'd text me, but he never did."

It hit Trish hard. Her mind began spinning. *Sleeping on the couch.* All kinds of theories began formulating, but nothing pieced together yet.

Mindy saw her face was blank. "Did I say something?"

"Charlie wasn't there..." Trish repeated out loud to herself.

"He probably wasn't. I always assumed that's why he wasn't shot. I watch the news, but you know how they never tell you all the details so they don't give the killer anything to work with? I assumed it wasn't important. So what's that mean? That Charlie had something to do with this?" Mindy suddenly seemed very concerned about who the man she'd been sleeping with really was.

"I don't know," Trish said. "You've been a big help though."

5

Adlar stood at his fridge and drank from a gallon of milk, chugging straight from the bottle. The fridge was filled with milk and few other necessities. Toby stared at the rows of milk, baffled. "You're a little milk-happy, don't you think?"

"It's not just for me," he said. "There's a cat that comes to the window."

"I definitely gotta get you out of here."

"I think we pissed Sal off," Adlar said.

"I'll take care of it."

Adlar nodded. "Sorry I pointed a gun at you."

"Happens all the time," Toby said. "I should go."

"You're not really dying, are you?" Adlar asked.

Toby stared at him a moment, calculating the harm the truth would cause. Adlar seemed hurt, but not angry. "No, I'm not."

"Then what's the deal? Were you going to end up...you know..."

"Killing you?"

Adlar nodded.

"I never planned on killing you, but I knew you'd die before me."

"Why did you use me then?"

"Because you're the only one I could convince."

"You really did use me then, huh?"

"That how you see it?"

"Well..."

"I brought something out of you. It was already there. Where the hell was your life headed Wilcox? Level two-hundred of Dragon Warriors?"

"There's no game called that."

"You have shitty parents. You were dating a shitty girl. No job. No money. I brought out potential. It might have been self-serving, but you can't say I didn't just hurry along what was going to happen anyway. I gave you a shot at it, and you still have a shot. You're a contender now and you have a better view of the field than I ever intended for you to have."

"You could have done it."

"No, I couldn't. It's not my niche. You're a rat and I'm a weasel. No one likes either of us, but for different reasons."

"Then why shouldn't I kill you?"

"Because it's still you and I against everyone else. We have different methods, but we're getting the job done together. The way I see it, we have an unspoken truce. You do your thing and I'll cover your tracks. I'll do my thing. When we're the only two remaining, the truce ends and whoever wants it more will take it. I have no advantage over you. All you have to do is kill a man who could never pull a trigger. You already know my game. Richard could end this if not for me. You need me, Wilcox, and I need you. At least until we're all that's left."

Adlar nodded.

"I should go," Toby said.

"Can I ask one more question?"

Toby sighed, already exhausted from the day. "Yeah, what?"

"Don't lie though. Just please tell the truth about this."

"Yeah, yeah, what?"

"Why not just kill Richard? Why'd you stop Sal? Why wouldn't that work?"

Toby smiled ironically, surprised Adlar had the stones to ask the question that seemed to be on everyone's mind, and Toby hadn't given anyone an honest answer, until now. "I don't know what you first did when Abby died. Probably ran your ass off. You know what I did? Popped the cork on a bottle of champagne to celebrate. And she was a cool cat. Nice ass too. Usually I have to resort to the dark side of people to get what I want. I used to think no person was beyond a dose of blackmail if you can bring their skeletons to light—find those inner demons and exploit em...works every time. Most people are pretty easy like that. Richard...I find nothing. I don't want you to kill him, because he's the only person I've ever met that simply doesn't deserve to die. Not by my hands. If it happens, it happens, but I'll have nothing to do with it."

"But he'll have to."

"Look at us Wilcox. You're a killer and I have thirteen more bottles of champagne ready to go. One is for your life. You and I are a couple of assholes."

Adlar nodded.

"I don't have regrets, but let's face it: if you or I had met Richard earlier in life, maybe we wouldn't be a couple of assholes."

Adlar watched him closely. He was thoughtful—sincere even. He snapped out of it and looked up in all seriousness. "But when this trial is over and shit really hits the fan, whatever happens to him, happens. Suckers get what they deserve..."

...Toby and Daisy exited Victor's office, catching their breath, surrounded by the environment of the seventh floor of Stone Enterprises. Toby turned to her with a blank stare, waiting as she took a sip of wine. She smiled at him, drunkenly. "There ya are. Now you have a weirdest place story."

"I owe you," he said.

"Tell the truth," she said, to his surprise. "Were you just saying all that to pick me up?"

"You're drunk. Lay down." He was surprised she was able to piece it together to that extent, but she was no threat to him in her state.

"I know, right? I only had two glasses of wine."

"It's strong wine."

"You should be drinking..." she started to say before her eyes rolled back and she passed out. Toby took the glass from her hand and set it aside. He crouched down to take a closer look. She was out. He stood and approached Victor's desk, ready to begin his search, but in that moment, his eyes went wide. The elevator across the floor was lit. Someone was coming.

He froze for only a moment before bolting across the room and diving into a stray office.

Toby stared through the smallest opening to see who was still in the building. Bernard Bell and Victor Stone stood side by side in the elevator. Ahead of them was a man carrying a briefcase. Victor gestured in, inviting the man into the building. The three men walked to Victor's office and disappeared inside, barely missing Daisy passed out nearby. Toby had an easy route to the exit, but stayed out of curiosity. Whatever was happening long after business hours intrigued him. He slowly made his way from one cubicle to the next, hugging the walls and staying in the shadows. He made his way to the office for a better position. Finally, he was able to find a sliver of a view but could hear every word clearly. In the office, Bernard opened his suitcase and the last man, Nikola, inspected the contents. Victor poured drinks and distributed them. Bernard leaned into Nikola's suitcase and inspected the contents with satisfaction.

Nikola spoke with a thick accent. "How about a demonstration?"

"No," Victor said. Whatever exchange was taking place, Victor had the least bit of interest. He even seemed troubled by the whole ordeal. Bernard, however, was eager to move forward.

"It's complicated," Nikola said.

"We'll do testing on our end."

"Then if you trust in me, we can handle the cost now."

"That's half," Bernard said. "When we're certain the merchandise is good, we'll set up the rest."

"Half?" Nikola said, taken aback.

"We need to authenticate it with our people."

"How long?"

They all stopped at a clatter coming from the lobby. All men halted mid-conversation as Toby ducked into the shadows. Victor, Bernard, and Nikola entered the lobby and followed the sound until they came across Daisy.

Victor gave Nikola an assuring look as he crouched down and shook her awake. She didn't move. She was out. "Relax," Victor said. "She's my secretary."

"Why is she here?"

"Yeah..." Bernard said, wondering the same.

Victor looked up. "I don't know." Then an idea came to him, and suddenly he stood and scanned the room, seemingly searching for signs of life. The others followed his lead. Victor turned to Bernard. "Put her in a cab. Take her clearance card. When she wakes up, tell her to find a new job."

"What do you think she's doing here?" Bernard asked.

Victor shook his head, equally confused. Bernard scooped Daisy in his arms and headed for the elevator. In a moment, he was gone.

Victor turned to face Nikola. "You have nothing to worry about. She's harmless. Seems she just had a few drinks. There's no way she could have known about this meeting." As he spoke, they reentered the office together. "She's just a receptionist who no longer has a job. I'll make sure our video is reviewed first thing."

Nikola was still uneasy.

"Let's just get this done."

"*Your partner took my briefcase,*" *Nikola said.*

"*No, he didn't,*" *Victor said, remembering Bernard's hands were full with Daisy. But then he looked and saw it too: No briefcase. The table was bare. Victor turned to the lobby and his mind wandered.*

"*Where is it?*" *Nikolas asked, raising his voice.*

Victor stepped back into the lobby and scanned the room again. There was no sign of life. He quickly shut the building down and called Bernard to warn him to look out for anyone coming out of the building. All his efforts failed though. Toby was long gone.

The next morning, Daisy sat on her couch, a box of Kleenex displayed in front of her and tears streaming from her eyes. Across from her, sitting on her coffee-table, was Victor and Bernard.

Daisy begged for mercy. "*I don't know anything else. I swear!*"

"*Daisy,*" *Bernard said,* "*your mistake has caused a shit-storm.*"

"*It wasn't my fault!*"

"*It is your fault,*" *Bernard said, his voice rising.* "*You brought a thief into the building.*"

"*He drugged me. I didn't know.*"

"*If we don't get that briefcase, there's gonna be hell to pay and it's gonna come back on you.*"

"*I know! I'm sorry!*" *Daisy yelled, squealing uncontrollably.*

Before Bernard could say anything else, Victor turned to him. "*We're done.*"

Moments later, they walked through the hallway toward the exit.

"*No one knew about that meeting,*" *Victor said, puzzled.*

"*I know.*"

"*Nobody knew anything was taking place at all.*"

"*It was a freak accident. A coincidence.*"

"*Guy talks a girl into helping him break in, drugs her, and takes the case? He was there for something.*"

Bernard banged his fist against the wall in a spurt of frustration. "*You think this guy's a professional? Someone who wants to take us down?*"

"*I don't know, but if he knows what he has, we'll be hearing from him.*"

Toby stared at a busty bartender's chest, an almost empty drink in front of his face. She threw a towel at him, to snap him out of it. "*Think you could be less subtle?*" *she asked with an eye roll.*

"*You're wearing a size too small and no bra. I didn't think I was supposed to be subtle.*"

"*Go away Toby. I'm busy.*" *She shook her head and muttered something under her breath. Toby finished his drink and wandered the bar once before growing bored of the scenery.*

 He left the bar and headed to his car. He hopped in the driver seat and put the key in the ignition. He stopped and turned to the passenger seat where the suitcase sat unopened. He pulled it toward him and struggled with the lock, unable to crack it open. He exited the car and popped the trunk, grabbed a crowbar and found his place in the car again. He'd tried gently opening it since the night before, to no avail. Now, he was ready to damage it. He carefully wedged the crowbar through the handle and began prying little by little. After some work, it shifted and the handle broke off. He opened the case and observed the contents, unimpressed initially. Then, he realized what exactly he was looking at.

 His eyes went wide as he scanned the contents. "Holy shit..."

...He walked down the street away from Adlar's building and started his car. Before he drove off, he looked up to the window where Adlar resided. Sure enough, a kitten walked along the ledge. He shook his head, thinking of the milk again and how pathetic Adlar was. He reflected on the day and allowed himself to forget his negative feelings. Adlar had saved him, and getting the best of Sal was fun. The important thing was that he was free to roadblock Richard once again, and when that was done, he'd pick up his game. Sal was right about one thing: He really only did have Henry screwing Maria and William working alongside Brian. Beyond that, not much progress with his chosen ones. But no good conman was without a trick up their sleeve, and Toby had a big one that he'd kept to himself.

 Adlar knew his game, but he wouldn't be a threat. Neither would Sal. Only Richard. Richard and his damn quest to end the game.

 He started his car and drove down the street, passing another car as he headed away. The car followed Toby there and parked long enough to pay attention to where Toby entered and exited. There was no doubt in Charlie Palmer's mind that he'd finally tracked Adlar down. He watched as Adlar leaned out a window with a saucer of milk, confirming the belief. His eyes narrowed and he let out a long overdue sigh of relief.

 He'd finally found the guy who shot his wife.

Chapter 15

1

Charlie awoke to the sound of birds chirping.

Later that night, when he'd reflect on how he'd killed Adlar, that's how he'd remember the start of the day. He'd slowly opened his eyes and let the world come into focus. His legs were outstretched on a rooftop. The smell of tar stung in his nostrils as the sun beat down on him. At his side was a rifle, purchased for the occasion. He sat up quickly and looked around, relieved to realize his sleep had been interrupted. He assumed the roof wasn't used often, but he'd hate to be found there with a gun.

He slowly crawled to the ledge and looked out at the apartment complex across the way. The window to Adlar's pad was covered with blinds. There was no movement inside. Still hazy from a hard night's sleep, he decided he couldn't just sit and watch the window all day. On the street, around a corner, a hole-in-the-wall breakfast nook sat. He'd caught a whiff of eggs and sausage the day before and mentally noted it was there.

He climbed down the fire escape after leaving his rifle covered with a tarp. He walked to the diner and entered. It was less than impressive inside and the waitresses were in no hurry to move people in and out. They treated everyone as if they were a burden, but Charlie didn't care. He wasn't in the mood to strike up conversations or have anyone ask him how he was doing every five minutes.

He ordered breakfast and told the waitress to bring him a pot of coffee. She scowled at him as if he said something wrong and waddled away.

At that moment, as if he sensed he was there, he turned his head and spotted Adlar Wilcox across the street, just entering the building, a gallon of milk in his hand. Charlie's eyes went wide as he stood so fast, his knees hit the table, causing it to shake with a rattle. The salt shaker toppled and the menu that stood upright fell to its side. Everyone turned, but Charlie didn't notice as he hurried to the door. He ran around the building and back to the fire escape. He climbed to the roof and pulled the rifle from its hiding spot.

At the ledge, he aimed the gun at the window and watched carefully. Seeing Adlar outside somehow made him believe Adlar would go to the window. Then, as if everything was lining itself up for Charlie, the window did open and Adlar peeked out for a moment before leaning out with something in his hand.

Charlie would have shot him then if he hadn't been curious to know what Adlar was up to. Adlar appeared to be talking to someone—or something, coaxing it to him. Charlie diverted his eyes to where Adlar was looking. A few feet from Adlar, the kitten walked along the ledge of Adlar's building toward Adlar. Adlar had found a friend—a way to keep busy while he was holed up inside. Mystery solved. He took aim again and closed his eye.

As he readied to fire, Adlar disappeared inside.

Charlie's eyes snapped open as he withheld an outburst. The opportunity passed. He fell to a sitting position, his back resting against the wall, rifle in hand. He waited.

In the sky, clouds rolled in fast and the wind began to pick up. Charlie squinted at the sky with the realization of what was coming. His mind began to spin. The venture had been difficult from the beginning and every moment he sat on the roof, he was closer to failure. He hadn't been aggressive enough.

Another light, presumably the bathroom light, went on. He stood and covered the rifle with the tarp, walked to the stairwell, and made his way down to the ground. He walked across the street, keeping his eyes on the light, which remained on.

He entered the apartment complex and looked up the stairs. The building was run-down and had a rusty smell in the hallway. Loud music vibrated from behind doors and the stench of pot drifted in the air. He climbed the stairs and made his way to the apartment he was searching for. From outside, he could hear the sound of the shower running. He reached for the knob and twisted. To his surprise, it was open. He walked inside...

...A car sped along a windy gravel road, kicking up a cloud of dust in its path. Inside the car, Abby Paterson turned to the man she'd fallen in love with. Charlie wiped a bead of sweat from his brow, distracting him just long enough to realize the car ahead of him was coming to an abrupt stop. He hit the brakes hard, preventing a fender bender. He let out a breath of relief, mixed with disgust.

"I guess when you're in Florida, you don't have to drive the speed limit."

Abby rolled her eyes. Charlie noticed.

"What?"

"You say the same thing in California."

"This is a new level of bad driving. These people are morons. There's no traffic. At least go the speed limit."

"She was going the speed limit. Any chance you can dial down on the cynicism in front of my parents? My dad especially won't like it."

"You basically don't want me to be myself then?"

"When did I say you couldn't be yourself?"

"When you started coaching me on how to act."

"I'm just saying be positive. It's a good way to be that way anyway."

"What will they say about med school?"

"Oh Charlie. They won't care."

"They'll look at me and see a failure who can't support you."

"Just tell them you're doing another year of rounds."

"They'll assume I'll fail again."

"You didn't fail. They're impressed you're trying. They know it's hard."

"I was supposed to be a doctor by now."

"So what? It doesn't mean anything. You're so much younger than everyone in your class."

"I still prefer we don't mention it. How about we compromise? I'll act all rosy and sunshine for you if you tell them I passed."

"When they find out you lied, they'll never forgive you, and they would find out eventually. That's not a lie you can carry too far."

Charlie nodded. He turned onto another road, which branched off from the main road. "Finally, we're not behind those morons."

"I wouldn't make fun of Floridans either."

"That's gonna be tough."

"They love it here and they love the people."

"What happens if they don't like me?"

"It won't change how I feel."

"I'm not trying to be cynical. I have a migraine."

"Another?"

"Same as yesterday. Hasn't really gone away."

"You need to see someone. This is happening way too often."

"They're just lapses from when I was young. It can't be fixed."

"I'm worried about you."

"Don't be. You know, it's not a big deal for me to be myself, but when my head starts pounding, it's hard to focus and every little thing that bugs me a little, bugs me a lot. I had a hard time focusing as an intern."

"I have aspirin in my purse."

"I'll be fine."

"Everything will be fine. Two days. That's it. They'll love you. Just be yourself."

"Myself without the lapses."

Abby frowned to herself, wondering what the comment meant. It was as if Charlie was Charlie ninety nine per-cent of the time, but there were moments—moments Abby witnessed—that something else controlled him. It was his migraines—migraines so powerful that Charlie couldn't be himself. He couldn't think about anything but the pain.

She turned to him. His eyes were fixated on the road ahead. Out of nowhere, he momentarily winced in pain. He recovered quickly with a few blinks...

...Charlie crept through the apartment, taking a look around the room at Adlar's living quarters. He contemplated where to sit—how to confront Adlar. He wished he had his gun. It would be easy to enter the bathroom and blow Adlar's brains on the wall.

A ding came from behind. He jumped, but caught his breath when he realized it was from Adlar's laptop, which sat open on a desk. He walked to it and crouched down, taking a look at whatever Adlar did to pass the time. A fantasy game was displayed on the screen, along with chat windows. He stared at them closely, reading the moniker Adlar used. "Archangel," he said to himself.

He minimized the windows and searched his computer, scanning the contents to get an idea of what Adlar was all about. Nothing there was noteworthy. He opened the pictures file. They were mostly pictures of Adlar with his parents. He stopped on one which centered Adlar as a child, seemingly innocent and happy. He sat with his parents, who smiled down on him with love. If those days really existed as the picture depicted, they were long lost.

Suddenly, the shower stopped and Charlie looked up, his concentration broken. He put everything back on the screen as it was and stood in front of the desk. He thought again about just how badly he wanted to end Adlar's life. He needed to make a decision quick. He looked at the picture of Adlar with his family again, closing his eyes with frustration.

When Adlar stepped into the room, it was empty.

2

"Do they do anything at all?" Eve asked, standing with Brian Van Dyke in the kitchen and watching out the window as Guy and Sandy sat at the patio furniture, smoking cigarettes silently.

"Nope," Brian said.

"Why don't you tell them we're busy?" she asked.

"Because we're not. And I can handle it."

"You're five orders behind and I've got people waiting."

"I know, and everything is coming."

Eve huffed with frustration, almost walked outside to tell them to get their asses inside, but decided against it and ended up back in the lobby.

Brian got back to work. He tossed two orders up in the time it took for three to be called back. When he finally realized he was in over his head, he was already drenched in sweat and out of breath. In the instant he was about to hurry outside and tell them he was getting slaughtered, the door opened and William entered. Without a word, he began helping Brian.

"I thought you were off today," Brian said.

"I am. I was passing by and saw cars in the parking lot."

"Really?" Brian said, surprised. His co-workers on the clock wouldn't even help and William detected Brian was swamped and hurried in. Suddenly, he liked William that much more.

"Yeah man. You should have called. You're getting killed."

"Yeah, well there's supposed to be three of us here."

With William's help, tickets were pulled at a much quicker pace. Brian pulled a ticket and called out to Eve. She appeared in the window, grabbed a plate, and gave an exaggerated sigh. "About time," she muttered and started to walk away. Brian wanted to say something to cheer her up, but it wouldn't work. At some point in time, their relationship had mutated. There was no more laughter, no more getting to know each other; Eve was uninterested in anything he had to say. At first, he assumed it was just a mood, but it'd been over a week since anything resembling a spark was present.

"Must suck having three waitresses to one cook," William said loudly, causing her to stop in her tracks and turn to him, confused. Eve waited until she had Brian under her thumb to start showing her true colors, but she made a hell of an effort to be liked by everyone else.

"What?" she asked with a confused smile.

"Don't worry about it. Just go collect your tips and wait around for the next customer while Van Dyke sweats his ass off back here."

Eve didn't know what to say. Instead, she stood awestruck and embarrassed to be called out. She knew she was being harsh, but it was Brian's job to call her on it. Except, she knew Brian never would. What she didn't expect was that Brian's co-worker would defend him so strongly. "Geez," she said, acting like it was never a big deal. "Sorry."

"Who's asking for an apology?" William asked. Brian backed away, afraid of the confrontation and hoping it wouldn't reflect on him. Secretly, he was glad Eve was hearing this. "If you're gonna be a bitch to Brian, you might as well go be a bitch to Guy and Sandy too. Your boyfriend's the only one actually working and they're taking a break. You planning on saying anything to them, or you just pushing Van Dyke around because he'll let you?"

Before Eve could muster a response and before Brian could react, Guy and Sandy entered. "Hey," Guy said, noticing William. "What you doing here?"

"Helping Brian cause he's swamped."

"You can go now," Sandy said without love for William. "We're here."

"For now."

"Excuse me?"

"I'll stay. Your next half hour break is in ten minutes."

"We got it," she said, shoving William aside. Eve used the opportunity to sneak away as Sandy stared William down and Guy got to working, watching from a distance.

William didn't stop. "The customers here don't plan their meals around your breaks twice an hour, so I might as well stick around and help Van Dyke, since he's taking all the heat from the waitresses when he can't keep up."

"What's your deal?" Guy asked, stepping forward. "Just go home."

William ignored him and helped Brian with the orders.

"We're allowed smoke breaks," Sandy said.

"Then go take another," William said simply. "We're faster without you guys anyway."

Brian watched as many things happened at once. Eve popped her head in and mouthed a quick "sorry" to him. Then Guy wedged himself into the mix and began working quietly as if the point was taken. There would be no more smoke breaks the rest of the day. Sandy didn't take the jab so well and told them if they didn't need her, she was going home.

The world was suddenly as it should be. There was something about William that Brian liked. It wasn't just the fact that William saw things as they were and said out loud what Brian could only think in his head. William was the guy Brian wanted to be—the guy who knew what to say and when to say it. He was in control. He was above this place. He could probably do anything he wanted. And he liked Brian. He considered him a buddy. It was a familiar feeling, something he'd had with Victor. Something he'd missed for a long time.

He looked up to William, even idolized him.

Most importantly, like Victor before he died, Brian found a guide.

Later, William proved his worth again when their boss rounded up the crew. "I'm very disappointed in you," Bob said. Everyone waited silently to hear why.

They watched Bob pace back and forth, shaking his head at them. Brian and William stood together, their faces completely mismatched. Brian was scared out of his mind, but William stared straight forward, bored and careless. Bob caught one of the waitresses smirking and did his best to sound hardcore. "Is this funny?" Her smile faded. He moved on. "I watched the cameras today. You know what I saw?" The group responded with silence. "I saw Guy reading the paper forty-five minutes followed by a fifteen minute break. In lobby, customers were ignored while Agnus and Melanie sat at the counter talking all day. Nothing was done. This is unacceptable. I expect productivity. I don't want to ever see this much laziness again, or there will be consequences. Do you understand?"

Everyone nodded, except William, who looked up at Bob with an accusatory look. "Who's watching you?"

Bob frowned, confused. Everyone waited in anticipation for what was about to come.

"Excuse me?"

"You said you watched us all day. Who watched you?"

"No one watches me. I'm management."

"That's too bad," William said. "It sounds like you got less done than everyone put together."

Bob fell silent and sneered at him. He looked from person to person, seeing the collective admiration for William and a mutual disdain for Bob. "My job is to keep you in check. If you have any problems with that, you can take that up with me in my office."

William didn't stop. "I don't know. Sounds like you're pretty busy in there."

Everyone tried to turn away, but some snickers escaped. Bob was furious, and directed all his anger toward William. "You've been here two weeks. Don't tell me how to do my job. Everyone's replaceable here. You got that?"

"Fire me then," William said with a shrug.

With no other reaction than to hide his embarrassment, Bob laughed cleverly as if William was ridiculous. From the expressions surrounding him, Bob knew he was the one who looked foolish. "Keep it up," he said, and tried to walk away.

"I intend on," William said.

Bob stopped for a second, but moved on without addressing the remark.

Brian played the moment in his head for the rest of the day, wondering how one person could be so destructive toward authority. Yet, somehow, even when William went face to face with his boss, he kept his job and made Bob look like a fool.

"You need a ride?" William asked as a car pulled up alongside Brian on his way out the door.

"I'm good."

"Where do you live?"

"Don't worry about it. I can take the bus."

"Get in the car," William said, with good-humor, but demanding enough that Brian obeyed. When he was in the car, William lit a cigarette. "Mind if I smoke?" he asked after it was too late.

"I don't mind." William proceeded to smoke in his care-free fashion. Brian watched for a moment. "That was pretty awesome what you said to Bob."

"It was true."

"Everyone always thinks that stuff, but no one says it. I thought he was gonna fire you."

"I wouldn't care if he fired me."

"Then why do you even work here?"

"I just want the paycheck, but places like that are a dime a dozen. You know how Bob said everyone was replaceable? Well, so are jobs, but he needs us more than we need him. If he fires me, I'll have the same kind of job tomorrow, probably with a better boss. Bob, on the other hand, has to advertise, rehire, re-train, only to get employees of the same caliber, sometimes worse."

"True," Brian said.

"It's the job replacement rule. If you have a minimum wage job, you can do pretty much what you want because you hold more value than your boss. If he calls your bluff, find something else. We're invincible dude."

"I still could never do that," Brian said.

"Of course you could. Don't go around picking fights. Just don't let people walk all over you." Brian nodded, but couldn't believe he was capable. "Let's grab a drink," William said.

"Nah, I can't."

"Just a quick one?"

"I would, but Eve would kill me."

William nodded and they sat in silence for a long moment, while William tried to think of a way to reach Brian. "The replacement rule..." he said. Brian turned to him. "Works for girlfriends too."

Brian had to hurry out to meet Eve for a double date with a couple old

friends: Neil and Miranda. Eve pushed Brian to introduce her to his friends
and that's what he came up with. He sat in the corner of a booth, the
awkward quarter of the group. Eve was at his side, with a friendly smile
that didn't fit her face. Miranda and Neil sat across from them, focused on
their conversation with Eve, which has been mostly at Brian's expense. The
red on his face confirmed his discomfort as Eve gave them the dirty details
on Brian.

"He'll seriously just wake up in the middle of the night and go to the
vending machines in the lobby and buy candy."

"I get, like, one thing," Brian said.

"No you don't. I see tons of wrappers in the garbage every day."

"You are getting fatter," Neil said.

Brian tried sucking in his gut as Eve went on. "I'm making him join a
gym."

"I have a gym membership already."

"No point in having one if you don't use it," Eve said. "A waste of
money."

"I used to."

"So you pay monthly for nothing?" Neil asked.

"They make you sign a contract."

"Well, we're gonna get you going again," Eve said.

Miranda stayed silent throughout, watching Brian grow uncomfortable
with the conversation directed at him and his weight. She couldn't take any
more and changed the subject. "When you coming back Bri?"

"Uptown?"

"Yeah."

"I don't know yet."

"What do you mean?" Eve asked.

"I was only supposed to be here one day."

"So you're only here temporarily? You never told me that." Eve
waited for an answer, seemingly offended.

"I already had the chance," he finally said.

"Really?" Neil asked. "When?"

"About a week ago."

"What did you say?"

"I said I'd rather stay. I mean, Eve's here."

Miranda frowned, surprised to hear this and disheartened, but she kept
quiet.

Eve smiled and scooted closer to Brian. "You guys should just see if
you can transfer too. We could always use the help."

"Not in the kitchen," Brian said. "We're fully staffed there." The last
thing Brian wanted was Neil showing up and taking everything from him

there too.

"Not if we get rid of William," Eve said.

"Why would we do that?"

"Who's William?" Neil asked.

"New guy. He's an asshole," Eve said, before Brian could answer.

"I like him," Brian said. "He's gotten Guy to help out more and he got Bob to back off today."

"All he did is tell Guy he's lazy, which is what I've been telling you to say all along."

Miranda looked away, unimpressed by Eve. What made matters worse was her own boyfriend throwing fuel on the fire. "Brian wouldn't do that," Neil said. "He's too nice."

"I'm not too nice."

"He's just too afraid to be honest with people," Eve said.

"Can we talk about something else?" Brian asked.

"Just saying..."

The conversation was diverted, but Brian's mind stayed on William. He was comfortable with him. This setting wasn't where he belonged. He wished he'd taken him up on his invite for a drink, but he'd risk losing Eve and Eve was the first real girlfriend he'd had in a while. He tried remembering everything William said in the car. He wasn't ready yet, but under William's wing, he might be soon.

3

Shiloh Reynalds returned to school. She was to start her drug trial in a week, but she told her mother she was feeling better and insisted on going to school. Trish already took the week off work, and when Shiloh left, she deep-cleaned the house, watched some television, and grew bored. She had the urge to go to the hospital. She'd spent so much time there lately that she felt guilty being away. Any day, there could be new developments and she didn't want to miss anything.

She'd also been distracted by the moments that led up to Abby's death. Charlie told the cops he was side by side with Abby in bed, but it turned out, he probably wasn't in bed at all. He was home...but not in bed. He could have been up late watching TV, or talking to Mindy on the phone, but no matter what the scenario, he lied to the police. Her police officer brain kept attempting to work the details out in her head. There were unanswered questions; answers known by two people: Charlie and Adlar.

She did go to the hospital, but this time, she sat in the parking lot, searching for Charlie's car. It seemed he had the day off work as well, which was surprising, considering he'd just come back. She drove to the Palmer household. No cars sat in the garage. Then, on a whim, she went to the hotel Mindy was staying. There, she found Charlie's car.

Mindy laid next to Charlie, who stared at the ceiling with the covers pulled over his chest. They lay tangled in the sheets, in silence. Mindy turned to him, and saw his blank expression. He was thinking about how close he was to Adlar, and trying to put together why he didn't go through with it. The answer was simple: He was no killer. Not even for revenge.

"So..." Mindy said. "That was a little unexpected."

"What was?"

"You and I. The sex. I don't know if you're moving on with your life or you're channeling your anger in bed."

"I don't need to channel anything."

"After everything you've been through, I'd understand..."

"I'm not."

"Whatever. Yesterday you wouldn't even have lunch with me." She stood and wrapped herself in the blanket and walked to the bathroom. The door closed and the shower turned on. Charlie rolled over in bed and stared blankly at the wall for a moment before his eyes caught Mindy's laptop sitting open at her desk.

He considered a few seconds before sitting and tampering with her chat menu until he figured out how to add a friend. He then added Archangel, not expecting much. He started to sit back and wait, but before he'd even gotten comfortable in his chair, a sign displayed and told him that Archangel accepted his friend request. Charlie leaned forward and slowly started typing. Before he could finish, a message popped up.

Archangel: Who is this?

The reality of what was happening sunk in. Charlie typed slowly, keeping in mind just who it was he was talking to.

GINNY70: My name is Abby.

He hit enter and waited a moment, literally on the edge of his seat. Finally:

Archangel: Cool. Did you find me thru the game?

GINNY70: No. I think I added you by mistake.

Archangel: OK cool.

Charlie contemplated what to say next, but nothing happened. The conversation seemed to be over, but Charlie needed more. Finally...

GINNY70: You wanna chat?

Archangel: Sure.

Charlie watched the screen closely for a moment and began typing...

...He sized up Doug and Layla Patterson, who sat side by side, their eyes fixated on Charlie. Abby sat by his side, waiting for her parents to say something. Their expressions were blank.

Finally, Abby spoke. "Charlie gets to see a lot of really interesting cases when he's doing rounds."

"Does he?" Layla asked.

Charlie nodded, relieved the topic was on work, an area he was comfortable. "Oh yeah. Most days aren't as fast paced as you'd think, but we're always running across interesting cases."

"Like what?" Doug asked. It didn't sound like he was curious. It sounded like he was challenging Charlie.

"Well, about a year ago, a guy came in with a screwdriver through his chest. Him and this other guy had been breaking into someone's car and he was using it to pull out the CD player. What happened is this guy hit the wheel hard climbing in and the airbag went off and the force shoved his hand into his body, where he stabbed himself with the screwdriver. It killed the guy."

Layla reacted in horror as Doug studied Charlie closely and waited for more. Charlie looked up and nodded at them to let them know that was it. That was the story.

"His partner went to jail," Abby said, trying to break the awkward silence. "Something about a law that has to do with committing crimes and if someone dies..." she stumbled with the semantics.

"If two people are committing a crime and one is accidentally killed, the other can be charged with murder," Charlie said.

"Well, I had no idea," Layla said.

"Have you selected a specialty?" Doug asked.

"I've always been fascinated by the dynamics of the human brain."

"Really?" Layla asked.

Doug nodded.

The only person surprised to hear this was Abby, who gave Charlie an odd look. This was news to her.

"What's next?" Doug asked. "More studying?"

"Two years as an intern and a surgical rotation. I'm trying to hold a career while learning the next step."

"He puts in ridiculous hours," Abby said.

"We work long shifts with very little sleep."

"Hopefully now you'll have a break," Doug said.

"Yeah," Charlie said, simply. It was as if Doug knew the truth and was trying to expose it. For some reason, the thought of Abby's father being able to see through him made him uncomfortable.

"Layla, grab Charlie a beer," Doug said. "I had a brother who did

what you do and it's not an easy feat to conquer." Layla began to stand as Doug readied his beer for a toast.

"Actually," Abby said, slowly, unable to let this go further. "Charlie still has a year left as an intern."

Doug turned to Charlie, whose face was frozen. "Yeah, one year left," he said.

Layla and Doug exchanged confused looks. Neither was able to ask the obvious question. Abby cut in instead. "Charlie has to retake the test."

"What happened?" Layla asked.

"It's just hard," Abby said. "Like you said, Dad. He was under a lot of pressure and wasn't feeling well in some of that time, but yeah, he's going to do another rotation and pass it next time."

Charlie looked down, ashamed at being caught in the lie, and angry that Abby exposed it. It was as if she wanted to oust him. He looked up to find Doug sizing him up in a new light, watching him thoughtfully.

Dinner was mostly quiet after that, other than some forced small-talk. Abby and Layla took over dishes and Doug disappeared upstairs, leaving Charlie on his own. He lingered in the kitchen where the women had a handle on things and then to the living room, where he waited. He looked at all the trinkets on their tables and then the pictures on the walls. He stopped on one, presumably Abby's sister. She sat on a horse in shorts that showed off her legs. He raised his eyebrows, impressed.

"That's Abby's sister, Stephanie," Doug said from behind.

Charlie closed his eyes in frustration. The whole night was beginning to feel staged, as if meeting the parents was supposed to be as embarrassing as they made it out to be in screwball comedies. He turned to Doug and tried to play it cool. "Yeah, I thought so. I was looking for the resemblance. I can see it in the face."

Doug nodded as he turned to the couch and sat. Charlie hung back.

"Grab a seat. Make yourself at home."

Charlie obeyed, willing to do whatever Doug asked at this point. They sat on opposite ends of the couch.

"First impressions are hard," Doug said, taking the words out of Charlie's mouth. "It's easy to go to work, go on dates, hang out with friends—all with practice—but meeting the folks is scary every time."

Charlie laughed to himself. "Yeah, it is," he said.

"God help us all if we're the same person all the time as we are when we meet the parents."

"I didn't mean to give the wrong impression. I was going to say something but I was running through my head how you'd react to me failing the test."

"You have nothing to worry about. I get it. In the same position, I

would have the same fear."

Charlie eased up a little at the old man's understanding. *"Good, because..."*

"I don't mind if you try to spare yourself the embarrassment at dinner, or even that you were checking out Abby's sister..."

"That's not..."

"What concerned me was how you told us about the man with the screwdriver."

Charlie eased up. Whatever this was, he could explain it. Only, what was this? *"I don't understand. That really happened."*

"Lack of empathy."

Charlie fell silent, shocked to be hearing this.

"Your job is different because it concerns human life. Doctors deal with life and death. It's a sensitive and very hard time for people."

"That's why I'm working to be a doctor. That's what I want."

"I'm not belittling your chosen profession. I'm questioning your sensitivity."

"I'm sensitive."

"My father was a mortician and his father before him. In those days, it wasn't as clean as it is now. He grew to be more dead inside than anyone I'd ever met. He even admitted to me on my twelfth birthday that when he sees living people, he sees them in a casket. His perception was that we'll all be dead, and if that's where we all end, that's what we all are."

"That doesn't relate to me at all."

"You're new to medicine. You're only an intern and the death of another doesn't strike a chord with you."

"It was just a story."

"You spoke of a man as if he had no name. You shrugged off his death as if it didn't matter. You defaced his life as an antidote."

"No offense Mr. Patterson, but I think you've got me pegged all wrong."

"Maybe I do. I don't know. But Abby obviously loves you and she's just about the most caring person I've ever known. I'm not saying that because she's my daughter."

"I agree with you."

"And if you can't return that..."

"The man I spoke of was a criminal."

Doug shook his head, hopelessly. Charlie was about to say more, but suddenly winced in pain as his head suddenly started throbbing.

"Everyone matters, or nobody matters," Doug said, getting to his feet. *"I have to get some sleep. You need a wake-up call?"*

Charlie was deeply distracted by the pain, but didn't want to make it *known. "Sure," he said. "I can set my phone alarm too. Doesn't matter."*

Doug nodded. His face was impossible to read. Charlie suspected it was deliberate. "Goodnight Charlie."

Charlie managed a wave and a smile, but the moment Doug turned away, he put his hands to his temples...

...**Archangel**: What do you do for fun???

Charlie thought for a moment and typed.

GINNY70: I'm a physical therapist and personal trainer.

Archangel: Cool

Charlie couldn't think of what to type next, but another message came through, saving him from forcing the conversation.

Archangel: You ever hear of Mid-evil Crusade?

GINNY70: No. What is it?

Archangel: A game. Wanna c? I got a link.

GINNY70: Sure.

Archangel: Where you live?

Charlie didn't respond. He wanted to keep teasing Adlar and give him hints as to who he really was without saying too much, or Adlar would disappear forever. A link eventually popped up. On it, a knight resembling Adlar, sat next to the word 'enter'. Charlie shook his head, disgusted by the sight of him.

He clicked on the link and soon was following the avatar as it ran through a village and obliterated other knights who attacked him. He was clearly a polished player as he effortlessly owned the game.

Charlie watched with fascination, growing angry at the sight of Adlar so easily killing man after man, as if it was nothing.

Archangel: Cool huh? That's me. The one with the gold sword. It takes a long time to get gold.

Video game Adlar ran through the village, stabbing one after another, sporadically telling Charlie about the game. Charlie leaned to his side and put his hand on his temple and began rubbing slowly as he zoned in on the screen, fake droplets of blood flying everywhere. He beheaded a jester.

Archangel: LOL!

Charlie winced and pressed his fingers harder, moving in a circular motion.

Suddenly the avatar stopped.

Archangel: Still there?

GINNY70: Yeah

Archangel: Watch this.

The character walked into a civilian hut. Charlie watched closely, his eyes plastered to Adlar, knowing what was coming. The character approached a family of civilians and began stabbing them, despite a warning across the screen that docked him points for failing his mission to protect the innocent bystanders.

He killed them all until all that was left was the woman. Adlar's avatar approached her and paused.

"Don't," Charlie said to himself, invested in a fictional character's life.

And then avatar Adlar stabbed the woman once in the gut.

Archangel: LMAO!!

Charlie closed his eyes.

When the bathroom door opened and Mindy walked out, she stopped and looked throughout the room. "Charlie?"

He was gone.

4

The next morning, at The Wasp, the kitchen brightened and the tone shifted as Brian, William, and Guy worked with perfect rhythm and the operation ran smoothly with the trio manning the kitchen. Life was going well for everyone, though Brian couldn't shake the change in his relationship with Eve. He wasn't sure what he was doing wrong, but she seemed to be upset with him often, and took jabs at everything about him. It was hard dealing with her at his apartment, but he saw her all day at work too, and usually she made him feel dumb in front of the guys.

She pushed through the door at the end of her shift, slinging her purse over her shoulder. "Brian, I need your keys."

"You're off?" he asked, surprised. He'd hoped she'd coordinate her day with his so he wouldn't have to bum a ride. He usually gave his car to her and found his own way home. He'd even taken the bus a few times. It seemed unfair, but he was trying to be a good boyfriend.

"We're slow. I'm leaving early," she said.

"Will you come back for me?"

"My parents are in town. Can you get a ride?"

Brian looked toward the group, who were within hearing range. He pulled Eve aside. "How long they in town?"

"Until tomorrow."

"Should I meet them?"

"Maybe if they're there later."

"Cause I want to."

"As long as you don't start telling jokes."

"What?"

"Those jokes you look up on the Internet and tell. My parents won't find them funny. So please..."

"K."

"And don't say 'K'".

"What?" he asked, flabbergasted.

"It's 'okay,' not 'k'".

"What's wrong with how I say it?"

"You make it sound childish."

Brian turned to see Guy and William eavesdropping. Both were amused, and it was clearly at Brian's expense. He pulled Eve aside quietly. "I can probably get a ride home."

"Good."

"Are you mad at me for some reason?"

"No, I just need you to listen better."

"K, but I wanna meet your parents if you don't mind."

"Fine. Call me when you're off and we'll meet up."

He handed her his keys. She smiled sweetly and kissed him. "Thanks."

She turned to William and Guy and cheerfully waved goodbye. After she was gone, Brian tried to avoid addressing their relationship with them, but he couldn't escape the clutches of Guy. "Everything cool?"

"Yeah."

"K," Guy said.

"K," William repeated.

Later, Brian stood against a counter, watching the door and waiting for William to finish up in the kitchen. He hoped he'd get home in time to meet Eve's parents, but it nagged him that she didn't say something sooner, that she didn't organize a meet and greet. It was as if she didn't want them to meet him. But why would she do that? A waitress finished vacuuming and turned off the last light. Bob rounded a corner and spotted him and trekked over.

"We're locking up."

"That's fine. Will's here."

"Listen, I need you to be more careful with orders or I'm going to have to start having some of that come out of your check."

"What are you talking about?"

"We had six dishes sent back yesterday afternoon."

"Yeah," Brian said. "From the grill."

"But it went through you. You need to check that and speak up if it's not to standard."

"I told Sandy not to send it up."

"You need to watch and make sure she's doing it right."

"She's been here longer than me though. Am I supposed to be training her?"

"Sandy hasn't quite caught onto grill yet, so I need you to oversee her."

Brian laughed to himself and shook his head in disbelief.

"Meat costs too much to be thrown away like that."

William approached, and caught the tail end of the conversation. "Bob, isn't there a chair in your office that needs to be warmed?"

"You're already on thin ice William," Bob warned.

"I've been on thin ice for weeks. Just let me know when I'm fired."

Bob backed away toward his office, repelled by a confrontation with William. "Keep it up Will," he mumbled on his way out.

"I'm going to keep it up Bob," William said back.

Bob hurried faster through the door and William turned to Brian with smile. Brian laughed and looked at William with nothing but admiration.

Moments later, Brian sat in the car with William and dialed Eve's number and listened, but he heard nothing but a ring.

"She answering?" William asked.

"No. She left a message on my phone. She's not even home. She's out. She has the keys to my place, so I can't even get in."

"You wanna stop somewhere and get a drink while you wait?"

"I better not."

"Well, I'll wait with you until she shows up," he offered.

"You don't have to..."

"I got nothing to do. You're not sitting alone outside while your girl has your keys. I'll wait."

Brian nodded, speechless at the gesture. He liked William—a lot.

Outside his apartment, they sat on a cement rail, their feet dangling over the shrubs below. They'd waited an hour, and there was no response from Eve on the status of his car. William stayed by his side like a loyal soldier. Something inside Brian told him that Eve's days were numbered, but William and he were just getting started.

"I hope this is grounds for dumping her," William said.

"We'll see what she says first."

"Man..." William said, with heavy frustration.

"I just wanna hear her side of it. She's probably just out with her parents."

"What the hell is wrong with you Van Dyke?"

"Look," Brian grasped for words. "I actually like what she does for me."

"Bitches at you? Steals your car?"

"She helps me improve," Brian said. "I grew up with a big family, alright? And they were all pretty successful. I was just a delivery guy.

Then, I met this guy who hired me as a driver and he was really successful. I was lost and he'd give me advice and tell me what to do and how to be, and I know that sounds pathetic, because it sounds like I just did what I was told, but he had good advice. He knew what he was doing. I needed a mentor and he did that and when I listened to him, I was happy. I figured stuff out. And I got more."

"Where's this guy now?"

"He died. I couldn't work for him anymore and I no longer had a mentor and now I work at The Wasp. I don't know what to do when I don't have a mentor in my life. But then Eve came along..."

"Eve tells you what to do. Guess what though. She doesn't know what she's doing. She's not a good mentor."

"But she is. Because like, if I say something dumb that annoys people, it's good for me to know."

"Yeah, except half of what she yells at you for is dumb shit, and she shouldn't be correcting you and publicly humiliating you. Everyone agrees with me too. Guy calls you the biggest pussy alive. So how exactly is she making your life easier? You're not some lost imbecile who needs to be told how to breath. People actually DO like you. You don't need to improve. You want a mentor? At least find someone who doesn't have their own best interest in mind. She's using you to make her life easier. She's your girlfriend, but where is she? Out with your car, and she'll come home and sleep in your bad-ass apartment tonight. She's using you. You think you need her? She needs you, because she just got out of rehab and has no money and no belongings, and you have all that, and she knows she can get you to do whatever she says because you're nice. But someday, she'll have money again, and she'll have her own things, and she'll dump you in a heartbeat, because you two aren't a good match and you never will be. The only way you're going to feel good about it is if you beat her to the punch."

"I just need someone to help me figure shit out. I'm not an idiot, but I missed out on a lot."

"I'll help you," William suddenly said, though he wasn't sure if it was because he was playing Toby's game or because he really wanted to help.

"How?"

"I got your back with Guy, Sandy, Bob, Eve... All you need to do is learn to take control. You've been saying you like that about me, right?"

"What do you get out of it?"

"Nothing," he said, as if it were that simple. "We're friends." Brian turned to him, touched. "She's a bitch. You deserve better. I'll get you girls ten times better looking by this time tomorrow night. Girls who appreciate a nice guy."

Brian smiled to himself, as if a weight had been lifted off his shoulder. William was right. Eve had been a bad influence. Victor was more like William: Smart and out for his interests with no ulterior motives. He looked up to find William was handing him something—a small white tablet. William popped one in his own mouth and insisted Brian swallow his. "Start with this," William said. "It'll take away your anxiety. Helps you relax. You'll wake up feeling like a new man."

"Is it…legal?"

"Depends on who you ask. It's not a drug. Just a way to mellow out."

Without giving it any further thought, Brian stuck it on his tongue and rolled it into his mouth, and swallowed. After a moment, he decided it was harmless. Eventually, the effect kicked in, but he'd mellowed too much to notice.

They sat silently, waiting.

5

The sun was setting and the sky was turning gray as clouds formed overhead. Charlie knelt on the rooftop, the moment closing in. A strong determination filled him as the kitchen light across the way turned on. He held the rifle at his side, ready to put closure to his wife's death once and for all. There would be no more second thoughts, no more humanizing a monster. The shadow inside started to move. Charlie raised his weapon and put the head of the shadow in the cross-hair.

He closed one eye and took a breath.

"Charlie!" Trish said from behind. He turned, and froze in place. There was no way to explain this situation other than the truth, but it didn't matter. Nothing would stop him—not even the threat of prison. He could hear everything she did behind him. He knew her gun was trained on his back. "Let it go," she said.

"Go away," Charlie said.

"You know I'm not going anywhere."

"Go take care of your daughter," Charlie said. "You shouldn't be here. She doesn't have the flu. I took a look at her charts."

"This isn't about me."

"You act high and mighty, but I looked at the roster of people that are on the anti-will side and you haven't gotten behind the Reverend. Why is that?"

"I haven't killed anyone."

"I haven't either. I know what happened the night Abby died. You have no right to be angry. You're equally responsible."

"You don't know shit about what happened."

"You weren't even in bed with her. You'd been fighting and you were having an affair. You held her responsible for your name being on the will."

"I never cared about that!"

"I know you loved her, but you had a moment of weakness Charlie."

"Then you know I don't have a choice."

"You'll always know that Adlar's attempt to kill Abby would have failed."

"Would have if what?"

"He didn't kill her. He shot her, but she had time and you know that. It would've been attempted murder for Wilcox. For you, it is murder. If you want justice for Abby's death, you're first in line."

Charlie's gun lowered. A tear streamed down his face.

"If you shoot him, that's two murders you have to answer for. Adlar will be dead. He'll never even know what hit him. And you'll pay for both for the rest of your life. And it won't bring her back, and she wouldn't approve."

His gun lowered, and he began to fall apart as a silhouette through the window opened the fridge and reached for a gallon of milk. Charlie watched closely and his eyes narrowed at the sight of Adlar. He suddenly raised his gun and regained his composure.

"Sorry," he said. He fired a shot.

The shadow disappeared quickly and Charlie was frozen in place. Behind him, Trish's hands lowered and she stared at the apartment window in shock. There was no movement. Nothing.

She thought she saw the bullet hit the window frame, but he could have hit Adlar, or Adlar could have ducked out of the way. A moment later, the mystery was solved as a gun appeared in the window and fired a shot in their direction…

…Doug crouched on the roof with a staple gun in his hand. He worked along the edge with a string of Christmas lights, carefully pulling himself along. Charlie exited the house below and looked up at him and called out. "They're making hot chocolate in there. You want me to bring some out?"

"I'll get some when I'm done," Doug said.

"You want some help?"

Charlie asked to be polite, but hoped Doug would say no. He didn't want one-on-one time with Abby's father and he thought it was mutual, but when her dad took him up on his offer, he ended up on the top of the ladder, trying to find his footing on the roof. It took him five minutes just to get onto the roof, and when he did, he had to work up the courage to keep himself leveraged before helping string the lights. "What can I do?" he asked, when he was comfortable.

"Just hold the lights and give me slack as I need it." He handed Charlie a handful of wires and they worked together, moving faster. "You came a long way from home," Doug said.

"Yeah," Charlie said, confused.

"When Abby said she wanted to bring you here, I was a little surprised. I don't get to meet many of Abby's boyfriends. When she called, we knew this was serious. About a year ago, she called home crying. Don't tell her I'm telling you this please."

"I won't."

"She was lost. She moved out there for a guy and that didn't work out. We kept telling her to come back. The night she called, all she kept saying was that she missed us and she wanted to move back home."

"I didn't know that."

"It was probably shortly before you two met. She was always searching for someone. She's a hell of a bright kid, but she always said she had to have a baby by the time she was thirty. You know how it is. She wanted to be a young mother. You're a nice man Charlie. You seem to have a good head on your shoulder and ambitious goals that you seem to work hard at. At least from what Abby's told me. It seems to me that you could become very successful."

"Thank you."

"But I have to be honest with you: You're not Abby's type. She probably knows it and won't admit it, but you're not."

"That's up to her to decide."

"I agree, but one of two things is happening here and I don't know which: One is I've misjudged you and I'm just a fool stapling Christmas lights to a roof. The other is that you met Abby at a time in her life when she was vulnerable and needed something to cling to."

"I've been with her eight months. I think by now, if I wasn't her type, she'd know."

"I don't know that she would."

"I know Abby."

Doug stopped working and positioned himself to face Charlie. "I'm not gonna sit here and tell you my daughter's too good for you. Every father thinks that by default. I just want you to know that if you're here because you want to ask me for permission to marry Abby, you don't have my blessing. Not now anyway. She's confused. One moment, she's crying and wanting to come home. The next, she's with a guy who was never her type."

"What's her type?"

"Compassionate."

Charlie paused, unsure of what he was talking about. Abby's father had nothing to base that assumption on. "With all due respect, I'm not sure you know me well enough to say..."

Before Charlie could say more, suddenly the gutter snapped and swung away from the house to the ground below, voiding Doug of his footing. Doug's feet dangled off the roof and his eyes went wide in horror. The only thing keeping him from falling two stories was his hands and bottom clutching onto the edge of the roof. "Pull me back!" he shouted.

Charlie scooted as quickly as he could toward him. From below, the door slammed and the women ran out and looked up for the cause of the commotion. Charlie positioned himself behind Doug, ready to pull him back, but suddenly his face went blank and he didn't grab him. He froze.

Doug tried to look back, but didn't have the ability to turn without throwing himself off balance. "Charlie, put your arms around me and haul me up," he said, trying to stay calm. He tried to turn his head, to see what Charlie was doing, but every movement made him slide further to the edge. He steadied himself, but caught a motionless Charlie. "Charlie..." he said, desperately.

Charlie suddenly reached out and interlocked his hands around Doug's chest, just as Doug's arms gave out. Charlie pulled him away from danger. The girls below let out a breath of relief as Doug recovered safely on the roof.

From behind, Charlie swallowed hard, in horror at what he'd almost just allowed to happen.

"Charlie's our hero," Layla said, approaching Charlie and wrapping him up in a hug. Doug stood back with his hands in his pockets, keeping to himself.

"Thank God you were there," Layla said, and Abby agreed with a proud smile. They turned to Doug who returned a quick smile. Layla invited Charlie back again and offered to bring him to Disney World on his next visit. As everyone said their goodbyes, Charlie stood awkwardly near Doug. He extended his hand and Charlie took it. They shook, but it seemed as if Doug was only going through the motions. Doug saw through Charlie, and that scared him, though he wasn't sure what there was to see. "Drive safe," Doug said.

"Will do."

He was relieved to be back on the road, far away from Abby's parents. Abby saw he was distant and pried to know what was on his mind.

"I'm tired."

"You're worried."

"Why would I be worried?"

"I don't know. They loved you. You probably saved my dad's life."

"I get the impression he didn't like me."

"He's hard to read...like you."

Charlie turned to her. Abby's eyes were glued to him, smitten with her mysterious man. He couldn't help but ruin the moment. "Are you only with me because you think you don't have better options?"

"No," she said.

"Then why?"

"Why are you compliment fishing?"

"I want to know why someone like you wants to be with someone like me."

"You're kind, funny, intelligent...compassionate."

Upon hearing he was compassionate, Charlie eased up, satisfied someone saw him in the way he liked to believe he was. He turned back to the road and found himself waiting for a car at a stop-sign.

"Why do you ask?" Abby asked.

He rubbed his temple for a moment, wincing. As if she hadn't said a word, he gestured to the car ahead of him with annoyance. "What's this asshole waiting for? Does he know the difference between red lights and signs?"

Abby closed her mouth for the remainder of the drive...

...A single shot was fired in retaliation before Trish pulled her weapon and fired through the window. She shot once, but it was all she needed. Charlie wasn't a marksman, but Trish had spent a good deal of time at the firing range. A split second after she fired, the window shattered and even from their perch across the street, the window was clearly splashed with blood.

"You're under arrest," she said.

"We need to go over there and see if he's dead."

"You're going to the station for the attempted murder of Adlar Wilcox."

"And what about you?"

"I fired back."

"That's not a police issued weapon. You're not even on duty. And I'll tell you something else: I looked at your daughter's chart. I know about your situation. I know why you're not helping Richard. You want the money."

She held the gun up, pointing it directly between his eyes. "I may need it," she said. She lowered the gun immediately and grew serious. "I told you to let it go Charlie. You better hope he's alive because..."

"Dr. Neomin is okay, but he's not great. I can operate. You won't have to worry about drugs or insurance or any of that bureaucratic shit that's killing Shiloh by preventing her treatment. What she has, I can handle. I have access to everything I need. You can keep pumping her full of snake venom or we walk away now and I help you save her. We help end the will and forget it ever happened."

She fell silent. Charlie had successfully made her an offer worth consideration. "You can do that?" she asked. "You'd lose your license."

"I don't want it anymore. I want to get out of this city. I want to walk away from all this. If I fix your daughter and help Richard, you let me walk away without any problems. Take me in, and I won't help you later."

Sirens sounded in the distance. They turned their heads slightly, and then directed their attention back to each other. Trish's gun was lowered.

"Decide fast," Charlie said.

She dropped her arm completely. As Charlie backed toward the fire escape, Trish turned to the apartment across the street one last time, searching for any movement. All she saw was a broken window and spatters of blood. She heard Charlie making his getaway, immediately regretting her decision from an ethical standpoint. As a mother, no one would have done anything different. To her surprise, she hoped Adlar really was dead.

He only stepped out for five minutes on a routine milk run. He was down to one gallon and his stray kitty demanded a lot of milk. When the apartment door swung open, something felt out of place. There was a draft and the sound of sirens were louder than they should have been in the confinement of the apartment. He didn't know they were coming to him. Then he saw the liquid in the kitchen, which was a mixture of red swirling with white on the floor. Many thoughts occurred to him at once. One was that the sirens were likely coming to whatever caused a man to be lying on his kitchen floor. Another was that the man, a stranger he'd never seen, had some sort of business with Adlar and it was a good thing he'd be out. Adlar left for minutes and had unknowingly escaped his death, but now, his eyes darted from the needle in the man's hand, to the milk container that was nearly all on the floor, to the gun laying near the man's other hand, to the stain of blood coming from the bullet-hole in the man's face—a man that only Royce Morrow would recognize.

Adlar grabbed his belongings and hurried from the apartment, leaving Bedbug's lifeless body behind.

Chapter 16

1

"You're the tuba player," Toby O'Tool told William. "In the brass section."

"Your analogies don't make sense."

"It makes sense," Toby said. William leaned against the wall and waited for an explanation. "I'm the conductor. That's why I'm not in the trenches. Every orchestra has a conductor and a pit. I'm present without an instrument, yet I guide the whole thing. You're in the pit."

"I'm more than that to you."

"You're a tuba player."

"You think if you say things with the right inflection, everyone believes they're true," William said. "You think you're special."

"I can't help it. I tapped into the cosmos and the gods chose to work their celestial magic through me."

"You said when this began, you went to see Wilcox and Van Dyke and you picked Wilcox..."

"Yes."

"Why?"

"He's controllable," Toby said, simply.

"Did you talk to Van Dyke for even a second? He's exactly that."

"We already have a Wilcox."

"Two's better than one. You obviously saw something in Van Dyke to make you visit him in the first place."

"I know you think that now, but watching Van Dyke try to advance in life is like watching a monkey try to fuck a football. He just can't figure it out. Fumble and twist and turn though he might, the end result is always the same, with everyone involved leaving frustrated and ultimately disappointed."

"Why'd you check on him then?"

"I believed his loyalty toward Victor could be a driving force, but we had conflicting viewpoints on what Victor intended."

"Why can't we change him? Adlar's already in deep. Everything points to him. Brian's invisible. He's so invisible that no one expects it. We can help him get away with whatever we want. He looks up to me. He wants someone to tell him what to do and he's been following everything I say. You think you're a conductor? I'm pulling every string on this guy. I can get him to do it."

"I don't think so," Toby said, without giving it any thought.

"I've spent the last two weeks working with him almost every day. He's Wilcox, but better."

"He's worse."

William stared at Toby, at a loss for words.

"He's inward. And you know what? I like inward sometimes. I like people who know when to keep their mouths shut, but he doesn't know when to act."

"He can be pushed."

"I'm sure you've heard of the proverbial ticking time-bomb. The bottling up of anger until one explodes..."

"And that's not Adlar?"

"Absolutely not. Adlar has no idea what a loser he is, but Brian understands his place in life and it frustrates him. Adlar will follow me around like a puppy and follow orders. Brian is the kind of dog that can be tamed, but one day he'll wake up and clamp his jowls on your throat. If you do happen to get him to follow your lead, you won't be able to control him. You'll get that pretty face gnawed off."

"Now I'm a dog trainer?"

"Dog training, tuba player."

"I know him better than you. I'm the one with my feet in the water. I deserve a voice in this."

"Yeah, you're also the one who brought Sal to the group," Toby said.

"He would have been an asset if you hadn't antagonized him. Is that what your problem with me is?"

"He was a mistake and you should have known that."

"What about Henry? He's been great."

"Fifty percent is still a failing grade, and Henry's not that impressive."

"He's done everything you've asked."

"Half of what he talks about is how much he wants to bang the ghost whisperer. Does he even know why he's here? You and him act like you love your fake lives. It's concerning. You're not here to get close to your assignments and become BFFs."

"Hey, we're waiting on you."

"You know my role."

"Yeah, you make judgments, but you don't know people as well as you think."

"Yeah?" Toby said without hesitation. "How's your son?"

William fell silent. He'd made a point to never tell Toby he was a father. He'd known him for over five years and the topic was never brought up, yet Toby said it as if it was obvious. He wondered how long he knew. "Yeah, so what?" William said. "You looked in my wallet. Not shocking you'd do that to a friend."

"Never touched it and I've never seen a shred of evidence other than your face and mannerisms every time the mere mention of children come up—especially boys. I knew from the moment I met you."

"Regardless, we're just killing time for one more week, and since you apparently want us to sit around and do nothing, and since we're not allowed to enjoy it in the meantime, I'm going to go ahead and see if Van Dyke is interested in money."

"Go ahead," Toby said, dismissively. "You'll find out he's nothing to us but an easy kill. I hope you catch on quickly, because the weak-willed people like him and Maria need to be out of the way fast so we can take time on the big dogs. We need to focus on the real challenges. Van Dyke is a test. He's practice. He doesn't scrape the bottom of the barrel. He doesn't even deserve to be mentioned in the same sentence as barrels."

"And if I'm right?" William asked, challenging Toby.

"I'll open my mouth in shock and awe and bring you the finest meat and cheese in all the land, but you're not. Brian Van Dyke is…"

…insignificant, sitting amongst four brothers and his mother. Dylan Van Dyke was the oldest and athletically built. Comparatively, he's far better looking than Brian could ever hope to be. Blake Van Dyke came next. He wore preppy clothes and sat calmly, only chiming into conversations when something intelligent needed to be said. He was smart and successful and Brian didn't say much to him because he never had anything to contribute that Blake didn't already know. Brian was in the middle, and below him was Taylor Van Dyke and Austin Van Dyke. Taylor was artistic. Austin was funny. They each had their very own personality— all of them labeled with their own flattering tag—except Brian. He didn't even have a negative label. There was no label other than…fat? Unintelligent? A follower?

In the middle of the table was a Birthday cake. The boys mother blew out the candles while the brothers cheered and jeered, and eventually gave her a hard time when she left a couple lit.

After the cake was cut, Brian announced he had a gift.

Eyes rolled around the table. Without knowing what Brian bought, the mutual reaction was that it must be pathetic. Brian didn't notice though.

"Alright, alright. Let's get Brian's out of the way," Dylan said.

Brian turned to his mother, ignoring the silent mockery at the table. "You'll like it." He reached to his side and came out with a neatly wrapped package. He handed it to her as she observed the terrible wrap job.

"Did you wrap this?" she asked.

"Yeah."

"It looks good," she said, unconvincingly.

Some of the boys exchanged smiles, all ready with jokes.

"Knock it off guys," Mrs. Van Dyke said, quieting them as she unwrapped Brian's gift. Inside was a watch, but not a great one. She held it up next to the one on her own wrist, which was clearly more stylish. She looked up at him. She didn't know what to say.

"I found it and I thought of you," Brian said. "It says Mom with a heart."

She turned it over and read the engraving. She smiled at how sweet it was, but didn't know how to tell him that she had no intention of ever wearing it.

"Do you like it?" he asked.

"I do," she said, leaning over and hugging him. He could feel his sibling's eyes on him, but he smiled anyway, satisfied to have found a gift from the heart.

"Alright Ma, the real gift is from the rest of us," Dylan said, causing Brian to freeze in the middle of a hug. The rest of them. They all went in on something together—Brian's four well-to-do brothers chipped in and bought her one gift.

"How come I didn't know about it?" he asked.

"A little pricey for you," Dylan said.

"I still would've."

"No offense. We went all out this year and we know right now doing the cab driver thing can't be too profitable."

"I'm not a cab driver. I work for Victor Stone," Brian said, annoyed that he'd had to remind them repeatedly.

"What's the difference?"

"He has money. I make a decent wage."

"You're still a driver."

"Yes, but for Stone Enterprises. Do you even know who they are?"

"So the guy who delivers mail to the NASA headquarters is an astronaut?"

"That's not the same thing. I didn't say I wasn't a driver. I'm just saying it's a decent living because I drive for a big company."

"Maybe it's time to move out of Mom's basement then," Lance

murmured from the side, highly audible to everyone. Their mother shot him a silencing glare.

"I love my gift Brian. You didn't have to chip in with whatever they got. This is special."

"Alright, let's do this," Dylan said. He stood and everyone followed as he led the way to the garage. Before he could even open the garage door, their mother came to a halt, disbelieving what she already knew.

"Oh no. You didn't," she said, overwhelmed with disbelief.

"Just come in," Dylan said.

Moments later, they all stood facing a sports car, which sat on display in the center of the garage, light reflecting off it's smooth surface. Their mother approached with shock, unable to bring herself to touch it. Brian watched in disbelief.

"From all of us," Dylan said with a smile. "Well...not Brian."

Brian watched the road as he drove, looking up at the rear view and listening to his mentor talk about things he wanted to understand. He liked when Victor preached, and believed everything he said, but it was always politics or topics that Brian couldn't comprehend.

"Politicians can talk all they want about eliminating waste, fraud, and abuse," Victor said. "But the truth is, we could pull the plug on the entire federal bureaucracy and it would barely make a difference. The real problem is runaway costs in Medicare, Medicaid, and Social Security. Until something is done to bring them under control before the baby boomers start retiring en masse, the rest is talk."

Victor stopped and looked up at Brian. He saw the confusion on his face. He liked talking to Brian because Brian listened—or tried to—but sometimes became aware and would ask him about his own life. "How did your mother like the watch?" he asked. He knew little about Brian, but Brian would mention small details from time to time—his mother's Birthday being one of them.

"She liked it," he said, but he didn't say it believably enough.

"But..." Victor prompted.

"My brothers bought her a car."

Victor frowned and shook his head. "You were upstaged."

"Kinda. I mean, mine was personal, but a car...you can't compete with that. Especially because she needed one anyway."

"Why didn't you contribute?"

"They didn't ask."

"Finances would have been a problem?"

"Yeah. They know I don't make what they do."

"You know, when you finish school, there will be internships within

the company."

"Yeah, well I won't finish. I didn't get the credits I needed."

"You said you had enough to transfer."

"I did, but I didn't pass two of my classes." Brian looked up into the mirror so he could read Victor's reaction. As expected, the man was disappointed.

"Why not?" Victor asked, a hint of irritation in his voice.

"Because I do this. It keeps me busy."

"This job?"

"Yeah."

"You sit in the car and wait for me for hours sometimes. You can study."

"It's not easy in the car. It's hard to focus."

"Why didn't you say this was interfering with your education?"

"I need the money. It's not just that though. I seriously have problems focusing. Sometimes, I just don't get what they're saying. If they had a course in what's outside the window I would have been head of the class. I still thought I'd squeeze by, but I didn't."

"Is that what you want? To squeeze by?"

"No, but I don't know what I want. I figured I'd get the credits and transfer to a four year and hopefully figure it out by then."

Victor fell silent.

"I haven't told my family but they'll figure it out soon, which is going to make my life hell"

"Will one more semester do it?"

"Yeah, but I don't know if I'm gonna yet."

"Why not?"

"I'll save some money and taking time to figure out what I want."

"Get the credits. You don't want to be in that rut. If you take a break, you won't go back."

"I would."

"You need direction Brian."

"What if I don't need a degree?"

"You don't come this far and quit. Get the credits. You need to figure your life out. You should want more than this. You need a destination. You need to ask yourself where you want to be in twenty years."

Brian tilted his head, thinking about the question. Victor watched him closely as he came to the conclusion that the whole idea was useless. He finally shrugged his shoulders and shook his head. "I dunno."

Victor took a deep breath, trying to withhold his frustration. "I'd like to get some work done," he said. "Put the partition up."

"K," Brian said. He pushed the button and watched Victor disappear

as the partition raised...

...He stood at the sink, running water over his hands and splashing his face. He rubbed his eyes, trying to cover any evidence of the night before. When he decided he looked his usual self, he warily exited the bathroom and walked through the diner and to the kitchen. He spotted Eve giggling with Emily. He watched for a moment with a solemn expression. Eve could be so happy—just not with Brian anymore. He stared hopelessly, wondering where everything went wrong.

From behind, Bob put his hand on Brian's shoulder. Brian jumped nervously and turned to his boss, a big smile plastered on his face. "Good news Bri-guy."

"K?"

"I decided to promote a head chef in the kitchen. I felt we needed more of a pecking order around here."

Brian began to smile, his day improving already.

"Anyway, Sandy's going to be running things back here from now on." His smile faded. "Sandy?"

"I wanted you to know so you can offer her your congratulations." Bob smiled and squeezed Brian's shoulder before turning to leave.

"But, she barely works at all," Brian said in disbelief. He had no intention of being confrontational. It just came out.

"She'll be picking up hours. I'm cutting some of William's."

"Why?" Brian asked, suddenly alarmed. "He's great."

"I don't think so. He's not really wanting to be part of the team."

"But he works harder than anyone here."

"Hard work means nothing if you don't have the right attitude."

Brian stared at Bob, at a loss for words. Bob gave him a reassuring smile in return. "Your hours are intact Brian. You've done a super job here. Sandy is the person. You need to accept that."

"I can't."

Bob was taken aback. His happy demeanor transitioned into disappointment. "I think Will is rubbing off on you. I think you'll see this is a great move for the company. I've got to run, but I expect everyone will pay Sandy the respect she earned." He left Brian on that note. Brian slowly walked to the window that divided the lobby and kitchen and looked out at Eve. She was still with Emily, laughing hysterically. She looked up momentarily and caught Brian's eye. He smiled at her.

She turned back without returning the smile.

2

In Kern State Prison, life for most cons had been routine since Donovan was put on desk duty. They woke up, exercised, had chow-time, shot the shit, and went back to their cells. It had been pretty peaceful because all guards were put on alert. There had always been someone higher up to enforce that everyone was treated humanely. Eventually, they'd slip back into the old routine. The cons would start turning against each other, the guards would use brutal force to keep them in order, and the heat would get turned up throughout. Lately though, everything had been calm. There hadn't been an incident in some time.

It was two weeks before Dent was able to step foot in the yard at Kern. Donovan was out of the picture and Ziggy was good on his word. Dent hadn't fully recovered, but when the sun hit his face, he closed his eyes and soaked it in with pleasure. He usually sat on a bench in the yard. Ziggy would give him space, but eventually join him. As days passed, Wayne pushed Dent for information, hoping to bring something back to the warden. Dent was vague with his answers, and though he claimed to have a plan, his sedentary routine convinced Wayne he'd be here forever.

"Wayne's asking a lot of questions," Ziggy said one day.

"Let him."

"You trust him?"

"Doesn't matter if I trust him. Trust isn't part of the equation. If I want something from him, I'll get it."

"I don't suppose you'll let me in on what you're up to."

"Like I said..."

"I don't need details. Just tell me what you need me to do."

"You've done what I need."

"It's not easy getting chemicals in here. I'm risking a lot."

"I know. You won't regret it."

"You're too sure of yourself Dent. You know that?"

"We're gonna walk out of here Zig. We're gonna walk out right in front of their faces. It won't matter if Wayne's with us or not and it won't matter if they know when and where we're gonna do it. It won't change anything."

Ziggy nodded, accepting Dent's truth. Nothing about what he spouted made sense. He believed him anyway.

Wayne constantly approached Ziggy with his concerns, while Ziggy tried to convince him that Dent might actually have a fighting chance out of this cage. Dent kept all plans to himself, but Ziggy trusted him. He simply got what Dent asked for. Dent spent most of his day meditating and keeping to himself. He was quiet and thoughtful—the perfect formula for a genius.

Dent's plan was damn near perfect, but he needed one more thing: something big. He needed himself, Ziggy, and Wayne to work in laundry. It was a matter of time before a window opened and a favor would buy his way in. He waited patiently for that window.

Dent impressed Ziggy, and Ziggy was true to his word. Donovan was out of the picture, business had increased ten-fold for Ziggy, and it was all set in motion by a man who took a beating just to win Ziggy's loyalty. Dent had taken his plan far—almost too far for his own good—and it paid off.

"Only way out of here is underground," Dent said.

Ziggy turned to him with a wrinkle in his brow. "That's it? We're digging?"

"That's it, but we won't have to dig. I've monitored every inch of this place. It's solid. Shift changes are air-tight. They overlap by at least five minutes. Most of these guards are buddies, so they talk."

"What's underground?"

"Kern's built on an abandoned copper mine. There's no way into the tunnels through the yard or holding area. There's three entries into the tunnels at different points. One we can reach, but it's through the main corridors, which we don't have access to. All doors leading underground are surrounded by offices—areas we could never get near."

"You got a way around that?"

"Working on it. If you can earn any favors, we need laundry duty."

"I hesitate to doubt you after what you pulled with Donovan, but you know how many screws have come through here? How many escape attempts? And we're not all dummies. There's plenty of good thinking men who have tried and failed. They've got weapons, high ground, technology...you know as much as anyone here knows and no one's successfully escaped."

"You know why a runner gets caught? The moment he's past the walls, the alarms sound. Heads are counted, search teams deployed, local and state police shut everything down. Getting over the wall isn't the hard part. Staying there is where they muck up."

"What you getting at?"

"What we need is a significant head start. We need to get ahead of those who have tried and failed before us and do something innovative. Every time a con exploits a weakness, the engineers in Kern find a way to strengthen it. Enough attempts and the guards get this place pretty secure. It's not about finding a hole they haven't plugged. It's about doing something unconventional."

Dent was pulled aside later when a guard told him he had a visitor.

Dent never had visitors. Then, he came face to face with a man he'd never seen before. He took a seat, sizing the man up, and picked up the phone on his end of the glass. On the other end, Richard Libby held his phone to his ear. "Christian Dent?" Richard asked.

"I know you?"

"I'm Richard Libby, one of fifteen people written into Victor Stone's will."

Dent didn't know how to react. "What do you want?" he asked.

"I wanted to tell you that in five days, a group of us are meeting. I was able to secure a guarantee that it can be invalidated if the majority are in support."

"Are they?"

"Yes, they are."

"Why are you telling me?"

"I'm giving you the opportunity to be a part of it."

"You pulling me out of here to do that?" Dent asked with a smile.

"I was given permission to confirm your support with a signature."

"You can forget it," Dent said.

Richard nodded to himself, disappointed but unsurprised. "What if I could help when you're up for parole?"

"You're looking ten years down the road."

"Ten years down the road, you'll be wishing ten years ago you'd said 'yes'".

"I have a feeling if I said 'yes,' in ten years, you'd have other engagements."

"I would clear my schedule."

"And what gives you that kind of influence?"

"I'm a reverend. I'm well known in my community and I can help you on your way to reform."

"You just need me to accept God into my heart. I get it. It's shoved in my face every day."

"I wasn't asking for anything but a signature, but since you brought it up..."

"I'm a bit of a skeptic Mr. Libby. I draw parallels between hope and faith, but faith is a fancy word for hope, and used by the gullible. All in all, the idea of a supernatural creator who demands worship and who has a certain list of rules that he demands we live by is pretty useless if he's not actually gonna make his presence known to the world and enforce them himself, right here on earth."

"I believe he is present."

"Who is present?"

"God."

"What if Russell's teapot got to you before the Christians? If you were a Roman, would you blindly follow the Pantheon? Would you worship a Coke bottle that fell from the sky if you were a Bushman? This is not thinking, this is instinctual response to stimuli. Brainwashing. Fear of the unknown. Group-think. People care about metaphysics, if not, you would all be sitting home on Sunday morning and we would all be living in peace. You obviously don't care about what happens, because you got your lazy default "my-god-thing-did-it" answer to everything if you can't suss it out with your inept reasoning skills."

"You've never believed in anything?" Richard asked.

"Maybe once. If there was indeed some big sky god that created all this craziness, it sure isn't still hanging around, playing puppet master and shaming its playthings into self-loathing. It most likely vacated the cosmos after setting its little doomed experiment in motion, wondering why the subjects never picked up on their free-will. If anything, this god thing looked back, saw what a colossal nightmare of vile idiocy its followers had become by carrying out the most heinous campaigns in its name, and hung itself from a shower curtain rod at the edge of the universe. That's just as plausible as anything in that dusty old foolish book that has been thumped on our heads for two millennial and counting. Why are science, technology and reason, so reviled by the churches? Oh, yeah, it puts those final nails in the stupidity of your organized cults of the doped-up faithful. Why is pleasure so detested when obviously so very necessary? Despite what you think, proselytizing and converting is hate. Entire races and civilizations, great and small, have been driven from the face of the Earth for being heathens, pagans and non-believers. Not many Aztecs, Incas and Mayans left, are there? So for you to say it is in my best interest to repent, relent, and surrender to what has caused great physical and emotional harm to the innocent is outright hatred..."

"Mr. Dent..."

"The thing about you Christians is that there are so many of you intolerant hateful opportunistic ones that the rest of you have to accept that you're hated because you're in bed with them. It just seems that you Christians get all fired up as long as there is someone or some group for you to get under your thumb and squeeze with your sanctimoniousness and whom you get to hate with God on your side. And then, when it's all said and done, we find the people helming these efforts aren't even practicing what they preach and, lo and behold, neither are the followers. Basically, you're full of shit and have no other goal than to have power over me, only I'm not being a despicable hypocrite about it and telling anyone I can get in my cross hairs that they're going to hell if they don't behave just so. Why aren't you out saving your own? Where's the opposing voice to all your brothers in that cult you stand behind? Why are you here trying to save one man that can't be saved instead of speaking out against the atrocities that your own commit every day? You get what I'm saying?"

"I do," Richard said with a smile, showing Dent that he couldn't get to him. "You're saying I won't get your signature."

"You won't get my signature," Dent repeated.

"A simple 'no' would suffice," Richard said, getting to his feet. "But I understand. You're lonely."

He hung up the phone before Dent had a word to say. Richard walked away, effectively leaving him speechless.

3

Brian noticed Miranda enter The Wasp and ready herself to work. She'd been asked to cover another waitress and Brian was excited to see her. He wanted to greet her, but Sandy suddenly entered the kitchen on the warpath and cornered him and Brian stopped abruptly, cowering at the large woman coming at him. He instinctively backed away.

"Van Dyke!" she shouted. "Has Bob gone over the meal rules with you?"

"Um, I think."

"Then you know you pay half price for meals and you know you can't just take what you want and eat it?"

He froze in place. He didn't know anyone actually cared about those rules, but apparently Sandy did, or she was power-tripping, using Brian as her example. Nearby, William watched curiously.

"I saw you make a sandwich and eat it. Did you pay for it?" she asked.

"Not yet."

"You weren't going to either, were you? I see you do it every day and it stops now."

"K," he said.

William shook his head, embarrassed for Brian.

"Bob has let too much fly back here, but we're going to watch our waste."

"K, sorry."

She turned and as she passed William, she added, "Same goes to you. If you don't know the meal rules, come see me."

"Say, Sandy, I do have a question," he said. "You wouldn't happen to get bonuses if you can cut down on expenses around here, would you?"

"That's none of your business." She walked away, leaving the two of them in the kitchen together. Brian turned to William, his eyes wide, clearly concerned. William said nothing, and gave him the cold shoulder instead. He shook his head in disbelief.

"You should say something to her," Brian said.

"Not this time," William said.

William quietly observed Brian most of the day. He thought about what Toby said—about how Brian was inward, and he saw Toby's point. Behind Brian's smile, there was always something eating at him. There was always an outburst about to come out. Under different circumstances, he would have coached a guy like Brian out of sheer concern. Oddly enough, as painful as it was to watch Brian struggle, it was exactly what was supposed to be happening. Brian was the perfect victim for what he was to do. Even beyond William's control, life just piled up on him. "Van Dyke," Emily said, entering the kitchen. "There's a guy out here to see you. Says he's your apartment manager."

Brian searched the lobby until he spotted his apartment manager standing in the entry, searching for Brian. "What's he want?"

"To talk to you," she said, in an obvious tone.

Brian walked to the lobby and approached. "Hey," he said. His manager turned to him.

"Who's the girl at your place?" he asked immediately. "She your girlfriend?"

"Um, kinda. How come?"

From off to the side, Miranda watched curiously.

"I just got a noise complaint and went to see. I knocked four times before getting my keys. I entered to find her in there with four other people."

The color drained from Brian's face.

"They were hiding something on the table."

"What did they say? Did you make them show you?"

"They said they'd quiet down and became very accommodating, but this isn't the first time we've had this problem, is it? You need to take care of this."

"K."

"Before I do."

"K."

His manager began to storm off.

"Sorry," Brian called out. He watched with frustration as he exited. Brian took off his apron and walked to another exit. Sandy stepped in his way.

"What you doing? Going on break?"

He said nothing as he passed her. William and Miranda watched from where they sat. William took a deep breath. Brian was as good as dead...

...His family gathered around, having multiple discussions. Dylan sat next to Brian, in the middle of a lecture on the value of education. "One thing I've found since I graduated is that, for the most part, it doesn't matter what your major is. Unless you are going for something very specific like accounting or anticipate going to graduate or professional school in your area, it doesn't matter that much. What you need to focus on is how to think. That sounds stupid, but it's true."

"What do you mean by how to think?" Brian asked.

"Let me give you an example: I majored in Neuroscience. I now am working towards a graduate degree in Math, and I work full-time as an engineer. Despite lacking a formal education in engineering and mathematics, I'm reasonably successful in those fields. This is because as an undergraduate, I learned how to think critically and learn. If I come across something that I'm unfamiliar with, I find a resource and learn as much as possible."

Austin had been eavesdropping, and cut in. "All of my friends didn't know what they wanted to be until about two years out of college. One guy who failed to get into med school worked two years figuring himself out, then went all-out and got into a med school. Another friend tried teaching and programming and bio-tech for a while before deciding to get a PhD and do Biology research. And there's me, who quit my bio-tech job and went into animation."

Brian nodded his head quickly as he was bombarded with advice from the elite of the family, but nothing registered.

"...On the other hand, there was this guy I went to school with: Doug Hertzfeldt, who spent all his time in high school making animated cartoons, went to Santa Barbara and majored in animation, graduated and started making animated films. Just ignore people like that. They are pretty awesome, but it will depress you if you compare yourself."

"Okay, but my job is really demanding, so I can't make time for that."

"Get a new one."

"K, but even though you guys think I'm just a driver, it's a pretty good job. I may not need school. I mean, just having my foot in the door or having a reference like Victor..."

"He's not that great of a reference," Dylan said.

"Unless you're applying for something illegal," Austin said with a laugh.

"He's not like that."

"If he was, he's not gonna tell you."

"Actually, he tells me a lot. I'm like, the only person he talks to about stuff."

"But not business..."

"No, but he's a nice guy. You'd be surprised. He treats me good."

"So what? If the manager at Subway is nice, you gonna make sandwiches the rest of your life? Hear me out on this: Your boss is at least by reputation, mixed up in things, and if he gets caught or something happens, you really think you're immune to taking the fall?"

"If I didn't know anything, yes."

"You're driving him around, probably to do his dirty work."

"You don't know that, and why wouldn't he be caught by now if he was doing something wrong?"

"Most of the time, these guys lawyer up like crazy."

"Yeah, and most are too shrewd to cross legal lines; they just dance along them, lingering in the loopholes."

"Stick around awhile if you want, but don't make it a career. For one thing, 'foot-in-the-door' is an overstatement. Stop thinking driving Victor around looks good on a resume. Aside from his reputation, it's still just driving. Get your degree and figure it out from there."

Blake, who hadn't been paying attention to their conversation at all, suddenly turned to Brian. "Hey Bri, coach Sheffield told me when you played football, you quit because you didn't want to take off your shirt in front of everyone. Is that true?"

"No," Brian said, defensively. "That's not true." Brian stood and began loading dishes in the dishwasher.

"Rinse it off first Brian," his mother said.

Brian tried scraping a piece of food with his finger, but it wouldn't budge. He picked up a worn down scratch-pad, but it was useless too. He rummaged through a junk drawer to find a better tool. "So..." he said quietly, "I have to do another year at community college."

The whole room quieted, except the sound of Brian rummaging in search of a scratch pad, his back turned to them.

"I thought you had enough credits," his mother finally said.

"I don't." Brian came to a stop as he spotted the watch he gave his mother, sitting against the back of the drawer, stowed away as if it had never been touched. He stared at it, thoughtfully.

"You didn't fail a course, did you?" Dylan asked.

"Yeah, I did," Brian said, his voice almost a whisper.

Everyone turned to each other for a reaction. Finally, Blake spoke up, unable to help himself. "Was it cause they wanted you to take off your shirt?"

Blake and some of the others burst into laughter. Brian didn't acknowledge any of it. He only stared at the watch...

...He sat against a wall, staring into space. He slapped a fly away from his face in annoyance. He'd escaped The Wasp and found a spot in the dumpster barn out back. Miranda peaked her head in and found him there, sitting on a crate. "Bad day?" she asked.

"No, I'm fine."

"Care if I hang with you on my break?"

"It's the dumpster," he said. "Why would you want to?"

"You're here." She crouched down, pressing her back against the wall. "So...what's been going on?"

"Not much."

"Things going okay with Eve?"

He looked at her, knowingly, as she gave him a look begging for an explanation. "You know," he said. "When I first met her, she was pretty nice. She changed. A lot."

"After first impressions, it's all downhill from there. So what are you doing Brian? Why are you with this girl?"

He thought about the question and didn't know how to answer. "I liked you," was all he came up with.

She nodded, confirming she knew.

"I thought I had a chance for a while."

"It was mutual."

"Yeah, and something got in the way."

"What? Neil?"

"Yeah."

"I didn't make a move with you, because in a year I'm off to school. I thought we clicked. I thought we'd work. I didn't want a reason to be held back. Maybe I wouldn't have gone to school. Maybe I would've held you back."

"If we chose that, we would've preferred it."

"I've studied to become a dentist for I don't know how long. I already relocated once for a guy and regretted it. We could have worked Brian. At least long enough that we'd both put our lives on hold."

"So what about Neil?"

"I was looking for something short term and meaningless."

"Doesn't seem that way."

"Cause it's not anymore. It started off that way, but we fell for each other."

"And now it's okay to hold your life back?"

"We're working something out. When I go to college, he's moving with me. It's not what we expected. Yes, I know it all seems hypocritical, but things happen even when we try to avoid them. I don't have any regrets, but I tried to be cautious. But none of that matters. What are you doing? I've met Eve twice and she treats you like shit. You can do better.

He nodded his understanding. He knew she was right. William was right. His apartment manager was right. But it wasn't easy for him to detach. Brian always had limited options. It wasn't often that women liked him.

He smiled and pulled himself to his feet. He didn't know what she said—maybe just that she was there with him—but he felt better.

"Coming in?" she asked.

"Another minute," he said with a reassuring smile.

4

Wayne stood before the warden, a guard at his side to monitor his actions. The warden ignored him while he filled out paperwork. He left Wayne in suspense, and a smarter man may have realized that was intentional.

Finally, the warden looked up, set aside his pen, and leaned forward.

Wayne hesitated to talk, but realized the warden was waiting for him to give him an update on Dent's plan. Unfortunately, Dent hadn't given him anything to work with. "Far as I can tell," he said, "he has a plan. Maybe not a big plan, but something."

"What do you know?"

"He's monitoring shift changes, train whistles, things like that."

"He planning a daytime escape?"

"I don't know."

"What do you know?"

"Well, he uses Zigfried to get him things. He won't say what and even Zigfried doesn't know his plan."

"You consider he might be stringing you along?"

"Why would he?"

"He doesn't trust you."

"I haven't done a thing to make him think I'm not with him."

"You think he needs proof? If he doesn't trust people, why would he trust you? Don't you find it a little uncharacteristic of him to be letting you in on this?"

"I'm his cellmate. He can't hide his going ons from me."

"Unless he's making an escape from your cell, he wouldn't need you to know a single thing. He hasn't asked anything from you, so tell me what he wants."

"I don't know. Maybe just needs someone that's been in and out of prison. I don't know."

"Let's make it easier," the warden said, a thought cultivating in his head. "Let's give him an opening. He needs supplies and favors. That's the only way to get things done. Let's give you some value. Let's force him to confide in you."

Dent laid on his bunk with a book in his hand, but couldn't focus on the words. He thought about Richard, the first beneficiary he'd met aside from Trish. Dent was a religious man, but didn't want Richard to have the satisfaction of his cooperation. Yet, Richard had the last laugh and planted a seed in Dent. He called him lonely. It wasn't the right analysis, but fell somewhere on the same playing field. More importantly, if what Richard said about the will being invalidated was true, then Dent escaping wouldn't mean he'd have the financial gain available that he once had. It didn't change his desire to move beyond these bars, but when he did, he'd have to work fast to prevent whatever they had in the works. His thoughts were broken when a guard approached the bars and looked in. He sat at attention, ready to answer to the man, but to his surprise, the guard spoke to Wayne. Wayne, who was just a useless pain in the ass with no significance, suddenly seemed significant to someone.

"Wayne," the guard said. "You're being pulled for questioning tomorrow."

"What for?" Wayne asked, getting to his feet. Dent looked up over his book, curiously.

"The Prescot boy you killed."

"I got nothing to say."

"You need to think it over," the guard said.

"I'll tell you what I told you last year, and the year before, and every year before that..."

"This week marks the tenth anniversary of his disappearance. They don't care about you. They just want to bury their son. It's no burden to you to point at a map. Why not do the right thing, buy yourself some good will with the warden, and tell us where you hid that body?"

"Get bent."

"Maybe you should hear what the warden has to say before you refuse. Around here, you need to learn to take what you can get. If you say nothing, another year will pass that you'll be deprived of something that you could otherwise have."

"There ain't nothing I want. I'm happy as horse-shit right where I am."

Dent leaned into the conversation. He wanted the guard to go away so he could talk to Wayne in private, before Wayne sabotaged the offer altogether.

"I'm just relaying the message," the guard said. "I don't care what you do. I'm here to tell you they're desperate. Probably thinking you won't ever spill it. They'll negotiate within reason. Thought I'd give you the night to think about that."

"I don't need the night. I got your answer right here." Wayne grabbed at his crotch, to the guard's disgust.

"Either way, the warden is pulling you tomorrow to talk about it."

"Good for him."

The guard momentarily hesitated, with more to say, but talking to Wayne was pointless. The moment passed and he walked away. Wayne rolled on his back as Dent sat up, his mind spinning.

Moments later, as Wayne closed his eyes, feigning sleep, he was unexpectedly jerked awake by a hand covering his mouth and another that grabbed his neck. His eyes went wide as he came face to face with Dent. He tried to make noise, but it was muffled. Dent did the talking.

"You yell for help and you're dead. Nod yes or no. Did you murder that boy?"

Wayne stared quizzically.

"Did you murder the kid the guard asked you about?"

Wayne shook his head yes.

"And you know where the body is?"

Yes again.

"Then you're going to tell them. You understand?"

Wayne didn't move. Dent slowly uncovered his mouth. "I don't want to see the family," he whispered.

"That's your problem and you deal with your shit however you have to, but you have leverage and if you want to be free of this place, you're going to use it. You're going to exchange information for a favor. Then you're going to give them what they want. You got that?"

Wayne pushed himself away and propped himself to an upright position. "What do you want me to ask for?"

"Laundry duty. For you, me, and Ziggy. It doesn't sound like much, but you get us there, I'll get you out."

Finally, Wayne had something of substance.

5

Brian didn't notice the relationship change. They'd shifted into a couple who disdained each other without reason. At least Eve did. Whether Brian did something to upset her, or a collection of incidents, the only thing he was guilty of most days was waking up. She stomped her feet through his apartment and didn't say a word, other than to tell him to hurry up. She was silent on the ride. When the car came to a stop outside The Wasp, she was out of the car first and walked ahead of him. He walked through the front door while she was clocking in. She brushed past him on her way to the lobby, blatantly ignoring him.

From the kitchen, William gave Brian a sideways glance. "Hey Bri."

"You're late," Guy said, from his corner of the kitchen, a newspaper sprawled in front of him.

"Sorry."

Eve appeared in the window. "Will, can you grab me some fruit? I haven't eaten." She was sweet to him, but avoided looking at Brian.

Brian opened his mouth to offer to help but Eve was gone in an instant.

"She's mean to you," Guy said.

Brian paused. "You think so too?"

"You're pussy whipped," Guy said.

Brian was constantly disheartened to hear he was such a push-over and Eve was so evil. "She's kinda like that, but most of the time, we have fun. She's always saying she likes that we can just sit at home and do nothing." Brian was lying. She'd said something like that early in the relationship, but it had been a long time since he'd heard anything resembling a compliment from her.

"She's nice when you get to know her. She's having a bad week."

"Oh, I agree. The only person she's mean to is you...her boyfriend."

At the end of the shift, Brian watched bitterly as Emily ran excitedly to the door to greet Eve, who'd changed clothes and was dressed up. She had a chipper demeanor. William stood at Brian's side and turned to him, as if to say it was his turn at the plate. "Gotta do it," he said. "She walks out the door now, you're putting it off another day."

"She's with Emily. Maybe I should wait until tomorrow."

"Sure, but let me tell you a story," William said. "One day in Hell, the Devil approached a man who loved the drinking parties there. The Devil told the man that as long as he was willing to quit drinking he could immediately go to Heaven, where he would forever have a better time. The man replied that although Hell wasn't so bad, and the parties were great, he preferred Heaven. The Devil told him that if he wanted, he could have a great send-off party now, and go to Heaven tomorrow. The man thought it seemed a good idea to have the best of both worlds, so he accepted the deal. The next day the man was reminiscing about how great the send-off party was when the Devil approached him and said he could have another terrific party right then and go to Heaven the next day. Of course the man accepted. Each day the Devil made the same offer, and each day the man accepted the party. Well, the Devil knew that the man didn't have what it takes to ever refuse a great party. The Devil knew he was weak. And you know where that man is to this day?"

A moment later, Brian was out of the kitchen, approaching Eve in the lobby. She gave him a sweet smile when she saw him. "Hey Bri," she said. He loved it when she called him Bri, and apparently she was being nice now, but he stayed on course.

"Can we talk?"

"Yeah, but make it quick."

Emily edged away, allowing them space.

"Why does it have to be quick? What's going on?"

"Em and I are going to a movie."

He doubted that was true, but dismissed it. "Alright, look, I don't want you to be mad, but I kinda get the impression you don't wanna be together anymore, so I'm just letting you know that it's fine with me if you want to break up."

Her face went blank. "What?"

"I know I'm not your type."

"You're trying to get me to dump you?"

"It seems like you want to be around other people and don't like me much."

"Are you kidding? So this is my fault?"

"No one's fault. I figured this is what you wanted."

"Well, I'll say what I want, so you don't have to figure it out on your own. Is that okay?" She slung her purse over her shoulder as if the conversation was over. He watched her try to exit, but stepped forward.

"Okay," he blurted, "but I want it."

She turned back; her whole disposition changed. "Want what?"

"I think we should break up."

"Whatever. We'll talk about it later."

"We can't. I want my key back because I don't want to sit around and wait."

She laughed. It was hard enough to stand up to her, but she wasn't reacting at all the way he'd hoped—the way he'd seen people react to Victor, or William.

"You don't want to sit around?" she asked with more laughter. "Even though that's all you do?"

"I don't know what that means. I work hard."

"At a dead-end job maybe, where it doesn't matter. All you do is watch TV and eat. That's all you're into."

"See what I mean? You don't even like me."

"Okay, well then, let's break up," she said with a good-humored smile. Apparently, it wasn't subjecting her to the same emotional turmoil.

"K."

"You're a loser anyway."

"You know, I inherited a lot of money," he said, without thinking.

William perked up, surprised by the direction Brian decided to take. Bob hovered nearby, waiting for his moment to calm the situation.

"Why would you say that?" Eve asked. "I don't know what that means."

"Look at my apartment. Look at my car."

"I know you have money, but you don't have money. You're a cook. You don't know anything and you don't want anything. So what? You inherited some money? It'll be gone in a year, if that."

"Yeah, and what do you want? To go out and have fun all the time?"

"That's a bad thing? Maybe if you knew how to have fun, you wouldn't be such a stupid fat loser. I'm not the only one who thinks so."

Brian's face went blank. He turned and looked around at his coworkers and friends, wondering who was on his side and who wasn't. His eyes caught William's and he tried looking into them, tried seeing whether he was his friend or thought low of him like everyone else. He couldn't tell. He turned back to Eve. "You're fired," he said, softly.

"You can't fire me," she said, laughing.

"I'd quit if she got fired," Emily said, cutting in.

Then Bob stepped forward. "Brian, you can't fire her."

Eve slung her purse over her shoulder. "Are you done dumping me?" she asked. He stood silently, all eyes on him. He couldn't win—not like everyone else won. He was a weakling, a loser, a fat nothing. "Good," she said. Then, she walked out...

...Victor sat quietly, scanning his work as Brian drove. He looked up every few seconds, ready to talk to Victor the moment their eyes met. Finally Victor pushed a button and the partition lowered.

"How's it going?" Brian asked.

"Very well, yourself?"

"It's going."

"Is there something on your mind?"

"Yeah, kinda. I wanted to tell you something without you getting mad."

"Go ahead."

"My family and I got into an argument about what I should do and I told them how I like working for you. So then I think they were trying to get me to go back to school, and they started saying how you were a criminal and that all those rumors are true."

Victor nodded, thoughtfully. "What do you think?"

"I mean, I like working here, and I think sometimes there are crimes

that are not really that bad, but also a lot of people who probably are jealous of you." He watched carefully through the mirror as Victor sat in silence for a long moment.

"You know," he finally said. *"I've done a lot of traveling, and there's something that always strikes me as odd: it's the way different objects in different cultures are described. Take something as simple as a key. Germans tend to describe keys with words such as hard, heavy, jagged, and metal, while Spaniards use words like golden, intricate, and lovely. Here in America, we paint death as male. Russians as female."*

"Really?" Brian said, politely. *"I didn't know that."*

"Every relationship that you have is different. How you perceive me is all that matters. I don't know what your brothers know about you and I don't know why they give you a hard time and describe you with words they do, but they're probably right. They probably have inside information that I don't—information that arms them with ways to pick on you. The thing is that it doesn't have any relevance to what you are to me, in this car right now, and I would hope that how others perceive me wouldn't change your opinion either."

"Just..." Brian started, but stopped abruptly. He had Victor's attention and decided to say what he'd been wanting to say since he figured it out. *"I know what I want to do with my life..."*

Victor curiously leaned forward. *"What do you want to do?"*

"What you do," Brian said, his face set in stone. *"I want your life..."*

"...Now, your life begins," William said.

"I know she was freaking out, but I dumped her," Brian said. "You're probably mad but..."

"I'm not mad."

"You're something."

"I'm not mad, but she was wrong and you were right and that's not how it looked from where I was sitting. It's unjust."

"I'm just relieved. It's a weight off my shoulder. I don't care how it looked."

"But you should. You should care."

"Why? It means nothing."

"Does anything matter to you?" William asked. Brian thought about the question and shrugged.

"Goodnight guys," Bob said, passing by. "Don't forget to lock up Bri-guy." Brian winced. "Sorry about Eve. I find it's best not to date coworkers. I've done it a few times myself and it never ends well."

"K."

"I know it'll be hard working with her, but I think the best way to get by is to consume yourself with work. Try extra hard and you'll get ahead."

"Am I not doing enough?" Brian asked suddenly.

"Of course you are. I'm just trying to help."

"You're exploiting me."

Bob blinked his eyes rapidly, taken aback. William watched with fascination.

"Sandy's my boss now? Where did that even come from?"

"Brian, you've had a rough night."

"You're, like, the worst boss I've ever had. You're here because what? You started when you were a teenager and never quit? That's not an accomplishment. Anyone can just stay put in a crumby job and become manager."

"I really think William is a bad influence over you."

"He's the only one who gives a shit about me," Brian said. From his side, William swallowed hard, wondering if there would ever come a day when Brian would realize William had only wedged himself into his life to end it.

"Tomorrow, if Sandy's not demoted, I'll walk out."

"What am I supposed to do?" Bob asked, nearly whining. "I can't demote her for nothing."

"I don't care. She's not my boss."

"Get some sleep and think..."

"I won't answer to her, and I'm not going to do any more work than everyone else around here. And my name's Brian. It's not Bri-guy. I'm not your fucking son."

Brian turned and walked out, leaving Bob awestruck and William with a proud smile on his face. He turned to Bob. "You really are a shitty boss Bob."

Moments later, Brian and William were on their way home in Brian's car. Brian was pathetic, but the journey to transform him somehow made William fond of his protégé. He was just a dumb kid who was socially inept, and the more he was formed into the man William needed him to be, the more he liked him.

"You got one of those things you gave me?" Brian asked. "Something to relax?"

"Yeah, you want one?"

"Yeah."

William thought about what Toby told him: Brian can be pushed, but he can't be controlled. The fat guy sitting next to William hardly seemed dangerous, but Toby was often right and Brian surprised him. He'd experienced a win. It was a small win, but Bob submitted, and if Brian would learn anything, it was how good it felt to win—to take control. And as he aggressively took control of his life, he'd simultaneously lose control of himself. William had a flash of fear as he considered what Toby said. If Brian really was a time-bomb, what would he do if he ever knew what William was really there for? He rummaged through his pockets and handed Brian a pill. He watched as Brian popped it into his mouth and swallowed.

"I know where there's a party," William said.

Chapter 17

1

Trish and Carlos sat in their squad car in a secluded parking lot. Carlos had a lunch-box on his lap and picked at a sandwich and side of carrots as Trish scooped the remains out of a yogurt. Her eyes diverted by movement near a shack in the distance. "Hey..." she said, suddenly serious.

Carlos followed her eyes to where Victor Stone stood chatting with an associate. "You know him?" she asked.

"Yeah..." he said. He couldn't remember the name, but everyone knew Victor's face, and he mirrored her reaction. Victor seemed out of place standing outside a shack in the middle of a field.

"He doesn't like me," Trish said. "I used to bother him. At first I was just doing it because no other cops would. Then, I did it for fun. Mostly, I can't stand these invincible assholes, ya know? But he's the one Paul works for."

"Really?" Carlos asked, surprised. "You never told me that."

"I'm not proud of it. Stone Enterprises is corrupt. I don't like Victor."

"Where do you stand with him now?"

"I hadn't seen him for a while, but then two days ago I pulled him over for missing a signal. He didn't say much. Just took his ticket and..." She stopped as Victor pulled a briefcase from behind a gathering of tall weeds and opened it. Carlos was equally enthralled.

"What do you think he's doing?"

"And why here?" she asked.

The associate observed the contents of the briefcase before pulling another briefcase and trading with Victor. When the mystery transaction was done, the associate scurried back to his car. Victor looked around cautiously. Trish and Carlos ducked, though they couldn't hide the squad car. They could only hope at this distance, they wouldn't be seen.

Victor walked around the shack and moments later, his car passed by in the distance. Instead of watching him, Trish turned to the associate's car, which was making its way onto the highway.

"I'm following this guy," Trish said.

"Follow Victor."

"If this turns out to be nothing, it won't look good."

"You think it's something?"

"Oh, it's something," she assured him. "We just stumbled upon something. And if this is what it looks like, then I may finally get this asshole..."

...Her stack of mail was composed of bills; medical bills for every test and visit. It also included her electric bill, phone bill, credit cards...

Her eyes filled with tears, as they had many times in the last few weeks. She dreadfully opened her bills and organized them. It was all crashing down, but she had bigger things to deal with.

Sirens flashed behind Anthony Freeman's car. He pulled over and exited the car, and waited until Trish reached him.

She sized him up on approach. He looked sick and exhausted. The lines around his eyes had deepened and he was seemingly stressed. "It's better to do it this way," she said.

"I understand."

"Let's get this over," she said. "I have somewhere to be."

She walked him to her car where she pulled a Breathalyzer test. He began relaying the story. "It was a few nights ago. I don't know for certain. I lost track of time. I'm not sure how much. It's a blur. Maybe we should go to the station for a blood test."

"If it's still in your system, there will only be trace amounts."

"I'm certain I didn't drink," Anthony said.

Trish tilted her head. "If the last thing you remember was being in a bar before you blacked out, then I don't need to tell you how to add two and two."

"I know," he said, hastily. "I know how it sounds, but after years of being sober, I would remember making a choice to drink. Maybe not when I was still drinking, but when you fall off the wagon, you remember why you did it and you remember the moment you decide to screw it up. That moment never came for me. Please spare me the grizzly details. I know where I was and how this appears."

"If you go to the hospital, they can do a urine test. It'll stay with you for eighty hours. That's your best bet if you need proof."

"This happened more than eighty hours ago. I woke up this morning and a week disappeared."

"Let me see the scar," she said.

He twisted his body and pulled his shirt up, exposing a long cut down his side, completely stitched up.

She inspected it. "It's a good stitch job."

"I know it is and no hospital has a record of my visit."

"I'm sorry Anthony, but there's nothing I can do for you. I have somewhere I need to be."

"You going this weekend?" he asked, off-topic, "To end this thing?"

"Absolutely. You?"

"You bet I am. We all need to see this through."

"Yeah," she said, unsure if she really wanted it to end. The timing was bad. Shiloh was sick and…

"How's Shiloh?" he asked, as if seeing the resistance in her face.

"I don't know, but I'm getting a second opinion and trying to sort some things out with my insurance."

"Everything will turn out okay Trish. Don't let your mind wander."

"That's naïve," she said. "Everything will turn out okay is a shitty cliché. Things aren't okay."

"At least it will be over soon."

"At a price. Shiloh's sick. Abby is dead. You relapsed without a cause or apparently, a choice."

"You don't know I relapsed."

"No, but there's no reason for any of this. Ending Victor's will won't make the world better or any less tragic."

"Where do you have to be?" he asked, concerned about how distraught she was. "I'll join you."

"No," she said. "It's a personal thing."

Since Trish caught the shooting in the news, she couldn't wait to visit to crime scene with her badge. Adlar Wilcox wasn't dead. It wasn't his blood on the curtains and he wasn't the shadow they'd seen in the window. Instead, a man she'd never heard of fell victim to the fatal shot Trish fired. The man had a gun, and later, it was determined he also carried a needle filled with a toxin that would have killed anyone that ingested it. Half the pieces fit together, but they made an even bigger puzzle. A random school-teacher from far outside of town was in an apartment to kill Adlar—who hardly anyone was able to locate—and instead of finishing the job, Charlie Palmer squeezed off a shot at the teacher. It all fell together nicely, if only the school-teacher made sense. He was connected to nobody on the will. He came up clean. He was a normal guy who apparently teleported himself into a shitty situation. And soon, someone would extract the bullet and trace it back to Trish and she'd have to explain herself, which is what led her to the crime scene.

She arrived at the apartment complex and looked across the street toward the roof where she fired the shot. She swallowed hard and entered the building, up two flights of stairs, and came to apartment 302, which was covered with police tape. She pulled it aside and entered, ready to flash her badge, but the place was practically empty. The scene looked fresh and not a lot of traffic had gone through. Murder wasn't investigated using all police resources on this side of town. In fact, only one officer stood in the apartment, staring out the window.

"Excuse me," she said.

The man turned and they both recognized each other at once. In full police uniform, Manny's brow crinkled and he smiled at her in recognition. Neither had seen each other in a long time. "I'll be damned," Manny said. "Trish Reynalds. Geez, you look good."

"Thank you, Manny," she said. "I'm happy to see you're still on the force. I wondered what happened to you."

"They tossed me on the south side in homicide. You know, I meant to give you a call. I saw your name in the paper when your partner got killed in that bomb blast. That was a damn shame."

"Yeah, it was. Big loss to the force."

"They catch who did it?"

"The bomb was traced to one of the workers inside. All evidence shows he wanted to kill himself and everyone inside."

"Open and shut case?"

"Supposedly."

"And you believe that shit?"

"Not at all."

"Good for you," Manny said. "Someone kills one of our brothers in blue, they deserve to have their windpipe ripped out."

She raised her eyebrows and pursed her lips together. She wasn't quite so passionate about revenge, but understood the sentiment. Manny turned away and stared out the window again, the friendly banter fading as he looked out toward the rooftops.

"Why are you on this case?" she asked. "If you work homicide on the south side, this is out of your division."

"This case hit me hard. Victim was a grade school teacher and a good guy. He shouldn't have been in this area, or in this apartment. He was far from home. And so he's in a place he has no business being, and a shooter across the street on the roof takes him out. Nothing really adds up. Cops around here are dumb as rocks, so I thought I'd take a look."

"Where are the investigating officers?"

"You know how they are over here. Useless. I'm going to the morgue today to take a look at the body."

"Mind if I join you?" she asked. The morgue was exactly where she needed to be. The body was in the morgue and her bullet was in the body.

"Why are you on this case?" Manny asked. "You transferred?"

"No, I'm bored. Made the mistake of going on leave to deal with some things and it turned out I had some downtime. I'm freelancing."

"Funny. The only two cops trying to solve this aren't even in their jurisdiction."

She smiled

"Anyway, we don't have the resources at our disposal. What I'm hoping is those useless rent-a-cops let me handle this myself. In their hands, they'll make a mess of it. If I get the bullet, I can run it in our database and link it to a gun. It'll probably be stolen, but it's a start."

Trish turned to face away, afraid he'd see the color drain from her face. She knew Manny was a good detective. She didn't know why he was here, but he'd always been the type to close cases—to follow evidence and find answers. "It'll come together," she said.

"Are there pictures?" she asked.

"No, I asked. They glossed over this like it was nothing. They took the body and assigned two officers to it. I ran into them on my way here and they said it was likely a gang shooting and wrote it off."

"Maybe that's all it was."

"Except for the teacher."

"It doesn't sound like anyone dragged him out here. He came here for a reason and I doubt it was on the up and up."

Manny scowled behind her back. She'd already seen his face though and detected sadness. She wondered what he was holding back. She wondered if he knew the teacher after-all and how well.

"Come on," he said. "I'll take you to the station. We'll check out the body at the morgue and get some real cops on this case."

They made arrangements to ride together, but Trish hung back and told him she was going to grab a coffee at the diner downstairs first. After Manny exited, she rushed to the window and ran her hands over the ledge. She remembered the shots. She knew where Charlie fired. One bullet was accounted for. The other wasn't. Getting her hands on the bullet that was still in the apartment would give her a head-start. She still wasn't sure who fired the fatal shot, and if there was a piece of evidence inside their corpse, Manny would easily link it to a cop. His mind might even take liberties of its own and connect a cop's presence who had no business being there. The day had to end with Charlie's bullet in that evidence-bag. She shuttered at what she was doing, but had no time to sort out the ethics.

She leaned out the window and ran her hand along the ledge. Charlie's bullet hit the frame. She saw it split. She found it wedged between two chunks of cracked wood. It was easy to miss if you weren't looking for it, or in the hands of incapable cops who were eager to write it off as a gang shooting.

She held the bullet between her fingers and displayed it for her eyes to see. She let out a breath of frustration, finding what she knew to be true already: It was Charlie's bullet she held.

Her own was about to be claimed by Manny.

2

Wayne sat quietly in front of the warden, tracing a circle on his desk with his finger. He had information, but still no substance. Dent could only leave him contemplating what his plan was, and the warden wouldn't be pleased with contemplation.

While Wayne tried to find his words, the warden spoke first. "A couple years ago, four inmates in a level five facility colored their clothes and disguised themselves as orderlies. They knocked out the guards one by one and stored them in a supply closet, hijacked a prison bus, and escaped. They were caught within five hours."

"I think what's going on," Wayne said slowly, "is he wanted to be in the laundry for chemicals. He knows about chemicals and talks about em and reads about em and I know Ziggy's been helping him get some."

"But you don't remember any of the names?"

"They were long. They had numbers in them."

"How about you get me those names?" the warden said, patiently. "I got you laundry duty. I've taken the heat off everything you're doing. It's starting to seem like you're getting a lot for nothing."

"I'm trying sir. It's like you said, he's probably dying the clothes..."

"That wouldn't work. All vehicles are on the east side. He wouldn't make it halfway there, but assume he's a step ahead. Assume he knows you're here with me now and that you've seen exactly what he wants you to see. Don't listen to what he's saying. Observe what he's doing."

"All he says is we're walking out right in front of the guards; A disguise sounds bout right."

The warden scratched his temple. It did seem that Dent thought he was going to throw on a costume and walk past everyone. He believed Dent to be smarter than that, but maybe Dent had nothing better. Maybe he'd overestimated him.

"You scared he can pull it off?" Wayne asked.

"I don't like the unknown," the warden said. "If Dent has a plan and its failure depends on you, you're gonna be real sorry if you don't get the upper-hand. Never assume someone's dumber than they seem. Only assume they're smarter. You're either right and you're a step ahead, or you're wrong and they fail."

Wayne closed his eyes with frustration. What the warden was asking was impossible. He could only hope Dent would try and fail.

"Get it done," the warden said. "If Dent gets out of here, you don't."

Dent and Ziggy dumped a bag of dirty laundry onto the ground and began sifting through, sorting it into separate bins. Dent caught a glimpse of a tattoo on Ziggy's arm, a pyramid with a crown of thorns around and the words: Phil. 4.13.

"You know," Ziggy said, "I've been trusting you with a lot, but you should know, these guys catch us in the act, they'll shoot to kill, and I ain't ready to die."

"You wanna back out, go ahead."

"I don't wanna back out. I got three daughters. They don't live far from here. I wanna see them and apologize for shit. Then I dunno what. This is the only way."

"The first place the police will go when you're missing is your home."

"I know."

"It wouldn't be wise."

"I know. I'd get the message to them and get out of the country."

Dent sighed and took a deep breath. "This isn't a good idea for you Zig. You got a chance at parole. You come with me and get caught and you'll spend the rest of your life in jail."

"What about you?"

"I'm here for the long haul anyway. I'm not equipped for this place. Most of my life ahead of me is scheduled in Kern. Not yours."

"I'll never get out either Dent," Ziggy said. "They act like I might, but I won't. They like having me here. I'll take my chances with you."

"Then focus on getting out and past the border. I'll have money Zig."

"Yeah? How much you looking at?"

"A pretty big inheritance. Seven or eight figures."

"No kidding?" Ziggy asked. "No wonder you want out so bad. I'm not asking you to tell me what you're doing, but how confident are you? I need to know."

"I make no promises. I can get out, but I don't got your back when we leave. That's all you gotta know and then ask yourself if it's worth it."

"I don't know what I'll do yet."

"Better figure it out soon."

"How soon?" Ziggy asked, studying Dent's face, which was lost in thought.

"Soon."

3

Trish and Manny entered the police morgue and found the body of Bedbug displayed before them. His face was clean, except for a bullet-hole that went straight through his cheek. Manny concealed his anger upon seeing his friend and forced himself to maintain some professionalism. They were followed in by the detective on the case, who didn't act like he had much invested in the truth. The detective brought them up to speed.

"Toxin analysis has improved but sometimes only luck reveals ingeniously administered substances. His needle held a lethal poison called polonium, which is a rare radioactive substance. He would've nearly gotten away with it if his target hadn't killed him first. If the other guy was found dead, nobody would have tried a highly unusual test for that kind of radiation poisoning, but of course he had the needle in his hand when he was blown away, so our shooter made sense of it."

Manny clenched his jaw.

"What about the gun?" Trish asked. "If he took precautions, why was there a shootout?"

"Probably because whatever qualm these two were having, a third person crashed the party. Very likely someone working with or protecting our apartment dweller."

"Who was the apartment dweller?" Manny asked.

"No idea. According to the building owner, that apartment was supposed to be vacant, but it's no surprise it wasn't. It was an office years ago, but this neighborhood took a turn for the worse and a lot of these places are empty. Usually the homeless or addicts occupy them until someone catches and kicks them out."

"You have any theories on what went down?" Manny asked.

"He came to kill in a professional and undetectable manner. Either someone knew he was coming or saw him and shot back, or there was a third party involved. Of course, that leaves out the lingering question of motive."

"How would anyone know he was there?" Manny asked.

"I don't know. I don't know who he was trying to kill or who killed him and there's a lack of actual living people who are around to tell the tale." He pointed to Bedbug. "This asshole's not talking. That's for sure."

Trish didn't notice Manny tense up. If she hadn't been there, the detective would've ended up on a table next to Bedbug, but Manny held his cool as the detective went on.

"Did you dust for prints?" Trish asked.

"Place was wiped clean."

Trish frowned, confused. She turned to Manny, suddenly suspicious, as if she'd had a revelation. She watched him closely, but he didn't react at all. He wasn't surprised there were no prints. Maybe he took care of that. But why?

"The popular opinion is this guy does this for a living. He's a grade school teacher by day, but all arrows lead to this being a contractual arrangement."

"You really believe a professional would get himself killed like this?" Manny asked.

"He would if a third party got involved, which is where the third party theory comes into play. No reason for the occupant to be on the rooftop unless he saw this coming. Something unexpected went down, but we only have theories at this point."

Another forensics expert entered, wearing an apron and carrying a case. He gave them all a look before approaching the body and asking everyone to stand back. They moved out of his way as he proceeded with his work.

"What are we looking for?" Manny asked.

The forensics expert raised an eyebrow at Manny, giving him a 'who are you?' look before answering. "We're digging for a bullet."

Manny took a step back and crossed his arms, watching intently. Trish stood at his side, hiding the fear in her eyes, grasping for ideas to get out of this mess...

...Sirens blared.

Carlos watched Trish as she exited the squad car and walked toward Victor's associate, who sat patiently in his car without a care in the world. Trish had been on pursuit of the associate for two weeks, and she didn't make much time for anything else. Carlos was annoyed, but her seniority kept him quiet. He watched Trish as she approached the car.

"What was I doing?" the associate asked without looking up.

"I clocked you going five over."

"Your thingy is broken then."

"Would you mind stepping out of the car?"

The associate sat still. His eyes rolled and gave her an estranged look. He slowly opened the car and stepped out. He turned and spotted Carlos lounging in the squad car. "You need me to step out for going five over?"

She looked into his car. The briefcase sat in the passenger seat. She eyed it as he watched her closely. "What's in that?"

A smile of disbelief curled at the corner of his mouth. "You really clock me or you looking for something?"

She leaned in and grabbed the handle.

"I hope you have a warrant."

Carlos leaned forward, alarmed by her actions. Trish pulled the case from the car and tried to open it without success. *"Where's the key?"* she asked the associate.

"You're making a mistake."

"Where is it?"

"I work for Victor Stone."

"Is that supposed to mean something?"

"When you realize I've done nothing wrong, you'll have to answer for it."

"If you've done nothing wrong, you don't mind opening the case..."

The associate chuckled to himself and pulled a key from his pocket. She snagged it from his hand and opened the case. Inside, were bundles of money.

"Nothing wrong, huh?"

"I don't see how having money..."

"What's he buying from you?"

"I want to talk to a lawyer."

Before she could answer, Carlos was out of the car. He joined Trish at her side and grabbed her arm, trying to pull her back. *"Come on."*

"Go back to the car," she said, pulling away from him.

"Officer Reynalds..." Carlos raised his voice. *"You're obsessing over this."*

She turned and met his eyes. After a few breaths, she calmed herself and turned back to the associate with a blank stare.

"Am I free to go?" he asked. He waited for her to nod him away. *"You'll be hearing from me."*

She scanned a database, studying profiles, one after another. She stopped on a profile of the associate and began to read.

An hour later, Trish and Carlos walked together in uniform down a busy pathway. Carlos listened as she briefed him on the associate. *"He's an investment banking analyst and he's been investigated for fraud twice."*

"So what?"

"Do you need me to draw you a picture?"

"Yeah, I get it. He's probably mixed up in some shit. I don't doubt it."

"And you expect me to turn my head?"

"There's a process you need to follow. You can't chase a hunch with no evidence. Even if you find something, you've already broken how many procedures? It won't hold up."

"We can worry about that later."

"Not we. I'm no part of this. You're cutting way too many corners."

"*I don't...*"

"*Let's not pretend like I don't know the law. I could make a list of ways you've broken the law.*"

"*Very small things.*"

"*Doesn't matter.*"

"*Half the department is taking bribes, stashing drugs and money in their lockers. I change paperwork to ensure a criminal is guilty instead of on the streets. Maybe you should channel your efforts elsewhere.*"

"*My father was a by-the-books cop and I honor that by doing what he would've done,*" Carlos said. "*I don't take bribes and I don't doctor paperwork. It's never okay.*"

"*You don't know that.*"

"*Of course I do.*"

"*You think I go home and tell Paul about these things? I tell him when we do something good. A month ago, we put away a suspect by convincing him to come in for questioning as a witness. On the book, he would've walked free after committing murder. I understand the need for a code, but that's the on-the-surface law that makes people feel like we have structure, but the truth is that criminals aren't by any book and that gives them an edge. You can't beat an edge unless you meet and exceed it.*"

"*Or find another way. A way to operate within the law.*"

"*Don't you understand that if every cop was like you, the criminals would own the city?*" she asked. "*We need to stop turning our backs on them just because they have the advantage.*"

"*And what? You go to Victor and try to lock him up? His lawyers will take you to court and he'll be back, only with a vendetta.*"

"*So you don't want to ignore it, and you don't want to take steps to prevent it. What exactly do you want Carlos? What exactly are you here for?*"

"*In only a year as a cop, I can give you a hundred times I made this city safer.*"

"*Temporarily. They all wind up back on the street. They don't change. I'm just not a parking ticket cop Carlos. I can't do this job and be that. Otherwise, what's the point?*"

She left him there and went straight to the office to wait for Victor or his associate, or any sign of illegal activity. She parked her car in the parking lot outside the building and watched. The lights were off and there was no sign of life. As the thought of Victor ate at her, she grew impatient. She struggled with what Carlos said, what Paul always said, what the job entailed and how to be effective. Ninety percent of her time was wasted. She made up her mind to proceed and exited her car...

...The forensics expert pulled the bullet from Bedbug and set it on a tray at his side, where Trish fixated on it.

Manny stepped forward. "I talked to the officers on this case. Doesn't seem to be a lot of interest in pursuing it..."

"If you're suggesting we're sweeping this under the rug..."

"Not at all. With all due respect, I knew the victim and he lived and worked within my jurisdiction. I would like to offer my assistance in handling this investigation."

As they spoke, Trish edged her way toward the bullet.

"We can handle it," the detective said.

"The crime scene was a mess," Manny countered.

"I'm sorry we don't have the lack of crime around here that you do in your corner of the city, but we have bigger fish to fry than some lowlife who got himself shot by being in the wrong part of LA."

"We both know this will be written off as a cut and dry gang initiation. That's what you guys do down here. When you don't know what happened; you call it gang related. There's more to this. You're blind if you can't see that."

"Then we'll find it."

"I'm offering my assistance."

"I'm telling you we don't need it. We know our reputation to your department and I'm here to tell you, we're plenty competent. Unless you want to put in for a transfer to this division and see the shit that we deal with—shit that would make your head spin."

Trish nonchalantly held the bullet up and inspected it. She slowly looked up and noted that no one was paying attention. The forensics expert stood nearby with his arms crossed, watching the argument, ready to jump in to defend his department if needed.

"You have an evidence bag?" Trish asked. The forensics expert walked off to grab one, and as he did, she tried shoving the bullet in her pocket, but her trembling hands caused it to fall to the ground. She quickly slipped Charlie's bullet in the bag instead and stood on her own bullet, blocking it from view.

"Do you know who I am?" Manny asked. "Do you have any idea who you're dealing with?"

Trish seemed to be the only person in the room satisfied that the conversation was heated. It gave her the opportunity to edge the bullet toward the drain with her shoe, until finally it fell with the tiniest of clinks. She let out a breath of relief. Her presence at the scene was erased. She only had Charlie left to deal with.

4

Billy Dilisio was a well-respected teacher at Conoga Park School. The faculty loved him. The students loved him. He was funny, engaging, and one of the kindest teachers anyone had ever seen. When the school learned that Billy was found with a bullet in his face, in an apartment in the slums, no one believed it to be true. Billy was a good man, no matter how the media was painting him.

Immediately, an assembly was called and members of the faculty honored him and the choir sang a song in his honor. As everyone gathered in the auditorium to remember the man who almost murdered Adlar Wilcox, but successfully ended the lives of many before him, Charlie Palmer struggled with how events played out on the rooftop. When he learned it wasn't Adlar who'd been shot, but a stranger he'd never heard of, he set out to learn as much as he could about the victim. Like everyone else, Charlie couldn't find the link between a teacher and Adlar. What he did know was that he was partly responsible for Billy's death. His may not have been the bullet that killed him, but he brought Trish to that rooftop and he fired the first shot. Now, all he was left with was to sort through how he felt about it.

Was it really that different than Abby?

He shook the thought. Of course it was. He didn't try to kill Abby. He stopped analyzing at that point, because to analyze beyond meant facing a hard truth. Instead, he stood in the back of the auditorium and watched numbly as tears were shed by hundreds of people who had no idea they were in the same room as the killer.

After the memorial, he drove past Adlar's house. There was still no movement and he didn't think there would be. If Adlar knew what went down in that apartment—and he probably did—he likely high-tailed it out of the area, which left Charlie at square one. He thought about tracking down Toby O'Tool and threatening him, but he was exhausted with the whole thing. Ever since Abby died, he had obsessed about killing Adlar. He had a chance and someone else ended up dead instead. He needed to focus on smarter ideas, like making sure no one traced him back to that roof. Everyone who knew Charlie understood he'd changed after Abby's death. He thought he could go back to his old self after he made things right, but he'd realized he was slipping. He was turning into the kind of guy that could end up dead or in prison for murder, and no one would be surprised. Charlie Palmer: bitter, angry, vengeful, out of control.

He went back to Mindy's house. She was surprised to see him. Their relationship had been nothing but a cluster of one-night-stands in the last month. Mindy didn't ask questions and neither tried to define the relationship. They just slept together. Charlie used her as an emotional outlet and he guessed she had her own demons and used him in the same way. It was a nice arrangement, but considering everything else in his life, it was starting to feel dark. He needed something good.

But then, he saw the look of disappointment on Mindy's face. He wondered what he could have done to upset a woman who seemed to never really care what he did.

"Who's archangel?" she asked.

"Who?"

"I was on my laptop and a message popped up. I don't even use messenger, so at first I was confused. Then I started talking to this guy archangel."

"What does this have to do with me?" Charlie asked.

"Because you installed it on my computer. And you added one person. And you told him you were your wife."

Charlie froze, partly because Mindy would demand an explanation for an unexplainable action, and partly because she called Abby his wife—present tense. Instead of bothering to explain the unexplainable, he let out a deep exhausted breath. "You know what? I won't use your laptop again. I'm sorry."

"How about telling me what's going on?"

"I don't need to tell you what's going on."

"Maybe I need you to."

"I thought you and I had a mutual thing. Why bring drama into this now?"

"I bring drama?" she asked with a laugh. "Within a week of seeing you, I find out you're married. Then, I find out you don't plan on being married long. I kept my mouth shut. I didn't want to be the other girl. I didn't want to have to think that maybe I was the reason you were going to end your marriage, but it certainly seemed like it, and I hated myself for it. Then, when I'm in the middle of figuring out how to handle that, your wife is murdered in the middle of the night."

"Don't talk about that."

"Oh, okay. Let's talk about how I'm the dramatic one then, because you Charlie…you're no drama at all. Lying, cheating, affairs, murder…you're just an average guy, aren't you?"

"Point taken," he said as he walked to the door and threw on his jacket.

"I don't care if you walk out, but tell me one thing: Do you know more than you say about her death?"

He stepped in again, looking into her eyes. She demanded an answer, but she looked afraid. "I can't even believe you'd ask that."

"I talked to a cop. I watch the news. You told everyone you were in bed with her, but you weren't. Innocent people don't lie. They do everything they can to help."

"Maybe I didn't want the world knowing I was having an affair."

"It's not as bad as the world knowing you're a killer."

"So that's what you think?" he asked.

"I don't know what to think," she said. "But I don't think you're innocent. Timing is everything. Yours sucks."

"What did you say to archangel?" he asked.

"I said I didn't know what he was talking about, and that he was mistaken."

Charlie nodded and then stood silently by the door. He thought about that one moment of weakness, and the lies he created because of it, and how everything toppled after. All because of Victor's will. "I have to do some things," he said, softly. "Can I come back later?"

"Tell me first. Tell me if you had anything to do with it."

"I didn't," he said, and immediately felt guilty. He could no longer tell people he didn't have anything to do with Abby's death. "I didn't shoot her."

His errand was something that had been in his head for the last few days. He visited Richard Libby to offer his support. He'd held back for reasons he hadn't completely sorted out. Abby was the victim of the will— so why eliminate it when he simply didn't care about anyone else? Even his own life seemed worthless now. In spite of the group, he was going to decline Richard's offer, but then he got to thinking about Victor, and that's when his mind changed.

Two people died in front of Charlie. He'd heard rumors of other deaths in association. The will was the cause of everything, and it was Victor's doing. If Victor's ghost was watching over them, he wanted it to know that his plan failed. It may have succeeded in killing one, but he wanted them all dead. He felt no moral obligation, or any need to be a team player. He simply wanted to shove it in Victor's face and say good riddance, and somehow find a way to move on. He got to thinking about what a miserable kid Adlar was. He was hiding, and maybe would be for the rest of his life. Charlie was starting to become content with that. Maybe he really could move on.

Richard was surprised to find Charlie at his door. He invited him in and offered him a soda. Five minutes later, they sat across from each other. Richard had a pleased smile on his face. "I thought you'd support me."

"Yeah, why's that?"

"Because you don't strike me as greedy. Troubled sometimes? Sure.

But not greedy."

"I'm not doing this for me or for Abby."

"I know," Richard said. And he did.

"Then maybe you shouldn't act so proud of me."

"I can't help but be proud."

"When this all goes away, it's like it never happened. And then, the only person gone will be Abby." Charlie looked down and his eyes began to water. "Why would Abby of all people deserve to be the only one?"

"She didn't deserve it. She was the casualty of evil. She was one of the good ones and she fell because the actions of the evil. Mr. Palmer, I understand that your decision to support me is based on your hatred of Victor, and your struggle is in finding a reason to believe this was all for something, but sometimes the reality is that good people are just pawns who fell for a greater good. The first man who died in any war had no idea what the outcome was, but each shot, each advance, inch by inch, second by second, they all eventually come to a head. All actions end in monumental moments, and the only thing that's important is the side you were standing on. Your wife would have joined us because she was good. Her life was cut short and it's tragic, but it was not for nothing."

Charlie wanted to believe Richard, and even though he couldn't get on-board with supporting their cause for any reason other than hatred, he'd be there and hopefully, one day he could look back and say it was the right thing. "Do you even know if you're going to win?" Charlie asked.

"I've got you, myself, Toby O'Tool, Tarek Appleton, Royce Morrow, Brian Van Dyke, Maria Haskins, Aileen Thick, Anthony Freeman, Adlar Wilcox…"

"Excuse me?" Charlie asked. "Adlar Wilcox?"

Immediately, he knew he made a mistake in expressing interest, but he couldn't avoid it. Adlar was the killer. The killer couldn't be there for support. Luckily, Richard misread his expression and smiled knowingly at him.

"I know," Richard said. "I thought the same thing. He was a little unexpected, but even if he's a no show, we still have a strong majority. I'd still appreciate your support, just in case. It would be fantastic if we were all there."

"I'll be there," Charlie said, but suddenly everything changed. Forgetting Adlar could be easy in time, but if what Richard said was true, Adlar wasn't on the run. He was ready to come into the open and face Charlie, and what Adlar knew about Charlie would end him.

5

Trish sat in the squad car with Manny, who visibly fumed as he stared out into the open. The longer she spent with her old friend, the more uncomfortable she felt. She chose her words carefully, wanting to be away from this man. "You don't need their cooperation to run your own investigation."

"The bullet solves the case," he said. "But since they'll hold onto all the evidence, that won't do much good."

"There's other ways. There has to be prints. The way it happened..."

Manny spoke at a rapid pace. "There's no prints because they don't know their heads from their asses here. A teacher goes to the projects to poison a fully stocked refrigerator filled with unexpired milk. Someone was residing there. What is this case to you exactly Ms. Reynalds?" he suddenly asked.

"Nothing anymore. I was just checking in but I'm uninterested."

"You're throwing in the towel?"

"There's not a whole lot I can do," she said. They sat silently while she mustered the courage to ask the same question. "What's this case to you?"

He turned to her, a dark expression in his eyes. They both could see through each other. "Billy and I were close friends," Manny said.

"And you didn't know what he did for a living?"

Manny's silence was the answer she needed. Finally, he spoke. "I don't know what happened, but someone needs to answer for it..."

...Trish strolled through the crowd of workers on the seventh floor of Stone Enterprises, making a straight line for Victor's office. His receptionist, a woman with a nametag that read Daisy, stood as Trish approached and gave her a hard time about needing an appointment.

"It's police business," she said.

"Do you have a warrant?"

"I can get one."

"You do that," Daisy said with fake cheer.

Victor opened the door and looked out as if he'd been expecting Trish. "You may let her in," he said.

Trish watched Victor disappear into his office. She was taken off-guard by his demeanor. She followed him slowly as he circled his desk and took a seat. He was comfortable with her presence. He seemed to see her coming. "Close the door," he said. She did. "What can I do for you Mrs. Reynalds?"

"I'm here to tell you I know what you're up to. I always knew, only I didn't realize how bad it really was. Securities fraud? Embezzlement? Tax

fraud?"

He smiled at her as she leaned in, slyly, sure she had the upper-hand. *"Do you have proof of this?" he asked.*

"It will take nothing to make this case."

"When you go to your department..." he said, prompting her.

"That's right."

"And how will you say you obtained this proof?"

"You think they'll care? The department will stand by me. Count on that."

"You mean, they won't care that you cut corners..."

"Not to take you down."

"Nine corners to be exact."

She shook her head at him, ready to debate, but grew confused. Why did Victor know everything she did so precisely?

"Count them up," he said. "It would have been ten had you walked into my office without my invitation. Of course, I don't need to explain search and seizures under the fourth amendment to you."

"What I do is nothing compared..."

"Compared to what? All I had to do is line myself up with where you were on one day. Do you really believe I'd conduct business in the open? I'm insulted by how stupid you must think I am."

Her smile faded and it all began making sense.

"You should dig again and see if anything turns up that wasn't placed for only you to see."

"Why would you?"

"To make a point. Turn every rock. Do what you have to, but you're standing in my office because you broke nine of your own laws to be here, and I did nothing illegal."

"You misled me. What was I supposed to do? Ignore you?"

"You harassed me long before this incident. I gave Paul a job that's provided you with your dream home and enough money to take care of your daughter for the rest of her life. I offered to leave you more upon my death, which you turned down, and that's acceptable, but you still carry a misguided grudge which I apparently can't escape because you'll abuse every power you have to get to me. I didn't buy anyone off and I don't ask for favors. If others are too cowardly in my presence, that's their issue, but you conjure crimes I haven't committed and I've paid you nothing but respect."

"Until now..."

"That's right. Yet, from the start, you've been on my back. You believe I'm a criminal, but ignore my contributions to the community, the ribbons I've cut, the organizations that stay afloat because of me, the jobs I create.

When you look into that, you'll find it far outweighs the stop lights I run."

"You gave me a reason to investigate, so I did."

"And broke more laws than..."

"My intent was decent. You want to know if I blur the line now and then to put actual bad people away? Yes, I do. So does every other officer on the force. But my intentions aren't selfish."

"Maybe not now."

"Not ever."

"Something tells me when you started your career, you told yourself and everyone else that the line will never be 'blurred', that you'd enforce the law with an iron fist, and never cut corners."

"My job teaches you pretty quickly that by the book doesn't always get the job done. Where we work, we know the truth: that to keep people safe, we have to do what it takes."

"For now."

"Forever."

Victor laughed.

"Is that funny?"

"Cutting corners is a gateway to the next thing. Yesterday you're by the book. Today you break some rules. What happens tomorrow? You see Mrs. Reynalds, you're going to find more ways to do your job the way you feel like it, until the day comes that you're not doing it to put away the criminals anymore. You'll look in the mirror and realize that you are the criminal"

"You think you know me."

"I understand people. When a petty thief skims the register at his workplace for food money and realizes how easy it is, he takes more, for clothes, for entertainment. Soon, he's taking every dollar he can get for all luxuries in life. It's human nature. We do what we can get away with when we're not being watched. Without fail, every time, it's what happens and you do it too. You've already evolved into a new kind of cop. Someday, you'll be covering your own ass. You'll never see what you really are, because you hide behind your badge and tell yourself you're doing something noble. And I'll be here, doing what I do, and I may be guilty of a minimal thing here and there, but I'll still have contributions that far outweigh yours ten to none for the rest of your life. And I'll still be the man that put the roof over your head, sent your daughter to college, and gave you the life you used to dream of. And what do I get in return? Pulled over on the way to my son's Birthday party because you have a vendetta."

Trish hung her head. "I'm sorry," she said. He nodded, satisfied.

"The bad guys never know they're the bad guys Mrs. Reynalds." He waved her off, as if to dismiss her. "That's all..."

"…You killed a school teacher," she said, facing Charlie across a booth.

He cringed at the words "you killed" as if she was completely disowning her own role.

"Charlie, the man you shot..."

"We shot," he said, coldly. He knew she would try to put it in his head through repetition, but he was far ahead of her, and she wasn't going to throw him under the bus. In fact, if Trish really fired the bullet that took a life, he might even have his get out of jail free card.

"You're the reason I was there. I was there to arrest you and fired when fired upon, I fired back. That's self-defense. How you'll explain being on a roof with a sniper rifle is your problem."

"Then why haven't you arrested me?"

"Who says I'm not going to?"

"We both know if this traces back to us, there will be a story to be told and your end of it doesn't make you completely innocent. I told you to mind your own business and you got in the middle."

"An innocent man died Charlie. At some point, enough is enough."

"Why would anyone else be there? Who was this guy to Adlar?"

"I don't know. I don't understand it yet. "I've done my research and there's no reason that man would be in that apartment with a gun, unless Adlar did something to him, but that raises more questions than it answers. If you're not the only one with a vendetta against Wilcox, who else does and how does a school teacher almost get the job done? I can't even say this incident is related at all to any of the beneficiaries. Look Charlie, right now, the only thing you need to do is honor your word. You help my daughter and I'll find what I can, but this mess is a result of your actions. This has nothing to do with our deal."

"You know," Charlie said, ignoring her. "You sound like you're asking me for a favor and setting me up at the same time. But it was your bullet and you already ran. You didn't stick around. If you'd called it in when it happened and said you fired in self-defense, you might have been able to stand on that. Not anymore."

"What are you saying?"

"Nothing. I'm just pointing out the facts."

"All you need to worry about is my daughter and our agreement. You need to see Shiloh immediately."

"What about this ordeal? You going to get rid of the bullet?"

She thought about the question. "I'll investigate, but we're talking about our agreement now. I let you go."

"I need to know that you're not going to throw me under the bus if it points to you. There's nothing that you have that I want, but you and I know this will hit you hard and you know I can help your daughter. You lose more than I do if this doesn't play out right."

"You'll lose your freedom."

"You'll lose your daughter," he said, staring at her with darkened eyes and a stern look on his face. "We can both have what we need and walk away from this. You've wanted to stop this thing from spiraling out of control? Well, one of these guys is a murderer. I'm doing you a favor by trying to rid us all of Wilcox."

"That's not the reason you're doing it. You're doing it because you and Wilcox are the only two who knows what happened that night, and Wilcox has a side of the story that you don't want told. You don't have the leverage you think you have. You're going to look at Shiloh. I'll pay for all the medical costs in time, but if she needs an operation, it has to be you, and it can't wait. I don't care how you do it, but you're going to do it."

"There's no way for me to do that without losing my license and legal action against me..."

"That's your problem."

"It's really not," he said, "because..."

"Your bullet killed him," she said. "I checked."

Charlie said nothing. He turned it over in his mind and studied her face. She wasn't bluffing, but she wasn't right. He knew what went down on the roof. He saw his bullet hit the window-frame. "I was off the mark. I knew I missed even before I took the shot."

"It's your bullet." The confidence in his face faded as he saw she meant it. "I know what you did to Abby and I know what you're going to do to Adlar, and I'm not going to try to stop you. You'll operate on Shiloh and I'll take the heat off of you. We'll invalidate the will and you can do whatever you want with Adlar. Then, we all walk away and forget each other. If you're caught, I won't defend you."

"And if I don't, you do what? Rat me out? Incriminate yourself?"

"No," she said. "I don't care about the rooftop. I care about my daughter. And if you don't save her, then I need to find another way to get her the treatment she needs. I'll see to it that no one meets with the judge. I'll see to it that the will is valid up until I'm the last of you."

6

Dent and Ziggy finished separating a load of laundry, folding towels meticulously and stacking them in neat piles. Wayne hung back, near the area Dent had his chemicals, trying to get a glimpse of the names and hoping he could remember enough of them that the warden could make sense of what they were. Christian looked over his shoulder at him.

"Get the metal box on the vent," Dent told Wayne. "In the box, there's a bag with two bottles and a dime. Bring them to me."

Wayne cooperated, taking the box from its hiding place and opening it. He scanned the contents. While Wayne was busy trying to make sense of everything, Dent reached into a drain and emerged with three masks he'd assembled from supplies he'd gathered in the cafeteria, the instrumental piece of the mask being the plastic bottoms of milk containers.

Dent grabbed the dime from Wayne's hands and walked to the wall where the pipe from the dishwasher ran. He began unfastening the screws around the pipe using the dime as a screwdriver. Ziggy stood by and watched in fascination.

"What are you doing?" Wayne asked.

"We're going."

"Now?"

The pipe came off the wall and Dent swiveled it into another opening: An air duct.

"I don't understand," Wayne said.

While Wayne pondered, Ziggy nodded his understanding in awe and full belief in Dent's abilities.

"Convicts try to escape," Dent said. "They try to sneak past the guards or hop fences. There's more of us than there are them. We outnumber them ten to one, but they've got weapons and high ground, so I asked myself how we could take the weapons—how we could control the facility." As Dent spoke, he started dumping the chemicals into the washer. Another chemical, he dumped into the compartment to be mixed upon the wash cycle. "What I'm making is essentially pentothol, sevoflurine, and midazolam...an anesthesia, running into every open vent in this place. These vents run into every corner of Kern. Everyone's exposed."

Wayne couldn't comprehend, but Ziggy smiled as he followed the pipe from the washer to the vent, wondering just what would be filling Kern in a matter of minutes.

"A forty-five minute cycle is all the time we have. Maybe another ten while the air clears and they're waking up. Like I said: We're walking out in front of their faces."

"Holy shit," Ziggy said.

Dent started the cycle.

"So what?" Wayne asked. "Something gonna happen to the guards?"

In the moments Dent explained to Wayne exactly what should be happening, a guard in the control room noticed another sleeping. He tried to wake him, but before could, his eyes began to sting and he ended up on the floor next to his buddy. From there, the air from the vents began spreading throughout Kern and one by one, the guards and convicts passed out before they even knew what hit them. Anyone remotely suspicious of an escape was knocked out before they could act on it.

Dent, Ziggy, and Wayne waited five minutes with the masks over their mouths, held securely in place.

Ziggy gave Dent a sideways look and a nod. Wayne wasn't quite so trusting, but held the mask to his face, afraid to take it off only to wake up and find Dent and Ziggy gone. If that were to happen, the warden would have his ass for sure. "We can't just go like this!" Wayne shouted, above the sound of the washer.

"Then stay!" Dent yelled back.

Dent and Ziggy ascended the steps that led back to the corridors. Wayne followed reluctantly. Dent and Ziggy gave each other a look, signaling they were ready. The last thing Dent thought before he shouldered his way through the doors was that he hoped this would work. This was his last chance at freedom.

Chapter 18

1

Dent didn't have a chance with the wall because there were always guards patrolling outside the compound, but when the evening shift began, right around shift change, the outside had no idea what was happening on the inside for three hours. Dent needed one hour inside without eyes on him.

He hurried through the hallways with Wayne and Ziggy at his side, holding their masks over their faces and turning from side to side to look at the guards who were slumped against the walls or at their desks. Ziggy and Wayne watched in amazement, seemingly shocked by what Dent was able to pull off. Dent only stared forward, focusing on his one objective. He navigated expertly.

"Where's this taking us?" Wayne asked.

Dent pushed through a large metal door and suddenly they were descending stairs into a dark underground room that was a jumble of pipes and wiring. He kept walking through, sure of his destination. "Seventy-five years ago, before this was a level 5 prison, it was just a jail. They kept head-cases and violent natured men with brain disorders. There wasn't a paper-trail behind any of it in those days. Some guy would off his family because voices told him to and they'd toss him in here and forget he existed. A group got together and began digging tunnels. Quite a few escaped but were later found and hung. The prison was restructured. Lockup was on the opposite side now and getting to the tunnels requires passing every guard on the way to the entrance, so the tunnels remain because there's no way to get to them."

"Guess they didn't count on being gassed," Ziggy said with a smile.

"Jesus..." Wayne said, unable to comprehend just how easy it all seemed for Dent.

Dent continued. "A few attempts have been made by small groups to overpower the guards. They add more security and cameras, but the door never had a chain and they never filled the tunnels because there's allegedly corrupt guards who used to sneak cons out at night under surveillance to see their families or get money they'd buried to pay them off for favors. This was seven decades ago, and not long after, most of this was forgotten. They built a brick wall in front of the entrance in the 60s and forgot about it. I doubt most of the guards know it's there, and the ones who do, assume the tunnels don't take you out of here, but the tunnels run into an abandoned tungsten mine."

"And you know the system?" Wayne asked with doubt. "How do you know they lead out? They could have collapsed. And how would you know the route? There's no way."

"I've studied the maps."

Wayne came to a halt. "I can't do this. I'm claustrophobic."

"Then go back," Dent said.

"How long you think we got?" Ziggy asked.

"By the time they come to, figure out what happened, and start counting heads, we need to be gone."

They turned another corner and all three came to a halt as they reached the brick wall. The brick was old and would easily collapse, but no one knew just what they would see on the other side. Dent started kicking and Ziggy followed his lead. Wayne made a half-ass attempt to toss the fallen brick aside, hoping the other side would be a wall of dirt.

A bead of sweat dropped off Dent's nose as he grabbed chunks of brick and one by one, tossed them to the side, grunting with every throw. Finally, the wall of brick collapsed...

"...How would you like your freedom?"

The question came out of the blue one day. Mitch was sitting in a chair with a bottle of booze in one hand and a cigarette in the other. A dumbfounded Christian, age eighteen, fell silent.

"You hear what I asked you?" Mitch asked.

"Why? You want me to go back?"

"No. I'm giving you a choice. Your daddy never gave you a choice, and neither did I. There ain't no chains on you and ain't no one gonna try to hunt you down if one day you're gone."

"I could have left whenever. I don't know why you're talking like this."

"You adapted to us Chrissy. I reckon now you might wanna think about returning while you're young enough do whatever you want."

"I'm not interested."

"Daddy was that bad, huh?"

Christian met Mitch's eyes and nodded.

"Something you should know," Mitch said. "I'm telling you like it is

when I say I want you to have your freedom, but I also think you should know that your mother is on her death bed. I've kept tabs over the years. Other day I found out she's got cancer. The kind you can't fix. It'll take her."

Christian felt numb. What little he remembered of his mother was that she was good and loving, but he resented her for the way his father controlled her. "How long she have?"

"Couple a months at the most. So if you wanna go back..."

"I do," Christian said suddenly. Mitch leaned forward, intent to hear what was on his mind. "I want to talk to her, but I won't be staying."

"If your mother sees you, or anyone else, coming back here would be pointless. They'd have every cop in ten counties searching for you."

"They ain't gonna see me."

"What about your daddy?"

Christian shook his head, dismissively. "I've got nothing to say to him."

Mitch studied his eyes. Christian had every intention of doing exactly what he said. He wanted to see his mother one last time, and that was respectable. It was a liability, but Mitch might have done the same if given the chance, and Dent had grown into an intelligent strong man. He could make his decisions and execute them well if presented with problems.

"I'll take you."

"Yeah?" Dent asked, surprised and relieved. It was a trip he needed to take, and not one he wanted to take alone.

"Yup. We'll drive down a couple days. You do what needs to be done and we'll return."

"Sounds good to me."

"Something else you should know. This business with your mother has won your daddy a lot of sympathy. Some people think he might make a run for Washington. He's popular with the folks there."

Christian sneered, disgusted by his father's positive reputation.

"His career's shaping up Chrissy. I don't want it rubbed in your face."

"What the fuck do I care?"

"Thought you might see it as it is. He's exploiting the circumstances. First, your disappearance and now he's about to be widowed. His rise in popularity is due to sympathy—to the strength they say he endured in hard times. You sure you're okay with this? He'll be around—campaigning and shit."

"I'm fine. I got nothing to say to him..."

...Clods of dirt cascaded down on the men as the brick toppled forward and scattered on the ground below. They stared at what they were up against. There was no doubt an opening, but the years had hardened the ground behind the wall and the opening was narrower than expected. "We need something to dig through this," Dent said.

Ziggy's optimism faded. It was a nice try, but there was no way of knowing what the tunnels would hold. He thought about suggesting they go back. There was still hope that everyone would wake up confused and not know what to make of it. Instead, he decided to follow Dent down. Why not? Kern had gotten old and Ziggy's life was closer to the end than the beginning. "I'll find something," he said.

"I'll go with him," Wayne said. "The cafeteria will have something."

They left Dent to keep working on the tunnels and went back where they came, reentering the corridor, where the guards were still out. It was a sight Ziggy never thought he'd see. If they were caught, the whole display was worth the effort put into it. Heaps of men slouched over their desks and sat in haphazard positions along the corridor as Ziggy and Wayne step over them. They searched frantically for anything they could use to dig through the pile of rock and dirt.

"We've gotta shut this off," Wayne said, his voice shaking. He didn't know how long the gas would last, but any moment, a guard could open his eyes and they would be as good as dead, and if not, Wayne would be stuck in Kern forever.

"That why you came along?" Ziggy asked. "You wanna talk me out of it? Just shut up and keep looking. We don't have time for this. We're not turning back."

"They'll kill us. We need to stop while we still can."

"I'd rather die getting out of here than stay another day."

Ziggy pushed through another door and Wayne reluctantly followed. They walked freely through the kitchen. It was surreal to have free reign in the building. Ziggy moved from one cabinet to another, frantically searching for what he needed.

He suddenly stopped as he found himself staring at a stack of pans. His eyes lit up as he grabbed three and stored them under his arm.

"It won't be enough," Wayne said.

"Then go back!" Ziggy shouted. He hurried past Wayne and maneuvered around a guard slouched against the wall on the way out. Wayne watched him from a distance.

As Ziggy hurried through the hallway without concern for whether Wayne was behind him or not, Wayne finally emerged from the kitchen and followed slowly at a safe distance. Ziggy turned back and caught a glimpse of him. "If you're coming along, hurry the hell up!"

Ziggy started to open the door back to the corridor, but before it swung all the way open, Wayne closed the gap between them and suddenly shoved it closed. As Ziggy turned back with surprise, Wayne grabbed Ziggy's mask and pulled it from his face. Ziggy's eyes went wide as he leaped to the ground to secure it back to his face before the gas got the best of him. He slipped it on and turned back to Wayne, ready to confront him, but was silenced as he found himself staring into the barrel of a gun. He realized he'd turned his back on Wayne long enough to allow him to snatch a gun from one of the guards.

"You don't have to go with us Wayne," he said, his voice shaking. "But at least give me a chance."

"This is my way out," Wayne said.

Ziggy knew it was the end. He saw the guilt in his eyes and knew Wayne had been talking to someone up high—probably the warden. He only had a moment to plead. "Wayne..."

Before he could say more, Wayne pulled the trigger. Ziggy's head snapped back and blood splattered on the wall behind him. Wayne turned away, unable to face what he did. He pulled the door open and walked through into the darkness, heading toward Dent.

2

With nowhere else to go, Adlar Wilcox went home. He couldn't face his parents or make amends with them. Instead, he went home while they were working and crawled in through a window. For two days, he wandered the house and played on his computer. At night, he stayed in his den, hidden in a small unused room in the basement, lying on a pile of blankets. He stealthily lived at home, and his parents never knew. It was a good place to hide if someone was after him. He followed the news and learned Bedbug's identity and was able to piece together a scary fact: So many people wanted him dead, now they were accidentally killing each other. He was lucky, but he was completely on his own, and he turned to where he felt safe, and sure enough, living in his basement made him feel safer than he had in a while.

If anyone was looking for him, the only trace of Adlar to his home was the small amounts of food he took from the pantry—so small they were unnoticeable—and the fact that during the day, the Internet was used. That would only be detected if one were to look for it, and Adlar assumed no one suspected he'd come home. What he didn't know was how resourceful those searching for him were.

There was no knock at the door, because the man who came for Adlar knew he wouldn't answer. Instead, Manny used his police skill-set to pick the lock on his front door and enter the house quietly in the middle of the day. From the upstairs dining room, he heard the clickety-clack of the keyboard as Adlar did what he did best. Manny descended the stairs and stared at the back of Adlar's head: The kid was toxic. Hard to find, hard to kill, but small and harmless. He was the King Midas of shit.

Manny thought about finishing what they were hired to do, but was intrigued by the situation. Royce Morrow wanted this guy dead? It made no sense. It made even less sense that this guy ultimately resulted in the demise of Billy. He couldn't comprehend what made Adlar so special and there was more to the story that he wanted. If not for that simple fact, Adlar would have been dead by now.

"Adlar," Manny said.

Adlar almost leaped out of his chair. By the time he turned and put himself together, he calmed down. The man in front of him was harmless. He had a badge and a calm demeanor. But he found Adlar. Was this the end? Prison? Maybe worse?

"Yeah, what?" he asked. He tried to play it cool but was terrified.

"I wanted to talk to you."

"You have a warrant?"

"For what? To talk to you?"

"Did I do something wrong?"

"No, but you may have been a witness to a crime. How long have you been residing here?"

"My whole life."

"Your whole life, huh?" Manny asked, doubtfully.

"Yeah."

"You like omelets?"

Adlar paused and squinted his eyes as if this was the strangest question he'd ever heard. "Um, yeah. I guess so."

"Couple blocks down there's a place that boasts good omelets. Get your shoes. I'll buy you one."

"Am I in trouble?"

"You don't have to be if you answer a few questions. I'm looking for someone and I think you can help me."

"I don't think I know anything."

"I think you do and I think you know it. And I think you don't wanna talk because you've done a few things you shouldn't have done. Am I hitting the right keys?"

"No," Adlar said, unconvincingly.

"What would you say if I gave you my personal guarantee that I don't care what you did? I'm only looking for the shooter on the roof. Don't care why you were there. Don't care who or why they wanted to kill you. Only want the shooter."

"Who?" Adlar asked, freezing up. Manny was looking into his eyes as if he could already see the truth. It didn't help matters that Adlar had no idea who Manny even was or how he was linked to the whole incident. It was just another stranger in a long line involved in a web of people who wanted him dead.

"I want the guy who killed the guy who was planning to kill you."

Adlar choked up, his body shaking with fear. Manny squinted his eyes at him suspiciously and a sly smile stretched across his face. "How bout that omelet?"

Adlar watched Manny shove a large chunk of sausage into his mouth. After Manny swallowed, he leaned in. "What about family? You got any family that would want you dead?"

"Yes," Adlar said, causing Manny to look up curiously. "Probably most of them."

"Why?

"They don't like me."

"That's not a reason. A reason would be that you're a direct threat to someone. That you've taken something from someone."

"I stole my uncle Ian's credit card once and he found out."

"He want you dead for that?"

"Probably."

"How much did you spend?"

"Well, he never knew it was me."

"Then..." Manny didn't finish his thought. Adlar wasn't very good at deciphering questions. "Look, being a pest isn't a reason to kill someone. You kill for revenge or gain. Who gains from your death? Who did you take something from? I need you to figure that out."

"Why? I don't know."

"Because you're lucky. Two unconnected people wanted to kill you and one killed the other, thinking it was you. You're alive because you're lucky. But there's one left and I want to catch him because he killed my friend."

"That guy couldn't have been there to kill me."

"He was. Read the news. You're the luckiest son of a bitch I've ever met, and you're walking around like it doesn't matter, or holding out because there's something bigger going on. Personally, I don't see how you can be connected to anyone or have made an impact big enough to be wanted dead, but I don't know. Maybe you do know. Maybe you know why you're worth more dead than alive. You're not doing much to prevent it from happening again, because if you're not completely dumb, you'll know they'll come at you until the job is done."

Adlar considered. "I guess I do stuff on-line sometimes. Not much lately, but I used to mess around and find ways to make money. Probably people just found out. But I never know their names or anything."

"Not good enough." Manny grew angry and his voice rose. "He was a teacher Wilcox. Does that matter to you? You got an ounce of empathy in you?"

"You said he was there to kill me, so I'm glad he's dead."

Manny's jaw tightened and his fingernails dug into the palm of his hands. "Maybe you knew he was coming," he said, coolly. I don't know how, but the only thing that makes sense is that you were on that rooftop."

"I wasn't," Adlar said, cowering.

"He's dead and you're alive. Maybe you're not lucky. Maybe it's not a coincidence. Am I onto something?" He leaned forward, forcing Adlar to meet his eyes. He analyzed Adlar's every movement.

"I brought the cat in and that guy was dead."

"Ah, right. You left for a couple of minutes and it all went down. Pretty convenient. Let me ask you something: Why were you even in that building?"

"I ran away and found that place."

"And you stepped out, two people tried to kill you, and you ran home..."

Adlar swallowed hard. "Yeah."

Manny nodded in disbelief. "I see."

"Can I go?"

"Yeah, as long as you know someone's going down for this. You've got at least two enemies in this world and I know one, but you're not getting that from me. Not yet. Maybe if you help me out, I'll help you out. But these people, they still have a bounty on you, and your life is still at risk, so when you figure out I can help you, give me a call. You're too incompetent to have been the shooter, but you better hope all roads point somewhere else. Someone will answer for this."

"It wasn't me."

"Call me when you remember something." Manny slid his card across the table. Adlar quickly snatched it and slid from the booth and away as quickly as he could. Manny watched him suspiciously as he shoved another bite in his mouth.

3

Sweat rolled down Dent's face as he clawed at the wall of dirt, pulling clumps aside piece by piece and counting the minutes in his head. Wayne and Ziggy were taking too long and a feeling of doom began to set in. Suddenly, a sheet of dirt fell in clods and collapsed inward to reveal the tunnel. He stared in wonderment at the underground pathway, ready to move forward. Something felt wrong. He turned back where he came and listened as the large metal doors closed in the distance. An echo traveled from the entry to Dent, and that was it. There were no voices, no hurried footprints; the silence was out of place. He stood and slowly walked along the wall of the room, waiting to be sure it was Ziggy and Wayne who would reveal themselves, but the quiet discomforted him.

From the stairwell leading to the boiler room, Wayne walked slowly, taking caution with every step, holding the gun close to his body. He kept his eyes on every bit of space revealed as he slowly walked toward Dent. He heard the same thing as Dent and it concerned him just as much: Silence.

Dent's eyes moved back and forth, trying to detect something. At a distance, he heard a footstep. His eyes narrowed suspiciously as he contemplated what to do. He turned and slowly made his way back to the tunnel and forced himself through the opening and into the darkness of the caves. Before going further, he turned back to see who would walk out of the shadows. He only saw one shape, and it moved slowly, as if trying to sneak up. He watched as Wayne approached the caves and looked into the dark, right at Dent...

...Sunlight shined through the windows of the car, blinding Dent as he squinted his eyes to see the scenery transform from the big city into trees and winding roads. It was a landscape that he'd long forgotten.

"This all familiar?" Mitch asked from the driver seat.

"Yeah. We lived on the edge of the woods. Had a river behind the house with a tree that fell and crossed it. My mother hated it but I used it as a bridge and walk across or just sit there."

"If we got the time, we'll see if it's still there."

"I don't wanna see it," Christian said.

Mitch quietly nodded. Christian seemed to have put his old life behind him and accepted that. "You might like being with me and my crew now, but someday things may go haywire, or we'll get too old to run shipments or the world will evolve and the drugs and transportation will change and we'll be replaced. You're taking a risk sticking with us."

"Why you still doing it if you feel that way?" Christian asked.

"Cause I suck at everything else. Could you picture me behind a desk?"

"I don't wanna be behind one either."

"You're different than me. That's for sure."

"How's that?"

"I chose this. That's how. You've got brains in your head."

"Yeah, because of you."

"Most people don't retain what you do. You've got a memory. Don't take your life for granted. I picture the relative brevity of life by imagining a laser-thin spotlight creeping along a gigantic ruler of time. Everything before or after the spotlight is shrouded in the darkness of the dead past, or the darkness of the unknown future. We are staggeringly lucky to find ourselves in that spotlight. However brief our time in the sun, if we waste a second of it, or complain that it is dull or barren or boring, it's a callous insult to those trillions who are never offered life in the first place."

"What the fuck is wrong with you?" Christian asked with a laugh. Mitch was talking in a way he'd never heard.

"Nothing. It's your mother. When my ma died, I resented her for wasting her life. I might not be doing what she'd want, but I'm sure as hell not wasting my time."

"She stayed with my dad. That's bad enough. Getting away from them was the best thing that ever happened to me."

"Yet, your father's made a name for himself. He works crowds and they celebrate him without knowing who he truly is. It should be you. You're better than him and you're as good as dead to the world. They probably don't even ask about you anymore or speak your name. Would he recognize you if he saw your face?"

"He'll get his someday."

"In a month, your mother will be gone. He'll have more supporters, just like when you were taken."

"And whose fault is that?"

"That's why I'm telling you to consider what you're gonna do next. Following me around and putting yourself at risk isn't something you should choose to do if you have better options. Go back to your river and your tree for all I care, but stop wasting your time with me."

Christian sat in silence the rest of the way, staring out the window and watching the scenery pass by.

The door opened, letting light into a darkened room. Christian stood in the frame, looking down at the woman in bed. His mother, Meredith Dent, laid there. It had been a long time since he'd seen her, but she'd aged a lifetime. Her eyes opened slightly, and she turned to face him. Her speech was slow and slurred, and he didn't understand what she said, or if she recognized him. He searched her eyes, but she was barely there.

He stepped inside, and his face came into the light. His mother's eyes widened enough to give him his answer. She stared in disbelief as he knelt at her side. "Mom..." he said.

Her eyes watered as she took him in.

She said something that was barely audible but he heard the word 'dream' and he smiled at her, making his presence known.

"It's really me. I'm here."

She managed a smile and looked into his face. "Safe..." was all he heard.

"I've been taken care of. My life is good."

Relief flooded her face.

"I heard you were here and came back. I'm sorry I didn't come back sooner."

"I knew you were..." she managed before whispering "alive."

"Yeah Mom. I've got a life in Miami. A good one."

"Dream..." she whispered.

"I always wanted to come back. I was going to get you away from him. When I was little, you know, I always knew if I stopped him from doing what he did, he'd do it to me. I always thought I'd come and take you away. Maybe do to him what he did for a while. Just, I always thought there would be time."

"You don't worry about me."

"You deserved better."

She found his eyes, and her own watered. "I knew you were alive. I only wanted you to be free. I didn't want you to come back to him. This is all I needed. The last memory I had of you..." Her voice faded to a whisper. Christian grabbed her hands and moved closer so she could whisper. "I drove you," Meredith said. "Let you put your hand on wheel...wanted to drive but..." She went into a coughing fit.

"It's okay. I know."

"I celebrated your sixteenth without you. I envisioned you in the sun driving with the top down...away."

"I was ma." Christian got choked up.

"You were better off..."

Dent couldn't decide whether it was a question, but he answered anyway. "They didn't hurt me. Didn't force me to stay. I'm always outside. I drive. I work. I didn't run away. I was taken, but I chose to stay."

She teared up again.

Dent searched for words. "I came back to apologize."

"No. I'm happy." She closed her eyes, seemingly at peace. He stayed and watched her for a long time, not letting her hand go. He shifted into a more comfortable position and sat by her bedside...

...Wayne stared into the darkness, wishing he had a flashlight. He could have been staring directly at Dent but wouldn't know.

"Dent?" he asked, his voice quiet. He waited for a response, but none came. What he was certain of was that Dent heard him. There was enough of an opening, but he couldn't believe Dent would move on without them—unless he knew something happened. He approached the cave opening and looked through the crevices that Dent would have had to squeeze through to move forward. He might have noticed Dent curled against the ground, pressed up against the ground, if there had been the faintest of light, but instead he was stuck with the decision to move forward without a guide, or head back and take his chances with the guards. The washer was very likely done with its spin cycle, but Wayne had no idea how long it would take for them to awaken.

Wayne stepped halfway into the dark and listened, keeping as still as he could. And then, after a long silence, he turned back the way he came.

When Wayne was gone, Dent began moving onward. He made his way like a man knowing where he was going. The openings became narrower. He squeezed through a cave wall, ducking, looking forward in the darkness. He kept Ziggy in the back of his mind, trying to contain the anger he had that the wrong man died today. He knew Wayne was stringing him along for quite some time, but didn't think it would make a difference in the end.

He stopped momentarily and put his hand up, staying still and waiting for a breeze. He detected a slight wind, but nothing like what he expected. He slowly pushed forward, unfamiliar with where he was. He turned his head, looking back where he came. The light from the opening was slowly disappearing.

Wayne hurried back to the halls and made his way back to the laundry, stumbling down the steps and approaching the washer. He looked at the timer and made his mind up. He turned the dial and shut it down. He turned and ran back up the steps.

Dent pulled himself through another opening, barely able to fit. He breathed hard, gasping for air and searching the area in hopes that the walls would expand. A drop of water fell in front of him. He looked up to see the faintest ray of light shining down on him. He reached up, weakly, but it was far and unreachable. His eyelids fluttered as he looked up toward the light. He tried to push forward, but it was too tight. Over the years, the ground had fallen in in too many spots. He closed his eyes in defeat. His one and only chance was fading fast. Going back meant facing the warden. Donovan would likely return. He wouldn't make it through the night. He rested his back against the wall and looked up at the sliver of sun light shining through.

Wayne entered an office and found Warden Sunjata on the ground. He grabbed around his waist and pulled him to his feet, desperately trying to wake him. The warden finally stirred and began rubbing his eyes, unaware of his surroundings. He started coughing and when he opened his eyes all the way, there were deep grooves and puffy redness surrounding them.

"What's going on?" he asked, confused.

"It's Wayne sir. Dent's making a run for it."

"How? What did he do?" The warden was still trying to make sense of what happened, while trying to get to his feet to act. He stumbled, his feet numb and his eyes stinging.

"He had some sort of toxin he released. He poisoned everyone. I shut it off."

"Where is he?"

"The caves."

"What caves?"

"Under the building," Wayne said. "There's caves."

The warden's face hardened and suddenly his confusion transformed into determination. He called for help and set out to get everyone back on their feet. When he had the manpower awakened and aware, he immediately had Wayne sent to the hotbox. He had another guard round up the population to take a head-count and took a dozen men through the corridor that led to the caves. He ordered a guard to make sure the population was back in their cells and Kern locked down.

They gathered outside the door that led to the boiler room. Slumped against the wall was Ziggy, his eyes still open and the blood on his face drying. The warden took the lead and positioned himself at the side of the door. He grabbed the handle and pulled it open. They stepped into the boiler room with their weapons drawn.

4

The floors creaked above and Adlar's eyes looked toward the ceiling, the only light on his face, the glow of his laptop. He wondered if his mom or dad was up late and moving around. He wondered if they thought about him anymore. Maybe they were happy to be rid of him. When he lived at home with their knowledge, he wanted to be left alone. Now, he was tempted to ascend the stairs and see whoever was there and tell them what happened.

He was afraid. The detective who visited him earlier put the fear back in him. Adlar had been digging himself a hole far too long and his actions came full circle. The only way to be truly invisible and hide from those who wanted to kill him was to live completely off the grid. He looked into his laptop screen and for the first time in his life, he wondered what life would hold for him if he closed it forever. His interest had always been gaming, but a decade passed and nothing changed, other than the games themselves, and they always would. He couldn't picture himself as an old man typing away on a keyboard. In fact, when he really thought about it, the games lost their appeal. He'd been doing the same thing for so long and he was tired. To be able to go upstairs. To sit and have a late night slice of pie with his mother or father and tell them something about himself, to find out something about them, sounded so freeing. He wondered what his parents did for a living. He didn't even know. He knew nothing about them. Not how they met, or what their interests were at his age. Everything surrounding Adlar had been a blur.

If he could find his way past all the trouble with Charlie, and Royce, and the man who died in his apartment sticking a needle in his milk...if he could find a way to make it right, maybe he could talk to his parents, find new interests, make friends, and a girlfriend. He suddenly wanted to have dinner with a woman, have sex after, go to the park with a friend; all the things he never cared about were suddenly colorful. To give up one thing he'd been so consumed with for every hour of every day, opened him up to so many things he'd never wanted—never believed he wanted.

In two days, Richard was gathering the group to stand before a judge to end the will. Adlar told Toby he'd agree to be there and back out, but now he knew he had to actually be there. He had to put an end to the document that tempted him, that distracted him and darkened him, that turned him into a killer. And maybe someday he could make things right for what happened to Abby, but he had to start with the will. When that was taken care of, there was no reason Royce couldn't have his box back. There was no reason Adlar couldn't put everything behind him and set his life on a better course.

He gently put his hand on his laptop and readied himself to close it.

Never open it again, he told himself and then tried to think of any last sites he needed to visit to tie loose ends. There was nothing. Just games with endless levels. They never ended. That was the point. Any child could start at level one and never reach a destination—only be distracted.

He fell asleep by the light of his laptop.

An hour later, from out of nowhere, the computer in the bedroom of Sharon and Gary Wilcox blinked and flashed before powering on. Sharon stirred. Gary continued snoring. The cursor moved on it's own, going through a series of actions as it opened file after file, changing them before moving on. Whoever was operating from somewhere far from the Wilcox home, finished within minutes before the computer shut down again. Neither Wilcox ever awoke.

As Adlar slept, the same movement began on his own computer before it too shut down. As it powered down, his eyes slowly opened. He warily rubbed them and looked up, confused. Upon seeing the blank screen, he frowned for a moment as if trying to separate his dreams from reality and let himself fall back asleep.

5

Guards rushed through Kern as alarms blared. Most were still hazy and confused, trying to piece together why exactly they all woke up on the job. Rumors circulated, but no one was sure who did it or how. They didn't have time to stop and converse. They had a potential missing prisoner to tend to. The convicts were lined up, each exiting their cells accompanied by guards. They worked their way up each tier and had only cleared half the ground floor. It wouldn't be long before they realized who was missing and where he was.

As the guards brought the convicts back to their cells from the cafeteria and other branches of Kern, the warden made his way through the tunnels with four guards who walked cautiously at his side, flashlights beaming through the tunnels, ready to jump in and protect him if anything unexpected happened.

"Who knows the cave system here?"

A guard stepped forward, volunteering himself.

"How many ways out of here?" the warden asked.

"One. Maybe none."

They came to a spot where the path split in two.

"Split here," he said. He pointed to one guard. "Go back and find out if and where the ground opens. I need to set up a search outside Kern if we don't find him in five minutes. We do not want to have to alert anyone, so find him."

"How could he have known about this?" the guard asked.

"I don't know, but be careful. We were all out. He could have a weapon. Until all firearms are accounted for, assume he has a gun."

The warden left his men and went straight to the population where the second tier was being taken to the yard, person by person. His eyes scanned the third tier, where Dent and Wayne's cell was housed. He shook his head in disbelief and walked straight to the yard and to the hotbox sitting against the far wall. He dismissed a guard and opened the hotbox door.

Wayne quickly got to his feet and eagerly awaited what he had to say.

"Did you kill Derrick Zigfried?" the warden asked.

Wayne nodded slowly. "Had to. Had to stop them."

"When we catch Dent, he'll know what you did. You can't see him."

"I'm getting out, right? I did what you asked."

"This went too far. You haven't done anything but help a man poison us."

"I didn't know he was fixing to go right away. You said you'd help me."

"I would've, but this is a real mess. We don't even know if he's in the caves anymore. We've got a dead con and Dent managed to overpower every guard in here simultaneously. You were supposed to be damage control. You were supposed to stop it before it started."

"I tried boss."

"Not hard enough."

Wayne repositioned himself and crawled toward the door, but the warden slammed it closed and latched it. Wayne called out, but the warden kept walking.

A guard caught up to the warden. "I've alerted all adjoining counties."

"Great," Sunjata said. "That's real great. How we supposed to explain this?"

"We had no way of knowing what was happening."

"We gave him the laundry. We let him have the supplies. We allowed his escape because we wanted to know how he was gonna do it."

"We'll get him."

"We have to. No one else captures Dent. Just us. Clear?"

"We have choppers on the way, dogs, the works."

"Shit."

"What do you want me to do?"

"Round up as many men as you can and find the mouth of that cave."

"I don't know where it is."

"Then find out!" the warden shouted.

The guard ran off and another one approached with new news. "Warden..."

"What?"

"We found him."

The warden suddenly came to a halt. "Where?"

"In his cell."

The warden closed his eyes with disbelief.

Moments later, he stood outside Dent's cell, surrounded by guards, all looking in silently as Dent lay on his bunk reading a book. He looked up to see a dozen men who wanted a piece of him.

"Where were you?" the warden asked, grinding his teeth.

"Right here."

"Right there, huh?"

"I did my job and when I was done, no one was around. Everyone was sleeping so I came back to my cell. What's the problem?"

"I know everything. You know the shit-storm you caused? I've got six counties on the alert and we have to explain that we don't have an escaped felon after-all. We've got a man dead..."

Dent's eyebrow cocked at that.

"...Forget what this shenanigan cost the taxpayers. Holy hell Dent, you just bought yourself a lifetime of pain. You're lucky we've got visitors on the way because you'd be dead five minutes ago if we didn't."

"Sounds like you jumped the gun a bit. Shouldn't you put out an alert only if there's an escape?"

The warden smiled at him menacingly. "You won a lot of people over around here. You've done a good job of getting what you want, but it's over. No more laundry. No access to supplies. You won't talk to suppliers. You won't talk to anyone. You will be watched every second of the day. You're going in the hotbox and you'll stand trial for the murder of Derrick Zigfried."

Dent tensed up, but held his voice steady. "Check the cameras. I didn't even know he was dead."

"We did check. Sure as shit you're the man."

The sly expression on Dent's face was replaced with something dark. If the men at Kern wanted to frame him, it would happen. He pissed them off enough to earn a lot of hell in the remainder of his time there, and his escape failed. The warden was the real winner today, despite everything about his demeanor that seemed otherwise.

The warden grabbed the bars and leaned in. "You'll spend a month in the hotbox. When you're out, you'll answer to Donovan, and the caves will be blasted to oblivion. You lost your one go at freedom. I'd have you killed, but I'd rather have you spend your life regretting the little privilege you had that you just tossed in the shitter."

The warden smiled, pleased with himself. When his back was turned, Dent said, "There's still the fence." The warden turned.

"Excuse me?"

"There's two ways out. The tunnels and the fence. You filled the tunnels, so when I do go, I'll use the fence."

The warden's face warped into a series of confusion, concern, and finally back to anger. He was unable to find the words. "You'll never see the outside of these walls Dent." He turned to a guard and shouted, "Get him to the hotbox!"

Two guards entered and hoisted him up. Dent went with them.

They tossed him into the hotbox only yards from Wayne. The hotbox was a small room made of metal and sized for one man to stand in. It sat in the middle of the yard, where the sunshine always came through. Dent's sweat would fill the vents below. The discomfort of standing in a confined space was bad enough. The heat was intolerable. The guards stared in at him for a moment until one man approached from behind and spoke up. "I'll take it from here."

Donovan stopped in the front of the group, a satisfied smile on his face. "This is a fine piece of architecture right here," he said, gloating. "Like being in a sauna all day long. You'll find yourself praying for a cloud in the sky or for the sun to set, but by the time the box cools, it's rising again. You know we've had men drink from their pool of sweat just to save themselves from dehydrating?"

Dent rose to his feet and fixated on Donovan. It took all his strength not to sound desperate, but he knew he did. "I have money waiting on the outside. I'm looking at ten figures, but I can't get it in here."

"I bet you are," Donovan said.

"We can work something out that gets us both out of this dump. You don't have to believe me, but see for yourself. Research Victor Stone. I'm a beneficiary in his will."

"How absolutely tragic for you."

"It doesn't have to be. I'm not offering a little bit of money. I'm offering you retirement for help. You don't want to work here anymore than I want to be here."

"I trust you as far as I can throw you Dent. You're all out of friends. You had your chance and shit, I'll give it to you, that was an impressive try. Caused a helluva stir around here and it might have even worked out for you if things went different, but that was your chance and now...now it's gone."

He slid the door closed and the clang echoed in the small space. The wall was suddenly bright, the surfaces reflecting off each other. Dent covered his eyes with his arms, but couldn't escape it. He slid as far down to the floor as he could go into a huddle...

...Reporters swarmed town hall, while Dent Senior walked among them and talked into extended microphones while they bombarded him with questions.

"Mr. Dent, do you have a comment on the allegations of Ipstein and the charges against them?"

"*I have proposed special commissions to investigate allegations of venality in the public sector.*"

"*Why hasn't anything been done until now?*"

"*Establishing such agencies include a leader's genuine concern with the adverse developmental impact of corruption and a perception that any effort to reduce corruption succeeds only through the creation of a special agency to expand customary police powers.*"

"*Do you believe they're guilty?*"

"*Drug companies and the psychiatric establishment have no kind of moral or political stake in these arrangements. They're in the game in order to protect the status quo. They just see, in the world's unhappiness, a chance to make money. They invented a disease so that they could sell the cure.*"

Among the crowd, Dent Jr. stepped forward with glasses covering his eyes and a hat riding low on his head. He held a microphone at his side, but addressed his father without it. "*Has the search for your son been called off?*"

Everyone fell silent. No one had dared to ask Sr. about his son for a long time—the day long gone that he'd gone missing. Dent Sr. studied the man. He saw something was off; he wasn't a typical reporter. "*You're with...*"

"*Channel 11.*"

"*Not that this is a memory I want to continually relive, but yes, Meredith and I have hired the best investigators and have done everything we can to guarantee Christian's safe return. We've kept him in our daily prayers.*"

Dent Jr. went on. "*Do you believe his disappearance as well as your wife's illness, have helped boost your public image?*"

More silence from the crowd. The question was unexpected, and cruel, if it had come from anyone but Dent Jr.

"*Excuse me?*"

"*Have you been elected on sympathy votes?*"

He stammered as he addressed the question. "*The accusation that I wanted any harm to fall on my wife and son is outrageous.*" He left the podium in a fury and hurried to his car as reporters bombarded him with questions. He dismissed them all and slammed the door of his limo before the car sped away.

Hours later, Dent Sr returned to his home. Before exiting the car, he turned to an associate. "*Make sure channel 11 clearance is revoked for future press conferences until I get a full apology and the remarks retracted.*"

"*You handled it well. They brought a sensitive subject to light. It won't reflect well on them."*

"It was a disaster. He planted a seed and everyone heard it."

"We'll control the fallout."

At the end of the day, as Dent Sr. replayed the encounter with the reporter in his head one more time, he pulled into his driveway. He'd heard a lot of rumors over the years. There were alleged sightings of his son, but as time moved on, he'd spent less time taking them seriously and more developing his career. He was once a family man. Then, his son was taken. Now, his wife would be gone too. A large part of him was sad to say goodbye to his past, but his star was rising and newer better things were on the horizon. He stood at the end of his driveway, a yard away from the front door, but before he reached it, a masked figure emerged from the bushes.

Dent Jr. watched his father's eyes go wide and dart in all directions as if trying to decide whether to run or try to make it inside. Before he could react, Christian hit him in the stomach, making his father double over in pain. "What do you want?" Sr. asked.

Jr. pulled him to his feet and hit him again repeatedly until the old man fell to the ground with a thud, in too much pain to move.

"This is long overdue," Jr. said.

Sr's eyes went wide in fear as Christian gave him a beating he couldn't escape. "You'll cancel every appearance or you'll tell them you're clumsy like you've had your wife tell everyone for years. I don't give a damn what you do."

"I never touched her," Sr. said, trembling.

Jr. hit him again. His head snapped back as a shower of blood crossed the ground between them. Sr. knelt on the ground and sobbed uncontrollably as his nose streamed blood.

"Let her die in peace," Jr. said. "Don't go back. You don't deserve it. If I hear one more mention of your wife or son in your campaigning, I'll kill you."

Jr. turned to walk away, but looked back as he heard his father's cough and wheeze. He stood there for a long time, considering whether or not to do what he knew he shouldn't. Finally, he pulled off his mask and stared at his father. Sr. managed to look up to see his attacker exposed. He started memorizing his face—likely so he could identify him later—and eventually found his eyes, but there was no sign of recognition. Jr. didn't know if it had been too long since his father had seen him, or if his vision was obscured by the blood on his face, but somehow he was disappointed. His father had completely forgotten his face, which enraged him more. Instead of attacking him further, he turned and walked away.

The sun beat down on Mitch as he leaned against the car, sitting on an overpass. He watched Dent approach with a stride. He looked rested and revived.

"You get what you wanted to do, done?" Mitch asked.

"Yeah, let's get out of here," Dent started toward the passenger door, but stopped. "Mind if I drive?"

"Yeah, I don't care," Mitch said, surprised by Dent's request. He tossed the keys and Dent caught them midair. He climbed in and let the top down.

"You're gonna burn."

Dent started the car without a response while Mitch stared at him, contemplating what Dent did. "Sure you don't want your freedom?" he asked. "You can turn back and have another chance. Before you answer, you gotta know, what we do Chrissy, we'd be looking at life if we're ever busted, and we're being looked at. We're getting a lot of heat these days and if the day comes that everything crashes down...I'm looking at hard time...maybe the electric chair. You stick with me and you may regret it."

Dent didn't acknowledge anything Mitch said. He started the car and put his sunglasses on. The car took off, headed away from town and toward the sunset.

Chapter 19

1

Adlar faced forward in the church, staring at the alter like he'd never seen one before. Behind him, Josh twiddled his thumbs, anxiously waiting. Adlar didn't know how people started conversations or developed relationships. Here was a kid not much younger than himself, and Adlar couldn't connect. Josh knew who Adlar was, but Adlar had no idea what Josh was doing waiting for Richard.

"Ever tempted by the money?" Josh finally asked. Adlar turned to him, bewildered. "Mr. Stone's money. You ever think about it?" he asked again.

"Yeah."

"It would be hard to ignore that much money, but I think it's cool what you guys are doing."

"Why does Richard care so much?" Adlar asked.

"Someone died. He wants to stop it."

Adlar swallowed hard. If only Josh knew…"So he's afraid?"

"I don't know. I just helped him with addresses and a bunch of legal stuff."

"Why?"

"I'm traveling abroad on a mission trip and he helped."

"Why would you do that?"

Josh thought about the question. The real answer wasn't so simple, so he gave Adlar the response he knew people were supposed to give. "To help people."

"You can help people here."

"Yeah, but there's so much shit here every day and everyone acts so entitled. This is a place that wouldn't throw away half their food in a restaurant or complain over the petty stuff people complain about. I get tired of people honking their horns and being depressed around here. Everyone is trying to be famous or getting plastic surgery and all this dumb shit. It's called Global Volunteer Network. I'm going to Haiti."

"Tomorrow?"

"Yeah."

"Our thing is tomorrow."

"I won't be there. I don't need to be. You know, you should do it sometime."

"What?" Adlar asked. "Go out of the country?"

"Volunteer."

"Sorry but I don't get it."

"Maybe you're perfectly happy then, because I can't figure out what to do. I still don't know. But the only way I'm gonna figure it out is by trying things that are outside anything I've tried before. And my parents suck."

"So do mine," Adlar said, but regretted it. The night before, he'd experienced something unlike anything he'd ever felt for his parents. He hoped to develop it, but needed to drop the victim act first. "Why do your parents suck?"

"They used to be cool people. Then, a few years ago, my brother drowned because we were out at Black Chasm."

"What's that?"

"It's on the coast. There's a bunch of caves and cliffs and stuff. We went there a lot to look for treasure when we were younger. We found this cave that we liked and used to hang out there. But then the earthquake hit and even though it wasn't a big one, the waters rose and filled the cave and pulled him out to sea."

"Geez," Adlar said. He tried to imagine, but couldn't sympathize. He never had a sibling. It was always just him.

"They were pissed because I didn't hang onto him or something. You know how people always act like if they had been there, they could have prevented something? But you know better because no one really knows how to react in the moment?"

"I dunno."

"Well, that's what happened. One moment he was there and in the middle of questioning whether or not we'd just felt an earthquake. Next thing I know, a wave hits us and when it pulls back, he's gone. I thought he was joking and hid or something and looked for him even after I realized what happened."

"Shit."

"So yeah, my parents hate me now."

"That's dumb. So if you died and not him, they'd hate him?"

"I guess that's how it goes. I'm not sure. They don't talk about it. We were inseparable, so I guess they can't see one without seeing the other. So I figured I'd get out of here. I didn't really want to go, but I mean, I guess I can't take them anymore. But I got in some trouble lately and Richard thinks I need to do something good. I'm too young to believe that I'm living through this defining time in my life where I either start being this charitable guy or end up in jail, but Richard said to act now—to try to save myself as soon as I can, while I still want to. But then he pretty much only cares about you guys and Stone's will, so who knows who's right and wrong?"

While Josh rambled, Adlar zoned out, but Josh's words hit close to home. Adlar thought Josh was a bit cheesy for his taste, but hadn't Adlar been in the same shoes? Hadn't he had a choice that ultimately led him to be where he was at this very moment? Hadn't he...

...sat back and played a video game. He shouldn't have been, but no one was watching. People rarely watched him at Stone Enterprises anymore. It had been rocky at first, and he'd even been bullied, but he'd found a way to survive. Every day, he took the parking garage elevator to the sixth floor, and went straight to his office. No one saw him come or go. Every other week, a paycheck sat on his desk. It was starting to seem as if he was invisible. No one visited or gave him any direction anymore. Maybe that was how they wanted it. Maybe it was all a tactic to make Adlar feel isolated enough to quit. He'd blackmailed his way into this job, so it wasn't such an unfair arrangement for everyone involved, but it was wearing on him, and after his encounter in the lobby with Jones—when he'd been humiliated and degraded far beyond anything he'd ever experienced—he was just buying time until Lawrence came back with new instructions. They'd evaluated the data Adlar provided, and never said a word after, yet, they still hadn't kicked down the doors at Stone Enterprises and arrested anyone yet.

What Lawrence did do was honor his agreement to provide Adlar with employment working in his organization, specializing in cyber-terrorism prevention. The job was more hands on. Adlar worked with a team to monitor any out of the ordinary Internet traffic. He wasn't sure if he liked it yet, but he certainly didn't feel invisible when he was there and he knew the Department of Integrity wasn't going to crumble one day and Stone Enterprises inevitably would. When that day came, he'd be standing with Lawrence and his men, watching as they marched Cory, Jones, Victor, and all their associates out of the building.

The phone rang for the first time in days. When Adlar answered, a voice told him to come to Victor's office now. The demand was so short and sweet that he had no time to decide who was on the line.

Adlar wasted no time, hurrying to the elevator. It wasn't until he was in the elevator that he realized just how scared he was. By the time he was in Victor's office, he could barely control himself from shaking. He even tried to squeeze out a "hi," but nothing came out. No one noticed.

"Are you familiar with the DII?" Victor asked without looking up.

"The what?" Adlar asked.

"Department of Institutional Integrity?"

"I don't think so."

Victor exchanged looks with Cory and Jones. "You're incredible," Victor said. "At what you do."

"Thanks?" He didn't mean to make it sound like a question, but it did. Everything he said, he wished he could go back and change his tone.

"I'm curious to see what else you're capable of."

"I can do whatever you need."

"Could you intercept communications from government run agencies without being detected?"

"Maybe. But they have people who watch their systems."

"So you can't go in undetected?" Jones asked. His tone suggested he wasn't a fan of bringing Adlar on-board with whatever they were up to.

"I mean, if I knew no one was there probably. I can get into any system," Adlar said, confidently. "Just, sometimes they have their own people like me who look out for guys like me." After a long moment of silence, Adlar looked from Victor, to Jones and Cory, and back to Victor. "Why? What do you want me to do?"

"Can we trust you?" Victor asked, leaning forward. Adlar looked into his eyes and all his worries went away. There was no accusation, no lecture, no nothing. They were going to do what they did the day Adlar became associated with Stone Enterprises—they were going to ask him a favor. It could be his way into their inner circle. If only he wasn't working for the same organization they wanted him to infiltrate. Before Adlar could answer the question, Victor moved on. "We have reason to believe we're under investigation."

"Is that bad?"

"As successful as we've been, every decision comes with challenges. In the past, we've made choices that may not have..."

"...they were illegal?" Adlar said, finishing Victor's thought.

Victor gave a slight smile to his partners and turned back to Adlar. "That's one way of putting it."

"Can you do it?" Cory asked.

"Yeah, of course. As long as I know what I'm looking for."

"Good," Victor said, satisfied. It interested Adlar to see that all they needed was his word and they believed in him. He'd proved himself as a cyber-genius. They'd treated him poorly, but they found value in him after-all. Asking something on this level would have to come with something

more—some kind of respect. "This responsibility will come with a very generous reward. That is, of course, if you're the type of person who can live with this. I suspect you are."

Adlar was. Only, he'd already made a promise to the enemy. Betraying one or the other would come down on him for certain. He made a mental note to list all the pros and cons of picking either side at a later date.

"I can do it. I don't get bothered by doing this stuff," Adlar said.

He meant it.

Two hours later, Adlar sat with Lawrence Curtola, the only thing between them was a pile of paperwork. Adlar's mind replayed the meeting in Victor's office. He felt guilty playing both sides of the fence.

"We're gonna set you up with a dummy file," Lawrence said.

"I can just tell them I can't get past the firewalls," Adlar said.

"That's the last thing we want. They trust you. We want them to hold onto the belief that you're capable."

"They'll kill me if they find out."

"They won't know. You've grown on them."

"No I haven't."

"You grow on people Wilcox."

"I do?"

Lawrence tapped his finger on the table for a moment and smiled. "Your personality needs a little tweaking, but your skills are hard to ignore. There's no organization in the world that wouldn't want you in it with your skills, which is why I'm gonna come through for you. You'd be a good fit in our cyber-terrorism unit. Don't let the name fool you. We investigate all things fishy from big business to teenage crackers working out of their homes."

"When Victor knows that I work for you..."

"When this is over, they'll be put away and the majority of their people will be searching for jobs. You'll be forgotten before they know it. They'll have bigger problems and you'll be a big shot around here."

"I won't have to go to court?"

"You won't have to testify. All you're required to do is protect our information and obtain theirs. Stone is suspicious of us and we of them. You're a double-agent. Do you understand what that means?"

Adlar nodded, wide-eyed.

"Between that and the lack of respect Victor has shown you, I hope the decision is an easy one..."

...Adlar and Josh watched Richard Libby walk through the church and head straight toward them. When he met up with them, he addressed Josh apologetically. "I'm so sorry I was late. What are the chances we can meet up a little later?" Josh tried to hide his annoyance, but it was visible. Richard noticed, but pretended not to. What he was doing was too important and everything was in place for Josh. There was nothing more than to say their goodbyes, but something happened in the course of the last few weeks. Josh was a different person.

"I leave tomorrow," Josh said, disappointed. "When are we meeting?"

"It's important that we put this together," Richard said. "You have everything you need. Can I call you later?"

"But he's a day early," Josh said, nodding toward Adlar. Richard turned to Adlar, who sat quietly. As Richard tried to think up a compromise, Josh let out a breath and stood and started to leave.

"May I call you later?" Richard called out. Josh shook his head but kept walking.

Richard watched him. "Did he say anything to you?" Richard finally asked.

"About what?"

"Anything."

"He told me he's going away."

After a moment, Richard focused his attention on Adlar. "What's so important?" he asked.

"Um, well, I was gonna tell you that that guy Toby wanted me to not show up and screw you guys, but I'm gonna come. He wants you to lose, so I was supposed to make you think I would be here and then not come."

Richard shook his head, not surprised. Disappointed, but not surprised.

"Why are you telling me this?"

"Because I don't want this anymore either."

Richard waited to hear more, but Adlar held back, with a look of shame.

"Is there something else you wanted to tell me?" Richard asked.

"Just um, after we win, can I do the thing where I tell you all ways I've uh..."

"Confession?"

"Yeah, and does that really make up for things wrong? I mean, even really bad things?"

"If you're sincere, then yes. We can do it now if you'd like."

"I just want to help end Victor's thing first. Cause otherwise..."

"It will end. Even if Toby's trying to sabotage our efforts, we have a lot of support. It seems most, if not all of us, will be there."

Adlar looked up, a thought forming. A thought that scared him. What if a specific someone happened to be there? Someone who might kill Adlar if he crossed his path. "Who?" Adlar asked.

"Anthony Freeman, Trish Reynalds..."

"Is the guy whose wife died coming?"

"Yes, he is."

Adlar's face changed, and suddenly he knew he wouldn't be able to make good on his promise. As badly as he wanted to contribute to the cause, he wouldn't be able to sit in the same room as Charlie. Even Royce would be there and give him hell. He'd let things get out of control and to the group, he would forever be the bad guy—the one who actually did what Victor wanted and murdered someone. He got to his feet. "Then if you have enough, maybe I won't."

"What do you mean?" Richard asked.

"You don't need me. So good luck."

He ran for the door and pushed through. Richard tried to catch up, but to no avail. When Richard reached the outside, he only had time to see Adlar disappear in the distance.

2

Anthony Freeman entered a bar, and took a seat. For the first time in years, he'd allegedly had a drink—and not just a drink, but enough drinks to be blackout drunk to the extent that he couldn't even remember his first drink. Most bar-stools still sat upside down on their tables and a woman mopped the floors, readying the bar for the coming day. She looked up upon seeing Anthony. "We're not open yet."

"I'm not here to eat. I was hoping to talk to the gentleman working last Wednesday night."

"He's not in until later."

"Do you keep credit card receipts?"

"Um..."

"I was here Wednesday night. I would like to see what I was charged."

"Why don't you check your bank?"

"I did, but there's no transaction other than my dinner. There may have been someone buying drinks. All I want to know is how many drinks were on his tab. I just want to pay him back. The gentleman working Wednesday night will confirm I was here with a friend."

"Oh," she said, no longer suspicious. "Well, he only works a couple nights a week and I'm not giving you his phone number or address or anything like that, and I can't give out other people's information, so you might wanna come back tomorrow night if you need to see him."

Anthony sighed and took a deep breath. "I'm a recovering alcoholic. I woke up with a hangover, and I don't remember the night. I don't even remember ordering one. I'm just trying to piece together the events that caused me to break my sobriety. I only want to ask him questions."

"How about I give him your number and I'll have him call you if he wants to?"

Anthony nodded. "You got a napkin?"

Later, he sat in a diner with his sponsor, holding a cup of coffee with both hands and sipping slowly. His eyes glanced at a piece of paper sitting between the two of them.

"I think you should face the facts," his sponsor said. Anthony shook his head and refused to submit. "Hear me out. Just hear me out. When we begin drinking, it's easy to count the first few drinks. Most people count and they lose track around five...six..."

"I didn't lose track."

"No, but by the end of the night, after so many, we don't remember the first."

"I know when I'm going to make a decision as monumental as submitting to my fatal flaw and breaking two years of sobriety."

"Then tell me what you think happened."

Anthony thought hard, but came up with nothing.

"There's alcohol in your blood. You don't recall the night."

"There's no hospital that put these stitches in me."

"But you're stitched. Someone did it. If you're refusing to admit to the obvious, you're left with the burden of proof. So you tell me your theory."

Anthony rubbed his temples, reflecting on that night as he had a hundred times already, wishing just one moment would come back to him. "I'm being framed," he finally said.

His sponsor laughed. "Framed for what? Being a drunk?"

"I don't know, but I know the conscious decisions I make. Come on Wes, you know me. After everything I've been through and giving you my word..."

"I'm not criticizing. Don't think for a second that I don't understand. I've lost two wives to my bullshit, but I take responsibility."

"I'm telling you with full disclosure, if I drink, okay, so be it. I'd be ashamed, but I'd admit it. I've had to admit it before."

"Why call me? To convince me? A moment ago, you weren't even sure yourself."

"I was stabbed. I told you about the will..."

"And these sound like stresses in your life. Why would anyone bother to force you off the bandwagon?"

"I don't know yet."

"We've been down this road. You need to take a step back and re-evaluate."

"That's it?" Anthony asked in disbelief. "I just acknowledge making a poor decision that I don't believe I made and start counting again? I would remember taking the first sip of the drink that ruined two years of sobriety!"

"Maybe you should stay out of the bars in the first place. Then we wouldn't have to have this conversation."

"I go for the atmosphere."

"The atmosphere is part of that addiction. You want my advice? Just work through the next couple of days. Don't let this eat at you. Get past it. Start counting."

"Yeah, great," Anthony muttered. "Start over…"

As Anthony began his count, two miles away, a car sped across the pavement, picked up speed, and crashed into a wall. The glass shattered and the car folded like an accordion. A body flew through the windshield and hit a wall, snapping in two.

After a moment, an alarm went off and a half dozen men rushed to the car and observed the scene, taking photos and writing on charts. Among them, Stan watched with amazement. His mind was on Anthony Freeman and what he did, and what he would have to do within the next 24 hours.

"Let's get her out," Stan's associate said. A crew of men worked on pulling the cadaver from the wreckage. The body was already white and drained of blood, dead long before the impact. They dragged her to a large laboratory, prepping the area.

"Looks like she was hot," one scientist said.

"She was married," another added.

"Not anymore."

"You can have her when we're done," Stanley said, taking a step forward. A few men awkwardly laughed. They couldn't tell if Stan was joking or not. His face never gave him away and he was a twisted man.

"Let's do this," their supervisor said, breaking up the fun.

As they ran tests, Stan's boss entered the room and pulled him away. Moments later, Stan's large frame filled the chair in his boss's office. Stan assumed he was there for business as usual, but a man in a suit stood behind them.

"Stan, this is Harry Hopkins from the SEP."

"Nice to meet you," Stan said, without turning.

"They want to shut us down," his boss said, a bitter tone in his voice.

"Why?" Stan asked.

Harry stepped into the conversation and began talking in a monotone voice. "Are you familiar with a study entitled Analysis of Air Resistance Effects on the Velocity of Falling Human Bodies?"

"I wrote it," Stan said.

"And published it?"

"That's right."

"It hit the Internet," Harry said. "Were you aware of that?"

"No, but it happens."

"In this particular study, a test subject broke into three separate parts..."

"One of my colleagues didn't follow..."

"There was a photo," Harry said, his voice rising above Stan's. "The family of the deceased received a link to the article and a picture of their daughter's scattered parts on the warehouse floor. They're suing."

"She donated her body. What did they expect?"

"There are regulations on concealing the methods in which we test."

"So what?" Stan asked. "This surprises them?"

"They didn't want to know. That's the idea. They sure as hell didn't want to find a picture on the Internet."

"We did nothing illegal."

"You certainly brought attention to us and now I'm going to look in every corner of this place and make sure you're following every code down to the tee."

Fernando waived his hand dismissively. "This is ridiculous."

"Only if you have something to hide," Harry said.

"Our funding is for scientific experimentation. Do you know how many lives we save? Every cadaver impact test we do improves airbags and brakes. Each test, on average, saves forty lives. They checked the little box that allows exactly that."

"I'm not here to debate. You're doing your job and I'm doing mine, and I'll expect your cooperation while I take a look around."

"Be my guest," Fernando said.

Harry wandered off, inspecting workers as he passed. Fernando addressed Stan. "What have you been working on?" he asked with accusation. He watched Stan, who stared in the direction Harry exited, displeased by his presence.

"I guess we'll find out," he said, numbly.

"And then what?"

"I'll lose my job," Stan said, simply.

3

Royce Morrow froze at the sight of Adlar coming his way. He finished a campaign speech at the library downtown and was making his exit when he saw him in the crowd. When he saw the look on Adlar's face—there was something innocent behind those eyes—he knew something changed? But what about Manny and Bedbug and their arrangement? Had they not been able to find Adlar yet? He assumed when they did, Adlar wouldn't live to tell the tale. He didn't want to talk to Adlar. He didn't want to have a reason to show mercy and have to reverse a decision that had already cost him so much.

He made a beeline toward Adlar anyway, who sat on a fountain bench, watching and waiting. Instead of a lecture, or a rude 'what do you want?', Royce sat next to him.

"Did you come to see me?" Royce asked.

"Yeah," Adlar said. He fished through his bag and came out with Royce's box. He set it next to him. Royce watched for a long moment, shocked at the gesture. He opened the box and observed the contents, just like they had been. It took a little bit of work on Adlar's part, but taking it back from Toby was necessary. He needed the peace offering, and now maybe Royce and Adlar could move past their problems.

"You can have your thing back," Adlar said.

"You know what this is?" Royce asked.

"A newspaper article and an award."

"And I presume you've concluded that this means something to me because it incriminates me and my friends in a crime."

"Yeah," Adlar said. "Did you do it?"

Royce paused. "Yes, I did."

Adlar managed a smile. "That's fine. I won't tell."

They sat silently for a long moment. "You sent a man to threaten me," Royce finally said. "Should I be worried about that?"

"I don't know what he threatened you with. I gave it to Toby O'Tool and he was doing some stuff. He wants the money."

"I intend on being there tomorrow," Royce said. "I would have been either way."

"That's fine," Adlar said. "I want to go too."

"Why don't you?"

"Cause I pissed people off," he said. "I made you mad and another guy too. I think he tried to kill me, or had someone else try to do it."

Royce registered the information, completely unaware of any other trouble Adlar had stirred up. But if someone tried to kill him…

"What happened?" he suddenly asked.

"I don't know. A guy came into where I was living and was trying to poison my milk but someone else shot him in the face and then a cop came to me…"

As Adlar recounted the events, Royce's face turned white. Could Bedbug have really made his move, and if so, what got in the way? And when and how was Royce going to hear about this? "Wait a moment," Royce said. "Tell me everything. From the beginning."

Adlar took a deep breath and started again…

…Adlar sat with the DII Cyber-terrorism squad in their meeting room, half listening as a speaker stood at the front of the room, giving a presentation.

"Internet traffic is directed by just thirteen clusters of potentially vulnerable domain-name servers. New dangers are coming. Weakly governed swathes of Africa are being connected up to fiber-optic cables, potentially creating new havens for cyber-criminals. And the spread of mobile Internet will bring new means of attack. The Internet was designed for convenience and reliability, not security. Yet in wiring together the globe, it has merged the garden and the wilderness. No passport is required in cyberspace and because police are constrained by national borders, criminals roam freely. Enemy states are no longer on the other side of the ocean, but just behind the firewall. The ill-intentioned mask their identity and location, impersonate others and con their way into buildings that hold the digitized wealth of the electronic age: money, personal data, and intellectual property."

He snapped his fingers at Adlar, who was slouched in his seat, bored. "Up here…" the speaker said, drawing Adlar back to the land of the living. Adlar sat up straight and the speaker went on. "About nine-tenths of the 140 billion emails sent daily are spam. Of these, about 16% contain moneymaking scams including phishing attacks that seek to dupe recipients into giving out passwords or bank details. The amount of information now available on-line about individuals makes it even easier to attack a computer by crafting a personalized email that is more likely to be trusted and opened. This is known as spear-phishing."

As the speaker talked, Adlar drifted off. From another side of the room, Lawrence watched him. After the seminar, as Adlar stuffed his books into a backpack and happily made his way to the exit, Lawrence caught up to him.

"Adlar…"

Adlar turned.

"What do you think?"

"Of what?"

"The job. Can I trust you to work with us?"

"Yeah," he said with an obvious tone. "I was gonna anyway."

"Then we need to move forward right away on Stone Enterprises."

"I'm still digging. I haven't found anything."

"Don't bullshit me. It's not something you're good at. You could

access the information in less than a minute. You're holding out."

"What? No, I'm not. I don't even like those guys."

"Then why don't I have what I want yet?"

Adlar shrugged and backed away.

"Look around you. You've got an honest to God job and a paycheck with a couple more zeros on it than most guys your age. Stone Enterprises will go down and you'll be caught up in the middle. Then what? You'll throw this all away?"

"I told you I'll get it. Geez..."

"You know what I think? I think you're playing both sides of the fence. I think you like feeling important and you're testing the waters and trying to figure out which one is a better gig. They want you to betray us and we want you to betray them and you just know that you'll be rewarded either way."

"That's not it. I don't even care about that kinda stuff."

"Then what is it? You're buying time. What? Because you're trying to figure out what side you're on?" Judging by Adlar's face, he hit the nail on the head.

"Wilcox, you're one of them or you're one of us. You've gotta decide. But you can't have it both ways."

"I know. I'll get it."

"Don't pick them Wilcox. Don't submit to the temptation of greed. Every day, I ask the question, why am I a responsible man and somebody else is in jail? The answer is pretty obvious. It's because I am obedient and subordinate to power and that other guy is independent."

"But aren't I here only because I broke the law?"

"I don't wanna overstep my bounds here, but I know where you're at. I used to raise hell in my day. And when I grew up and I was handed a few opportunities, I felt a sense of injustice, like I didn't deserve them, like I was one of the bad guys. But you just gotta get over that. You are what you want to be. You want the cubicle with the rest of the group and you want to help clean up the mess that you used to start, then do it."

Adlar nodded his understanding. Lawrence turned to walk away, but turned back.

"You won't regret it..."

...The next visit wouldn't be as easy. Royce only wanted his box back and to believe Adlar was no threat, and apparently, as soon as Adlar filled him in on his recent brush with death, Royce had other things to worry about. He could safely say that he was one person away from being free from his sins. Unfortunately, stealing personal property was more forgivable than murdering a man's wife, but Adlar still had some control over Charlie. He still knew Charlie wasn't completely innocent. Charlie may never forgive him, but he certainly could agree to a stale-mate and harmlessly hate Adlar from a distance for the rest of their days. It was the hope that they could learn to live in the same world together that brought Adlar to him. He didn't find his courage immediately. Instead, he walked around Banner General twice before entering, sat in the lobby and watched TV for an hour, and finally entered the hallways, wandering aimlessly in search of an encounter.

When he found Charlie, he was in the cafeteria. Adlar had played all possible encounters through his mind. He'd found comfort in knowing Charlie would probably be busy, or surrounded by people, and he could safely gauge his reaction before talking. If Charlie's eyes burned with fire, Adlar could simply run away. If there was resolve, he could pull him aside and apologize. Adlar didn't expect to find Charlie sitting alone in the cafeteria, staring at nothing. His window was wide open. If he didn't find the courage, there would never be another.

Adlar slowly approached from the side. He tried to decide whether a slow or sudden reveal would be more effective. He didn't have much time to think about it. He was at Charlie's side, and he stopped thinking altogether and let himself talk instead. "Charlie?"

Charlie did a double take. Adlar read his eyes. There was no fire, no resolve, only exhaustion. Charlie appeared to weigh his options for only a moment, but went back to his lunch. Maybe he was wise enough not to make a scene in a public place. Maybe he'd just decided to drop the whole thing. Maybe moments after Adlar sat, he'd have a steak knife sticking in his heart, but he sat across from Charlie anyway. Charlie continued eating and didn't look up.

"Charlie?" Adlar said again.

"What?" Charlie said, in a dry monotone.

"I'm sorry."

Charlie looked up. "For what?"

There was no way for Adlar to complete that sentence and he would do everything he could to avoid saying what they both knew to be true. Instead, he moved past it. "Tomorrow, everyone is going to that thing. I was going to be there."

"Why?" Charlie asked. "You obviously want the money."

"No, I don't. I mean, it could help, but I'm trying not to want it."

"It's a little late for that."

"Just tell me what you want me to do and I'll do it. Things were bad for me, but I'm making them better."

"Good for you," Charlie said without sympathy. "I'm glad things are better for you."

"Look, I know I did what I did, but you tried to kill me and you killed some other guy. And then also everyone thinks you were in that bed, but you weren't, and all that time passed. You think I'm dumb, but I'm not. If you kill me, then you get in trouble too. I want to stop all this."

"Do you think you deserve that Wilcox?"

"I know I'm a screw-up," Adlar said. "I've always been. Everyone knows it. But you're an adult. You're a doctor. You're the one who everyone is gonna be surprised about and you'll be in all the papers and maybe TV. If I screw up, no one cares. We'd both go to jail. So what's the point?"

Charlie laughed to himself. "Why do you think you're sitting here now?"

"Yeah, but that was you who tried to kill me, right?"

"You don't know as much as you think."

"I don't need to. I'm tired of this. I just want to go home to my parents. If you want me to do certain things or be a certain way, I'll do it. I put away my laptop. I'm quitting all the dumb stuff I did, but the only thing I did wrong, you did wrong too. You can't be mad at me and not yourself."

Charlie wanted to scare Adlar, or make him feel like shit, but he was speaking a truth that Charlie knew for a long time. He'd already considered letting Adlar live out his life. He'd embraced some of what Richard said. Everyone made mistakes, and Abby wasn't coming back. But Adlar walking free and living out his days—possibly as a normal happy carefree adult—it was too much to fathom.

"Tell you what," Charlie said. "I'll be there tomorrow too. I think you should come down, we'll vote to end it, and then, you turn yourself in."

"Why would I do that?"

"Trish Reynalds already knows it was you. She knows everything that happened that night, but I've got a pass, so your threats are empty. You turn yourself in, take what you deserve, and I'll forgive you and support you."

"That would ruin everything for me. That doesn't help."

"Face it Wilcox: You have nowhere to go. Your parents don't want you around. More than one person wants your life. You won't be successful, and if you grow to have any decency, you'll live with the regret of what you've done forever. The only way for your life to be any good is to own up to your actions."

"I just wanna go home."

"And what will you do when the next bullet for you hits your parents? Or would you even give a shit?"

"Just leave me alone."

"Look at you. You don't even think you deserve to pay for what you did. You want to be one of the good guys now, when you've got nowhere to go."

"I never wanted to do what I did."

"It's too late to turn back. I'll never forgive you, and you'll never be safe. And neither will anyone in your life. Go back to running like a coward..."

"I'm not a fucking coward!" Adlar shouted.

"You walked through my home in the dark and fired a shot into a blanket and ran. You couldn't even look her in the eye."

Adlar wiped away a tear and ran his fingers through his hair. Charlie watched him with pleasure, satisfied to see Adlar begging for mercy.

"It's your decision. I'm not going to touch you, but there are others who want to."

"I've already taken care of that."

"You'll never be free from what you did," Charlie shouted as Adlar got to his feet.

"Neither will you," Adlar said, a darkness overcoming him. "I shot a stranger, but you killed your wife. You're a thousand times worse than me. And if anyone else tries to kill me again, I'll come back and kill you."

4

A group of people took turns discussing their encounters with their addictions. One man held the floor, everyone's eyes glued on him. No one noticed Anthony enter the room and join the crowd.

"...I miss the smoky atmosphere, the tinkle of ice in the glass. It was pure sophistication, but most of all, I remember that first sensation of the warm whiskey radiating throughout my body. I drank so much that night that nobody believed I hadn't been drinking all the time, and I belonged."

Nods of recognition resonated throughout the room.

"...Despite my active church and school life as a child, I had never really felt comfortable; I was actually very nervous and insecure around people. But this night in the bar was like no other time in my life. Not only was I completely at ease, but I actually loved all the strangers around me and they loved me in return. I thought, all because of this magic discovery. Alcohol, what a revelation!"

Some giggles and murmur of support spread. The man smiled and stepped down as they applauded him. A few faces turned and recognized Anthony, surprised to see him. A woman at the head of the room stood and addressed Anthony, welcoming him to the group. Everyone turned and smiled warmly upon seeing an old friend. There was something else in their eyes: Concern. If he was in their meeting, there was a reason.

"I didn't drink," Anthony said, answering the question on everyones' mind. "I believe I didn't."

"What happened?" the woman heading the room asked.

Anthony didn't want to go on. He knew how unbelievable his story sounded, and how much worse it was about to get. "I...was at a bar...drinking club soda. Next thing I know, I wake up at home smelling of alcohol."

"We've all been there," a man in the group said.

"I don't know how to describe this. I had no desire to drink. I don't remember ordering that first drink or any after. I remember having a conversation with a gentleman, and he left, and I went to the restroom. And then nothing."

"But you were in a bar..."

"I sometimes sit there for the atmosphere. Sure, I'm tempted, but I think of the last time I drank; I count the days. Two years, two months, three days..."

"If you smelled of alcohol..."

"I have a cut on my side and it's stitched up. How can I have been inebriated enough not to remember, but make it to the hospital and home without anyone stopping me? Without remembering any of it?" The more Anthony talked, the more sure he was of himself.

"Why are you here?" she finally asked.

"Because..." he said, thinking about the question. "I had nowhere else to go with this. I feel as if something beyond my control is happening. I feel as if someone else is behind this, trying to sabotage my efforts."

"Who?"

He shook his head in defeat.

"Mind if I make a comment?" a man in the group asked. Anthony nodded. "I did something like that once. I hit a record number of days without a drink. I was proud of myself. Then one night I did, and for no reason. I had one drink. I didn't even have a buzz. And the next day, I kept right on counting like I didn't do it and told myself it didn't count because it was random...a one-time thing...that there was no consequence. I couldn't accept that I did it without reason. No bad day at work or anything. Just up and did it like a fool."

Though Anthony knew this wasn't the case, he let the suggestion process, questioning what he knew again and coming up with the same: Everything happened just as he believed. He wouldn't be able to convince the room. He sounded the way every alcoholic did and he wouldn't believe himself either if he was listening from the crowd. Instead of objecting, he nodded and sat back, silently listening for the remainder of the meeting.

Stan led Fernando and Harry into the darkened storage center that acted as his personal workspace. Stan knew what they would come upon, but didn't hold back. The end for him was near and there was no point in prolonging the inevitable. He had other opportunities that he was more focused on anyway—opportunities that would come to fruition soon. The lights turned on and the men stepped in, staring in fascination and disbelief.

"What the hell is this?" Harry muttered. They turned to Stanley, waiting for an explanation. Before he could answer, Harry's voice rose. "Don't tell me you're doing your own work on cadavers!"

Before them, a cadaver was sprawled, wires and tubes sticking out of ever orifice. Stanley turned with demented eyes. Something had always been off about him. He'd always had a morbid fascination with his work, but this was beyond anything Harry had imagined.

"You don't know what this is," Stan said. "I had the resources to..."

"I don't want to know!"

"It's energy."

"Energy..."

Stan continued. "The circulatory system is a circuit...it's in the name. Blood is a current which flows continuously while we're alive."

Harry followed the wires with his eyes, hooked up to various electronic devices: light-bulbs, a toy train, and even a computer.

"What the hell?" Harry said.

"If I hit the switch, I can send a flow of liquid with the same properties as blood through the circulatory system and power everything within a mile radius."

"Are you insane? You're talking about using corpses for energy?"

"Donated corpses. Consider the future of energy. I'm not talking about just the deceased. I'm talking about living breathing humans able to power everything around them."

"You're crazy," Harry said.

"Think about every human being as energy for everything around them. You can prevent your body from overheating or cooling. A stroke or heart attack would trigger an alarm at the nearest hospital."

"Get your shit out of here."

Stan turned to Fernando. "I'm fired?"

"Now, you're only fired," Harry said. "But we will tear this place apart and find out exactly what you've done. I came here to make a case against you, but you've done a fine job of that all on your own." He then turned to Fernando, who was awestruck. "As for you, send your people home. I'm shutting this place down and doing a search of the premises."

"We're fully funded. You can't shut down the impact div..."

"One phone call and I'll have this place filled with police and FBI and I know you don't want that." He gave his attention back to Stan. "And don't go far. This is only the beginning for you."

5

Adlar hid in the basement. He avoided opening his laptop and curled up in a sleeping bag instead. The upstairs was quiet. He heard murmuring in his parent's room, but then silence. Tomorrow, he would talk to them and tell them he was home. He'd get a job. He'd try to restart. He'd even show up with a smile at The Coop. Richard had a meeting room set aside for the group and if Charlie had anything to say, Adlar would take him down too, but Adlar guessed Charlie was too cowardly. He might have wanted to kill Adlar, but he wouldn't do it in a crowded place. When it was over, Adlar would move on, eventually move far away from Los Angeles, and put some distance between his past and future.

He turned the light off and dozed off.

He didn't know how much time passed until the light turned on and Gary Wilcox stood over him. When Adlar's eyes opened, his first reaction was relief. Now, he could make it known he was home, with nowhere else to go, and show some humility and ask his father if he wanted to see a movie over the weekend and have dinner with his mother. Then, he saw his father's face. Disappointment. Anger.

Adlar sat up suddenly. He didn't want to hear what his father had to say. He didn't want everything to be undone.

"Get out," Gary said, sternly.

"Sorry," Adlar said in protest. "I was going to tell you tomorrow. I had to go somewhere."

"I lost my job today because of you and your constant shit," Gary said.

"Wait a second..."

"You've been back, what? Less than a week? It took you less than a week to ruin my life?"

Adlar swallowed a lump. He didn't know what to say. Whatever got his father canned probably did come from Adlar's computer, and no amount of protest would sway his father from believing otherwise. Only action. "I'll throw away my computer," Adlar said. "I'll never use it again.

"I've heard you beg and plead every time you're about to lose privilege and act like a shit otherwise. I'm done with you."

"I'm your son. You can't just kick me out."

Gary grabbed Adlar's ear unexpectedly and without mercy. He pulled him to his feet and up the stairs while Adlar tried to loosen the grip. When

Gary had him at the front door, he unlocked it and tried to pull him out. Adlar noticed his mother sitting in a chair, watching expressionless. The decision to rid themselves of Adlar was mutual.

"What do you guys want me to do? Just be homeless? I have nothing. I didn't even do this. It's this other kid I know who is trying to make me look bad."

"You're a fucking liar."

"Dad," Adlar said, his eyes begging. "There's a lot of stuff I'll tell you. There's a lot that's happened and it isn't just my fault. I did a lot of things, but there are things that you have to understand."

"I don't care anymore," his father said. "No excuse you have is going to get me my job back. You're on your own now…"

"…You worthless sack of shit."

Adlar looked up. Jones looked down on him with disdain.

"Uh…what?"

"You said you could get it."

Victor stood at his side, studying and analyzing Adlar's face.

"I could if there was something to get," Adlar said.

"We didn't say we thought they were looking at us. We said we knew."

"I guess you were wrong," Adlar said.

"Bullshit," Jones said. "You need to look again."

"I'm not lying. I looked." He couldn't maintain eye contact. Victor and Jones gave each other a knowing look before Victor exited the room.

"Tell me how you're an expert hacker who can't break their firewall," Jones said.

"I don't know. Maybe they keep their stuff in another place. That happens. Or maybe they don't keep anything at all in case you try to do what you're doing. They didn't leave it where I can find. They find new ways to cover things cause of spies. Their security is better than ours."

"And you're supposed to know how to bypass that."

"Look, spies used to risk arrest or even being killed by trying to smuggle out copies of documents. But the ones in cyber-world don't have that risk. It used to be a good hacker could steal a few books worth of material but then they'd restock the shelves. Then the hacker would steal it again and they knew they couldn't just restock. They'd have to find a whole other place. You know what I mean?"

"Yeah, I get it. You're telling me you're worthless."

"At this, yeah."

"That's a comforting thing to know from a guy who works for us."

"That's not my job anyway. I do my job."

Jones got in Adlar's face, and Adlar backed away, but Jones continued to step toward him, invading his space and backing him into a corner. "Let me tell you something, loser: There's not an employer on the planet that would find use in your Space Intruder gaming skills."

"There's no game called that."

"Ten, twenty years from now, no one will give a shit about your worthless life. Your time at Stone Enterprises will expire and I'll be the first to show you the door."

"Why are you so mean?" Adlar asked.

"Because you're not worth the attention you get around here."

Later, Adlar walked through the DII office with relief. He passed a crowd of agents who applauded as he walked through. He turned from side to side at the approving smiles as they showed their approval. An employee passed by and patted him on the back and called him a rock-star.

"What did I do?" Adlar asked, confused.

Lawrence stepped out of the group and greeted him. "It was your ability that led us to Elroy."

"Who?"

"Yesterday's meeting."

Adlar still didn't understand.

"It was what you said: Hacking used to be about making noise. Now it's about staying silent."

"I said that?"

"Yeah...yesterday."

"Cool."

"Elroy would wrap encrypted submissions in layers of junk data to obscure their size and origin, then route them through servers in Sweden where it's a crime to disclose a source. He's been able to stay under the radar because we never knew where he'd pop up before he did. But you gave us a profile. He wasn't playing rock-n-roll cyber-space cowboy like we'd expected. When Elroy was twenty, when he was first starting out, he hacked into the master terminal that Nortel maintained in Melbourne and began to poke around. When you told me you like to revisit your roots, I informed the international subversives to visit the master terminal frequently. Normally he hacked when they were semi-dormant, but he didn't think a Nortel administrator was signed on. He realized his mistake right away and tried to update the systems to buy the administrator's loyalty and even told him he did no harm and asked not to tell, but he was reported immediately. Agents picked him up last night and are bringing him here now."

"Oh yeah?" Adlar asked, but didn't really care.

"Listen Wilcox, I know you didn't exactly get this job on merit, and

maybe when you stepped foot inside, you thought you were in over your head. Hell, I thought you were, but ya know, you can fit in here. Hell, we may have stumbled upon a valuable asset. With or without our case against Stone Enterprises, you have a place here."

"Can I go to my desk now?"

Lawrence smiled at him, hopelessly. "You're doing something monumental. Even though you don't see that, I hope you can come to appreciate what you've been given."

The rest of the day, Adlar had a hard time getting work done. He was given accolades by everyone in the office. He even tried his hardest to impress the cute girl in the cubicle next to his own. He had her attention, and desperately tried to hold it. "The hackers and virus-writers who once wrecked computers for fun are gone and replaced by criminal gangs trying to harvest data," he told her. He tried to sound smart, to live up to the reputation he accidentally built for himself, but before he could go on, a commotion stopped the conversation. Adlar and the girl turned as two agents escorted Elroy—the infamous hacker—into the building.

Elroy walked through slowly, and Adlar looked at him with sympathy, staring at what could be a mirror image of himself. Elroy's hair was messy, he sported dark clothing and careless demeanor. Adlar looked down at himself in his white shirt and tie, his hair parted neatly, suddenly feeling out of place.

As Elroy passed, he and Adlar made eye contact. Adlar looked up at him, and saw desperation in Elroy's eyes. After Elroy passed, the girl in the adjoining cubicle gave her attention back to Adlar, but he was gone. The only thing remaining was his tie.

"I was working for them," Adlar said. "They made me do it."

Victor sat across from Adlar with his hands folded in front of him. He contemplated for a long moment, at a loss for words. Adlar fished through his pockets and pulled out a memory stick.

"I can tell you everything they've done. I can clean up everything they're looking for here."

Victor's expression went through a range of emotions: Anger, confusion, and finally compromise. "Why are you telling me this?" he asked.

"Cause even though you don't think so, I fit in here. I'm not one of them..."

...Romey stepped outside his home for the first time in a week. He kicked aside half a dozen pizza boxes just to get out of his basement. When he was outside, he faced Adlar, as he'd expected. "I'll call the cops," he said. He was in no mood for a confrontation.

"You sent another virus."

"Talk to Toby. This has nothing to do with me."

"You sent it."

"I don't have a choice. I told you that."

"My dad lost his job. And I got kicked out."

"Well," Romey said with a shrug. "Sorry. I don't want to be doing this either but that guy pretty much could screw me over if I didn't. So talk to him."

"What does he want?"

"Come on," Romey said, walking back into his house, leaving the door open for Adlar. Adlar followed him in and to his den, where he had equipment set up everywhere. Adlar stood at a distance while Romey talked over his shoulder.

"He said you'd come here," Romey said. "He said to tell you to remember what you're supposed to be doing. Like I said, that guy is using all these things against me. I don't know how he knows it, but I'm doing what I have to, which I know you understand because I know who you are and we play the same games and do the same shit, ya know? Whatever you guys have going on, he said you need to be out there. He didn't tell me to tell you this, but he doesn't want you to be comfortable or like your life or anything like that."

"How good is your setup?" Adlar asked.

"Since the last time we talked I've made a dozen improvements."

"What if I go to the police and say you sent a virus?"

"I'd deny it. I seriously have state of the art stuff. Nothing will link us. Sorry." He turned to his computer and booted it up, readying his equipment for Adlar. "But you should talk to Toby cause I don't want him to bother me either."

"You can give him a message from me," Adlar said.

"I'm not your messenger. I'm only doing it for him cause…"

That's when a cord was thrown around his neck and his windpipe cut off. Romey threw his hands up and waived them haphazardly, grabbing at air hopelessly. His eyes went wide and his arms flailed more as the panic set in. He tried to talk, but it tightened and he tried to grab the cord instead.

Adlar stood behind him with hatred in his eyes. "I'll take care of Toby myself," Adlar said. "I told you to leave me alone and you didn't and you don't know what you've done. All you had to do was leave me alone."

Adlar shifted him by pulling the cord back and to the side so he could look into Romey's eyes, which plead for mercy. His face was white and his body weakened with every second. Adlar watched as his eyes went red and the life was taken out of him. He dropped him to the ground and let out a breath. He stared at Romey's body; his eyes were still open.

"You did this," Adlar said. He pulled himself to his feet and found Romey's eyes again, which were bloodshot. This time, he felt no guilt or regret. For most of his life, Adlar chose a life of isolation and he suffered for that, but this was different. This time, Adlar tried to reform, but he no longer had a choice. Some people are destined to be the bad guy, and as the day came to a close, Adlar accepted his place in the world. He dropped the cord at his feet and exited Romey's house and stepped into the dark.

6

Richard had ten that were sure to be there and he only needed eight. If Adlar decided to show, he would have eleven. He recruited everyone but Dent, and that was more than satisfactory. He sat up the night before, proudly scanning his list. A life was lost, but fourteen would be saved—at least the lives of those who chose to help. Richard tried calling Josh one last time, but he didn't answer. All he could hope was that Josh would meet up with the rest of the group going on the mission, learn something, and come back a changed kid. Richard believed he did what he could with Josh—what he was capable of doing while he orchestrated the event. If Josh harbored bad feelings for the little time he spent with him, he would get over those soon enough when he had a chance to help people far away and gain more perspective on the world. Though Richard had conquered what once seemed like an impossible task, he still lay awake, feeling guilty.

Charlie Palmer's eyes were wide open too. Mindy slept at his side, her hair a tangled mess on the pillow. He had his arm around her and her body pressed against his. It was a familiar feeling—laying next to someone he was intimate with—but it felt different. Wherever he and Mindy were headed, the time was coming they'd end up there. The will created a mess of Charlie's life, and when it no longer existed, he'd look back and take an inventory of how much it took from him and what it also may have given him. Charlie had been through a lot, and at one time, his demons didn't exceed insecurities and doubt. Somehow, those traits were a thing of the past and Charlie had turned into someone else. Now, all that mattered was getting through the next twenty-four hours, taking what he could get, becoming a brilliant surgeon, and learning to cope with the collateral damage that was caused by one moment of weakness. When he finally fell asleep, a jumble of nightmares filled the night. He repeatedly found himself back in his bedroom, a dark red stain growing on Abby's white nightgown. He tried to tell her he loved her, but he was breathless as her beautiful eyes stared at him, waiting.

Shiloh Reynalds curled up in her mother's bed. Trish watched her
sleep, her mind dominantly on her daughter's health. Shiloh had felt a
hundred percent better in the last couple of days, and while Trish counted
the hours that passed in which Shiloh seemed to have recovered, she feared
the day it would resurface, and questioned how she would financially get
through it if that time came. There was no doubt that from the beginning,
Trish wanted nothing to do with Victor's money, but when her daughter's
life was on the line, her mind kept wandering back to such a simple
solution. After tomorrow, the awful temptation would finally be scrubbed
from her life and she could focus on how to right herself again. She would
be there to help end Victor's will. Carlos was gone. Her daughter was sick.
Paul had turned out to be an even more irresponsible father than she'd ever
known. It seemed as if in the short amount of time since Victor's will was
read, her whole life was poisoned. Her awareness of what she was
potentially throwing away was heightened. If Shiloh had only weeks left,
and saving her came down to a matter of dollars, Trish wondered if she
would regret doing this. As she thought about her answer, she drifted off.

Toby O'Tool put all plans on hold. Unless a miracle happened,
Richard was on course to win. Toby tried to find dirt on the judge, but
came up empty. He gave Henry and William the simple tasks of preventing
Maria and Brian from coming, but it seemed as if both intended on being
there. He had other plans in motion, but put them on hold as well. Toby
contemplated being a no show himself, and if he could find his way out,
he'd leave before the judge arrived, but needed to measure the situation
first. If he could simply prevent Brian and Maria from being there, and
make up his own excuse, the will would live and breathe and he could
cross the next road when he got to it. Adlar was still a question mark and
he could probably approach any beneficiary and try to sway them, but as
the hours passed and time closed, he decided he wanted to see where the
chips fell and let the game play out.

Aileen Thick was good on her word. She would be there, but was sad
to see the end, if only because it was something that both her and Jason
were a part of—an opportunity to connect again. When she heard Jason
wouldn't be there, she stood by her decision to be there anyway. Jason
wanted to keep distance between himself and Victor's will and Aileen
respected that. With her son living in Hawaii and this chapter of life
coming to a close, she accepted that she may never see him again, and if
their relationship would never be mended, then the only good thing she
ever accomplished was forever gone. She would live her life with regret,
and she needed anything decent to grab onto. Being there to end the will
was something she would be a part of. She knew she'd never have the
money and she certainly didn't want to die. She slept easy, ready to have a

coffee, some conversation, and walk away with the chance to start a new chapter—hopefully a better one.

Brian Van Dyke felt he was betraying Victor, but Victor was gone, and a group of people who had constantly seen him in a bad light—as if he was Victor's groupie ready to carry out his legacy—were counting heads. Richard insulted him, just as Anthony and Trish had. He'd been looked at as a suspect for every bad thing that happened, even as he'd heroically tried to save Anthony the day Ira Moore tried to kill him. There had been no thank you and no one bothered to include him in the group. They, like everyone else, refused to see him as he was, all because he was loyal to Victor. He apologized out loud to Victor, as if Victor's soul would know and forgive him. It was partly real guilt, but partly the beer and pills that William hooked him up with. He spent the night before at a party that William brought him to. William was pushing the alcohol, but Brian resisted enough to keep himself fully conscious for the next day. William was disappointed, but Brian needed a night off. After three beers, Brian made his way to the bedroom and crashed while the party went on in his suite. Unknown to him, William stepped inside with his arms crossed and watched for a few moments, contemplating what to do to keep Brian from The Coop.

Maria Haskins was dealing with the same issues with Henry. She had every intention of supporting Richard. She didn't know if it was for the best, but nothing had happened to Royce as she believed it would and time winded down to sixteen hours until the end. She couldn't logically find a reason why being there with the group would get Royce killed, but she couldn't shake the vision: Royce laying on the ground in a pool of blood. Henry continuously made plans for the day, but Maria consistently told him she'd be busy. Henry pried but she wouldn't tell him. She didn't want his opinion on the money. She was afraid he might want it, and Henry's opinion mattered to her. It was best that he never knew the truth. She wanted to end the will and start a life with the man she recently fell in love with. She put her arm around Henry in bed. She sensed he was awake and whispered "I love you" into his ear. He didn't respond, as if he wanted her to believe he was sleeping. She knew he wasn't.

Royce Morrow searched for answers after Adlar's visit, and pieced events together little by little with the help of his private investigator Malcolm, he linked Manny's address to the homicide division of the LAPD. Royce assumed that meant he was a decent guy who was just moonlighting for money on the side—detached from the people whose lives he ended. He couldn't find a link to Bedbug, or where Bedbug was, but he fully intended on calling off any execution on Adlar. He'd pay double, or triple if it was necessary. He drove to Manny's neighborhood and tried to knock on his door, but Manny didn't answer. He followed the smell of smoke to the back yard and saw Manny from a distance, a bottle of liquor in his hand and a bonfire at his feet. He drunkenly murmured, and sifted through his work. From a distance, Royce realized that Manny wasn't the decent guy he'd encountered in the past. He was dark and angry and seemingly troubled by something. It wasn't the time to confront him. The time was during the day, when Manny was working—right before he met the group at The Coop to put an end to Victor's will. A visit in a public place, a generous financial proposal, and he could wipe his hands clean.

Anthony Freeman ran his hand up and down the scar on his side. He cut the stitches out himself and pushed at his skin, trying to find the source of the pain inside him. He stared at himself in the mirror and held up his hand, watching it shake as the arthritis crept into his bones. Since the will came into his life, he'd been stabbed, dealt with the death of Abby Palmer, and somehow, fallen off the wagon. He was happy to see the end of the will. It meant they beat Victor, but not at a low cost. He held his side again, and pushed his fingers inward, fishing for anything out of place. Then he felt something unnatural.

Tarek Appleton was the last sure supporter, making the count a solid ten. He hadn't given a lot of thought to the will. He'd only watched the chaos he created among the press without apology. The public went wild and started digging into the lives of those he mentioned on the air.

He planned on being there the next day too, but his mind replayed the fun his career had become. He entered his suite, whistling a tune, and flipped on the light. Then, sitting in his chair, a familiar face. A flood of memories came back. His early days in standup...the man who was sent to intimidate him...Victor had told him he fired that man. Now here he was, with an invested interest in Victor's affairs and no longer the man who was put together so well so long ago. Now, he was a coated with poor maintenance and lack of hygiene. Stanley Kline sat in a chair facing Tarek, gun in hand.

"You're...Victor's guy..." he said, keeping cool. "What do you want?"

"I want you to hear my story," Stan said. "Sit."

Tarek obeyed, afraid not to obey. Stan looked deranged. His eyes seemed expressionless, as if someone else was driving him from within.

"Shortly after I met you," Stan began, "Victor decided to do away with my position. Months before that, he told me about his will. I loved and supported the idea, and when he executed my employment, shut me out, and ruined my life, I decided I would like to be a name on his will. So I went out of my way to piss Stone off, and what I did to him..." Stan laughed as he reflected. "...he put me on there with the rest of you. Then, he died, and low and behold, I wasn't called in for the reading. Lucky for the rest of you, because you'd all be history by now if I was. So whatever…I wasn't included and I'm left to improvise, only, I only know your name is on there, but you're a stubborn bastard. You ready for this?"

Tarek nodded, a frown set on his face. He already suspected what was next.

"Your friends sold you out. Tony Tadesco and Rick Marcus. They were supposed to bring me names. They managed to do everything except what I asked, which is why I killed Rick."

Tarek closed his eyes as his world was turned on its head.

"In the end, Tony's loyalty saved your ass, but I still didn't have the names…"

"I won't give you the names."

"I've got a name: Anthony Freeman."

"He's less likely than I am to talk."

"Tomorrow at two o'clock, he'll be with the majority of your group and he's wearing a tracking device, among other things. The way I see it, if everyone who wants to shut it down are going to be in one place, I might as well eliminate them all together. Lucky for you, I still need a guy that can collect the money, and you're my guy." Stan rose to his feet. "You know, I had a great job. Yeah, we did some sick shit, but I had nothing going for me until he picked me up and had me do his scut work. Then you came along and put the scare into him and Stone abolished the very tactics that kept me in business. This is your chance to make things right."

"You should have taken that up with him. I didn't tell him to do anything. I ditched that act. I was a nobody. You had no business coming to me. If you would've left me alone, it wouldn't have escalated like it did. You'd still have your job."

"This is my fault?"

"You threatened me. You came to me, and on the command of a man who screwed you in the end."

Stan ignored him as he grew emotional. "You know after I lost my job, I lost my wife, my daughter, everything I had. Then, on top of it all, Victor didn't add me to his will. He probably knew I'd have that money in a week and couldn't fathom the thought. It's all I had left to rely on. I even celebrated when the bastard finally died. I thought about killing him myself. But no letter…no phone call…I couldn't even successfully become his enemy."

"You want money?" Tarek asked. "I've got money."

"What I want is for someone who's listed to collect when everyone else is dust. You're that man. You're spared. You may not like it, but the alternative is worse."

"If you walk into that place and just start shooting…"

"Not shooting," Stan said with a Cheshire cat smile on his face. "You know the blood that flows in our veins runs like a current in every single one of us? An electrical current? If you were to insert an actual device into a human being, it can be done and as long as the blood flows, you could power anything."

Tarek's forehead wrinkled. He didn't know where Stan was headed, but his confidence was scary. He had a plan—either a workable plan or one he believed to be, but it wreaked of destruction.

"But if you fabricate mesh containing a circuit of silicon after thinning the silicon until it's flexible...well let me tell you about that." He paced around Tarek, who was stiffened in fear. "You could deposit the silicon circuit into a silk to provide the structural support without sacrificing flexibility, take the silk from a silk-work cocoon that's been boiled to create a solution that could be deposited as a thin film..."

"What the hell are you talking about?" Tarek asked. Stan ignored him.

"...and when the film containing the circuit is placed on biological tissue, it would dissolve naturally and leave behind the circuit itself, attached to the tissue by capillary forces."

"You're intelligent. A man like you shouldn't need to..."

"I lost the last job I'll ever have today, but it doesn't matter. See, Anthony Freeman's body houses the bomb that will kill every last one of them, and anyone else in the building." Stan laughed at the visual.

Tarek flinched. Somehow, he'd figured it out just as Stan said it.

"It can't be disarmed, except with a number code that I have, but only after cutting into him. It can't be taken out. The flow of his blood is the circuit. If the flow is cut, just as a light-bulb lights up, so will he, and it will swallow everyone around him. It's the simplest damn thing in the world."

"I'll pay anything you want to go away and forget this."

"It's too late for that. No matter what happens, Freeman won't have an open casket funeral, and neither will anyone else who decides to try to put an end to that will." Stan pulled a remote device from his side and flashed it in Tarek's face. "We're going to get ourselves a front row seat to the end."

"You don't need me there."

In a blink, the gun was in Tarek's face again and pressed against his forehead. "You have no idea what I've been through and I don't have time to play cat and mouse with you. Only one person can live and it's either you or it's not."

"I'm not helping you with this."

"I'll give you three seconds to change your mind."

"Wait!" Tarek said, sweating profusely.

"Three..."

"Let...just..." He stammered, trying to find his way out.

"Two..."

"Jesus! Just listen to me!"

"One...

Chapter 20

1

"Victor," a voice said in the dark. "Pack a suitcase. We're leaving."

Victor Stone, twelve years old, sat up in bed and rubbed his eyes. "What?" he asked, confused to see his father Franklin standing in the doorway.

"Only take what you need. We're leaving the rest behind."

Victor stared at his father with dread. "Is it Nicolas?" he asked.

"Nicolas and I are all that's left," he said. "He won't waste time."

"I'll kill him if you won't," Victor said. He stood and faced his father with a stern look. His father might want to run away, but Victor wanted to face Nicolas; he wanted his father to be the last man standing.

Franklin stared into his son's eyes and saw he was serious. "Don't talk that way."

"It's self-defense if he's coming to kill you."

"I have family in Canada. They know we're coming. He won't find us there."

"We shouldn't have to run," Victor shouted, tears forming in his eyes.

Franklin took a moment to come to his son and put his arm on his shoulder, comforting him the best he could. "We'll come back someday."

Victor buried his head in his father's chest and sobbed until he was dry inside. Later, he could stop and explain everything to his son, but they had little time—Nicolas was desperate, much more desperate than Franklin had ever believed.

They hauled their suitcases down the walk outside the house, which was falling apart. It was run-down—the kind of home Victor would never live in again. Lightning flashed in the distance and droplets of rain began to fall.

"Why can't we call the police?" Victor asked.

"Let's go. Come on."

"We can't just leave. I have friends here. What about your shop?"

"We don't have a choice." He threw the suitcases in the car and just before he shut the door, the sound of a car-door from the street sounded. Both turned. Franklin froze. It was too late. "Get in the car," he commanded.

Victor hopped in the passenger side without a word and ducked, watching through the rain-streaked windows. He tried listening, but could only hear the murmurs of the men outside the car.

Outside the car, Franklin faced Nicolas, a tall man with glasses and a walrus mustache. Nicolas held his hand under his raincoat. "Where you headed at this hour?" he asked.

"What are you doing at my house at this hour?"

"You know," Nicolas said slowly, a smile forming on his face.

"We were friends."

"You know it's not personal. I didn't want this. You think I was happy that your name was included? I want you to know that I plan on making sure your son is taken care of."

Franklin sneered at him. "I don't want him to have this money. You kill me, but stay away from Victor."

Nicolas pulled the gun from his raincoat. Franklin watched him closely, swallowing hard. This was it. He tried to pull himself together—to prepare for the inevitable. "May I say goodbye to my son?"

"Of course," Nicolas said, in a kind voice.

Franklin walked to the car, opened the door, and faced Victor, who sat low, shaking in his seat. "Dad, get in. We can go," he said, desperately.

Franklin shook his head slowly and looked into his eyes, telling him everything would be okay. "He won't hurt you. You have to forget about this. You say it was a break-in and you didn't see the shooter."

"Dad!" Victor protested.

"Vic, you're too important. If he'd go this far for that money, nothing will stand in his way. You have to back off because it's too important to me that you go on living. I'm okay if you keep living. Be brave."

Victor nodded, tears streaming down his face.

"I love you Vic," Franklin said, putting his hand on his son's cheek tenderly.

Victor tried to speak, but Franklin closed the door, leaving him alone. He looked up for only a moment, but decided he couldn't see it happen. He closed his eyes and crouched down in the car and prayed that something would change—that the man would get hit by a car or have a change of heart. Anything would be better than the inevitable: that once Victor was able to emerge from the car, he'd find his father face down, just like all the others. Franklin's friends were all dead in a short period of time because they were all a part of some game—something his father had repeatedly told Victor was harmless.

Victor tried to block out the muffled sound of voices outside the car. Maybe Franklin was talking his way out of the situation. Maybe there was hope...

Then a single gunshot—a quick pop and silence. Victor's lip quivered and he sank deeper to the ground. He tucked his head down to his knees, afraid to look up. He could feel eyes on him from outside the car as a shadow covered the light coming in and paused there. Surely, Nicolas was watching and weighing what needed to be done about Victor. Finally, a car door and motor. And in a moment, the man who killed his father was gone...

...Maria Haskins rushed through her kitchen, multi-tasking between getting dressed, applying make-up, and cleaning. Henry watched from the table, eating at a slow pace. "What's the hurry?" he asked, annoyed at the way she went about everything so dramatically.

"I have too much to do today."

She hurried from the room. When she was out of sight, he opened his cell and sent a text to Toby. His only job was to prevent Maria from leaving the house, but she was too damn stubborn about this and he was forced to inform Toby that Maria would be there. As he finished the text, she rushed back in and stopped long enough to look at his plate, which was only half eaten, though he was finished.

"Eat it all," she demanded.

"I'm full."

"Animals give their lives to feed us, so it's on us to eat every part of them. It's a form of respect, and it's a better way to live than just treating meat as a disposable commodity."

"It's a half strip of bacon," he said in disbelief, though it was more than that.

"Eat it," she said, quickly.

He bashfully shoved the bacon in his mouth.

"I have to go," she said. She leaned in and took the time to give him a passionate kiss. "I love you."

Henry hesitated, smiling to replace a response. "Have a good day," he finally said. He watched her make her way to the door, contemplating his next move. Without thinking through a plan, he blurted, "can I get a ride first?"

She turned. "Why can't you drive?" she asked.

"I'm having engine trouble. Last night it was cutting out on the way home."

"Why didn't you say anything?"

"Didn't think it was important."

"I have to be somewhere," she said.

"You make your own hours."

She lingered in the doorway, searching for a way to say no. "Where do you need to go?"

"The library. Then, I thought I'd come hang out with you at work."

She paused for a long moment. Should she tell him the truth? Of all days to be clingy, Henry hadn't picked a good one. She wondered how he'd feel about the will. Maybe he'd overreact. Maybe he'd forbid her from going. "I have something personal to do," she said.

Henry stepped toward her and looked in her eyes. "You keeping secrets?" he asked.

She was at a crossroads between a lie and the truth. She didn't want to lose his trust, but was afraid of what he'd say. She searched for a truth that didn't tell him everything. "I'm meeting some friends today," she said. "It's a group of people and we're working on a project."

"What project?"

He wasn't going to let it go. "I'd rather not say," she said. "It's nothing bad. It's not even my thing. I just said I'd support it."

"Where you meeting them?"

"Henry…"

"It's fine," he said, with a dismissive smile. "Can I just get a ride?"

She let out a breath, relieved to end the line of questioning. They left together, mostly driving in silence. Maria loved Henry. She fell hard for him, and though in the past, she'd always claimed each guy was different, Henry really seemed to be. He did everything right. Sometimes, she thought he did everything too right. It was an unusual feeling being with a guy who was accepting and gave Maria his full attention. But he still didn't love her…or didn't say he did. She was sure he'd say it back eventually. He was too passionate with her—too into her. When she dropped him off at the library, she watched him walk away. He turned, smiled, and waved. There was something about his smile. It seemed…rehearsed. It dawned on her that she was thinking too hard about Henry and how he felt about her. Over-analyzing was the death of too many relationships. She reminded herself to just be happy for now. She started the car and began to drive away. She caught a glimpse of Henry in the mirror as he pulled out his cell phone. She wondered whose number he was dialing before shaking the suspicion from her head.

Toby stood in the doorway at The Coop with his cell to his ear. He watched Richard Libby and Anthony Freeman from a distance. They had a room reserved and sat deep in conversation. They were four hours early and apparently set the whole day aside to seal the deal. Toby watched with disgust at the duo as they happily sipped their coffee and passed the time until they destroyed Toby's dream—unless Toby could pull off a twenty-fourth hour miracle. He desperately tried to block Maria and Brian via Henry and William, but it seemed neither would come through. He had another trick up his sleeve, but would only resort to it if they were one beneficiary away from failure.

"Find a way," he said. "I don't care what she says. Just do your job." He shut his cell and watched outside for a short time while rain started to fall.

After Richard and Anthony were up to speed, Anthony grew quiet and began letting his mind wander. The rain changed the tone in the building as people began coming in from outside. The sky turned dark as it clouded over and for a short time, it sounded like static as the rain hit the roof.

"What happens if we don't win?" Anthony asked.

"I believe we have an overwhelming majority," Richard said.

"On paper, sure. But we're winding down and those who believed they could support this have very likely been dosed with reality, fueled by adrenaline. It's that superhero-esque, eleventh hour, fourth quarter realization."

"Faith," Richard said with a smile.

Anthony responded with a scowl, which Richard noticed. "You're not a religious man, are you?" Richard asked.

"Faith is a word that man invented. To believe what we can't see can't be proved or disproved and if it could, the word wouldn't exist. Faith and its definition contradict each other—unless you deny it."

"Non-religious people, children even, have been rescued from hopeless situations, and later recounted a higher power helping them through it."

Anthony laughed. "Miracle logic dictates that every missing girl who wasn't fortunate enough to be saved, was being punished or neglected. People believe what they're told Richard, despite the evidence. In one of my college courses, our instructor showed us a moving picture of a collision between a bicycle and an auto driven by a brunette, then afterward, we were peppered with questions about the 'blond' at the steering wheel and other details that weren't in the film at all. Not only did the class remember the nonexistent blond vividly, but when we were shown the video a second time, we had a hard time believing it was the same incident we recalled so graphically." Anthony tapped his temple with his finger. "Power of suggestion."

From behind, Toby appeared. "I took a college course once where the instructor constantly made me yawn really powerfully and my arms would stretch and shake. It was similar to this conversation." Toby plopped in a seat. He didn't bother to prep himself with his fabricated agreeable persona that he'd allowed Richard to see ever since Abby died. He was truly bummed out, and he couldn't hide it.

Anthony greeted Toby with a smile, uncertain of what to make of him. Anthony had thought about Toby a lot—occasionally as a suspect behind the lottery—but as big of a dirt-bag as he was, Anthony couldn't see him as someone who could inflict violence.

Toby turned to Anthony and shook his head in disbelief. "You really pulled it off."

"I won't be satisfied until it's done," Anthony said.

"I was just telling Mr. Freeman to have faith."

"Ah yes," Toby said. "I'll have faith that Abby Palmer will throw her full support behind your endeavor today. I hope she can find the time and energy to be here. I have faith that she will."

Anthony smiled to himself. Richard was outnumbered, but it didn't seem to bother him at all. Anthony added to Toby's point. "You know Richard, this is the final countdown for at least one or two of us. Someone wanted the money badly enough to set up the lottery, to murder Abby…someone with power and money. It's not entirely implausible to believe somewhere someone may have a plan to prevent today from happening."

"We have to believe it happened for a reason," Richard said. "Victor's vision kills all but one of us. We may not be able to call this a victory, but it was better than the alternative. I'll be happy if we can get this done."

"Saying it's not bad because it's not as bad as it could be is like praising syphilis for not being HIV," Toby said. Anthony chuckled and even Richard smiled. He understood their perspective, but guilt and sorrow could sit on the shelf for another day. Anthony was right. This was their last chance and the focus needed to be in one place.

"Since you asked though," Toby said, "I'll give you a sermon from the church of Toby, and listen up because I'm only doing one service and it will be the most profound shit you've ever heard: Every religious group, atheists included, have a bunch of good intelligent people, and a bunch of absolute smacktards, so I don't waste my time on petty battles where there are no winners or losers, and even if there were, no one would care. Especially because when you're wrong, you don't actually know you're wrong. It's called the Dunning Kruger effect: People who don't know much tend not to recognize their ignorance and fail to seek better information. I don't care what any of you believe. My guess is millions of years from now, after western civilization has fallen and the Earth has raptured and cooled and been reborn and a new life form has taken over the planet, if any of them happen to stumble on any evidence of all the stupid shit any of us so strongly care about: Silly straws, Coco Puffs, Justin Bieber, or even the book Anthony managed to publish, they'll sum up the passing of our culture in two words: Good riddance."

Richard silently watched as Toby and Anthony tag teamed him with conversation.

"Great writers do double-takes on received wisdom," Anthony said. "Sometimes I think of the world as impregnated by centuries of fiction and self-fertilized by science swelling out in new forms of consciousness. It's gotten well beyond the literary imagination. I've learned to make my own views clear. That's all anyone can do in this enterprise. People who write have their own strong conception of how things should go. In fifty years' time, presumably the oil will be gone, in a grossly overpopulated world with too many people and not nearly enough food or water, millions more species of animals will have disappeared forever, alongside the places they lived, natural resources that we need to survive as a civilization will be long gone, attempts to save them will have been too little, too late. The things we do don't matter in the long run Richard. I don't need to have faith because we're all here today to get what we want, and if we don't, it's not because it was meant to be. It's because the majority of us are greedy."

Richard laughed unexpectedly. Anthony raised his eyebrow at him.

"You're both intelligent," Richard said. "No doubt about that, but the apocalyptic references are all I needed to sum you up. A hundred years ago, they predicted a world just as dire and would have had just as much evidence for it. Apocalyptic thinking isn't new, but it's always wrong. So is Utopian thinking though. We have a need to believe that our problems are unique, and that we will be the generation that sees the final tipping point, mainly so that we can believe our deaths will be the deaths of everyone. A part of you hates the idea that the world will simply grind on as it always has, but it will, long after you're gone. In four hundred years, three gentlemen will be sitting in this very spot having a similar conversation, and the only difference between them will be the question of whether they were brought to this very spot, or if they decided they wanted to be there."

"Richard..." Anthony said softly, but Richard carried on.

"I don't care if your life has a purpose or if it's meaningless, and I don't care that you don't see good anymore. You can't take it away from the few of us who still do."

Toby gave Anthony a sideways glance and before they could say more, Richard's phone rang. He took the call outside the room while Toby and Anthony sat in silence. As he listened to Benjamin on the other end, he shook his head with disappointment. A plane took off that morning and Josh was supposed to be on it, but wasn't. Richard had played it safe with Josh, making a point not to get too connected, and it was apparent that Josh didn't appreciate that approach. He hadn't had the time to feel guilty and he certainly couldn't prioritize making Josh feel better constantly while juggling other responsibilities. If only the mission trip had been one or two days later, Richard could have managed to ready him and see him off. He put his phone back in his pocket and sat again, ready to open a new conversation. The day was supposed to be about one thing, but his mind kept wandering back to Josh and just what he was doing.

2

Manny sat amongst his crew at the LA homicide unit. Everyone was mid-conversation, laughing and talking with vulgarities. Manny only stared forward, blocking out the noise, his mind on his fallen friend, Adlar Wilcox, Royce Morrow…trying to play scenarios in his head. It was unlikely the shooter on the roof was Adlar or Royce. A third party made no sense. No one would know Bedbug would be standing in that spot. It only left the possibility of an accident. This was no breaking news. Manny called it an accident from the beginning, but tried to sway himself from that belief, because an accident meant Bedbug was damn unlucky and when it came to Manny's moonlighting activities, luck wasn't supposed to be a part of the equation.

"Manny! You got a walk-in!" a receptionist shouted. Manny didn't want to be working. He didn't want to do much of anything that distracted him from putting the pieces together, but to maintain his secret, it meant maintaining the Manny who everyone saw during the day. Manny was well liked in his crew. He always brought pastries and coffee to the group, came armed with new jokes from Maxim and Playboy, and asked questions as if he was genuinely interested in the lives of others. He was good at being chipper. He was smart about his persona. And then Bedbug died and faking became a chore.

He forced himself away from his thoughts and walked to the lobby. When he rounded the corner, he stopped abruptly as he came face to face with Royce Morrow. He managed a friendly smile. "Can I help you?" he asked. When his world became a puzzle, Royce was one of few who could hold the answers. Adlar was too dumb to understand the storm he was in, but Royce might have some insight, and if he didn't, he was the initiator and the consequences fell on him.

"We need to talk," Royce said, scanning their surroundings. He still couldn't understand why a man of the law was also a contract killer, but he supposed that made it easier. He wondered which one Manny was first—which one meant more to him.

"Do you have information about a case?" Manny asked.

"About Bedbug," he said, under his breath.

Manny paused, but held his composure. "I've got an unbelievable workload here," Manny said, pulling Royce off to the side. "Maybe we can talk in private."

Royce nodded, taken aback at his composure. Manny was too calm and collected. It was as if it didn't worry him in the least that Royce knew the real Manny. "I don't know what happened to him," he said. "I didn't say a word to anyone. Whatever happened on that rooftop had nothing to do with our deal. I didn't call it off, but I intended to. I don't want Adlar harmed and I don't expect anything. I had a knee-jerk reaction to a hardship, but I assure you that I've come to my senses. I also wanted to assure you that I had nothing to do with what happened. Adlar is the type of person who makes enemies easier than he makes friends, but I don't know anyone he associates with and can't offer a resolution, other than to say I'm willing to forget this happened, you will have profited heavily, and I'd also like to offer my condolences."

"I already know you didn't kill Bedbug. You don't have to explain yourself."

"You told me that if anything went wrong..."

"You were not the cause."

"Do you know the cause?"

"Not yet."

"I assumed you'd be upset."

"I am Royce, but until I have the whole picture, I don't plan on pointing the finger. Maybe you can help me out with some of the details though."

"Like I said, I don't know Adlar very well."

"No, and normally I wouldn't ask, but due to the circumstances, I think we need to talk about why it is that you came to me."

Royce nodded while contemplating. He could easily tell Manny the truth without telling him that the end of the will was near. They'd been cautious about who was in the loop because the last thing they needed was outside influences after the money. In four hours, the will wouldn't exist and given the circumstances, it wasn't a big deal for Manny to know. But then what? Would he find the person who really did go after Adlar and kill them? Or was he just looking for an arrest?

"The men who came to you were friends of mine. We all spent a good deal of time together living on the streets of LA. At one time, we were harassed by a man and he pushed things too far. Things came to a head and the man became too big of a threat. We didn't mean for it to happen the way it did, but there was an altercation and the man ended up being killed. Adlar is an angry young man who broke into my home and threatened my wife and I because I have money. He left my home with something that incriminated my friends and I. It would have come down on them if exposed and I couldn't let that happen. When I told them, they said they knew a guy who could get my personal belongings back. I didn't know…the nature of what it is you did. But the point is that Adlar was destructive, and he didn't think about what he was doing or how it impacted people."

"Then why did you call it off?"

"What happened in that apartment seemed to scare him. He came to me and apologized and gave my property back. I don't know much about him, but I know he's made some poor decisions and faced some hard truths. I can't offer anything more than that. I want to put this behind us and move on. Can we do that?"

Manny thought for a long moment. Royce was clearly telling the truth, but unfortunately, in Manny's eyes, it wasn't that simple. "I'm about to look at a crime scene and wrap up a case. Come along for the ride."

Royce wanted to cooperate with the man. He wanted to do whatever was necessary to put this chapter of his life behind him, but he didn't know what more Manny could want and he was afraid to find out. "I have an appointment," Royce said.

"Only take about half an hour. You came all the way to see me. Go on a run and I'll have you back asap."

Royce studied Manny's face, which held a smile that he couldn't read. He tried to think of what the worst Manny could do would be, and again questioned the morals of a lawman who doubled as a hit-man. "I've got half an hour," Royce finally said.

At the end of the block, three buildings from where the group was to gather at The Coup, Stanley Kline reserved a room on the third floor of the hotels housed on the corner of the block. With Tarek Appleton as his guest and a view of The Coup from the window, Stan's day was up and running. He'd already seen a familiar face enter the building: Anthony Freeman, who met another man. Everything was falling into place nicely. His weapon was the first to arrive, and by two o'clock, whatever group was in support would be blown to pieces, leaving very few remaining beneficiaries to deal with. Timing was everything, and the timing felt right, down to the loss of his job which put him in a desperate situation. The silver lining was the money—money Stan intended on having soon. He turned to Tarek, who lay on the bed staring at the ceiling.

"You'll owe me a thank you when this is over," Stan said.

"I'll be sure to do that."

"You would've been in that building."

"Well, thank you for not murdering me," Tarek said. "Remind me to thank Hitler and Atilla the Hun later too."

"Everybody dies Appleton. Might as well get what you can while you're still here."

"How did you know I'd be on his will?" Tarek asked.

"Above all, Victor cared about loyalty, and I saw what you did to him."

"You assumed I was on it? That's it?"

"I assumed right, though I assumed I'd be on it too."

"You know I won't collect the money for you, right? You can't force your way to the end of this with me at your side. I'm high profile. I bet if you turn on the TV, you'll see I'm already missing. Not everyone's going to be there today. Hell, you've got a guy in prison on the list. What's your plan to get to him? Tony already knows who you are. There's no way you can do everything you need to do and then waltz me into a bank to collect the money."

"We're going to work fast," Stan said. He tossed Tarek a notepad sitting by the phone. "Write all the names."

"I'm not writing the names."

"Last night, you said you were in. I won't count to three this time."

"You counted to one, down from three."

"So what?"

"It's different."

"We've got at least three hours together. Your distractions won't buy you the time you wish you had."

"What makes you think I wish I had time? I'm not trying to talk you out of it."

"Cause you don't got a chance."

"Look, if you wanna think you're forcing me into this, then good for you and good for me, but don't talk down to me as if I'm supposed to be afraid or as if my role is to talk you out of this. You threw me off-guard. That's all. But I don't care that we're here doing this. It's a smart idea. I'll give you that. But you're not doing me any favors. I would've gotten the job done whether you were here or not. You're just making it quicker and easier for me. I have no problems giving you a cut if you're going to take the burden off of me, but you're not going to be a royal prick all day about it."

Stanley stared out the window and blinked hard while he registered what Tarek said. He turned to him with a raised eyebrow. Tarek sat carelessly on the bed, seemingly unaffected by Stanley's plan. "What are you trying to say?" Stan asked.

"I've tried several things," Tarek said. "Some worked. Others, failed. I had Anthony Freeman stabbed. Did you hear about that? But he survived. I've managed to eliminate one."

"What are you talking about?"

"Abby Palmer. She's the only one on the list who's dead. Her husband will be there."

"Yeah, right. Tony said someone died. You expect me to believe it was you?"

"I don't expect you to believe anything," Tarek said. "Believe it or don't. Just do what you're gonna do, I'll give you the names, and work quickly if you want a cut, because if you're caught, I'm not giving you a dime."

Stanley didn't usually allow people to talk to him the way Tarek was, but he was dumbfounded—too dumbfounded to find his response. Tarek has proved to be a clever man in the past, but in a life or death situation, he was uncharacteristically cool. Stan let himself toy with the idea that Tarek really was behind some of the bad things that happened to the beneficiaries. Someone had to be. "Why would you do it?" Stan asked.

"Same as you," Tarek said, simply. "For money."

Stan turned back to the window and watched across the way silently. He clearly had the upper-hand and there wasn't anything Tarek could do to stop him, but he couldn't help but ask himself what Tarek's intent was here. If Tarek really was in the same boat as Stan, what did that mean for him? Did it make him a bigger liability? Was he just messing with Stan? A car pulled into the parking lot of The Coop and Charlie Palmer and Trish Reynalds exited. No matter what Tarek said or did, the building would be obliterated by the end of the day. And then, Stan would finally take back the life that Victor stole from him...

"...Knock knock," Victor said, leaning into the doorway.

Stanley looked up from his desk and sized Victor up before going back to his work. "Read the sign on the door."

"The door was open."

"Business is closed though," Stan said, pointing to the sign.

"I only ask for a few moments of time," Victor said. "I'll make it worth your while."

Stan motioned for Victor to sit. "You looking to hire me for a job?" Stan asked. "Because I'm moving to St Louis the day after tomorrow and I've got a lot of packing to do."

"Why are you shutting down?" Victor asked.

"I'm losing my license."

"Why?"

"Because some people don't like the way I get things done. Most people don't like to hire detectives in the first place. Usually I'm out to prove someone's being cheated on or occasionally track down a long lost whatever. No one needs me if they just run a Google search or know their significant other, but nowadays I have so many restrictions on what I can and can't do, you might as well just call the police instead of me."

"Were you caught?"

"I have eyes on me and if I don't close shop, they'll shut me down anyway, so I'm leaving town and starting fresh."

"How about one last job?" Victor said.

"I'm not agreeing to anything until I hear what it is."

"Twenty-five years ago, my father was murdered. I know the name of the man who did it, but he left the country shortly after. He could be anywhere in the world and I wouldn't have an idea of where to start."

"Sounds like a more than forty-eight hour gig."

"It is if you stick around and work it."

"I can't take this to St Louis?"

"Absolutely not. I would need access to you."

"Well, then the answer is no."

"Why do this? Why be a private investigator?"

"I like being my own boss."

"It can't be good money and you said it yourself: Restrictions."

"Yeah, well, not much else I can do."

"What if I employed you? You'd be making a lot more than you make doing this and you'd be under only my supervision. My only demand would be that you continually search for this man. I have no expectations. It could take years."

"Why me?" Stan asked with suspicion.

"Your reputation. The very reason you may lose your license; because the very methods that are frowned upon are necessary."

"All you want is to find this man and bring him back? To face trial?"

"To face me."

"Before we go any further, if I humor you and consider, assuming you can offer stable work for worthwhile pay, I don't take any job without full disclosure. I don't like surprises and I don't like finding out later that I didn't have the information I needed to make decisions."

"He killed my father," Victor said. "I don't intend on giving him the luxury of a trial."

"At that point in time, what happens to me?"

"If you're a worthy investigator, and you spend sufficient amount of

time on this, you will always have a job at Stone Enterprises."

Stan found Victor's eyes and suddenly stood as he realized who he was conversing with. Victor smiled.

"You'll be paid generously and you won't have to run away. You'll be paid under the table, but I'll be sure to finance all the perks of being a salaried employee, and if and when the time comes, I'll be sure to send you off with a resume and all the accolades you'll need to do whatever you want."

Stan smiled. It was as if Victor knew he'd been down on his luck. Victor was saving him from a decision that he never wanted to make. Not only that, but within moments, his life changed for the better. Stan needed to rebuild his credit, find a nice place, a girlfriend, maybe get married and have a few kids; he needed to get his life on course. They had yet to discuss the compensation, but something told Stanley this would be worth his while, and in time, he'd discover he'd underestimated just how much money he'd make.

"All I ask is for your loyalty," Victor said. "And you will have mine..."

...Trish picked Charlie up at the hospital after working the graveyard shift. She offered to buy him lunch at The Coop while they waited. They sat in the corner of the bistro in two leather chairs, with two drinks between them and a file sitting on the table at their side. Charlie opened it and looked at the x-rays he'd already closely observed, and spoke carefully, still trying to grasp his diagnosis. He pulled the first x-ray and placed it on top of the stack.

"This one shows the tumor clearly." He pointed to an off colored area in the brain. "Neomin probably went over this with you."

Trish nodded.

"He has the right diagnosis. Does he treat this with any sense of urgency?"

"He's doing what he can."

"Did he recommend the trial?"

"Yeah, why?"

"No reason, but the drugs he's giving her is killing it at a rapid pace. Almost miraculously."

Trish frowned. "I didn't know that."

"You should. In fact, he should be shouting it from the mountaintops. This venom thing is a new development with some positive results, but in Shiloh..." He pulled the next x-ray and pointed to the tumor. "This is amazing. Too amazing."

Trish let out a breath of relief.

"I assume he's trying not to get your hopes up, but this is all very positive Trish. When this is over, don't be surprised if your daughter is the poster child for this kind of treatment."

"Is it really that effective? I mean, what are the chances of full recovery off the trial alone?"

"Slim to none. This drug isn't believed to kill the tumor. Just stop the spread. What we're looking at may suggest otherwise though."

"Now what?"

"Keep doing what you're doing. Stick with Neomin for now and I'll look over her treatment too."

Trish had a thought, and suddenly eyed Charlie with suspicion. "Are you trying to get out of our agreement?"

"Not at all. Talk to Neomin and he'll confirm this. He may be downplaying it for your sake, but he'd be outright lying if he didn't look at this x-ray and call it optimistic. He's a good doctor. I don't know him well, but I hear good things, and it seems as if he's taken an interest in Shiloh."

"Is he not this way with all his patients?"

"I don't know. He could have a soft spot for children or maybe he likes you."

Trish looked away.

"Neomin's single by the way," Charlie said. "In case you were wondering."

Trish laughed as if the notion was ridiculous, but had appreciated everything Neomin did for Shiloh, and after this news, all she wanted to do was see her doctor and express gratitude.

"Look at that guy," Charlie said, nodding toward the entry where Toby spoke on his cell phone.

"What about him?"

"Surprised he's here. He's an instigator."

"Why do you say that?"

"I ran into Victor's attorney shortly before we met on that roof. His attorney tells me that guy was asking about Abby's history with Victor and so his attorney gives him some old personal things and then leaves them at my home for me to find. I followed him to get to Wilcox."

"Why would he do that?" Trish asked.

"He's just starting shit."

"Toby O'Tool was the one who wouldn't stop talking the day the will was read," Trish said. "And he didn't make a secret of the fact that he wanted the money."

"So why is he here today?"

Trish watched Toby closely as he spoke into his cell, visibly upset. "I don't know."

On the other end of the line, William explained his side of the story. Brian passed out the night before, though he hadn't had much to drink. William was going to wake up and stall him and do whatever it took to distract Brian into not coming, but when William woke up, Brian was already gone. He'd tried the uptown and downtown Wasp, but he was nowhere to be found. He could be out for a drive, or on his way to The Coop, but with Brian missing, William had no way of preventing him from throwing his support Richard's way. Hopefully, he'd think better of going or forget.

"I don't know what to tell you Toby. You're sitting there with the group. Why don't you leave?"

"Because I need to count heads and sway them when the count is in Richard's favor."

"I'll keep calling Brian, but I don't have any control over it."

"You've worked with him for almost a month," Toby said. "You should have your hooks in him by now. I've been very clear that he can't be here today."

"Well, if he gets there, let me know and I'll find a way to get him out."

"Unreal," Toby said, and hung up the phone.

He watched out the window as the rain slowed and picked up again. He watched Charlie and Trish in the reflection. Five people were already at The Coop and it was still early. Maria was presumably on the way and maybe Brian. Aileen, Royce, and Tarek were sure to be there. He was fighting an uphill battle. He considered playing his wild-card but decided to wait. He still had his trick up his sleeve—only to be used if absolutely necessary.

He changed his composure back to his cooperative self and entered the meeting room, just as Charlie and Trish stood and entered. There were greetings all around and after a few moments, they sat in a scattered circle around the table. Toby continually watched the door and when a familiar face finally arrived, it wasn't one he expected. "What the hell is he doing here?" Toby asked.

Everyone turned as Bernard Bell made a beeline toward the meeting room and entered. He didn't look at anyone or say a word. He was clearly angry and everyone fell silent, unwilling to ask what he was doing there.

"Who's all coming?" Bernard asked.

"Everyone but one or two," Anthony said.

Bernard let out a loud sigh. "This is ridiculous," he said. "You're all going to stomp on Victor's final wishes?"

"You don't have to be here," Trish said.

"Actually, I do. I'm the executor and I hold the will. I don't want to be here and I think it's absolutely stupid that anyone's here, but my day is ruined by this. Thank you all."

Toby raised an eyebrow. Bernard always had a motive but he wasn't hiding his anger toward the situation well, and his very presence in the room made the group uncomfortable. Before anyone could get around to starting a conversation, Bernard began preaching his disapproval of what they were doing, calling names, belittling, and anything he could do to make it intolerable for them to be there.

And after a half hour of Bell's ranting, it started to work.

3

Stan was buying the charade. From his vantage point, Tarek saw the conflicting emotions bouncing around in Stan's head as he stared out the window. Tarek's eyes kept making their way to the clock, but he forced himself not to be too anxious. Before Tarek was a talk show host, he had a sitcom. Before that, he was a comedian. Before that, a ventriloquist. What most people didn't know about Tarek was that before that, he went to school to be a psychiatrist. He'd studied Sociology for four years before he decided to give it all up and hit the stage, but he'd used his skills throughout his career to get what he wanted. He was good at picking at people, at finding their weaknesses, at making them believe they had what they desired while silently holding the upper-hand.

Stan didn't expect Tarek to pursue the money. He'd expected resistance, fear—and Tarek would give him the opposite. If Stan's guard was lowered, Tarek might have a chance at getting the best of him. Since he'd learned what Stan did to Rick, the only thing on his mind was to beat him and see to it that he went to jail for his crimes. To win him over, they first had to be on the same side. Then, he needed to introduce a new element into their relationship. He had to do it quickly, but without raising suspicion.

Stan turned to Tarek thoughtfully. "If what you're saying is true, this is going to work out better than I thought. You know Appleton, you're the reason I lost my job and my life fell apart. I've always despised you for it, but this is your chance to make it right. As long as you're being honest and don't have your own agenda, then we'll take care of the remainder of these guys, split everything fifty-fifty, and go our own way."

It was time for the next stage of Tarek's plan. He searched for a serious tone and found it. "We're not splitting anything fifty-fifty," Tarek said.

"No need to be greedy," Stan said. "A tenth of Victor's money is still a retirement fund."

"That's about how I plan on splitting it," Tarek said. "So there shouldn't be a problem."

A grimace formed over Stan's face as he studied Tarek. The man was a stranger to him, and though he now believed Tarek, a new problem was developing. Tarek was on board, but now he wanted too much. "You're fucking around, right?"

"I already had everything under control," Tarek said. "You think cause you come along and try to hurry things along, you deserve anything? I can get this done without you. I don't need you."

Stan looked genuinely hurt, but mostly shocked. Inside, Tarek was applauding with glee, but he kept his expression in place.

"Too bad Appleton. You may not know it now, but I'm doing you a favor. I'm willing to negotiate the cut, but it ain't ten percent."

"It sure as hell isn't fifty."

Stan grew defensive and walked away from the window. "What the hell does it matter to you? Fifty is more than either of us could ever spend."

"On principle, you don't deserve a dime."

"I'm about to eliminate half, or more, of the list. What have you done? Killed one and failed on others?"

"I wasn't in a hurry."

"You should have been, because they're meeting down there right now to end this. What was your plan then?"

"They can't end it. You think anyone's going to show for that thing?"

"They're already there. Look, I'm not going to argue with you. I'm doing all the work."

"I didn't ask you."

"Too fucking bad."

"Here's the thing Stan: You can't do anything to me because you need me, but the first chance I get, I'll turn you in, and what can you do about it? You're right. You are going to take half the group out, and that's a pretty sweet deal for me because all I have to do is sit in bed and watch cable on your dime. Then, when all is said and done, when the police find me, I can tell them I was taken by you and your prints and whatever skills you have to put a bomb inside someone—all the shit that will obviously prove you're guilty will come crashing down. You'll be arrested and I'll finish the job and collect my money. By the time you're out, you won't even begin to know where to find me."

"What the hell is your deal Appleton? We can work together on this."

Tarek kicked his feet up on the bed and fell back onto a pillow. "Do what you're going to do, or don't," Tarek said. "At the end of the day, I really don't need you."

"Then maybe I'll recruit someone else."

"You sure you've got the time to do that? You sure you can ever get this many of us in one place again? You sure that if you wait, it will even be a legal document tomorrow?"

Stan had no answers. He was thrown off-guard by Tarek. He was prepared to justify himself all afternoon, but instead, had to justify why he deserved a cut to a man who wanted it more. Tarek closed his eyes with a smug smile, allowing Stan to do his dirty work while he waited, and Stan wondered if Tarek really would get his way in the end. He wondered if there was a way to get through. This wasn't the battle Stanley was prepared to fight, and it wasn't one he was sure he could win.

And inside, Tarek had the same struggle. He didn't let his act slip, but he caught the clock on the wall. An hour and a half until the judge arrived, and when that happened, Stan would push the button. An hour and a half for Stan to hand the control to Tarek. So far, he was on task, but Tarek didn't know Stan any better than Stan knew Tarek. He didn't know just how far Stan would go…

…Stan made a good living working for Victor. Over the course of two years, he met a woman who was pregnant with his child two months later. They married two months after that, and by the time two years passed, she was pregnant again. Stan was the proud father of a boy and a girl, husband to a lingerie model, and owner of a house with a deck and pool. Stan always hoped to become successful, but never anticipated this. All thanks to Victor, who kept Stan around and made good on his promise.

Stan spent that time trying to find Nicolas without success. He'd stumble on a lead here and there, but never tracked the man down, and with nowhere to begin, didn't have a lot of optimism in doing so. Victor rarely asked about Nicolas, but Stan saw it when Victor looked at him. There was always a new hope in his eyes, as if he was waiting for Stan to deliver news that never came.

Stan considered Victor a friend. They'd been to each other's homes, met each other's families, and shared drinks together on more than one occasion. Stan was asked to do a lot of things for Victor that weren't always legal, and somewhere during his employment for Stone Enterprises, Stan became the muscle—an intimidation tactic. It wasn't his dream, but it wasn't long before Stan realized it was fun being that guy.

The honeymoon lasted four years before Tarek Appleton came along with his song and dance about corruption at Stone Enterprises. First, Stan was assigned with strong-arming him off the stage. Then, Bernard Bell tried paying him off. It was Victor who eventually hooked Tarek up with an agent, but before that happened, a fear was put into Victor and he had to reevaluate the structure of Stone Enterprises. It was a hard conversation for Victor, but necessary. He invited Stan into his office at the end of the day, poured him a drink, and gave him the bad news.

"That ventriloquist...he made a puppet that resembles you," Victor said.

Stan laughed, confused. "What?"

"He's mocking you now. He's portraying you as a thug."

"I'll talk to him again."

"No," Victor said. "A local newspaper picked up on what he was doing and published a story."

"So what? The guy had an awful show."

"It's getting attention. People are asking who you are and what you do for me."

"I'm not worried."

"I am," Victor said in all seriousness. Stan grew quiet. "We're growing Stanley. I've been under the microscope for some time and there are people turning every stone in the company to see that we're doing everything right."

"Well...let's be careful then. We can lay off some things."

"Stan..." Victor said, as Stan turned away from him and shook his head. He tried to prevent what he knew was coming. "I don't have a place for you here anymore."

"You promised me employment," Stan said, his voice rising.

"I kept you running for years," Victor said. "The search for Nicolas seems to have been nothing but a dead end and I have no room for you. People are already asking questions. This is best for everyone, including you. You don't have an education. You're an ex private eye who lost his license. What do I tell people you do for me?"

"I don't know. Open something like you did for Haskins. You're always pulling favors for underdogs. Please Victor, at least hook me up with something."

"I can give you seed money to get yourself started," Victor said.

"Jade and I just got a place. She's not working. What about the kids?"

"You're capable," Victor said. "This was never your only option."

"You promised loyalty. I'm living in my means and now you're cutting me off? Then what? I can't make what I make here anywhere else. Shit...shit..." Stan paced back and forth and ran his hand through his hair. He turned back to Victor. "I'll find Nicolas."

"I'm sorry Stanley," Victor said. He didn't budge from where he sat. He looked up with sincerity and let Stan know his mind was made up. "There's too much to lose..."

…Toby fell into his seat, staring at nothing in particular. He barely noticed the portly waiter approach. "Excuse me, but you left the counter without paying," the waiter said.

Toby rolled his eyes and pulled some bills from his pocket. He counted it and compared his amount with what was written on the check. "Spot me a couple cents?"

"What about the tip?"

"What about it?"

The waiter walked away, shaking his head.

Trish gave Toby an unimpressed look. "That was mean," she said.

"Haven't you heard? Mean is the new nice."

"I didn't think it was nice."

"You see how disgusting that guy was?"

"No."

"Sure you didn't."

"He was overweight. It doesn't mean you should act like that."

"Yeah, I bet you date guys like that all the time."

"I'd date a guy like that before I'd date a jerk."

"Thinness is an outward sign that a person has a degree of discipline and self-respect."

"I don't think he needs you telling him that."

"He thinks he's smarter than he is," Aileen Thick said, approaching the group. Toby shook his head to himself as the group greeted her. All except Bernard, who glared at her as she added to the headcount.

"You two know each other?" Trish asked."

Toby said "no" and Aileen said "yes" simultaneously, piquing Trish's interest.

"From before the will?" Trish asked.

"We have history," Aileen said.

"You weren't…" Trish started.

"No, I wouldn't touch him."

"If by 'wouldn't,' you mean 'I did occasionally', and by 'touch him', you mean 'drove me to have black out orgasms,' then you can pretty much take her word," Toby said.

Trish shifted in her seat awkwardly as Aileen glared at Toby. "You came to me," Aileen said. "Let's not forget that little detail."

"Why are you here Toby?" Trish asked, confrontational.

"That's not obvious?"

"From what I saw, you seemed interested in the money," Trish said. Charlie leaned in awaiting an answer.

"He's here to be the opposing voice," Aileen said.

"I'm backing Richard," Toby said, simply.

"Really…" Trish said, doubtfully.

"Richard's threatened me with an eternity of damnation and promises me thirty virgins when I die. Not that I believe anything would have ever come of this…"

"What about Abby Palmer?" Trish asked.

Charlie cocked his head.

Toby went on. "Would've happened either way. Victor was trying to promote fear. Not violence."

"You're working with Adlar Wilcox," Charlie said, bringing silence throughout the room.

"Adlar who?"

Charlie didn't bother to say it again. He shook his head. Toby shifted uncomfortably, but was saved when Bernard started ranting again. "This is pathetic," he said. "If everyone is going to be here to end this, then how is anyone a danger?"

Anthony tried playing the opposing side, but Bernard was hostile and unreasonable. Trish and Aileen left the meeting room for half an hour because they couldn't listen to him talk. Richard distracted himself by making calls to find out what happened to Josh. Benjamin didn't know, but told Richard he'd contact Josh's parents to make sure he was okay. Toby didn't offer much to the conversation and focused on texting his recruits. When Maria Haskins entered The Coop, he began grinding his teeth with frustration. Maria brought the count to seven. Richard had half. If another showed up, it was over. The word was out on Brian and Adlar, but Tarek and Royce were most certainly going to arrive. As a last ditch effort, he texted Henry and told him he needed to get over here now and get Maria out of this place. He offered no reason Henry would have to show up, but he was desperate.

Toby rubbed his temples as he realized Bernard was still talking down to the group. He closed his eyes and tried to sleep, but couldn't block him out. Anthony gave up trying to reason with Bernard and walked to the restrooms. It was there that he ran his hand over his side and poked around for the bump he'd found near his stitches, just under the skin. He decided when the day was over, he'd get himself to a hospital and get an x-ray to find the source of discomfort.

Charlie studied Shiloh's folders from time to time and talked with some of the others in brief spurts. He managed to get an apology from Maria for coming to him before Abby's death. He'd forgotten about that and tried to ignore the fact that there had been some truth in what she said. He simply told her not to worry about it and went back to his thoughts.

Half an hour passed and it was a lot of the same. Random chatter, beneficiaries trying to escape the belittling of Bernard, and clock-watching.

In an hour, the judge would walk through the door and it would be over once and for all.

Henry arrived about that time and Maria was surprised to see him. They found their own table and Henry played it off as if this was a big coincidence. He asked her what she was up to and she finally told him why she was there—what she was doing. He pretended to be surprised and searched for an approach to get her to leave.

Richard heard back from Benjamin, who told him he spoke to Josh's parents and they told him he was likely at Black Chasm, the caves along the coast where his brother died. He went there often to think and was probably throwing his usual tantrums and feeling sorry for himself. Richard felt bad to leave Josh in that state. He felt worse than ever that he'd kept him at a distance, in fear he'd turn out to be like every other person Richard had tried to fix in the past. He reminded himself why he was there—to lead the charge to end the will. He thought about Victor— thought about what Victor wanted and believed. When this was over, he would spend more time giving, helping people, and fighting battles he may not win, but be satisfied to be trying. He would lead by example. The more he motivated himself, the more he thought about Josh, sitting on an island of rocks and inviting death to come for him. That's what he was doing after-all. The sky was turning dark again and Josh decided to give up on the good he was going to do and give in to whatever darkness he had. Maybe to defy Richard. Maybe because it was who he was. Either way, Richard looked around the room and felt like he was in the wrong place for the first time in a while. Everyone looked miserable, bored, or as if they were only there to prove they were good. Bernard wouldn't shut up. The sun literally wasn't shining. It seemed as if the tone of the day was the perfect metaphor for what was happening in The Coop. It was supposed to be a happy ending to a bad chapter, but everyone looked as if it was a burden.

But the most intolerable of all was Bernard, who spit his words, as if desperate for the group not to go on. Some thought he was just trying to be loyal to Victor, but others watched him suspiciously, wondering why this meant so much to him. The mutual bond in the room was that everyone wanted him to shut up. They would have to endure another hour of his ranting and raving, and it would only get worse when the tie-breaker showed up.

Anthony watched the door with the dreadful feeling that there would be no tie-breaker. Brian and Adlar would probably be no-shows, but Tarek said he'd be there. Most importantly, Royce wouldn't miss this for anything. In fact, he was surprised Royce wasn't here yet.

4

Royce watched the raindrops hit the windshield and get cleared away by the wipers repeatedly. He turned toward Manny, who kept his eyes focused on the road. Manny took him on the freeway heading south and kept going until they were out of Los Angeles and headed toward Orange County. As time passed, a bitter taste filled his mouth. They'd been driving for an hour more than what Manny promised. Most of the ride was in silence and Manny's face had a permanent frown. Royce was afraid to ask where they were really going, but he couldn't take it anymore. He needed to make conversation to ease the tension.

" Why do you do what you do?" Royce asked. "I mean, on the side."

"Why do I do what I do?" Manny repeated, as if asking himself. "I was a cop first. I just kept coming across these crime scenes where it was easy to catch the guy who did it because they're all sloppy and stupid. It makes you contemplate how you can get away with what they can't, as if you're trying to convince yourself that you're smart. It's like this job I had in High School, working the drive through. I realized you can delete pieces of the order and do the math in your head and make a few bucks off every car that comes through and pays cash. Then, I'm using coupon scams and soon, I figure out how to make it seem as if there never was an order. A few bucks per car added up, but I didn't do it for money. I was just trying to be smart. I was the fast food guy who was going to the bars every night and buying drinks like a big shot. When I became a cop, I obsessed over the same shit. A fool tries to kill his wife so he can collect life insurance and attempts to make it look like an accident, I see the flaws in his plan, I brainstorm how I would've done it. So then one day, I just had to know if I had what it took. We look for means and motive and patterns and witnesses and we ping cell phones; I know the tactics, so I work around the tactics."

"So you murdered someone just to see if you could get away with it?"

"Absolutely. Then, I felt bad for a while, but did it again. Just random people with no pattern. It was entertaining watching the police running in circles. I worked one of my own homicides once. That was a thrill. They had a serial killer on their hands and had no idea. They didn't even link two together. I used different weapons, in different neighborhoods, at all times of the day with different signatures. Serial killers like to make the police think they're smart, and then they get caught and they still have that proud smile on their face when they sit in front of a judge, but what do I care what some lawyers and a judge thinks? I wanted to be smart for me. I wouldn't trade letting the world know how smart I was for a jail cell. But then, I got bored. I realized I could do it but didn't have a reason, but I didn't want to stop."

"What about protecting the law? How can you be a cop and do what you do?"

"Good question Royce, and the answer is that I don't know. I liked being different. People are either brutal madmen or decent people and I was an enigma that no one knew existed. But I'll tell you what kept me going: I patrol the streets and see people shouting for no good reason, trying to sell me shit in the tourist destinations, shoulder to shoulder foot traffic, street traffic, no parking anywhere in the city, little rich bitches yelling at each other because their dogs are barking at one another. There's too damn many people in this city. When I'm in bumper to bumper traffic, I wish the whole fucking line of cars ahead of me to just be wiped from the earth and I get to thinking, what if I killed the guy in front of me tonight? I'd be one car ahead. It ain't much, but it's a start. I'm just sick of the clutter. People are disgusting for the most part, and I hate human nature, so I used my skills to make some money on the side and it turns out, there's quite the demand for what I do and there's good money in it."

"How did you come to work with Bedbug?"

"Met him in a bar and accidentally spilled my line of business when I was drunk. I started thinking I might have to kill him too, but he was excited about it and wanted to kill someone that very night. Bedbug and I hit it off right away and wrote our own rulebook on how this is done. There are guys out there that are maybe a little more or a little less professional, but we made damn sure to keep our bases covered. You weren't the first and you won't be the last to fuck up."

"Where are we going?"

"There's a debt Royce. Some debts don't have monetary solutions and this is one of them."

"I had nothing to do with what happened."

"You may not think so, and maybe you don't, but I believe you set it in motion. I told you from the beginning that once we've reached an agreement, you turn away and forget you did it. But you broke the rules. You went searching for Adlar, hired a guy to find him, tried backing out."

"None of that puts you at risk," Royce said. "I wanted you to forget about him."

"We sat down and I gave you until the end of the day to call it off, and you didn't. We figured out where Wilcox was and Bedbug went on a routine assignment and next thing I know, he's shot in the face from across the street."

"I explained…"

"Yeah, you did Royce. You explained, but it doesn't change the outcome. I don't care if you're innocent. I kill innocent people by the week for nothing, but you're going to be the collateral damage for what happened."

"Where are we going?"

"Just sit back and enjoy the ride."

Royce stared out the window. He wished he'd gotten out of the car when traffic was heavy, but the freeway turned into hills and desert and soon, they drove along the coast where trees covered the land. Royce waited for Manny to pull off the road to a secluded area, but he kept driving. Maybe he was just trying to put the scare into Royce. He still held on to too many regrets. At the end of them all stood the only thing he cared about in the world: Sandra Morrow, who would be sitting at home waiting for him, calling and texting, worried. Royce had to buy his way out of this, or talk his way out. He considered all the possibilities as to what could have happened to Bedbug, but he was as lost as Manny was. There was no sense in what happened, and Royce was the only logical person for Manny to take it out on.

Royce looked up at the clouds and told himself it couldn't end like this.

With less than an hour left, Tarek couldn't sit back carelessly anymore. He had to keep his plan moving without raising suspicion. It had been convincing because he'd made a point to show Stan that he didn't care what he was about to do. If he started talking in a hurry to fulfill his agenda, Stan would notice the urgency. He kept hoping Stan would open the line of communication, but Stan was waiting it out and Tarek's bluff was only good until Stan pushed the button.

"Less than an hour," Tarek said. It was a stupid comment and sounded like he was trying too hard, but Stan didn't notice. He was lost in his own world, watching the building down the street.

"Why haven't you written all the names down?" Stan asked.

"Security. When this is done, I'll give you the names."

"Why when this is done? When are you going to get it through your head that we need each other?"

"I don't need you."

"You wouldn't have gotten the job done," Stan said. "You don't got it in you."

"I already proved that I do."

"Four months and you got one. If my name had been on his will, you would've all been dead by now."

"Guess you didn't piss Victor off enough."

"Oh, I did," Stan said. "He told me about his will. His father had been a part of a similar idea and got himself killed. When you and Victor ruined my life, I made damn sure to do what he'd never forgive."

"Maybe he knew you'd kill us all and the money would be yours," Tarek said. "Maybe his revenge for you was to exclude you from the will."

"Maybe. Probably. I don't care."

Tarek looked at the clock. It was time to start making suggestions and hope Stan didn't see through the plan. "I guess this worked out well for me then," Tarek said. "You'll get your ten percent and be happy, I sit back and do nothing, you get your hands dirty and risk prison, I retire with my ninety percent."

"We're still not settled on the cut," Stan said.

"We don't have time to negotiate and we both know I have the upper-hand," Tarek said.

"I don't see it that way at all."

"You're going to do what you're going to do, and wipe half these guys off the playing field. Then, I have to walk into the bank with that money. Face it Kline: You're desperate. You'll take what you can get. That's why you're stuck doing all the dirty work and I get the reward."

"When did you become such an asshole?"

"When you told me you murdered Rick."

"Rick wasn't invited to the party."

"Neither were you."

"What? I killed your friend and now I get the hard end of the bargain? No way Appleton. If you want me to do this, you're going to be a lot more grateful than that."

"I'm indifferent Stan. I told you, if you don't do this, I'll do it anyway. Stay and help or let me take care of it, but the funds will be put into my account and I'll decide how I want to disperse it. If you're lucky, you get ten percent. Take it or leave it."

"How about you put your money where your mouth is?" Stan said.

"I don't have to prove myself."

"You sure the hell do. What's to keep me from just killing you after they're all dead?"

"Access to the money. You're as dumb now as you were when we first met. Victor used you up and threw you away when he was done with you, and I'm going to do the same damn thing."

"You're going to push the button Appleton."

It's working.

"The hell I am."

"You're going to prove yourself."

"If you hand me that thing, I'll throw it out the window."

"No, you won't," Stan said. "Freeman's wired. All I need is his heart to stop. I don't care if I trigger it or put a bullet in the guy, but you're going to push the button, or I'll put a bullet through your head." Stan pulled his gun as if he was ready to use it. He stared at Tarek with disdain. His expression frightened Tarek, but he was eating up everything Tarek was putting down for him.

"If I push the button, it doesn't change any of what I said," Tarek said.

"You're making this harder than it has to be. How much money do you really need? I could take ten million and my life would be set."

"Then what's the problem?"

"Principle, we're splitting everything fifty-fifty. We both contribute to the kills and we split the money. Then we walk away. You do it any other way and we'll have nothing but complications. I would find and kill you eventually or I'd implicate you in this and we'd both be in jail." Stan's voice began to rise as he grew passionate. "I was supposed to be on that will. If I had been, you'd be dead. You may have had that money eventually, but whatever misery your life is in, whatever end you're looking for, you can have it in a week. Ten million is the same as ten billion when you're just trying to get out of here. I want out too, but you're not going to treat me like I'm useless. Not after the blood and sweat I've put into this from day one."

Tarek pretended to think about it, sizing Stan up. He applauded himself on the inside for his Oscar worthy performance. Stan bought the whole thing, but it wasn't over yet, and even if Tarek could dodge the bullet today, what would Stan do tomorrow? He hadn't thought that far ahead. He'd only thought far enough to prevent a bomb from killing everyone in that building.

"Alright," Tarek said, finding Stan's eyes. "Fifty-fifty."

He fell back onto the bed and planted himself there, but before he could get comfortable, Stan held his hand out with the remote trigger. He was looking for insurance, and Tarek had successfully made him believe it was his idea. Tarek reached out and delicately took the remote from his hand, afraid to drop it or of an unexpected shift in his hand. The simple act of pushing a button brought so much tragedy to his life, but it was better in his hands than Stan's. "If you do anything other than push that button, you'll get yourself killed," Stan said. "Don't forget that. If I have to kill you, I'll improvise."

"That won't be necessary," Tarek said. He grabbed a pillow and walked to the window. He propped his elbows on the pillow and watched the building. "Half an hour and you'll know what I'm capable of." Tarek's face was set in stone, but inside, his heart was thumping. He watched out the window as another beneficiary pulled into the parking lot, giving Richard the advantage.

Though he said he'd be there from the beginning, no one was sure Brian Van Dyke really would be. Toby especially was irritated to see him and cursed William's name again. Bernard swore up a storm upon seeing Brian and told him Victor would be disappointed, trying to play Brian's emotions.

Brian took a look around and counted the heads with the realization that they really were going to invalidate the will. He wished they wouldn't. It didn't seem right, and he always liked the thought of having those riches one day, assuming he happened to live the longest. It was also a weight off his shoulders though. He wouldn't have to worry about his life being cut short. He didn't know the likelihood of that happening, but he didn't want to be the guy that didn't show up, and when he realized he was the beneficiary who gave the group the majority, he smiled proudly, hoping someone would notice. Richard and Anthony seemed relieved, but there were no thank yous and among the conversations throughout the room, Brian couldn't find one he could wedge himself into and be a part of.

He stood against the wall near Trish and stared at her for a moment, trying to force a conversation. "I'm glad this will finally be over," he said, though it had less truth than his tone implied. She looked up, ready to say something, but noticed his face...his eyes. She shook her head at him.

"Really?" she asked, and he didn't know what it meant until she went on. "Have you looked at your eyes?"

He tried to cover them, but knew they were bloodshot. Within moments, he'd given himself away and Trish saw through him. He hated that he said anything to her and wished he'd stayed sober the night before, but it was too late. At the very best, they could end the will and he could walk away forever, hoping everyone would forget them.

Toby noticed his discomfort and wanted to add to it. Maybe he could convince Brian to dart from the room, but it wasn't likely. Between Trish's jab, Bernard's ranting and raving, and Toby digging into him, maybe they could make the situation intolerable. "I knew you'd be here," Toby said. "Van Dyke's the most likely to get killed. Fire a gun in four directions and three of those shots are likely to hit him."

No one laughed, but no one defended him. Brian looked around the room with the realization of what he'd seen in doses, but was now seeing the whole picture: No one liked him. But he stayed, and watched the clock, and hid from the group. He thought about getting a pastry, but he wasn't hungry. He realized he hadn't been hungry much lately and his pants were starting to get loose. Strange, because he wasn't on one of many diets he'd tried in the past with less success than whatever was making him lose weight now. He bought a water and returned and sat in a corner, waiting for the day to be over. If someone else arrived and they didn't need Brian anymore, maybe he'd use it as an excuse and leave.

By the time he made up his mind that that was exactly what he was going to do, Trish's phone rang, she answered, talked a moment, and suddenly began gathering her things. She hung up and stepped toward the group. "I'm really sorry, but I have to go."

Richard, Anthony, and Charlie were suddenly on their feet, and for the first time, Bernard fell silent. "My daughter…" she said, but stopped herself from volunteering any more information.

As Trish told the group she was sorry, Bernard leaned in to Toby. "You need to walk out of here right now."

"Why would I do that?" Toby asked.

"Because you don't want this to be over and if you walk out now, they lose the majority."

"Until Morrow and Appleton arrive."

"IF they arrive. If they don't, you would have passed up the chance to prevent this."

"I think you should keep insulting the group instead. Give that approach time to work."

"You know Toby, there was a time when you were at war against me and Victor, and even though you were stirring the pot, we knew you were exceptionally good at manipulation. Even when it was only you against us—you held your own just fine, so how the majority of the group is here right now is beyond me. How you haven't prevented anyone from being here…"

Toby looked around the room, soaking in the words. In one corner, Henry was desperately trying to reason with Maria, but she stubbornly refused to leave. Brian kept looking at his phone. He was receiving texts but ignoring them. Whatever William was saying wasn't enticing enough for Brian to up and leave. Toby swore his allegiance to Richard, if only to protect himself, and if he walked out now, what Richard knew could potentially turn them against him, but so what?

"I'm seeing it through," Toby told Bernard. "Trish is on the way out. Maybe one of the others will change their mind."

Toby and Bernard watched as Trish made her exit, bringing the count down by one. Toby's eyes fixated on the door, wondering when Royce or Tarek would appear.

"Not good enough," Bernard said, and was suddenly on his feet in the middle of the room. They tried to ignore him, but his tone sounded reasonable, and for once, he had something to say that everyone wanted to hear. "Has anyone asked Toby why he's here?" he asked, giving Toby a smug smile to let him know he was about to be a target.

Silence.

"At one time, when Mr. Libby made his first attempt to invalidate this will, Toby O'Tool compromised his attorney into dropping the case."

Richard looked down and shook his head.

Charlie stood. "He spends time with Adlar Wilcox," he said, walking toward Toby. "He exposed secrets between Abby and I that damaged our marriage."

Maria looked up and watched Toby quietly. Brian frowned and thought to himself of all the times Toby came to him and seemingly tried to convince him that the money should be his. "Yeah, he messed with me too," he said quietly. "Almost got me fired from my job, like that's what he wanted."

Bernard smiled and took over the room again. "Toby shouldn't be here, but he is, and it's very likely to sabotage your efforts. With what we do know about him, consider everything we don't."

Henry hid his face, afraid they'd see through his existence.

Anthony's eyes narrowed. Could Toby have set up the lottery after-all?

Aileen leaned forward too. She'd never liked Toby, and knew his nature, but how many of the incidents could be tied to him?

"I just want to be clear," Bernard said, "that if this lives to see another day, you better keep your eyes on this guy."

Toby opened his mouth to say something, but no words came out. Before he could speak, another interruption saved him.

"I'm leaving."

Everyone turned and to their surprise, Richard walked to the door. No one knew what to say, or what it meant, but the man who'd crusaded against the will from the beginning was tired of being there.

"Wait," Anthony said, and caught up to him at the door. "I don't understand."

"You take this," Richard said. "I have a friend who may need me right now."

"Who? What are you talking about?"

Richard searched the room and studied the faces. Bernard Bell and Toby O'Tool, Brian Van Dyke, Maria Haskins, Aileen Thick, Charlie Palmer—all bored, hostile, unappreciative, or indifferent. No one truly cared to see the end. Richard had been warned about that, but tried anyway. He only knew of one person who was crying for help.

"Richard," Anthony said. "If you leave, we're one behind. Victor wins."

"Victor didn't win," Richard said. "He made a poor decision, but this isn't what he wanted."

Anthony didn't know what to say, and he wanted to reason with him, but Richard's mind was made up. Everything he did until this moment only wove a new perspective for him. It wasn't worth ending—not on his watch.

"I hope you see this to the end," Richard said. "But this isn't my battle…"

"…Have you heard about this Morrow guy?" Bernard asked, sliding a newspaper toward Victor with a feature on Royce. "Guy's a bank manager now but said two years ago he was on the street with nowhere to live. A stranger gave him fifty bucks one day and told him to use it to increase his worth instead of on booze, and now he's an up-and-comer. Amazing…"

Victor frowned thoughtfully at the familiarity of the story, but before he could piece it together, a knock at the door brought Bernard and Victor back to attention. Jones popped his head in with a smile. "We got him," he said.

"Got who?"

Jones's smile gave Victor the answer. Instead of speaking, he stared into space, unable to comprehend what to do next. The hunt for Nicolas spanned more than three decades and they hadn't gotten so much as a lead.

"How?" Victor asked.

"We had some feelers out there. We were contacted by a guy who said Nicolas flies a charter plane in and out of the country from time to time to check on some dealings he still has here in the states."

"Who contacted you?"

"A guy who knows one of our guys. Doesn't matter."

"Where is he? You have him?" Victor had a thousand questions and didn't know where to begin. He also didn't know what he would do when the time came that he'd confront Nicolas. He'd been convinced for a long time that the day would never come.

"We have him in his hangar. It's leased under another name but we linked it to him. When he landed, we grabbed him and cuffed him in his plane."

"He's there now?"

Jones nodded. Victor turned to Bernard and back to Jones. He didn't know what to do.

"I can handle things here," Bernard said.

Victor walked to his office and spent half an hour alone in the dark, reliving the night his father died for the first time in a while. All he'd ever wanted to do was come face to face with Nicolas and the time had come. He was simply too stunned to react, but as he thought about laying in the car as a child as the shadow of the man who killed his father passed, his adrenaline began building and by the time he walked out, he was determined to see the man, look into his eyes, and watch his life drain away.

Jones drove Victor to the hangar, which was an hour north of LA. He sat in silence the entire drive, focused only on the task at hand. When they pulled into the parking lot, Victor sat in the car another ten minutes, just staring at the building as Jones waited silently.

Finally, Victor spoke. "In the plane?"

"Yeah. You want company?"

"No," Victor said. "Thank you Jones."

He exited the car and began walking to the hangar; every step felt heavy and slow. The building was empty. The setup was perfect. Victor could stay as long as he needed and walk away whenever he wanted undetected. Nicolas' discretion worked against him in the end. He'd hidden for so long that no one knew who he was or where to find him. They'd find a body and know nothing else.

He pulled a chain that forced the garage open and inside, in front of his eyes, an airplane centered in the garage with the door open. Victor circled it once and stepped inside. He slowly passed the cockpit and looked into the aisle. There, a man he hadn't seen since he was a child was bound and his hands cuffed to opposite sides of the plane, on display for Victor, laid out for slaughter. The man had aged many years, but there was no mistaking the eyes.

"Nicolas..." he said, and pulled the gag from his mouth.

Nicolas' eyes moved up and down, studying Victor. "Who are you?" he managed to ask.

"Franklin Stone's son."

Nicolas looked him over again, remembering who he was and realizing why he was there all at once. "The boy in the car."

Victor said nothing. He stared at the man for a long time, trying to make up his mind. Was it really going to be this easy? Over in a moment and the scales tipped back to how they should be? "You were his friend," Victor said.

"It was never personal Victor. I heard what you did for yourself. You have no business coming at me like this. You made out well. I'm just an old man. There's no reason to do this. I'll apologize, I'll give you whatever you what, I'll disappear forever. I'll do what it takes to put this behind us."

Victor never heard the words. He wanted to kill him more than ever. The man had no remorse. He'd lived off the compensation given to him by his father's blood for so many years, and he expected to walk away. Victor walked to the cockpit. He found a six pack of beer. Nicolas spent his years flying, drunk. He hoped that meant he was tormented by his actions, but guessed he just enjoyed himself. He picked up an empty and smashed it against the seat. He slowly approached Nicolas, taking his time so the man would have a long moment to realize what was happening.

"I told my father to kill you that night," Victor said. "I didn't care about the money and neither did he, but I wanted him to kill you in self-defense. I knew if he didn't, you would murder him. He was packing our things, running from you and starting over."

"Smart man."

"He wouldn't hurt you. That's why we're here. He was above that."

"And you're going to honor him by killing me?"

"Absolutely," Victor said. "Because you spent your life in paradise because of what you did. Every moment after that, you didn't deserve."

"Victor, I promise you it hasn't been paradise."

Victor raised the shard of glass to his neck. "Whatever it was, you didn't..."

"Stop!" a voice shouted from the door of the plane. Victor turned. Stanley stood with a gun aimed at Victor's forehead. He hadn't seen or heard from Stanley in over two years. For a while, the giant of a man harassed him for his job back, but finally disappeared. And now here he was, but why? He was the informant...the man who found Nicolas and delivered him. But why?

"Stanley..."

Stan smiled, satisfied at the scenario. "Step aside."

Victor slowly obeyed.

"Drop the glass."

Victor looked at his hand, which had a trickle of blood oozing down his wrist. He'd held the glass so tight, but hadn't noticed. He let it fall from his hand. "What are you doing Stan? How did you find him?"

"I'm a good detective. I was anyway. Now, I'm working on corpses—testing crashes and military helmet impact tests—making about a fifth of what I made with you. Lost the house, lost the wife, lost the kids. You didn't return my calls, so with nothing left to do, I set out to finish what you had me start, only this time, no loyalty."

"I'll pay you for your time, but..."

"That's not going to work." He uncuffed Nicolas, who massaged his wrists for a moment before walking toward the cockpit, giving Victor a smug smile on his way there.

"You found him to rub in my face?"

"Why not?" Stan said. "What's the difference? I changed my life for you. You gave me everything and then took it away."

"I explained myself."

"You've got a whole slew of people with no qualifications who work for you because you like them. Me, you dropped, but not before lecturing *me on expectations of loyalty. Get off the plane."*

"You can't let him walk away," Victor said. "You know what he did."

"You can handle this however you want," Stan said with a smile. "I'll be back in a couple weeks. Kill me, have me beaten, ruin me further, I don't care. I just gave you everything you ever wanted and took it away. How does it feel?" Stan stepped close to Victor and their eyes fixated on each other for a long moment. Victor had nothing to say, but seethed inside. "Now, get off the plane."

Stan pulled Victor down the aisle and shoved him down the steps. Victor hit the ground below and looked up in time to see the door close. The engine picked up and the propellers turned as the plane began to roll out of the hangar, onto the tarmac. Victor stood and watched as Nicolas and Stan disappeared down the runway and into the air. That evening, he added Stanley Kline to his will...

"...Twenty minutes," Bernard said to the group. "In twenty minutes, you will all pass up the opportunity of your lifetime." He looked around the room as the beneficiaries tried to ignore him. He took a step toward each, trying to make his case. "This was his final wish. You're all on it for a reason. He gave you an opportunity and you're throwing it back in his face."

"Abby already lost her life over this," Charlie said, numbly.

"Victor didn't do anything to her. Someone broke into her home. If just one of you has the balls to walk out of here now, it won't be over. You'll still have a chance, and you won't be stomping on the memory of a man who was only trying to improve you."

Bell turned to Anthony as he chuckled at the notion. One by one, he turned to each, hoping to find a glint of understanding. Maria, Charlie, Brian, Aileen, Toby... "Even that asshole Libby had the sensibility to walk out."

Suddenly, Toby was on his feet, and for the first time in a long time, won the respect of the room. "Does Stone Enterprises hear pitches for new investment ideas?" he asked.

"What are you talking about?"

"If I came to you with a pitch for a product, would you invest if you liked it?"

"We don't have time for this."

"Then maybe we should talk about something else. How about a building that you own on Vine? Maybe we should talk about pharmaceuticals instead."

Bernard smiled at Toby, challenging him. "You and I had an understanding to..."

"There's a lot of things I thought we had an understanding about," Toby said. "For example, yes, I did block some of Richard's efforts..."

Everyone leaned in, silently.

"...I made no secret of the fact that I would like to have that money. I'm also no killer, and the next time you see Richard, you can ask him about how our relationship evolved. He knew what I did and would have exposed me if I didn't support him, so here I am. A few of you, I talked into being here, so to say I'm out to have you all killed is contradictory to my very presence. But I'll tell you this much, before I even knew that Victor had a will, Bernard Bell was at my doorstep, giving me the dirt on all of you. He knew what was going to happen and I guess he wanted me to use my talents against you. I didn't even know about Richard's efforts until he warned me and told me to stop him, but I guess that's what Bell does. He's the man behind the curtain who tries to act like his efforts are valiant. He tells you he's here to honor Victor's last wishes, but if you spend enough time with him, you'll know he hated Victor, so what's HIS real reason for being here? Anyone? Anyone have a guess? I'll tell you what it is…he's rewarded for moving things along, but most importantly, when Jason Stone finally bites the dust, who will run Stone Enterprises? What's the best way for Jason to exit the picture? For the wills intended effect to take place. Now, you can all call me an asshole because I want that money. You can even call me an asshole because I would pop a bottle of champagne open for each and every one of your death certificates to be submitted, but you won't find a gun in my hand and I won't give anyone a dollar to murder any of you, and so what does that make me exactly? A guy who hopes to outlive you. That doesn't mean I want your lives cut short. I just hope to live the longest. So how about we talk about my idea Bell? I call it The Marriage Patch. It works in a similar fashion as the Nicotine Patch, but instead, it deters people from getting married. How many times have you been married Bernard?"

Bernie watched him with hatred in his eyes.

"I'd lose count too if I were you, but no need to answer. We all know you're in the five or more club, so you'd be perfect for this. My target demographic will be middle-aged men with a lot of money and no personality. Every time they hook up with a broad and are naive enough to believe she likes them for something other than their wallet, he just pops on his trusty marriage patch and it sends signals into his body that remind him that the only reason anyone would show any interest in a man with no sense of humor, intellect, talent, good looks, or ability to succeed without riding the coat-tails of others, could only be because of the cash flow he was lucky to stumble upon at the expense of others, and when she wants to hook up in Vegas or have a romantic court-room wedding, he's reminded it will last just long enough for her to take his money and walk away because no self-respecting woman would actually want to spend more than a few hours listening to this man try desperately to be included at the cool kid table. The Marriage Patch—what do you think Bernard? I think I could get this thing rolling with four hundred K."

Everyone watched Bell. Some tried to hide smiles as he chewed on what Toby said. Instead of responding, he fell silent for the next twenty minutes and waited for the judge. He felt defeated, and so did Toby, but at the end of the day, Toby allowed himself to feel okay with what was happening. He may never be a billionaire, but life had always been fun, and always would be. He'd find another way to keep himself wealthy, and wouldn't have to resort to acts beyond what he'd ever wanted to do. Richard was a good man, and some of the people in the room were alright too. Bell was a monster, and when the line was drawn in the sand, Toby refused to be standing with Bell. It was the lesser of two evils.

Fifteen minutes later, a car pulled up outside and the judge exited. Everyone held their breath.

Tarek hoped Stan wouldn't realize it was the judge, but his eyes went wide and his smile widened. He patted Tarek on the back and told him to get ready. He'd done such a good job of turning Stan to his side that Stan considered them buddies. The buildup had been perfect, but the execution would need to be flawless. The trigger would need to be beyond Stan's reach, and Tarek had one chance to make that happen.

He already had the pillow, which would serve a cushion. He didn't know how delicate the button was, but all his efforts would be useless if the button accidentally activated the bomb. He rested his elbows on the pillow under the guise of discomfort. He'd unzipped the pillow where all the cotton stuffing was housed. Everything was ready, and seemed so simple, down to the fact that Stan had no idea where Tarek's loyalties lay, but they were down to the wire. When the judge entered The Coop, Stan was as good as ready. Tarek scanned the area and eyeballed the window—his last obstacle.

Stan shrugged, as if to say he supposed now was the time. "It's about as good as it's gonna get in there."

"There's still five minutes until two," Tarek said. "Might be a few that show up right at the time."

Stan nodded without realizing the stall tactic. Tarek was only trying to get the most bang for his buck. He could appreciate that. "Fifty-fifty?" Stan asked, confirming their agreement.

"We split all responsibilities, then yes," Tarek said. Then he unwittingly said the wrong thing. "If you're loyal to me, I'll be loyal to you." And although it was a good line, and although there was nothing suspect in the words, it made Stan think about Victor, and suddenly he was willing to take the brunt of the work, even if it meant his cut went down.

"I'll push the button," Stan said. "You don't have to worry about it."

Tarek paused. Did he say something wrong? He turned to Stan, who held his hand out.

Now or never.

A moment of hesitation would give Tarek away. It had to be done in that moment.

"What's going on?" Tarek asked. "You trying to cut me out of what I have coming to me?"

"No," Stan said. "I want to be in control."

Before Stan could say another word, Tarek shoved the trigger into the pillow and in one swift motion, threw his shoulder into the window. It didn't shatter as he'd expected, but it did break the frame and the window fell to the ground below, where it did shatter. Stan's eyes went wide as Tarek tossed the pillow to the roof. A lot of things happened in the next few moments. Stan realized he'd been played and Tarek's heart sank as the pillow slid down the roof with the rain and fell to the ground below. It landed on the lawn, but no explosion followed. They were safe until the moment Stan got his hands on the trigger again. Until then, Tarek wouldn't make it easy.

"That was all bullshit?" Stan asked, unable to comprehend.

Tarek smiled and feigned addressing an audience. "I'd like to thank the academy," he said.

The gun was shoved into his side. "Go," Stan commanded, giving him a shove. "If you say anything to give us away, you're dead."

They walked into the hall to go after the trigger.

5

The landscape at Black Chasm was filled with rocks jutting outward to the ocean below. The waves sloshed as the rain hit the water. Richard walked along the edge, searching for Josh on the rocks below, but didn't believe he'd find him. Josh would have to be crazy to be standing down there, but supposedly it was where he went when he needed to clear his head. When he did see Josh on an outcropping of rocks which was practically an island, it didn't seem he was thoughtful at all. It seemed he was inviting death. Richard watched for a long moment, hoping Josh would turn and see him, but they were too far away and the rain drowned out all sound. He took a breath and searched the rocks for a path down. There was no path, only footholds and enough surface area that Josh must have been able to navigate his way down. For a spry kid like Josh, it may have been easy. For Richard, it was more of a challenge, but he found his way slowly, stopping to yell for Josh every time he'd made a significant gain, but the boy only stared at the waves as they crashed at his feet.

Richard found his way to an opening in the cliffs which looked as if it had once been a path, but the rock had smoothed and shifted into a steep slide down to the ocean. He carefully made his way down, wincing as the drops of rain hit his face. He slid the rest of the way and plunged into the water below, but was able to stand and make his way across the sharp edges of the rock floor under the waves. He hugged the rocks at his back and made his way toward where the rocks jutted upward and Josh stood. He called out. This time Josh turned, his face frozen on Richard. Richard approached, stepping high to move through the waves.

"Leave me alone!" Josh yelled.

Richard climbed up the island and stood at his side. "I heard you didn't make the flight. I came to check on you."

"Who told you I was here?"

"Reverend Benjamin talked to your parents."

"Today's your thing. What happened?"

"I don't know. It should be starting about now."

"So you're coming here to blame me for that?"

"I'm not blaming you for anything," Richard said. "It's not meant to be."

Josh made a point to laugh. "That's all you've obsessed about."

"Yeah, you're mad," Richard said. "I don't get it. I'm a stranger to you. What did you want me to do?"

"Help me."

"I pointed you in a direction. I get it. It's not what you wanted. I pushed you and I probably did it to get you off my back, but today I realized I've been making a decision for thirteen people and they can make it for themselves. I haven't been strong enough glue to hold it together, and maybe it wasn't supposed to be."

"You did it because you said you had to—cause Victor is forcing them to kill each other."

"No, he's not. We have that choice. We participate or we don't. I'm won't hurt anyone."

"And if they hurt you?"

"Then that's what happens. We all stand exactly where we stand because of the series of choices that were made before us. Some of us land on a net, some in a river of gold, and some of us, on rock, surrounded by waves. What are you doing here anyway? The storm is supposed to pick up and I don't see a way up."

"Well, that's the point. There's not."

"You're going to let me help you up, but after that, you're on your own. You can come to me, talk to me, vent, whatever you need to do, but you're not going to stay in this spot. This isn't where you end up."

"Why you acting like it matters all the sudden?"

"I'm pushy to a fault, but I'm going to tell you why and pay attention because you're a miniature version of me: I think too big. I'm always looking for a purpose so that when I exit this world, I can feel like I gave my life to something. But I'm too old for that burden and you're too young. Those other guys can kill each other, possibly kill me, but where I'm supposed to be is right here, right now, because I think that one life can matter more than all that. But purpose is relative. You're comparing yourself to people who have done great things, but who's to say because they did A and you do B, you don't matter? That's not how you should be thinking. I've taken on more useless crusades than I want to count and usually it blows up in my face and I ask myself what the point was, but here it is: If you're a decent person, all the little things you do throughout the course of your life add up and you may not see the result of them, but that doesn't mean you haven't made a monumental impact on the world. Of course, you can do the opposite. You can lie and steal and cheat through life, hurt people, ruin them, poison them with bad temperament, and that will add up too. A lot of people do that, and we need people on our side to even the score.

But one thing I know is that you can't choose between being good or not if you're gone before your time. You may not have the slightest idea, just as I don't know if I ever really bettered the world by spending time on my brother who over-dosed, Micky Miller, Victor Stone, you... Maybe, maybe not. I certainly didn't see the positives if there were any, but if you're truly decent, you're not keeping score. You're just blindly doing the best you can and when you exit the world, I hope you have a moment to reflect with a smile because you just know..."

Richard couldn't tell if it was rain hitting his face or tears in Josh's eyes, but something broke through. Something changed in him in that moment. Maybe it was something Richard said, or maybe it was the rock bottom a person feels when they invite death and reach a low that they can only bounce back from. Looking out into the waves, even Richard felt something unlike anything he'd ever felt. This was what the end would look like. "We have to go," Richard said.

"There's no way up."

"I'll boost you. When you get past that last drop, hoist me up."

Josh looked up with doubt, but the waves were crashing at his feet and they didn't have many options. They moved toward the cliffs, the water waist-deep now and waves completely covering them, the force throwing them against the wall. Richard cupped his hands together and Josh stepped on them, reaching for an outcropping to pull himself up.

Richard thought about the group at The Coop. He wondered if anyone else showed up and if it really was over. It didn't matter much. As Josh hoisted himself past that final drop to the ground and to safety, Richard felt a sense of relief wash over him. This was exactly where he was supposed to be.

The car finally pulled to the side of the road and took an exit through the trees. Manny drove silently as Royce watched the trees go by. He swallowed hard as it grew darker and the vegetation thicker. Soon, there was nowhere left to drive and the car came to a stop.

"Get out," Manny said. His tone no longer concealed the anger. This was it. Royce knew what was happening and he didn't have the energy for a plan. He wouldn't overpower Manny and there was nowhere to run. All that was left was to accept the situation. Except, he couldn't just leave his wife to never know what happened.

"I will give you anything if you allow me to call Sandra."

"Sorry Morrow. That's not an option."

"I don't understand this. This shouldn't fall on me. I'm not responsible."

Manny impatiently exited the car and walked around. He opened the passenger side and pulled Royce from the seat and shoved him to the ground. "Start walking," he said. Royce did as he was told and as they made their march through the trees, Manny started talking again. "Early on, I have this husband who wants to off his wife. So I go to the wife and in those days, I thought it was appropriate to allow them a chance to reflect on their life, so I'd tell them face to face what was happening. I tell the wife and she starts crying and telling me what an abusive asshole her husband was and begs me to show mercy and kill him instead. And guess what; I did. Killed the guy, but not before he starts making a lot of noise and shit. So his death is a clear cut murder scene and it falls on the wife. She gets arrested and two days later, she's found hanging from her cell. You know the moral of the story? You live by a rules and you never break them."

"Will you make sure my body is found?"

"No can do. You're not getting any favors. I don't have an ounce of mercy for you." They stopped. Both were concealed by the trees. They were about as in the middle of nowhere as they could be. "There's only one thing that matters now, and it's the debt. Someone owes it. Someone will pay it. That falls on you."

"Manny…" Royce began, but before he could go further, Manny lashed out with his gun, striking Royce on the side of the head. It cut open immediately and Royce was blinded by a flash of light. Manny started circling him, his emotions running wild. He punched Royce in the gut and he toppled over as blow after blow, hands, feet, an elbow to the back, flattened Royce to the ground. His fingers found the grass above his head and he tried to squeeze it, if only for something to hang on to. "You son of a bitch," Manny said, his voice shaking. "Billy didn't have it coming!"

"I didn't…"

Another kick to the ribs and his words turned into a coughing fit. Royce kept his head to the ground, blood and spit hanging from his lip and Manny held his gun over his head. He pulled the hammer back and placed it against the back of Royce's head. Royce closed his eyes, ready to accept the debt.

Stan froze as the elevator door opened and a group of people stepped in. Tarek gave them a winning smile as they stared at him in disbelief. "That's right," Tarek said. "Tarek Appleton. I'm headed outside for autographs. Bring the family."

Stan reached and hit a button. The door opened and they exited on the second floor. "Shut the fuck up," he said, pushing Tarek toward the stairs. "You do that again…"

Tarek turned to a maid who was passing in the hallway. "Tarek Appleton, Late Night with Tarek."

He was shoved through the door and almost toppled down the stairs as they worked their way to the bottom floor through the stairwell. Tarek was gambling on Stan needing him too much, but his fear was they'd reach the pillow and Stan would hit the button. He hoped someone found it and took it. A pillow on the ground outside would be out of place, but everything was happening quickly. He needed to stall. He needed a crowd. Stan was moving too quickly. He would reach it and do something drastic before Tarek could draw attention. He tried coming to a halt, but Stan's beefy hands were too strong. He grabbed Tarek's neck and gave have another shove which sent him toppling the rest of the way down the stairs.

Anthony watched the clock as the second hand passed the top. It was two o'clock. The judge leaned forward and addressed the group. "Anyone not listed, please step outside."

Henry walked out, but Brian, Maria, Toby, Anthony, Charlie, and Aileen sat in place. Bernard watched quietly, holding the folder containing the will in his lap. By his count, there were only six. He didn't know what judge Proctor would do without Richard, but he was prepared to fight in his place.

Richard watched Josh clear another outcropping and look down. It was too far for him to reach Richard, but he moved on anyway, intent on finding help the moment he reached the top. A wave hit Richard and he was almost pulled out, but he grabbed at the wall to secure himself. The island of rocks was mostly covered. If they hadn't moved to the cliff, the water would have washed them off by now. He searched the area, but there was no handholds or outcropping as far as he could see. He turned his attention to the ocean and looked into the distance. The sun hid behind the clouds and lightning flashed in the sky. He realized how beautiful it all was and smiled to himself. He took out his phone and dialed a number.

Anthony asked the judge for a moment as he walked to the corner of the room and answered. He listened as Richard spoke.

Royce repeated Sandra's name as Manny started to squeeze the trigger.

Stan pushed through the door and stood outside, holding Tarek's neck between two fingers. The pillow sat ten feet away. Stan shoved Tarek to the side and hurried toward it and scooped it up, quickly shoving his hand into the stuffing. He fished around for the remote, which fell further into the pillow. Tarek called for help, but Stan was consumed with the task at hand. He would kill Tarek in a moment, but not until the button was pushed. Then, he'd run for his life and come back when it was safe, find the next beneficiary, and use them instead.

His hand found the trigger and he pulled it from the pillow just as a crowd of people began to gather.

Josh reached safety and looked down…

"…I didn't think I'd ever see you again," Victor said, smiling at Richard. "The last time I saw you, you said you'd speak with Stanley Kline…that you'd convince him to come to me with an apology." Victor shrugged as if to point out the obvious: Stan wasn't there. "What do you want Richard?"

"I went to meet him and do you know what I found? The man is in rehab. He lives out of his car. He works two jobs and still has no money. Victor, why would you expect an apology from a man who has nothing? He's already ruined and you eat just fine."

"You don't know what he took from me," Victor said.

"Maybe not, but I know what you took from him."

"*Why don't you accept that you don't understand the situation Richard? Walk away and forget me. You're a good man, but you and I don't mesh well.*"

"*I do know the situation. Someone hurt you and you hurt him back and you're going to do that dance until the end of your life. Vengeance is poison Victor. No one knows where the hatred begins because it traces back before you can remember, but the only way to stop it is to choose to stop—to forgive.*"

"*You're preaching.*"

"*You don't need religion to understand pain. Forget what I do and who I am and ask yourself if this is really the legacy you want to leave behind. Your will only spreads this poison and you're a man who is capable of doing so many great things. I've seen it in you Mr. Stone. I've seen you try to be a good man and struggle with demons that have darkened your soul and you've given up the fight. You've let them take over, but you're still a good man deep down somewhere and I have faith that you can do the right thing.*"

"*You question why my will is written the way it is. My father died the same way. He was a decent man. That's what I remember…just…decent. I never saw the man angry in my life. He told me he was a beneficiary on a will and it would all go to the last survivor. In the beginning, he told me not to worry, that he believed in people. He thought they'd all just wait it out. He prayed every night and he would sit me down and force me to pray alongside him and he always prayed for those who were written into the will with him—that their hearts be pure.*" Victor laughed, as if mocking the concept. "*But they turned on each other and after a while, only my father and his best friend remained. So tell me why my father deserved to die at his hand and why the man responsible has been free and wealthy since that day. The man had money, fame, women, popularity, he went on to have a family…my father's death was a second page headline and the police spent a week on it. You talk about faith as if we all just have to believe everything works out in the end, but those of us who aren't naive have a good understanding of the balance in this world. Good doesn't prevail. I don't believe there's a plan and it doesn't bring peace believing there's a greater good. It does the opposite. It makes me angry. It makes me hate God.*"

"*I don't blame you for what you feel. I like to believe that everyone, even your father in death, served a purpose. Maybe you don't know it. Maybe you're the man you are because of that defining moment in your life and because of it, you can reach more people, but it's up to you what you do with your power. You can be the man who killed your father, or you can be like him, but you don't have the right to be angry at the killer if you're going to spread that hatred on to the next group of people. If you want to honor him, redraft your will. You have to ask yourself if God, in some mind-bending way, was answering your father's prayers by failing to answer his prayers."*

"He was wrong!" Victor shouted. His voice carried in the room, but he didn't care who was listening. "That's what you don't seem to understand. He should have fought to be the last. He should have fought because he had me. Even if it meant doing what he had to do so that a horrible man's life would end and his could live on."

"He had integrity. The best kind. He wouldn't take a life because he stood against it, even if he had to give his own. He died for his convictions."

"He chose to die like a coward."

"You can't justify what you're doing."

"I allowed you the chance to make it right and you didn't!"

"All you have to do is forgive him."

"He's not asking."

"He doesn't have to. You need to have faith."

"There's no such thing. You don't even believe it. If you did, Stanley would have…"

"Then put me on it instead," Richard said, abruptly.

Victor fell silent, unable to respond. He found Richard's eyes. They were serious. The last thing Victor wanted to do was corrupt a good man. "That doesn't solve anything," Victor said. "I understand your view, but I…"

"Take his name off and replace it with my own."

"I'd never do that to you."

"You're not doing anything to me. Faith is believing in the unknown. I know I'll be okay because I believe that before your life comes to an end, you'll dispose of your will. I believe you have it in you."

"And what happens if I don't?"

"It won't change anything. I won't die by your hands. I know that. And it won't matter if I do. What will matter is the man I am when I die. I have a vision of who I want that man to be. Your will is what is left of you Victor. It's what you leave behind in this world. You're worth more money than most of us have ever seen in our lives. What you leave and the manner in which you leave it, is going to be what defines you. You can hate the man who killed your father, you can hate Stanley Kline, and anyone else you've written into that garbage, but when you die, let it die with you. If you pass it on, that will be who you are. If you want proof, take Stan out and put me in, and come see me when you rip it up…"

"…Something happened to Richard," Anthony said, addressing the group. "I apologize, but I have to go."

Bernard smiled and Toby's eyes lit up, but everyone else was on their feet, trying to stop him. They tried to object, but Anthony hurried from the room and to the front door. He stepped out in the rain.

Manny's cell rang and he released the trigger long enough to look. It was a local number, but he didn't recognize it. He answered. Royce listened to one side of the conversation in disbelief. "Yeah, I remember you…that depends…are you willing to repay the debt left by the death of my colleague?…You have impeccable timing Wilcox. Someone owes you a thank you."

The call ended. Royce didn't look up. He waited for Manny to say something, but no words were spoken. He slowly looked up when he heard a branch crack in the distance. Manny walked casually back to the car without a word.

Royce squeezed his eyes closed and let tears fall.

Stan looked up, trigger in hand, a moment away from blowing the building to pieces. He stopped abruptly in disbelief as Anthony hurried from The Coop and moved a safe distance from the building. If one thing could stop him in the moment, that was it. What was Anthony doing outside? He was supposed to be where the population was, but if he pressed the button now, he'd effectively kill only one. He paused for a long moment, hoping he'd go back, but Anthony hurried to his car instead. Stan fumed in disbelief as he wondered what the hell was happening. With Freeman gone and the bomb safely away from the group, he turned back to Tarek and pulled his gun, but Tarek had rounded up a crowd of people, and even the police were approaching.

Stan was left alone with a gun and a useless bomb. The whole plan failed. He turned to run, but he had nowhere to go. He looked toward The Coop where business had likely already started. Everything he'd planned ended in failure. Everyone was safe and in a short amount of time, he would be captured and thrown in jail. He closed his eyes and made an inventory of his options, but came up with nothing. He needed sleep. He needed time to reassess his options and he wouldn't be able to focus on the run. He had to admit defeat, take a step back, and come back when he could make another go of it.

He opened his eyes and walked back toward Tarek. Tarek backed away slowly, but saw Stan posed no threat. Instead, he extended his arm with the trigger and handed it over. He leaned in and spoke so only Tarek could hear. "Deactivating this is as simple as taking the battery out," he said. "It's just a garage remote. You can tell Freeman that to deactivate the actual bomb, he'll need it surgically exposed and a code entered. There's no other way."

"What's the code?"

"Here's the thing Appleton: I was supposed to be on that will, but someone did you a huge favor by excluding me. Now, unfortunately, I need one of you pieces of shit, but you need something from me. I'll keep it that way for now."

"If he has a heart attack or…"

"I wouldn't recommend an open casket funeral," Stan said. He turned and started walking toward the police. They became quickly aware of his presence and asked him to stop. Instead, Stan pulled his gun from his jacket and began to raise it. Two shots later, he was on the ground looking up into the sky as the rain fell down on him.

6

The judge pulled his copy of the will and Bernard sat alongside him, talking into his ear. No one could hear what Bernard was saying, but his desperation was clear and the judge considered what he was saying.

"Here's what we're going to do," Proctor finally said. "Mr. Richard Libby hasn't bothered to be here at the designated time, and we clearly don't have the majority, but this document does leave a bad taste in my mouth, and for that, I'm going to make this real simple. If you do not want to be included, speak now and I will see to it that your name is removed."

Everyone silently exchanged glances as they let the proposal marinate. It all came down to a simple yes or no, and suddenly, a few perceptions in the room changed—mainly Toby, who realized if everyone simply released their name, his job would become much easier.

"I'll go around the room and ask everyone once." He pointed at Aileen. "Your name and what do you want?"

"Aileen Thick," she said, and then bit her lip. She turned to Toby and saw him leaning in, anxious to hear what she'd say. "I think we should all do what Toby does," she said, and everyone in the room seemed to agree.

"Wait a second," he said. "You clearly don't want to be on that thing."

"You said you didn't either," Charlie said, challenging him.

"He's not asking me what I want. He's asking everyone what they want. Just answer his question."

The judge turned to Toby. "Which one are you?"

"Toby O'Tool."

"Do you want to be a beneficiary on Victor Stone's will?"

"I need to consider."

"I'm not saying a word until Toby answers," Aileen said.

Everyone else followed suit and as they went around the room, Toby desperately tried to talk each into doing the right thing and taking their names off, but no one did, forever sealing their fate and getting the best of Toby in the process. After the judge was gone, Bernard left immediately without so much as a goodbye. Toby lingered long enough to tell them all they made a mistake before making his exit. Though there had been satisfaction in the whole display, most of them wondered if there was truth in that statement.

7

Helicopters circled the cliffs and the coast guard slowly edged its way along the waters, but the search was in vain. The ocean calmed and the rocks below emerged, but there was no sign of life. Divers and police swarmed the area, but the search was exhausted and came to an end three days later. Richard Libby was declared deceased—washed out to sea.

8

The funeral was held two weeks later. More than twelve hundred people attended. The Reverend Richard's death came as a surprise to everyone and whole services were dedicated to people relaying their stories about how Richard helped them personally. Josh and his parents attended, as did Richard's family, who came from all over the states.

Anthony arrived and sat in the back of the church, looking around the room for familiar faces. One by one, he spotted the beneficiaries, all except Dent and Wilcox. After the funeral, he walked with the crowd to the cemetery, where a plot was put together, in memory of a man whose body would never be found. The plot would never hold a body.

Anthony wasn't sure he could put together the whole group, but set out to do just that. He tracked down Trish, who stood with Shiloh. He arranged a bonfire at the cliffs of Black Chasm afterward for the group to get together in honor of Richard and to hear what Richard told him before his phone cut out. Trish spread the word and Anthony drove to the cliffs to ready the fire for the night.

As the sun set and the waves began crashing below, Anthony parked his car and opened the trunk, where beverages were displayed for anyone who wanted to stay. He unloaded lawn chairs, blankets, firewood, and newspapers to keep the fire going. He sat and waited, hoping for some kind of attendance.

He watched in the distance as a car pulled up and Jason Stone and Todd Mason stepped out. They shook hands and made conversation until Royce arrived, the bruises on his face still healing. He'd been telling people he was mugged since he came back from his close encounter with Manny. No one asked questions, and no one believed him.

Trish arrived with Shiloh in tow. Shiloh kept herself busy with her phone and IPad while Trish sat and had a beer. Tarek joined the party, followed by Brian, Aileen, Charlie, and Maria, who had Henry at her side. Finally, though he didn't speak to the group, Toby showed up with a bottle of jack. He sat on the ground and stared at the ocean.

When they were all together and the sun was setting beyond the ocean, Anthony threw more paper on the fire and addressed the group.

"Richard Libby was vocal about his disapproval of Victor's will from the beginning," he said. He held up a file, stuffed with papers. "This is everything he was working on to invalidate the will, from research to contacts, anything relating. We all know Richard walked out without seeing it through. If he hadn't, we'd very likely be free of the will, but we still can be. We have everything he was doing right here, and I believe if we appeal to the judge, we can have another go at this, but before we decide, I want to share with you my last conversation with Richard. He was in this very place, standing in the water because he decided there was someone else who needed him more than we did. I don't know exactly what happened, but one of the last things he did was call me and he told me two things. The first will come of no surprise to you, but it's worth keeping in mind: He told me not to trust Bernard Bell."

Nods of agreement circulated the group and even some jokes at Bell's expense.

"The second was that he no longer believed the will should be invalidated."

Everyone was surprised to hear this, and would have called bullshit if anyone else had been saying it.

"He had a feeling, he said, that we were exactly where we were supposed to be, that there are deeper things at work and we need to come together. Without the will, we no longer have the bond, and that concerned him. He didn't say what he was talking about, and my beliefs are very different than Richard's were, but I feel the same thing. I feel that there is something at work here, and if we're wrong, I'm still willing to honor Richard's last wishes. With the exception of Dent, only one of us is absent today, and I don't believe that person is a threat to us. If we can all be here right now, then we are safe from each other. If anyone disagrees, speak now. If not..." Anthony held the file over the fire.

No one said a word.

He let it drop, and as it slowly caught fire, everyone watched with fascination as the wind picked up and the embers swirled in the air and scattered along the rocks and blew out toward the ocean. They sat silently for a long time, but as the sky darkened, they started talking. Soon, they were laughing, telling stories, getting to know each other.

At midnight, Brian said he was getting tired. He'd been trying to avoid William's texts, but suddenly felt like he could use something to relax. Maybe they'd find a party, have some more drinks, meet some girls…the usual stuff. Before he walked away, Jason sized him up and told him he looked much thinner. Brian knew it was true, but was surprised it was so noticeable. Whatever he was doing, he'd keep doing it, and William seemed to be the key. He nodded to Toby as he made his exit, but Toby said nothing.

Shiloh fell asleep in a blanket, which was Trish's cue to leave. She picked her daughter up and said her goodbyes. Charlie stopped her to ask how she'd been in the last week. Trish told him it was touch and go and Charlie promised again that he'd look into her case. Trish told him the investigation into Bedbug's death hit a brick wall and won't likely be pursued. She told him if it was, she'd have his back. He nodded in appreciation and said his goodbye and went his separate way. As Trish tucked Shiloh into her bed, Charlie went back to his own home instead of Mindy's. He fell asleep on the couch, unwilling to go into the bedroom. In time, just as Trish and Adlar wanted to let go of the past, he thought he could learn to forget too. He suspected he already was starting.

Maria had some drinks and watched with adoration as Henry charmed the group. She mostly stayed silent, but he constantly included her in the conversation, bragging about her talents and making her fall harder than she ever had before. Through him, she grew comfortable with the group as a whole and them with her. They made their exit around one as it grew colder. Toby gave Henry a look as he passed and Henry understood that the game was ready to go to the next level. When they got to the car, Henry told Maria he loved her. They fell asleep in each other's arms.

No one said anything to Todd about his disappearance. Instead, they asked questions and stated they were glad he was okay and asked what he would do next. He told them he wasn't sure and that he'd like to return— that he felt optimistic about returning, but wanted to make sure his wife and kids were safe. No one knew for sure what that meant, but didn't ask. He and Jason had an early flight out and had to get back to the hotel. Before Jason joined him in the car, he stopped by Aileen and stood with her looking at the ocean below. "You were there in support, huh?" he asked. She nodded. "Good for you. I'm proud of you." After he walked away, Aileen's eyes watered. Despite the circumstances, it was the best moment of her life.

Royce made polite chatter, but was distracted by thoughts of Manny and Adlar, and whatever they would be doing together, but he brought his focus back to Richard. He said his goodbyes and assured everyone he was okay. He walked Aileen to her car and went home to Sandra.

Tarek and Anthony talked until three. Tarek told him everything he knew about Stan and they discussed the bomb inside Anthony and what he would do next. Anthony had no ideas, but said the next step would be to talk to Stan. He would do it when he was ready, but now wasn't the time. He thanked Tarek again for handling Stanley. Tarek told him all he did was stall, but if Anthony hadn't exited when he did, they would have all been dead. After Tarek walked away, Anthony reflected on the statement. He only walked out of The Coop because Richard's phone cut out. He thought about Richard's words again: *I am exactly where I'm supposed to be.*

It was hard to argue with a man who saved them all by exiting. When his phone cut out, Anthony walked out of The Coop, taking the bomb with him. If that hadn't happened, Stan would have pushed the button, and that would have been the end. Anthony hoped Richard knew what he did. He wished he could tell Richard. Instead he looked out into the ocean for another minute and thought about Richard.

The fire was almost out and the night had grown quiet. Only Toby was left, staring at the sky as if no one else had been there at all. Anthony approached. "How long you staying?" he asked. Toby didn't respond. "Trish's girl was asking why you weren't talking to anyone."

"She should have asked me. I could have explained that she should mind her own business."

Anthony smiled and nodded. "We should talk about what you said at The Coop when you were addressing Bernard. Something about a building on Vine and pharmaceuticals?"

Toby was silent. Anthony saw something in his eyes: He was deeply conflicted and irritated to have someone interrupt him while he sorted things out. "I'll let you go, but before I head out, I wanted to tell you that it's perfectly acceptable to want Victor's money and mourn Richard's passing simultaneously. Nobody is one thing Toby."

Toby scowled and Anthony walked away with an amused smile. After he was gone, Toby boosted himself up and took a deep breath before pulling his cell from his pocket. The time was coming to get back on task and Richard's death was motivating, though he couldn't find the energy to celebrate. He dialed a number. Henry and William knew what to do, but he still had his wild card—the riskiest plan of all. He had a buzz and didn't care that he woke the man in the middle of the night to tell him what was next.

"We're still going," he said. "But lay off her for a while. She's got another surgeon looking at her daughter, so make sure you've got your shit in order."

Neomin sat up in bed and rubbed his eyes and forehead, stressed by the situation. "We need to call it off," he said. "We're not going to be able to do this. There's no way to keep going with this without being discovered."

"You've done fantastic so far," Toby said with a slur in his voice. "Let her mother think she's doing better for a while and I'll get this other guy out of the way. Then, we'll really back her into a corner. Get back on the horse Neomin. If you want your little secret to stay that way, you'll make Trish Reynalds believe that the only way to save her daughter is with a whole lot of money."

He shut his phone before Neomin could object. He pulled a bottle of champagne from his side—one in thirteen he'd reserved for the death of each beneficiary. He held it up in the moonlight, ready to pop the cork. Instead, he stood and walked to the edge of the cliff and tossed it into the ocean.

If you liked my book, even if you don't, I encourage you to go to my Amazon page and leave a review at: http://www.amazon.com/Mr.-Brian-Darr/e/B00K7UBSNQ/ref=sr_ntt_srch_lnk_1?qid=1400826397&sr=8-1

I love feedback and being an indie writer, knowing what you like/don't like, gives me the opportunity to constantly improve. Thank you for taking the time to read The Eye of Providence. If you enjoyed reading it half as much as I enjoyed writing it, I consider that a victory.